C_MANTIS

THE PATH OF ASCENSION

BOOK THREE

aethonbooks.com

Aethon Books
www.aethonbooks.com

Print and eBook formatting by Josh Hayes. Artwork provided by Fernando Granea.

Published by Aethon Books LLC.

ALSO IN SERIES

Book One

Book Two

Book Three

Book Four

1

Matt looked to Liz and Aster and, in unison, they all Tiered-up. There was no need to go to a higher Tier rift and use its essence to help with compressions. After all, they had already delved a Tier 7 rift. Their cores were as compacted as they could be at Tier 5.

Looking inward, he inspected his recent cultivation. He had been allocating most of his directed cultivation to mind, senses, and proprioception. Now, his greatest problem was keeping up with his boost from [Mage's Retreat]. It would only get harder from here, as he would be able to pump more mana into the skill as he Tiered-up.

In the past month, he had gotten the skill into his core spirit and was slowly expanding its capabilities to increase his endurance when using the skill. Once he was done, he would take the skill out of his core spirit and start absorbing the other skills he had collected. He planned to try and make them cheaper so he could use them earlier.

With the three of them now Tier 6, they quickly packed up their camp and flew into the air. Matt took one last look at the island they had camped on, and the neighboring one where they had done their rift experiments.

It was a bittersweet sight. He felt like he had passed a pivotal point in his life. Money and essence no longer meant as much to him as they had before this moment. His time experimenting had also given him a better impression of enchanting and of its benefits.

He felt like he was a different Matt altogether compared to when he arrived on this planet, only a few short months ago. It only took a glance to see the half-dozen rifts that he'd left. They were the best of his creations, and it gave him a bit of satisfaction to think of how valuable the island would be in the future. Especially once people saw there was both a Tier 7 rift and one capable of producing endless Tier 5 natural treasures for mana cultivation.

One would eventually Tier up the planet, and the other would create near-endless wealth.

The other rifts were the ones that produced growth items most often, or consistently had valuable rewards. Liz's herb rift would probably be a hot commodity in the future for an alchemy guild.

He smiled as he thought of the faces of the people who would find their little retreat.

With a thought and flex of his spirit, Matt turned and flew toward the gathering point. It was set in the middle of nowhere on the planet's fourth continent. It was a weird location, but he assumed it was selected by the imperial army instead of the kingdom. Otherwise, it would've been in one of the two teleporter cities.

It would take them a few hours to reach their destination, but the message calling them together had a countdown timer. They had nearly a full day until the countdown reached zero. Neither he nor Liz had any idea what the counter represented, but they didn't want to get caught out of the city if it indicated the invasion point and start time of the war.

Matt didn't think it likely, as this was more a training ground than a real war, but they hurried anyway.

As they flew, Matt increased his max mana pool to 80, and then immediately downed one of Aunt Helen's mana concentration potions. He almost fell but was able to keep his flying sword steady with the aid of his AI. After checking and finding that his mana concentration was now 1.3, he was slightly taken aback. The potion had given him an increase of 0.15 mana concentration, even more than the 0.08 that the first one had provided at Tier 4.

After reflecting, it made sense that a Tier 30 plus mana concentration potion would do more than a max mana of 20 could handle. With the realization that he would get more out of Aunt Helen's potions when he had more maximum mana to sacrifice, he decided to save the potions for the higher Tiers and regretted his decision to take the potion now.

Putting it out of his mind, he focused on returning his maximum mana to his new cap of 80. The doubling of mana gave him a massive amount of wiggle room in his spell casting.

A quick test of [Hail] showed his AI that he could create a much larger area of coverage. When given a larger portion of MPS, it also created more ice. By doubling the initial mana cost, it nearly doubled the area affected by the spell. That was nice, but what made it amazing was when he noticed that the increased ice density remained without increasing the upkeep cost. When he increased the channeled mana to his full mana generation of 80 MPS, the skill appeared more like a wall of ice than a natural storm.

Aster took control of it from his backpack and created a few ice sculptures that floated around the flying trio. He didn't miss that most were rabbits and hearts, but he laughed at her antics. From her mental pushing, he knew he would be making rabbit rifts for her anytime they stopped in a single location for too long.

It was also tempting to instantly absorb [Fireball] just so he had a skill to cast like a normal mage, though he would need to use the mana stone trick he had with [Hail]. In the end, he decided to wait until [Mage's Retreat] finished its modifications and was out of his core spirit.

It would still be much faster to modify the skill when he absorbed it, rather than doing it the slow way. The small voice that said he could buy another [Fireball] was easily crushed. Even if he could do that, it was just too wasteful. The skill once used was gone forever, and as much as he had changed, he still remembered the lack of skills on his home planet of Lilly.

I can change that.

Matt didn't know what he would be doing in the near future with their management team still being assembled, but he started listing reasons in his AI about why going to Lilly and making some low Tier rifts for the populace was a good thing.

He brought his mind back to his skills. [Mage's Retreat] had already been calculated but, with his increase of mana concentration, it was nearly thirty percent more effective at increasing his strength for the same mana cost. The same logic applied to [Cracked Phantom Armor]. Matt sighed as he realized that, while he would have the advantage in mana concentration at the lower Tiers, he would fall behind at the higher Tiers due to his reliance on potions. That is, if his math was accurate.

Matt quickly searched for the actual scaling for mana concentration. Finding nothing, he turned to ask Liz, "Do you know the actual way mana concentration works on skills?"

She shook her head. "No, I just know it's good."

Turning back to the KingdomNet, he finally found a source that seemed well-rated and spent the money to get hard numbers for his math.

As it turned out, his notion of how mana concentration worked was slightly off. Instead of being a direct multiplier to effectiveness, it was logarithmic in nature, doubling the strength of skills for every ten times concentration he encountered. So, instead of thirty percent, his skills would be about eleven percent stronger than 'normal.' It also meant that mages his Tier would be stronger, but not by *that* much.

Before he knew it, they were nearing the marked location, and both he and Liz paused in their flight. The others that had been flying near them did the same at the impressive sight in front of them.

Where there should have only been an unexplored continent and a grassy plain, a full-bore *city* waited for them, albeit made of stone rather than metal. It was a dozen times larger than the cities the Seven Suns had built around the teleporters.

At first, Matt swallowed. If this was the queendom's invasion force, they were well and truly screwed, but he quickly noticed the flying patrols were all in the army's color-shifting uniforms. Even with their full camouflage disabled, they still seemed to blend into the background, making them hard to notice at first, and harder still to keep an eye on.

"What is this?"

Liz was close enough to hear his question and called out, "I don't know, but it's impressive. I can't imagine how difficult it would be to create a city that large in that time frame, but only the army could do it. Look at the wall. It's covered in defensive formations."

Matt caught the faint shimmering of the enchantments and nodded as his eye caught something else as well. "And look at their cannons.

They're massive. I think I could stand up inside of that barrel. What are they expecting?"

Liz circled back to him and shrugged. "Maybe it's a show of force to the vassals. Something like, 'Look at how strong we are, don't try and fuck with us.' I don't know for sure, though."

"Well, it's working on me. The walls must be two hundred feet tall, and the buildings make them seem small."

Matt was thoroughly impressed. Even from here, the city was all a uniform brown that implied that it was created with [Earth Manipulation]. Before he could look into it deeper, he saw that his AI had registered an EmpireNet. They hadn't had access to it since they left the vassal kingdom's capital.

They followed the stream of people entering into the city, and Matt ogled the triple layers of walls, each over fifty feet thick. From the surrounding sounds of water, he assumed there was a moat above the tunnel and between the first and second wall.

It would have all been useless if not for the flight inhibiting formation over the entire city. Liz tried to peek over the crowd, and found that while her flying device worked, it only got her an inch above the ground before she was shoved back down.

The expense was mind boggling. Excluding everything else, just running the formation must cost thousands of mana per second for a city four hundred square miles, by his AI's calculations. Matt wasn't thrilled about the implications of needing a city this large, but he still asked Liz about it while she was pressed against him in the crush of people.

"How many people are they expecting to show up?"

He had to repeat himself another three times before she nearly shouted in his ear, "Gotta be ten million-plus. Have you checked the CityNet?"

Matt hadn't explored it yet, so he did so at Liz's suggestion, and quickly saw what she meant. The CityNet was tied in with the EmpireNet, but it had more local information. Everything seemed to be about people taking sides in the upcoming war or trying to find ways to profit from said war. There were thousands of stores and individual crafters trying to sell their wares or services.

But what caught and held his attention was the information that listed the war's rules of engagement.

This city was a designated neutral site, and all fighting was prohibited under imperial law, except in designated fighting arenas. No one would be allowed to break the peace, and the army was there to ensure the rules were followed.

The second thing was that all newcomers from The Path of Ascension would be entering through the city, before either side would be able to recruit or transport their personnel. It was also the location of all reward distributions for every participant.

As Matt was looking for more information, he received a message from Juni with a location to meet at. If he was reading the message right, the kingdom and queendom had set up buildings across the street from each other.

It screamed of creating conflict and trying to ensure that people fought, but Matt assumed the Empire knew what it was doing. It couldn't be the first time they had done this, after all.

The location they needed to reach was so deep into the city, they decided to take a cab. The price of a Tier 6 mana stone to go anywhere in the city made Matt's inner poor kid cringe, but he still paid it. It let them escape the mob of people, instead of trying to move through the street or waiting for public transportation. Once they were in the air, he was able to see how the crowd quickly dispersed into the massive city as the area surrounding the gate was cleared. As they flew through the high-rises, the true scope of the city came into perspective, and Matt disregarded the expense.

The city was gorgeous. There were flying islands that looked like parks and meditation areas. Some even seemed to be elementally aligned, and he made a note to find one for Aster to play in. Even if the aura wasn't any good for refining her mana, she would still enjoy spending time with other ice aspected people.

As they flew, he saw massive floating platforms that were clear combat arenas. Unlike the normal standard arenas he had seen, these were scenario-based ones. From the few he saw, he could tell there was a variety of combat arenas from false cityscapes to elemental battlefields. Each one was hundreds of feet wide, and several of them held people actively fighting. He tried to get a better look, but the cab moved too quickly, and the buildings cut off his view as they sped along.

The use of all available space was impressive, and Matt couldn't help but stare.

When they started to descend, Matt noticed what he thought was a massive teleportation area. But instead of having runes, it was a clear area that was nearly a mile wide in the middle. No teleportation platform could be that big. The larger they were, the greater the cost, and that was thousands of times bigger than the ones that jumped between planets. It would bankrupt even the Emperor if it was a teleport formation.

He nudged Liz to ask what it was, and she looked at him oddly. "It's a spaceport. Oh, right. You probably wouldn't have seen much of them. Teleportation platforms fall off in usage pretty hard after Tier 15, when people can more readily navigate chaotic space, something that's impossible without a Concept. You can't even really *see* properly without a Concept, so you need someone high enough Tier to fly a passenger ship through chaotic space without a teleport set up, and they usually have better things to do with their time than spend day in and out ferrying people around.

Teleportation platforms are great for small volumes of people, but they're way too expensive for long distances or moving in a hundred thousand people at once. If they're bringing Pathers in from all over the Empire, it makes sense they'll fly them in rather than push them through the teleportation network. It's actually… Ask me later. Looks like we've arrived."

The building they were meant to enter was obvious when he saw it. It was a mirror to the building on the other side of the cleared area and colored in the Seven Suns Kingdom's colors of gold and dark red, while the queendom's building was colored in silver and light purple.

There were also guards in each of the factions' respective colors, which Matt assumed were from the respective kingdoms. The fact that there were people manning the queendom's side was slightly alarming. Had the invasion already started, or were they an advanced party sent as an emissary?

Matt was constantly thrown off by the fact that this wasn't a true invasion. If it was a real war, they would break through at the teleport location and build a teleporter of their own, so that more troops could be quickly funneled into the planet.

Or wait, with what Liz had said about ships, would they use ships instead of making a teleporter? Or would they just travel through chaotic space directly? He knew the higher Tiers could do things like that, so why even bother with ships? Or…

Matt shook himself out of his pointless musings and climbed out of the cab to march up to the Seven Suns building. It wasn't like the Empire would publicize how they attacked people in a real war, so it was pointless to check.

They were stopped at the stairs by the guards and told to wait until someone could vouch for them. After a message to Juni, they were immediately let through with an apology.

They were given directions to a room in the middle of the massive building that was so awkwardly located, Matt wondered if Juni had a falling out with the prince. To his surprise, they found a massive topographical table map of the planet, with hundreds of fortifications of different designs and colors, with a dozen or more small groups inspecting various parts of the map.

Matt and Liz walked around the set-piece while Aster curled up in the backpack, uninterested in the boring human goings on. Juni quickly came over and shook both of their hands.

"Thanks for getting here early. Things are a little crazy right now."

"Yeah, we noticed with the out of the way location."

Juni flinched hard and said, "Don't mention that. Even though the prince isn't here, he's a little touchy about that. We've also had a few…" he paused, "incidents. Princess Sara, the queendom's leader, is Tier 7 like the prince."

Matt was shocked by that and checked Juni. He found that the prince's right hand was now Tier 7.

He interrupted by asking, "Sorry, but you advanced? I thought you both had quite a bit more to go."

Juni laughed at that, "The king is giving us everything we can think to ask for, and the army said we couldn't bring more Tier 7s to the planet. They said nothing about making them here with essence stones. Apparently, the Empire is reimbursing everything they spend on this, and the better the battles and war, the more the kingdom will be rewarded. If the rumors are true, that extends to both personal rewards for the king, and rewards for the entire kingdom. He's sparing no expense and giving everything he can and plans to advance a lot of people. Last I heard, the king intends to move up something like twenty million Tier 5s and 6s."

Liz whistled. "That's a lot of people. What are they all going to do?"

"Fight, I suppose, I'm sure the king would send more, but that's the limit for the kingdom to send. Anyone else will need to be recruited from the Pathers. Speaking of Tier, I see you all worked hard. From mid-Tier 5 to Tier 6 means you were busting ass."

Juni looked around and then pulled them to the side. "But back to my point, the queendom's leader is a Tier 7, Princess Sara. They had a meeting last week where she instantly and very publicly declared she would marry the prince."

The man looked incredibly awkward as he finished. "The prince tried to play it off as a joke, but she bet him that if she won the war he would have to go on at least a dozen dates with her. To the prince's dismay, both sides' parents agreed to the condition. I believe the king wants to pressure the prince to not lose, and it's working. The problem is, for as much of a physical monster as Princess Sara is, she's unexpectedly crafty as well."

"She's already gotten packages into the prince's bedroom twice and crashed meetings like this with extravagant gifts *four times* in the last week. In fact, just this morning the prince woke up to find his room filled to the brim with roses." The man was looking more frazzled the longer he talked. "We still haven't a clue how she did it."

Matt had to give credit where it was due. "That's impressive."

"It is, but it's also a sore spot for the prince, so we've been moving meeting locations to random rooms, and it seems to have worked. So far, at least. Just don't mention her, please. Especially around the prince when you see him later."

Moving the conversation along, Matt pointed at the map and asked, "What are the little castles?"

Taking advantage of the change of topic, Juni smiled. "So, while the Empire hasn't released any information officially yet, we know a few things. The army is busy building locations that have strategic value, or at least simulated strategic value. However, they're still finishing with a few locations. It will be reminiscent of a game of capture the flag, where the longer one holds the location, the more points that side accrues. It's technically a secondary objective, but not to the king. In fact, it's his highest priority. The war ends when one side controls the entire planet for a full month. But from a few rumors, some of the prizes are allegedly worth more than the Tier 20 planet to the kingdom, so it's of vital importance to hold the positions. The king has even said that he'd rather lose the war if we got him enough points."

"Is there not a bonus for winning?" Juni nodded in response.

"Of course, but the problem is that no one knows how much it's worth. It could be worth millions or five mana stones. That's too far above us, though. As long as you're okay with it, you will be back with the team that assaulted the golem fortress. We'll be filling out the group to about five hundred over the next few months, with the best of both Pathers and kingdom fighters. We'll be acting as the quick reaction force and doing a lot of the hard work when it comes to taking and holding important locations. I suggested to the prince that we take the fighters from the golem war and make them our team leads for the best fighters. So we want you three to lead one team."

Matt shrugged. It seemed like a good opportunity to earn more points. He said, "We don't mind taking a team leader role." He looked at Liz, who nodded at his unspoken question. "This just feels wrong. I get that this is a curated war, but it feels a little too much like a game. The queendom is already here. Why wouldn't they just attack?"

Juni looked tired and sighed at the question. "Yeah, but we can't do anything about it. When the countdown ends tomorrow, we believe the war will officially start. The queendom will appear in the city that correlates with their teleport location, and they will start moving in. We don't know exactly where that is yet, though. And we're unable to preemptively take control of any of the valuable points. We've been limited to the areas near our cities, but that leaves nearly two-thirds of the planet uncontested. Once the war starts, we'll be scrambling to try and block the queendom off, and it won't be easy. They can appear anywhere and attack a single location with their full force, but at least our defending advantage won't be completely nullified with the Empire's restrictions in place."

Matt took a look at the map and noticed that the cities with the teleporters were surrounded by blue forts, while the rest of the map was gray. There were also larger, city-like structures strewn about.

There was one on each of the five continents, and one near an isolated archipelago chain on the other side of the planet

"What are they? Fake cities?"

Juni shook his head. "No, they're cities that the army made like this one, only a lot smaller. They also have teleportation formations in them that will allow the cities to reinforce themselves. We expect that the queendoms' teleport location from their planet string will drop them in one. Sadly, they can only be teleported to when the war starts, and they've already been captured by one side."

Matt tried to take it all in but was distracted by the sheer scale of it all. Twenty million people were being brought in for the first wave, and that didn't even account for the Pathers that the Empire would be *literally* shipping in.

To his surprise, he was actually excited and itching for a fight. Unlike with the golem fighting, lives weren't on the line here, and there were goals to fight for. He didn't miss the forts situated around rift clusters and natural resources. If his guess was right, there were a few artificial resource nodes in areas that would otherwise be unimportant.

His competitive blood boiled, and he wanted to get out and take the fight to worthy opponents. Matt had no doubt that there would be strong people in both the vassal forces and among the exceptional Pathers.

Juni kept telling them about what to expect, but it all amounted to not much of anything. They would have to wait until tomorrow for the truth of the situation, when the war would officially start.

"What should we do now?" Liz's question re-focused him once Juni excused himself to make more preparations.

"Well, we don't have any responsibilities until the war starts, and our team isn't assembled yet, so I doubt we'll do anything tomorrow. This all seems to be progressing much slower than I would've expected. We have a room set up, but I'd like to visit one of the enchanters around the building. I want to get a second opinion on the pattern I made for my sword, so I can enchant it before the fighting starts tomorrow."

"Whelp, let's go. Our room doesn't seem to be in a dorm-style, so at least we can enjoy our off time in between fights."

She stretched, showing a bit of her midriff where her shirt rose.

"That is, if we have much down time. Somehow, I expect this will be more like the golem war, and we'll be running from place to place to put out fires."

Matt laughed and shook his head. "Yeah, but without the risk of death, this should be pretty fun. There's gonna be plenty of other Pathers to fight, and lots of vassal people to round out the numbers."

Liz shrugged, and they wound their way out of the building to find one of the Tier 7 enchanter locations. Unable to find one near them, they wandered in the direction of the crafter's district, until Aster leapt out of Matt's arms and scampered off into the packed crowd.

Following his connection to his bond, he found her hanging off a man's red and bushy fox tail, who looked at the arctic fox with bemusement.

He met Matt's eye and chuckled over Aster's growling. He shook his tail, causing the fox to sway. The man lifted his tail to waist height, bringing the troublemaker attached along with it.

"I take it she's your bond."

"Yes, I'm so sorry. I have no idea what got into her. She's never done this before, I swear."

Matt moved to pull his bond off the man's tail, and noticed that he was wearing an army uniform, and was traveling with a squad of others. Of course, Aster had to attack a Tier 15 or above soldier.

"It's fine. I'm assuming I'm the first fire fox she's met, and our elements clashed. I can't blame her. I'd be a hypocrite of the highest order."

Matt finally wormed his finger into his bond's growling jaw, and finally freed the man's bushy red tail from her teeth. Even if Aster couldn't hurt the man, it was incredibly rude to bite someone, so he scolded Aster telepathically as he apologized to the man out loud.

"Really, I'm so sorry." As Matt was going to continue, the man shrugged and scratched Aster's ears.

"Don't worry about it. Once she calms down, she'll have better control over it next time. I remember my first time meeting an opposite element. I bit his ankle and refused to let go. Good times."

With that, the man left, and Matt looked to a mortified Liz.

"Do you know what that was?"

"Sadly, yes. Opposite elements can have reactions of hate and anger. Fire and ice in this case, but I didn't think Aster would be affected like this. She's never reacted to me, and my bloodline is fire-based. Sorry, I never even thought about it."

Probing his bond, he could tell that the problem mostly stemmed from the man being a fire aspected *fox*, rather than being a fire aspected individual in general. She clearly felt that all foxes should be ice aspected, and anything else was bad. It was all that she was thinking about.

Matt soothed his bond until she calmed down enough for him to get a message through to her.

"Aster, you can't do that. You can get hurt or in trouble. You had me worried!"

"Fox ice. Fire bad. Fox ice!"

With as stern an emotion he could push to her, he said, "Aster no. Foxes can be anything. They don't have to be ice aspected."

He was interrupted with an inquisitive, "Aster fox. Aster ice. Ice good." Like she had explained the most obvious thing in the world.

Matt wanted to pull out his hair.

Is this how it feels to raise a kid?

Suddenly, he was happy to have been fined for having his birth control implant missing. It would have been incredibly unlikely, but if this was how it was to raise a child, he wanted nothing to do with it.

With a sigh, Matt and Liz tried to explain how not all foxes were like her, and that she needed to treat them all with respect, and especially not bite them.

She insisted that she was right with the inarguable logic of repeating herself endlessly.

It was a long walk to the enchanter's building.

2

Matt carried a pouting Aster to the enchanter shop and found that the building was spatially expanded to at least three times its normal size. It was so large he couldn't see the opposite wall of the building, even though it should have only been a dozen feet away. It shouldn't have surprised him, given it was a Tier 10 enchanter's shop, but it seemed excessive.

While he started walking toward the back to speak with a salesman, Matt got distracted by the rows of enchanted items. All of them were in protective glass, and some cases blocked his spiritual sense while others he could feel through. After scanning one of the items that was protected, his AI told him that it was a special item made by the owner of the shop.

Matt didn't know if that meant the proprietor designed the enchantment from scratch, or if they had just modified something existing, but it was interesting.

The item in question was a flying hairpin that had an armor-piercing enchantment. The hairpin was displayed using a wigged mannequin head. It secured the hair in a bun, leaving the mannequin's long neck exposed. With a sudden thought, Matt popped up and peered over the rows of shelving. He caught a glimpse of his redhead bobbing in and out of view two isles over, so he called out to Liz.

"Hey, come look at this. I think you'd like it."

Liz meandered around on her way to the container and half nodded, and half shook her head.

"They're pretty, but it's not practical. I have armor on when we fight, which covers my head."

"I was thinking about when we aren't preparing for a fight. I at least have my sword in a spatial ring. This would give you something to defend yourself with around the city or wherever we are."

Matt kept a straight face. The argument wasn't wrong, but it wasn't his primary motive. Liz typically kept her red hair in a long braid that fell to the side of her head. She rarely tied her hair up, which was a shame, because she had a long elegant neck that he couldn't resist. Liz was a weapon in and of herself and didn't need any further protection, but if she bought his excuse and got the hairpin, he'd get to enjoy the view of her seldom seen neck.

Liz ran a finger over the glass, then started to play with her hair, raising it and spinning it into a bun before she shrugged.

"Yeah, I can make it work. It's not a bad idea. It just seems kind of expensive. It's a Tier 7 mana stone for a Tier 6 item."

"I don't see us advancing that quickly in the next few months, so it's a good investment."

Matt didn't *say* they weren't lacking money, but they really weren't. Now that they were Tier 6, it was no longer economical for them to delve Tier 5 rifts for growth items. However, they still had made more than most guilds could have earned in a comparable time. So, they were insanely wealthy for their Tier in both mana stones and empire contribution points.

With a mental fist pump, Matt watched as Liz picked up the little slip by the glass container and slipped it into her hand cart.

As they wandered the store together, Matt made a few mental notes for things to try and recreate. A bracelet that created a bubble that blocked rain while flying seemed easy enough, while also being useful, so he set his AI to research the design. With his extra mana regeneration of 80 MPS, he had mana to spare. He figured while he wasn't fighting, it was a good way to stay productive.

He reached the clerk, put on his best smile, and asked, "Hi, is the enchanter in?"

The man seemed unimpressed and stared at Matt blankly for a moment before asking, "Why?"

Not used to the curt attitude, Matt cocked an eyebrow but answered truthfully, "Well, your LocalNet listing said there was a Tier 10 enchanter here that was on the Path. I wanted to get his help and look over an enchantment for a weapon I bought."

"So, you want a weapon enchanted," the clerk replied in a bored, monotone voice. "Put it in the bin over there, and Kelley will get to it in the next few weeks. For an additional Tier 6 mana stone, you can be bumped up to a higher priority."

Seeing where the misunderstanding came from, Matt smiled at the man. "No. I need to enchant the weapon myself, but I want to see if there is anything else I can get out of the weapon, and possibly have the enchanter watch me lay the enchantment."

"So, you want a lesson?"

Seeing as how the man seemed incapable of understanding what he wanted, or at least didn't care to, Matt just nodded. "Sure. When can I meet with him?"

The man lazily swiped at the pad in front of him for what felt like a year and finally said, "He can do an hour lesson now for a Tier 7 mana stone. Standard disclaimer applies. He'll teach you what he wants, no matter how much or little that is. Though he'll target your wants or desires."

Just wanting to end this pointless discussion, Matt nodded and sent the payment over with his AI. He didn't carry that much money on hand; they kept it stored in their team's bank account for safety reasons.

The clerk looked disinterested to the extreme as he led Matt back behind the counter and to a room with a metal banded wooden door. With a loud rap, he waited. When nothing happened, he started to pound and kick on the door until it opened abruptly.

The clerk only said, "Lesson," before he walked away.

The man, Kelley, Matt assumed, looked wild with his beard and hair spiking in every direction.

"You here for a lesson?"

"Not really, but that was the best way to get past your receptionist."

Kelley glared at the wall and growled, "Sorry, he's my sister's kid. So, what do you want, if not a lesson?"

Matt cut to the chase and summoned his weapon from its ring, holding it parallel to the ground so the enchanter could inspect it.

"I have a growth sword that only I can enchant, but it's got a few advantages."

He didn't get any farther before the Tier 10 man snatched the weapon and turned back into his room, shouting, "Shut the door when you come in!"

Matt did as he was told, sending Liz a message to keep her in the loop. Aster, who was still in his arms, stopped pouting and started sniffing around while still being held.

The enchanter had his sword on a table with a light so bright, Matt had to squint. He pulled out his and Aster's sunglasses to spare their eyes.

Kelley hummed over his blade for a while, and without looking up, asked, "It's a Tier higher than you? Is that intentional?"

"Yeah, I can handle the physical weight, and I figured the spiritual weight isn't a huge problem if I just keep the enchantments at my own Tier."

Kelley tapped at the blade then ran his finger down the flat, as if he was inspecting something through feel.

"You can remove the enchantments, right? Hmm. Yeah, I can feel that. I can also feel that only its owner can do the work."

He looked up at Matt and shrugged. "While this whole thing is interesting, what do you want?"

"I have a blueprint here bought from the Empire Market, and wanted to get it inspected. It was done by a lower Tier enchanter than yourself. If I had known this city was going to be here, I wouldn't have wasted the contribution points."

Kelley looked at Matt in a new light. "You already have access to the Empire Market? Huh, must be a seeker."

"Something like that, yeah. Can you help?"

The Tier 10 glanced at a pile of armor and then firmly nodded. "As long as you aren't total garbage at enchanting, I think I can walk you through the process. I have some scrap iron you can practice on. And I don't want to work on that armor anymore, so you're a useful distraction."

Kelley asked for the blueprint and inspected it, finally asking, "Can you afford these enchantments? They're pretty standard, but this sword doesn't have a slot for a mana stone like a crafted one would, so it's unable to have its own reserves."

Matt carefully said, "Mana isn't a problem for me. Act as if I had a functionally unlimited supply of it for the purposes of the sword's enhancements and skills."

That earned him another odd look, but the man was a part of the Path, so he knew that everyone had their own secrets. Matt didn't expect him to ask anything more, but when he did, it was a question he hadn't thought of.

"When you say unlimited supply, do you mean as a stream? Or as a pool? I can do some interesting things depending on each answer."

"As a stream. Think regeneration, not capacity."

It was more than he wanted to share, but Matt was intrigued by the enchanter. Besides, he had already accepted that the man would get a pretty good guess of his Talent when he watched Matt enchant. It was a price he was willing to accept for his new sword, and he was okay with it since the enchanter was a Pather. Kelley wouldn't be under any actual restriction, but Matt felt that anyone who made it to Tier 10 as a crafter would know how to keep their mouth shut.

If he had to, Matt would ask Liz to throw her parents' names around if Kelley tried to blackmail him.

"Oh, that's interesting. You want the standard runes for repair, durability and sharpness. This has them all as major runes. I'd drop the repair one to a minor one and save the space."

Seeing Matt's skeptical look, the enchanter explained, "All growth items can repair themselves to a degree. As long as they're mostly intact, they can fix themselves. I've seen swords be shattered, then fix themselves with a little time and metal, if most of the pieces are gathered back up. The point is, we can free up some space and add either another rune or a skill. You have a second advantage with this being a growth item. It doesn't need the rune to take in your personal mana, which gives us *just* enough room to fit something else."

The man pushed things around until he uncovered a pad of paper that served as a desk mat. Ripping off the top and stained sheet, he started sketching with a pencil he pulled from nowhere.

Catching Matt's puzzled look, the man smiled cheekily. "At Tier 10, you can handle a small, specially made spatial ring. If you know a Tier 30 enchanter, they can make a cubic foot of space into a ring if they're good. But be prepared to pay out the ass in contribution points. The only reason they do it is so that lower Tiers buy things for them."

"Wait, what?"

The man looked at Matt's cores and asked, "Did you just Tier up?"

"Yeah, why?"

"Go and look at something at Tier 5 that you've seen the price of."

Matt checked his AI and found a growth item that he knew was seven thousand contribution points. He was shocked when he saw that the price had doubled in its value.

"Why the fuck is it fourteen thousand contribution points?"

Kelley grinned evilly at him. "When buying an item under your Tier in the Empire Market, you take a penalty to the cost. Double the price for the item for each Tier it is under your own. It prevents higher Tiers from monopolizing the market. But it also means that some things can get incredibly expensive for higher Tiers. At least for low Tier things, like growth items that only sell on the market. Most of the time, you can buy things with mana stones. But when you need a particular item, it can be worth it to offer services in exchange for an item, when dealing with a lower Tier person. I had to spend around forty thousand for a Tier 8 rare item to trade for this ring. Its original price was only ten thousand, but it was two Tiers lower than me. The Tier 30 who also wanted it would've had to spend almost one and a half *billion* contribution points."

Matt's jaw dropped, "That's an impossible number."

"Yeah, it's absurd, but that's why he traded for an item. This little beauty is worth around a hundred thousand contribution points, but no one makes them. They're incredibly hard to make, and it needs a Tier 30 or higher. But who's gonna spend that much for an item that they'll only use for five Tiers at most? I was lucky to come across someone offering to make one in exchange for an item."

"What item was it?" Matt couldn't think of something that would be so rare that it was worth the cost of a ring like this, and also interesting enough for a Tier 30 to buy.

"A Tier 8 rift reward. That's all I can say. The Tier 30 made it a condition of the deal. But don't expect that to happen all the time. If it's not unique, or so rare that it can't be bought, good luck. A Tier 30 would rather spend mana stones than contribution points for something below their Tier. And most people would rather have the money, as you don't get ten times more contribution points when selling to someone a Tier higher. The extra is just lost."

Matt wanted to slap himself for Tiering up. He had wanted to buy other things and hadn't seen it as an issue. But now, anything Tier 5 and below was incredibly expensive. He didn't know what to do.

"Fuck me. I didn't know that. I would have bought some more shit while I was still Tier 5."

Kelley had gone back to sketching, but still answered him. "Eh. It's not that big of a deal. Tier 5 is the lowest Tier that shit is really sold on the market, and that's for growth items. After that, there's a lull of stuff sold, as most things aren't so valuable that there isn't a standard market. Most would rather get the mana stones anyway. Services dominate the market until Tier 14."

The man paused, "Well, Tier 10 has the special Concept bottles for sale, but they're expensive. Although, if you're on the Path at Tier 10 and don't have your Concept, you probably don't have enough contribution points."

Kelley tore off the sheet of paper he was drawing on and tossed it to the side, then continued, "Everyone on the Path gets access to the market at Tier 10. Tier 5 for crafters on the Path. It's how I knew you were a seeker. They always get access early, which gives us crafters a market to buy from and sell to."

"All right, look at this." The enchanter held up a drawing of his swords with runes and formulas he only half understood, "If we made the suggestions I said earlier, we can either supercharge the runes to handle more mana by expanding them a little or add something else. A fire enchantment is always popular."

Matt thought that over. He'd avoid fire out of respect for his fox, who was still watching everything with bright eyes. But the idea didn't really resonate with him either. He was already adding [Mana Charge] and [Mana Slash] to his weapon. He'd rather increase their efficiency and double down on what he was good at.

He could look to add another rune, and he had explored that option before. He still thought that expanding his sword was a lackluster ability, as the expansion was made from mana, not real metal. Adding an element to his attacks had its advantages, as it could enhance his overall damage output. If there was something that he wanted, it was a way to make things bleed more for Liz.

But that wasn't a standard rune in any database he had seen.

"Can you give the blade a bleeding effect?"

Kelley paused in his drawing for a heartbeat before shaking his head. "Nope. I know of a rune for it, but it's at least Tier 20, as that was the weapon I saw with it. None of the databases I own have a bleed rune in them either."

"That's what I expected. Can we make the two skills more efficient then?"

"Maybe. But that would mean putting a higher Tier skill on it, then crippling the skill. It will be better than the Tier 6 skill pattern, since it would technically still be a Tier 7 skill. That's only possible because the weapon is already Tier 7, by the way. But sure, we can manage."

"Let's do that then."

With that, Kelley showed Matt a page with a drawing of his blade, along with the runes and their approximate locations. He was messaged with a much more detailed version of the design that showed the runes interacting in three dimensions.

It was more complicated than anything he had done before by a mile.

"I don't know if I can do that."

Kelley looked surprised at that. "I thought you said you've enchanted before?"

"Yeah, a few things that my AI created, but nothing this complicated."

"Can I see?"

Matt didn't see why not, so he sent the man a recording of his few tests, including his weapons enchanted from the golems' fortress.

"Huh. This is an interesting light rune. Tell me more about it?"

They went off on a tangent about how AIs tested and tried to create their own runes.

They became fully sidetracked once Kelley tried to quickly remake Matt's light rune.

"It's not very efficient, but it's very simple. It also produces a bit more light than the one we use."

Matt's rune was lighting up the entire room in a blinding fashion.

Even when Kelley threw a blanket over the rune, it still illuminated the surroundings.

Kelley was an amazingly knowledgeable person, but Aster quickly grew bored of his talk, so Matt let her out and told Liz he would be here a while. They had already blown over the hour the lesson was supposed to last, and had no sign of slowing.

He and Kelley talked about runes for another three hours, until they started testing Matt's ability to enchant.

Matt didn't think he was that bad, but Kelley nearly laughed him out of his shop when he saw Matt's mana control. It was embarrassing, as he had been working on it during their breaks. But, apparently, he was woefully behind what a normal crafter at Tier 6 would have.

It took five attempts on blanks for Kelley to allow him to try. The first two failed and destroyed the slab of metal, but the final three succeeded. The last two were even passable, according to Kelley.

Matt was nervous when he enchanted his blade, and botched the first attempt almost immediately. Unlike the standard items, it didn't fall apart when its spirit was damaged. Instead, the blade refused to allow him to modify its spirit until he fed it a few thousand mana. It was like watching a crack in a wall expand, but in reverse. The crack slowly closed and smoothed out. It was as if it never happened.

In his second attempt, Matt finished the entire enchantment in a single go. It took nearly forty minutes, and almost 200,000 mana to enchant the blade. He half-expected Kelley to say something about the absurd amount of mana directed into the blade, especially without tapping into the city's reserves. But the man pretended like nothing was amiss, which relieved Matt.

When the weapon was finished, he squashed the idea of testing the skills, and settled for testing the runes. When they held mana, to his and Kelley's satisfaction, he sent some mana into the skills, but just enough to see that the mana flowed through the proper channels. He let it dissipate instead of releasing the skills.

Shaking the man's hand, Matt asked, "What do I owe you for the enchantment work and help?"

Kelley looked slightly insulted when he waved Matt off. "Don't worry about it. It was a fun distraction, and I learned something new with that light rune, which is worth way more. Let's just call it that

Tier 7 mana stone my nephew charged you. Don't be a stranger, though. When you want to talk shop, swing by, or message me."

Matt smiled at the Tier 10 man. They had only known each other for a short time, but he felt as if he was friends with the man already.

It wasn't hard to agree, and he hurried to find Liz.

To his dismay, she was across the city, and had just sat down for dinner with Aster.

Giving up on joining them and telling them to enjoy themselves, he grabbed food at a food cart, and went back to their room in the Seven Suns building.

Along the way, he was intercepted by Juni, who carried a bag with him. "Everyone is to wear Seven Sun colors apparently, so do you want a full suit made? Or get your armor colored?" Seeing Matt's disinterest, he added, "We also have arm- or headbands."

That made the choice easy, but Juni looked disappointed with Matt's decision.

The gold and dark red armbands were simple enough, and seemed large enough to tie onto Aster's armor as well. He wondered if he could get her to wear it as a headband and laughed at the mental image.

If he played his cards right, he figured she might even go for it. A little flattery worked wonders. Besides, he really did think she would look cute in it.

He quickly changed before finding a training room to test out his new sword.

Matt stood with nearly four hundred other people in a field, across from an equal number of people from the queendom. They weren't here of their own free will, but because they had been called here as the counter neared zero. Matt was just happy he had enchanted his sword yesterday, and hadn't decided to wait.

This was an assembly called by the Empire's army, and Colonel Thorne was addressing everyone while he hovered ten feet above the crowd. "Today is the day that the queendom's main force is entering the planet, which nearly coincides with the first wave of Pathers. There will be five waves of Pathers joining us from across the Empire, who will arrive in the next three months. There will be about fifteen million Pathers joining us here over that time. But since the war is starting when the queendom breaks into real space, I want to cover a few things."

Matt tried to listen to the man, but something was nagging him. There was a resonance with his Concept as the man stood there and hovered over everyone.

His musing was interrupted as the Tier 33 continued, "As this is intended for training and not actual bloodshed, my soldiers will be pulling people out of combat. We will be assisted by a second planetary level AI that will be linking with your own AIs. We will only be reacting to the information about whether or not you can survive any attack. If you wish to keep something hidden, feel free to restrict your AI. But don't bitch to me when you get pulled out because of an attack you think you would have survived. I. Don't. Care."

There was a murmuring at that, and while the Colonel let the crowd buzz, he felt something at the man's feet. It seemed close to his Concept, so he used his own to probe the area. It caused the Tier 33 to immediately glance at him. He was afraid he pissed the man off, but he got a grin instead. Suddenly, what the Colonel was actually doing became more clear to his spiritual senses.

The man was using his Concept to harden the air, so he floated. It *felt* like a standard ability that all Concepts could do, much like how monsters could lock down fighters in a rift, if they had general Concepts.

Matt flexed his own Concept, but instead of willing mana regeneration to those around him or repulsing objects, he willed the air to harden in front of him. He tapped it with a finger and felt a slight resistance, before what felt like a plane of glass broke, and his hand went through it.

He looked up to see the Colonel nod at him as he continued speaking. "This is a game meant to sharpen the weapons that you will become. To that end, you will earn points like in any real war. However, unlike in a real war, if you sacrifice all your accumulated war points, you will be able to buy back your 'life', and rejoin the fighting."

Thorne held up a hand and said, "You may choose to *not* rejoin the game, and cash out your points, but know this. If you're dead, you can't spend your points unless you cash out. However, you *can* spend your points as you wish while you're alive. Yes, that means you can spend your points right before a big battle. The Empire even encourages that. That comes with a second caveat as well. If you have zero points, you can't rejoin the fighting. You need to give up at least one point to rejoin. For those on the Path, note that you can choose to leave the side you have chosen for the cost of twenty thousand points. Good luck to those who choose that route."

The man glanced to the sky. Following suit, the gathered crowd all witnessed ships ripping through space as if they came from behind some hidden screen. Matt counted four different designs, but as he watched, hundreds, and then thousands of ships arced down to the clear area in front of the two buildings.

Right in front of their two groups.

"Those are our Pathers. Welcome them, try to recruit them, fight for your side for wealth and glory. Good luck."

Like that, the man vanished.

Juni called out to everyone, "All right. We have access to the ship's logs and have cross-checked them with the people arriving. We will highlight anyone who chose our side blue and anyone unchosen as green. Do your best to sway them to our side. The kingdom started with a number of contribution points to hand out, so anyone who brings someone over to one of the kingdom representatives will get one point. Anyone who directly recruits someone will be given ten points."

He turned away and moved into the mass of oncoming people.

Matt just looked at Liz. "That looks like a pain. Want to skip this and go wait on the side?"

She didn't even wait for him to finish, already disappearing into the crowd.

3

Matt sat with Liz and Aster on a nearby stone wall while everyone else scurried around, accosting the few people highlighted in green in his HUD. It was more like a school of fish swarming around prey than any normal human interaction.

Seeing nothing interesting, Matt started working on his Concept again. With an effort of will, he hardened the air in front of himself and tapped at it, causing the plane of solid air to crack.

"What the fuck, Matt!?"

With a questioning look, he turned to Liz, who pulled at her hair as she glared at the area in front of his hand.

She poked his ribs and growled at him, "How are you doing that?"

He tried to get away from the finger of doom, but as he wiggled away, she scuttled after him.

"That hurts! And tickles. Stop! No fair! I'm running out of wall."

Liz finally stopped but still pouted at him.

"How are you doing it?"

Matt noticed that for all her joking attitude, she was serious about her question.

"I just felt what the Colonel was doing and tried to sense it. When he felt me, it became clearer, so I copied it. It's not strong enough to stand on yet, but it really doesn't seem hard to do."

Liz mixed a glare with a pout for a truly odd sight.

"You can't really do that until Tier 10, though…" She let the statement trail off as she watched him recreate the plane of solid air. "At least that's the common convention."

She started poking the air in front of her, but he felt nothing with his Concept.

Liz gave up after two more attempts. "I don't know if it's my Concept being internal or what, but I'm finding nothing here. What are you doing?"

Matt thought about it for a minute before replying, "I'm just recreating what the Colonel did. I felt him hardening the air, so I just wanted the air to be solid. I didn't really find it hard. Why? Is it normal for people to not be able to do it?"

Liz leaned back and started ruffling Aster's fur while dodging playful nips aimed at her fingers.

"Yeah, most people can't do it at our Tier, as they don't have the willpower. Maybe you're getting a benefit somehow with your image, but I honestly don't know. It's impressive that you can do that already, though. I'm proud of you."

Matt let the compliment bolster him as he added a ruffling hand to Liz and Aster's game, but he still wanted to help Liz. To that end, he tried to explain further. "I'm doing what you do when you resist monsters in rifts from trying to restrict movement. It's like that, but instead of countering their own will over an area of effect, I'm recreating what they were doing. I'm *willing* the air to solidify."

Liz looked up from their game of 'tease the fox' and poked at the air once more, before raising an eyebrow at him. "But I don't do that. When I resist a monster's Concept with my own, it's with my body. I force my way through it, so it's not able to slow me down or restrict me. I don't counter their Concept; I fight through it."

"Huh. I didn't know that." He really hadn't known that she hadn't used her Concept in that way. He had always assumed that she was using it just how he was.

In his mind, when someone tried to push you down, you resisted in the equal and opposite way, or you redirected the force. That way, it wouldn't be able to apply the intended effect on you. It was exactly how one would resist a physical blow they were unable to dodge.

He did it constantly every time he fought.

That was when he realized why he might be able to make the change. With a thought, he turned the Concept from just hardening the air into willing a plane to exist and resist his forward momentum. The harder he pushed, the more it resisted. It was like his Concept's repulsive effect but facing him.

The new resistance was also much easier to produce in comparison. With a flat palm, he shoved hard and slid backward until the back of his knees pressed into the wall. It drained some willpower, but as the area was a small, flat plane, and not a sphere around his entire body, it wasn't that bad. The cost still increased with his force, but it was a good starting point.

Aster nipped a too-slow finger, and he returned his attention to where it belonged. With his family.

From a hidden, warped area he had formed with his Intent, Colonel Thorne watched as the boy played with his Concept and his friends. He was about to leave while mentally noting that the boy was good, but not exceptional, when the boy's methodology *changed.*

Suddenly, the boy did something that shouldn't be possible at his Tier and experience.

He quickly brought up a profile on the boy, and was about to set up an offer for army recruitment and personal tutelage, when his body froze. It wasn't an attack, but an overwhelming pressure of a greater cultivator. It was a second later that his spirit cried out a warning that a monster was looming over him with jaws wide open.

His instincts gained in countless battlefields over his last nine thousand years in the army cried out for him to flee, but he was caged by a will stronger than his own. His Intent was gently rebuffed and forced down. It was a terrifying realization that also brought some comfort, because if someone that strong wanted to kill him, he wouldn't have even noticed his death. The horror of being this close to a monster was something he hadn't felt since his Tier 20s.

A purple-haired woman floated in front of him, and he received a message verifying the woman's identity as Luna. She was surrounded by two other people who stood close by, but said nothing.

With an air of pure authority, she said, "These are mine. Go find your own clay to mold."

This was a Path manager in the flesh. He had never met one before, and he already wished that he hadn't.

"I didn't mean to interfere, ma'am. I can…"

She didn't seem to hear him, continuing as she sent him a second message with coordinates. "Also, make this island your base. But if you ruin the rifts there, I'll take it out of your hide."

Thorne cringed internally at the order, as he would need to move his entire operation, but this woman was at least Tier 40, and had the Emperor's ear. Technically he had no obligation to follow her orders, but for something this small it would be dumb to refuse her. It was a harmless change that wouldn't impact their plans so he would do it to avoid trouble down the road if nothing else.

He waited for a dismissal quietly. He didn't want to leave before he was dismissed, which might anger the great lady. It was unlikely that she would harm him, but even in the Empire, catching the ire of someone this highly placed was never good for career advancement.

As Thorne listened, his expression grew confused.

"This idiot boy. What is he doing? He could be getting fourteen percent more out of his Concept if he added a bit of firmness behind his repulsion. Lessons in physics are in order. This is shameful, her boy toy is using Concept manipulations, and she can't."

The man handed what looked like a piece of paper to the ranting woman while he wrote on a floating notepad. The woman read it for a moment, then it vanished in a puff of void. "I don't care if she has an internal Concept. It's only a little harder for her. She could do it if she put in the work."

Thorne felt bewildered. Internal Concepts made it nearly impossible to harden the air or carry oneself without flight spells. Almost anyone who truly wanted Concept flight from their internal Concept would wait for Minkalla. From the testimonies he had heard, doing it naturally had taken positive ages in figuring out how to lift their bodies up. It was at least a hundred times harder than flight with an external Concept, which by itself was quite difficult.

This woman wanted the girl to do something he had only heard of two internal Concept users accomplishing without Minkalla? The difficulty of the task was only matched by the reward for actually figuring the methodology out. Internal Concepts sacrificed the ability to use manipulations like that for increasing the user's power. But if they were able to learn to reach *outside* of their body, they got the best of both worlds.

The man turned to him and nodded a dismissal.

Thorne cast [Teleport] and escaped from the crazy manager. Anyone who pushed their charges that hard was someone whose attention he didn't want to garner.

Those poor kids.

Just in case, Thorne marked the trio to be watched. Any special treatment would earn him some demerits due to their Pather status, but he didn't want to be surprised about their movements.

With an internal sigh, he started the arduous task of moving the army base to the island selected. He would personally inspect the rifts, as they must be unique for the Tier 40 to take an interest in them. He also didn't want any potential dangers near his camp, no matter how unlikely a few Tier 1 through Tier 7 rifts were to be a threat. The Tier 1 rift was particularly unusual on a Tier 6 world, but it was no real cause for concern. The Tier 7 rift was notable as well. Rifts growing to a Tier higher than the planet was normal enough, and indicated that the planet would be Tiering up in a mortal generation or two. But he still would need to check them both out as outliers.

They played with Aster until a commotion drew their attention, and they all peered over at the noise.

"Albie! Albie over here!"

A huge woman, with an incredibly muscular frame a little over six feet tall, walked in through the crowd to where Prince Albert sat at a recruiting desk. She called out loud enough that it carried to where he and Liz sat, "Did you get my flowers? Were you surprised?"

She had a glowing, menacing lance that she used to trip the two guards that tried to intercept her. Matt didn't miss that Juni moved behind her but stayed in the crowd.

Prince Albert crossed his arms and replied with a stiff face, "Yes I got them. Very…" He paused for a long moment, clearly choosing his words. "Considerate of you. Although, in the future, I would prefer if you delivered them to the front desk, and not break into our headquarters. I should report you to the Colonel for violating our sovereign territory before the start of hostilities."

Princess Sara laughed. "With your outdated security it was hardly breaking and entering. But you like the flowers? That's great. My team found this great out of the way rift that was full of them. It had these awesome vine monsters that spread seeds if you didn't kill them fast enough. From what my team told me, they should put up a good fight. If you want, I can take you to the rift. Besides the vine monsters, it's very romantic. Nice and isolated, on the edge of a cliff that has a great view. What do you say? Could be fun."

While the princess was speaking, she worked her way through the crowd until she stood in front of and looking down at the prince, who looked flustered.

Uncrossing his arms and standing up, the prince took a step back. "If you're done playing games, I think you should leave. As you can see, we are very bus… Hey!! Stop poking me!!"

"What? I thought you like being poked with a stick! You know, considering the one lodged firmly up your ass."

Liz pulled him forward, saying, "Oh, I like her. Or at least, I like that she's annoying the Prince. Dude's an uptight prick."

"Yeah, it's kinda nice to see him all flustered after all the shit he pulled during the golem incident." Matt enjoyed the exasperated, non-in control look the prince had on his crystalline face.

They pushed through the crowd in time to see Princess Sara hit the butt of her lance against the ground. "Come on! Let's ditch this place. How about this? You come with me to the rift, and I'll let you know where we're entering the planet."

"Like you would betray your queendom or mother. She would have your skin."

Sara shrugged. "She would chew me out, but I've been chewed out before. It can be worth it if the cause is just, or the person doing the chewing is the right person. Do you want to be that person? You could put that cut jaw of yours to good use."

Matt wanted to laugh at all of them. He wasn't sure if it was a ploy to get the prince flustered, or real affection. But the woman was shaking the prince up well and truly. The royal didn't look like he knew how to handle the woman's advances.

If she was serious, Matt was impressed with her determination and forwardness. If she really liked the prince, she was pursuing him directly. Whether that would work with the kingdom's seemingly backward morals or not was to be seen, but it was an entertaining sight to behold.

"I would ask you to stop your antics and leave. Against my better judgment, I've already agreed to your proposal if you win the war, and that's the last I'll hear of it until a victor is decided. Remember that I get twelve percent of your income from delving for a year if I win. I would also appreciate it if you stopped encroaching into my kingdom's territory before we begin."

She shrugged and called out to the watching crowd, "Then get better security! We have quite a few unsigned Pathers here. Why don't we have a spar to show them their potential leaders? If you want to win the war, you will have to do better than your current attempts at recruiting. A good fight, best of ten engagements."

The prince laughed. "And let you take the advantage with your higher attacks? No, if we fight, it will be until one surrenders. I won't let you take advantage of your burst damage like that."

"You want to spend more time with me? Perfect!" She clapped her hands together and twirled slightly. "Let's fight then."

The prince looked once again thrown off his plan with her change in tune, but quickly he settled himself.

Matt expected for them to clear an area right there and get to it, but one of the floating platforms moved over. It was a flat grassland with a single tree covered in brown leaves. It had a thick, green trunk that contrasted with the burnt orange hue of the grass.

Even the princess looked at the weird flora of the arena with a cocked head, as it gently landed in the lawn. The prince shook himself out of his trance first, and he climbed to the grassy arena, taking a position on one side of the circle. To Matt's surprise, he was nearly half the size he should be, and the grass came up to his knees.

Is everything here spatially expanded?

The cost seemed extravagant, but Matt paid attention to the prince's armament. He had upgraded from the last time the trio saw him fight. Now, the prince had a blue sword and yellow shield combo that seemed to meld with the armor that grew from his skin like liquid metal.

It wasn't metal though, Matt's AI identified it as the skill stopped forming. [Living Crystal] wasn't bad but wasn't amazing either. Its major downside was that the crystal was brittle, and restricted movement of the caster's body. It had its advantages in that it rendered slashing attacks and most magical attacks all but useless. The skill was essentially relegated to those who couldn't afford better, or those that could either leverage one of its advantages, or negate its downsides.

The prince was clearly in the second category. His Talent was obviously something that made him crystalline. But the odd thing, at least to Matt's mind, was that the man's skill had clearly merged with his Talent. It made him bulkier, but without the rigidity that the skill normally imparted.

Princess Sara hopped into the ring with much less armor than her counterpart. Her arms and shoulders were covered in a heavy armor set, but the rest of her armor was either leather or light mail. Her shoulder pauldrons extended up nearly a foot, and were angled in a way to direct blows over her armored head. Matt took note of them, as he had never seen anything like that in an actual battle before.

It was an interesting combination that seemed to revolve around her lance.

Lances weren't standard foot fighting equipment. It was usually used by mounted attackers, or those with a lot of speed. As the princess didn't have a mount, Matt expected the reality to be the second option, and he was proven correct as soon as the fight started.

Sara launched forward with incredible speed that cut a swath through the oddly colored grass. She bolted in a straight line for the prince.

Her glowing polearm led the way, but the prince simply set himself into a defensive stance, clearly willing to take the attack head-on instead of dodging. His reasoning was proven correct, as when the princess got within fifteen feet of the prince, she reappeared on his right side, momentum intact.

Matt wasn't sure if it was a teleport variation or something more unique, but his AI took note of an important clue. Her current location relative to the prince had maintained a perfectly circular arc when compared to her previous position.

Albert then stepped forward while spinning, with his blade cutting across at Sara's neck level, and his shield reaching over to block the glowing lance.

The sword and lance were both blocked by their wielder's respective armors. Sara's shoulder pauldrons perfectly meshed with her helmet when her arm was extended, and caused Albert's blow to deflect up and over her head. At the same time, her glowing lance was knocked to the side by the prince's shield.

Sara moved through and out of the prince's range, but it was too late for her to completely dodge the [Earth Spike] that Albert created and kicked at her retreating back.

As she passed the fifteen-foot range, Sara vanished, then charged at Albert for a second time. Now, she came directly at the prince from directly ahead. He hadn't expected a frontal assault, so his pivot toward the wrong direction in anticipation was costly. He turned his head to face the princess just in time to watch the glowing lance catch him in the side, testing his skill enhanced skin.

To Matt's surprise, the kingdom's leader was neither cut down, nor pulled out of the ring by the hovering referee. He only had a deep gouge cut from his crystal armor that had slowly begun to heal itself.

This time, Sara moved through the fifteen-foot radius, and kept going until she was fifty feet away.

"Mhmm that's so hot, Albie. No one at my Tier has ever taken one of my attacks so casually." Even under her helmet, she cocked a cheeky grin and asked, "Why won't you marry me? We could do this every day."

"I barely know you!? I'm sure you can find someone else with a strong defense if that's your largest criteria."

"Yeah, but none of them would have your chiseled good looks," the princess replied with a smirk.

The prince now looked cool and collected in the face of the woman who stood outside of his range.

Liz whispered, "Oh, she has him now."

Matt was turning to look at Liz when an explosion rocked the stadium.

As the dust settled, the now soot-blackened prince charged out of a crater with his shield leading the way.

Sara seemed unprepared for this and was unable to create enough distance to effectively use her lance.

Albert wasn't in any better shape, as half of the crystalline armor on his lower half was shattered. It had only just started growing back to cover the exposed skin as he started his charge.

Sara backstepped and cast [Twister], causing a funnel of swirling air to launch at the prince. He paused just long enough for her to pass through the fifteen-foot radius around Albert, and she reappeared at his sword side in another charge.

Their attacks proved ineffective, but neither tried to use more than the skills they had already shown. There were enough aborted movements from both royals to indicate that they were each clearly holding back reserves of skills and abilities.

It was smart, but it caused the fight to stalemate rather quickly, and the referee called it a draw after a few more ineffective engagements.

Neither side looked entirely happy with the outcome, but they weren't upset either. The prince and princess both put on charming smiles and headed back to their respective sides. The princess didn't try to start any other shenanigans, and with that, she was gone.

The battered and soot-covered prince smiled while he called out, "A good fight! Ah, yes, where was I? Mr. Polovesnty, we were talking about what you would gain by joining my faction."

Matt and Liz turned back as Albert was swarmed by green outlined people trying to join the kingdom's side. Apparently, his little showing was more effective than Matt would have guessed.

It didn't escape his notice that Sara had an identical scene around herself on the other side of the landing area.

Matt and Liz returned to their room, and by nightfall, were joined by three other people to round out their squad.

They all sat around in the little common room that linked their five doors into a suite.

The first was a man who looked slightly older than them and had the beginnings of stubble on his face.

He introduced himself, "The name's Conor. I'm peak Tier 6 and twenty-two years old. I primarily tank, with a few special properties that allow me to use [Demon Zone] without hurting myself. I'm a solo Pather, so I'm going to have to change some things up to work with y'all, but I can make it work."

Matt looked closer at the man and nodded, he knew the skill and its limitations, as he was looking at getting it himself back on the training world, but that hadn't panned out yet. It was an incredibly rare Tier 8 skill, since it wasn't valuable enough to farm rifts for.

Liz nodded and said, "We're familiar with the skill, and Matt at least can work inside without issue."

That caused Conor to look closer at Matt. They would need to have a good spar and test each other out. Melee fighters needed to be familiar with one another's fighting styles if they were going to work efficiently in each other's vicinity. The best way to accomplish that, obviously, was a good fight.

Matt looked away and nodded at the next two people who sat close to each other.

They were identical twins. Even Matt's AI had a hard time telling them apart when they left his sight. It didn't help that they purposefully styled themselves in the same fashion, but they took the hint and introduced themselves.

"I'm Emily."

"And I'm Annie."

Emily continued, "I'm a burst mage with mostly water and lightning spells."

Annie went on without missing a beat, "I'm an assassin with invisibility."

Like that, she vanished. Even the indent where her weight pressed down on the couch was gone.

Matt spun and guarded his and Liz's rear, ready to activate [Cracked Phantom Armor] at the slightest indentation of the short carpet.

From behind him, Annie questioned, "What are you doing?"

Matt turned around to see that the woman hadn't moved.

"I half-expected some teleport or [Blink] with a move like that."

The woman looked wistful when she said, "No. I wish. It would be an amazing combination. Sadly, we're just too poor to buy a skill like that."

The other twin, Emily, continued, "We're both peak Tier 6 and twenty-five. We were going to Tier up to 7 early, and keep ahead of the curve, but we held off with this little war. We had the time, and even without the rewards, the combat experience isn't easy to come by."

Matt waved slightly and said, "Matt. Low Tier 6. I have [Hail] as my only real offensive skill. I'm a longsword melee fighter with an armor Talent that lets me take hits a Tier above my own. I also get a strength increase with the skill."

Conor and Annie looked interested, so he flicked his armor on for a moment to give them a look. He was going with the same excuse that he used during the golem fighting, as he was sure that Juni had it registered. There was no need to blow a cover that was already provided for him.

Liz continued, "I'm Liz. Blood mage who can act like most water mages, as I'm sure you already know. Emily, we should see how your lightning works with me. I absorbed some blood iron, so maybe we can do some combination attacks there. I'm good at sustained and long fights, as the more people bleed, the more free blood I get to use. I can take down Tier 7 foes with my skills."

Matt held up Aster, who had walked by him, and introduced her, "This is Aster, my bond, and the third person on our team. She's an arctic fox who uses ice spells. She's just starting to talk, but she's only really at two-word sentences, so cut her some slack. She loves eating ice cream and hearts."

The latter caused everyone to pause slightly, but no one questioned it. He also purposefully didn't say their ages. While Liz was six months older than him, she still wasn't quite nineteen. While not *unheard of,* it was an incredibly fast pace to reach Tier 6 by. They were hoping that little tidbit would be overlooked.

Aster looked around and asked everyone present, "Ice cream? Where? No smell."

The others smiled at that, but Emily asked, "While I don't have a problem with it per se, why are you three in charge? You're weaker than us, and younger by a good margin."

Liz answered that. "Well first, we've been in the kingdom for a while. We came in as a part of the subjugation mission for this planet. That involved fighting in the golem battles when we were Tier 5, and we took both first and second places for our contributions when taking the fortification." She let that settle for a moment before she tacked on, "We were only mid-Tier 5 at that time attacking peak Tier 6 monsters. We're on the Path as well."

The last was added as almost an afterthought, but Matt had to smile at how it caused all of them to re-evaluate their perceptions of the trio. Liz, for all her bitching about high society, had a knack for handling people.

Conor nodded. "That's impressive enough. I won't complain."

Annie asks, "So, you've been here longer. Why choose the kingdom over the queendom?"

Matt shrugged a shoulder casually. "We were already here and actually like Juni, the prince's right-hand man. Also, we wanted to delve in peace during the downtime between the announcement and attack."

They had since confirmed that it was a good call, as anyone who chose to swap sides had been confined to the cities for the duration of the countdown timer. They were stuck there until the neutral city had been built. Matt didn't want to know where they would be if they hadn't had the time off to increase their wealth and strength before the announcement of the war.

Liz checked her watch and said, "We were told that we wouldn't be deployed until tomorrow, but I'd like to get some light sparring and team tactics training in tonight. Nothing crazy, since we don't have a healer. But enough so that when we get started, we don't have to fight together blindly."

No one disagreed, so they went to find a training room, and saw that mostly everyone had the exact same idea. All of the training rooms they came across were already occupied.

The Golem Battalion had been nearly fully staffed with the arrival of the Pathers. It didn't escape anyone's notice that there were no teams consisting of cultivators on the Path and kingdom cultivators together. They were always in separate groups.

They stood around for nearly ten minutes, until Conor asked, "Does anyone know how the challenge areas work?"

Liz caught on faster than Matt and called out, "Brilliant! I challenge you three to a duel."

Matt laughed as their AIs asked for confirmation. When they accepted, they got a notice that a platform would be sent to their location shortly and showed a four-minute timer.

Annie looked at the other man and nodded. "Good thinking. I wouldn't have thought of it on my own."

Conor looked unperturbed. "Saw it in a movie, so I can't take the credit."

They milled around, and to the shock of the other teams nearby, boarded the platform when it descended. They got a marshy swamp area; Matt felt bad for anyone who didn't have a skill to keep out murky water and foul stenches.

The teams who were huddled around the front entrance of the kingdom's building put two and two together as they watched the group of six. As their platform rose, Matt was able to see four more platforms moving in their direction.

Summoning his sword, he began moving forward, only to stop when a hovering woman appeared to ask, "What's the challenge for, and what win conditions do you want?"

Matt quickly said, "We'll be using the platform for round-based three vs. three with team swapping and breaks."

The woman shrugged and vanished while echoing, "Well, let me know when you all are done."

Almost as an afterthought, she added, "Do you care if people can see or watch in?"

Liz quickly added, "We would like our privacy, please. From all but you, of course."

The edge of the area seemed to shimmer in the air like a heat haze. Seeing that they were protected, Liz withdrew her spear and said, "Well, let's test each other out some, shall we?

Matt readied his blade. They had a war to prepare for.

4

Matt flew in formation with his team to their objective. It was a fort, a part of a larger chain of fortifications protecting a mountain chain. They had been called upon at 4 AM their time, but the sun was shining high in the sky where they had teleported to on the planet.

Their side had captured three of the neutral and newly made cities, for a total of five on their side. The other two were under the control of the queendom. Their cities were being flooded with personnel who would staff and defend the city, since the kingdom used them as teleportation platforms.

It was incredibly expensive to do the intra-city teleports, but the kingdom still sent their strike forces through as fast as they could load them onto the platforms.

Their team had been called up not long after they went to bed for the night. Thankfully, as Tier 6s, their need for sleep was lessened compared to the unawakened.

Their advanced scouts had noticed that the queendom was mobilizing forces to these forts. From their mission brief, the kingdom was assuming that the enemy troops were trying to create a chink in the outer layer of the city's defenses. It seemed that they were trying to claim a foothold, so that future operations could be initiated from the base in order to break through the defensive layers. Defending this forward base from the queendom was the kingdom's war AI's decision. They weren't entirely sure why this singular base was being targeted, but their trajectory didn't leave much room for debate.

According to Juni, they needed to move quickly, so they were out on their various flying devices only minutes after being roused from their sleep.

They would need to hold the fort until reinforcements could arrive and take over.

Matt didn't understand why the queendom was trying to take the base without the surrounding area being controlled. Still, from the limited information he had about the ongoing war, it was mostly a game of sending out small token forces to gather control of as much territory as possible.

There were points given to each side depending on the amount of territory they held. The territory's worth was determined by the value of available rifts and natural resources like metals in the controlled area. Both sides were overextended to cover as much land as possible, while also contending with teleportation costs and traditional travel times.

The queendom hadn't advanced very far past capturing the city neighboring the one they had arrived in, but they *did* have to gather their forces from their own territory after all. Their interplanetary teleporters were constantly active to help consolidate their strength. The lack of initial push from the queendom meant that they had less than a quarter of the planet's area under their nominal control to start. The kingdom could have pushed their initial advantage, but it was considered a waste of resources to try and contend with the queendom over the territory directly around their cities.

The attack that Matt's team was intercepting was just part of a larger offensive on the part of the queendom. As an opening move, he felt it was a little lackluster, but he didn't know what their greater plan was.

Even if they took this fort, it was surrounded by other controlled territories, and they had no teleporter to get reinforcements through.

In the end, Matt decided that it didn't matter. They just had to sit on the fort and defend it while earning war contribution points.

They would earn ten apiece for taking and holding the fort, along with an additional point for each hour they held it. It wasn't a large amount, but it was better than nothing, like the team's current point total.

Matt glanced at the map that was overlaid on his vision, and spoke to the team over voice coms. "We're two miles out. I'm going to scout ahead."

His flying sword was the fastest of the group's devices, so he moved ahead through the air and performed a large loop around the fortress. The landscape mainly consisted of scrubland that gave little cover, but he kept half a mile above the ground just in case of a hidden ambush. The sky was clear, which protected him from surprise attacks from above.

Seeing nothing of note, he pushed an all-clear message to his team. He landed in the three-story fort and started to inspect it for any hidden enemies.

He didn't run into any opposition as he cleared empty floor after empty floor. The forts that the army built were barebone stone fortifications and were clearly meant to be filled out later by whichever force took them over.

On the bottom floor, Matt found the item that he was looking for. With a quick scan of the room, he walked over to the head-sized crystal and started to pump mana into it. A few seconds and 1,000 mana later, he pulled his armored hand off the crystal as the base's systems came online. The fort's preliminary shielding and anti-flight formations activated a moment later.

It only took a heartbeat for Matt to get a ping asking if he wanted to claim the base for the kingdom. As he walked to the door, he mentally selected yes and stepped back into the light.

His team landed in the clearing around the fort, and he saw Conor step off his flying carpet. He moved to check the fortification's doors while his carpet rolled itself up and flew into his bag.

Liz and Emily started to climb the tower stairs to get in a position where their ranged attacks would be the most optimal. Annie pulled out a chair and sat behind the parapet, looking out into the open land around them.

Conor was moving to the opposite wall to do the same, so Matt went back inside. After deactivating his armor, he started to get a good charge on the mana reserve built into the fort.

They had been sent with fifty Tier 7 mana stones to charge the fort quickly. That was a Tier 8 mana stone worth of value, but the pile of little crystals had 40,000 mana in total. It always amazed him how much value an increase in Tier could make. From Tier 7 to Tier 8, the mana capacity only increased from 400 mana to 500, but the cost was fifty times larger.

Even with the economics explained to him during his schooling, such an increase felt strange to him. The mana stone value was set from the top down, with the stone's value being more representative of their worth as the Tiers increased.

Matt charged the stone himself and pocketed the money. The job was being done either way, and he felt no guilt in taking the stones for himself. To the kingdom, a single Tier 8 mana stone's value wasn't anything of note, but that was a few nights at a really nice hotel for Matt, Aster, and Liz.

Five minutes later, he exited the fortress and took up his position on the wall. Being the last one out, he got the worst spot of them all. It was built up the side of the mountain, and he had to crane his neck just to observe his section of the wall. Luckily, it wasn't all that bad, as he just leaned his chair against the inside wall to recline.

Not even ten minutes later, a message from Juni came through, asking about their situation. Liz quickly reported in. There was nothing to see, and they were told to sit tight until they were relieved or given other orders.

With little else to do, Matt let his AI use most of his available mana running simulations of their team fighting various opponents or completing random tasks. While his AI worked, he alternated between practicing his mana manipulation and using his Concept to make fields to stand on. The first task was actually going well. While his new mana generation rate was hurting his mana control, he was picking it back up.

On the other hand, using his Concept to will the air to repulse him was nearly nonfunctional. With his weight pressing down on a disk, he just sank through what little resistance he could muster with his Concept. It was like standing on quicksand. It was enough to slow his descending foot, but it wasn't anywhere close to keeping him aloft.

As he continued to practice, he kept most of his attention on the surrounding area in front of his position. Even his AI was analyzing his vision for any anomalies. Two hours later, he was still wrapped up in his distractions when Annie messaged them through their team channel.

"Got something on my side. Scrub grass moved perpendicular to the wind for a moment."

Matt wanted to turn and look but kept his vision on his area instead. He hopped off his chair and changed his position. If there were hidden lurkers, he didn't want to be an easy target for an archer.

Liz's next words gave him a little more detail on the situation. "The one I highlighted?"

"Yeah."

"Okay. We see it."

A second later, and there was a thunderclap that echoed off the mountain cliffs and fortress walls.

Someone jerked in front of Matt, and an arrow slammed into the crenelation beside him. He and everyone else called out variations of "Hidden enemies!"

Matt summoned his sword with a thought and started charging it with mana. As it neared 2,000 mana, he swung his sword forward while activating [Mana Slash]. The crescent-shaped mana attack rushed forward, but dissipated before it could cover the two hundred-foot distance between him and his retreating attacker. He cursed his impulsive use of the skill. If he had used his crossbow, he might have hit his target when their camouflage was disrupted.

Conor asked through their voice chat, "Do we engage?"

Liz answered immediately, "Our orders were to only engage if we thought we had a chance." She paused before continuing, "Besides, they look to be retreating. Let me call in."

During the lull, Matt scanned the area around the rocky outcropping where his attacker had disappeared. He didn't quite fancy fighting in those tight quarters. Flying would be iffy, as the anti-flying formation spread out for nearly half a mile, and unlike the city's formation, this one couldn't tell friend from foe. It was a trade-off for its cheaper operation cost.

After another minute, Liz came back on and said, "We are to pursue and try to capture the attackers. Note that if you do so much damage they would die, they'll get pulled away by the army, and we won't get to question them. Watch out for suicide. That's been a common tactic of theirs to avoid capture."

Matt took over at that point. His AI had been burning mana by the millions since their spars last night. He had run simulation after simulation with their group in every scenario he could think of.

"Annie, go invisible and see what you can find. Watch out for traps to cover their retreat. We'll form up and forge a path behind you."

"I know what to look out for." Her tone wasn't snippy, but it was a good reminder that his team knew their jobs better than he and his AI did. He wasn't too worried for the woman. From what he could glean after their spar, he didn't believe that her Talent was solely invisibility. No matter what she said, [Invisibility] and its lower Tier variants didn't stop water ripples, or weight creating impressions in soft mud.

When they practiced in the sparring yard, the woman didn't leave these, or any other indications of her presence when invisible. No matter what she said though, he didn't buy it. But that was okay. She had the right to her secrets. It wasn't like he didn't lie about his own Talent.

If his AI was right, she could have a cracked skill variant that gave some form of invisibility and intangibility. That, or her Talent did something even more unorthodox, like make her entirely unnoticeable. He didn't think the last option was very likely. When he checked an area she had walked through an hour afterwards, there were still no signs of disturbance.

Either way, she would be fine if she didn't walk into an ambush. That was what took her out in most of his simulations. He didn't have enough data on her ability to detect traps to accurately model her actions. It was an oversight that he intended to correct when they got back to the neutral city. There had been training rooms dedicated specifically for stealth and reconnaissance, and he wouldn't mind picking up some of those skills himself.

The rest of them gathered at the front entrance and unbarred the door. It left them vulnerable, but anyone who wanted to come in after them would need a way to scale the twenty foot wall. Even with their enhanced bodies, jumping that distance was nearly impossible to do without a climbing rope or a ladder.

Either way, it would take time, and they had their orders to sally out.

Annie sent a message ten minutes later that she had found the rendezvous point where their attackers retreated to. It was half a mile away and just outside the no-fly zone. Matt nodded and lowered the locking bar behind his team as they exited the fortress. Running, he climbed the stairs and jumped down from the wall with a crash of dust.

They moved at a pace only made possible through their bodies' enhancement from cultivation. As they neared the location marked by Annie, they slowed and watched the AI updates from their teammate. While it was unlikely that they had the ability to detect the hidden AI frequencies, it wasn't impossible. So, whenever she sent a message she moved to a new location.

Matt was impressed that he didn't need to warn her about that. He hadn't even known it was a thing until his meeting with the Path investigator.

They saw three people with crossbows loading their bags in a hurry and with their flying devices laid out. It didn't look like they would have time to do more than rush in if they wanted a chance to stop the retreating team.

Matt sent a quick attack order to his team and charged forward, while cranking [Mage's Retreat]'s throughput to 50 MPS for its seventy-five percent boost. The team of three all looked at him and froze for a moment. That moment cost them their freedom.

As Matt and Conor charged, the mages attacked the flying devices. It was unlikely that they would destroy them, but it caused the fleeing group to backpedal away from their means of escape. Conor proceeded to tackle a woman to the ground, while Annie appeared from nowhere and threw a rope around the second man's neck.

Matt punched out at the last man, who raised a glowing dagger to defend himself. The man crumpled under the blow to a degree that even Matt cringed at. He *felt* the man's rib bones crumble under the strike. He had checked before he attacked, and felt that the man was Tier 6. He figured that he would have to strike with his full strength for his blow to have any effect. But before he could worry about potentially killing the man, a woman in army fatigues appeared and quickly vanished, along with the downed man.

Matt refused to freeze up from seeing the man get pulled away for medical treatment, so he moved to help Annie restrain her captive.

They struggled for a moment, but the man was taken down after Matt kicked out his knee from behind.

He was much more careful with his power this time, and was sure to only send the man to the floor, instead of whatever hospital the army was using.

Conor had his woman already tied up with her hands and feet restrained behind her, forcing her to arch in an uncomfortable position.

The mages arrived soon after, and Liz started mouthing words, already communicating with someone back at the neutral city or one of the captured cities.

She came back to reality and looked at the two downed captives. "Okay, you have two options. One."

"Fuck you. Just kill us and get it over with."

Liz just nodded while Matt debated the ethics of kicking a captive man. He decided it would be cruel and unusual, but interrupting someone while they were talking was his pet peeve. *Especially* when the someone being interrupted was Liz. Besides, by the look on the man's face, he intended to do it again.

Liz shrugged. "No. We aren't doing that. The kingdom knows your side is doing some sneaky shit, since you have less area to defend and can send out parties like this."

"We won't tell you anything." It was the woman this time.

"Listen to me first, please. If you interrupt me again, I'm breaking something nonvital."

Both prisoners blanched at that, but as the man fixed his mouth to call Liz's bluff, Conor placed his foot lightly on the man's bound hands. That quieted the captive down, and Matt nodded at his teammate.

"We won't kill you. We're going to capture you and hold you for points or prisoner swaps."

She let the realization that their capture would mean weeks or even months out of the fight sink in. Once the desperation started to take hold, Liz offered them a lifeline.

"If you tell us what you know, we're willing to let you go after a few days. If what you tell us is really good, we'll kill you now, and move to try and stop whatever it is your side is planning."

The man cracked first as the woman tried to yell at him to stop.

"They're attacking another fort deeper in the mountains as a diversion as well. I don't know more than that, I swear."

Matt looked at Liz and sent her a message, "He's not lying, but I don't believe it. Seems too easy. Shit, we don't even know other groups' movements."

Liz played along with the two and nodded while driving her spear into their chests lightly. It was recorded as a way to 'kill' someone without needlessly burdening the healers. They would be out of the fight as if they took a spear through the chest, which meant at least two weeks of downtime, but without the cost of healing a massive and deadly wound.

A heartbeat later, they were both grabbed, and their scattered belongings vanished as well.

Matt was about to open his mouth when a series of notifications from the planetary AI appeared in his message window.

Prior Total (last updated 0 days ago): 0 points.

TEAM MERITS:

(Calculated for Tier 6 Combatant).

- Enemy vassal killed, Tier 5. Worth 1 point. Performed 0 times.
- Enemy vassal killed, Tier 6. Worth 5 points. Performed 1 times.
- Enemy vassal killed, Tier 7. Worth 25 points. Performed 0 times.
- Fort defended from attackers. 4 points.
- Enemy vassal captured and interrogated, Tier 6. Worth 8 points. Performed 2 times.

PERSONAL MERITS:

(Calculated for Tier 6 Combatant).

- Enemy vassal killed, Tier 5. Worth 1 point. Performed 0 times.
- Enemy vassal killed, Tier 6. Worth 5 points. Performed 1 times.

- Enemy vassal killed, Tier 7. Worth 25 points. Performed 0 times.

ARMY MERITS:

- Items and equipment looted but returned. Worth 4 points.

UNACHIEVED MERITS: For reference purposes only.

- N/A

SUMMARY OF GAINS:
Team Merits:

- **Raw Total:** 25
- **Team Multiplier:** 1x
- **Category Total:** 25

Personal Merits:

- **Raw Total:** 5
- **Personal Multiplier:** 1x
- **Category Total:** 5

Combined Merits:

- **Sub-Total:** 30
- **Total Multiplier:** 1x
- **Grand Total:** 30

New Gains: 34 points.
New Total: 34 points.
Pather Team Ranking (Kingdom of Seven Suns): 20,781st place.
Estimated Daily Stipend: N/A.

. . .

34 war contribution points wasn't bad, considering they were added to the 10 points received for capturing the fort, along with the additional 3 they earned for guarding it in the meantime.

It was a good start, if Matt said so himself. He also liked that he seemed to be able to double dip with personal achievements and team points.

Annie whistled softly. "Wow. I need to do more covert shit. I got 10 points for discovering the ambush and then another 40 for tracking and discovering the base."

Matt had to agree. It was a nice haul and was 10 points more than what he got in total, most of which he assumed that she got as well.

Liz interrupted their chatting and said, "Juni wants us to push into the mountains and check the other forts, but be wary of traps. He agrees with us. Something is funky here."

Matt used his AI and scanned the area, but neither of them noticed anything that stood out. It wasn't like there would be an obvious spot that said, "Trap here!" In the end, they just decided to fly around and look for obvious changes in the terrain. If they got lucky, they might be able to find enemies on the move.

They all removed their flying devices from their spatial bags and took to the sky without much more talking. They inspected the other unoccupied forts for nearly two hours, and found nothing. The only other kingdom occupied fort in the chain had been attacked, but after wounding two of the defenders, the queendom's troops retreated without trying to take the now lightly defended fort.

Together, the six of them hovered in the air high in the sparse cloud cover, where they were unable to be observed or easily ambushed.

Matt's AI had noted a slight discrepancy in the fort's coverage. It wasn't obvious, as the fort's anti-flying formations weren't active, but the designed overlap had a small gap in it. The space coincided with a valley that was closed off from a landslide on one end. If the formations could pass through rock, they would be covered, but their effects were reduced with physical matter obstructing the Path. Thus, the debris from the landside created a slight gap.

The gap would be obvious when the formations were up and running, but since they were still shut off, none of them would have noticed the discrepancy. It was the best place for a party of ambush troops to be hiding. They had flown past it in a test, but they had seen no evidence of human presence or signs of a hidden base.

Emily said over their voice channel, "The logic checks out. This *is* a good location for a hidden base, but they don't seem to have one set up." Her sister tried to interject, but was punched in the shoulder for her trouble. "And no, I don't think it's a good idea for my sister to scout by herself. We'd be so far away that she would have zero back-up."

Conor nodded along with everything the twin said and added his own two cents. "I think we report in, and strike at the area hard and fast. We should tear the place apart. Either we find an enemy and fight them, or we find nothing. We can always retreat if they have a numbers advantage, and if we find nothing, we won't lose anything but some time."

Matt liked the man's idea, but from how Liz cocked her hip in the air, she didn't agree. As Liz expanded on the ways that it could backfire, he ran the scenario with his AI.

Their impromptu team was strong for their Tier, and the other three had all run Tier 7 rifts easily enough at Tier 6. Unless the base was chocked full of Tier 7s, they should be fine. If the queendom was doing the same thing as the kingdom, they would have broken open their vaults and given each Tier 7 a full kit of weapons and armor at their Tier, with a single Tier 8 item for attack or offense, depending on the person.

While those on the Path of Ascension were unable to partake of the free gear, they all hit above their Tier, so they should be able to handle a kitted out Tier 7 fighter. They would only have problems if they encountered someone who hit above their Tier and was also well equipped. If they fought someone on the level of the princess, they would be distinctly at a disadvantage. There was no rule that said all of the powerful fighters had to be on the Path.

"I think we can do it. The risk is minimal." Seeing that Liz had stopped talking, Matt took his chance to interject. "There is a risk. But it's unlikely that the queendom would send a massive commitment for a small base like this. At worst, we'll face an average Tier 7 overseeing a group of Tier 6s. It's not impossible for us to fight and beat a squad of that caliber."

"There's still a chance that this is a larger play by the queendom.

They don't have as much territory and they aren't as spread out, so they have more wiggle room to send out stronger forces. We could very well fight a full team strong Tier 7s. I don't think it's worth it if we die now. There's a lot of free points to gather in the first few weeks."

Matt didn't really have a counterargument for that. It was risky, but it wasn't guaranteed that they wouldn't run into a situation larger than they could handle.

Matt could overrule her if he wanted to, but he didn't want to do anything that drastic. They had already decided that he was in command of any combat operations. His AI was simply able to process more information than hers at any time, which let him plan fights better. Liz took charge of their interactions with the kingdom and was the official leader.

He looked at her armored form and shrugged, throwing the ball into her court.

Finally, Liz said, "Let's do it, but we have to be careful. We'll fly over first. Then we can go in at a hover. The anti-flying formations aren't active; they don't even reach here anyway. So we should be fine to make a quick getaway, if need be."

With that, they dropped like rocks with the power of their flying devices. Matt kept with his team as they made an arc into the valley.

They did as Liz said and did a slow and careful search of the valley. Finding nothing once again, they moved to search closer to the ground.

They almost finished their sweep when Aster noticed something. Matt only got a warning through their bond, as his fox sent a message to everyone else in their chat.

"Smell human."

They all went on alert, and Annie flew behind a tree. With a thud, she vanished into the sparse trees.

Liz looked over her shoulder and asked, "Where's the scent strongest?"

Aster sniffed around and led them to a tree that looked like any other in the area. At least, that was what Matt thought until he looked closer. The surrounding trees were in the early signs of spring with small buds of green, whereas this one looked to be in the full bloom of summer.

Matt called out at the same time that a hatch in the side of the tree opened with a ringing sound of metal on metal.

Conor dropped to the ground, which kept him from tumbling like the rest of them did when an anti-flight formation activated. Matt landed with a thud, but rolled with the impact and joined Conor in holding the entrance.

The man's [Demon Zone] was a red haze that encompassed the entrance.

Matt mentally ran through the skill description of [Demon Zone]: 5 MPS base cost. A portion of all damage dealt while in the area of effect would reflect back to the damage dealer as physical damage. There was a percent chance for any damage dealt in the area to affect all occupants. No designation of friend or foe. The user would take fifty percent damage from all reflected damage. The skill couldn't be recast for two hours, and channeling time didn't count toward cooldown.

The skill was slamming energy blows against Matt's [Cracked Phantom Armor] as he countered an attack from a woman. She escaped the tree and moved around Conor to flank the two of them.

Matt smiled as what felt like a hammer blow landed on his leg. His armor completely absorbed the damage, but the woman's posture crumpled as the unexpected reflection hit everyone in the zone.

Not willing to let the opportunity go, Matt stabbed forward and took the woman in her lightly armored gut with a thrust. As he withdrew his sword, she was suddenly gone.

Pivoting, Matt moved right beside Conor to help hold the entrance. As much as he hated to admit it, his new melee teammate was a better fighter with more weapons than Matt. He was more skilled with a longsword, but the man was a miracle worker when he used any one-handed weapon with his shield.

Whether it was a mace, a short sword, or anything in between, the man struck with lightning-fast blows. Each had a chance to strike everyone in the aura. The light blows weren't meant to cause any real damage, just to disorientate. Any time [Demon Zone] reflected someone's attack to the queendom's fighters, Conor used [Momentum Strike] to finish off the nearest opponent during the moment of disorientation.

When they sparred, Matt had only been able to hold his own, but without battering the man down with spell cast after spell cast, he had been forced to call it a draw. Unless they were willing to go all out, there was no clear winner in their fights.

It made them an amazing frontline duo. Matt wasn't bothered by the light reflected attacks with [Cracked Phantom Armor], and Conor had never encountered someone who could effectively guard his side with his skill active.

They cut down another two Tier 6s before a larger presence moved up and out of the entrance like a charging bull. Conor retreated and let the man escape the confines of the tree façade.

The Tier 7 tried to turn and attack Conor, but Matt thrust his sword into the man's side, causing him to abort the attack. The armor he was wearing was Tier 7, which meant that Matt's blade was the same Tier, and would be able to pierce the armor.

The man was unwilling to take the blow to land one of his own.

Matt pulled the man away from Conor and engaged the queendom's Tier 7 on his own. He wielded a white-hot war hammer equipped with a glowing blue spike. It also felt heavier than the man to his spiritual sense, indicating that it was a Tier 8 weapon.

Cursing the worst-case scenario, Matt settled in to defend against the man, and looked for an opportunity to finish the fight with a single, decisive blow. It was either that, or batter the man down with a few dozen [Mana Slash]es and [Mana Charge]s.

Liz ducked under a barrage of [Water Bullets] cast from near the top of the tree and thrust her spear into an attacking Tier 6. The man bled an unhealthy amount before he vanished, leaving only more blood to use.

Aster jumped out of her backpack, and before Liz could worry about her, the world went white.

Everything was suddenly flash frozen. From the trees, to the enemies, and the grass. Everything was covered in frost that slowly grew roses.

Chancing a look back, she saw Aster anchored in ice that grew up her legs, while more ice-covered her body in spikes. The nine enemies around them had it much worse than the surroundings. Each was encased in thorny, blooming vines that sapped both life and mana from them. It was a visible process that withered them and all the frozen foliage to nothing.

Emily looked as shocked as Liz felt. She knew that Winter's Embrace was strong, but this was beyond her expectations.

Seeing that her partner was okay and handling the small fry, Liz gathered the blood. She pulled all of it to her. If this was back when she first met Aster, she would have been unable to control frozen blood, but now it was only slightly harder than the liquid variety. It was still blood, after all.

Pulling it together, Liz created a modified version of her blood golem, while Emily fried a group of Tier 6s who tried to attack Aster and her ever-expanding zone of frozen death. The now-empty vines reminded her that for all the blood spilled, no one was dying today.

After Matt had crumpled the Tier 6's chest in a single blow, she had been hesitant to use her full force. She knew he was, too.

Taking a barrage of skills on her heavily armored golem's head, she punched hardened arms and feet into the metal tree and started to climb. It took only a minute for her to reach the screams above her. Once she got to the top of the tree, she found a crudely built palisade disguised as tree branches.

Liz let loose with tendrils of blood that broke bones and spilled more of her red dominion. She was nearly blasted off the tree when a Concept infused [Wind Blade] took her in the side. The man was Tier 7 and had a Tier 8 staff that glowed with light green energy as more wind built up around the staff.

She didn't have time to savor the look of shock on his face as he realized his sneak attack hadn't worked. Infusing her own Concept into her blood, she struck out, intending to swat the man away, but he was pulled away by a force greater than her own.

With the realization that she might have been going a little too hard, she toned it back as she finished off the rest of the mages on top of the tree tower. She was a mage, yes, but in the end, she was building her body more than most mages. She was going with a forty sixty split with magic taking the larger portion, but she got more damage out of building her blood than most. After the addition and upgrade of the Blood Iron, she was debating whether to transition into an even split of essence.

After all, the stronger her body got, the stronger her main weapon was.

Pulling a little blood from her glove, she moved it to the tips of her arms and started to spin her limbs like drills. It only took a minute until she was able to pry off the top of the tree, and she fell into the mass of people still trying to escape from the tree's front entrance.

Annie moved through the forest with her Talent keeping her hidden from everyone.

When she found the back door, she slipped in and carefully weaved through the escaping queendom people.

She was here for information gathering and to assassinate any leaders running the show from inside the hidden base.

It was a shock when she found a teleporter formation built into the floor. There was a pair of Tier 7s standing at a row of pads and talking as they watched the fighting outside. "We need to consider this a loss. Both Adam and Bret were taken out."

The other woman cursed, "Fucking useless. Neither of them lasted more than a minute. Disgraceful."

The first woman shrugged. "This clearly is a very strong Path team. Better to learn about them now than during a more pivotal moment. We now know how strong they are, so we can start planning to counter them."

The second woman spat on the floor but nodded. "Do we pull out with the teleporter, or do we destroy it?"

"Set the bomb, and we'll teleport out before it goes off."

Not liking the sound of that, Annie debated whether she could take the two women. They were Tier 7 and might be able to sense her if she wasn't careful, but she liked the idea of being here when a bomb went off far less.

She took careful, quiet steps before she drove her dagger into the leader's armpit, activating the enchantment at the last moment. She twisted and jerked it out before ducking low and stepping around her victim. As the second woman tried to attack, Annie hip-checked the leader into her path, causing the second woman to stumble slightly.

That was all Annie needed to throw a dagger into the woman's throat. In under four seconds, both women were gone, removed by the unseen referees.

Annie started to download everything on the pads to her AI and took careful scans of the teleporting formation. It might lead to other hidden bases, and that could be worth a boatload of points.

She checked her sister's AI and saw that they were doing fine up top. It was weird to be in a team with others. Annie had expected to have to carry the team, but after their sparring yesterday, she was forced to acknowledge that her new teammates were heavy hitters.

Conor's [Demon Zone] perfectly countered her, which was infuriating in and of itself. If she entered the zone and moved too quickly, he could feel the disturbance. If she attacked him, she would take a blow in return. If the blow was strong enough to kill him, it would probably do the same to her, as she was much less invested in heavy armor and durability. She was working on growing her Talent to counter that, but it was a slow process. If the man wasn't so attractive in his quiet way, she would be even angrier.

Matt, Liz, and the fox, Aster, were another story together. Annie had missed it at first, but Emily had noticed that they were kitted out with growth items. It wouldn't be suspicious if they weren't on the Path, but as it stood, it let her know that at least one of them was lying about their Talent. She had met a seeker before, and they were the only ones able to gather that much wealth while on the Path.

Neither she nor her sister could figure it out, though. Matt's Talent seemed straightforward enough, and its effects were obvious. Blood was rare enough that it seemed unlikely to be Liz, but that just left the cute fox. The problem with that was, with the fox being a beast, she would only have standard racial Talents until Tier 25.

Overall, their best guess was that they had a fourth member at some point, or one that wasn't participating on the frontlines of the war.

She had expected paper tigers who relied on their items to fight, but the trio was as strong as her and her sister were, if their training duel was any indication.

So far, she was happy with how things were going in this little war. She and her sister had a little more than a year before they needed to advance to Tier 7 and stay on the Path. But with these four new teammates, gathering the points needed to slingshot themselves ahead of the Path seemed more of a certainty than a possibility.

They were doing fine as a duo, but they both saw this as an opportunity to gather skills and items that would normally be out of reach for the lower Tiers. The Empire was generous with the rewards for war contribution points. And they intended to leverage those rewards to reach the end of the Path of Ascension.

Matt gave up after the first two exchanges and simply charged up both [Mana Slash] and [Mana Charge]. He let the first strike out in a light blue crescent of mana, before following it up by releasing the stored mana in [Mana Charge] on the Tier 7's gauntleted forearm.

Before he could see how much damage he had done, the man vanished, so Matt moved forward to help Conor once again. The man was still holding the entrance as the masses tried to push through him.

The fighting ended as Liz climbed up the tree tower and cut her way through the metal, and dropped down on their enemies as if she were a blood goddess.

Only a minute later, she called an all-clear, quickly echoed by everyone else. There were no more enemies remaining. They had won.

Not to be disappointed, Matt saw the notifications rain in.

Prior Total (last updated 0 days ago): 34 points.

TEAM MERITS:

(Calculated for Tier 6 Combatant).

- Enemy vassal killed, Tier 5. Worth 1 point. Performed 0 times.
- Enemy vassal killed, Tier 6. Worth 5 points. Performed 30 times.
- Enemy vassal killed, Tier 7. Worth 25 points. Performed 4 times.
- Enemy base captured. Worth 50 points. Performed 1 time.

PERSONAL MERITS:

(Calculated for Tier 6 Combatant).

- Enemy vassal killed, Tier 5. Worth 1 point. Performed 0 times.
- Enemy vassal killed, Tier 6. Worth 5 points. Performed 5 times.
- Enemy vassal killed, Tier 7. Worth 25 points. Performed 1 time.

ARMY MERITS:

- Various information gathered from enemy base. Worth 100 points.
- Items and equipment looted but returned. Worth 87 points.

UNACHIEVED MERITS: For reference purposes only.

- N/A

SUMMARY OF GAINS:

Team Merits:

- **Raw Total:** 300
- **Team Multiplier:** 1x
- **Category Total:** 300

Personal Merits:

- **Raw Total:** 50
- **Personal Multiplier:** 1x
- **Category Total:** 50

Combined Merits:

- **Sub-Total:** 350
- **Total Multiplier:** 1x
- **Grand Total:** 350

New Gains: 537 points.

New Total: 571 points.

Pather Team Ranking (Kingdom of Seven Suns): 12,312nd place.

Estimated Daily Stipend: N/A.

Matt smiled. Now that was what he called a haul. 537 points for the fight, 487 from the team, and 50 from the personal merit. The benefit of double dipping between team and individual points was on display again.

Not bad for half a day's work.

5

Matt kicked his way through the debris while holding a tuckered-out Aster. His bond was exhausted from freezing half of the valley during the fight. He mentally reminded himself to thank Emily personally after this was done. She had protected Aster while a number of enemies tried to rush her.

Her protection lasted long enough for Winter's Embrace to spread and capture a few more enemies, and for Aster to blast away the few that remained free of the ice's grasp. Emily's lightning was twice as strong as it should have been, according to his AI's review of Aster's recording of the fight. It also picked up that the mage always alternated between her water spells and her lightning spells.

It was an oddity, but nothing a Talent or cracked skill couldn't account for.

Either way, he was grateful for her help.

He was currently walking through the hidden base with Liz and refilling their mana reserves with his Concept. When anyone else came too close, he turned it off, but he still had them almost full after ten minutes.

Liz was inspecting her handiwork from the battle when he asked, "Was there anything you didn't wreck?"

She looked profoundly smug when she said, "I didn't mess up the floor."

Matt looked at her blankly while he kicked a fallen metal wall to the side. It revealed four scratch marks in a circle.

It made him pause while he questioned what they reminded him of.

When it hit him, he laughed and asked, "Are you getting a little flighty with your golem form?"

She looked confused, which made him laugh harder. "Do you not even realize what you're doing?"

Liz still looked confused, which pushed him over the edge.

"Liz, your golem form has bird feet."

She flushed hard as she stared between the floor and her feet.

Her spluttering made him laugh all the harder. "I d- d- do not! It's ahh…uhh…someone else! Yeah, it's someone else. It's a good way to keep a grip on a slippery floor! Yeah, that's it."

She tried to stop his laughing by covering his mouth, but it was just too funny. For all the bitching she did about her bird-brained mother, she was slipping into the form unconsciously. He couldn't wait until Tier 15, when she got her beast form. He was already preparing bird jokes to tease her with.

Half an hour later, there was a flurry of activity as forty people descended from the sky in a wave. Juni was one of the first to land. After he saw Matt, he walked over with a sardonic grin and shook Matt's hand.

"You always surprise me, Matt. The oddest things happen around you."

He scratched Aster's head while shaking her paw before moving on to repeat his actions with the rest of Matt's team. For all that Matt was ambivalent to the prince, Juni was charismatic, and knew how to integrate into a group.

Matt followed the man into the underground bunker and watched as the people that came with Juni started plugging into various banks of electronics.

Juni kicked a piece of the fake tree exterior over as he asked, "How did you even find this place?"

Liz took that as her cue and explained everything that happened.

When she was done, he asked, "Can you do an escort mission to the rest of the forts? We need them staffed sooner than later."

Annie moved forward and spoke for the first time, asking, "What are our rewards looking like for this?"

Laughing lightly, Juni shrugged the question off, "We'll see when we plunder this place. I have little doubt the teleporter formation will be next to useless. I'm sure they moved any bases this place was linked to, or at least the ones that we could've gotten intel from."

"So, we should get credit for all of those things, right?" Conor's question caught the prince's right-hand man off guard for a moment.

"That's a fair point. The problem is, we don't know how much that's worth. I can do 500 points but, in the end, it's all speculation. Maybe you stopped the great threat that would have led to the collapse of our entire defenses. Maybe this was just an outpost meant for spies to get into our territory easier. I have limited funds that I can spend and giving your team 3,000 points is already pushing my authority. Once we review everything, maybe I can get you more. The prince has control of the kingdom's wallet, not me."

Matt shrugged; it was a good point. The information was hard to quantify, and they had already made a killing from the points they had earned so far.

Juni continued as he pried open a panel and started shining his light at the innards of the console. "These were your first points earned, right? You should check the marketplace. You should all have at least a thousand points. You can afford some of the cheaper things already, as you're slightly ahead of the pack when it comes to earnings."

"Wait, people have done better than us already? How?" Emily's question mirrored Matt's own thoughts.

Juni pulled back and gave them a funny look. "Your group is about top thirty at best. There's some other Pather, a Tier 5, that rushed the queendom's main city and killed a dozen Tier 7s before he was driven off. Not killed, mind you. Just driven off. Killing two Tiers up gave him 125 points per person. Matt, Liz, Aster, I know you're strong as hell, but there are some *monsters* running around this war."

He slid back under the console after tossing them a small bag, and dismissed them with a simple, "If you want more points, escort the teams to the other forts in the line, please. There are the crystals you'll need. It's the best I can do right now. I wouldn't worry about it too much though. This war isn't expected to last a few months, more like a few years."

They moved out and escorted the teams to the forts throughout the mountain range, and Matt repeated his trick of filling the forts with his mana instead of using the provided mana stones. He always converted one stone so he could scatter some dust around, but that was it.

In between forts, Matt flicked into the Empire War Contribution Points Market.

Now that he had points, he had access to the listings of items in the war version of the Empire Market.

Matt searched through the registry, hoping to get a good feel for what everything was worth. He was surprised to see Tier 8 skills listed for 2,500 points apiece. It seemed expensive, but seeing how generously the Empire gave out points for fighting, they were in reach for most people. Even for Tier 6s, skills were still hard to afford otherwise.

Even growth items were available, though admittedly at 25,000 points instead of the normal 5,000 on the regular Empire Market. Still, Matt could see how it wouldn't be impossible to earn that much over a few months, as the fighting heated up. A single battle had netted them 500 points, and it was a small-scale engagement. If they had to siege a city, Matt could see the numbers increasing massively.

Sorting by cost showed that there were Tier 14 skills available, and Matt contemplated which ones they could use as a team. Liz and Aster were easier to search for than himself, as his mana reserves limited the skills that he could use. The Tier 14 skills mostly had a higher base mana cost that accounted for their greater effects.

He still wanted to get [Flamethrower]. It was a channel spell, and he could imagine just burning everything that came close to him endlessly. Aster would hate it, but he was willing to bribe her to accept it. The Tier 14 skill like most of the higher strata of skills listed were double the points of the Tier 8 skills, which made them expensive but within reach if they did well.

He stumbled upon a seemingly hidden repository of rune crafting made by the Empire crafters for internal use only. It was worth a solid half million points by itself, but it would make his rune-crafting so much easier if he kept it in a partition. It could do anything a Tier 25 enchanter could do with regard to planning rune layouts and utilizing their practical applications. Most guilds had a version of that already, but he expected the Empire's own to be the best.

The repository was the only way to progress past the Tier 5 level that was commonly available. And from its description it wasn't able to be shared with anyone.

One of the most expensive things for sale was [Side Slide], a Tier 14, short-ranged teleport. The skill was so rare, it was more myth than anything else, which explained its one million point cost. If he and Liz didn't have their bonded rings, Matt would be tempted to get it, but the skill didn't do anything that they couldn't already. If they were willing to expose their trump card, that is.

The second most expensive item was the Tier 20 skill, [Cracked Breach]. The Cracked effect drastically reduced the minimum cost for the skill, making it possible for someone even of Tier 6 to utilize it. But the cracking made it impossible to further lower the cost. The original spell was a siege-level spell intended to attack enemy fortifications and batter down shielding.

Its original 500 mana base cost was reduced to 100, but it could then be charged up a hundredfold for added damage. With the Cracked version, which meant it could take up to 10,000 mana for a devastating long range attack.

Matt salivated at the thought of that skill. It seemed perfect for him. The cost of one and a half million war points was prohibitive, but nothing he couldn't handle.

Finally, the most expensive item being sold was a void dragon bond egg for a whopping five million points.

The last listing was a shock, as Matt expected something like that to be used, and not up for sale. A bond egg was always received from a rift as a reward, after all. How would you get something so absurdly rare and choose to sell it?

Not to mention that the price was as absurd as the item itself.

"Liz, is selling an egg like this, okay? I feel like the beast kingdom wouldn't like that." Matt asked his question on a private channel and caught Liz's shrug as she flew in front of him.

"Why would we care?"

"There's a bond in there! What if an asshole gets it? What about the person who found it?"

"An asshole won't get it. I'm sure there's a high-level beast guarding the egg as well. They will vet the prospective owner, I'm sure. Also, if the person who sold it was actually willing to sell it, that means they weren't the right person for the bond. If the person meant to bond with the little dragon is here, they will come across the points needed. There is also no rush to hatch the little lizard. Bonds from rifts can stay in their egg indefinitely without issue."

Matt flew in a daze for a solid minute as he tried to process that ridiculous statement. "Fate? Are you leaving it up to fate? Something that has been proven a million times to *not* exist?"

"These things work out, Matt. Beasts have been doing this longer than the beast kingdom has been around. It's not perfect, but it's pretty good. However, I have no idea why someone wouldn't want a void dragon as a bond. Can you manage the potential of that little lizard?"

Matt still felt the practice was odd but couldn't think of anything better. Someone had to bond the egg for it to hatch, but he still felt selling the unhatched dragon wasn't the most moral thing to do.

He kept quiet as they moved through the forts. It was a small issue, but it bothered him, nonetheless. Liz's blind acceptance of 'what they always did' also rubbed him the wrong way.

Liz, who flew next to him and rubbed his shoulder, said, "Matt, you're thinking about this like a human. I know you care, which is sweet, but think about Aster. What would've happened to her if you didn't advance?"

"She would've..." Matt trailed off as he thought of it, "She would have stayed a normal fox."

"Or she would have left you when her instincts drove her to advance. Giving the egg to someone driven enough to earn such an absurd number of points will ensure that the dragon has a partner able to keep up with its frankly absurd powers. Void beasts are rare and aren't like normally affinitied beasts. Void eats away at everything. When I say everything, I mean it. They need special healing while they're under Tier 15 to keep themselves from burning out from the inside. As long as they advance quickly, they can keep ahead of it. But more than one void user has developed some questionable personality traits from struggling to find an outlet for the destructive forces inside of them. After Tier 15, it's not such a problem, but void affinitied people and beasts pay for that power."

"What about healing?"

"Healing works, for sure. And it's a common enough tactic, but how long can a healer be dedicated to taking care of one person if they refuse to advance and fix their own problem? Maybe the person this little dragon gets paired with is an asshole or something, but at least they'll be strong and able to keep up with their bond. If the person who gets them is on the Path, they'll be given the strongest advantage you can manage."

Only slightly mollified, Matt continued their job of escorting teams to the forts without further complaint.

After they finished up, they flew back to the army-built city to catch the teleporter back to the neutral city. On the way, Liz privately messaged him. "You heard what Juni said about the kingdom's war points, right?"

"Yeah, so?"

"I think we should try and squeeze both vassals for their points."

Matt was interested, so he motioned for her to continue.

"We have a few dozen Tier 5 mana cultivation potions left. But I still have a spatial bag full of the dried ingredients, just waiting for me to make them into something useful. We could sell them with Samuel acting as an intermediary. If we sell them in an auction, it will force both sides to bid for them. They're only good for Tier 5 people, sure, but if one side has them, they would have a stronger base. It would start a bidding war. We could get all the points!"

Matt actually liked the idea. There were quite a few things they could buy that would help their combat effectiveness, if they were clever.

Liz continued, "Did you see the healing skills? There's like thirty cracked healing spells listed. Some are even pretty good. Think what we could do with a healing spell or three."

With a quick thought, he was on the page and saw what Liz was talking about. It was frankly absurd how many different cracked skills there were. Matt had a fleeting image of someone with a pile of healing skills, smacking them one at a time with a hammer, then tossing them away. He shook his head to clear the ludicrous thought away, then looked at the options once again.

[Ranged Heal], the most common healing spell, normally had a base cost of 100 mana, which put it just outside Matt's ability to cast. But at Tier 7, they could have a healing spell in reserve, which would make any future delving much safer. They still had to deal with the healing cooldown from magical healing, but it was better than having to pay for a healer or fighting through injuries in a battle.

Ideally, they would get the less expensive cracked versions, and get a skill shard for each of them, but they were expensive. If they took the [Cracked Ranged Heal] that only healed skin, it would be a waste. Why that was even an option, Matt didn't know. But he guessed that there was probably someone who could use the skill to great effect, somewhere out there.

With the plan set, Liz went to rent out an alchemy room, and Matt found Samuel at an auction house.

When Matt explained their idea, the man looked hesitant, until he took out a vial of the potion for him to inspect.

The man then turned giddy.

Holding the murky potion up to the light, he said, "The auction houses were already kind of planning something like this. They were going to hold a huge auction of goods for the people coming in this week, right after the second wave of Pathers comes in."

He winked at Matt. "Speaking of that, I know you kept back some skills in your little bucket. Have any more you want to sell? I expect things will go for a premium in the first auction."

"We still have some, but I think we want to save them. For now, we're more interested in potions. What do you expect them to sell for?"

Samuel wiggled his hand back and forth. "I'd bet the starting bid goes for at least 100 war points. I'm not really sure. If they were Tier 6, it would be more, but at Tier 5, they're for the fodder troops. They might want to buy with money instead of points as well."

"We don't need the money. We'd like to only sell for points."

"Sorry, Matt. If you want to guarantee that they're sold for points, you need to put them on the market. But there aren't that many Tier 5s in the war. If you spread them out, you can probably get a few more points, but the auction house can't force the vassals to bid with points. A percentage of any bulk items needs to be sold for mana stones."

Samuel shrugged. "How many are you looking to sell? That's really what will have the greatest impact."

Matt wasn't sure but tried to give a best guess. "Maybe two hundred-ish."

"Hmm. Maybe we can work that into an only points sale. If we put a bunch out, maybe fifty, then ration the rest over the next few auctions, we could get them to spend points. You should put at least another fifty on the Empire market itself, though."

Matt dropped off the five potions Liz had with Samuel and left to go join in some team training.

During the next week, they took various small missions, but with the reinforcements of kingdom personnel, the menial tasks like fortifying the thousands of forts had dried up. It was a small income they were sad to see go, but more than one fort had been seized, or at least attempted to be taken, earning points for everyone involved who had survived.

There was more talk of increasing operations, but the news of all the auction houses holding a joint auction derailed any plans that either side had. The leaked items had sent everyone into a tizzy, and no one was willing to risk their points with something like that coming up, so everyone was overly cautious.

Matt and Liz were both peeved that nearly half of the items were ones they had sold to the auction house in bulk previously. They schemed about making their own auction house and putting them all out of business, but their joking quickly fell apart when they started looking into it. There were simply far too many logistical problems to even think about, especially for something so petty as revenge for reselling items that they didn't even care about.

As he was in the gym getting some solo weight work in, his AI pinged him. He was so surprised, he nearly dropped the weight he was benching.

Melinda and her team had arrived. He hadn't been sure that they would come, but the thrill of seeing his friends again after so long sent him running to the shower while sending them a message.

"You guys came? I hope you didn't choose the queendom! Haha!"

Even if they did choose the queendom, it wasn't a big deal, but it would be nice to fight with his friends. Fighting against them could be fun, too, but working with them as comrades was clearly the better option.

Liz was mixing a potion when Matt messaged her that his friends had arrived on the planet to participate in the war, and he set up dinner with them.

"Dinner with Melinda's group. They just arrived. They said they can be ready in half an hour."

"Fuck!" Her surprise caused her to add too much reagent and ruin the potion. She hardly cared about that, but the fact that it caused a bitterly sweet smell to waft over her and the table was a different story. She knew that she wouldn't have time to clean up and still join up with them at the time they set to meet.

Cursing, she quickly scrubbed at the table while throwing her borrowed glassware into the cleaning station. She'd pay a premium for the cleaning, but the Tier 7 mana stone meant much less to her than making sure she made a good impression on Matt's friends.

They were the closest thing to family that he had. They exchanged messages at least once a month, and she was determined to earn their approval.

If they are Matt's friends, that means they could be my *friends.*

The thought caused her to stumble into a table. Aster looked up from her cooling bed with a questioning yip.

"New friends! This is exciting, Aster. People that like me for *me* and not my parents."

Aster curled back up, but Liz didn't give her the chance to nap again. Aster had it easy, and only had to nap on the ice blanket to passively increase her ice aspect, but Liz had no time to let the fox continue to lounge around. She had friends to make.

She ran out of the room with Aster in her arms, only to stop when she passed some glass and saw her reflection.

Her hair was a mess, and she had soot around her eyes.

Checking the time, she cursed again. "Fuck! Matt, why didn't you give me more time?"

She ran to the closest public restroom and scrubbed her face while running wet fingers through her thick unruly hair, before giving up and deciding to braid it when she got in a cab.

Aster just yipped unhelpful advice like, "Relax." And her ever overused pun, "Chill out."

Where she learned that one, Liz didn't know. But anyone who taught the ice fox such a bad joke was on her shit list. The little faker also refused to say it around Matt, which Liz took as a conspiracy against her.

She arrived at their room to catch Matt coming out of the shower and looking at her like she was crazy.

"What's with the rush?"

Liz wanted to scream. "I have two minutes to get ready! That's the rush!"

His eyes flicked back and forth in a motion that she recognized as him thinking, and not using his AI.

"No reason to rush," he carefully replied. "We still have an hour and a half before we meet up with them for dinner. Didn't you see my second message?"

Liz checked her messages and saw a follow-up that arrived not a minute later, saying he pushed it back so everyone had time to settle down.

She kissed his cheek as she ran past and let the relief flow through her. If she wasn't so happy about the extra time to get ready, she would've been pissed that he didn't say all of that in a single message. He let her get all worked up for nothing.

Aster started to struggle as she noticed Liz cranked the hot water all the way up. She didn't have time for a separate bath for the fox, who obviously preferred ice baths.

They were doing this together.

Matt sighed as he avoided the latest disaster caused by the hurricane that a nervous Liz became. He assumed that she would want to get ready, which is why he pushed their dinner reservation back. He also assumed that Melinda's team would need to get settled in with the queendom. He hadn't expected Liz to miss his second message and work herself into a worry.

He picked up her discarded armor that was strewn in a line across the room and started to rub it down. There was a sickly sweet smell coming off it, and he knew she would hate that. Besides, he had little else to do as he waited.

Ten minutes later, Liz and a pouting and wet Aster came out of the bathroom. Aster ran over to him, projecting mental anguish that she had been forced to take a *hot* bath instead of a cold one. Activating [Cracked Phantom Armor], he dried off his sulky bond while complimenting her on how nice her fur looked. That instantly turned her mood around, and she preened as he brushed the water out of her fur.

They were ready an hour later, with Liz in the nicest clothes she had, a newer set of her under armor wear. Matt thought she looked fantastic, but she was worried about the slight wear and tear on the stretchy material.

Her armor was in his bag, along with his presents for them, in case he could talk his friends into a spar. He thought it unlikely, but he wanted to show them how much he had grown, and to test them out. He didn't expect to win, as they had an amazingly balanced team, but it would be like old times, which was enough of a reason for him.

They had chosen to meet up in between the opposing factions' buildings, at the edge of the landing platform. Aster noticed them first, as she jumped out of Matt's arms and rushed toward them through the crowd.

Unlike last time she did that, he wasn't worried. He found her wiggling happily in a tall blonde's arms, while receiving pets from another five people.

He called out, "Hey, guys!" and joined the group hug. He noticed Liz was just standing there, nearly wringing her hand and clearly unsure of what she should be doing.

He pulled back and hooked an arm around her waist and introduced her to everyone present.

"Everyone, this is Liz. Liz, this is Melinda and Mathew." He pointed at the now older couple. Mathew was nearly his own size and seemed bulkier. The man was as wide as a door at his shoulders, with large thighs and calves to even him out. Matt made a note to ask for his workout routine. His calves could use a little work after all.

Continuing his introductions, he pointed in turn to the people on Melinda's right. "This is Sam and Kyle." Kyle looked lean but brimmed with strength. Matt wanted to wrestle the man and see how he fared. With [Mage's Retreat], he thought he might stand a chance, unlike before, when he was turned into a pretzel anytime they fought.

Sam was still shorter than everyone else and smiled as he pointed at her. Her hair was now a vibrant green and cut in a swoosh, with one side longer than the other.

She interrupted, "Is that Angler's Reagent I smell?"

Liz flushed red, but before she could say anything, Sam continued, "I hate working with it. One drop spilled, and you smell for days."

"Oh, you practice alchemy as well? We'll have to chat about it." That point of familiarity seemed to set Liz at ease, so he continued to the last two people in Melinda's team.

"The last two are Tara and Vinnie." Tara was still as thin and lean as she had been in the PlayPen, but Vinnie had slimmed down a little into a more whipcord build.

They looked good and healthy.

There was a wave of relief that washed over him, as he was able to see that they were okay in person. Just the occasional message wasn't enough.

"Come on. I reserved a table for us to have dinner. Let's go."

He quickly called over a taxi and flew them to one of the nicest restaurants in town that wasn't catering to the immortals.

When they stepped into the flying car, Melinda said while holding Mathew's arm, "Matt, you look really good. Too good, really."

Seeing his confused look, she quickly clarified, "I can see damage done to people with my Concept. It's like monsters made of dark mist. The only people who don't have it are those who are Tier 15 or higher. You look like you're halfway broken through. It's weird. I can't really explain it."

Matt laughed. "We met up with a seeker who pointed us to a Tree of Perfection after we helped him out a little. It brings a single aspect of your body to Tier 15, or nearly so. I ate the body root. I guess you're seeing that."

"That makes sense. Let me heal all of you, though."

Liz protested, "Oh, there's no reason to waste your mana like that."

Melinda shrugged and cast her spell twice at them, and then onto Aster, who was sprawled over her, Sam, and Tara's laps. Her thoughts were on her time as a kit and getting pets and affection from them at the PlayPen. She was in a state of mental bliss that bled over into Matt's own feelings.

"I'm happy to help. It'll make sure you don't have anything wrong lingering with you. I don't see anything, but a heal a day will keep sickness away."

That caused all the girls to start chatting, so Matt slid over to Mathew and asked, "So, what *are* you doing for your calves? Whatever it is, I need to start doing it, too."

After that, they launched into descriptions of their various workout routines. Their chatting lasted until they reached the restaurant, and Melinda immediately began protesting.

"Matt, we can't afford this place."

He shrugged her concern off. "I'm paying. And it's only one dinner. We made more in the last few months here than you can imagine."

When Sam looked to protest, Liz said, "We sold more than one growth item while we were at Tier 5. Let us treat you to a nice dinner. Shame my Aunt isn't here. Now *that* would be a good dinner."

Tara seemingly teleported next to Liz and nearly shouted, "I'm gonna marry her!"

While he and Liz looked at her in confusion, the rest of their group groaned. Melinda grabbed the archer's arm and started to drag her along.

"Ignore her. She's delusional."

Tara protested as she was dragged to the door. "I'm not! Really, I'm not. She's amazing and I'll marry her one day!"

Matt thought the idea was ludicrous, but Liz looked amused. "You're going to have your work cut out for you. Aunt Helen's list of suitors probably spans the known…well, everywhere. She's broken a lot of hearts over the ages with unreciprocated feelings, and I'm pretty sure she's accidentally started a war at least once."

Hearing Liz's comment, Tara looked even more determined, and seemed like she wanted to argue her case. Liz continued, "But go ahead and try. Maybe you'll be the one. How did you guys meet her, though?"

That caused their procession to stop again halfway through the door, but Kyle, who was in the front, grabbed Melinda and dragged her forward, bringing in half of their group. When they were seated, Melinda thanked them.

"As I was trying to say, thank you for the shard. It got everyone else on the right track to discovering their Concepts. I don't know how to repay you."

When he and Liz went to protest, she held up a hand and stopped them. "This is massive for us. It's not a small trinket, but my family's ticket to immortality. Not everyone can take that first step, and they eventually die. I just fell into mine without knowing what I was doing, and how much it would separate myself from them. Just…thanks."

Vinnie smiled and said, "I was the first to get my phrase. These dummies took a lot longer."

"It was a day before the rest of us, which was over a year behind Melinda you rube." Sam's comment cut Vinnie down, and in the group's usual theatrics, he fell over and started to smother her.

Their waiter came over, and when they didn't order enough, Matt just ordered the larger party platters in addition to their meals. When they protested, he repeated his earlier statement.

Liz activated her earring, which gave them privacy and made it so the entire table was covered.

Once they weren't in danger of being overheard, Matt reached into his bag and withdrew the two growth items he had saved for Melinda's team.

"I'm glad I didn't send these to you the slow way. Otherwise, they might have missed you."

Tara looked at the quiver and asked, "I can always use a new quiver, but this feels weird. What does it do? Also, thank you."

Trying to not let the smugness and pride creep into his voice, he said, "I'm proud to give you both growth items that are perfectly suited to each of you."

Vinnie nearly dropped his bracelet as Matt said that.

"Man, this is too much. I can't afford this."

"It's no big deal. I wasn't joking when I said we pulled more than one growth item."

He and Tara pushed the items across the table in unison. Tara said, "It's too much, really. You should sell them and propel your team to greater power. Buy some more skills or something."

Matt rolled his eyes, trying to downplay the gifts. "Guys, at least hear what they do first."

Tara looked longingly at the quiver and said, "No, don't do that! It will hurt even more knowing."

"Okay. Think about it for a minute. You guys know what my Tier 1 Talent does. Have you ever checked my Tier 3 Talent?"

The murmur of yes was universal, but no one seemed to understand, and he could see everyone checking their AIs. Mathew whistled, saying, "Same as last time. It's impressive as all hell, but I don't get it."

"How are rifts made and powered?"

It took a moment, and he felt a mix of pride and satisfaction at the looks of incredulity on the group's faces as they pieced together what he meant.

"So, you can just…" Sam waved a hand around, pointing at the pair of growth items.

"Yup!"

"And it's just that easy?" Kyle didn't seem like he believed Matt for a minute.

"Yup!"

"That's amazing…" Melinda trailed off, but it was broken as Tara and Vinnie lunged for their items in unison.

"Okay, what do they do? I need to knooow!"

Matt laughed. Giving presents like this was addicting. Seeing how happy they were made him tingle in a way he had never felt before.

He pointed at Vinnie "That bracelet increases the range of all earth skills cast while wearing it."

Vinnie nearly fumbled it as he slipped the metal and rope band around his hand. It cinched down as it was bound to him with a perfect fit.

Tara hugged her quiver and gave him puppy dog eyes.

"That"—he pointed to her and as she nodded rapidly. He drew out his silence, and as she looked to be ready to vibrate out of her seat, he finally continued—"is a quiver that acts like a spatial item, and it can also create arrows over time. It also enchants them if the arrows remain in the quiver while it gets fed mana. I thought it was perfect for your style."

Tara started bouncing around and lunged over the table, knocking over two thankfully empty cups in the process.

"Oh, thank you! Thank you! It is perfect! I love it."

The others looked happy for their friends and didn't have the least bit of displeasure on their faces, which only reaffirmed to Matt that they were good people.

To finish it off, he brought out their bucket of skills.

"We also got a ton of skills if you want something. It's mostly the ordinary ones, but a few might help. Take and trade anything if you want. We already kept what we wanted."

Mathew smiled and clapped Matt on his shoulder. "You sure know how to give wedding presents!"

"Wait, you guys got *married*?"

6

Matt was surprised that his friends had gotten married, but their clear happiness was enough for him. He was slightly jealous and had to make a conscious effort not to look at Liz. Marriage was a nice thought, if a little scary.

Melinda stuttered, "Matt, this is too much. It's…it's…"

Her voice trailed off as he shrugged his indifference. It really was nothing to him.

"Guys, take what you want. We already sold a bunch to the auction house. We don't really need them. These are just the more basic ones that we kept around to perform more rift experiments on when we got the chance."

Seeing their confusion, he explained, "Rift making isn't just throwing mana into an area. Well, it is, but we learned that you can put stuff inside and use aspected mana to influence the rift and its rewards."

Looking for an example, he pointed at Tara's quiver. "We made that by using wind mana and putting a bow and arrow set into the area where we created the rift."

Liz poked him and said, "You're getting a bit loud, Matt."

Matt grinned in slight embarrassment and, after checking his volume, said, "But, yeah, we learned a lot while we were able to experiment. Got a lot of items and money from it. Even skills."

Liz added with a wry smile as she leaned into him, "And investigated for cheating."

He enjoyed the little spike of fear that crossed his friends' faces. It was what he felt in the moment, but now, after everything was fine, it was more funny than scary.

Kyle blurted out, "Wait, what?"

Matt waved it off. "Oh, it was scary as hell at the time, but we got access to the Empire Market. It's like the contribution point market for the war, but with a seemingly more universal currency. You can buy some amazing things. The investigator was reasonable and heard us out."

He was going to explain more, but the air bubble popped as their waiter came in with two massive trays of food. He let the matter drop for now.

It smelled divine, and for its absurd price it had better taste as good as it smelled. It still stung to spend this much money, but he consoled himself with reminders that it was a special occasion and kept the pain of his slightly lighter wallet off his face.

As the meal progressed, he started to rehash the adventures that he had been through with Liz and Aster. Most were things that they knew already, since he had shared stories in their messages back and forth, but it was more fun to share in person. It was really nice to hear about how simple and calm their lives had been. It was fun to see the other side of being on the Path.

As dinner wound down, with most of the plates only half-cleared, he suggested they move to a park and continue the talk there. He had seen the waiter pass by twice, and the restaurant was full. He didn't want to hog the table when they could talk long into the night in the nice city air, without bothering anyone else.

They chatted well into the night, and as it was winding down, Melinda stretched with an exaggerated sigh. Her party seemed to take their cue, as they started getting ready to go.

Matt said, "We should spar tomorrow morning. Like old times. It would be great to see how you have all grown."

Melinda smiled. "We'll spank you around like we did at Tier 3."

He waggled his eyebrows and said, "Ah, but I was only Tier 2 then." In an overly pompous voice, he said, "We are now the same Tier. Now, I have the power to defeat you!"

As they said good night one final time, he smiled while thinking about how good it was to see someone from home. It had been so long, and they had all grown so much.

Aster was nearly asleep when he picked her up, and he walked arm in arm back to their room with Liz. She leaned on his shoulder as they walked back.

When they were halfway there, she said, "Your friends seem really nice."

Matt resisted the urge to fist pump the air. He had been trying to make sure Liz was included in the conversations throughout dinner, but once he saw her talking to Sam about alchemy, he stopped paying attention.

He was unable to prevent his excitement from coming out in his voice. "You like them? Really?"

He had to make sure but felt confident that he would get a good answer.

"Yes, they seem kind and intelligent. They also treated me like one of their own, which was AMAZING!"

She shouted the last bit, which caused Aster to kick in her sleep. Matt felt like he was on cloud nine as he floated down the sidewalk. Things were looking up in the best way possible.

Liz wasn't sure that sparring was the best idea for friends that hadn't seen each other in years, but with how casual they all seemed, she didn't say anything.

She was just hanging back as they all talked, watching them. They all seemed so happy. Sam even made sure to smile at her as the others got ready to board the fighting platform.

The woman was knowledgeable with alchemy, and Liz wanted to collaborate with her to use the leftovers she had from the herb rift that Matt had made for her to practice with.

She was debating how to best ask the woman, when someone appeared next to the referee and shooed him off.

That oddity caused Liz to instantly go on alert.

The unknown man said, "I'll be refereeing this match."

Matt looked irritated when he asked, "And you are?"

His attitude matched Liz's own. She didn't like unexpected occurrences like this. Something was off, and she could smell it.

Liz barked out, nearly at the same time, "What authority do you have to do that?"

The man seemed un-bothered and calmly answered, "I'm Baxter. Over Tier 40 and a healer in the employ of the Emperor. I can keep any secrets you might reveal in a fight just that. A secret."

Liz was about to start screaming and sending messages at the blatant lie. The Emperor had only one personal healer, not the multitudes that this man implied, and she knew the Emperor's healers. He was *her* healer growing up.

This young man was *not* the Harvest Moon. Moon was old and wrinkly. She only knew him from her time in the palace, which wasn't an extensive period of time, but she had spent a few weeks visiting Uncle Manny now and then. She had met and interacted with Moon enough to know that this wasn't him.

As she was creating a message to call for help, she received a message from her Moon, "I'm undercover, so don't blow it for me."

Liz paused. It sounded like the Moon she knew, and faking messages was incredibly difficult. A quick check showed that the ID matched her Moon's old ID, so she sent him a testing question.

"How many times did I break my arm, and how many times did *you* heal me?"

The man's lip twitched as he replied, "You broke your leg twice falling from the same roof trying to fly, once with a bedsheet after the first attempt without one failed. And you landed in my garden in the imperial palace. *Twice*. Don't try and test *me* child."

Liz swore she caught the slightest glimpse of a wink as she finished reading his message.

She smiled at the memory. She'd thought that if mom was a bird, then she should be able to fly as well. When the first attempt hadn't worked, she realized that she didn't have wings, and that *had* to be the problem. So, she grabbed a bed sheet to make the jump a second time. Her logic at three years old was flawless.

Moon was one of the few who knew that she had broken her leg trying to fly. Uncle Manny and her parents knew, but no one else. While he could still be a fraud, albeit one with a good information source, she found it highly unlikely.

His voice messages sounded right, and she trusted the little test she had done.

She said out loud for the benefit of the others, "Oh, okay. That's fine."

Liz was unable to stop the grin that crept onto her face.

Moon, or *Baxter*, she corrected herself, glared at her. She sent him on the side, "I'll have dad flood your garden if you're mean to me."

His lip twitched for a second time. But he didn't rise to the bait and instead asked her, "Now that you know who I am, convince your friend that I need him to do what I asked."

Matt laughed as he said something to his friends that she missed while talking to Baxter, but Liz messaged her teammate, "You can trust him."

He paused and looked at Baxter questioningly with a raised eyebrow.

Liz shrugged and sent another message, "Don't tell anyone else, but that really is one of the Emperor's personal healers undercover, don't tell anyone else who wasn't here. But you can trust him."

It was a long moment later that he seemed to reluctantly nod, glancing at Liz.

Taking her spot off to the side with Aster, she waved the fox's paw at everyone and called out, "Have fun!"

She watched as Matt exploded forward while casting [Hail] and shooting at one of his friends with his crossbow. The crossbow golem arm had taken up Matt's free time while he tinkered over the last week, and he was as proud as her mother after a molt with his new toy.

They intended to sell them at the auction, but they were going to hold off until after he used them in combat at least once. They wanted to show their creations' value to the queendom and start a bidding war as the kingdom, more specifically Juni and the prince would already know their potential.

Matt had snatched a few dozen of the arms. But, apparently, it wasn't easy to modify them for human use while keeping their enchantments whole. Still, he had figured it out after some tinkering.

Liz was surprised when her partner ran Mathew through with his sword and started to shout at Matt for taking it too far, only to find that she was in a Concept bubble. She raged at Moon through the soundproof wall of will. She tried to resist it with her own Concept, but she only got a headache for her efforts.

If she knew this was what he wanted from Matt, she wouldn't have agreed to push Matt into it. It also explained why he looked so unsure.

Seeing that she had no way to stop this shit show, she forced herself to calm down, and watched as Matt decimated his friends.

She cursed again at the healing downtime he was causing as he slaughtered his way through them.

Liz would have been impressed with how strong Matt was, but the stomping seemed to be more from a lack of coordination and training on her new friends' part.

A simple [Hail] was able to shut down their archer, Tara, for nearly the whole fight, and Sam couldn't even pierce Matt's armor with her dagger. She knew that [Cracked Phantom Armor] was strong, but that result fell far below her expectations. Matt had talked them and their achievements up all night. She expected to see Matt get slapped around, not to watch him toy with them.

And toy with them he did. She saw it as he fought with Sam and Kyle. Why Kyle used a ridiculous metal slab to fight, she didn't know. It looked incredibly unwieldy, even though he seemed to handle the weight better than she would have been able to.

She knew of other fighters that used massive swords like that, but not without a flight skill or a Concept to anchor yourself. The counter forces were needed to swing that much weight around, which meant it was an ineffective style until the later Tiers.

Matt took much longer to take down the duo than she expected, going by his earlier performance. He could have ended it with the skills enchanted into his blade with two swipes.

As he chased down Tara, Liz got her first and only surprise. Tara could injure him, which was impressive in and of itself, as he could nearly handle Tier 7 attacks at Tier 5. Now that he was Tier 6, she didn't expect a Tier 6 to be able to punch through his armor.

She noted Tara as the strongest on the team.

When the fight ended, she ran out and kicked Matt in the butt and Baxter in the shin.

"What the fuck!? You seriously injured them!" The redhead turned to Baxter and yelled, "And you! What the fuck as well!? You shouldn't have let them get limbs cut off. They'll be out of commission for weeks with that healing downtime! How amateurish are you? You should know better! Idiot."

She had already cemented the idea of burning down his garden the first chance she got in her brain. This was incredibly unprofessional of him. Melinda's entire team would be out of the fight for weeks, even after Baxter healed them.

Melinda stepped forward and placatingly said, "Don't worry, my Talent gives all healing spells I cast Overhealth. We'll be fine."

Liz paused and recalled what Matt had said about his friends and Manny. One of them had a Talent that he wanted enough to message them at their PlayPen. She was unable to keep her face straight when thinking over just what that Talent was.

A Talent that gave every healing skill Overhealth both explained his personal interest, and explained his sending the top healer for what she assumed was a mentorship for Melinda.

Overhealth was just too useful, and being able to cast every spell with it was unheard of. She was sure Manny was watching Melinda with a hawk's eye. He probably updated his copy of her Talent every time she Tiered-up.

Liz hesitated for a moment after she broke out of her trance. She debated telling them about her parents, but a small part of her was afraid that they would see her differently. She only had a single night of them treating her as a friend and didn't want to give that up so soon.

It wasn't fair to withhold that information after a revelation like Melinda's, but the fear kept her mouth shut about her parents. She was mad at both herself and Moon. She glared at him- it was a lot easier than self-reflection, after all.

He couldn't have told her about his plan, but he could have told her not to worry.

"Matt's friends are the perfect team on paper. They have all the traditional rift delving roles, but with Melinda's Talent, they've been coasting and wasting their potential. They needed a wake-up call, which is what I asked Matt to do. I also asked him to play it up. I have to say, you found an amazing friend there. I assumed from the giant 'Do not touch' on your profiles that he was strong, but even I'm surprised."

His message was written in a calming tone that didn't register with her. Liz also didn't let Moon's praise of her Matt distract her.

She could be proud of him later. She snapped back, "What if they hate him now? That's not okay!"

"They won't. I made sure to steer the conversation in a way about how they could be better. And from what I overheard, it worked."

Matt looked hesitant as they asked for a rematch.

Liz moved back to the side and watched a repeat of the last fight. Matt bounced an arrow off the ground to hit Vinnie, who hid behind a raised slab of earth to protect his torso. After the only person who could trap him was gone, this bout was handled as quickly as the previous one.

Baxter then nodded to Liz and sent over a message. "I need you to hammer it home that they need to work hard. One fight, please, and I'll leave you all to train or do whatever."

Liz gave Aster to a sheepish Matt and took the field.

Their armor had rents and blood splattered over it, but their flesh was perfectly intact. Liz understood how they could be so mediocre while staying so far ahead of The Curve.

Melinda's Talent was absurd on so many levels. She knew all about Overhealth and just how rare and powerful the Talent was.

Liz closed her eyes for a moment and calmed her mind. She would repay them for what she was about to do after their fight. She could see the hope in their eyes. They thought Matt was the exception, and the team's heavy hitter.

They were wrong.

If they were to learn and grow, she needed to show them there was more power at Tier 6 than they currently possessed.

She opened her eyes as the countdown hit zero and reached into her glove. The well of blood was like a pool, and she withdrew it all in a wave.

The initial surge of liquid deflected the first arrow that Tara launched, and she flowed with it as she pushed the blood and herself forward. She quickly washed over Mathew and directed the blood to slit his throat with a gentle hand.

He was gone before she cut more than half an inch, which she was grateful for. She would have been pissed at Moon if he forced her to truly hurt them.

More arrows tried to punch through her iron-reinforced blood, but with a thought, she formed her blood into a more humanoid form and cast five [Blood Bullets] at the remaining members of the team. She didn't hesitate and followed it up with five [Blood Spear]s aimed where she expected each of them to dodge.

Between the two attacks, they were all 'dead' and teleported out less than fifteen seconds after the start of the bout.

She withdrew all of her blood back into her glove and stood there in the silence. No one said anything until Baxter announced that he would let them train privately.

Hopefully, that didn't discourage them.

Melinda called out with what Liz interpreted as grim determination to do something she already knew the outcome of.

"We need to fight Aster as well."

Aster looked confused, but after Matt whispered something to her, she scampered onto the field.

When the countdown hit zero, she jumped up and forward, calling ice down in front of her. She copied Matt's use of [Hail] to block Tara's arrows. Taking advantage of her small form and agility, she worked her way into the center of their formation. When she reached the center, there was a flash of frost as the entire team was frozen solid, entombed by the thorny vines. Roses bloomed as life was drained from them. It was a beautiful sight.

They were out of the ice and moping off to the side as Aster ran over and tried to bring their mood up with her usual antics.

Matt joined Liz and quietly asked, "You don't mind helping them, do you?"

She glared at him but softened her gaze. He wasn't the one who she was angry with, and that particular individual had vanished at the first sight of the fight concluding. She was sure that he was lurking around somewhere, but she would never be able to find him if he wanted to stay hidden.

Liz marched over and was met by a very stern-looking Melinda.

She spoke before Liz could, "We suck compared to you."

Liz didn't want to agree, as that would be in terrible taste, but it was true.

"We got this way by pushing ourselves and training."

Matt picked up where she ended without a pause. "And we can help. We can spar without worrying about injury or mana cost."

Liz inspected Melinda's team's faces and internally sighed as Mathew stood up first. He said, "This is a good thing. We found a weakness and a perfect opportunity to correct it. This war won't be short, so as long as we try and get better when we have free time, we can fix it."

He looked awkward as he asked, "I don't want to presume, but we can spar after this, right?"

Liz gave him her gentlest smile as she said, "What are friends for if not helping each other?"

Luna watched her charges spar with a list of a million suggestions and critiques. She was momentarily impressed with Matt's use of his Concept. He hadn't practiced that in combat yet.

But then, the drive to improve her charges took over, and she started noting the flaws in his usage of his abilities. Moonie told him to play with them, so she didn't note how he extended the fight, but he could have been smoother about it.

Cleaner.

Her other hand wrote down a laundry list of what the other team could work on. They needed help, and the need to help them fulfill their potential ate at her.

It was only her long practice in controlling her compulsions that allowed her to hold herself back from rushing down and forcing them to be better.

As the final fight ended, she paused, hearing what Liz said.

"What good are friends for if not helping each other?"

She paused her pens and stopped writing for a moment. Harvest entered her sphere of influence and sat next to her quietly, letting her enjoy a moment of calm.

They were old friends, and he knew her well enough to enjoy a rare moment of peace together.

She ground out, "Are you going to be taking their manager position?"

"If they make it to Tier 10, maybe. Where's the rest of your team?"

"Kurt and the new girl are taking a break."

Luna shook her head. She had to resist the urge to change into beast form. The healer next to her radiated the same feeling that moons gave off, and she was named for her love of that feeling.

She had lost her bond, Nora, to old age from not advancing quickly enough and not pushing herself. It was what drove her to make sure others met their potential.

With an effort of will, she stopped herself from retreating to the past and focused forward.

She *needed* to prevent others from making the same mistake that she and Nora had. That was why she pushed her teams so hard. Nora had died from not having a Concept, and not being able to break into Tier 15. When she first started in this career, it was enough to stay sane. But as she advanced to better teams, it was no longer enough to quiet the caged animal inside that demanded everyone's best efforts.

No, she needed them to push harder and faster. The better they were, the more they could advance, and the stronger they could become.

Seeing wasted potential was like being stabbed, and watching the little healer's team was like being shredded. The waste of potential was *that* bad. They had so much to offer, but they threw it away like it was worth nothing.

Little did they know, it was worth everything and more.

She was mollified slightly by the fact that her team was taking the initiative to help, and that the healer's team was also trying to correct their mistake. Friends were the only thing that kept you going after becoming immortal, and too many people lost theirs along the way. Too many were too engrossed with themselves to look outwards. She was happy that her charges were willing to help.

She looked at Harvest and said, "You look stupidly young."

He rolled his eyes. "It's too much effort to change back and forth. Deal with it."

It was difficult for him to just change how old he looked? The man was Tier 47! Making cosmetic alterations to his body should have been as easy as breathing. Possibly easier, if he actually breathed anymore. Luna idly contemplated a few body modification exercises that he might benefit from, before settling on a set that the man would *most* benefit from.

When she handed him the paper, he just looked at it for a moment, and in a flash of moonlight it was gone. He gave her the finger and said, "You're obsessive."

She didn't have a retort for that one.

They watched as the children started to spar while getting corrections from Matt and Liz. Their corrections weren't perfect, but Melinda's team didn't need perfection. She could see the mix of embarrassment and anger driving them and made a note to check if they continued to push forward. She had to know if they would make the improvements she thought they could.

"She's going to change warfare for the Empire, isn't she?"

He sighed next to her. "She has that potential. More than we did."

Luna thought about that. She had created thousands of powerhouses, and he had forced the other Great Powers into a new agreement about healing stations after his was attacked. He slaughtered the attacking army in a single night during the planet's autumnal equinox. It was where he got his moniker from.

Harvest Moon was more literal than most realized.

"I hope this little wakeup call works as intended. She has an incredibly useful Concept that she refuses to use as well. I just hope she can use this to grow."

Luna moved them forward until she was in the blonde's face. She inspected her with both her spiritual sense and eyes.

"She looks driven. At least right now she does. We'll see if they can keep it up. War is coming, and she could be of use."

Harvest looked at her and bumped her shoulder. "Your new ones are just as impressive. Maybe more so. I can see an *endless* list of things that his Talent could be used for, if it works how I think it does. Even the non-combat potential is wild."

She ignored his bad attempt at a pun and moved them back to a higher vantage point.

"He could be great. I intend to make sure he lives up to it."

"Have you told Mara and Leon that you're managing their daughter?"

That caused her to laugh. "The airheads have been avoiding me after I critiqued their play fighting when it moved over my house. It covered my sun bathing spot so I went up there and put a stop to it. I made Mara act as my heat lamp for a week. Apparently, it brought back bad memories of their time under my tutelage, and they've avoided me ever since."

She smiled at that. She was proud of her work with the duo. She was proud of what she had molded them into. Their daughter looked to be everything they were and more. Where they had amazing combat potential, despite their conflicting affinities, they had little room in their heads for anything serious.

Their daughter was both strong, and a thinker.

Luna intended to rub that into her once protegees' and now friends' faces.

She turned into her cat form and curled up under Harvest's aura. Seeing friends help each other was enough to calm the raging desire long enough to get to sleep.

Sleep was so rare for her, but she cherished it. When she slept, she dreamt, and when she had dreams, she had Nora.

Matt moved around Kyle's slash and slapped the flat of his blade into his inner thigh. Kyle didn't yelp, and instead tried to hit Matt with an aggressive backswing.

They were sparring and working on his style, as Matt was the only one who could match his pure strength.

He still felt bad for what he had done to them and had apologized to each of them. None of them seemed angry at him, but more so with themselves.

It also put their progress in another light for him. They had stalled, and while they were ahead of him in cultivation slightly, they should already be fighting like Tier 7s with their Talents. He knew it wasn't fair when you considered that they had limited mana to spend on delving, but they should have been able to fight up a Tier if they worked on their combat prowess.

Their fight had opened his eyes to the harsh reality. When he started the duel, he expected a challenging fight where he struggled to hold his own. When his starting crossbow shot and [Hail] took both

Vinnie and Tara out of the fight, he was surprised that they didn't expect a quick opening.

When he was able to lift Mathew off his feet to negate the man's Talent and run him through, he was disappointed.

As Melinda stood there frozen, he understood what Baxter wanted from him.

He hadn't really believed the man when he said that they needed a wakeup call and had only done it because Liz had vouched for the man. While Baxter hadn't said it, Matt expected that he was filling in for the same thing as his own still forming management team and was trying to push them.

So, he tried to show them exactly how far behind the power curve they truly were. He toyed with Sam, Kyle, and Tara. He hadn't liked playing it up; in fact, he hated it. But he had hoped that it would drive the point home.

He hadn't even needed to use his AI to predict their moves, as they didn't vary off the most obvious choices. After the first few exchanges, he turned it off and found that it didn't hamper him at all.

Thankfully, they seemed to have learned their lesson, and were trying to improve. The team had taken the initiative to share their Talents and skills with Liz, who did the same. She was as shocked as he was at how well-rounded they were while being so weak.

They agreed that Melinda's team should, in theory, be beating them more often than not. They had so much utility and damage to leverage. They simply relied too heavily on their cultivation and Melinda's healing. They had the essence, but not the experience.

Matt was determined to help them advance. He contrasted the team that worked so hard in the PlayPen with the team that was unable to do anything against his own. He saw the hurt looks in Sam and Vinnie's eyes, and anger and pain in the rest of the team's. There was what he thought was determination, but he wasn't sure if he was just hoping to see that.

Still, he was determined to help them where he could. He contemplated throwing them into freshly made rifts, to help them get used to fighting without a guide. He understood using it to reduce danger but, apparently, they *needed* guides.

Them being on the other side of the war was suddenly looking like a good thing. He knew their side had some powerhouses, just from the golem war. There were a lot of people on both sides that Matt could see them practicing their abilities and skills on.

He and Liz also decided to try and get the rest of their new war squad to come to a spar or two. It would mean hiding his and Melinda's Talents, but it would be good to show them other strong Pathers.

They sparred for hours, relying on Matt keeping everyone full of mana to burn, and [Endurance] to keep going when exhaustion would have forced them to stop normally.

"Let's go get showered and meet up for the auction. I hear it's going to be crazy."

Vinnie said while glaring at the floor, "We don't even have points to spend. What's the point?"

Matt didn't like the defeatist tone his friend had. "Things will be sold for mana stones as well. Also, it's useful just to see what is for sale. Our point of contact and leader implied that the kingdom was buying items to exchange for missions that had a high chance of death, as a form of compensation. You might see something you like."

He bumped Vinnie and grinned at him. "Come on, if nothing else, it should be a nice little party."

Melinda stood and brushed her armor off. "We only have the skills you're giving us to trade, and we can do that without being there in person. I think we need the night to ourselves."

She looked at him, and while she did look sorry, she also looked determined. "Sorry Matt. Next time. And let's plan for some more sparring tomorrow. Okay?"

Matt wanted to say he could buy them whatever they needed, but he was pretty sure that he was running close to what he was allowed to give as a seeker equivalent. He also didn't think they needed, or even wanted his money. Being there to help them train seemed like the better option.

While he didn't regret his gifts from the way Tara and Vinnie looked at their items, it seemed to only make them feel worse for not keeping up.

The last thing Matt wanted to do was replace one weakness with a dependency on him to keep them competent. He knew they could be great on their own.

Matt just hoped that he didn't do more harm than good with his gifts. His friends looked like deflated balloons after their fight, and they only seemed slightly recovered after their sparring.

With that settled, he and Liz quietly went back to their rooms. Their moods were somber as they walked away from where the arena platform dropped them off. Even Aster seemed to sense the mood; she didn't even beg for ice cream when they passed a shop.

Neither said anything until Liz asked, "Do you think that could happen to us?"

Matt looked confused. "What do you mean?"

"I mean if we didn't get investigated and we didn't get the management team. Would we have stagnated?" Liz clarified with a troubled look on her face. Matt wanted to immediately deny it, but he paused.

Would we have?

Because of Melinda's Talent, they got sloppy. He remembered the time before they had their Tier 3 Talents. They were much more diligent. While Matt's Talent didn't make injuries a non-issue, it did allow them to gain a large amount of essence in a very short amount of time, with minimal risk if they only delved at their Tier.

Now that he thought about it, they were already forming bad habits. If the manager hadn't forced their hands, they would have skipped out on this war. They would have stayed at Tier 5, playing with rifts and delving for growth items, simply for wealth.

Matt slowly replied, "As much as I want to deny it, yes. During our break, I was already beginning to back slide. Without the manager, we would have stayed at Tier 5 longer than we should have. With Melinda's Talent, they would really benefit from having a manager. Baxter seems like he's trying to fill that role, but maybe he doesn't have the authority to tell them what to do? Otherwise, why would he be asking for our help?"

After a moment of contemplation, Liz responded, "Yeah. You're probably right. I felt it, too. Getting investigated was more of a blessing than I thought."

They walked in silence for another moment when Liz said, "You know, I wanted to say something about my parents when Melinda shared her Talent. I just froze up and the moment seemed to pass me by. Sorry."

He grabbed her hand. He hadn't expected her to share until she was comfortable and didn't expect it that soon. She was working on it, but it wasn't as if she was cured of her fear just because she told him about them.

"You have nothing to be sorry about, so don't worry about it. It's pretty understandable. When or if you feel ready, that's the best time to tell them. Besides, it's not like they really need to know."

"I know, but it didn't seem fair to me. Melinda shared her big secret, and I just couldn't bring myself to reciprocate. But they're good people. I can tell that much already. I'll definitely tell them. I just need to work up the nerve first." With her mind clearly made up, Liz squeezed his hand and pulled Aster from his arms.

When they arrived at their suite of rooms, they found Emily, Annie, and Conor lounging.

As they walked in, Emily called out, "We've been waiting for you. Are you coming to the auction?"

Liz nodded, saying, "We were sparring with some old friends. We'll be ready in ten minutes."

Conor checked his watch, "Should be enough time. I hear that it's being held in a special location, and that transports will start moving at the top of the hour. That's in fifteen minutes, though. I don't want to be the last to arrive."

Annie popped to her feet and added, "Yes! This is our first auction like this. I hear if you have more than 1,000 points you can have a room for yourself. We can pool our points to stay together, right?"

Emily rolled her eyes, and Matt noticed that Annie hadn't taken her eyes off Conor, who still had the far-off look of someone interacting with their AI.

Matt decided to help her in her ploy for the man's attention.

"I think that's a great idea."

Annie grinned at him and threw him a thumbs up hidden away from Conor.

"Well hurry up and go shower, then. We don't have time!"

7

Conor had been right about the area being packed. The entirety of the massive landing area where the Pathers' shuttles came down was chock full of people.

There were easily tens of thousands of people waiting. Matt took a quick glance down the streets and couldn't see anything but more people standing around. Considering they had just walked those streets, he was flabbergasted at the sudden appearance of the crowd.

They moved down the steps and fought their way to the edge of the grass platform. Annie tried to say something, but the noise of the mob around them was too loud to overcome.

Giving up, she shrugged and swallowed what she wanted to say. Apparently, it wasn't important enough to message their AIs for.

They waited for nearly ten minutes before everyone started to look up, drawing Matt's gaze along with them. They watched as a swarm of flat shuttles flew through the air. They looked like flying stone platforms with railings.

The stone platforms hovered over the crowd, and ladders extended out of them, allowing people to start climbing up. Matt felt for the platforms with his spiritual sense and found that each platform's aura felt as dense as a Tier 15s. These things were spiritually heavy.

He and his team were near the last of the people to get on the platform, and they were pressed up against the outer railing. The flying platform took off with a smoothness that surprised Matt. There was a shield that seemed to stop the turbulent wind, but it also removed drag somehow. It was an interesting formation. Matt was trying to find where the runes were, wanting to see if he could make heads or tails of them.

To his surprise, he actually found them, but they were obfuscated with some kind of security formation that seemed to make their forms change every time he looked at them. As he tried to peer through the obscuring layer, he was immediately hit with a headache and a roiling stomach.

Realizing it was futile to continue, he pulled his attention back to looking over the edge of the platform and enjoying the view of the ocean flashing by.

He called out, "I grew up in a city by the coast. My parents' apartment was facing the waterfront. I loved watching the waves pass by. It was always soothing."

The rest of his team didn't take much notice of his sharing that, but he didn't miss the look of surprise from Liz. He never talked about his parents. He just smiled at her and went back to looking at the water whipping by. His time on the islands had given him a renewed appreciation of the view that he hadn't known he missed until it was gone.

Emily added while following Matt's gaze, "We went to play at the beach quite a lot. We grew up on a planet with more islands than anything else. Kinda like a resort planet, but not quite. Water is as peaceful as anything. Most nights, we'd fall asleep while listening to the water running over the rocky beaches."

Annie looked to Conor, who added after a moment, "I grew up on a Tier 25 planet, so I lived in an inland city. I didn't really ever see the ocean until I joined the Path, after I went to a world without the ability to defend the cities. I spent a half-year delving a water rift with lots of little attacking fish. They had an amazing fish soup thing, though. I think I ate it every day for a month."

The large front liner sighed, and everyone looked at Liz. Matt did as well. He was interested in what she would say.

"I grew up in the capital."

Annie and Emily's eyes went big as they interrupted her in near unison.

"The *capital* capital? Like of the Empire?"

"Wow. That's a Tier 47 world."

Conor just raised an eyebrow, asking the same question. Matt was interested in how she would play it. He didn't think that she would tell them about her heritage. He was surprised she had even shared this much.

Liz shrugged like it didn't matter.

"If you're not the child of a powerhouse, most of the planet is played out and locked down."

Conor nodded like he understood that, but Annie and Emily looked interested, so Liz explained, "There are the three great guilds, who each have two Tier 47 rifts. The Empire controls the rest, with six for the independents who refuse to take part in worldly affairs, and the rest under their direct control. Even then, it's still a Tier 47 planet. There just aren't any rifts below Tier 40. It's too hard to keep the mana and essence out of them, so you can't really advance if you're young and don't want to absorb ambient essence. Most of the kids are taken to another planet in the Soren star system."

She waved her hands around and had them orbit in a circle, as if they didn't know how planets orbited.

"The capital has a dozen planets orbiting it, each trying to Tier up to Tier 47 by using the essence that radiates off the capital itself. One of them is still only Tier 15, which lets them use in-system teleporters, and that provides the kids rifts to delve. But even then, it's not really accessible for most. There's just too many people and a limited number of rifts, so most get sent off-world to nearby lower Tier planets. I was lucky enough to be offered a spot on the Path and got a place to delve. Once I was Tier 3, I got out as fast as I could."

Annie said, "It must be amazing, though. Have you ever seen the Emperor, or one of the royals?"

Matt had to stifle a grin at that. Liz didn't so much as give anything away, but she froze for a moment before saying, "Once or twice. It's not that special. I've found the planets that aren't just giant cities way more impressive. Or at least, more varied. It can be lonely being a child surrounded by people thirty Tiers or more higher than you. I didn't really have many people near my age to play with."

He reached over and rubbed her back. Matt was proud of her for sharing that much.

Before they could say more, their flying platform angled downward, and they smoothly submerged beneath the waves. Matt was surprised because if he hadn't seen the change, he would have had no idea when they moved from air to water. The flying platform didn't change its pace at all.

He reached out to touch the rushing water, but Liz pulled his hand back and with a mischievous smile and said, "Watch."

He and his team did so. Not ten seconds later, someone else reached out and put their hand through the barrier just to be sucked out violently.

Liz giggled, and when she saw the looks of shock, she pointed at the dozen or so people who repeated the same action. "I've used these types of shuttles before when I visited my uncle. There were always a few tourists who got dragged out. The shuttle pilots even made a bit of a competition out of it. They would deliberately fly near schools of fish to tempt people to reach out."

Seeing their looks of shock, she rolled her eyes, "They'll be fine. Really, if they're taking us underwater, they expected this. There, look. The collection team."

As the people were fading from view, they saw another platform scooping them up and bringing them to safety.

Now that their lives weren't at risk, it was actually kind of funny. Matt laughed while also looking at his own fingers. He would have tested it without hesitation. It just would have been embarrassing to arrive soaking wet at the auction.

Before long, Matt saw a massive dome surrounded by a few dozen smaller ones branching off, connected by clear tunnels. It was a shining beacon of light in the inky waters.

Their platform passed through a shimmering barrier, and they were in dry air once again. Matt should have expected the area to be spatially expanded, but he hadn't. When they arrived in one of the smaller edge bubbles, its outer dimensions had only seemed to be that of a large building. The inside was actually a huge expanse dripping in luxury.

The edges were lined with balconies that wrapped the entire sphere. There was a circular area in the center that held a floating statue, seemingly made of light. It was sculpted into the shape of a ballerina, frozen in a moment of their dance.

Matt was mesmerized for a moment until the bustling crowd

bumped into his back. They didn't have to climb down the ladders this time, as the bubble had dedicated moorings for the shuttles. With the exit made apparent, the passengers poured down the ramp in a wave.

The signs bombarded him with advertisements for all kinds of extravagant goods and experiences. There was everything from rare wine tastings to specialty cheese shops.

"Wow."

Conor's exclamation matched Matt's own thoughts. Annie broke him out of his stupor with a poke to his side.

He looked at her in confusion, before she pressed her hands together with three fingers each and split them off.

Matt grinned at her. He decided to throw her a bone after noticing the eye roll from her sister.

"This place looks amazing. We should split up so we can cover more of it. The main auction starts in three hours, so we have time. I'll make sure we get a box like we said earlier. Why don't Conor, Annie, and Aster go together, and the rest of us will do our own thing. We can message each other about anything amazing we might find."

Aster jumped up into Annie's arms and yipped a yip Matt knew all too well, so he headed that off with, "Only give her a small bowl of ice cream. I'm sure she'll want more at the banquet that they're holding after the auction."

His fox's ears dropped, but Annie kissed her in between the ears and said something that caused them to perk back up.

Matt ignored the foreboding implications and turned to leave with Liz and Emily. Before they left, he made sure he put the kingdom's colors armband on Aster, which she refused to wear as a headband, so he had to settle for a scarf.

They all had their own on as well. While it hadn't been a hard rule, it had been suggested strongly for anyone attending the auction.

Annie's sister scoffed when they were out of range of her sister, leading Liz to ask, "Do you not like Conor?"

Emily sighed. "No, it's not that. Conor is actually much better than the last few crushes Annie's picked up. One tried to get us to have a threesome with him. Like, come on."

Matt's face scrunched up at that.

Liz threw an arm around the shorter woman and said, "Then isn't it a good thing Conor doesn't seem to be that type?"

Emily nodded at that but accompanied it with a shrug. "I guess, but none of them started out being weird. Just call me a pessimist. I haven't seen him checking me out when he thinks I'm not looking, at least. That's something more than I could say about most of her crushes."

The brown-haired woman perked up and changed the topic. "What are you guys interested in checking out? I looked up some of the amenities, and there's a spa section that has a massage parlor. We don't have enough time to *really* enjoy it, but we have enough time for a half-hour massages and mani-pedi."

Liz jumped at the idea. "Yes! My feet are always in boots. I'd love that."

Matt agreed. "It won't hurt, that's for sure. But I'll skip out of the mani-pedi. I would rather have a longer massage."

They moved through the bubble, down toward the center of the concourse. They made their way down a tunnel set at a declining angle, with a gravity nullifier that allowed for faster transport. It was fun to throw himself down the tube and catch himself at the end with a flip that let him land with a solid *thunk.*

He was tempted to go back just to experience the weightlessness once again. It was exhilarating.

Seeing that the women wanted to move on, Matt shrugged it off. They were in the central bubble, and the sheer size of the area boggled his mind. The entire center was carved out, so that the balconies had a clear view along with the progressively larger boxes that trailed up the side of the inner area. Near the bottom, there was a section of what looked like standing platforms that Matt wanted to avoid being placed in.

They found a booth to reserve a private auction box, only to find out that they already had one set aside for them. Or at least, Matt and Liz did. Emily didn't, which they found odd.

Guessing what happened, Matt sent a message to Juni asking if he did that, and almost immediately received a response with a laughing face and 'You'll see.'

He and Liz didn't think they were being set up in a bad way, so they decided not to push for more information. They reached their reserved massage appointment after three more transfers through the weightless tunnels.

The massage was everything Matt had thought it would be and more. The worker dug into his back with fingers of soft steel, while two others attacked his hands and feet at the same time.

He was glad that he had a towel covering his face, because he was pretty sure he was drooling by the end of his appointment.

The three of them bonelessly moved to a bench near a wall to watch the fish and other underwater creatures slither and swim by.

"Do I still have feet?" Matt lifted his now rebooted feet to the giggles of the two women.

He went along with it. "I'm just pissed that I've never done this before. I always figured that it couldn't be worth the money. Damn, was I wrong."

Seeing something in the reflection of the wall, Matt turned in confusion as he noticed a massive turtle walking up behind him. Upon further inspection, he was taken aback a second time from the discovery that the approaching figure really *was* a turtle.

Standing around four feet tall from floor to shell, the turtle was short but stocky. The sections of his shell were more spiky than normal, appearing like small, sharp hills on its back, instead of the smooth humps he had seen before on the mundane variants. The turtle's exposed skin looked more scale-like, reminding Matt more of a lizard than of a turtle. As the light played over his shell and scales, it reflected like dull metal.

Liz noticed him looking and turned to glance as well, saying, "Ah, a mountain metal tortoise. Poor guy was born in beast form, which kinda sucks. At least he seems to have a friend."

Matt looked and saw that there was a woman with purple hair and a wide-brimmed hat talking with the tortoise. How Liz knew it was a male, he had no idea, but he went with it. It was a good reminder that the Empire was wider than he really knew.

"Why do they do that? It seems cruel."

Liz sighed. "I'd agree personally, but there are advantages. One is litter births. You can have more children if done in beast form. Tying in with that, there's an increased fertility that comes with both parents being of the same species *and* both in beast form. Also, there's the belief that children born like this are stronger or have better Talents. It's not really confirmable, but there is enough anecdotal evidence to make something of the rumor."

Seeing the queendom's colors on both, Matt sighed in annoyance. He had no idea how to fight a turtle. His shell looked to be thick and made from metal. He was glad that he had a blunt weapon at his Tier, but he honestly doubted that it would do him any good against a shell made for defense.

"Wouldn't their Talents be set by their species? Like Aster?"

Liz rotated her hand back and forth and said, "Yes and no. They have human minds, so they have unique Talents, but they tend to be somewhat related to their racial Talents. Although, completely different Talents have been known to show up. It's a practice that's become somewhat taboo, but it still happens."

After they recovered from their massages, the three of them wandered around and snacked on the various samples of food that the shops were offering. After an hour or two of eating, drinking, and lounging, they moved to their assigned auction box, and Matt realized why they had one already set aside for them.

As he leaned out of the box to inspect their surroundings, he saw that their box and all of the surrounding ones were covered in screens showing highlights of the golem war's battles. He and Liz were featured on their box, with clips of them shredding golems cycling on the screens in a short, repeating scene.

Matt was profoundly embarrassed by the display but had to admit that the entire stretch of boxes decked out and displaying the kingdom's top fighters from the golem fight gave off an imposing air.

He retreated into the box and activated the privacy barrier that the area was equipped with.

Emily gave them shit for nearly five minutes, until Liz flicked water at her and started a mini-war, with the plate of hors d'oeuvres serving as ammunition.

Conor, Annie, and Aster came in shortly before the starting time. As they entered, Annie looked at Matt and grinned at him, which he reciprocated. He didn't think Conor was a creep, and Annie seemed to like him, so he moved seats so they could sit next to each other.

As the time ticked down, a man with a magnificent beard came on to the stage.

His appearance was projected to a smaller pad in their room, but they had an unobstructed view from their box.

"Good afternoon, my young friends. I am Javier, Tier 29, representative of the Empire auction house, Deep Sky Auctions. We are the ones who provided the structure you are in now."

There was a clatter of applause, which he smiled through. Once it died down, he said, "We could not do this alone. We are partnered with a number of local auction houses from the kingdom, and one from the queendom. Please, give them your thanks when you see the number of smaller auctions after the main event. They were gracious enough to provide those items and have each broken into their own vaults to bring out some truly *scintillating* prizes."

The cheering was much louder after that proclamation.

"Ah, but let me also thank the king and queen for attending at my humble request."

The view on their pad transferred to a shot of a man in expensive-looking fabric sitting with Prince Albert. The man looked like an older version of the prince, with the same eyes and hair color, and similar shapes to their faces.

The queen was a woman with silver and pink hair, surrounded by four other women sitting slightly behind her. Princess Sara was next to her, clearly indicating her status as the heir.

Javier continued, "Many wonder why the vassal countries are going to such lengths for this small Tier 6 planet. Perhaps this will serve as an answer."

Two cases were brought to the stage, both covered in a blanket of each county's colors.

"The Emperor, in his wisdom, had these items custom made for each respective ruler if their side earned enough points during the war. He wished these to serve as an incentive for preventing the war from stalling out or becoming stagnant."

With a motion of Javier's fingers, the first cover was knocked off.

"First up is the kingdoms item; a staff of Tier 37 make. It will multiply all manipulation skills' effects in both a damage boost and an equal reduction of mana cost. It also acts as a storage device for materials of the wielders choosing."

The staff was made from metal and what looked like liquid darkness in a swirling pattern that made Matt's gaze slide off the weapon.

The announcer tapped his nose and added with a wink, "It does a few other things, but I won't spoil them. Let's just say, the good king should enjoy them."

The king in question had leaned forward as if to get a better look at the staff and had a smile on his face that appeared chiseled on. He glanced at his son, who nodded at his father's look. It was apparent that he wanted the item and was making sure that the prince knew it.

"The queendom's item is no less impressive."

A repeated flick of his fingers caused the other cover to go flying.

Under the cloth was a gauntlet made from what looked like forged and solidified light.

"We have here a Tier 37 sun gauntlet. It was forged from the remnants of a dying sun. This little gauntlet will condense and store light for future use. Along with the amplification of all light-based skills and spells channeled through it. As with the king's weapon, it has a few more functions, but we'll let the queen figure them out."

Princess Sara's mother licked her lips and flexed her right hand as if she was already wearing the gauntlet. The naked desire on her face was a clear indication that she was just as interested as the king had been.

Both items vanished with a wave of Javier's hand.

"Finally, the reward for winning the war."

The clamor of the previous items vanished, as a heavy weight seemed to press on everyone at the auction. Both vassals' rulers were intently watching the auctioneer, who seemed unbothered by the Tier 35's scrutiny.

With a wry smile, the man said, "As you can see, they haven't seen the rewards yet either."

When no one laughed, he continued on. "Unlike the other two weapons, this reward is slightly different. It has not been made yet. No, no. The reward for this war's winner is an item crafted to the exact specifications of the victorious ruler, fully financed by the empire and expertly fabricated by none other than Madam Renaissance herself!"

Matt didn't know what that meant, but by the changes in the king's and the queen's faces, it seemed important.

Javier laughed at their expressions. "For my friends under Tier 25 or so, Madam Renaissance is the Empire's best crafter. Her detractors say she is only the best-*known* crafter, but do not let those criticisms distract you. Hidden masters aren't making items for anyone. Madam Renaissance is a Tier 46 crafter, proficient in everything from smithing, to tailoring, and enchanting. She can do it all. Her items have massive markups, and the wait time to even get on her *list* is counted in thousands of years."

Matt whistled. That sounded impressive.

"To prove her skill, allow me to say just this. She has Tiered-up through crafting seven times. Yes, I said seven. *Seven* times she has Tiered-up through inspiration. That includes her last two Tiers. All achieved through her crafting. She is a woman of prodigious ability!"

On the pad, both rulers looked to their heirs with naked command. They both *needed* to win the war, and Matt could see that neither would accept a loss, especially with the rewards now revealed.

Matt turned to Liz and asked, "Is all of this as impressive as I think it is?"

Everyone turned to Liz, and she laughed. "More, probably. Madam Renaissance is more of a crafting legend than anything else in the capital. I've heard rumors of her crashing classes and giving impromptu lectures. Rumor has it when she did it last, half the class had inspirations during it. The other half had one within a year. When Javier said that the wait to get on the waiting list is measured in thousands of years, he wasn't joking. I heard they actually need to stand around and wait in a line. They do it happily! Even though the cost is said to be an arm and a leg, sometimes literally."

Matt tried to picture that. If the woman was that good of an all-around crafter, it didn't surprise him that her time was so valued. He tried to think what it would be like to wait in line for thousands of years, but he just couldn't wrap his mind around it.

After a long pause, Javier smiled at both rulers and said, "With appetites and desires aflame, let the auction begin!"

A woman brought out a flower of purple and yellows, and Javier kicked off the auction. "Our first item! The Tier 8 Flower of Miraculous Life. Anyone who eats this little beauty will gain wood-aspected mana. If you can find a skilled alchemist, it serves as a key ingredient for a potion to obtain the much rarer life aspected mana. The aspect is desired by healer and growth specialists everywhere. We'll start the bidding at 200 war contribution points."

The bid quickly shot up to 920 points before the item was sold. Matt wanted to buy it for Melinda, but he would have burned through all of his points while also doing exactly what he decided not to; give them another crutch. He did send her a message with the item and its purported abilities, so she at least knew that it existed.

The next item was one that Matt recognized from the batch of items they sold to Samuel at the auction house. “This is a Tier 5 rift made sword that increases swing speed and damage massively when mana is run through it. The sword is rated to Tier 7 strength. Bidding starts at 50 war contribution points.”

Matt looked at Liz, and they smiled at each other, seeing where this was going. A lot of the items they pulled were like that one. They were useful, but not what they wanted, so they sold them in bulk to the auction house. It was slightly painful, as they had gotten mana stones out of it, which were much less valuable than the war contribution points they were selling for now.

More items flew by, with nearly a quarter of them being ones that they had sold. Matt reaffirmed his intention to only sell through the Empire Market to avoid something like this. It twisted the knife to see his items go for so much higher than they had sold them for.

They watched in disinterest until their first mana cultivation potion went up for sale.

“This pretty little thing is a potion that our alchemist confirmed will increase each of the consumer’s three mana cultivation aspects. It’s balanced to give a slight increase to both Mana Regeneration and Maximum Mana. That’s not all, it uses most of the potion’s effect to give a Mana Concentration of 0.1. This is the first batch up for auction, and it contains 10 potions. Like all of the following ones, they are for Tier 5. Fighters, if you want to firm up your base, these little beauties are the way to do it. Starting price of 100 war contribution points.”

There was a buzz that ran through the audience.

Someone called out, “Are you selling any singles?”

Javier pointed into the standing crowd and answered the question. “Yes. The final and best ten will be sold in single lots at the end. If you don’t get one here, I believe the war market will have some of them for sale as well, but their price will be set according to the final bidding price”

Matt leaned forward in his chair in anticipation. They would be getting these points, so he crossed his fingers and hoped their price rose to the sky.

"125."

"150."

"180."

"210."

"250."

"300." The final price was called out by the prince, and Princess Sara immediately snapped out a counter.

"350."

Matt wiggled in his seat.

Finally, after a long moment of deliberation, the prince called out, "400."

"500!" the princess didn't hesitate in the slightest when she raised the bid again.

Matt didn't think 50 points apiece was bad for the worst potions that Liz had made. While the others' attention was all on the unfolding drama, he smiled at Liz, who looked to be on cloud nine.

He was proud of his partner and all of her accomplishments.

Looking across the stage, he saw Sara smiling and getting a pat on her arm by her mother.

Sara was nearly out of her seat, while the prince was more collected and calmer, as if none of this bothered him in the slightest.

Their third batch of potions, with a Mana Concentration of 0.12, had just sold for 600 war points, when a skill shard was brought out.

Javier stroked the case holding the skill and called out in his sonorous voice, "This beauty is [Cracked Mana Bolt]." At the murmur, Javier laughed and spoke over the crowd. "This is a marvelous cracked skill. Unlike most mana bolt skills that are neutral in their attack, this one randomly changes its aspect to anything. Shoot it enough times, and you punch through any armor type."

Emily was out of her seat and had her face pressed against the privacy formation.

"The starting bid is 200 is points."

She immediately shouted, "1,000!"

Matt was shocked by her spending nearly all her points, but he was blown away by someone else immediately bidding higher.

In just a moment, the price was at 2,500 points, with smaller and smaller bids being placed.

Emily looked at them, and after a brief internal struggle, said, "I need to get this skill. I'll pay you back with interest, but please."

Seeing their hesitation, she blurted, "Look, long story short, my Talent basically lets me repeatedly double the effect of any skill, as long as it's a different aspect than one I used in the same chain of spells. Once I repeat anything, it resets. This is *perfect* for me. I *need* it."

Matt looked at Liz, and they nodded.

At nearly the same time as Conor, he said, "We have 3,000 you can use. No interest needed."

"I have 1,000."

Annie looked at her crush with doe eyes, and Emily turned and shouted, "3,000."

Someone else called out when the countdown was at one, "4,000."

"Fucking fucker. I need this. You brain-dead idiot."

"5,000!" Her voice was overly controlled when she spoke through the screen.

Matt leaned forward with anticipation as the countdown reached two, then one. It felt like an eternity when it finally clicked to zero, and Emily was the winner of the auction.

She dropped to her butt at the edge of their box. "I think I'm going to vomit."

Matt patted the woman's arm and pulled her up to her chair, where she bonelessly sat.

"Thanks, guys. I really owe you for that one."

Matt was interested in her Talent but didn't want to press. He carefully asked, "Don't answer this if you don't want to, but if you can double the effect of a skill if it's a different element, why don't you have something common like [Fireball]?"

She stretched and sighed. "We grew up on a water world, and it didn't have a lot of fire skills. It's why I have two water skills and a lightning skill that we were able to trade for. I intended to buy a [Fireball] here with some points, but that's kinda shot for now. Thankfully, it's pretty common, so I should be able to get it in a few weeks. Well, after I pay you all back, of course. I *really* appreciate it guys."

Matt looked at Liz and raised an eyebrow. He was leery of giving more help after seeing what happened to Melinda's team, but he had an extra [Fireball] that wasn't reserved for himself.

Liz shrugged, putting the ball back in his court, but nodded slightly as well.

He thought over her suggestion. She was okay with it, and the more he thought, the more he had to agree it was different from Melinda's party. Annie and Emily were strong in their own right. They held their own in their fight. And one extra skill would, if he understood her Talent right, take her from a four times multiplier to an eight times multiplier. That was massive, if paired with her [Bolt] skill as a finisher.

Hoping he wasn't making a mistake, he withdrew and tossed the still boneless Emily a [Fireball] skill. "Here's a [Fireball]. No reason to wait. Just giving us the standard value in mana stones or points is fine. Better to have it now if I understand your Talent right. An eight times stronger [Bolt] would be devastating in a fight, and it'll help our team build up points faster."

She looked up from the skill shard that she scrambled for, and with a hard look in her eyes, said, "I won't take it if you wanted to sell or trade it. Even if it would help me, I won't slow you down to do it."

Matt debated taking out his bucket of skills to shock her, but only brought out his other [Fireball]. "I have my own. We were going to sell it, but we'd rather sell it to you instead of someone else. In the end, we get the same payment, just a little later."

Emily didn't protest further, simply nodding to him and then to Liz and Aster. "Thank you. This really does help, and your math was right. With the [Cracked Mana Bolt], as long as I don't get fire, water, or lightning, I can pretty much get an eight times damage bonus; possibly more if my luck is good."

Matt shuddered at that thought. It would undoubtedly rip right through [Cracked Phantom Armor] at that high of an increase in power. He looked at Annie and Conor and said, "If either of you are looking for specific skills, let us know. We can help you try and get it."

Conor raised his drink and said, "To new friends and growing stronger."

They all drank to that.

8

They started ordering drinks from the auction staff as item after item got brought out to the stage. They were all poor now, so watching new items come out was more a game for them than it was actual shopping. Matt hoped that this wasn't the best the auction houses had to offer, because no one but the actual factions had earned any substantial amount of points at this point.

Besides the odd item or two, most things went to the prince or princess, who had access to the points generated by capturing and holding various forts and cities.

It made the auction boring; nothing was going to the little guys.

So, they drank.

They were ordering Tier 6 liquor and were thoroughly tipsy by the time the auction was coming to a close. None of them had to be told to not go overboard, but they were riding the edge of feeling good, and actually getting drunk.

Matt was trying to keep Aster out of the sour apple brandy that apparently smelled too good to resist, when an item brought on stage caught his attention.

While a small vial was displayed on stage, Javier called out, "Here, as one of our final items, we have a Tier 10 bottled Concept. Unlike most…"

Matt lost interest once he heard that it was a bottled Concept and said, "Psh. Who cares? It's just a bottled Concept."

Annie shushed him, as did her sister. Even Conor got up to watch the auctioneer, with only a slight wobble.

Seeing that he was outvoted, Matt quieted down and listened. "Even a Tier 6 can use this. Yes, truly a marvel of alchemy. This is a triple attribute Concept. Yes, *Three.* "

After a slight pause to accommodate the murmurs of interest, Javier raised his arm, flexing his bicep as he continued, "Strength."

He lightly rapped his knuckles against his chest and said, "Durability."

He casually reached out with an open hand, demonstrably closing his fist as he finished, "And Regeneration. This is the ideal bottled Concept for anyone trying to build a more physical combat style. It can be used to bolster your defenses, or it can help you lean into the offensive a little more. Starting bid of 5,000 war points!"

Matt's new teammates all made sounds of disappointment when they heard the price and returned to their chairs. Matt felt Aster lurch out of his arms but was distracted by Liz.

She scoffed at them and said, "Just make your own Concept." She burped in the middle of her sentence while still holding her beer but continued after a moment. "It's *waayy* better."

Annie flicked the condensation off her glass at Liz, who spluttered at the droplets' sneak attack. The twin said "It's not that easy. You need…"

Liz threw up her hands. "I can teach you!"

Matt missed what was said next as he noticed the lack of his bond in his arms. He looked around to find her muzzle deep in his once half full glass of alcohol he had placed on the table.

He pulled her back to get a burp in the face, and a pushed thought of, "Apple!"

Oh, that's not good.

Aster went into a tirade about apple-flavored hearts and ice cream, which Matt ignored while she started kicking slower and slower as the liquor took effect. He glared at everyone who could have seen Aster going hog wild on his glass but sighed in defeat. After all, it was his own fault in the end.

He was brought back into the conversation by Emily, who kicked at his leg and yelled for him. "Maaatt!"

"What!?"

"I asked if it was that easy. I want my own Concept."

Matt thought for a moment, until the topic of conversation came back to him. "It's not that hard. Do you have your…?" He looked at her for a few blinks until the word came to him. "Phrase! That's the word. Do you have your phrase? Or at least an idea?"

Annie shrugged. "How would we know if you already need a Concept to tell?"

"Damn, that's a good point. Shit! I don't know…" Matt shrugged and joined everyone as they looked at Liz, who was now sitting primly. If her cheeks weren't flushed so bright red, she would almost look authoritative.

"It's easy. I'm telling you. I can get you a Concept. Fifteen minutes."

Even Matt booed her, and she corrected herself. "Okay, okay fine! Maybe not fifteen minutes, but before the war is over for sure. You guys fight well, and I'm betting that if we push you really hard, you can figure it out."

Annie called out, "I want a stabby Concept!"

Everyone stopped to look at her, and she defended herself while holding her glass like a shield. "What? I can already do the sneaky part. I just need to do the stabby part better."

She mimed stabbing someone, and when she sloshed her drink over her hand, she started trying to lick the alcohol off it. Matt failed to stop himself from laughing as Conor's gaze was cemented on her actions. He slowly flushed while watching her probably unintentional display.

He made a note to tell her about it later. It was a good sign, but he was distracted by Emily loudly saying, "I want a Concept of power!"

Even Conor was drawn out of his staring when she said that. He countered, "That's not a real Concept. It's too vague. You need to start with spell damage or something."

Emily glared at the other man and pouted into her drink when he didn't seem to notice.

Liz added another nail in her coffin. "Power isn't a Concept, that's an Aspect. I think I heard of someone using that, or at least something like it."

She pursed her lips and was suddenly distracted by a cheese wedge that Matt was in the middle of eating. She snatched the remaining half for herself with a devilish grin at her crestfallen partner, and added, "I think they started with bodily strength, then bodily control for their Intent, and finally used bodily power to round it out. There's nothing stopping you from going for a spell version."

Emily wiggled in her chair with a dreamy look on her face.

Conor shrugged and leaned back with a large sigh. "No clue what I want for my Concept. First, I need a way to take hits better. Reflection does nothing to me, but my Tier 3 Talent gives me a slight bit of sustainability. Do I lean into that, or go for more tanking? Maybe I can transition into more of a hybrid like you, Matt."

Matt tossed out, "What do you see yourself doing? Do you like being on the front line?"

Conor chewed on an olive while he pondered the question. "I don't know. I was given my skill by my sponsor when I joined the Path. They pretty much set me down the path toward my current build." The large man paused to think about it for another moment, before finally adding, "I don't mind it. But being defensive will only take me so far on my own. Rifts are slow fights for me most of the time. I need either more damage, or someone else on my team. I've gotten this far by choosing the rifts that I counter, but eventually, I'll run out of time. It's so nice to fight with all of you, where I can just keep a defensive posture."

Annie looked like she had a brilliant idea, but she was silenced by her sister, who swiftly lunged to cover her mouth. Annie struggled for a moment before starting to lick her sister's hand. Emily must have been used to that trick, as she maintained her muzzle on her sister and eventually persevered. Conor glanced at them with a puzzled look but ignored their antics. He looked back to Liz, asking, "How do you intend to help us with our Concepts?"

Liz looked up from the near-empty tray of snacks and shrugged as she half leaned over Matt and Aster to get at the other plate of hors d'oeuvres.

"It's not that hard. Matt and I—well, really just Matt as I have an internal Concept—can restrict you with his Concept while sparring. It's not guaranteed to work or anything, but it's a good start. You'll start to resist it naturally, and that can give you a glimpse into your phrase."

Emily, with her hands still covering her sister's mouth, called out,

"Yeah, okay, how is that different from fighting in a rift that has monsters with Concepts?"

As if she had expected the rebuttal, Liz countered with, "How often do you *actually* fight monsters with Concepts? At Tier 5 and 6, rifts have like, what? A three or four percent chance to have monsters with Concepts? Faster to avoid them and fight the easier ones."

That actually made sense to Matt, who nodded his agreement. During their rapid rift-making months, they had only fought a few rifts that contained monsters with Concepts. But *they* didn't have that much issue with those monsters, since they had their own Concepts.

Liz had suggested something similar when they started training Matt for his Concept, letting him feel her own more than once during their training to get a grip on his phrase. Once Connor and the twins got their phrases, it was only a matter of time until they created their images. The hard part would be the first step.

Matt's attention was brought to the stage as a copper bowl was brought out to be displayed.

"This little beauty will allow you see anything in a mile radius, at the cost of 200 mana per cast." When people seemed disinterested, Javier added, "It's better than you might think! It's incredibly hard to spot by the observed party. If you have this, your scouts will be much more effective."

For once, the item didn't go to the prince or the princess. They actually let the bowl go for only 2,000 points. Matt assumed that they didn't care, as long as the other side didn't directly get it. Anyone who spent that many points wouldn't be willing to give it up, and would only use it for themselves, limiting its effect on the war.

Both sides' leaders had seemed to understand that they were the only ones with any appreciable amount of points, and they started letting the lower floors take an item if they started to bid. Their benevolence didn't extend to abstaining from raising the price of an item that they figured the other side wanted more.

Not long after, the end of the action came to an explosive end. Streams of fire and multi-colored light burst out from the stage. It startled them enough to stir them from their conversation.

Matt stretched as he stood. "About time for dinner. Ugh. All the snacking just made me hungrier. I heard they have a huge layout planned."

Annie, finally freed from her sister's clutches, asked, "What's a layout?"

Matt was too buzzed to care and shrugged it off. "Layout of food… I can't think of the word."

Liz scooped up the still groggy Aster and said, "Who cares what it's called? I want food."

As they all stood, Conor muttered, "A menu. It's called a menu."

They trooped out of their box to mingle with the crowd. From the loud calls, it seemed that they weren't the only group that had turned to alcohol when they ran out of points to spend.

As a mass, they trooped down the winding stairs, until they reached the standing room area. Unlike when they entered their boxes, it was now totally clear, with the previous occupants now seated on floating tables that lifted off once they were full.

They got a table for the six of them, which promptly took off into the air once they were all seated. Not long after that, the food was delivered. Everyone got a plate that suited their individual taste. No need for them to order it seemed, as Matt was given a honey roasted lamb haunch. Aster, who had only just now woken up, had a plate of rabbit legs lightly battered.

Liz was face first in a plate of something Matt thought was Alfredo, which was confirmed when he stole a forkful. The twins followed his lead, leaving Conor as the odd man out. Matt cut a few slices off his lamb and shoved it over to him, causing everyone to share choice bits of their plates.

After trying everyone's food, he had to say that Conor had the best meal. He was served a pressure-cooked bird of some kind that he didn't recognize but wanted to try again.

All in all, the floating meal turned out amazing. Matt had no problem admitting it. The idea of eating on a flying table sounded cheesy, but it was more fun than he would have thought.

They floated up and down through light constructs that cut through their table as they drifted around. When they finished eating, they talked for a while longer. When the conversation wound down, the table gently lowered itself and landed, as if it knew they were ready to leave.

As a group, they moved to follow the crowd of other exiting diners who had finished their meals. Two bubble changes later, they found themselves in a bubble with recordings of the various fights playing on banners that streamed down from the ceiling.

One banner on a raised platform caught Matt's eye. It was accompanied by a smiling young man, who couldn't be more than seventeen, with dusky skin. He looked smug as a recording of his fight played on the banner behind him. On the recording, the young man attacked a city's walls with blades of wind that cut down a number of people that tried to rush him. As the recording progressed, Matt saw more than four distinct wind spells being used. A quick spiritual glance revealed that the man next to the banner was Tier 5. It told Matt everything he needed to know after hearing Juni talk about a Tier 5 rushing a queendom city.

Annie scoffed. "Idiot. He gave away everything he had on day one. Now, if anyone sees him, they're gonna throw an [Earth Spear] at him, and he'll be dead. Showing you only use one element is asking to be countered. Better to be subtle about your arsenal, so people can't counter you so easily."

They walked around through the sea of banners, separating and rejoining each other as they saw banner recordings that caught their individual eyes. Matt, Emily, and Conor stopped by a woman in studded leather playing an upbeat chorus on her guitar, with an ever-growing crowd around her. She seemed to be able to read the mood of the people surrounding her, as she leaned in to sing to a particular section, which caused more cheers.

She cycled through three popular songs before they moved on to scan some of the other highlight banners.

One that caught Matt's eye was of a woman who seemed to dance around long range attacks as she defended a fortress wall. As the wall was destroyed in an icy blast, she leapt down in a flash of lightning. She had tossed what looked like electrical grenades that caused sparks to fly across the ground that moved like living spiders as they exploded and spread.

Contrary to what he expected, she dove into the field of electricity and started to dismantle the charging opposition with a metal rod. It seemed to be used as a mix of cudgel and spell amplifier, and she shot what looked like [Bolts] out of it. In under a minute, she had taken out nine attackers on her own, and seemed to absorb the remaining lightning arcing along the ground.

Seeing that she was on the kingdom side, he made a note to try and seek her out. The grenades she used seemed effective, and he wanted a few for his own use. If they worked the way he expected, he could pre-charge them and use them as an area denial tactic while fighting.

Matt commented to Liz, who had joined them, "How do you even counter someone like that?"

"Range. But even then, she took a few hits that I think should have been fatal, so she might have something to counter that. Thankfully, she's on our side."

Liz pulled him over to a banner that showed a tattooed fourteen-year-old. "Watch this one. He looks young, but he's strong. queendom's side, so we should watch out for this one."

They looked far too young to be more than a newly awakened Tier 1, but with only a recording, Matt had no way to tell their Tier. In the recording, the queendom fighter seemed to flicker around in their battle with three people.

Matt watched as the man appeared in two spots, faster than he could blink. He said, "It has to be a short-range teleport."

Liz asked, "A part of his Talent? I can't see an actual teleport skill being given out, as it is too valuable and strong for a starting skill gift. It seems to be limited in range as well. It feels like a Talent."

As they watched the young man use devastating kicks to dismantle a party creeping through a dense underbrush area, Matt had to agree on the Talent idea. If it was a skill, they seemed far too young to be that proficient in melee combat. They were a kicking monster, and Matt didn't even notice a skill being used. One missed kick dented a tree to the point that slowly toppled over.

What impressed Matt the most was when the fighter disarmed someone, and proceeded to use the sword with the same grace as when they used their legs. Matt wasn't sure he could be as proficient if he split his focus to more than one fighting style.

"We can just have Conor fight him."

Matt nodded at Liz's suggestion. The Melee style would force the man to eventually take a hit from [Demon Zone], and that could allow Conor to finish the man if the blow stopped the teleporting.

Seeing their melee teammate, Matt split off from Liz and watched the banner Conor was trying to dissect. The fighter seemed ordinary enough, with the exception of violet hair and incredibly pale skin.

The recording started in the middle of an already ongoing fight, as the man moved through a pack of kingdom embossed fighters like they were cheese. When an attack seemed to land on their uncovered back, a turtle shell of what looked like mana flashed to protect him. The shell seemed thinner than a normal skill's density, so Matt speculated that it was a Talent. Suddenly, the fighter flashed forward with ghostly, tiger-like claws, and disemboweled the defenders' leader in two brutal swipes.

Matt expected the recording to end there, but the fighter was attacked by a humanoid-looking tiger. They proceeded to exchange nearly a dozen blows with claws, before both retreated with deep cuts over their exposed arms and chests. Before the fight had a decisive end, the recording looped back around to the start.

When he saw his teammate standing next to him, Conor asked Matt, "How would you handle him? He seems to have a defensive form and an attacking one. Emily would probably be able to blast him, but he moves quickly. Might be hard to hold him off. Don't know if I could do it if he was determined to move around me."

"I might be able to slow him with my ice spell, but even that wouldn't do much more than hold him off for a few seconds. Shit, there are a lot of strong people here."

Conor nodded at that. "I thought I was hot shit, but apparently not. Average of the better fighters at best."

Matt had to agree. He knew they were good, but just the people on his team all had the abilities needed to counter him. Annie would hit him from behind, and if she timed it right, she could penetrate [Cracked Phantom Armor] while it was weakened from defending another attack. If she got a dagger skill, she might not even have to wait for that. Emily could just pepper him at range until her skill got eight times stronger and blast him into ash.

Conor was an easier fight, but only because his main skill was countered by Matt's armor. He was still a better melee fighter than Matt was. While Matt was better with his longsword, Conor had a much better understanding of more weapons and that gave him versatility.

The war was showing Matt that he wasn't as special as he thought he was. It was sobering.

When the entirety of the team met back up, they agreed to move on. As they left, they passed each of their own banners. The first showed Liz tearing through the metal tree, and they paused to watch out of morbid curiosity.

The group of them all shifted awkwardly as the next banner showed the footage of Aster and Emily wiping out nearly a dozen people in as many seconds. To top it off, Annie was shown to stab two women from behind, but the video thankfully made her visible, which meant most of their trump cards were still hidden. Although, it made Matt wonder which of the other banners were similarly edited.

The three banners were in a row, and they hurried past after watching each once. Matt grinned at Conor, who returned it as they realized that they hadn't done anything to rate the banner treatment with their less flashy fighting styles. Matt didn't mind, and Conor didn't seem to be bothered about being out of the spotlight either.

It was a good reminder that people were always watching, and without anyone truly dying, there was no way to stop information from getting back to their enemies.

They sheepishly moved out of the bubble of banners after that, too embarrassed to remain.

The next area they wandered into was a casino, and Matt and the others got to watch as Liz won round after round of poker. Matt had heard how good she was, but seeing first hand was another thing altogether.

Annie asked, "How is she that good?"

Matt didn't have an answer but felt a little background wouldn't be amiss. "I know she beat a Tier 24 in poker a few times. She's just good."

Emily and Annie loudly whispered to never play Liz, then started wondering if they could bring her to an actual casino.

The table made everyone wear an anti-AI bracelet to restrict things like card counting, but it didn't seem to slow Liz down, and she continued to win. She didn't win every hand, but if she raised the ante, she was more than likely to take it.

Matt had heard about her skill with cards, but seeing it first hand was both amusing and terrifying.

Sadly, they weren't playing for points or mana stones, but instead various raffle prizes that she could try to win. Considering there was no buy-in, it was fair enough, but Matt wanted to see Liz at a real casino now, and wondered if the twins had the right idea.

The others eventually left, but Matt was interested enough to stay and watch as the game progressed. He was only able to pull her away when the table bled off its remaining players, as they ran out of tickets and had to move on. No one was interested in taking their places, with Liz reigning supreme.

Liz came up from the table with fistfuls of tickets, and she danced around to their congratulations as she cheered. "Let's go see what we can get!"

The ticket counter was staffed by half a dozen people, but they were still swamped as they tried to process people's purchases. In the end, Liz threw all her tickets on the lottery for what was called the 'Mundane Living In Rough Conditions Skillset'. It had six skills in total, intended to make life easier when delving for long times or away from amenities. It had [Create Water] for its obvious usage, and [Cleanse], which would remove dirt or contaminants from something at the caster's discretion. It didn't destroy the contaminants, just moved them away, but it was a skill that Matt still wanted. They hadn't been able to find one during their own delving.

[Alarm] would wake the caster if anything passed over a set area. It was a niche skill with a function that could be handled by technology but being too careful never killed anyone. He didn't think it was a bad skill to eventually get. [Perk Up] was a skill he had never heard of, but after reading its description, he made a note to get it. It was apparently like caffeine, but without any of the side effects. It was much cheaper than [Endurance] and could last for hours.

[Cook] and [Chill] were a pair of food-related skills that he had heard about, but no prideful chef was allowed near them. [Cook] simply heated food until it was safe to eat for the caster's biology while killing any parasites or viruses in the meat. No finesse or care for taste. [Chill] had its usage for preserving food or cooling down drinks, but most used it with [Cook], giving it a bad reputation.

Matt's cooking instructor had spent nearly an entire class lecturing why the skills were a mockery to the culinary art, and not to be used.

He didn't have any use for those skills, but the rest were useful enough to warrant picking up.

They wouldn't know the results of the raffle until the end of the week, so they ended their walk around after finding one of the smaller auctions and sitting down to enjoy the bidding. They were selling various small arms, but Annie said that her dagger was fine for her Tier. So, they only lingered long enough to watch a few items get sold before they moved on to the nearby duel arenas. There various people fought in what appeared to be some entertaining bouts, judging by the crowd.

It only took a quick search to see that the prize for any duel was a flat 100 war points for the winner, and 25 for the losers. Also, winners would get thirty percent of all points bets, while losers would get ten percent. It was profitable enough. Matt looked to his teammates and asked if they wanted to try their luck.

Emily looked interested enough but shook her head. "No. I want to keep what I can do under wraps for as long as possible. The early points are nice, I'm sure. But I don't think the vassals are dumb enough not to have people watching the fights to compile builds and such."

Conor nodded and agreed. "Shame, though. I could always use more points."

They did stay to watch a few more fights, but only one caught Matt's eye. There was a massively overweight man who slung spell after spell as he gradually grew thinner and thinner. Eventually, he ended the fight with some type of AOE skill. It sent his opponent flying into a barrier that encompassed the fighting arena. The payout for his fight was massive, as he had been given horrible odds by the watching crowds. Being that overweight usually meant that they were sedentary, but it was clearly a skill or Talent. If Matt had to guess, the man stored mana as extra weight. It was interesting, and from the number of skills he used during the fight, pretty effective.

The prize of nearly four thousand war points was almost enough to make Matt take the stage, but he kept walking with his friends as they moved to finally leave. They had wandered through most of the bubbles that they wanted to see.

With no points to spend, and not willing to give up more information about themselves by dueling, they boarded a platform and exited the underground leisure land. As they left, there was a banner that offered special Tier 5 and Tier 6 rifts to delve for 1,000 war points apiece. Matt didn't put two and two together until the banner changed, and an ad for a newly discovered Tier 7 was advertised for 4,000 points a delve slot.

He and Liz met each other's gaze and smiled. They knew that the rifts they left would be of great interest, but he hadn't expected the army to camp on them and control their access. It made sense when he thought it over. A rift a Tier higher than the planet was an asset for the faster Tiering up of the world. While he wasn't upset that they were selling access, he wished he could get his hands on a list of the rewards that people got from them.

They tried to delve the rifts a good bit, but they were nowhere close to completing a true rift drop table by the time they had left.

Matt rode the platform back through the sea and to the city with a busy mind. After a day of sparring and high emotions followed by a long night, Matt was exhausted. By the time they arrived back home, he flopped into bed with Liz and Aster. None of them even bothered to undress, and they just fell asleep in a pile.

He woke up the next morning with a dry mouth. Seeing that everyone else was still asleep, he started cooking. He still had some monster meat from their time spent delving, and it was going to go bad sooner rather than later, as he only had a basic mana powered fridge in his spatial bag.

Going all out, he cooked a massive breakfast and moved around the little kitchen like a man possessed, determined to wow with his breakfast feast. Annie and Emily came out of their rooms at nearly the same time, just to argue who would use the bathroom first. They ended it with a round of rock paper scissors, which left Annie bouncing from foot to foot as her sister took her time in the bathroom.

Liz and Aster were the last to arrive, after Conor, Annie, Emily, and he had already finished their plates and then seconds.

Now that Aster was awake, he pushed laughter at her as she was experiencing her first hangover. She was not enjoying it. She yowled at him until it exacerbated her headache, causing her to curl into a miserable ball. Picking up his bond, he fed her a pain killer and waved bacon under her nose until she ate it, before setting her down in her personal freezer bed.

Liz wasn't in nearly as much pain since she used [Endurance], but she was eating slowly at breakfast. While she finished eating, Matt went to the gym with Conor. The two of them only lifted weights and avoided sparring. They were only there to do some strength training.

Their rewards for the selling of Liz's potions arrived, along with Emily's skill shard. They earned a whopping 5,603 war points after the auction house's cut. Matt rubbed his hands together at the influx of points, and immediately put up a bounty for anyone with mana aspects that he didn't already have, or different variants.

He posted it as a crafter looking to aspect rechargeable mana stones. It was true enough, even though he wanted to use his growth item instead.

With a look at Conor, he asked, "Hey, is your mana aspected?".

Conor looked confused for a second and responded, "No. I've thought about getting mine metal or earth aspected, but I couldn't afford the potion. Why? Are you thinking about getting yours aspected?"

Matt didn't want to lie but didn't want to give away his Talent or growth item either, so he told him part of the truth. "No, I dabble in enchanting. My sword requires me to do the enchanting work myself, and for other work, the books recommend getting as many mana aspects as possible to create synergies."

With a casual shrug, he added, "The aspected mana stones cost an arm and a leg for even the common aspects. With how many millions of people are here, *someone* with a rarer variant has to be here, and it costs them nothing to inject a little mana for me."

"I've been thinking about getting a gauntlet that I saw up for sale at a shop. I was wondering if you could give it a look. I don't know enough to know if it's a good deal."

"Happy to help. What's the item?"

"A bracer that acts as a kinetic energy storage, which can be blasted out as a short-range attack."

Matt was surprised and said as much. "I expected you to want a longer range spell. I know I did."

Conor shrugged the comment off. "I don't see it as that important anymore. At least not for the next year. We'll be fighting in teams, and while it would be nice to round out my damage in a rift, I don't see it as a good way to spend my money right now. Better to be a more capable front liner and earn my team, and therefore myself, more points."

Matt liked the man's approach. If he still had [Copper Skin], and knew it didn't have side effects, he would've given it to the man on the spot. He was right, and the better he was as a defensive shield for their mages, the more Matt could go on the attack as a melee damage dealer. Right now, he was a hybrid, which he didn't mind, but focusing on the attack would allow his abilities to shine.

They reached the store in question, and Matt inspected the gauntlet Conor was interested in. It was made by a Tier 7 crafter who obscured his work, so while Matt wasn't able to get a perfect look at the item's runes, he was able to get a feel for its general craftsmanship.

He was honestly impressed with the item. It was good, solid work that seemed to have the runes completely integrated with the metal, but not in the way he was used to seeing. After checking the price, Matt understood why Conor was hesitating.

At a Tier 8 mana stone for the Tier 7 item, it was expensive. Matt could only give his opinion and leave it up to the other man to decide.

"I think the price is worth it. It's well made and will last you a while. It's also a great defensive item if it does as it says and absorbs attacks that land on your off arm. The price, though…"

Matt let himself trail off, and after another few minutes of Conor pacing, he finally bought the item.

As they walked back to their headquarters, Conor offered an explanation. "I had a lucky rift before I came here, but that was most of my liquid assets. Hard to jump off the ledge like that."

"I understand. Look at the bright side. It should last you well after this war, and with its durability and repair enchantments, it should last a good while longer with minimal spending. I think it was worth it. Oh, by the way, we should probably get the girls together and do some sparring when we get back."

They were nearly back to their rooms when their AIs were pinged. Their party had a mission in three hours.

9

The two of them ran the rest of their way back, and Matt noticed there was a great deal of bustle for both sides. It seemed that everyone was rushing to make up for lost time, compared to the slight lull that had happened before the auction.

It could also be the rulers pushing each side to earn more points. They have to both be desperate to win the staff and gauntlet. I can't say I blame them. Those items seem incredible, and they weren't even made for me.

Matt and Conor burst into their suite of rooms and saw that everyone else was already getting ready. Liz threw Matt his under armor clothes, which he slipped on, and he slung his bag over his shoulders in a swift moment.

Conor took longer with his full metal plate armor, but his teammates helped to expedite the process. In five minutes, they were on their way down to the teleporter room, only to find a mass of people milling around the entrance.

The door opened, and a woman's voice called out, "Quill's team, you're up."

There was a shout from a small group, then a shoving as they made their way forward.

The same voice shouted out again, "If your scheduled time isn't in the next hour or less, go away. Come back then. The teleporter is busy, so we won't be doing early jumps."

"Fuck!" Annie looked ready to fight at the realization.

Liz shrugged and offered, "Want to go back to our room for the next two hours or so?"

Emily kicked at the ground and added her two cents. "Or we stand around like these guys. I guess the three-hour time slot was an actual time to leave, and not a suggestion."

Matt felt dumb as they trooped back to their room. He knew it wasn't true, but he felt like everyone they passed was watching them. It was just in his head, but he felt foolish for their rushing.

They all sat awkwardly around their common room for a while before Liz threw on a random show for them to watch. Conor was the only one who removed any of his armor, only his chest plate. It was, as Matt knew from his training at the orphanage, the most uncomfortable portion of plate armor to wear for a long period of time.

It was the first time Matt truly understood the phrase, 'hurry up and wait' from all the war movies he had seen. They were rushed to get ready for combat, then expected to wait around for their time slot.

Two excruciating hours later, they backpacked Aster and headed down at a more sedated pace, just to wait in line now that their teleport time was closer.

They still had to wait another forty five minutes for their exact time slot. From their observations, it was obvious that the in-planet teleporter only worked every five minutes, severely limiting the number of teams able to go out.

"Team Bucket? Your turn."

There was a noticeable air of confusion at the team name, and as Liz kicked at the dirt, she sheepishly mumbled, "I thought it was funny. Sorry."

Now that Matt knew what it was, he started laughing. It was funny. He liked the bucket of skills they had and how ridiculous it was.

They moved forward and through the crowd to reach the door and entered the same teleporter room they used last time.

A woman walked beside them and hastily barked at them, "The objective is to tie down the medium fort and keep the defenders from leaving. If you can take the fort, do so, and you will be doubly rewarded. More information is in the AI packet." She took a single breath before she asked, "Questions?"

None of them said anything, and they were then guided to the circle of runes that would teleport them to the nearest city.

They arrived in a flash and were hurried out of the city center by a uniformed official. They quickly jogged to the entrance of the city before boarding their various flying devices and taking to the air.

Matt was reviewing what he knew of the medium forts and comparing it to what his AI had on file about them. They were larger than the forts they had charged previously, and usually protected a strategic asset, whereas the smaller forts acted like a fence to guard the more valuable areas.

The medium forts were wider and covered a larger area with both their physical walls and their protective formations. According to the information survey, there was a simulated, high-value ore vein slightly to the west of the fort. It was in the perfect position to provide the occupying faction control over the area, and an opportunity to collect points.

The fort itself was fifty percent larger than any they had encountered in the war thus far, with an interior tower two stories higher.

Overall, he thought they could take the fort if it was staffed by the usual number of guards. They just needed to draw the defenders out, and let Annie use her invisibility to sneak in and start wreaking havoc. She could even just open the gates for them. Ideally, they would be able to lure at least a small number of defenders to protect the simulated mine. According to the rules set down, any simulated resource had to be protected in order to keep generating points, as any real one would.

The reward for taking a medium fort was listed at 5,000 points, and Matt was eager to collect. Taking it as a solo team, Matt expected even more when it was all said and done. That didn't even take into account the number of defenders they would be killing, or the additional rewards from the kingdom.

The largest catch of the assault would be at least one Tier 7 guarding the fort. If they were lucky, there might even be two or three. It was how the kingdom was deploying them, and their intelligence report suggested that the queendom was doing the same. Still, it wasn't anything they couldn't handle, which was why Matt started briefing his team about his idea as they flew.

Matt lay behind a short bush atop the hill overlooking the simulated mining site. It was about two miles away from the target fortress, and the queendom had created a small wooden wall around the simulated mine. He peered through the sparse underbrush and watched as people stood around the building next to the hole that was the mine.

There was a guard station in the small wooded palisade that the defenders had erected so they wouldn't be out in the open.

Matt breathed slowly and deeply as he kept watch.

Their plan was laid out. They just were waiting for the signal.

"I'm in place."

With that message from Annie, he slithered back down the hill, and with Conor's help, pushed the boulder they had prepared beforehand. They got it right under the crest of the hill and set their feet before looking at each other around the backside of the massive rock.

"Ready?" Matt grunted out the question. Even with [Mages Retreat] active, this rock was still just over three feet tall, almost halving Matt's six and a half foot frame. On top of that, it was made from Tier 4 material. While the boulder was lighter than it would be if it was of a higher Tier rock, it's still incredibly heavy. Thankfully, it was only rock and not metal as rock didn't get as heavy with Tier as metal did.

Conor didn't respond verbally and just started to shove, and Matt quickly joined him. They grunted as they struggled forward, and slowly, the two-and-a-half-ton boulder crested the hill and began rolling on its own.

The pair of front-liners watched the boulder pick up speed as it started racing toward the bottom of the ravine, heading straight for the wooden wall.

Breathing heavily, Matt summoned his blade and started sprinting after the bouncing boulder with Conor right behind him. They screamed with what little breath they had left as they raced forward, futilely trying to catch up to the careening boulder as its multi-ton weight bounced around.

The rock had been their answer to the wooden walls that they didn't know how to get around, but as Matt watched it bounce down the slope and build up speed, he worried that it would actually kill someone. The rock was now hurtling through the air at a frantic pace.

They struggled to keep from tripping as they ran down the steep hill, but Matt managed to see the rock obliterate the wooden wall. It passed through as if the barrier had never existed. Wooden splinters flew everywhere, and the rock flew through the building and out the other side of the wall. It continued to roll and skip up the far slope before it lost most of its momentum.

Matt cursed their luck and choice of rock as Liz sent a message. "What the fuck was that!?"

"We did the boulder plan."

"Ascenders' balls, that was a shit ton more than we wanted!"

Matt and Conor rushed the fort and started to fight the defenders who were still standing. Of the nine that were in the base, five met them with weapons drawn. The two of them limped out with clear injuries and fought at their worst, while the others had escaped the improvised missile.

During their planning phase, Emily mentioned that if they instantly wiped out the mine's defenders, the rest would just hole up in the fort and not risk sending more people to an ambush.

That was why it was just the two of them attacking the mining base. They wanted to appear to be part of a foolhardy attack by rogue elements hoping to earn some easy points.

Liz, Emily, and Aster waited in a bush situated along the most likely path that the defenders' reinforcements would come through. In the end, it all depended on Matt and Conor's acting skills.

Through the shouting and clanging of weapons, Matt heard the orders being shouted, "Hold them down and don't let them deeper in!"

"Hold the entrance!"

Someone else shouted, "For Ingrid! She got blasted by those bastards' boulder. Give them no escape!"

Matt parried a blow and returned with what he hoped would come off as a lucky thrust through the defenses of the spear wielder.

They screamed and were suddenly gone as if they were never there.

He caught sight of Conor downing his opponent and pushed forward enough for them both to get surrounded individually. Matt was trying to seem overeager after downing one of the defenders, hoping to draw more attention to himself.

Finally, the message they were waiting for arrived. “Ten people on the move. I slipped in while they went out.”

Matt grinned and burst forward with his full strength as he felt Conor’s [Demon Zone] activate. He grabbed the Tier 5’s sword with his armored hand and thrust his longsword through their weaker chest armor. As he withdrew the blade, they vanished, and he lunged at his other attacker, taking their mace attack on his exposed head.

The queendom fighter was too weak to damage him through [Cracked Phantom Armor], and Matt pounded them in the face with the pommel of his weapon, breaking their nose as he transitioned to a thrust toward the leader.

In three moves, three more people vanished as they were taken away by the army watchers. Matt smiled, pleased that the plan was going so well.

Conor stood over a few spots of blood, and he saw the man return his grin from under his helm.

“Let’s go help the mages.”

Conor scoffed at Matt’s suggestion. “They don’t need our help. I bet they’re already done with the reinforcements.”

Matt shrugged; his fellow melee fighter was probably right, but they still hurried to their teammates’ AI reported locations.

They were only halfway there when they received the message that they were expecting. “Reinforcements dealt with.”

When they met up with the mages, they moved to the edge of the fort’s line of sight as a group of five.

Matt was the combat leader, so he sent a message to Annie. “Annie, what’s your situation?”

“Sitting over the gate. There are five people here, and they’re debating what to do, since their links to the others all vanished. I can take them, but it will be noisy.”

Matt thought it over and had his AI run the simulations.

“Go for it. Take them out, and we’ll rush the gate at the same time. We can batter it down if we have to, but the defensive shielding will slow us down. If you can get the door open, we can back you up.”

After a long pause, they received a message. “I’ll move on your order. I’m ready whenever.”

"You'll hear us."

Matt looked to his teammates and explained his plan. "Conor and I in the front, blocking the archers. Stay close, and we rush them as fast as we can."

Emily cursed quietly. "I hate these anti-flying device formations. It would be a lot easier if we could attack from above."

"It would be but stay low and behind us."

Matt returned his longsword to his ring, and after digging into his spatial bag, withdrew the shield that he had used during his time as a frontliner storming the golem fortress. Conor was already in position, and they started out onto the cleared field surrounding the main fort at a steady lope.

They were a quarter of the way across the mile of cleared area when the arrows started to rain down on them. At first, it was the occasional plink of metal on metal, but as they reached the halfway point, it was like a torrent as the defenders tried to force them back.

A blast of fire impacted his shield, but Matt pushed through it and kept in line with Conor. They were nearly at the fort when a glowing blue arrow punched straight through Matt's shield. It was stopped by [Cracked Phantom Armor], but his AI calculated that whatever skill the archer used would punch through if he gave the archer a clear shot.

It wasn't as strong as Tara's Tier 3 Talent that pierced armor, but it was strong enough to be an issue.

All at once, the rain-like sound of arrows disappeared, and they were under the entrance of a tunnel that was covered in arrow slits. The large wooden door was slightly ajar, and as they reached it, they could hear fighting from the inside.

Matt dropped his shield and ripped the door open as Conor rushed through with his shield and shortsword raised.

Emily was the next through, with Liz right on her heels and with Aster in her backpack looking over the blood mage's shoulders.

Matt resummoned his longsword and joined the others, only to see a floor covered in blood and Annie looking as if she had just fought Liz. His AI told him that she only had a single, light cut on her hip, which meant that it was her enemy's blood that covered the entranceway. He didn't know how many people she had fought, but he was thoroughly impressed with her results.

Liz took a moment to gather the blood and moved to the entrance that led into the clear area between the fortress walls and the fort itself.

"I'll go out in golem form and move right."

"Remember to watch out for the archer with an armor-piercing skill. They'll punch right through your golem. Use your [Blood Shield]."

"Will that block her?"

Matt waited for his AI to run the calculations before replying, "No, but it'll make it nonlethal."

"Got it. I'll go out spell heavy and try to take out the remaining defenders on the wall."

Liz exploded out of the little cover they had to a peppering of arrows and a [Fireball].

Matt and Conor gave Emily cover as they left the tunnel through the wall. To his surprise, Matt found most of the queendom's guards already retreating back into the fort itself. Liz had seen that as well and engaged the retreating archers. Aster was in the golem with her and was sending shards of ice to anyone trying to flank Liz's blood golem. Matt noticed that the pair was attracting attention from two queendom archers on top of the fortress roof.

Matt cast [Hail] on them, and as the near-solid wall of ice fell, it forced the archers to retreat. The remaining defenders raced to join the mass of people trying to all fit through the small entrance at the base of the fortress. Annie had already reactivated her Talent in the chaos to see if she could sneak into the building.

There was shouting, and they turned to try and stop Matt and Conor's charge as Emily cycled through sending [Water Bullet]s and [Bolt]s at the mass of people.

Every time the lance of lightning illuminated the inner courtyard, someone was teleported out. Matt wished they had more time for Emily to absorb the two skills she had, as it would take her from a two times damage multiplier to an eight times multiplier. If she was killing a person with each shot now, he marveled at what she could do when she got the extra effect. [Bolt] could chain if it had enough damage left after impact, or if there was a large amount of metal near the target. The mission had just come too soon; she had only received her [Cracked Mana Bolt] this morning.

They slammed into the mass of people who had the door shut on them, and Matt and Conor started hacking down at the queendom fighters with large, heavy blows. Blood flew, and flesh was rent with each attack.

The screams in front of Matt were overpowered by screams coming from his left where Liz had gone to rout the archers and other ranged defenders causing Matt to glance over quickly.

Otto looked on in horror as the red monster ran out of the gate's guardhouse. He didn't know what it was until Lesley loosed a glowing blue arrow at the monster, which caused him to do the same.

Her arrow sunk deep into its shoulder while his skittered off as if the monster was made from stone. He made a mental note to adjust his shots as if this was an armored target.

Otto prided himself on being the second best archer in their group but the lack of an archery skill was showing its flaws now.

"Aim for her head. It's sticking out of the thing's chest."

As Lesley said that Otto noticed the discrepancy and loosed his own arrow at the pale face surrounded by living blood.

He had to force down his bile as the monster cut through the other archers. He knew them, spent time with them, cared for them. Otto watched them get cut to pieces.

As he withdrew and notched another arrow, he was mesmerized at Harvie's leg flying through the air and spewing blood before it all vanished. Or the flesh did. The blood was pulled into the monster as it looked up at them overhead.

With the rain of ice keeping Lesley and him pinned to one side they had the perfect view of the monster as it ran at them.

Otto repressed the twinge of fear as the golem of blood reached the base of the fort where it met the outer wall's walkway. It was the second floor out of five and while they were on the roof the monster was unable to reach them.

His elation halted as the monster seemed to stick to the wall as what seemed to be frozen blood latched on and it started to climb up. The first steps were halting, and it slid down twice but as he and

Lesley launched arrow after arrow on the thick shoulders of the monster it grew nearer and nearer.

"We need to run!" His voice cracked which caused him to repeat the statement again only to see Lesley ignoring him.

After five useless arrows, the monster had reached the halfway point of climbing the wall and he repeated himself for Lesley to nod and turn toward the front of the fortress.

They had gotten a single step each, Otto froze along with Lesley as the sight sunk in.

They were trapped.

The ice skill which they had avoided by moving back was still producing at a prodigious rate and had accumulated a foot-deep pile of ice that grew each moment as more fell. The problem was it was covering the front half of the fort's roof. Where the trap door was.

"Fuck!" Their exclamations were said nearly in unison.

Otto withdrew another arrow but fumbled it as he leaned over to launch his arrow.

The monster was only a foot beneath them.

Yellow eyes met his.

He stumbled back but that was the only thing that saved him from a whip of blood that cracked the air with its passage. The snap was so high pitched it hurt his ears and then it was too late.

The monster was on the roof.

Lesley had retreated and loosed her [Charged Shot] skill enhanced arrow. His Tier 6 team leader's shot was deadly and at this range she couldn't miss, and the skill made sure it couldn't be blocked.

Until today.

The arrow was deflected off a flat plane of blood and ice causing the shot to careen off to the side of the woman's head. He saw a wince as two tendrils of blood lashed out and Lesley twisted to avoid them.

He, still on his back, scooted away and notched another arrow before his legs stopped working.

Otto looked down to see why he wasn't moving to find his legs were gone and then the pain hit.

He screamed.

Through the pain he tried to loose the arrow but found a bird claw descending toward his face.

Otto's last sight was of Lesley being impaled from behind as the ice on the roof rose, and a rain of blood like bullets killed his friend.

Suddenly, the pain stopped, and he was momentarily disoriented in a wave of purple then laying in a hospital bed with a view of Lesley's hole filled body and glassy eyes staring back at him from one bed over.

He overheard someone saying they got overwhelmed and cursing followed but his eyes were locked on Lesley.

Her mouth moved and she tried to say something to him, but it was lost in all the other screaming.

Otto reached out to help her, but she was swarmed by people in healer's robes and suddenly he was surrounded as well.

"It's okay now." An older man stood over with only his eyes visible from his sanitary clothing.

His eyes were a kind brown that spoke of the soft soil of his family's backyard. It felt so far away and so long ago that he had seen it last.

Otto felt everything going cold and wondered if he was going to die.

The healer said something, but he missed it.

What does a dead man need words for?

He didn't die. The pain receded not long after and he looked down to see his legs were now attached and the healers gone. He wiggled his toes and found everything still worked.

A nurse, a tired-looking man, reached out with a hand and said something he missed.

Otto focused on the man's uncovered mouth and finally pieced together what he was trying to say.

"Come with me. We have a nice peaceful place to stay."

He was led to a comforting room that looked like a garden mixed with a petting zoo.

At his guide's instance, he sat by a tree where a curious rabbit wandered over to him and then climbed into his lap.

He idly stroked the soft fur as the events replayed themselves over and over. Blood and pain.

Otto pulled himself out of his thoughts and looked around. A few people in healer's robes moved from person to person but he was confused at their purpose as some stopped to talk and others moved on. It didn't take long for him to realize that they were checking up to the people who were breaking down and talking to those that needed it.

He refused to be one of them.

His pride won out until he remembered the taloned foot descending onto his face. If the watcher had been any slower…

He swallowed hard and focused on the soft fur in his lap until Lesley was led in and he noticed her clothes were replaced with a white set he hadn't noticed himself wearing either. Everyone was but he had somehow missed the change of clothes. He didn't know why he was focusing on that, but he was unable to take his mind off the incongruity.

That was until Lesley saw him and burst into tears. His strong resolute team leader slumped to the ground in front of him and wept into the soft grass.

Otto couldn't hold it in any longer and did the same as he watched her. Great wracking sobs tearing out of him.

He didn't know who moved first but they were embracing, they weren't close friends, but they had grown close over the last month of war preparation and then the week of standing guard. As her second in command over the archers they spent a lot of time together.

In the end it just felt good to be held and that just caused the emotions to pour out faster until both of them were finally drained.

Matt brought his sword around and cut into a hip. Most of the defenders, who were locked out of the fort by one of their faster comrades, were Tier 5 and unable to stand up to a group of Pathers a Tier higher than them. A few of them were Tier 6, but they fared no better, as Matt ignored their attacks that simply bounced off [Cracked Phantom Armor]. He used the openings from their failed attacks to finish them off.

After a minute of frantic fighting, they were standing alone, only left with the sound of blame being passed around inside of the fortress.

Matt smiled when he heard the shouting. Two of the people who made it in blamed the other for closing the door too early, and the other insisted that they saved them by shutting the door early. It had been them or the people outside, after all.

Stopping [Hail], Matt began charging his blade with mana, and as it reached 1,000 mana, he brought the glowing blade around on the door. He released [Mana Charge] onto the wood and metal just before impact.

The door cracked and splintered at the loud explosion but held. The fortress had a reinforcement enhancement that allowed it to resist more damage, but thankfully, the shielding formation was only on the outer wall to prevent ranged attacks. The inner fort had to make do with the simpler rune.

As he readied a second attack, Annie messaged them. "Got a line to the second floor."

Matt paused for a heartbeat and said, "Conor go with her. Emily and I will keep their attention down here."

Half a minute later, he slammed another [Mana Charge] into the door, causing another loud explosion.

He unleashed three more attacks before a hole appeared at the top of the door, and a [Fireball] greeted him. With his reflexes perfected beyond the norm for Tier 6, Matt was able to duck the attack, and Emily returned the spell with one of her own.

The [Bolt] caused a scream that indicated someone else was out of the battle.

He checked everyone's overlays and found that Emily, Liz, and Aster were all at around half mana. It would cause them to start rationing their spells. Conor was the one who surprised him during his check. The man had mentioned that his Tier 3 Talent let him sustain mana, and he was currently sitting at around seventy-five percent. His AI made a note that he was able to hold the mana hungry [Demon Zone] for so long, which meant that his Talent gave him back quite a bit of mana.

The next blow of his sword blew away enough of the door for him to see that the defenders had stacked tables and chairs over the entrance. This time, Matt charged a [Mana Slash] that he used to cut through the debris. Its penetrating power was stronger, while [Mana Charge] had more blunt damage.

Another scream came from inside the fort, and after charging his sword once again, Matt jumped through the now broken down door.

He was immediately met by another [Fireball] to the face. It washed over [Cracked Phantom Armor], but wasn't able to break through, only straining his control over the skill. From the feedback his skill gave him, he guessed that the mage was a peak Tier 6, or a weak Tier 7.

He landed with a skid, as the floor was slick with something, and he tumbled across the room as another wash of flame hit him. The oil he slipped in caught fire with him, but its slower damage was far easier for [Cracked Phantom Armor] to handle. The flames from the oil were nothing compared to the skills that ate through the mana flowing through [Cracked Phantom Armor]'s structure.

He stood, and with the fire blocking his vision, relied on his spiritual sense to find his nearest enemy. His AI indicated that it was the mage who had lit him on fire, so he decided to return their gift and tackled them into the still burning oil. With a thought, he created spikes on his armored fists.

It took three blows for the person under him to vanish, and Matt was quickly running low on air. His armor would block the flame, but the fire was burning all of the oxygen around his face, and his already taxed muscles were growing desperate for air. If he had known this would happen, he would have taken their underwater breathing broach. He could have used it to expand his breath-holding abilities.

Drawing from his rechargeable mana stone for a full mana pool, he quickly cast [Create Water] over his head before his active skills drained him down to one percent of his maximum mana. There, his regeneration could handle the costs of his core skills that were constantly running.

With the fire extinguished, Matt let the water skill run, as the mana cost to continue was nothing to him. The first breath was sweet as his armor filtered out the smoke, and he finally saw a burnt-out bottom floor of the fortress.

Matt went to move up the stairs, only to get messages from Liz and Annie in almost unison, causing him to pause.

"Top floor is clear."

"Conor and I cleared the middle floor."

Matt sent back, "Bottom floor burnt out but clear. That leaves a floor between each of us." He thought for a second before asking, "Anyone kill the Tier 7?"

At the chorus of no's, he said, "Annie and Liz, clear the floor between you two. Emily and I will clear the floor between you and us. I expect Tier 7 to be between the top floor and the middle one."

Emily was now in the room, with a wet cloth wrapped over her mouth and nose.

She private messaged him, "The fuck are you made out of? I saw you burning."

Out loud, he responded, "My armor is great for low damage over a long time. What it can't handle are single big hits."

She nodded at that and turned to the stairs leading to the second floor.

"Ready?"

Matt didn't verbally respond, he just moved forward after finding his blade along the far wall. The staircase ran along the outer wall, and they rushed up the stairs and to the door, only to find it unlocked and unbarred. He burst through and found not a single person inside. From the fighting he could hear from above, he assumed that Liz, Conor, and Annie were fighting the remaining defenders.

He and Emily ran up the stairs, but the fighting was already over when they arrived. Their team was simply standing around, while the floor was covered in blood and debris.

Matt went over to Liz and Aster and asked, "What happened?"

As he approached them under the pretense of scratching his bond, he activated his Concept, but Liz grabbed his wrist and privately messaged him.

"No. Don't do that. It's too obvious right now."

He did as she asked. She was right, the others could see her mana pool's percentage, and if it rapidly filled, it would be far too obvious. He sighed as Liz explained what she and Aster had gotten up to.

"Aster and I fought our way along the wall, then climbed to the roof where we could fight the other two archers. Good call on the shield skill. The archer was on the roof and got a good, skill enhanced shot off, but with my Concept reinforcing the spell it blocked the arrow. After that, I cleared the roof, then Annie, Conor, and I fought nearly a dozen people in this room. The Tier 7 was a melee fighter, so it wasn't that bad. I just flooded the area of the room he was in."

He looked to Annie and Conor to hear about their floor.

"We had a few people in the middle floor, since it had a door leading to the wall, but nothing crazy. Easy enough that there's nothing to report."

Matt nodded. "Liz, report in for us while Annie gets her hip looked at. Conor and I will go repair what defenses we can. I think we'll be told to hold this location, so let's prepare for that."

Emily was already looking at her sister's wound, and he and Conor moved to the bottom floor, while Liz and Aster moved to the roof to message someone back at headquarters.

Matt couldn't wipe the grin off his face. They had only been expected to harass the fort, but they had managed to take it.

As he and Conor boarded the gatehouse back up, they discovered that the door was cracked and didn't sit right in its frame. Neither of them knew how it happened. They could only speculate that it was when Annie managed to get the door open for them. Breaking the door wouldn't have been a bad move for the defenders if it kept them out.

After that was taken care of to the best of their ability, Matt left Conor to go charge the base's mana stone located on the second floor. It still had half a charge, but he topped it off with his own mana. Meanwhile, he drained a single mana stone to spread some dust around the crystal and hide the fact he filled the fort's power reserves himself. It was some plausible deniability, at least.

Liz messaged everyone while he stood around the fort's mana stone. "They want us to hold the fort. They didn't expect us to take it and are scrambling to get us reinforcements."

"Did they have an estimated time?"

"Three hours at the earliest."

That wasn't that bad, and Matt moved back outside to join Conor and watch their surroundings.

While keeping watch, he checked his messages from the army AI, and smiled at the points he had earned.

Prior Total (last updated 3 days ago): 537 points.

TEAM MERITS:

(Calculated for Tier 6 Combatant).

- Enemy vassal killed, Tier 5. Worth 1 point. Performed 40 times.
- Enemy vassal killed, Tier 6. Worth 5 points. Performed 11 times.
- Enemy vassal killed, Tier 7. Worth 25 points. Performed 1 times.
- Mining site captured. 500 points.
- Medium fort captured. 5,000 points. Two times normal points are awarded for solo team capture. 10,000 points.

PERSONAL MERITS:
(Calculated for Tier 6 Combatant).

- Enemy vassal killed, Tier 5. Worth 1 point. Performed 19 times.
- Enemy vassal killed, Tier 6. Worth 5 points. Performed 7 times.
- Enemy vassal killed, Tier 7. Worth 25 points. Performed 0 times.
- Medium fort captured. 5,000 points.

ARMY MERITS:

- Items and equipment looted but returned. Worth 624 points.

UNACHIEVED MERITS: For reference purposes only.

- N/A

SUMMARY OF GAINS:
Team Merits:

- **Raw Total:** 10,580
- **Team Multiplier:** 1x
- **Category Total:** 10,580

Personal Merits:

- **Raw Total:** 5,035
- **Personal Multiplier:** 1x
- **Category Total:** 5,035

Combined Merits:

- **Sub-Total:** 15,615
- **Total Multiplier:** 1x
- **Grand Total:** 15,615

New Gains: 16,239 points.
New Total: 16,776 points.
Pather Team Ranking (Kingdom of Seven Suns): 132nd place.
Estimated Daily Stipend: N/A.

Matt couldn't remove the grin from his face. He had earned 16,239 points, just from this mission. Beyond that he had little doubt that the kingdom would also reward them for their surprisingly successful operation.

The fact that they got double the expected points from taking the fort made him want to dance on the walls as he kept watch. Getting rewarded for taking the fort as a team and as a personal merit was interesting, but it was enough to make him start planning the next mission.

If they repeated this feat a few more times, they would have more than enough points to get the Tier 14 skills they wanted, along with some of the top tier items in the price range of hundreds of thousands of points.

He spoke to Conor as they passed each other on their opposite paths of walking the wall.

"We made out like bandits on this one."

Conor grinned and fist-bumped Matt as he passed. "We need to see if we can do this again. I could use the points."

Matt laughed at him and called out over his shoulder, "Great minds think alike. I can't resist the lure of these points."

The six of them watched the fort for four hours with the expectation that their reinforcements would arrive soon. They had been told it was taking longer, but they were already an hour late.

None of them minded the extra wait. It was free points, after all.

Liz, on the top of the fort with Emily, called out, "I see something."

Matt looked where she was pointing, but it wasn't from the southeast as he expected. No, it was from the north. Queendom territory.

"How many?"

"I can't tell. I only got a glimpse. They were flying low."

Matt thought hard. "Call it in and ask about the state of our reinforcements."

A moment later, Liz said, "We are commanded to hold. Reinforcements are fifteen minutes out."

Matt nodded. It seemed like a reasonable call. The approaching enemies would take time to get here, and he doubted they would engage immediately, allowing their reinforcements to scare them off. He doubted that either side was sending more than the fifty people who usually held a medium fort.

They would just need to defend the fort for a short while.

He and Conor moved to the front gate to see the approaching attackers. There were nearly one hundred people. Far more than he expected, but with the defender's advantage, he expected that they could hold them off until their reinforcements arrived.

There was a special irony about defending the fort they just took over, but he tightened his grip on his blade and watched as the group of queendom fighters advanced.

He looked to Conor as he stood next to him and said, "You know what the queendom defenders did?"

"Yeah?" Conor didn't look away but sounded confused as he replied.

"Yeah, we're gonna take that, and do the opposite."

10

The approaching small army stopped at the edge of the tree line and spread out. It wasn't a full wall of people, but it was wide enough to alert the attackers if Matt and his team tried to escape from the fort by climbing over the back wall.

It was a good strategic decision that he wished they hadn't made. If they were incompetent, this would all be a lot easier.

At least their reinforcements were only a few minutes away. Matt looked to their north and found nothing, but knew they had to be somewhere, racing across the horizon. They just needed to hold these guys off for a little while, and they would get harried from the rear, trapping them between a rock and a hard place. At that point, he hoped that the queendom would give up on retaking the fort.

Annie raced over toward them, under the area where they were standing on the outer wall.

"Any chance I can sneak out?"

Matt looked around and asked, "Can you drop down without your invisibility breaking?"

Annie was silent for a minute. "Not if they have a Tier 7. And the drop would be hard to hide."

Matt reached into his bag and withdrew his modified golem crossbow, along with the three quivers of bolts he kept for the weapon.

"Maybe you can make use of this."

He paused and asked, "Wait. Are you any good with ranged weapons?"

Annie shrugged and said, "It's not my favorite style of combat, but I have the ranged module for my AI, and there isn't much wind, so it should be fine."

Matt cursed internally, but they had little recourse. He was needed to guard the broken fort's door with Conor. It was very obviously broken, and he doubted that the attacking force would be caught unawares about their reinforcements. That would only lead to them sending a single, strong push to break through the weakest point. They would be hoping to secure the fort before more kingdom fighters could arrive.

It was a gamble on being able to overwhelm them with sheer numbers. With Annie on the walls, and the three mages attacking from the high ground on the fort's roof, he hoped that they could hold through one or two waves.

The attackers would need to storm the fort quickly with everything they had, if they hoped to overwhelm them. Unless they had siege equipment with them. Then things would get a little dicey. Especially if they had the means to climb the twenty-foot stone walls. Ladders would take time to make if they didn't bring them because of the limited space that lower Tier spatial bags had to offer. Grappling hooks were harder to use, but easier to carry, so there was a distinct chance that they were equipped with a few. He made a note in his AI that they should have brought grappling hooks with them. It would have allowed them to avoid the front entrance.

As he watched Annie vanish in the light of the setting sun, he received a message from Emily. "My [Bolt] is too short-ranged to use from the top of the fort. I need to be on the wall."

Matt's initial thought was to curse, but as he rechecked his surroundings, he noticed that it wasn't that bad of a situation. They would need someone on their left flank to protect from attacks holding them down and allowing a token force to scale the walls. Annie could handle one side, being both invisible and ranged, but that left their other side undefended. This could work.

"Take the left flank." He ran the simulations and then added, to his distaste, "Take Aster with you."

His bond was a better pair with Liz and synergizing blood with ice, but she didn't quite have the range that Liz did. Even then, the situation was still less than ideal. Liz was basically a water mage, who were mid-range at best. An archer would be ideal to cover them from above, with Liz guarding their rear, but they would have to have her take both roles.

Aster would be better on the wall, helping to keep people from climbing it.

He checked his AI and its internal clock. Fourteen minutes and seven seconds. They could hold out for that long.

The first row of attackers moved forward with quick steps and set up what looked like a stubby tube. Matt was confused until the image registered with his memories from the war movies that he'd seen. It was a siege cannon.

To his horror, they were pouring mana crystals into the rear holder from a spatial bag, as if they were water.

He and Conor seemed to register it at the same time, and they dropped off the wall. A split second after they had the chance to hunker down, the concussive force of the spell shattered the air. The world seemed to shake as the dust settled. Matt stood before Conor, with the world around him ringing and blurring. The man was mouthing something while working his jaw. Matt's ears had been mostly protected from the concussive force by his armor, but Conor wasn't so lucky.

With two steps, he was in the little gatehouse and staring at the door that was little more than remnants of hinges clinging to the blackened stone.

His AI had already identified the model of cannon and done the math. They had used at least 10,000 mana in that blast. That was fifty Tier 5 mana stones, essentially the value of a Tier 6 stone, if not its mana equivalent.

Matt was aghast. He created mana at an absurd rate, but that single attack was the production of a Tier 5 rift run eight times, if the average reward was given. It just seemed wasteful when that much mana could have sustained a crafter making a permanent weapon or powered a city for hours. If they converted that mana into personal mana for their mage's mana pools, it could have completely refueled four or five mages.

Matt wasn't able to think anymore, as the enemy had charged

forward in unison with their first wave and were now only steps away from the annihilated entrance.

He cleared his head and realized that he had been instinctively charging [Mana Slash]. The blue crescent quickly lashed out with an eager bite. Two people vanished as they tumbled in a spray of blood and still-settling dust.

Conor appeared next to him as the attackers reached the doorway. The other man stood at his shoulder and thrust his shield forward, blocking a descending mace. An idle part of Matt noticed that the man was using a short metal truncheon instead of his sword, or longer mace.

Matt kicked an attacker in the knee and immediately noticed that they were only Tier 6. The way they crumpled under his full power almost gave him pause, but he had no time to think, he could only act with power and speed.

The door was four people wide, which let him swing his longsword around without any hindrance, but it also meant that he was always fighting at least three people while they cram their way in. A shield was split under his Tier 7 blade as he braced himself and swung at the nearest enemy.

A screaming howl of wind tried to knock him off his feet, but Matt instinctively used his Concept to anchor himself to the ground. It knocked everyone else to their asses at the same time, and Matt noticed the mage and five archers standing behind their fallen allies. He didn't know when they moved forward, but they were now only fifty feet away, so Matt rushed them.

As he stepped over the rising bodies of the queendom forces, he kicked an armored head and winced as the man vanished. Head wounds were dangerous, he tried to avoid them if he could, and only hoped that the man had been pulled out before any significant damage was done.

The archers and mage hadn't missed the opportunity created by their comrades falling, and the archers loosed their arrows. He didn't know if it was a miscommunication or not, but they all aimed for Conor's still prone form instead of splitting their targets.

That was their final mistake.

Matt was close enough to get off a [Mana Slash], which he realized right as he was nearly halfway across the distance separating them. A [Wind Wall] sprang up, protecting the mage in the center and an archer on either side of him. The others were just gone, and as Matt slammed his ever brightening blade into the defensive spell, he understood why.

They were only Tier 5.

He almost felt like a bully, but they were a part of a mixed force, and therefore fair game. His feelings didn't cause his blade to slow as he reared it back, and with a bright explosion of blue light, broke through the mage's defenses.

The wind mage just dropped to the ground, with blood running from his nose from the rebound of having his spell forcefully shattered. But Matt still had two archers to deal with. They hadn't been dumb, and knew they were stuck behind the [Wind Wall], but they hadn't sat still.

Once the barrier fell, they both fired arrows at Matt. They were good shots. One went for Matt's face, and the other at his chest, making them exceedingly difficult to dodge or block at this range.

Matt ignored the arrows as they bounced off his armor and bounded toward them. He cut through both of them in a heavy horizontal slash.

As they fell, he noticed another group of attackers forming up at the edge of the woods, and more people mulling around the cannon. Matt sprinted back to the safety of melee combat with his enemies and started slashing at them from behind.

Conor was back up and had taken most of them out already. He had four arrows sticking out of his shield, and another in his shoulder.

They retreated into the hall and peered out as the attackers prepped their cannon.

"Can you pull this arrow out? It's stuck in my shoulder joint, and I can't reach it."

Matt reached up, and after checking the direction of the arrow, pulled it out. To his surprise, it only had a small drop of blood on it.

"How didn't this hit you?"

Conor shrugged with his now mobile shoulder. "No clue, I was just huddling behind my shield when I saw the backline. Got lucky, I guess."

Matt tossed the arrow and asked everyone else on his team for a report.

Annie responded first. "Two small groups of people tried to scale the wall. They were going more for stealth, so it was easy to deal with them."

Emily said, "A full team with ladders tried to scale my wall, but I managed to kill them and destroy the ladders."

Matt cursed and asked, "Did they look made here, or professionally made?"

"Rough, Sticks and shit lashed together."

Matt breathed a slight sigh of relief. It wasn't ideal that they were making them, but they at least hadn't come prepared with them.

Liz noted, "People were sniffing around the back wall where it meets up with the fortress, but I was able to keep them away without much effort."

Matt peered out of the tunnel and saw that the enemies were actually pulling back their cannon and assembling a larger force. It looked like they were gathering everyone that hadn't been a part of the last rush or the encircling force.

Scared to see how much time had passed, Matt checked his countdown. Seven minutes fifty-seven seconds left.

Matt sighed. They were practically guaranteed their victory when their reinforcements arrived.

If his initial guess of one hundred people was correct, he estimated that they had sent twenty-five or so people to surround them, with another twenty-five in the last attack through the three places they tried to gain entrance. If they attacked with everything they had, it was at most fifty people, if they wanted to keep their encirclement up.

At five people abreast, if they all tried to cram through the front entrance, they could probably do this. They didn't need to kill all of them, just weaken them enough. When their reinforcements arrived, the queendom fighters would either flee or stay pinned between two attacking forces.

The party of fifty people moved forward in a ragged formation, with shields in the front and the archers and mages behind them.

Matt slapped Conor's side to get his attention, and they moved to either side of the opening. A quick glance at his AI showed him that Emily and Aster were slightly forward, but still guarding their side. Annie had mirrored their actions, and Matt steadied his breathing while he peeked around the corner.

The approaching unit was peppering the tunnel with arrows, trying to keep them pinned down. But with the thickness of the wall and construction of the gatehouse, there was little chance of him or Conor being hit.

Matt looked to his left and nodded at his fellow melee fighter when the group reached the fifty-foot mark. They both burst forward as the attackers did the same.

With how close the groups were, there was no chance of stray arrows taking them out, and they wanted to have the whole entrance to retreat back through.

Together, they took the charge head on, and stopped it dead in its tracks, but it wasn't without cost. Matt took a spear to the chest, and while it wasn't able to punch through his armor, it stymied the swing of his sword. The weakened blow only cut into one shield and got stuck halfway through. He kicked out and freed his sword, but he took three chopping strikes in retaliation.

As he was bringing a [Mana Charge] empowered blade around, he felt a phantom blow on his shoulder. As everyone in Conor's [Demon Zone] also flinched at the same time, he knew it was the chance for an attack in the zone to reflect to everyone. With [Cracked Phantom Armor], he was unharmed by the weak blow, but everyone else was unprepared for a sudden blow, and stumbled under the force.

When his blade slammed onto an unbraced shield, the soldier wielding it and the two people behind him were gone in a flash of light. They might have used 10,000 mana to break down a wall with the war cannon, but Matt used 1,000 mana to obliterate three people with his enchanted weapon.

With Conor at his side, Matt fought on. They were mostly in a melee, with few spells being cast. Most of the skills used were weapon enchantments or melee skills. Anything that needed range was simply too hard to use in such close quarters. After what felt like an hour of fighting, the battle began shifting to a more and more defensive struggle as the minutes dragged on.

He was breathing heavily. Even with [Endurance] running at a full 2 MPS, fighting was hard work. And with stakes this high, Matt was giving it everything he had.

A glance at his AI told him everything he needed to know.

Time until reinforcements: minus three minutes and four seconds.

They were pulling back because they were retreating, with their retaking of the fort a failure.

Matt checked his team's status and found everyone except himself and Aster with slight injuries.

Conor's leg was flashing red, causing Matt to reach for him and pull him back deeper into the tunnel.

"What happened?"

"Sharpness enchanted blade got my thigh. Didn't hit anything important, but I can't put much weight on it."

Matt internally cursed while he pulled out a clotting potion and just dumped it onto the bleeding leg. It had an anesthetic effect, which would help Conor remain active. Though, without full use of his leg, the man would be essentially stationary for anything they needed to do next.

Annie, Emily, and Liz all had shallow cuts on their upper body, and Matt wondered about how they sustained. But what was more worrying was their mana situation. All of the mages were all sitting at around one-quarter of their maximum.

Matt left Conor propped against a wall at the entrance to the tunnel at the man's insistence, and moved to the wall to get a better view of what was happening.

He expected to see the enemy retreating, or fighting off more forces, but his brain ground to a halt when he saw none of the above. They simply retreated, with around twenty people, back to their encirclement line.

In the group chat, he asked, "What's going on?"

Liz snapped back, "Our fucking relief went dark, and no one can contact them, but they know they aren't dead."

Matt froze at the unexpected situation. He just didn't know how to comprehend that. Afraid to attack a wounded party of roughly equal numbers? Who would make such a call? Even if they just wanted to play it safe, they could have fought their way to the fort then joined Matt's party in the walls.

"What?"

It was only half-coherent, but Liz seemed to understand.

"I've been talking with Juni, and he's as mad as we are. My best guess is the reinforcement group is led by a coward. Headquarters is trying to find us help, but they already had to scramble to get us that idiot."

Annie said, "Okay, so we're fucked. Same with this fort. I vote we get the fuck out of here."

Matt nodded. "That's the best plan. I'm not dying just for the kingdom to still lose the fort."

They still had to figure out what to do with Conor, but the man seemed to understand and said, "I can't run to keep up, and I'm happy to try to buy you some time."

Matt had already run the simulations and found a course of action where he didn't need to do that. They only needed to fight their way out of the fort and to a mile away, where the anti-flight formation didn't have an effect. If he could've simply shut down the formation, he would have done that while still inside, and just had them fly out from here. But, sadly, that was impossible.

"I don't think that will be necessary. We can carry you with Liz's blood and get us all out of here."

Matt looked around and said, "How's everyone else? Any problems?"

At the chorus of no's, he peered over the battlement at the attackers. They were performing triage on their wounded, though there weren't that many. Most had either 'died' and were teleported out or didn't take much damage.

They needed to escape. And they needed to do it now.

Matt was quickly joined by Annie, Emily, and Aster, while Liz made her way down to them. In just under ten minutes, they were ready to leave. Conor's large frame draped an arm over Liz while being held up by tendrils of blood.

The six of them were getting ready to make a break for it, when another group of queendom troops came through the woods.

This time, it was easily more than the one hundred that first came to the fort, and Matt saw their chance to escape vanish when he noticed that the far-off figures had spread out to make the encirclement stronger.

He cursed, "Fuck! Back into the fort."

It was their only chance, and it was a bad one. At this point, they had to hope that they could hold on to the smaller and more defensible fort itself.

Matt had an idea percolating but wasn't happy with it. Still, it was their only chance.

He wasn't willing to tell anyone about his Talent, it would paint too large a target on him. But he *could* reveal his Concept. Giving mana was rare, but not unheard of, and it was limited by willpower. It wasn't an unlimited resource, so it wasn't as dangerous to expose.

With a few carefully crafted lies, he could keep them going while giving them a chance to hold out for more reinforcements. As long as they held the inner fort, the queendom would need to dedicate a sizable force to prevent them from sallying forth and attacking their rear. A hundred kingdom fighters not led by a coward could easily harass this border fort enough to make it too costly for the queendom to continue to bleed troops in a losing position.

It was a faint hope, but it was all they had, and Matt refused to give up. If retreat wasn't an option, they had to stand and fight.

They entered the fort and slammed the surviving half of the door shut.

Emily hurt. Everything ached, but her spirit was growing more and more sore with the repeated use of her Talent. It wasn't exactly as she had told everyone at the auction. While that hadn't exactly been a lie, it wasn't the full truth either.

Her Talent didn't *exactly* double the power of spells, but it was close enough especially at the start.

She looked down to her wrist as they came into the fort. If she stopped absorbing the [Cracked Mana Bolt] and let it settle into her spirit, her [Bolt] would do four times as much damage. The problem was, if she did that, the skill would be at her outer spirit, and the mana cost of the skill would go up. While she could fix its location, it would take months of meditation to move the skill through her spirit once the initial absorption of the skill ended.

If her and her sister's lives were actually at risk, the choice would be easy, but with only a fake death, it didn't seem worth it. They would lose their points, but this war wasn't going to be short, and they could be earned back easily enough.

She once again cursed herself for starting with [Cracked Mana

Bolt] instead of [Fireball]. She wouldn't care about dumping that skill into her outer spirit. It would only be used in conjunction with the rest of her chain, not for its damage. She had more water spells that would be better to cast later.

[Water Bubble] also got an increase in effect, and it was an amazing defensive choice if she needed it.

They were about to get screwed over because some kingdom leader was a coward. If they had arrived an hour ago, when they were supposed to, this wouldn't be a problem. If they had arrived and attacked the rear of the enemy, they could have easily held the fort against two hundred people with fifty.

Matt grabbed her attention as the door slammed shut. He quickly spoke, "My Concept gives mana. Most of it is focused inward."

She almost didn't believe him. Melee types like him always went with hitting hard. It was the best way to increase damage, but as she thought about it, it made sense. The man always sat near empty with his mana, but that made sense if his Concept was feeding him mana.

She felt her spirit churn as mana flowed into her from somewhere. It was like water was being poured down her metaphysical spine. Not uncomfortable, but a completely new sensation.

"I can't do this forever, but I can get you all back to near full, then I'll run out. I'd appreciate you keeping this quiet, but I can't let us die when I might be able to make a difference."

Emily nodded to herself. That was a sign of trust. It also explained how he cast things like [Hail] without his mana changing its level. But with an armor Talent that made it free, she could see the logical steps to giving his excess mana to his mages and turning that into a Concept. No, now that she thought about it…it was a flawless move.

She knew the man was smart, but that was out-of-the-box thinking.

"I won't say anything."

Her sister echoed her sentiment, and Conor nodded his agreement. He was clearly using [Endurance] with the free mana to heal quickly, and had his eyes closed while rubbing the area around the wound.

Annie, the first to reach full mana, said, "I'm going to slip outside and try to create some havoc."

Emily was going to protest, but Matt beat her to it. "No. It's better to have you do that in here."

Emily didn't like that either, but it was an improvement, so she held her tongue.

They peered through the destroyed doorway and saw the queendom fighters moving forward.

Liz said, "We already blocked the second floor door with some stone rubble. We can hold and bleed them as we climb upward when we get pushed back. Headquarters seems to want to hold this place, and they want us to hold out while they get another team here."

Her sister spat, "Yeah, because that went *so* well before. Fuck them. When we get back, I'm finding and stabbing that coward of a leader."

Emily agreed with the sentiment, and from Liz's curled lip and Matt's armored stance, they seemed to as well.

At the pounding of feet, Emily turned to the door and shot out a [Water Bullet], quickly followed by a [Bolt]. Her Talent increased the effect of the last skill, and [Bolt] normally had a slight chance to jump from person to person, if there was leftover energy. When it was twice as strong, the spell almost always took out two people. She wasn't sure if that was the army watchers being cautious, or if it would take more hits to really kill someone.

It wasn't a pretty thought, but she was pretty sure that with both [Fireball] and [Cracked Mana Bolt], she would be hitting seven times harder. That was a jump of nearly a Tier and a half. It was a scary, but exciting thought. She needed to find a way to solve the problem of spiritual strain and mana cost.

Her mental eye went to the blue armored man in front of her guarding her front. With Matt's Concept, while she couldn't cast indefinitely, she could get as far as her spirit let her. The thought that she needed to keep close to him was quashed ruthlessly. She wasn't her parents, who used everyone near them. She liked Matt, and firmly made up her mind to never ask the man for mana.

He was a friend not a resource.

It was still a welcome novelty, as she cast without care to her reserves. She didn't worry about saving her attacks for the optimal attack and just cast [Water Bullet] and [Bolt] as fast as her spirit let her.

Two queendom fighters shoved their way into the door, and Matt and Conor stood firm, taking blow after blow. They were more a makeshift wall of skill and steel, but they held admirably.

She cast her combo once again, and the front two people vanished.

They were settling into a rhythm when Annie messaged them all, "They're breaking into the second floor. Earth mage or something."

All of them cursed, and a rain of [Hail] burst out on the door, causing a pile-up as they all ran to the rear and up the stairs.

Matt threw himself at a man who, even when cut nearly in half, didn't disappear, and instead quickly fused together with a burst of lightning. They were entangled, and Emily had no idea who would come out on top. She cast her combo at another two people and watched as they vanished.

Conor intercepted a man in armor with a pink undershirt who cast [Force Bolt] at the frontliners' armor joints. Conor took the hit without a sound, even as she saw blood fly. She tried to give him a hand, when the world went white.

Everyone froze, and all of the enemies were encased in white, while Aster stood at the center of the growing ice attack. The other queendom fighters were covered in frost, which grew to ice, then roses. It was so pretty, but while she wasn't affected personally, the display was a reminder that her fox teammate wasn't just a cute mascot, but a dangerous mage in her own right.

Matt disentangled himself from his opponent, and as everyone encased in ice vanished, Liz stepped into the second floor. She was being pushed back from her position holding the first-floor attackers off.

Aster broke herself from her spell, and they all ran up to the third floor, where they would only have to defend a single point of entrance instead of the two on the second floor.

The door was slammed shut, when Emily noticed that her sister was nowhere to be seen. She cursed and was about to go back out for her, when Conor stopped her with a hand on her shoulder.

If it was anyone else with her sister's Talent that had stayed behind, she would have expected they would run and abandon them, but not her sister. Annie had always taken the burden from her.

Annie pressed herself in the corner of the room's ceiling and waited. Watching Aster flash freeze half a dozen people was impressive, but she still saw the way things were going. They were left out to dry, and they were all fucked if they didn't do *something*.

Matt had a good point about holding out, but she didn't think it was likely. The commander was throwing everything they had at this assault, and from the way the fights were going, she noticed at least two groups of Pather's being sent ahead to clear the building.

No, if any of them wanted to get out alive, some chaos needed to be spread.

She waited until a mass of queendom fighters came, and then slipped down to the first floor while the stairs were clear.

She didn't know what Liz had done, but the room was painted red. There was blood dripping off the ceiling in a disgusting display.

Annie picked her steps carefully. While her Talent allowed her to remain invisible and mostly intangible, it wasn't perfect, and bloody footprints would give her away. Even if she could walk through most soft objects without disturbing them, liquids were still beyond her for now.

Carefully picking her way out of the fort, she found a wounded man and scooped him up while using his body to cover her kingdom arm sash. She had learned long ago that blending in was more than not being seen. Sometimes, being seen was far better, so she abandoned her Talent without hesitation.

She stumbled like her leg hurt and started to move the man out of the fort, where there was a triage station set up. No one wanted to be killed and lose their points if they could avoid it. She also noticed the leaders camp right next to the aid station.

As they limped closer, she inspected the healer. It was a party healer, which meant that they were fair game. She formulated her plan, and as the healer reached out to help her and the man she was caring for, Annie thrust a knife into the man's chest, and pulled the three of them down.

She didn't go for his heart, but his lung. Without the ability to hold air, the man couldn't scream. The man next to her was dispatched by touching her dagger to his throat. Both of them vanished.

Annie reactivated her Talent, and half crawled away and under a table. She waited until someone noticed the disappearance of their healer and ran to report to the leader. When she identified the man in charge, she prepared to slink away.

From her spiritual sense, the leader was Tier 7 and might be able to see through her Talent. So, she fell into step right behind a Tier 6 woman as she brought the leader a scrap of bloody cloth as evidence of the healer's death.

When the aide was a step away from where Annie thought she would stop, she kicked the aide's forward-moving foot behind her planted one.

As the woman flailed out, the leader instinctively reached out to steady the falling woman.

Annie jumped into action and had just enough time to see the man's eyes widen as her dagger took him in the throat.

Annie didn't bother to run. She was surrounded by people and used her dagger to slash out at the other people who seemed important.

Her blade met flesh until she was too slow and took a dark, black, mana made chain through the chest.

She flung out her dagger in a last defiant attack but was in a hospital bed before she saw the result.

Matt brought his blade forward in a thrust.

His head was pounding, and he felt like deactivating his armor and just letting someone split open his head to relieve the pressure. He had never overused his Concept this much before, and keeping the mages over half mana was all he could do.

It was the only reason they were still fighting strong. Emily was continuously blasting people away, and if not for the force of people pushing from behind, Matt knew that no one would be willing to face the embodiment of a lightning blast.

Liz and Aster took potshots while Emily caught her breath. She was panting as if she was running sprints and clutched her rib as she cast spell after spell.

Matt was angry.

They were only in this situation because the kingdom had put a coward in charge, and he had every intention of breaking his bones for a few weeks straight.

A [Wind Blade] shot up the now cleared stairway, and Matt took it on his chest with a wince. That was no normal Tier 6's attack. They broke his armor for a second but were unable to punch through his lighter inner armor with a single attack.

Mentally thanking Keith for his armor-breaking training, Matt quickly reformed the spell in his spirit, and had it ready for the next attack.

The mage realized that they weren't getting anywhere after three more attacks and gave up.

The only thing Matt could hear was heavy breathing from around him and from the floor below.

A scream behind him caused him to whirl, only to see what looked like a physical shadow behind them, and a bloody Emily vanishing.

Matt lashed out with a [Mana Charge], but Liz beat him to it with a rain of [Blood Bullets]. The blood attacks didn't do much to the living shadow, but Matt's mana empowered blade cut a rent out of the man, and he vanished.

It was already too late, though. The man had done his job, and people poured around a vanishing Conor and flooded the room.

Liz lashed out with whips of blood, but a glowing barrage of arrows took her out of the fight. Matt heard a yip and felt a flash of pain that only hammered the steel of his rage even further.

Standing alone in a sea of bodies, he slashed with large rending strokes. Bodies vanished, but more always appeared to fill in the gaps.

Matt fought on his own for what felt like years, but his AI said it was closer to fifteen minutes. They kept sending bodies at him with little strategy, and the fighting turned primal. Strategy and technique were discarded for power and bloodshed. The queendom fighters stepped forward and one by one he cut them down as he was slowly pushed back into a wall.

His armor was broken through more than once, but he was always able to reform it before taking more than shallow cuts. Rage fueled him more than stamina or mana could at this point. In his anger he discarded [Endurance] and put everything he had into [Mage's Retreat] and [Cracked Phantom Armor]. They had harmed his family, and he was going to make sure they paid for it.

With his back to a corner, Matt felled a dozen people in queendom uniforms. When they pulled back, a shorter man with dark hair and a blue tint to his skin replaced them.

Matt panted heavily as a wave of what looked like ink flew out at him in a wave. Matt tried to sidestep it and charge forward but felt himself lifted off his feet as the pressure increasing on his armor. The dark water mage was squeezing him until he popped.

He ignored it and tried to think. He had no leverage, and his only option was to use his teleporting ring. But it felt like a waste to give up his trump card so easily.

As he tried to think of a way out, he swung his sword through the water ineffectually. The glowing blade gave him an idea but with nothing to hit he couldn't release the mana stored in [Mana Charge].

Bringing his blade around to his leg Matt let the blast of mana out. It was unfortunate but without striking something the skill couldn't be triggered, a safety measure he intended to remove after this.

It broke [Cracked Phantom Armor] and mangled his leg, but it also shattered the spell around him, and he dropped down into a watery puddle. Matt awkwardly lunged forward, but someone else stepped up to protect the mage, and stabbed him while his armor was still coming back.

The leg he used [Mana Charge] on wasn't working properly, but Matt pushed through the pain and ripped the shield forward with a guttural roar.

He brought his fist down on an armored head, even as he felt metal bite deep into his back and chest.

With a final punch and roar, the man under him vanished.

A moment later, and with an ever-growing cold sensation through his chest, he did as well.

11

Ash stood panting, staring at the pool of blood the man had left behind. This was why direct combat should be avoided; ambush tactics were so much more *refined.* Ash's Tier 1 talent allowed them to use any skill as though it were Blackwater affinity, a high-level mana aspect that primarily contained water and shadow.

The tool kit it granted them trended very strongly to ambushes and fighting from the shadows and made them far better at assassinations than anything else. It was why Ash was teamed up with Thayden for this little war after all, to deal with hard-to-hit targets.

Why the two of them were sent to take back a fort in the middle of a siege was a mystery. They worked better as a strike unit, used for infiltration ahead of the main assault, focused on taking out a leader or sabotaging gear and defenses.

Attacking head-on was stupid, but they had their orders, and had to comply if they wanted to be rewarded by the Empire war AI. Purely suicidal missions weren't permissible but, apparently, 'kill that monstrous team' wasn't enough to be considered suicide.

Ash didn't consider it suicidal either, until they had all nearly died. Thayden had a brilliant idea of going through the window by mixing their abilities with shadows to let the man turn intangible.

Sadly, the attack hadn't worked completely, and Thayden was dead. On top of that, the attacking force was down to twenty-odd fighters.

Still, they had won, and the reward for taking a medium fort would be hefty.

But killing the final armored man was a task that they weren't sure was even worth it. The man had fought like a monster in human flesh. Or perhaps more accurately, in impenetrable skill armor. Archers were unable to get a good enough shot to kill the man because of the tight space, and the melee fighters were utterly dismantled as they came into reach of the man's blade. Still, they were ordered to capture the fort, so they had, despite the cost.

Even so, Ash had to burn a Tier 7 mana stone to charge their fast converting mana stone. The stone was an ace in the hole for emergencies, one recommended by their sponsor. It could convert mana near-instantly, but the efficiency was awful. 400 mana invested had yielded in less than 30, but they had figured that it would be enough to restrain the armored man and finish the fight.

They had never expected that the kingdom fighter would blow off their own leg after being hoisted off the ground. Ash didn't even know that it was possible to disrupt a blackwater skill like that.

Ash had only survived because a random queendom guard had jumped in the way of the armored man's last lunge. Ash hadn't been sure they had defeated the man until he was teleported out. And that was only after everyone stabbed the man in the back. Repeatedly.

Screams disrupted Ash's musings, and through the window they saw a stream of kingdom-colored troops fighting the encirclement group outside of the fort with a second group of at least twenty entering the building. Before the queendom defenders outside could do anything useful like group up, they were quickly subdued in small packs. Unable to use their near equal numbers to good effect.

Everyone still alive on Ash's floor simply dropped their weapons, too tired to put up any sort of fight, as a smiling woman with dull brown hair entered the room. She had a rainbow-colored parasol spinning behind her. Her cheer seemed out of place with the blood and gore splattered around.

Her armored dress was a fashion statement that Ash had never seen before, and looked as impractical as it was flashy. Apart from her dress, she was as plain as could be.

The woman surveyed the queendom fighters and spoke with a

clear, bell-like voice, "Felix dear, please dispatch these ones. Thank you."

One of the Tier 6 melee fighters who had survived spat at the woman's feet, saying, "Fuck y—"

Before he could finish, the woman in command turned around and viciously kicked him in the face. Blood from the man's nose arced through the air, splattering the other captives in the face. The woman's dress had hidden it, but she wore practical combat boots under all the finery. That must have hurt.

"Now there, I'll have none of that." she said with a gentle smile on her face. She looked down and saw the blood that had landed on her dress, "As if this day couldn't get any worse."

Looking at the queendom fighters she continued with a sigh, "Honestly, I expected better from the best and the brightest the Empire had to offer. I guess all that glitters is not gold. Well, I thank you for your efforts, substandard as they were." With that final statement she closed the parasol with a snap, placed the tip on the man's forehead, and pushed it back. With a brief flash of blood and light the man disappeared.

"Now, I must be off. I'm sure poor little Albie will want to have some words with me and it's best if I can make some plans before that happens." The woman spun away while waving her hand at the rest of them in obvious dismissal.

Ash looked at the hulking man behind the woman as he gently touched a sword to Ash's chest, and they were gone. The last thing they heard was the snap of a parasol.

Luna watched the show that her little Pathers put on. She was impressed.

Other managers were more or less *hands-on* than her, depending on their ideals, but her approach was always to stay in the shadows until she thoroughly understood her subjects. No two teams were the same. She had learned that lesson millennia ago.

She watched. She evaluated. She planned.

Once all that was done, she made suggestions on essentially everything for the children placed under her care. In her early years she'd had plenty of teams that wouldn't follow her advice and would simply leave most of the time. It was where she learned to be selective and more stringent with her team choices.

But some teams *could* take it, and she would push harder and harder until she squeezed every ounce of potential out of them.

It was so rare for her to find the true gems these days. It was the reason she had stopped taking children under her paw.

For all she had watched, Luna had to admit. She was impressed.

The three were strong and had fought well for being unaware of the treachery at play. Combat between intelligent combatants was always a shock to people only used to rift delving.

They were falling prey to the normal machinations that these little wars brought out. She had watched these skirmishes time and time again. More often than not, betrayals like the one the little Rainbow Peacock Alyssa was cooking up were a middle-level commanders' first moves.

The girl thought she was clever for her ploy when it had been done millions of times before her. It had already happened five times on this very planet and was currently happening on another three battlefields.

She made a note to watch out for Alyssa and Liz's first meeting. It would be the first time she would meet someone with a purer bloodline than her, outside of her parent's protection. Not many could claim that, but there certainly were a few out there. High-purity, high-existence, like dragons and phoenixes, cultivators born of dual beast parents were rare, but they existed.

Luna's senses easily stretched across the entire planet, so she could see everything going on in this…*game.*

Would Liz back down? Or stand and fight? Could Liz handle not being the best at something as intrinsic as bloodline purity?

Her claws tried to stretch out of her humanoid fingers as she thought of the coming drama.

What direction would the young Pathers take with the ill-treatment of the two vassal states?

Her favorite was when the Pathers created a third faction and started wreaking havoc. It was always so very fun to watch those wars unfold. Sadly, she doubted that would be the outcome this time. Both of the royal brats were taking steps to prevent that exact scenario, but Luna could hope.

She sent a message through her hated AI to April and Kurt. She had both of them getting the various materials and training facilities ready. Or, in Kurt's case, tracking down the people Luna felt could best train the trio. Her mute protege was making a list of where they were, and the best order to have the children visit them in.

Luna had to resist forming a tail to swish as she thought of the kids' faces when the prices of those facilities were revealed to them.

When she was a young liaison, she thought it was dumb to make the Pather kids with management teams pay for everything they were to use. But after a time, she came to understand.

The resources at her and her fellow managers' disposal could turn a turd into a diamond if given the proper guiding hand. Competent strength was expected of anyone able to successfully complete their training. Success in the challenges they would face while on the Path would hardly be impressive if everything was given to them.

The *real* monsters came out when the added incentives a management team could provide were acted upon. They drove the children harder and helped to advance faster. It pulled the best out of them.

She had one young woman who slept outside to save on even that little expense. Annabelle had done well for herself and already ascended. She hadn't completed the Path, but she had gotten close and gone on to make a name for herself in the exploration communities.

One of Luna's earliest works. One of her best.

She was already calculating cost to account for Matt's Talent, but it would just inflate prices. It wouldn't change the relative timeline that they were expected to maintain. Keep them mostly in line with the other Pathers. The help was meant to be earned with effort. Even with her increasing the price they would be paying less than it would normally cost to hire Tier 25s or higher for personal training. The Empire gave tax breaks for those who helped Path teams after all. That was worth far more than the paltry sum the teams paid.

Luna's major restrictions were items and skills. She couldn't give them either. They had to earn those themselves.

It shouldn't be a problem with Matt's abilities, but their earning potential was greatly lessened with them now being Tier 6. She would recommend that they sell full Tier 5 rifts to a few select guilds for first dibs on growth items once they hit Tier 10 or 15.

She wasn't sure which. It would depend on them.

Luna floated around the fort for another moment, rewatching the battle from memory.

Watching Liz shred thirteen people on the bottom floor had been a special treat. A well-laid trap was always a joy to watch. The damage her little blood mage had put out was well beyond her Tier.

It was also the first time she had been forced to help the army personnel assigned to the battle. They were overwhelmed by the sheer number of casualties her team had inflicted. Liz's slaughter of over a dozen people at once was more than they could handle. A Tier 15 could handle at most two people, and with the rate her team had been killing people…

If Luna hadn't stepped in, someone could have actually died.

The blender of blood wasn't a bad trap at all, and Liz used it to… decent effect.

She made a note to remind Liz that she could've ensnared fourteen people with a little more patience. Letting the first person come up the stairs would've allowed two more to enter the bottom floor. After killing everyone on the first floor, she could have easily handled the remaining person from the higher steps.

Her plan hadn't been bad, but it wasn't perfect either. Little Liz had room to grow, but Luna could see the gem waiting to be polished up. She just needed time, and a little pressure.

Matt had surprised her. She hadn't expected him to tell his team about his Concept, while still hiding his Talent. It was a surprising move, from what she had seen of him so far.

She made a note that he was more devious than her first impressions had indicated. It was good. She hated the blockhead melee fighter stereotype that too many let themselves fall into.

After watching him savage nearly thirty people on the third floor, she was afraid that might be the case.

He had failed to use his [Hail] skill as she expected. He could have used it to fill an entire room with ice, and effectively block it off. Or he could've used the skill during his melee, when he was forced back into a wall.

Either use could have been explained away by the reveal of his Concept. He already said that it mostly affected himself.

She sent another note to Kurt to find a few spy specialists. They could be useful for all three, but getting Matt to use a bit more lateral thinking would be their top priority. His mana situation gave him too much variety and that could be a problem in the future if he didn't learn to use more than a handful of spells.

Aster got most of Luna's praise today, though. The fox had used her growing intuition and intelligence to protect the mage, Emily. And she took out the little wannabe hive mind, Nael. Without a fire spell, he would have taken them all out in a few minutes, while the damage they inflicted failed to stop his regeneration.

She hoped that Liz could fight the young man in the future, since he was a good counter to her. Blood counted as biological material, and he would simply absorb all of her attacks.

But no. Aster noticed what everyone else had missed and froze the whole room. It was clever. The fox acted so quickly, Matt didn't even notice the oddity of the Pather that he was fighting.

They each needed help and guidance, but they had potential. Oh, so much potential.

Seeing the carnage, she made a note to monitor their mental states after this. This was the first time any of them had taken heavy wounds, and they would have died if not for the army's intervention. She had a few experts that she could call if they seemed to slip into some kind of depression. Harvest Moon would be her last resort, but he knew his way around the mind.

She wouldn't let her new toys break because of mishandling. It wouldn't be the first time she broke her hands-off rule before she introduced herself. She had done it before and would do it again. The long-term gains always outweighed the ruination of her information gathering.

Luna scanned the rest of the battle and made hundreds of notes identifying where they could do better.

A shiver ran down her spine. A delicious one, the likes of which she hadn't felt in at least a few thousand years. They would turn into her best work yet.

She could taste it.

Albert watched the projection of the planet as if it spun by his command. Various upgrades he could buy for mining sites or forts appeared in his vision as the globe spun—all things to spend the kingdom level points on.

He ignored them.

He was mad. No, he was angry.

He thought about it for a moment. No, it was worse than that. He was monumentally pissed off.

First, his father forced him to bank half of the points their side earned. His father didn't trust him, so he hampered his progress, then used that as proof he was right. Thankfully, it was only for the first few months, but it completely negated the defensive advantage he had. If his father hadn't done that, he would be out earning the queendom instead of being slightly behind.

Albert could disregard his father's orders, and there would be nothing the king could do while the army was here. But they wouldn't be around forever, so he had to acquiesce to his father's orders.

That had pissed him off already, but the day had only gotten worse as it went on.

The real problem was that the Pathers were too damn good at their jobs, and too many of his mid-level commanders were only concerned about their own points. The larger strategy of the war as a whole was lost on them.

It was the Ascenders-damned point system. It rewarded the individual more for *taking* a fort than *holding* it. However, for the kingdom as a whole earned hundreds of times more points for holding the fort. The incentives were *fucking* contradictory.

That caused his relief teams to hold back until they could take a fort back for themselves and split a larger amount of points between their squad. Breaking a siege was only worth a quarter the points a capture was worth.

A message beeped at him.

Alyssa had taken over a fort.

He checked the logs and slammed a crystal fist onto the table in front of him.

The loud noise frightened a few of the aides as they moved back and forth, so he mumbled an apology.

Another Pather team had taken a fort, only to have their reinforcements purposefully delayed, so they could take the fort back themselves.

The more he read, the worse it seemed. The leaders of the team had been a part of his golem disaster.

Matt, Liz, and Aster. He vaguely remembered them, and his AI provided the relevant details. They had been the top earners during the final push, while only being Tier five.

Now, they were Tier 6, and with three others, had single-handedly taken out a medium fort, then almost held it from an assault by three hundred people.

A quick check of the casualties showed that the attackers had lost a little over two hundred people, with Alyssa taking out the others. He read between the lines and through the provided metadata and found that most of the people she killed were simply Tier 5 perimeter guards.

Solely for her personal gain, she was screwing one of his top ten teams over.

He could only blame himself, really. This being the first day after the auction, and the beginning of true hostility on both sides, the orders had been over-optimistic.

Having the Path teams harass forts was one thing they expected to be easy. They had added 'take forts if possible' as an idle thought, hoping one or two might succeed.

But no. The Pathers were overachievers on both sides. Nine forts had been taken, and they had only prepared reinforcement teams for the first three. After that, it was digging deeper and deeper into the barrel to find more. After the seventh, they weren't scraping the bottom of the barrel. They were turning it upside down and shaking.

That was where Alyssa came into the picture. Albert hated the smug woman and had given orders for her not to be used unless necessary. The order had only been half because of his personal feelings and half because she really was the worst blend of competent and vindictive. Best to keep her involvement to a minimum.

The fact that it had come to that only drove the point of the kingdom's desperation home. She and her little band of nobles were worse than useless most of the time, as they had so readily proven.

If she hadn't always been self-centered and conniving, he would have suspected his political rivals of trying to influence the war. He didn't think it likely, as his father would take anyone's head if they ruined his chances at winning the grand prize. But it was a possibility.

His only solace was that the queendom was having the same problem. Albert had to grin internally. While the queendom took nearly sixty percent of the Pather fighters who came in from the greater Empire, the kingdom had clearly gotten more of the quality troops.

The queendom had unexpectedly only taken six forts to their nine. His side might lose out slightly in numbers, but powerhouses could win wars if the quantity difference wasn't too severe.

Albert was brought out of his musing by the sound of the door opening. After a quick glance back, he found Juni poking his head in, nodding at him.

That wasn't good. It never was.

Albert moved into a private meeting room, and found Juni slumped over a table with his head in his hands.

"That bad?"

Albert didn't really want to know. But he had to know. His position demanded it.

Juni mumbled into his hands, "It's bad. Really bad."

Albert moved over to sit next to his friend. It was a break in royal decorum, but they were alone, and it was the only reason that Juni would do it.

Finally, Juni pushed back from the table and paused. "The eight fucked over teams are pissed."

"It's nine now. Alyssa."

Juni froze for a moment, then turned and punched the wall. A flare of gravity caused the wall to distort for a moment as Juni started wailing on the wall.

"That stupid bitch! I knew she went dark, but I was hoping she just got ambushed or something. I spent weeks working on that relationship, trying to fix it after the mess with Zoey. Fuck! And now I bet it's all down the drain."

While Juni didn't and never would say it Albert could read in between his friend's words. He had wanted to use the excuse of the golem fight to remove some political snakes and spies planted in his retinue, but Juni had advised against it.

Albert had insisted and that decision was still biting him in the ass today. It was the reason he didn't have full authority to remove worthless leaders without questions which would solve his problems in one fell swoop. But because of his blunder he now had noble families ready to question every time a commander position was changed. Asking if he was trying to purge their young. Or, worse yet, slight their honor.

"What do you think the chances are that they'll leave?"

In contrast to everything else that could be purchased from the shop, the 20,000 cost to switch sides was the only item that could be bought on credit. The cynical side of Albert knew that it was so the vassal states couldn't hold the Pathers hostage, but it rankled.

"Lysandra's team is definitely changing sides. But the others are in the air. I think I can offset it by getting the team that took over Kelsor's fort to jump ship. They got fucked hard by the queendom. Everyone else is on the fence, waiting to see how we react."

Albert thought about that. He already intended to put a stop to this, but how he did it would need careful handling. Especially if he didn't want more of his best teams to defect.

"What about…" he sighed, "Team Bucket?" Why, by all the Ascenders, did one of their top teams have to choose such a stupid name?

Juni flopped back onto the chair and spun it.

"I've only looked at the quick review, but they seemed to get hit pretty hard. Worse than we expected."

Looking at his right-hand man, Albert waited for him to continue. "I'm sure you noticed that the numbers don't add up?"

"Yes. Is it what you expected?"

Juni stopped spinning, "I'll need to confirm, but their mages lasted far longer than they should have. Especially after taking the fort in the first place. I already got some information from our sources in the infirmary. They went in fast, hard, and with nothing held back. No way they should have been able to keep up that mana expenditure. Even with the fast converting mana stones, they would have needed to burn tens of thousands of mana to get back to full. No way they burn money for us."

After a moment, Juni continued, "I think Alex's feeling that Matt has a mana Concept makes sense. He only has a phrase, but he said that he felt something when everyone was asleep back during the Golem fight, and his mana came back faster. He woke up to piss and felt it, that is something which would fit the criteria."

They had collected information about all the heavy hitters during the golem siege and Matt's team had more mana sustainability than expected. Up until now it had just been a tidbit tucked away.

"That means that it's limited to a small squad level, though." Albert trailed off. A Concept for giving mana also explained how the man could cast [Hail] for so long. It was the perfect support ability. Odd for a melee frontliner to have it, but nothing unheard of. Concepts didn't always conform to normal team archetypes. And a mana Concept wasn't new. Just incredibly rare.

It could be useful for sieges though, so Albert made a note of it.

Juni cut into his thinking. "We need to keep them. What do you intend to do, Albie?"

Albert thought on it for a moment longer and said, "We don't have the points, but reimburse the teams who got screwed. It will eat into our coffers, but better to handle this now rather than later, when it becomes a greater problem. Also, tell them I'll make the various team leaders give them personal explanations. Do you think that will be enough?"

His father demanding that half the points get set aside made things tight, but Albert could make it work if he spent his personal points for being the overall commander.

Juni was already walking to the door. "I'll make it happen. I might have to push the limits a bit. I just got a report that Amber is trying to poach our teams as well."

As Juni disappeared, Albert thought long and hard before coming to a resolution. Amber was Princess Sara's right-hand woman, but he personally felt that she was less efficient than Juni.

No, that wasn't his problem.

He had read the reports of old Empire sanctioned vassal wars for Pathers and wanted to head off the worst-case scenarios. If they lost control of the Pathers, both sides could lose everything.

It had happened before.

If things got bad enough, the army would step in, but he had a few plans. One was increasing the kingdom-side payments for jobs correctly done. If he matched the Empire's contributions, it would incentivize people to think tactically, not personally.

He could also publicly punish people for screwing over their allies for personal gain.

He could even increase the points earned for holding forts. He was sure that he could get a few Pather teams to stand guard with that.

The problem was spending the points. It would help resolve problems, sure. But he still needed to make sure that he didn't allow the queendom to get ahead in points, solely for strategic level spending. A few upgraded forts could go a long way into fortifying their position on the planet and making it nearly impossible to win the war.

But if he warned her of his intentions, he could force her hand into doing the same, if only so he didn't look like a better side. If they did it together, it would ensure that they lost a near equal number of points.

With a sigh, he started a video call with Sara.

Matt's vision went from the stone floor to a blinding light.

He tried to reach up to block the light, but invisible bands of force resisted his movement.

"You're okay, son. Just lay there while we heal you."

Matt checked his AI to make sure that his teammates were okay. Specifically, Liz and Aster.

His fox bond was currently moving in circles, but Liz was still. Since he didn't have a map of the area, he could only guess at her situation, but her AI showed that she was alive and being healed.

A second check showed all his teammates were being healed or were already healed. Annie and Emily were together already.

Matt twitched as he felt something in his back start itching. As it turned to tickling, he started to struggle against his restraints.

"Try not to move."

In between gasps for air, Matt got out, "It tickles."

"Oh, sorry."

The tickling stopped, and he was back to just the weird itching.

"Sorry about that. Happens to a select few people. Gotta change my methodology."

"How bad is it?"

The healer was looking at Matt's stomach, but even with the mask on, he saw their eyes wrinkle.

"Bad enough I'm questioning the judgment of the Army personnel. You are *fucked* up, kid. You have nearly no meat left on your leg. Not to mention half a dozen stab wounds."

Matt was kind of surprised. He hurt badly enough, but he didn't think it was that bad.

"I think they let me finish beating someone to death first?"

He lilted it off in a question. He wasn't really sure.

"Are you the armored fellow? Had more than a few people cursing you and your family line for a dozen generations."

A burning sensation started to crawl through Matt's stomach, but after a moment, he got it under control and answered, "Maybe. We got pinned in a fort we had just taken, and then had to fight our way deeper. Finally, they took us out."

The healer just nodded. "Yeah, you're not the first team to have that happen to. Apparently, it's a pretty common event at the start of training wars."

What felt like a bubble was filled in his guts, and a loud fart was inadvertently released.

Matt would have been embarrassed, except the healer nodded and said, "Okay. Stitched up your intestines."

He looked at Matt and asked, "How ya feeling?"

"Not that bad. It just itches and feels like hot water's moving around in there."

The man nodded. "Good. Good. The pain blocker is working. How are you mentally about your death?"

Matt shrugged. "It wasn't a real death. More angry than anything else."

"Oh?"

Noticing that the man wanted more, Matt half changed the subject. "On a completely unrelated note to being left out to dry, what's the worst thing to deal with while healing? Maybe a particularly painful thing to break?"

The healer laughed. "I'm not going to help you get revenge. I'm worried about your mental state. A lot of people don't handle knowing they would have died without the intervention very well. It can be a pretty heavy moment when you're forced to recognize your mortality."

Matt thought about it, while what felt like bugs crawled down his right leg. There was a pop that sounded like a tree branch being snapped apart, but he barely felt a thing.

"I think I came to the realization that I could die a long time ago."

At the single raised eyebrow, Matt continued, "My planet and city had a lot of rift breaks, and a lot of people died. I knew a long time ago that I only lived because I got lucky. Today, I got unlucky. It might happen again. Fighting people is a lot harder than fighting rift monsters. The skills…"

Matt trailed off. The fighting had been more than a spar or anything else. Even the battle at the hidden base. No, this was brutal and primal.

He made a move, but his opponents made a move to counter him at every turn. He had to be stronger, faster, and smarter. All things he hadn't been at the fort.

Matt felt a burning desire to not only beat their reinforcement's leader's ass but prove to everyone that they had only died because they were unprepared. If he had known…

He forced that line of thinking down. He should have been prepared and expected…well, everything.

If this was a real war, he would have actually died, and not woken up in a healer's room. Matt needed this experience against people with skills and tactics.

Being forced on the defensive was hard. He had tried to make plans, but the enemy commander had been a step ahead the whole time. He had felt clever when taking the fort, but now understood how the defenders had felt. He was outmaneuvered, and unable to plan for the enemy's strategy. Even the things they *had* planned for didn't turn out as well as they could have.

"It was a good learning experience."

Matt finished with that, and the healer let it drop. He started telling tales about his younger days.

He was thinking about how much harder it was dealing with thinking people when one of the stories caught Matt's attention was the story about how he tried to heal a femur. The man in question was in so much pain, the healer needed to sedate them to heal the bone. Apparently, it was the worst bone to break, with pain levels not seen anywhere else in the body.

Matt started planning on how to break both of someone's femurs at once.

He had to smile at the healers' roundabout way of helping him get a little revenge.

Before he knew it, he was guided up as the bed bent forward.

"Back to rights. You're out of all combat for two weeks." The unnamed healer pulled down his mask and met Matt's eyes with his own. "I'm serious. No fighting at all. If you need to be healed again, your body might not be able to handle it. The mana cost was already increasing toward the end. Whatever you did to your body is making you stronger, yes but harder to heal. Give me your word."

A petty part of Matt wanted to say that his friend could fix the healing downtime with a single spell, but he took the healers' good intentions as they were meant. No one else knew of Melinda's Talent, and even if he did get healed by her, it wouldn't get him into the field sooner.

He did make a note to get her to heal at least Liz and Aster, though. Just in case there was a lingering problem. It was also good to know that his near perfect body was making it harder to heal. That was a side effect he hadn't thought about.

"I promise. Thank you for the patch-up."

Matt stuck out his hand and shook the healer's. The man didn't let go until Matt added, "And I won't get into a fight or anything until after the two-week healing cooldown."

The healer grinned, then let him go, saying, "My assistant will guide you to a relaxation room. Take your time and let your mind wander for a bit. You need to spend at least an hour in there. Enjoy it. There are rabbits and all sorts of cute critters to cuddle."

Matt froze.

"Did you say rabbits? And everyone had to be in there?"

"Yeah?" The healer seemed confused.

Matt started to run to where his bond was still doing circles.

He could only imagine what his playful bond would do with a room full of traumatized people and cute fluffy animals.

Aster! Please, don't be mutilating the support animals!

When he arrived, he found a forest meadow with goats, sheep, and rabbits bouncing around. It was full of people in white clothes matching the ones he was somehow wearing. What he didn't see was his bond, or any bloodshed.

After following his AI, he found Aster holding onto a rabbit's tail with her teeth, while the plump bunny bounded around in circles. His bond was bouncing around behind said rabbit getting kicked in the head with each leap.

He would have been worried if his connection didn't show her having the time of her life finally with a rabbit who wasn't too weak to play.

Matt facepalmed.

12

Matt quickly scooped up his bond and the abused bunny. It took more than a little gentle coaxing to get her to let go of the fluffy whitetail. Once he did get the bunny free, it jumped from his arms, to rush toward what it expected was freedom from its tormentor.

Instead, it jumped up and kicked his bond in the head before bounding away twice, then turning and wiggling its nose at her.

Aster flew from his arms and raced toward the disappearing bunny.

Allowing the two to play, he turned back to following Liz's AI marker. He found her talking to another group of delvers and was waved over once she noticed his approach.

"Matt, this is Amy, Gerald, Franklyn, and Dee. They got screwed over as well."

As she spoke, Liz entwined their fingers, a little firmer than their usual hand holding. He squeezed her back. While he had been assured that she was fine through their AI, it was still good to see her up and moving about. He assumed from her hard grip that she felt the same way.

Amy was closest to him, and proffered her hand to Matt, which started a round of handshakes all around.

Amy had an odd accent that Matt couldn't place, but he sympathized with her words. "We got a mission. They told us to take the fort if possible, and our reinforcements just went poof. Never arrived. It was fucking bullshit."

Dee leaned in and added, "But guess who we found here?"

Matt just raised an eyebrow along with a shoulder to show he had no clue. He would have expected her to say one of the people they fought, but his short walk through the relaxation area showed him that it was only filled with kingdom personnel. Separating people was a good idea when they had nearly killed each other, after all.

Gerald fell back and punched at the air. "A friend of mine, Jen. Dead like us. She was a part of a cobbled together relief team, and their commander forced them to hold back and wait until the team they were supposed to relieve had died. That way, they could earn the points for capturing the fort themselves."

Matt gaped toward the still standing members of the team and said, "No fucking way. They just threw you to the wolves?"

"Yeah, fucking pricks. I…"

Matt missed what Dee said after that as his thoughts slipped to their own team's situation. Heat seeped into his veins like molten metal. A glance at Liz was returned with a nod. She believed that they had been screwed the same way.

Wanting to see the full extent of the damage, Matt brought up his AI messages.

Prior Total (last updated 0 days ago): 16,776 points.
TEAM MERITS:
(Calculated for Tier 6 Combatant).

- Enemy vassal killed, Tier 5. Worth 1 point. Performed 72 times.
- Enemy vassal killed, Tier 6. Worth 5 points. Performed 130 times.
- Enemy vassal killed, Tier 7. Worth 25 points. Performed 7 times.
- Medium fort defended. First wave: six vs one hundred. 2,500 points. Five times normal points are awarded for difference in numbers. 12,500 points.
- Medium fort defended. Second wave: six vs two hundred. 2,500 points. Ten times normal points are awarded for differences in numbers. 25,000 points. Failed.

PERSONAL MERITS:
(Calculated for Tier 6 Combatant).

- Enemy vassal killed, Tier 5. Worth 1 point. Performed 13 times.
- Enemy vassal killed, Tier 6. Worth 5 points. Performed 58 times.
- Enemy vassal killed, Tier 7. Worth 25 points. Performed 2 times.
- Medium fort defended. 2,500 points.

ARMY MERITS:

- Items and equipment looted but returned. Worth 2,834 points.

UNACHIEVED MERITS: For reference purposes only.

- N/A

SUMMARY OF GAINS:
Team Merits:

- **Raw Total:** 13,325
- **Team Multiplier:** 1x
- **Category Total:** 13,325

Personal Merits:

- **Raw Total:** 2,840
- **Personal Multiplier:** 1x
- **Category Total:** 2,840

Combined Merits:

- **Sub-Total:** 16,165
- **Total Multiplier:** 1x
- **Grand Total:** 16,165

New Gains: 18,999 points.

New Total: 35,775 points.

Pather Team Ranking (Kingdom of Seven Suns): 52,312nd place.

Estimated Daily Stipend: N/A.

18,999 points lost. No, Matt corrected himself. They had also lost the 16,776 points from taking the fort in the first place. 35,775 points vanished into thin air, as if they had never existed. That was without the 25,000 they could have received if they had been able to hold onto the fort.

The heat that rippled through Matt cycled with his mana. He wanted to break someone, and the leader of their reinforcements had a lot of explaining to do. He doubted that they could explain their decision to his satisfaction, but he'd give them the opportunity. *Then* he would do some breaking.

Matt wondered how many times he could challenge them to duels before the army would force him away.

Liz pulled him from revenge fantasies when she excused them from the group. It didn't take long to realize why. Annie, Emily, and Conor were at the door and glancing around at the colorful, animal-filled area in something between wonder and bewilderment.

He understood the oddity of the situation, but it didn't stop him from running a hand through a sheep's silky curls as it brushed up against his leg. He still didn't know how he had gotten here before all of them. His fight had lasted longer, and he had died after them. His only guess was that their wounds were less severe, so they were a lower priority.

Liz reached forward and grabbed their hands, pulling them forward. "We need to talk, and we can't do it in the doorway."

Annie seemed completely distracted as a butterfly larger than Matt's head gently fluttered past. It took Emily forcefully dragging her with them to keep her from running off.

They found a secluded grove, and all sat in a circle.

Liz started them off. "We got fucked. Hard."

The three recent arrivals looked confused, but it quickly turned to anger as Liz explained what she found.

"The relief commanders were playing fucking games with us. They intentionally let us die so they could get more points for a capture of the fort. I talked to two other teams who died in the same way."

Emily looked ready to spit fire, which matched Matt's feelings. "What fucking pricks! I lost thirty-five thousand points! If this is true, I'm out. I'm switching sides and killing that mother fucker as many times as I can."

Matt was about to agree when Liz held up a tempering hand. "I was thinking the same thing, but two things are keeping me from going through with it."

Seeing all of their displeasure at that, she continued, "Juni wanted to talk to us. His message was short, but he seemed just as mad as we are. Second, if we change sides, we lose the leverage we have over the prince, and more importantly, Juni."

Annie shrugged, unconcerned. "I don't think that anything they say can convince me to stay. If we stay, I won't get the chance to kill whoever failed us."

Conor, surprisingly, spoke up, "Not necessarily true. I talked to my healer's assistant. It's what made me take so long to get here. Apparently, the army has a system for assassins, and they don't have any restrictions on who you kill as long as you give them a heads up. You just need to pass a practical test or something. They didn't know much more, but I think haunting the leader for weeks then killing them could be worse."

They all looked at Conor with blank stares. He hadn't yet shown such a dark side of himself.

Annie looked like she had discovered a new facet of the man and wanted to gobble him up after seeing how ready he was for her to do wetwork. So had Matt, for that matter. He had underestimated the quiet man.

"I'm pissed as well." He answered all their unspoken questions with a shrug. He didn't look pissed as he scratched a raccoon's head.

Liz nodded. "That's a good idea, but I don't think there were just the other two teams who got fucked over. I think this was pretty widespread. Historically, there are a few things that Pathers do in retaliation. One is to form their own faction and make a third or fourth party in the war."

Matt liked that idea. And images of burning down the prince's plans gave him quite a bit of pleasure after all the man had bungled.

But Liz shot that down. "That isn't likely to happen. There needs to be a whole lot more corruption for us to get to that point. What we can and should do is form a sort of Pathers' union, with Pathers from both sides. If we do that, we can get more bargaining rights. If we do that, we can try for a few better things, but I need to network a bit more before I can make it happen."

The others looked at Liz like she grew a second head. It was long enough for her to get uncomfortable and ask, "What?"

Emily shrugged and asked, "Where did you learn this? Seems like you're always two steps ahead."

Liz scoffed. "No! I bought and read Ingrid's Path Vassal Wars. It's dry reading, but it explains almost everything we need to know about this. This has all played out dozens of times before, and the rules are purposefully lax, so problems arise. They aren't just testing us but the various leaders on both sides. If things got so bad that we, the Pathers, weren't getting a good war out of this, the army would step in and impose harsher rules. But that's only happened once."

Still getting odd looks, she scooped up a passing puppy and held it like a shield as she cuddled it.

"I thought it was interesting, okay?"

Matt knew it wasn't, as she had read parts to him when the war was first announced, but it was the best sleep medicine.

Emily said, "Well, first we need to decide if we're going to move in a group or not."

Conor just shrugged. As the lone solo member. He was free to do as he wished.

Matt threw his two cents into the ring. "I don't know all of what Liz has planned, but I think we should move as a group. I know we won't stay together after the war, but we work well together. While we may have lost at the end, we kicked major ass before we went down. I don't really want to risk being separated if we don't have to."

He didn't want to step on Liz's plans, but added, "I wouldn't mind leaving the kingdom side, but I also think we should hear Juni out. We've known him for a while, and he's done right by us so far."

No one else had anything major to say, so they just sat together, trading stories about how they went down while petting the animals who wandered past. No one bothered them until they received a message requesting a meeting from Juni.

They accepted it as a team, and a conference call started.

"Oh, good. You're all up. Is this a good time? Or would you rather I call back later?"

Liz spoke first. "No, it's fine now. We expected your call."

Juni winced, and his AI translated that into the image of him projected to them. "You and everyone else. Today was a disaster."

Liz and Emily both opened their mouths, but he cut them both off.

"I'm not blaming you. Unless being competent has become a bad thing in the last few hours, and I hadn't noticed. You deserve an explanation to start, though. First, your own success was against our expectations. Or at least, the chances of the Pathers' success *as a whole* was significantly underestimated. We, the prince and his headquarters staff, added the line about taking a fort as a throwaway. We expected maybe a team or two to succeed, but we've had nine, including yourselves, take their assigned forts. It's been a disaster."

"We had three relief teams ready and waiting, but that obviously wasn't enough. We were forced to find bodies, but they weren't the leaders we originally wanted to use for a reason. By the time your team needed reinforcements, we were scraping the bottom of the barrel, and your team suffered for it. I apologize."

Juni sighed and continued, "Fortunately, or unfortunately rather, this petty bullshit wasn't limited to the kingdom. We have intelligence suggesting that four out of six of their Pather teams were wiped out, just like you were. Their Pathers just weren't as good as ours and didn't take as many forts. We lost six teams from the nine forts we captured. You should talk to the queendom fighters you're recuperating with to verify."

Emily took the man's pause to ask, "So, how are you going to make this right? I assume that's your intention. And if you thought there was a chance of our reinforcements bailing, you could have told us to leave and not risk it."

Juni didn't look bothered by the interruption and pressed on. "The prince intends to reimburse every one of the points you've lost if you choose to come back into the war. And yes, we could have ordered a retreat, but Alyssa was supposed to get there a lot sooner, making it a likely capture."

Annie opened her mouth, but Juni spoke faster, "Even if you wish to leave our side, we will still reimburse you."

Annie shook her head. "Good to know, but not what I wanted to know. I want to know who fucked us over."

Juni looked surprised for a brief moment but answered her question readily enough, "Alyssa. She's the daughter of a Barron and has an incredibly pure bloodline. She's a manipulative piece of... Well, let's just say she's a piece of work. Believe me, she's the last person in the entire kingdom that we wanted to send, but we were backed into a corner."

He looked to the right and said something to someone else that wasn't transferred through the conference, before looking back to them. "Sorry. I'm handling a dozen things at once right now, and wanted to start with some familiar faces. The prince will also be pushing through changes in the way points are handled. He can't do anything with the army AI, but he intends to reward those who think strategically, and those who can see the bigger picture."

Liz nodded and gave a noncommittal answer. "We'll need to think it over. Getting our points back helps, but we're still on medical leave for two weeks. That's not nothing."

"It's not. And if you want to do some grunt work in the headquarters or working a station, we'll be happy for the extra hands. But that's optional, and not worth a ton, really. I can't do much more than that right now. All I ask is that you hear the prince out before making a decision. I know he has a few ideas that he's bouncing around, and you can always choose after with little issue."

"If any of you have more questions, please let me know. I just got word; Prince Albert will be having a meeting in two days, when everyone can leave the hospital. And the people responsible will be in attendance so you will have your chance at revenge. And while we can't force them to accept a duel, you might be able to pressure them to accept a challenge. Maybe even offer a large enough bribe to get them to risk it. You can't fight for two weeks, so you should have plenty of time to figure it out."

With a few more pleasantries, Juni ended the call.

Emily said through gritted teeth, "Did you notice how he didn't say there would be personal punishments for the bitch?" She reached out and strangled the imaginary person in front of her before turning to her sister.

"What are your chances of getting a license to kill thing that Conor heard about? Passing the test or whatever."

Annie looked around, and to Matt's surprise, she looked slightly panicked. "I don't know. Pretty good, if it's a practical test. But I don't know. The idea sounds amazing, but I don't want all the pressure on me."

Matt had never seen the team's rogue be quite so vulnerable.

"It's harder to work in a city than most people think. There are more layers to security than just getting into a door. Even while invisible, there's a dozen things to bypass. It's not that easy."

Liz brought their focus back to the main topic. "Are we all okay with the kingdom's proposal? We'll get half our points back, and…"

"Half!?" It wasn't just Matt who exclaimed. Why would they only be getting half the points back?

"Did none of you read the actual rules? Go try to buy back in."

Matt did as Liz said and found a message greeting him.

You have accrued 35,552 points since your last death.

If you choose to leave the war, you will be able to spend all of these points, but will have one standard day to leave the world, and will not be able to participate in any fighting.

If you choose to stay in the war, you will have to spend all of the banked points. Half will be lost, and half will be saved until you choose to leave the war. The half that is set aside will not be accessible in any way, shape, or form, until you cash out. If you die once again, half of those points will be added to the cash out pool.

Your current cash out pool is 0 (17,776).

Please, think carefully. All decisions are final.

Stay in the war?

Yes. No.

Matt looked back to Liz. Once she saw that she had everyone's attention, she repeated Juni's words. "*The prince intends to reimburse everyone for the points lost, if they choose to come back into the war.* He said the points lost, not the points earned. So, if someone cashes out now, they would get nothing. If someone comes back, they would pay half the points we had. It makes us whole, but it's not perfect either. That's why I mentioned the time we lose with the healing cooldown. It was a long shot, but I was hoping for more points."

Matt wanted to sigh but refrained from it. Those kinds of word games were exactly why he hated dealing with people in power. He would have completely missed the difference that Juni's phrasing made.

It was one of those things he just never wanted to deal with. But a smaller part of him whispered that he needed to at least *try* to learn some of Liz's interpersonal skills. If he read the book she bought, like she suggested, he would have known that they kept half their points upon dying.

He had taken the army leader saying that they lost all their points at face value. He figured that they were permanently gone. Not half of them gone, and the other half put into what was essentially a savings account.

The revelation also changed how he saw the overall strategy of the war. Dying still was something that should probably be avoided, if for no other reason than to not build bad habits. But it wasn't so strong a detriment that it was to be avoided at all costs.

Even if they had died and lost half their points, standing their ground had earned them quite a few as well. It mostly meant that teams with fewer points could make more desperate stands, as they had less to lose.

Matt redirected his attention back to the conversation just as Liz finished her thought, and he missed it. His teammate was on a warpath, getting teams together and bargaining for support. He agreed that amassing their political power was a good move. At the very least, they could demand points being returned for unjust deaths going forward. But from the look in Liz's eyes, she had more planned.

"What do you need us to do? How can we help?"

Almost everyone she approached seemed interested. Even Annie had stopped pestering Conor to stay engaged. Emily was also locked in. They were all far more engrossed in Liz's appeals than Matt himself.

Liz nearly glowed while she was the center of attention. "We can't talk to the queendom side until we're out of the rest area. It's a pretty reasonable restriction, considering we just killed each other. But, if you could all talk to the other Pather teams, that would be great. A word of caution, though. When I approached a team, I got a warning from my AI, but now I know that we can skip that step. Don't approach anyone if they look to be in distress or talking to a therapist. Honestly, I'm going to make one round here, then move into the rec rooms. This is meant to be a mental health recovery room. Actually, now that I think about it, we probably shouldn't talk to any more teams here. I kinda got ahead of myself with that one."

She pulled herself back to the topic at hand. "Anyway, my idea is, we get as many of the top teams together as we can. Then, we argue for better terms for ourselves, and harsher punishment for anyone who purposefully abandoned allies for points. Although, if the prince is having a larger meeting, he's probably already planning something along those lines. It would be silly to gather everyone and show leniency toward the people responsible. It would be like asking for a riot. Still, we can demand our own terms. I'm not certain on what exactly I want, but if we talk to the other teams, we can come up with something appropriate."

The crowd appeared as if they were ready to leave, so Matt motioned for everyone to sit down.

"Before we go, I think it's important that we all talk about how we did in the fight. We should address what went right, and what went wrong, too."

Annie snapped, "We got fucked over. That's one."

Emily bumped her sister's shoulder with her own. "Yes, but we still weren't perfect. I'll start. The timing was awful. I didn't have time to fully absorb my new skills, and selfishly chose to continue absorbing the skill I was on, even though it would have doubled my damage output had I stopped. I prioritized getting it to my core spirit over the team as a whole. Sorry."

She was looking down and pulling at the grass by the end of her critique. Matt didn't hold her decision against her in the slightest.

Conor spoke first, though. "I doubt you would have chosen that if real lives were at risk. In the end, this is a game. I don't blame you."

Liz patted her knee. "It would've taken months for you to fix that. Don't feel bad. Anything else?"

The mage twirled a blade of grass around for another moment

before she added, "My synergies with Aster were good but not perfect. Same with all of you. [Bolt] isn't the perfect skill for aiming, but it's my highest base damage skill. I'm happy with how I handled the wall, though. I had never done anything like that, and I was able to hold my position when they were shooting at me."

Annie went next without prompting. "My lack of range fucked me over pretty well. I need to spend time at an archery range soon. We never really needed it before since I usually protect Em. But now, I don't need to block for her. I could do a lot more damage if I had a ranged weapon."

As she paused, Matt offered, "Feel free to keep the crossbow. I have a few more. Besides, the bolts are standard, and pretty cheap. I can offer a little training, but I'm no expert."

"Thanks." She grinned at him and said, "I think I might take you up on that, but we'll see. For what went right… Hmm. I'd like to think my killing of the healer and leader went really well. It would have been better if I got away, but I never expected that to happen."

Conor, who sat in between Annie and Matt, took her finishing as his cue.

"My lack of range is always a problem, but same with my defense against range and magic. That was what finally got me. An arrow went through my thinner stomach armor. Speaking of that, does anyone know what happened to our gear?"

No one knew, so he continued, "I was pretty happy with how I handled myself, since Matt and I held the entrances, even though we aren't ideally matched. We made a good wall. Even when he went on the offensive, I was able to hold my own."

Matt nodded. "I could have mentioned my Concept earlier. Sorry, mana is basically money, and people get weird about it. If we had more mana at the start, we could have done a little better, I think."

He paused to think, and Emily looked as if she wanted to say something, so he nodded toward her.

"I don't want to nitpick, but you could have also flooded a room with ice, and Aster could have frozen it solid. If we thought of that, we could have just held up on the third floor with the second and fourth rooms solid. Then, we could've been nearly impossible to attack, and would've been able to rest and attack at our leisure. Eventually, they would have blown the building apart or chopped through the ice, but it would've been a lot better for us."

It only took him a minute to agree with her. She was completely right. "You're right. I need to think like a mage, and that's new to me. I've been blade only for a while, and when fighting monsters, I mostly use [Hail] to give Aster free ice. I should be treating it as the full skill it is. Any chance I can do some mage training with you?"

She looked surprised, so Matt explained, "Liz is more of a mid-range hybrid, and she relies a lot on her manipulation skill. That's not the kind of fighting style I need to work on."

Emily looked pleased at his asking for her help. Matt really could have asked Liz, but he knew that she wanted to push her plans of creating a Path union forward. "I'd be happy to help. I'd also like to buy a crossbow and do some training. It would be good to see if my Talent works with enchanted bolts. Even if it doesn't, I could still save some mana with it."

Liz was last up. "My blood spells were useful, and I was able to set up quite the trap downstairs on the first floor."

Annie interjected, "Yeah, I meant to ask. What did you do? Even the ceiling was covered in blood. Shit, girl."

Liz flushed slightly. "I left pools of blood and waited for them to come to the floor, and then I just started spinning it as fast as I could, with my Concept strengthening the blood. I made it sharp. But it could have been a lot better by using skills instead of [Blood Manipulation]. It's expensive, and I'm not used to having skills to take up some of the burden. So, I fell back to what I was *used* to instead of what I *could* do."

The five of them talked for a while, but when they exhausted their suggestions for each other, they all got up and followed Matt and found Aster half asleep in a pile of bunnies.

When he asked her what she thought she could have done better, he only got, "No mistakes. Good kills."

He debated grabbing his bond for a better answer but, in the end, left her in her pile of fluff. She was having fun, and could always find him when she wanted. He also knew that with this being a hospital, no one would harm her or be mad at her for foxing out. For all her increased mental intelligence, she was still a child.

Matt half-expected to find more hospital beds on the other side of the relaxation room, but there they had a temporary suite for teams to bunk in. They were small rooms with three tall bunk beds, but they would work for a single night of sleep. He dreaded sleeping in them later that night. He doubted that he'd be able to roll over with how narrow they were.

No one was allowed to leave the hospital until they were examined the following morning.

This dorm area contained a distinct mix of vassal teams. There were even a few people that he remembered from their fighting. It was mostly eyes, chins, or body shapes, but he was ignored for the most part, due to his lack of armor.

Liz was not. It seemed that she had made quite the impression, as more than one person flinched from her gaze as they passed by.

Meanwhile, the gym was calling Matt. He wanted to work his body and make sure that nothing was amiss, but he put his urge aside and held Liz's hand. He wasn't sure how she would respond to the attention. She did have a particularly visceral combat style. Getting sliced apart was one thing, but being eviscerated with your buddy's blood was another.

"You okay?"

Liz thankfully didn't play dumb. "Eh. This hurts a bit, but nothing I wasn't prepared for." She patted his arm with her free hand. "I'll be fine. Really."

They had a light dinner together. Neither of them really wanted to separate, so Matt hung out with her as she started to talk to the other teams. He tried to ingratiate himself with them as well, but it took effort, and he wasn't half as good as her.

Liz walked up to nearly any group, and after a little introduction, was chatting as if she had grown up with them. Once she did that, it was easy for him to talk to them as well. But when a second group sat next to the one they were talking to, Matt's attempts to do the same yielded lukewarm results. Where Liz got a firm yes to her proposal, he got maybe's.

When he asked her, Liz said, "You needed to look at them, and their body language. I'm avoiding the unapproachable teams. They either don't like us, or they don't agree with our ideas. The worst thing we could do is get into an argument with someone. We don't need everyone's support, just a decent amount of them. So, I'm going for the low-hanging fruit first."

She surveyed the room, and as she pulled him forward, said, "You'll pick it up as we go. Don't worry."

I hope not. This political shit's exhausting. When can I sneak away?

13

Matt swung his sword back and forth. Blow after blow carved through the enemies before him. As he killed one, two replaced them. He tried to escape, but his feet felt stuck in the ground.

The crab monsters slowly morphed into horses with teeth of fire. He stood his ground and continued to cut through them all. In the distance, he heard a faint cry, and fought in that direction. He just couldn't move.

He and his blade were one as they mowed through the thousands of winged rats that replaced the crabs turned horses. With his skills fully charged, Matt made quick work of them, but the more enemies he killed, the farther away the voice sounded. Soon, he was unable to move, and the voice seemed to be moving away from him.

As he looked on, the landscape beyond was just a flat, blank slate full of monsters—an endless struggle against faceless obstacles.

Unable to move, Matt stood his ground and slaughtered anything that approached him. He desperately searched for the pull in his spirit that seemed to lead him toward the distant voice. He tried to drive himself forward to no avail, failing to find the source of the noise in the endless sea of enemies.

Liz retreated through her parent's home. They were nearly upon her. A hard left turn led her to the hall that connected to her parents' second dining hall. She was panting, and a quick glance behind her told her she'd escaped.

Her heaving breaths sounded far too loud in the empty corridors. Each step on the polished wood flooring sounded like weights being dropped. Every echoing sound added to Liz's growing dread of being found again.

Another noise caused her to take off running again, pushing through the sore and aching muscles. The pain was nothing, and she would prevail. If she found her parents, everything would be okay.

She paused. That wasn't right. She didn't want her parents' help. She was strong on her own.

Liz opened the nearest door to find Kelly, the young girl from two apartments down.

"Kelly!! Have you seen my parents?"

"No, but can you help my parents? They just need a little money. Mommy's potion shop isn't doing well."

She looked around for her parents. They told her to always find them if someone mentioned money. But she liked Kelly, so she offered up her allowance of a few dozen credits.

"Is that it? It's not enough!" There were tears running down her face. "If she doesn't get more, the bad men are going to take her store away. Aren't you rich? Why won't you help my mommy?"

Kelly threw the small, glowing currency down, and stomped on it as she turned large and angry. Flames escaped from her eyes as she screamed that it wasn't enough.

Liz ran through the door and slammed it shut. She breathed heavily into the cool wood. Before she could process what had just happened, she was already opening the next one.

Dominic, her hairdresser, snipped her hair shorter on one side after she saw it in a movie.

"You know, the preserve of Jastor Nath fish is nearly extinct. That means they will be all gone soon."

Liz gasped in the boosted chair. Extinction was bad. She had learned that word in school last week!

"That's not good!"

"Yeah, it's really bad. I'm a part of a charity that's trying to save them."

"That's so cool! Can I help?"

"Yes. You just need to get your parents to donate."

Liz tried to find her mother, but she was gone. She had to find her. She got up and ran toward the exit. Again, she found herself in the long hallway.

The next door had gold filigree around the edges, and when she opened it, she wound up playing with some blocks that she found at the edge of a party.

"Aren't you just the sweetest little thing!"

Liz looked up at a matronly woman. "Thank you!"

She didn't know what she had done to earn the compliment, and she was slightly miffed that it wasn't about her blocks. She had a perfectly presentable tower halfway built. Her work was what deserved to be complimented, but her dad always said to be polite, so she thanked the lady.

"Not like those common rabble. When I ruled my house, they didn't let the filthy commoners into the capital. No, it was well kept, and only for those of the peerage. Those of superior blood and breeding. You should come with me. I have a nephew your age who would be perfect for you."

The woman reached for Liz's hand. Liz was scared. She didn't like this woman.

She pulled her hand away and ran, noticing that she was suddenly taller as she crashed into the arms of a handsome young man on a ballroom floor.

Liz leaned into the chest of a sixteen year old Hedon. She stared up at him, eyes fluttering. He was handsome, charming, and soo dreamy. All the other girls were jealous that she was dancing with him. And at twelve Liz was smitten.

"So, you'll come to the autumn ball for society youth with me?"

Liz wanted to frown but refrained herself. She hated social events, but for Hedon she agreed. "Of course. I just need to tell my parents about the change of plans."

Hedon laughed. "Oh, no it's okay. We can sneak out. It will be great fun."

Liz turned her head, looking for her parents, and when she turned back, Hedon was gone. She was back in the hallway. She moved down to the next door before she paused. She could barely grip the handle with how hard her hands were shaking. But she pressed on.

She opened the final door, only to find herself standing on the battlement and fighting off hordes of attackers. There were endless crowds in the queendom's colors of purple and silver. She whipped out a line of blood and cut half a dozen people in half.

She fought until her mana ran dry, and she resorted to her spear. When her spear broke, she clawed at them with her fingernails. When her fingers were worn away, she bit and tore chunks away from them.

Everything turned fuzzy as she watched Matt and Aster succumb to the horde of enemies. She watched as they were dragged under, to never rise up again.

Still, she fought the horde, even as they screamed at her how she was the real monster for how she brutally killed them. It was a mantra repeated each and every time she vanquished another foe.

Finally, she stood alone on a balcony, and an archer stood across from her. With a mental effort, she tried to gather the blood around and on her, but with no mana to back it up, the blood didn't respond to her call. The arrow split a dozen times while in its flight toward her.

She had no fear, as she knew her parents would save her.

The arrow came closer.

Liz tried to turn away. She could save herself. She could save her friends. She could…

The arrow slammed into her.

Liz died.

Matt was on his back, gripping a giant mouth that tried to descend and eat him.

With a start, he jumped up into the descending mouth, causing him to nearly hit his head into the bunk above as he jerked awake.

He slipped out of bed to be eye level with Liz as she tossed and turned. She was sweating through her clothes, and the expression on her face was enough for Matt to reach up and shake her awake.

She startled up with a quiet gasp. Aster, who was on the bed with her, jerked up at the sound. Liz popped up, and Matt didn't miss how her shirt clung to her from the sweat. Even her hair was wild and clinging to her face, as if in a parody of blood.

"Sorry, bad dream."

"Yeah, me, too. I heard you and thought I should wake you up."

Liz pulled the confused fox into a brief hug as Matt heard her say, "Okay? Scared, sad, bad?"

He nuzzled her head from behind as Liz held her and projected, "It's okay. Just a bad dream. It's all better."

Liz plucked at the shirt that clung to her flesh. "I need a shower." She sniffed at herself and recoiled, "And I fucking reek. Ugh."

Matt checked himself and decided it would be a good idea to do the same. He was drenched, too.

The three of them quietly moved out of the room and into the shower rooms, where they washed the night terrors away. Aster stayed outside of the dreaded hot water, but pushed encouraging thoughts Matt's way and yipped a few times at Liz.

When they were done cleaning off, they moved to a lounge area, where the bright lights chased away any lingering thoughts of monsters that tried to manifest in the stitching of the couches.

Matt sat and patted the couch next to him, and Liz sat close, with Aster taking her position on their laps. His bond spun twice before she settled down in a ball, with her tail blocking out most of the light.

Liz petted the circular ball of fox, and they all sat quietly.

She looked like she wanted to say something but, in the end, she refrained. Matt spoke up instead. "I might have been a little too cavalier about my death. From the nightmares, it hit a bit harder than I expected. I was fighting endless opponents. It's getting fuzzy now, but I *needed* to go somewhere. I just couldn't get there."

Before either of them could say more, an older woman came into their room with a steaming teapot and cookies.

That would have been weird enough, but she was in full healer's robes. As she dropped off the tray, she offered, "If anyone needs to talk to a therapist, we're always open to listen. You can find us in the relaxation room or send a message to the hospital AI. We know this can be hard to process."

With that, she was gone, and the three of them sat there quietly. Matt leaned forward and started to pour the tea and passed the little cups around. He didn't know what type of tea it was, but as he drank, the hot liquid had a soothing effect. Soon, he found himself relaxing into the couch. He idly wondered if the tea had been spiked, but he felt fine. Just calm.

Matt looked to Liz, who had seemingly had the hardest night.

She shook her head after sipping from her own cup.

"It was mostly memories. But twisted into weird patterns. Things I'd rather not think about too much honestly."

She paused for a long minute as she dunked the small biscuit into the tea before asking, "What about you?"

"My dream was fuzzier. Something about not being able to move. I'm not sure. There might have been a voice. It's all fading."

Matt rubbed her back while he took control of the room's wall screen and started playing an old comedy show. It was mindless background noise, but it was enough to get a few chuckles from them.

Liz stood on a couch back with a hand holding Matt's to stabilize her. She probably didn't need it, but he felt better offering it. They were back in a neutral meeting hall, gathered early at Liz's request to plan their approach for dealing with the various sides' negotiations.

"I got a message for a private meeting before the larger general meeting. I'm sure they'll try to offer us a pittance for our hardships. If everyone argues for the maximum amount, they'll know that we aren't leaving until we've had our pound of flesh."

There was a murmur from the hundred or so gathered Pathers from both sides.

Liz nodded at what she heard. "They aren't dumb, and they're moving quickly to try and stop us from doing exactly what we're trying to do. If we stick together, and argue as a group in the larger meeting, we can get much more. Just don't give into the short term rewards at the cost of long term ones."

"But they gave us our points back!" Someone said from the general crowd.

Liz nearly spat at them, "They gave us half of our lost points to counter their fuck up. No. We shouldn't be content with shitty handouts disguised as rewards. Rewards should be prizes in and of themselves."

Liz looked as if she was about to say more, when Matt received a message that their meeting slot was up.

As she dropped down, Liz reminded everyone, "Don't accept their scraps. Argue that you want more, and that we'll only negotiate as a group."

The six of them were pulled into a meeting room with Juni, who sat there and smiled tightly at them as they entered. He stood and shook each of their hands as they passed each other, and took a seat on the opposite side of the long table.

Matt tapped it as they sat. The table's wood gave a strong, sturdy feeling that he wasn't sure of, but after examining it with his spirit, he guessed that the material was at least Tier 10.

Expensive for a meeting room. Or a statement.

"Sorry about everything. We just wanted to speak with the individual teams before the larger meeting and see how we can make things right. This is your chance to air your grievances."

Matt and the others all let Liz take the lead as she leaned forward and said, "I'm not sure you can. We're out twenty thousand points and two weeks' time, which could mean far more points than we've already lost. It's a significant blow to our point generation."

Juni nodded and said, "We are punishing the guilty parties as much as possible. To our regret, the Empire doesn't allow us to fine points from anyone. Even our own people."

Liz seemed as unconcerned as Juni was while she countered, "Remove them from the war. That would send the proper message to any would-be offenders."

The prince's right hand man actually frowned at that. "We would if we could, but the army heavily limits the number of Tier 7s we're allowed to have, and the spots are not transferable. As much as we hate what was done to you and your team, it's not feasible to cripple our limited Tier 7 powerbase. So only two from each side were removed completely. It was considered fair, as they had no remorse, and openly stated they would do it again if given the opportunity. But since each side punished an equal number of people, it keeps either side from gaining an advantage."

He gestured to the side, "We've arranged for you to talk to the people who have harmed you. It's the best we can do right now. Please remember that you'll get in trouble for attacking them without a duel, and you all are on healing cooldowns. Also, there's no way to force a duel."

Liz held up a hand. "We'll want to talk to Alyssa. Don't doubt that at all. But first, we want to hear your offer."

Juni's smile returned. "As I mentioned before, we will be matching the points earned from the Empire, if the points earned were the result of the proper orders, and if no allies were betrayed during the process. We feel that is fair compensation, and incentive to have everyone act appropriately."

Matt actually felt that his offer wasn't too bad. If they earned double the original amount, that could equal quite a lot of points in their pockets.

Liz ignored the gesture to say, "Our team, and the other Pathers who were affected, will want to negotiate for more than that during the joint meeting. But we'll be happy to see Alyssa now."

Juni didn't seem willing to push for more, and simply looked to a second door. The one they hadn't entered through.

Alyssa sauntered over to them, using a multi colored parasol as both a cane and a baton. One moment she was leaning on the parasol, and the next she was twirling it through the air. She was a plain woman in everything except her clothes. Her brown hair and eyes matched perfectly with her unremarkable facial features.

Her clothes reflected her parasol in their loud and bright colors.

Matt felt the tension in the room skyrocket from his team, and briefly placed a hand on Liz's leg under the table, to ward any explosions off. The rest of their team came up and flanked them, creating a wall against the woman who had screwed them over so badly.

Juni made introductions and then fled the room. "Alyssa Clairmont, Team Bucket. Team Bucket, Alyssa Clairmont."

Alyssa came up and smiled brightly at them all. "Well, good to meet you all. Shame it couldn't have been yesterday, but with you all dying, it made it a bit difficult."

Annie snapped out, "Ohh, you have nerve, woman. I'm going to…"

Alyssa waved them off. "Don't be crass, dear. It's unsightly."

Liz, calmer now, said, "It's unsightly to throw allies under the bus for points. If you had done your job yesterday and backed us up, we would have met then, so don't try, and turn this around on us."

Alyssa didn't seem bothered in the least, and waved her parasol around as she said, "Oh, don't be that way. Those that can, do. And I can. I did what was best for me at the time." She shrugged. "If I had known you were so competent, I would have moved in between the two waves of attackers. I thought you would die on the first attack. I wouldn't have done that if I had known, but we all make our decisions, and we must sleep in the beds we make."

She twirled her parasol once again, before catching it over her shoulders with a flourish at the end of her statement.

Matt's attention quickly latched onto that colorful rainbow of light that was emitted from the fabric and felt something like his growth mana ring. Her parasol had multiple aspects of mana flowing through it.

He was awoken from his inspection by a pinch on the leg from Liz.

Realizing what his inspection looked like, he clarified quickly. "Your parasol feels interesting. It's full of random aspected mana. It feels more like a weapon, though."

The woman beamed as if she had won a prize, "Oh, this lovely thing? I got it from a wannabe suitor from the Empire. My darling here is a growth item as pretty as I am. We match so well, don't you think?"

Liz wasn't impressed and moved back to Alyssa's last statement. "You had better watch yourself, or you'll get a taste of your own medicine sooner or later."

Alyssa looked unconcerned with Liz's not-so-subtle threat. "What goes around comes around. I'm not particularly worried about it. What will be, will be."

Emily said from her end of the table, "We want a duel from you."

Alyssa looked overly put upon and sighed dramatically. "The same thing little Albie asked for. No, I won't duel you. I did nothing wrong. Was I selfish? Yes, without a doubt. Do I care? Not really. It really wasn't anything personal, and I've already been punished quite harshly. It's just a game."

She sighed dramatically and said, "If you want someone to blame, blame math. It was simply worth more points to let you die. We aren't friends yet, so I had no incentive to help you. Besides, you're all getting lucky with Albie's bribe. Most of the other Pather's aren't so lucky. My little birds have been flitting about and learned that most teams won't be getting nearly as good a deal as you were offered."

She smirked at Liz and met all of their gazes before she stood and sauntered out the door, calling over her shoulder, "Well, I'll be on my way. After the next meeting I have a mission where I'm sure I'll be tragically ambushed. I'll see you at the little group therapy session in a bit. Tata!"

Annie shrugged as the door closed. "I don't give two rats asses about what makes me look bad. I'm going to kill her the minute I can get away with it. She can decline our duels all she wants, but she can't decline an assassination. She can bitch all she wants after the fact, but it won't do her any good with a dagger in her throat."

Matt was pretty angry himself. "I'm going to break both her legs. The healer said that was the most painful thing to break. Think you can work that into it?"

Annie bobbed her head around a little and said, "Yeah, probably."

Matt threw her a thumbs up.

Maybe after Annie kills her a few times, she'll be willing to duel us to get the assassinations to stop?

Matt wasn't sure it would work, but he liked the idea.

Conor broke him out of his reverie. "While I hate to break up your revenge fantasy, I think we should draw the line at actual torture."

Annie shot Conor a betrayed look, similar to the look that Aster would give Matt when he cut her off from eating ice cream.

Conor looked at Annie with an almost imperceptible smile on his face as he explained, "Sure she was being selfish, but she had a point. She was just gaming a flawed system, and she had no real reason to help us or the kingdom. Which, from everything I've seen and heard, is total dogshit. And she can clearly get out at any time, if her suitor comments are true. She had no reason to play nice."

He shrugged. "I think a single death will be sufficient. She'll lose half her points and be out of the war for two weeks. Same as us, except she won't get those points back."

Annie countered zealously, "She should die six times. One for each of us."

Matt ignored the bickering. He wanted to hate Alyssa, but maybe Conor was right, and he and Annie were going a little overboard with their plans for retribution.

Juni moved to the prince's side as the meeting hall filled. "Things were worse than we expected. No one's taking the bait. They all demand to collectively negotiate for compensation."

Albert shrugged. "It was always a possibility. We'll pay more up front but, in the end, they can't gather up every time one of them dies. It will work itself out."

Juni hesitated for a moment and said, "We'll have to cancel the strike on Alyssa. She knows about it already."

He wanted to curse the woman. For as much as she was a pain in the ass, she was good at networking and getting spies into places they shouldn't be. It was good that he had bugged all the meeting rooms beforehand, or he would have missed that she was already aware of their ploy.

Albert didn't look surprised at that. "We both knew that it was a long shot. If we just pause the order, we might be able to cause her to worry, and that could be just as bad for her."

Juni wasn't so sure, but as Princess Sara walked forward, he stepped back and started observing the crowd for the upcoming negotiation. No matter how this turned out, he needed to identify the major players and start learning their weak points, so the proper leverage could be applied.

Matt stood with about one hundred others in a large meeting hall. They were all Pathers who had been screwed over in various ways over the last few days.

The groups weren't only the teams that Liz had spent all morning recruiting for her plan. No, there were at least a dozen more teams that had been abandoned by their vassal allies and other preventable disasters.

The mood of the room was sour, and getting worse by the minute as they waited for the prince and princess to arrive. No one seemed to have taken the small bait offered in the individual meeting, which seemed to only piss the other teams off even more.

Something Alyssa had said sent Liz into a messaging frenzy, and she had spent the entire time after their meeting typing at her pad and sending messages to various parties. It was like a fire had been lit under her.

That was what led to more than half of the room being distinctly crowded around their group of six. Both sides were present and mixing without the enmity Matt might've expected.

He hadn't needed to ask Liz after he thought about it for a little while. In the end, calling the Pathers here to fight as mercenaries wasn't wrong. Their fights with each other were the reason for the war, sure, but it was also a game. And the vassals were screwing it up.

None of them had been able to sleep much before the meeting, so Matt had read parts of the book that Liz had recommended. While he didn't find it as interesting as she had, he certainly learned a few things. Mostly, he learned that if the vassals didn't stop these problems now, they would, at least historically, spiral out of control. At least until a third faction was formed, or the army stepped in and laid down new rules.

Matt was very interested in what those new rules would be, as he thought that they could be a good starting point for arguments. But two things killed that hope. One was that there was no record of what those extra rules could possibly be. Anywhere. He had searched high and low on the EmpireNet but had found nothing.

The second was that Liz, when he mentioned it to her, said that it was a last resort for a reason. They were meant to deal with these things on their own. It was a test for both the Pathers and the vassal faction's young leaders.

His musings were interrupted when Sara and Albert walked onto the raised stage. Matt wasn't sure what he expected, but they seemed unconcerned by the array of angry faces aligned against them.

"Good afternoon. I wish this meeting was under more joyous circumstances."

The prince's opening statement was met with a hiss of anger, which he nodded toward and spoke over.

"Yes. As I said, these are not ideal circumstances by any means. While I had hoped that the individual meetings would allow for more personal negotiations, Princess Sara and I are more than willing to hear everyone out."

Princess Sara took over. "Is there a speaker for everyone? It would be easier that way."

Calmly, Liz called out, "The offer of points is a bandage for the greater problem. And that's not good enough."

All around them, there were murmurs of, "Yeah."

Princess Sara looked unsurprised as she asked, "And what is it that you want? More points? Money? A duel we can't force?"

Liz smiled right back at the woman looming over her. "No. We-" she spread her arms out, encompassing the small faction she had created. "-and a few thousand of our friends don't like how we're being treated and want a change."

"You don't have…"

Sara started to speak, but Liz cut her off. "Oh, I assure you we do. We have both the authority and the leverage to demand what we want. On my side, I have the top ten percent of earners for the Pathers." She paused to emphasize her words and finished with, "From both sides."

Liz's voice echoed out as she continued, "We're all angry, and most of us have two weeks of healing cooldown. We have nothing better to do than trying to drum up support for our faction."

Princess Sara looked miffed, but asked, "And what are your demands? If you think you'll be able to create a third faction, you overestimate how badly we've mistreated the Pathers as a whole."

Liz laughed and said, "No. What we want is a cut of the profits, and a seat at the table."

Albert looked genuinely surprised at that and asked, "How so?"

Liz looked like a shark that had found its prey, and with a wicked smile, said, "We want three percent of the points earned by our various factions. Given to the teams with the greatest contribution based on percentage. According to the point totals published by the Army, which should be adequate compensation. If you want us to fight, we need some skin in the game. We also want a voice in all decision making and command sessions going forward. We want a council created for all war decisions."

Princess Sara looked slightly green at the suggestion, and Albert looked stonier than usual.

Liz jumped on their hesitation. "Don't think we didn't notice that not all of us have been reimbursed. More than one team was simply told to go pound sand. This isn't okay. We, right here, are a pretty good representation of the best that the Path has to offer. If we don't look out for everyone else now, we'll all be screwed over sooner or later. And in two weeks, we can have everyone on The Path refusing orders. If you're willing to treat *us* like this, how much worse will it be for the lesser Pathers?"

The princess finally said, "We can't do that. It would disrupt our plans too much, and I don't believe that you can get enough of a faction together to force our hands. That would cripple our point production and slow down every decision to a crawl. It's an outlandish, childish desire."

Liz was about to speak up when, suddenly, Alyssa's voice rang out from a corner as she walked to the edge of the stage. She sat on the edge and said, "I and the people I represent agree to this, but we want in on it as well. And I want a seat on any decision making council."

She looked at the prince while twirling her obnoxious parasol. "I've been talking to the crafters in our outlying cities, and they aren't happy with how things are being handled. I'll be taking over as a voice for them." She waved a hand around and nearly took out someone's head with her parasol. "Mana shortages and such. I can solve them, if given the right incentive."

Albert didn't look happy, but after a brief whisper with Juni he nodded. "I see you had your fingers in that pie already."

Alyssa beamed at him. "Oh, I knew you would try to freeze me out Albie. I took my own measures. But remember that I didn't cause the mana problems. You shouldn't have only spent your points for mana for the defensive formations. You know how much mana the crafters use, and how they can get when there isn't enough of it. That was *your* lack of foresight. I just strolled around and heard *oh so much* juicy gossip. Same with your cities, Sara. I have agreements with both sides' poor, forgotten crafters to negotiate on their behalf."

Liz looked like she was about to spit fire at the other woman, but she didn't let it show as more than a clenching of her fist. Still, she didn't look half as mad as Sara, who realized that a kingdom representative had the ability to speak for her crafters.

Princess Sara spat out, "It's Princess Sara to you, and I'll see your hold over my people broken the second I leave here you venomous, slithering, snake."

Alyssa seemed unruffled by the threat and just smiled demurely. "I'm *sure* you will. I look forward to meeting them, *Princess* Sara."

Liz was perfectly calm and collected, and she took advantage of the change in conversation to agree with Alyssa's counter offer. She replied with a clear voice, "If we're going to split the points over such a large population, we need a larger percentage. Five percent minimum."

Matt's currently most hated person leaned forward on her parasol with a genuine smile and added, "One percent of that five to be spread equally to everyone. The poor crafters don't get out much. Hard to earn points inside a city. The other four are to be spread to those that earn it."

Liz nearly growled out, "*To those that earn it.*"

With the two of them in agreement, the entire room's focus shifted to the two faction leaders on the stage. Somehow, the argument had turned from the two vassal leaders, to an argument between Liz and Alyssa, then back to the royals just as quickly.

Albert and Sara leaned in and conversed in whispers for what felt like an eternity. The crowd started to murmur after the first minute and, after the fifth, there was an audible growl in the air.

The discussion between the two leaders turned quite heated, and they took turns glaring at both Liz and Alyssa, before they removed their privacy barrier and came up from their huddle.

Sara spoke for both of them. "We can agree to these terms, with the added stipulation that there be no more hesitation or backstabbing on either side. If there is, the offending party will go on a planet-wide blacklist and be given no help from their own side. A higher reward will also be paid out to those that kill them."

Albert, who had been glaring at Alyssa the entire time Sara spoke, finally looked away and added, "Speaking of prizes, we're both creating a leaderboard. Or rather, we're using the Empire's rankings, and we'll be giving out rewards to anyone able to take out the highest impact people on either side."

Liz just smiled at the royals and said, "The Pathers agree. We don't mind a challenge. We mind being betrayed for personal gain." She ended her statement with a glare to Alyssa, who just beamed back at Liz.

Out of nowhere, a man appeared, hovering in the air between the two sides. It was the army leader Colonel Thorne.

His voice boomed around the small building as he said, “The army has seen and heard the agreement. It shall be put in place effective immediately. Any further arbitration will have to be agreed upon by the three sides comprising the agreement.”

As suddenly as he appeared, he was gone.

The two royals quickly left following the pronouncement. Their act was mirrored by everyone else remaining in the hall.

Matt figured that everyone was trying to leave before the deal changed further.

Annie looked around and said, “I don’t get what happened.”

Liz stomped lightly and responded, “We got helped by that bitch is what happened.”

Emily scrunched up her face and said, “I don’t follow. What does that mean for our idea? Seems like we did better than the original offer. Or am I wrong?”

Liz seemed unconcerned about the points and was still glaring at the door Alyssa had used to leave the building. “Now, we get a percentage, which should help us in the long run. It’s split more, but with four percent going to the top earners, we shouldn’t see much of a difference. At least by rough calculations from the official totals. Overall, we, the Pathers’ Union, did fine. I’m more mad about that woman stepping in to help me. To make matters worse, she somehow seemed to know about our idea, and used it for her own benefit. Fuck! I hate that bitch!”

They filed out of the stuffy meeting hall with the rest of the Pathers, into the cool city air. Most were happy, but Matt heard more than a few people plotting revenge against their betrayers.

Matt didn’t really care about looking like an asshole, and was trying to figure out how to pin down the clearly crafty woman, and get her to agree to a duel. No matter what Annie did to her, or how much Alyssa helped their cause, he was going to break something inside of her before the war was out.

He did take Conor’s warning to heart though, and would keep his revenge from turning into torture.

Sara looked over the retreating audience from the side door. Today, despite the tense atmosphere, had been very beneficial, and she was quite pleased with the result. That redheaded Pather's little ploy had worked quite well. Her profit sharing point system effectively removed the incentives for her commanders to be greedy little shits.

What benefited the queendom, benefited all. The only real thorn in her side was having to form a ruling council with the Pathers. But so long as the Pather representative was capable and saw things her way, it should be a minor issue.

I expect that the redheaded Pather will be on Albie's council at some point. What was her name again?

She checked her AI and found the woman's profile that her people had put together. She saved a deeper look for later, only grabbing her name.

Ah, right. Elizabeth Moore. I'll have to keep an eye on her. She seems promising.

The beneficial rule changes aside, Sara was most excited about her interactions with Albie. It was perfect, she had kept him in a call for hours, and gotten him quite relaxed around her. It had only taken a little complaining about how his Pathers had done better than hers.

Which wasn't hard to fake, as she was quite peeved about that. She was getting more Pathers than him, and the fact that they had lost in overall quality was concerning. She also had quite a great time planning ambushes for all of their back-stabbing, and handling the problematic commanders that they hadn't been able to remove.

Speaking of which, Albie had sent her a message regarding Alyssa's ambush. The conniving snake apparently knew about the ambush, and it had to be rescheduled. Given what she knew of her, Sara wasn't surprised that she found out.

How did she even get all those kingdom and Pather crafters to agree to her plan?

Alyssa's scheme had been amazingly well timed, and she fully expected Albie to have his hands full with that one. It wasn't perfect on her end either, though. She now needed to find a capable and loyal representative that her crafters would accept. It was never easy to replace a chosen leader but she couldn't let Alyssa remain the public face of her crafters.

But, overall, today was a good day. Except for one nagging issue Alyssa brought to light.

Why was Albie spending all of his points on mana for defensive formations this early in the game? Is he expecting a siege?

That wasn't like the Albert she knew. She corrected herself. That wasn't like the Albert she *thought* she knew. In every interaction she had with him, he seemed intelligent and cognizant of his situation, and how to best take advantage. It was one of the reasons why she was so enamored with him. He would make the perfect co-ruler.

Neglecting the crafters was a rookie mistake. Everyone knew that there were two kinds of people you never piss off: healers and crafters. No one wanted to be blacklisted from either of their services. That was why his actions confused her.

With a flick of her fingers, Sara sent a message to her intelligence team. With one last, long look at Albie's retreating figure, she began walking back to her headquarters with a pensive look on her face.

Oh, Albie...I hope you'll forgive me when we take everything from you.

14

Matt and his team were left at their wits' end once the meeting was over. They didn't know what they should be doing with their free time. They couldn't even spar, in case they injured themselves. So that was out of the question for at least another week, and without the ability to go on missions, Matt felt adrift.

With little left to do, Matt offered, "I'm going to pester an enchanter I know. Does anyone want to come?"

Annie sighed. "It's too early to work. How about we go get pedicures? Maybe a full message? Treat ourselves a bit."

No one else wanted to do work after that suggestion, and Matt wasn't going to be the odd man out when he wouldn't mind the distraction.

They found a nice place and were pampered into an absolute mess of luxury. The place was so fancy, they were treated to haircuts as well. His hair was buzzed back to nearly nothing, as he didn't want to deal with it during a fight. Conor had taken the same approach as well.

Liz and Emily both had their long hair merely trimmed, but Annie had taken her shoulder-length hair to a style only a finger-length long. She said that it would only get in her way, with all the sneaking she planned on doing.

Aster had her coat brushed and shined. The finishing touch was the array of ribbons that she had woven through her fluffy tail, along with a matching pair of bows by her ears. She pranced around, showing off her cuteness to everyone they passed as they walked around the city. Eventually, they stopped in for a light lunch before they went their separate ways just after noon.

Annie and Emily were going to visit a friend, and Conor was doing the same. Liz just pushed Matt to go visit Kelley, the Tier 10 enchanter that he had made friends with. She was going to start preparing for the upcoming changes and try to get ahead of what she expected was coming.

He offered to help, but was very kindly told he wouldn't be of much use to her.

It was actually a relief, he really didn't want to play nice with people that he didn't know. All he wanted was to do some enchanting.

Kelley was waiting at the front desk next to his nephew when Matt walked in. Matt hoped he would be. He had messaged the man earlier, and then once again when he was on his way.

"Oh, you're here, good. Let's head back. No girlfriend or Aster today?"

Matt shook the Tier 10's hand and laughed. "Nah. We died yesterday, and after a spa day, we have nothing to do for the next two weeks, until we can safely spar again, which is at least a week out."

The man looked positively gleeful at the news, and he half dragged Matt into his workshop.

"That's perfect. I've been playing with the light rune you gave me. I think I figured out how they can be linked together to create an array, but the efficiency loss is still a little higher than what's practical. To make it commercially viable, we need it to be as bright or brighter than the standard rune, at the same mana per minute level. Not the high end of mana cost, where it already wins. But I think I'm close."

Matt snagged a pair of dark-tinted goggles and peered through the blinding light, looking at and recording the string of runes that Kelley had set up.

At 80 MPS, Matt's AI started parsing through what Kelley had done, and began testing modifications from both the base rune and the one the older man had adjusted.

"I think we can work on this. First thing I see is…"

The sun was peeking over the horizon and illuminating the giant walled-off city. The tips of the skyscrapers glowing like candles as Matt walked down the street to their rooms in the headquarters building.

On the way, he ordered breakfast for everyone and returned to their room with warm bags in hand. He had just finished setting the plates when Liz came out of their room with a sleepy Aster. She still had the ribbons in her tail, but not the ones by her ears. Considering how much she moved in her sleep, he wasn't surprised in the least.

Liz just yawned at him and asked, "How'd it go? I was surprised you didn't come back last night, so I figured it either went really well or really badly."

Matt grinned at her around his face full of egg.

"It went really well, actually. Well, kinda. Kelley and I mostly worked on the light rune I gave him, and we managed to solve the problem of the rune being too inefficient. But it only works for single runes, and not for strip lighting. We'll work on that later, after we both have time to think on it. After that, we mostly worked on enchanting various bits and bobs he had lying around."

Liz looked vaguely concerned at that. "He isn't taking advantage of your mana, is he?"

Matt waved his fork, "He isn't. Or if he is, he's either really bad at it, or working an extremely long con. He didn't ask, and when I half offered, he waved me off."

They ate in silence for a while, until they both finished their plates. Eventually, Matt asked, "How did the prep stuff go?"

Liz grinned at him. "*Gooood.* But I need you to stand the first watch for me."

"Watch? What watch? And where? And when?" He cocked an eyebrow and said, "I'm willing, but confused."

If Liz needed someone to do something fast, it was much easier for him to step in and take over for a while, than to scramble to find someone else. The only question was what exactly it was that she needed him to do.

"We need someone to staff the situation room and basically see if they're trying to send Pathers on suicide missions because of terrain or anything." Seeing the expression on Matt's face, she hurried to add, "It's not meant to be hard. We're still working out the exact details, but we don't expect it to be more than that. Or at least not much more. We're thinking about rerouting all Pather communications through the offices we are setting up, but that seems like a little too much for a single person to handle."

"Wait, back up a bit. Who is we?"

Liz looked confused but finally understood. "Sorry. Yesterday I was talking to Juni, and afterwards, Talous. He's the one of the top Pather team leads on the queendom side, and we're making sure we get everything we can from the two royal heirs. Anyway, he and a few others on both sides who are interested planned out a lot of things yesterday. Some of us are dead, and some aren't."

"The idea is, we'll always have a top fifty Pather in charge, and on the council that the prince is making. If no one in the top fifty is dead, the top ten need to send a representative. It's not ideal, as it will screw up some missions, but it's the best we can work out for now. None of us want to do it permanently."

Matt wiped his plate with his toast and asked, "And that means someone needs to be in the situation room?"

"Yup! That's where most of the big decisions are carried out. I think you'll at least not mind it, even if it isn't your cup of tea. The map shows everything that's going on, and the various upgrades that can be bought from the points that the kingdom is earning. We'll get someone else to do it soon, but we all need to start today."

He looked at their room with longing, but blasted [Endurance] at 80 MPS for a few seconds to banish any fatigue he was feeling. They left the food out for the others, and they quickly moved downstairs, where they separated.

Matt found himself in a brightly lit room with row after row of massive screens, and people tapping at them while interfacing with their AIs. He was surprised by how quiet the room was with that many people talking, and by their gestures, some discussions were getting rather heated.

A quick inspection of the room with his spiritual sense showed him a series of enchantments surrounding each workstation. It was overlaid with an obscuring rune, making it murky and twisty to his senses, but the application was obvious.

A petite young woman with bright pink hair came over to him and introduced herself. "Jessica, watch commander for the first shift. I assume you're the Pather assigned here."

"That's me. Though I admit, I'm not exactly sure what I'm supposed to be doing, or how any of this works. Any help would be greatly appreciated." He grinned at her, trying to show that he wasn't going to step on her toes or try to take over somehow.

If that was Liz's plan, he had no idea how he would even begin to go about that, so he just kept things honest.

Jessica looked at him questioningly, then motioned around after finding what she wanted. "This is the relay section and where we communicate with the various teams who are out in the field. From those that are defending the lowest level forts to those defending the cities."

"Not an AI? I know we didn't deal with one, but I'm surprised by that, with how many teams are out there now."

The Tier 7 woman shook her head. "The hundred people we have are generally enough to handle the volume we get. It's usually a lot of small calls that only take a minute, but we don't let an AI handle the communications simply because the teams don't like that." She shrugged and continued with, "Apparently, it's been tried and doesn't go over well. Even though most of the operators are relaying information that an AI is giving them. Don't ask me about the psychology. I can't explain it."

Matt raised his hands slightly and took a half step back. "Oh, I understand. I'm sure someone figured out the most optimal way a million years ago. I was just surprised."

Jessica laughed lightly at that. "Fair enough. Sorry, that's something that some of the other nobles were upset about. They thought it was wasteful that we requested their people for such dull work." She made air quotes with her fingers and sarcastically chimed, "Menial labor that an AI could do. And they always seem to complain during my shift."

She guided him forward to a glowing, projected globe ringed by panels, with levers and knobs inlaid.

"That's the big boy. That isn't our work; the Empire put this together for us. It lets the prince spend kingdom level points to upgrade various forts or cities throughout the world." She pointed to a counter on a side wall and said, "That's the overall points total, and where we're earning our points. Everything can be interfaced with your AI if you're in this room. Feel free to poke around. You won't break anything, since none of us have permission to do much more than view the files and processes. Only the prince has the ability to spend these points. And while he can delegate things, only like three people have been given the right. But I'm pretty sure that all three are really just Juni."

Matt laughed at her attempt at a joke and said, "Yeah, the prince seems to trust Juni, and he's always busy with various things. Though, I've only worked with him for a little bit, so I'm sure you know him better."

Jessica grinned and responded, "The running conspiracy is that Juni's Talent makes it so he doesn't need to sleep, since no one's ever actually seen the man sleeping. It would explain how he gets so much done."

Matt paused to think about that; he hadn't seen the man sleep either. Juni always was up and about, constantly doing something during the golem attacks, and afterwards. He doubted that it was actually the man's Talent, but it could be.

She looked at the map and said, "You aren't a part of the kingdom, but Juni has a reputation. He gets things done. People have tried to pin assassinations and sabotage on him to the prince a million times. If he does things like that, he's never been caught, or at least left substantial proof. He's also insanely loyal to the prince, though that one makes sense if you know their history."

"Oh?" Matt was officially interested and tried to pry some more information out of the shift commander.

"Yeah. The prince ran away when he was around five, I believe. How he got away from his minders, no one knows, and more than a few heads rolled for that lapse. But he found Juni's house and was taken in by the family. He pretty much lived there for a few days before anyone found him."

Seeing Matt's look of incredulity, she nodded. "It was a new backwater world. Tier 3, and no one there was strong enough to scan the whole place, so it took a while. Either way, they apparently became fast friends, and when they were to be separated, Juni said he would follow his friend. Five or so years later, Juni shows up at the prince's birthday celebration after crashing the event by climbing down a chimney. Right in front of the king and everything. He swore his allegiance to the prince in front of everyone and was granted a knight title by the king himself. Lifted his family right out of peasant status with one move. They've never been separated since."

Matt wasn't sure how much of that he believed but nodded along with the woman. It just sounded too fantastical. A prince without a Tier 25 bodyguard? Or one so incompetent that it took days to search an area that an unawakened child could escape into? No, he didn't believe any of that.

It was an interesting look into Juni's history, or reported history, if nothing else. He made a note to relay it all to Liz later. She was more likely to be able to weed out the good information than he was.

Jessica's head jerked away from him, and she said over her shoulder, "Gotta work. If you have any questions, find me once I put out these fires."

Matt walked over to the huge map and inspected it. It seemed to be a larger version of the one he had seen with Juni when they had checked in with the man.

There were five continents with a city each. Two of them on nearly connected landmasses were red, with the surrounding forts colored in a similar shade. The map clearly showed a series of large forts surrounded by a ring of medium forts, with the walls of smaller forts creating something akin to border walls around the cities.

Little resource icons flashed, but any in the queendom's territory were dim, with not much information provided. He could only see what the resource was, and its expected value in both points and material yield. Though it was just an estimation based on the information gathered before the queendom took over the land. Quickly swiping over to a kingdom-controlled area, he found a Tier 6 iron mine that was producing two tons of material a day. The mine wasn't simulated, as he expected. Instead he saw that there were upgrade paths in the map where automated miners could be purchased. But the kingdom seemed to have invested in actual miners.

After some spinning of the globe, he found a virtual mine by finding the medium fort his team had taken over. It produced aluminum; or it would have, if it was a real mine. Instead, it was simulated, and produced a set amount of virtual aluminum, which could be converted to real aluminum for free, or converted into points.

That mine was creating points at an astonishing rate. Three thousand points a day as it was now. If they upgraded it, they could double that. It seemed incredibly unfair when you considered that it was one of the thousands of medium forts, but two things still caught his ire.

The first was that they were kingdom level points, and not normal points. They weren't the same, and couldn't be converted except at a pretty massive loss. Even when converted, it couldn't be done without the army's approval. Matt suspected that it was the reason why Colonel Thorne was there for the meeting.

The second was that upgrading everything was absurdly expensive. It cost thirty thousand points to upgrade the fake aluminum mine to the next level of production. Ten days of production wasn't bad in and of itself to double the mine's output, but that was nothing when looking at the cost for fort upgrades.

For a small fort to have the cheapest upgrade, which was to improve the gate to a Tier 7 metal banded wood, cost eighty thousand points. To raise the wall another five feet taller and increase its stone to Tier 7 cost two hundred thousand points. Adding a set of mini defensive ballista on each side of the front gate cost half a million points. Upgrading them to mana cannons was another million points on top of that.

And those prices were all for the smallest of forts. The prices only scaled further for each level of defensive structure.

Increasing the defensive rating of the wall around a city cost fifteen million points per section of wall. That meant one hundred and fifty million points for the smallest city, and two hundred million for the larger cities.

The cities were the only structure that could increase the Tier of their defenses to Tier 8, but the cost was so absurd, it was nigh unreachable. Upgrades for each section cost half a billion points.

Still in shock, Matt flicked to the other defensive upgrades that various places could get. True magical shielding was on the list, but it was only available for medium forts or larger. He didn't even feel that the price was all that high, at least for the initial price. Two hundred thousand points was relatively cheap, until he looked at the specs for the shields. It cost 15 MPS as a standing price, and had a battery of half a million mana, which would be drained to sustain itself when absorbing damage.

That wasn't bad. The king was Tier 35, and clearly invested in the prize for winning the war. A Tier 35 mana stone had two hundred fifty billion mana, and the man had, or at least should have, the ability to get them quickly. There had to be a few nobles he could shake down, if nothing else. One stone could power everything itself.

That was his perspective on things until he looked at the outgoing costs that the kingdom was incurring. Nearly two-thirds of their income was being spent on mana. A little searching showed that the Empire had realized that a single, higher Tier mana stone could turn the tides, so they forced the kingdom to buy mana with points.

A single point bought 10 mana. That meant that it would cost fifty thousand points to fill up a shield's reserves. That wasn't a small investment. It changed the light in which he viewed the mana stones he pilfered. That wasn't a small investment, though he doubted that the army was handing out lower Tier mana stones. It would make more sense if they had a few Tier 45 mana stones, and just slowly drained them. At five hundred trillion mana, a single one might fund the entire war a few times over.

That would be a fortune to everyone in the vassal kingdoms, of which the strongest weren't even Tier 36. But it would be nothing to the Emperor, who had Tier 47 rifts to delve.

It made sense to limit the outside materials that could be brought in, as it rendered the various mines on the planet actually valuable to the war effort.

Matt tried to think of how he could use that to his and his team's advantage, and spent the next two hours reviewing various functions. In the end, he didn't see any way to exploit his mana regeneration. The easiest way would be to create a rift where iron was present in the ground, as there were two Tier 5 rifts being delved for that purpose. A team went in with miners who, after it was safe, started mining the rift over and over. The rifts had a limited number of instances, so they could expertly mine the ore and leave.

He was pretty sure that he could make a rift like that, but how he would own it would be a separate problem. If he said he made it, he didn't know what would happen, but the questions he imagined being asked would be less than ideal for his continued anonymity. He also didn't know how he would be able to claim a rift at all. He was pretty sure that they were considered a part of the planet, unless you were a guild or noble family.

It wasn't like he needed the money, but he did want to increase his point generation. The two weeks of forced downtime sucked, and he was anxious to earn enough points to buy the [Cracked Breach] skill. He half suspected that it was placed there explicitly for him. It was just too perfect of a coincidence, otherwise considering that the skill could accept an absurd amount of mana with a relatively low upfront cost. But he could cover upfront cost with the help of a mana stone next Tier.

Some of the upgrades just felt weird. Why spend points on a moat when you could just dig one out? After some consideration, Matt figured that this actually *was* the army's intent. You could spend an absurd amount of points, or you could build whatever you needed yourself.

Things like the teleporter setup for large forts seemed impossible to build on one's own, but considering the strategic value of something like that, it seemed kind for the army to provide them at all.

That didn't change the fact that the kingdom was raking in points like they were hotcakes. A single small fort generated ten points an hour, and there were tens of thousands of them. The medium forts generated one hundred, and the large forts were worth five hundred points an hour. A city generated *ten thousand* points an hour.

If he decided to become a mana battery, he could make 6,912,000 mana a day.

Matt paused as the realization sank in. That was worth 691,200 kingdom level points per day. If he sold his secret right here and now, he could buy everything he could ever want out of the reward shop. All it would take was a few days of sitting back and relaxing. He was sure that the conversion wasn't one for one, but that hardly mattered when he never ran out of mana.

I could change the course of the war with a few days' worth of giving mana. That's enough to redirect points into upgrading a fort or two.

Matt was almost tempted to try and work out a deal.

No. Fuck that. I'll earn more points than that by fighting. I'll carve out a deeper impact through my actions, not my mana. I will not and will never be reduced to just a mana battery. I'll kick down a city's walls solo if I have to, but I won't devolve into nothing more than my Talent.

Still, the scale of points was mind boggling.

He received a call from Liz as he was idly scrolling through the numbers. Since it was the first contact he had had in five boring hours, he quickly picked up. "Check to see if 54°21'56.0"S 36°34'45.6"W is a bad spot to send a team."

Matt found the spot and saw that it was a cold and mountainous region near the pole of the planet. There was a single medium fort defending a palladium mine. The fort was distinctly far away from cities, and acted more as a beachhead for the queendom, located on the southernmost continent. It was half-covered in ice caps, with a large fort built at the center, with a small ring of forts around it. The continent and fort were both otherwise isolated from the main forces of both vassals.

After thinking it over himself and having his AI simulate the situation, he responded, "Seems clear enough."

After a long moment, Liz finally asked, "Okay, good. How are things down there?"

Matt shrugged, even though she couldn't see it. "Fine, I guess. Mostly boring since there isn't much for me to do other than observe. From the lack of communication so far, I guess you can handle everything from your end?"

Liz seemed apologetic when she said, "We got set up with a full office, and it has most of the capabilities I thought we would need someone down there for. Sorry. I didn't think it was worth your time."

"Don't worry about it." Matt tried to reassure Liz, who he could tell was genuinely remorseful about leaving him out.

"I thought we'd need a lot of oversight, but the kingdom has been super helpful and hasn't tried to double-cross us or anything."

"So, do you need me here?" He tried to keep the eagerness out of his voice. While he had not minded this little break, and had learned quite a few things, he'd much rather be doing something else.

"For now, yes. I've got a replacement on their way. If nothing else, we at least have a face down there, so that should keep anyone from getting ideas about changing orders or something. Sorry I have to go. Someone's at my door."

Matt almost reluctantly disconnected and spent the last hour of his shift planning out his next steps. He started on his idea for posting a reward for unique mana aspects. He would offer 10 points per person who had an aspect he lacked.

He wasn't sure if it was enough to attract people, but he felt it was more than fair for someone spending a few points of mana to charge his ring a bit.

That was an hour's worth of standing guard but for a few minutes of effort.

To his surprise, by the time his shift ended, and a young woman came to replace him, he had half a dozen pings responding to his posting.

He eagerly sent them each a message to meet up with him at a public park and hurried his way over to find six people milling around.

"If you can line up, I just need to input mana into my refilling mana stones."

That was Matt's answer to hiding his growth ring. He bought two dozen small and inefficient mana stones that could be recharged, and intended to simply have the people add their mana into one, then move on.

Steam, cloud, iron, tree, plant, and finally ice were the aspects of mana that he added to his collection. He was about to refuse the ice person but decided to take it anyway. The young man was Tier 5, and had a scraggly look about him that Matt recognized from his days in the orphanage. It reminded him of the kids who were falling into depression. That haunted look along with the young man trying, and failing, to hide his eagerness caused Matt to ignore the fact he had Aster's ice mana.

"Thank you all. If you know anyone who has unique mana, please let them know that I'll take a copy."

The cloud mana woman was the only one to stick around and asked, "I assume that you're a crafter?"

Matt just nodded to her question. He did craft things, after all.

"If you have anything that reduces weight, I'd love to buy it. No one else has it at a reasonable price."

"Head over to Kelley's enchanting shop. He has a Tier 7 earring that does that. Price is seven Tier 7 mana stones. At a thirty percent reduction, it's well worth the price." Matt only knew of it because he had helped Kelley create an earring last night once they moved on from the light rune. The earring they had made wasn't the same one he was telling her to buy, but Kelley had shown him the weight reduction one as a reference. The one they made was a custom job to reduce wind resistance but crafted in the same shape and style.

The woman winced but nodded. "Better than most others I saw. It's even better if it's Tier 7. It's just expensive. Do you know what the price is in points?"

Matt paused. Kelley didn't actually have points listed in his store, so he wasn't sure if the man even accepted points. But considering that the only reason he was on the planet was for the contribution points, he would surely take them.

"I think so, but I don't know the cost in points, sorry. I don't think it would be more than a few hundred. But I really don't know."

With that, they went their separate ways, and Matt pulled out the nearly empty mana stones.

The first five were quickly absorbed into his ring, and he cleaned off the old mana signatures by ensuring that the stones were fully drained.

Matt was about to just empty the ice one, but he decided to try absorbing that one as well.

It was worth the points to see how repeated mana aspects would be handled by his ring.

To his surprise, his ring absorbed it without a problem, and didn't overwrite Aster's ice aspected mana. They sat next to each other as near twins, but with a subtle difference between the mana types.

Aster's ice mana was a more *cold* ice, whereas the young man's mana was more of a *slow* ice. Or at least, that was the fuzzy interpretation he came up with from comparing the two.

He immediately edited his posting about asking for anyone with aspected mana to come and visit him, no matter the type.

Spending ten points was nothing to get extra unique mana types. He wasn't sure if that type of difference in mana aspects could make unique rifts, but he was itching to find a secluded place and test his theories.

For now, he intended to try and make a new item with a slowing ice effect, instead of increasing the cold damage. Kelley was Tier 10, and probably could go for another all-nighter.

Probably…

15

Matt and Kelley were sitting around two pairs of gauntlets, one with a cold rune etched into the back of the hand, the other with a slowing rune.

They just sat there and stared at them together. Their half a day of testing had finally paid off.

The same mana aspect could be subtly different, which led to subtly different results. With some manipulation of the standard cold rune, they had created a rune that, when cold-based skills were cast through, created a slowing effect. The effect wasn't minor either, with a near thirty percent effect.

All from creating the rune with the cold aspected mana.

The second pair of gauntlets with a slowing rune were designed to slow anyone struck with them. With the slowing cold mana, it was nearly twice as effective as the base, though it was still limited to melee attacks.

"Hit me again."

Matt did as instructed and lightly backhanded the Tier 10 enchanter.

The man dropped an apple with his off-hand and drove to catch it with his other hand. It was like he was moving through honey for about half a second, then the effect stopped, and his hand shot forward like a snake, catching the apple.

It would have lasted longer if the man's Tier wasn't so much higher than the rune.

Inspecting the apple, Kelley repeated himself for the sixth or seventh time. "I can't believe we got it to work."

Matt looked at the floor covered in ice from their test with [Hail], the only cold skill between the pair, and the cold slow enchanted gauntlet. He repeated himself as well. "Neither can I."

Kelley kicked his way through the ice, over to his workbench, and pulled out a bottle and two glasses.

"Careful with this. It's Tier 10 liquor and will put you on your ass before you know it."

He poured them each a drink. Matt's was noticeably smaller, more so a shot compared to Kelley's nearly full glass. The enchanter raised his drink and said, "To learning something new."

"To getting an edge on the competition." Matt knew what Kelley really cared about and couldn't resist teasing the man. He would work for free if everything was provided for him. Selling his wares was just a means to buy more things and fund his projects.

They both downed their glasses. Matt nearly died as the potent alcohol kicked him so hard, his teeth hurt. He had to brace himself against the table while the fire burnt its way down.

Kelley's two fingers of liquor went down much easier than Matt's, if his lack of reaction was to judge.

"Shit, this changes everything. I mean, I knew using aspected mana can improve certain runes, every crafter worth a damn figures it out, but..."

He was about to curse the man out a little for not warning him more when he noticed the man staring at his glass with a thousand-yard stare.

Matt's Tier 10 friend started rolling his glass around idly. "Aspected mana comes from five places. Innate bloodlines, Talents, carefully cycling ambient mana, special techniques involving cycling essence and mana through materials, and finally, natural treasures. The main aspects are easy to find: air, water, ice, fire and so on. It's that secondary property that's hard to capture. It's more unique to how each person views their aspected mana. An abstract idea like 'slow' doesn't exist outside of Talents as a full aspect of mana. These extra layers are essentially 'understanding' made real. It's like a concept. No, a *Concept…*"

There was a rippling in the air that Matt didn't dare disturb, and after what felt like a year, "Fuck! It explains so much! Concepts do the same thing. They can change your mana to better reflect your understanding. Someone with an ice Concept could use it to aspect their neutral mana into ice aspected mana, but that would just be the main aspect, the same as if they used an ice natural treasure."

Kelley paused for a moment, grabbing one of the gauntlets. "Unless their Concept isn't found in nature, but as long as the person's Concept is the same as the natural treasure, it's no different. The inverse applies as well. Unique aspects could appear from peoples' Concepts. They would need to use their ice Concept to introduce the slowing secondary property. It would let their mana reflect the abilities of ice as they understand them."

Kelley started to chew his lower lip as a faint strum rippled through the air.

"If you understand the Concept well enough, you can add that secondary property. The right…" the enchanter seemed to search for the word, "*sub-aspect* to the main mana aspect. You multiply the effects greatly. That must be one of Ascendent Crafters' guild secrets, it explains how their products always out perform with the same runes and materials. They must have huge libraries of aspected mana. I can do the same."

Kelley uttered, "I make the rune. I can find the best aspect and sub-aspect for the rune. I can change…"

Matt felt the air and surroundings vibrate like a bell was struck. Matt's Concept and his cores of essence vibrated to a frequency that was not his own. But it still sounded discordant.

Kelley was rapidly thinking his way through forming his Concept, but there was something more happening. Matt had felt when his and others' Concepts formed during the ascension, but he had never felt the essence responding like this before.

"I can change the aspect. I can choose the rune. I decide its properties. I can change. I am the sculptor and the stone."

With each phrase that Kelley uttered, the vibrations were brought closer and closer to harmony. Matt's Concept vibrated in what felt like sympathetic resonance, but before the sensation settled down, Kelley said, “I am *change*.”

It was like a bomb went off, as everything fell into place and a smooth harmony rang out in a melodic fanfare. Essence started to rush into the room as if there was a vacuum pumping it in. And now, Kelley was absorbing the ambient essence at an absurd rate. Like a starving man at a banquet, he kept pulling more and more in.

The pressure built until Matt felt like he was underwater from the sheer volume of essence that was being pulled in. As the quantity increased, a resonance started to expand out through the essence as more and more rushed inward, condensing within the enchanter.

Once the entire room was vibrating from the resonance between man and essence, there was a moment where the torrent stilled. His enchanter friend was no longer Tier 10, but Tier 11.

Kelley’s first word was, “Huh.”

Matt kicked the man. “Huh!? Is all you have to say for yourself!? That was an inspiration! You just had an inspiration! By every Ascender.”

He had no idea how to react, honestly. It wasn’t just mind-boggling. It was beyond that. Inspirations were rare, and Matt had no idea how rare it was for a crafter to create their Concept at the same time.

Matt had no idea why it had taken so long. The movies he had seen depicted an inspiration as lasting only a minute at most, but this experience had lasted five already. The real oddity was that this planet was only Tier 6, while Kelley was Tier 10. The essence shouldn’t be useful for the man, but he still felt the essence condensing as it neared the enchanter.

Or at least, that was the feeling he got from his spiritual sense. It would explain why the man was pulling in so much essence. Quality had to be created from quantity.

Kelley hardly rocked from Matt’s kick, and just started laughing until he had to wipe his eyes from the excitement.

“I can’t believe it either. Fuck! It’s kinda hard to believe. I-I don’t know.”

The newly-minted Tier 11 vibrated with excitement before he broke out into an awful dance.

“I need to test…everything!”

Matt wholeheartedly agreed. He didn't ask about the man's revelation. From the little he knew about inspirations, which was solely based on a movie or two, asking was considered incredibly rude.

So, he asked about the man's Concept instead. "What about your Concept? What did you make? What do you think it can do?"

Instead of answering, Kelley picked up a scrap of metal and looked at it. Matt felt out with his own Concept and felt nothing. After a few minutes, Kelley looked up and said, "I have no idea. How did you tell?"

Matt felt flabbergasted, but half shrugged. He had just flexed his Concept, and it had worked.

"I don't know. It just worked for me when I interacted with it. I felt there were two things it could do, and it was pretty easy. If I had to guess, try something related to the image. I assume it's crafting related, so try that."

The Tier 11s stylus appeared in his hand, and he started carving into the metal bar in his hand. The rune was familiar to Matt, as they had just been working on it. After a minute, the outline of the slowing rune appeared, and Kelley started to imbue the rune with his own mana.

Matt was about to offer to do that when Kelley grunted out, "Mana. Please."

Throwing his Concept onto the man, Matt watched as the enchanter imbued his rune and then inspected it with a grunt.

He waved off Matt, who was still refilling the man. "I'm good now, you can stop."

Matt didn't and just asked, "You figured something out. What was it?"

Kelley looked happier than a kid on his birthday as he said, "I got myself the ability to somewhat influence my own mana with different properties. It's almost like copying what I learned from the cold. But it seems that I need to know how the aspect and sub-aspect work."

He tapped Matt with the bar, then from Matt's perspective, rapidly cleared the workbench up. By his AI count, the effect had lasted one and a quarter seconds, but it had felt more like fifteen.

Matt nodded to the man. "It worked, but not as well as the slowing ice aspected mana."

Kelley nodded. "It also burned a lot of my own mana to convert it to both the aspect and sub-aspect, while also eating a ton of my willpower. I have a headache like you wouldn't believe, but I think that if I practice this, the mana conversion will get a lot better. Something feels off right now, but I'm not sure."

"So, what are you gonna do now?"

Kelley looked at Matt like he was dumb. "I'm going to keep testing! At the minimum, I'm going to copy your idea with normal converting mana stones. It will cost me an arm and a leg, but I'll need to at least test with them. I bet the large guilds have pre-made libraries already, but I don't. It will just take some time and searching."

Matt offered, "Why not try and hire a few Tier 5 teams to run the rift I got this from? It was dropping dual typed mana stones until I got this."

Kelley was interested, so Matt explained how the army was selling the rifts.

"It's a good idea, and it's worth a shot. I doubt I'll get a growth item like that, but there's a one in a few trillion chance I get lucky and get something similar."

With that, they went back to creating various applications of the ice mana. Matt wanted to make an addition to Aster's collar to get her more cold damage from her own mana aspect, and the ability to slow things down with the other mana aspect.

If it worked as intended, he'd see about making one for himself.

After three hectic days, Matt finally saw an exhausted Liz for more than five minutes. She had been working twenty-hour days trying to set everything up, and had finally finished most of her preparations.

He had been bringing her food three times a day after he noticed that she had been skipping breakfast and dinner.

She was so busy, he hadn't seen her with a free moment at all when he brought her the meals. He offered to help, but while she asked him to run an errand or two, it wasn't much more than her trying to make him feel better. So, he just gave her an open offer and left it at that, while trying to make sure she ate regularly.

After those three days, she was able to cut down her responsibilities with managing the Pather side of things to about half a day's work. She said she expected it to be even less as time went on, but she was still effectively running the show.

While the trickle of points was quite nice, it wasn't crazy. As a top fifty team, they earned about a thousand points a day. Unfortunately, as their ranking fell, so did their points. It got to the point where, a week after their death, they were only earning a measly seventy points a day.

It was still something, so no one complained. Well, nearly no one. Liz had ranted about how someone had called to complain about the new point system, and how it would let other people buy things faster, and therefore make acquiring the limited goods even more competitive. That, and people were mad over others getting points while doing nothing, even though it scaled to contribution. At least they had expected *that* complaint.

As dumb as it was, that particular gripe reinforced the reason why everyone was here. To earn gear or skills beyond their normal means.

Just mentioning it was enough to piss Liz off, though, so it was a topic avoided by everyone.

Now that it was a week after their deaths, they could safely train with light sparring. Matt, Liz, and Aster were still intent on helping their teammates get their own Concepts.

It would have been safe for them after three days, when Matt had Melinda come by and give everyone a 'checkup' with her Talent. But he couldn't explain that to Annie, Emily, and Conor, so he settled for knowing that they were properly healed.

They all faced off against Annie, who blocked blows from both Conor and Liz while he and Aster tried to force the assassin to stillness with their Concepts. It was like fighting through molasses for her, and while they all pulled their punches, it was a losing battle.

That was the point, and as her desperation grew, the hope was that she could start to resist, and therefore find her own Concept.

They were an hour into things, and the training wasn't going as well as Matt had hoped. He knew that he was overestimating how effective standard training would be, but a part of him believed that it would be as fast as training with the reality shard had been for Melinda's team.

Objectively, he knew the idea was stupid and unrealistic. If it was as easy as fighting someone with a Concept for a few hours, everyone would have Concepts. But his new friends were strong and competent, so he felt that they should click with it.

Kelley had been Tier 10 without his own Concept, and was not only successful, but also considered well ahead of his peers. It was just another indicator of the truth. Concepts were hard to create, and some people never managed to form them. There was a reason that the Empire restricted knowledge until people hit Tier 10, and had already used the two bottled Concepts. It was for their own good.

Even at Tier 10, a cultivator would have a lifespan of seven hundred and twenty years. At Tier 14, it was double that. Compared to Tier 4, with a lifespan of around one hundred and thirty years, it was a massive difference. Without the bottled concepts, the average lifespan of a cultivator would be drastically reduced.

As Matt commanded Annie to halt with his will, he thought about what it must have been like before the bottled Concepts. He tried to imagine what it would be like if Annie, Emily, and Conor grew old and died while sitting at the peak of Tier 4. Unable to advance as they grew older and older, with Tiers ahead of them to reach immortality.

He thought of Melinda, Mathew, Vinnie, Kyle, Sam, and Tara. Even with the help of the reality shard, they were still stuck at their phrases, and only slowly progressing.

Annie panted out, "Break." and he and Aster released their hold on her. Aster was panting slightly, and Matt understood. It was hard work on their end, even if they were sitting on their butts while the others fought.

Liz flopped to the ground as Matt stood. Emily stood and glared at Liz, who was manipulating her blood to cover the twin in a thin film. They had quickly realized that Liz couldn't exactly recreate what he and Aster did with their Concepts.

She could resist them trying to slow or stop her easily enough, as her Concept was internal. But she didn't actually have the ability to project her Concept without her blood. Because of that, she needed to cover the person in blood to hold them.

On the bright side, she was able to fully lock down a person on her own, letting Matt and Aster get a break, but it wasn't pleasant for the one resisting.

As Liz sat with her eyes closed, Matt repeated her mantra. "Find what you are and what you want to become. Find what resonates with you."

He sidestepped a bolt of mana that was tinged yellow-brown and felt like an earth element. With a stick, he slapped Emily's side and rotated around her.

"Think about how you see yourself, and how others see you. Find where you want to go from there."

A strike from Emily was less than half speed, but Matt blocked it with a raised forearm. "Find an idea that represents yourself, or some aspect of your fighting style. Find it and visualize it."

Emily kept a fierce expression as she shot another [Cracked Mana Bolt] at him. Matt had tried to absorb the mana from her attack into his ring to get free aspected mana but hadn't found a way to efficiently absorb it. The skill simply dissipated on contact after expending its energy in the initial hit.

It was incredibly disappointing, as her skill could create any elemental type. They were still working on the numbers, but it seemed like fifty percent of the time it was a basic aspect like wind, water, fire, or earth. Thirty five percent of the time, it was a higher level of aspect like ice, lightning, wood, or metal. The remaining fifteen percent was broken into weirder elements and effects that they weren't able to document very well.

Matt was pretty sure that they felt a bubble aspect on one of the bolts, but how those percentages broke down would take a lot more testing than they had done so far.

He changed his mantra to something more specific to Emily as he struck out again, "Your Talent lets you double things. Maybe you're a bacterial growth in a petri dish, with the skill being food. The more food you can add, the more you can grow."

She ground out, "I'm not bacteria, Matt. Fuck you."

Since she had the ability to talk back, Matt hit her thigh and then her extended arm. She sent a bolt of lightning at him. This one stung his shield, as it was within her window of doubling time. Matt kicked some dirt at her in retaliation.

It was kinda mean to compare her to bacteria, but it was the best doubling thing he could come up with at the moment.

"Think about standing on a pyramid where…" Matt halted in his diatribe as he felt something. It was faint, but his Concept felt a resonation from the blood-covered girl.

They all watched as Emily sat cross-legged. Conor and Annie, from their panting positions, each scrambled to a spot where they could see Emily. Liz stopped resisting the women's movements and watched with everyone else.

After about five minutes of nothing happening, Emily opened her eyes.

"I lost it. I had something, but I lost it."

Annie crawled over to get right in front of her bloody sister's face. "What did it feel like? And what do you think triggered it?"

Emily opened her eyes and mockingly glared at Matt. "It *definitely* wasn't bacteria. There was something about the pyramid, but I don't know what."

Liz fist-pumped. "Well, see? I was right! That's the first step. Now you know where to start. We just need to do more training."

Conor hopped to his feet when Emily retreated back into herself to examine her slight breakthrough.

Matt hoped it was a sign of things to come, but it wasn't. No one had any more progress, even when all three of them were out of will power and had blinding headaches, forcing them to stop training.

It wasn't much progress, but it showed that the end goal was possible.

Matt was pulling apart his golem crossbow arm in a workshop while half-listening to Liz and Sam work behind him. They had rented a general workspace for half the day, as it was cheaper for them to all rent the room.

He could have crashed Kelley's workshop, but the man had been so busy with his Concept and engrossed in his research, that he hadn't even noticed Matt showing up or leaving.

So instead of risking bothering the man, he rented out a workshop to convert his golem arm crossbows into ones wieldable by humans.

When Liz and Sam finally started to meet up to practice alchemy together, they needed a room as well, so they rented one out as a group.

But Matt wasn't fully concentrating on the item in front of him. No, he was much more focused on listening to Liz complain about running the Pather side of the war.

"I have people always coming up with *great ideas*. It's always just coincidental that the idea only helps themselves or their friends. These people clearly think I'm an idiot, but I still need to hear them out."

Something clattered, and Sam said, "Just tell them to take a hike."

Liz groaned, and Matt had to resist turning around. She hadn't shared any of this with him. She had played things off like it was mostly busy work.

"I can't. I need to hear people out at least marginally. It's even worse now because people are complaining to me about the missions they get. I only approve the missions that the AIs suggest if it looks viable. I can't help that the Tier 5 teams are outmatched for most things other than guard duty, or being a part of a larger group. Am I supposed to make the other side weaker and only send Tier 5s as well? No, that's fucking stupid. Ugh! It's just frustrating."

"People suck."

"Yeah, but I need to lead them, which makes it worse." Liz sounded incredibly tired.

Sam said something Matt didn't hear, and Liz responded in kind.

Matt wanted to go over and ask her what else was wrong and try to help, but it wasn't like she couldn't have told him. They hadn't seen that much of each other in the last week and a half, but things had been hectic with them playing catch up on training and Concept work.

They had all been busy with their own thing, but he was slipping as Liz's friend and boyfriend.

That night Matt asked Liz as they were settling into sleep, "Everything okay?"

"Yeah, it's all fine." She murmured her answer while stifling a yawn.

Matt waited, but when he got nothing, he pressed, "Even with the leader gig?"

"It's fine."

"I heard you talking to Sam."

Liz groaned, "Dammit. I thought we were quieter than that."

"You mostly were, but when I was changing arms, I was able to hear."

Liz rolled into him as she said, "I've barely seen you, and it feels like all I do is complain when I *do* see you. I don't want to burden you as well."

Matt poked her under the rib. "I'm happy to help."

"See, that's the thing. You like to fix things, but this isn't something that can be fixed. I just wanted to complain and bitch to someone new a little. It's shitty sometimes, but it's not all bad. I've met some really nice and grateful people. It's just turds that taint the whole bowl sometimes."

"Well, I wanted to let you know I'm here to help."

She patted his chest. "You are helpful. Time spent with you is time I don't have to think about all the bullshit I need to work on the next day. Thankfully, we only have two days off left, and things are heating back up, so we'll have more time together."

He kissed the top of her head, and they lay there together.

Matt wasn't happy that Liz was dealing with everything on her own, but at least they weren't having any problems as a couple.

How can I help?

As he drifted off to sleep, Matt kept thinking about the question.

Matt took a fist on his unarmored forearm and felt [Mage's Retreat] flare slightly in response as the skill moved more mana through the area that increased Durability. He concentrated on stretching that area out. Just slowly.

If he moved too fast, the skill would actually start pulling from the Strength boost it gave. But if he was slow, he could slowly stretch the skill structure out like taffy. Adding his manual manipulation while getting hit doubled the effectiveness of his training.

His normal meditation was better for feeling out the skill, but he knew [Mage's Retreat] as well as he knew [Cracked Phantom Armor.]

Matt's AI pinged him. It was nearly time.

Shutting down and retreating from the training aid, he sat. With two hours of meditation, he moved [Mage's Retreat] out of his core spirit and into his inner spirit, with [Endurance] and [Hail].

It was right at the edge, but he needed the free slot for [Fireball], which he was currently absorbing. When it reached his core spirit, he would quickly modify it to reduce the mana cost while it was still malleable.

He checked his AI's timer, and found that [Fireball] had another three hours before it reached his core spirit. Then, he could perform his modifications to the skill.

It was enough time for a little more testing. He had practiced for the last week with the cube he and Liz had used to train for modifying [Endurance], and the time was nearly upon him.

Still, it wouldn't hurt to test the modification once more. He had the time.

Matt connected his AI and sent his spiritual sense into the cube and started to simulate the process.

In the last week, he had doubled down on his skill training. Normally, he spent an hour or so a day doing it in the morning or before bed. But with the abundance of free time, he had been focusing on pure meditation training, and adding in skills training while using them in sparring matches

He knew it was just another side effect of his Talent that he hadn't appreciated. Annie, Emily, and Conor all commented on how his refilling their mana regularly let them use their skills more, and actively expand their capabilities.

They were usually forced to only meditate on the skill and try to eke out whatever increase they could get when fighting or sparring. Even then, they were normally only able to do that once a day, as it took them a day and a half to fully regenerate their mana naturally.

His keeping them topped off let them train much harder than normal.

It was still a weird thought for him, as some small part of himself still thought of his Talent as useless. Even though it gave him and people around him advantages he could never have dreamed of.

With a soft chime, he stopped his wandering thoughts and focused inward. [Fireball] was close to the edge of his core spirit.

The longer it took him to make the modifications, the longer the skill would have time to sink deeper into the spirit, and therefore increase the time it would take to move back into the inner spirit.

He wanted to be quick.

As the skill breached the dividing lines between the spirit layers,

Matt started to shrink the entirety of the skill down as much as he could.

He condensed it along the x, y, and z axes, along with shrinking the inner tubing that made up the skill's structure.

The first bit was easy, but as the skill shrank lower and lower, it was harder and harder to compress. Matt even felt some of his willpower going into the task. His task became increasingly more difficult as the skill continued to shrink.

As the skill stopped moving and its malleability diminished to normal, he inspected the skill. He hadn't been as fast as he wanted, but the results looked good.

The skill was nearly half the normal size.

And at a base cost of 10 mana, he was hoping to get the skill to a mana cost of about 6 when it was removed from his core spirit.

Still, his modification had worked perfectly.

Standing, he went back to the training aid and turned on [Cracked Phantom Armor] at the lowest draw possible. He filled a mana crystal up before refueling his mana pool. He only had 80 mana for a second, as the 1 MPS of his armor and AI slowly drained his mana pool. His regen was next to nothing if his current mana was over ten percent of his maximum.

Still, he sent mana into the new skill in his spirit, and with giddy excitement, watched as a fist-sized ball of flame appeared, then launched in the direction he was thinking of.

He missed the training aid, and the [Fireball] splashed harmlessly over the back wall.

Not caring in the slightest, Matt launched half a dozen follow-up [Fireball]s and laughed his best evil laugh as the vents needed to pull the heat and smoke from the room.

After half an hour of testing his new skill, he checked his AI for the results.

In his core spirit, the skill cost 4.1 mana, more than the ideal 3 mana cost that would allow him to use the skill endlessly at Tier 8. Matt didn't think an item could reduce the skill enough. He had learned from Kelley that mana reduction items were hard to make, and worked off a percentage. Essentially, he'd need an amazing item to get him under the cost of his one percent max. A thirty percent reduction wasn't impossible, but it was rare.

At Tier 9, at one percent of his max mana, he would have 6 mana, which would make the skill perfect for his inner spirit. Skills in the core spirit were thirty percent cheaper and far easier to manipulate than the inner spirit, which was considered the baseline.

He decided to move the skill out of his core spirit until he was Tier 7, so he could continue to work on [Mage's Retreat] some more. But he was going to commission Kelley for a Tier 8 mana reduction item. Matt winced for his bank account. Even with the Tier 15 mana stone from the sale of the growth item, it was going to be an expensive item. Tier 9 or 10 materials at least, to help the efficiency get to thirty percent.

It wasn't a huge problem, considering the value of the Tier 15 mana stone that he had. But Matt really hated spending money, and it felt incredibly expensive as a Tier 6. In the end, he refused to take advantage of a friend, and that won out.

Still, the skill worked perfectly, even if it was at a little less than half power after his modifications. He could make up for quality with quantity.

Deciding to let large decisions be a problem for tomorrow, he cleaned up and headed out. Tonight, he would celebrate with everyone for the success of his new fire spell.

Matt paused. He should get some ice cream for Aster. She was going to hate his new spell. But he loved it.

16

Matt flew through the air with his team, interspersed throughout the standard guard team.

A month after their deaths, they were pulling secret escort missions. While neither glorious nor high earning, the missions were necessary. Nearly half of the kingdom's resource shipments from the outlying forts were being stolen. The third city was being plucked at from all sides, and the thefts were costing the kingdom valuable resources. The prince had personally asked them to escort the shipment while hidden inside of it.

Matt was in forest drab armor, with a long staff at the ready. The prince's espionage staffers excelled at disguises and his face was made up to the point that he didn't even recognize himself. His cheeks were filled in, and his hair dyed brown, completely changing his appearance at first and even the glance.

Liz underwent the same treatment, and now had ink dark hair, which contrasted with her pale skin. He loved her red hair, but the black hair was new and exciting. It caused them to both to muss their disguises quite a bit before the mission. The espionage staffers who had to redo their makeup were less than enthused.

Liz was also in 'heavy armor' with a new spear. The former helped conceal how thick the backpack that she was wearing was. It was only necessary because Aster had flatly refused to dye her fur red. She'd rather die than take on the visage of a fire fox. After that horrible suggestion, she refused to change into a fox of *any* other element, while adamantly maintaining that ice was the best. They really shouldn't have started with fire. Matt tucked that lesson away for future reference and ordered an illusion collar instead; it would turn her into a dog.

It wasn't the dyeing that irritated the fox. No, they had been able to make that seem fun to her, and she dyed the tips of her ears purple. What set her off was the people thinking that she used fire. That was an indignity too severe, so she chose the backpack when they gave her the option between it or the dye.

A large backpack with a white fox was synonymous with their team, so it had to be made to look like a much slimmer backpack, forcing Liz to wear the fake armor ensemble.

Conor was in what Matt felt was the most dangerous position. He was keeping his own role as a heavy melee fighter, but his armor was too distinctive, so it had been swapped out with a second set. It apparently wasn't sitting right no matter how much they adjusted it. That wasn't exactly an ideal way to go into battle, and Liz intended to hurry to his side as soon as things kicked off.

Annie and Emily had simply done the same as Matt and Liz. Emily was acting like a basic mage, equipped with only a [Fireball], just like Matt.

Annie was using one of the golem crossbows he had made in bulk and sold in the monthly auction.

The sales had netted them nearly 5,000 points, which while not a ton, was still a few days' worth of their idle share of the kingdom earned points. Their team sat around the fifth spot in the rankings when they could hit big missions back to back. Their death all but grinded their momentum to a halt, sliding them back to thirty-second place. It was a setback from which they still had hardly recovered from.

The six of them were infamous for a guaranteed death, so most teams preferred to surrender rather than take the death when they showed up. Losing half your points to buy your freedom and prevent a two-week death timer was a *much* better option than losing half your points and earning a two week wait to get back in the war.

They were hoping that this ambush would allow them to get back on track, due to a distinct lack of forts changing hands after the

Pather's meeting. Without orders to take a fortress, they couldn't earn points from the army war AI.

That left them with an ambush mission.

Twenty guards were interspersed throughout the shipment. They flew in formation around a messenger with a spatial bag stuffed to the brim with Tier 6 gold.

Or, at least, that was the information that the kingdom had purposefully leaked. Usually, the courier was given both the package and the fastest flying sword. But today, the courier was bait. He was paid well, especially for the second phase of the ambush, which they knew was lying in wait somewhere nearby.

Matt was the actual courier because he had the fastest sword. His Tier 7 sword was made for speed after all. It was better than the ones that the kingdom was allowed to bring, and what most people could afford. His [Cracked Phantom Armor] also played a large part in his role, as he could activate it and take a hit that would incapacitate most of the others.

And they didn't intend to *just* survive the ambush. No, Team Bucket was going to find the ones responsible and kill them, then destroy any and all infrastructure that the ambushers had established.

As they flew around the target fort's anti-flying zone, they heard a shout from the neutral zone, and Matt readied his staff while turning. So far, this was precisely how the other ambushes went down. They pinned the teams against the anti-flying barrier, and either pushed the team in when they had the height advantage or chased the team down if they tried to flee.

Three teams of ten people had flown up behind, beside, and in front of Matt's team. The ambushers must have thought that they made a safe bet with the ten extra fighters. They were wrong to think that they could win through sheer numbers.

Matt and Emily flew up with the courier and three other guards, while the other fifteen guards rushed ahead to entangle the ten fighters flying in front of them. It was exactly as every other escort team acted.

The five guards with the courier were meant to help him break through any subsequent ambushes.

Matt cast a [Fireball] at the nearest group of mages as they flew up and over, and smiled at the staff in his hands.

An average staff either reduced the mana cost of a spell, or increased the recovery speed of the spell diagram in the spirit, allowing the mage to cast faster. His weapon increased the damage of all fire spells channeled through it. Not exactly a rare effect, but it put his weakened [Fireball] just over the strength of a normal [Fireball]. The staff enabled him to go from the fist-sized ball of flame that normally appeared by his hand to a head-sized one that now appeared at the top of his staff.

With a satisfying woosh, the [Fireball] raced out and slammed into the head of a melee fighter, who wasn't able to get into contact with the kingdom troops. That unfortunate soldier was teleported out, and the explosion's blast wave sent the two nearest fighters tumbling as they lost control of their flying devices.

Matt kept his place in the formation as the six of them flew up and over the forward-most attackers and escorts. His AI indicated that Liz, Aster, and Conor were fine, but he still worried for them in the madness of the battle.

Annie was off his radar, as she should be. Her role was to go invisible and shadow their group until the enemies fled from the failed ambush.

Not even two minutes after their escape, they flew into the expected second ambush, just as they slipped through a slight gap in anti-flying formations.

Ten more people flew up from their concealed positions in the underbrush below. Eight Tier 6s and two Tier 7s now faced Matt and his group.

Matt launched five [Fireball]s in quick succession, then started to fill the mana stone he had in the band on his wrist, before draining it and launching more.

The bracelets of mana stones were their team's newest idea. Normally, Matt kept his team of three going with his Concept, or manually filled their personalized, fast converting mana stones. Their current formation made that infeasible, so they had the idea to make bracelets with ten personal mana stones and charge them before their fights.

The extra 2,000 mana would enable them to fight longer than anticipated. Filling this many mana stones wasn't usually done, as it took a typical mage about a day and a half to refill their mana pool.

Very few people could afford to spend that much time away from any real fighting. At least, not people who were trying to push themselves. Training was just as important as combat, after all.

Yet with Matt able to refill his team's mana pools with his Concept, it was fine for them to sit around for an hour and bank the 4,000 mana needed for the bracelets, while also having mana to train with.

Their preparation had some flaws, though. The mana stones in the bracelet couldn't be linked to act as one big battery. So, they had to individually access each stone and then draw from it. From their testing, ten stones around their wrists were the max they could use before they couldn't efficiently withdraw mana. With more training, they could probably increase that number, but for now, ten was the best they could do.

The strategy was still infinitely cheaper than throwing a higher Tier mana stone into a rapidly converting mana stone, which usually had a near ninety percent loss rate. Those stones were only to be used in emergencies, or by the uber-wealthy. Even Matt used them sparingly. The standard, personal converting mana stones were more efficient, if you had the time. Even the ordinary fast converting mana stones that they commonly used were better, if you had at least a minute or two. The rapid type was only beneficial when near-instant conversion of rift mana to personal mana was necessary, or when you simply didn't care about the cost.

The effect of having an extra mana pool was more pronounced with Emily, who didn't have to ration her four spells as much. Consequently, she became a terror on the battlefield. Even now, as she rapid-fired [Fireball]'s alongside Matt, he was impressed at her speed and accuracy. She hit most of her shots, even on the evading fighters, which he routinely missed.

Together, they removed four of the Tier 6s. One of the Tier 7s flew to them, and the other led their five remaining Tier 6s to attack the melee fighters.

"I got him."

Emily nodded at Matt's AI voice command and retreated with the other group.

Matt readied himself to block the short sword swing with his staff and used his foot to brace the end of the staff on his flying sword.

When the wooden staff met metal, it wasn't destroyed as the melee Tier 7 expected.

The staff he was using had metal bands running up the sides to give it more sturdiness, and it was enchanted with durability. If the Tier 7's weapon had been Tier 8, it might have done more damage, but with their weapons being equal, it was a stalemate.

The Tier 7 flew up and to the right slightly as he swung down at Matt's lightly armored head, but Matt had already started moving as well.

To the melee fighter's ever-growing surprise, Matt flew into him and started to grapple with his free hand. The man's smirk quickly faded when he realized that Matt wasn't the weak mage he had expected. He probably thought their first exchange was simply a difference in flying equipment, but he should have thought twice about a *simple mage* attempting to grapple him.

When Matt held his opponent's sword arm at bay, it was already too late. He drove his dagger into the enemy Tier 7's armpit and twisted the blade as he removed it. It wasn't *instantly* fatal. The man had about a minute before he bled out enough to fall unconscious, and two before he died.

The Tier 7 could have fought through the pain and retaliated, but the wound was damaging and painful enough to force the man to clamp his arm down. It was a futile attempt to staunch the arterial bleeding.

The man's instinctive movement left him open to a second attack. He was teleported out just before Matt moved to slice his throat in a backswing. As his blade neared the man's neck, the shock on his face was evident. Even as he was teleported out, he still didn't seem to believe what had happened.

The army watchers apparently decided enough was enough, removing the Tier 7 before more work was given to the healers.

Spinning with a flick of his hips, Matt faced the back of the melee and started launching [Fireball]s. In under a minute, the ambushers decided that their mission wasn't worth it. As a unit, they disengaged and flew off.

None of the defenders flew after them. Matt and Emily decided to act after they heard from Annie. The encounter wasn't exactly ideal; they hadn't gotten the other Tier 7, who had a chance of seeing through her Talent. Still, he trusted her. After all, she *had* passed the assassination test of the army, killed Alyssa, and torched her closet. All without getting caught.

The Tier 7 woman, to their mild annoyance, had been more upset about her wardrobe than her death, as she had apparently expected it, and had already spent her points. She had mildly reprimanded Liz about it, saying that killing her was one thing, but destroying her clothes was a step too far. Although, in the next moment, she ended up thanking Liz for the excuse to buy new clothes. The next day, she showed up to headquarters looking brighter than ever. It seemed like nothing would keep her down for long.

Matt threw Alyssa out of his thoughts. The less he thought about her the better.

It was just a waiting game now. Annie would track the bandits to their lair, and they could hopefully take down a large central hub, earning enough points to set them back on top.

The five of them continued on with their mission, with one of the melee guards having been killed and removed from the fighting. Together, they flew the remaining distance to the city and dropped off their payload, earning a decent chunk of points. They hoped that the points for the delivery would be dwarfed by their taking down another secret base.

He and Emily didn't dawdle to sight see, and immediately flew back out of the city toward the first ambush site. Liz, Aster, and Conor were waiting for them.

As they pulled up, Matt asked, "How was your ambush?"

Liz answered with a shrug. "Fine. They didn't try to do much more than hold us back, just like the reports said. What about yours?"

"Everything went as we thought. The ambushers retreated once they took decent losses. Annie's following them as we speak."

They moved in a group to follow their rogue's trail. As they did, Matt threw his Concept on at full blast. Everyone was full according to his AI, but he couldn't see their reserves.

All of their mana dipped by about 200 before filling back up, with them having used some mana stones in their fights. Once they stopped emptying their mana after being restored, he cut off his Concept and fully concentrated on chasing after the retreating team.

To his surprise, they didn't abruptly rush in. They dismounted and walked through two separate anti-flying fields, then another mile into queendom territory, before turning back around into kingdom controlled land. There, Matt's squad walked through a few more anti-flying formations near a small fort. Finally, they found the hill that Annie was inside of.

They didn't see an entrance despite their careful observation, but they sent a low priority message to Annie, who simply responded that she was handling it.

Two minutes later, she popped out of a grass-covered hatch and waved for them to come down.

"It's all already taken care of. There were only three people inside besides the few who retreated. Easy enough to take them out one by one. They never even saw me."

"Oh."

Matt was incredibly disappointed. They went through all that trouble, only to not even get a good fight out of it.

Aster popped her head out of the backpack and mirrored Matt's sentiment. "No fight? No fun."

She shot a glare at Annie, who shrugged. "Sorry. It was easy. Also, I doubt this is the only center of operations. It's just too small. I'm sure there are others out there."

Emily said, "Maybe we can get points for that, but this was a colossal waste of time." She quietly grumbled, "It's gonna take a week or more for this dye to wash out."

Matt agreed, it felt shitty that they had gone through so much preparation to get nothing.

Together, they walked to the small fort and informed the leader that there was a bandit camp under his nose.

He looked green at the discovery, and none of them bothered to comfort him. The man was in for a talking to at a minimum, or getting sacked at worst. His best and only defense was that it was a hilly area, but an enemy encampment not even half a mile away from his fort was inexcusable.

They were halfway back to the city when Aster started sniffing, hard.

"Fire? Fire!"

At her message, they flew higher until they were able to see the curvature of the planet. At that altitude, they were able to see the medium and large forts that were part of the circular protection around the city being besieged, bypassed, and set ablaze.

From their vantage point, they also saw the mass of people moving through the anti-flying zones on foot.

This was a full invasion.

They didn't need to speak, and rushed forward to the city perimeter, where they encountered its anti-flying formation. They immediately dismounted and sprinted for the entrance. They weren't the only ones. A message was being sent to everyone in the vicinity to either retreat to the city before they were surrounded, or retreat to one of the large or medium forts.

Reinforcements were already pouring in from the neutral city, according to the Pather network. An urgent call went out to everyone ambulatory to get to a teleporter and move to this city, before the queendom could set up the spatial locks.

Once those formations went up, all teleportation would be shut down as the space inside the city got locked down. After that, the defenders would be on their own.

The six of them ran up the stairs to the fifty-foot tall walls, and peered out over the battlements. Together, they stood and watched as the large fort in their view was simply surrounded and bypassed. In fifteen minutes, the front gate was surrounded, and a thin wall of people encircled the city. They had even more concentrated numbers around the city's other entrance that Matt could see from his vantage point.

The city had four at each cardinal direction, and the queendom forces seemed to be moving quickly to block all of them off. Small teams moved out to chase down any kingdom teams who strayed too close.

With a noticeable rumble, the door under their feet slammed shut.

"Well, fuck a duck. This was shit timing." Annie spit over the edge of the fort after saying her piece.

"What?" Matt looked to her and said, "This is amazing timing. Who knows if we would've been able to join if we missed the initial start. We're gonna earn a shit load of points for this."

Annie didn't look convinced. "I doubt it. There are thousands of people, and we'll need to outperform them all. We're gonna get like twenty points for this."

Her sister slapped her shoulder. "Come on. We're far better than that. Matt and I can probably hold this entire city ourselves. Easy peasy."

He didn't quite agree with that statement, but before he could retort, Conor started to strip out of his armor. Matt and everyone else, realizing what he was doing, followed suit.

None of them wanted to fight an important battle with gear other than their own. Matt was faster than everyone except Annie, who also wore light armor. So, he moved toward Conor and helped the man with his full plate armor. By the time they were finished, the rest were also done, and the six of them moved their borrowed gear into their spatial bags.

They looked out beyond the ramparts and watched as a trebuchet was assembled at the edge of the queendom formations. Piece after piece was pulled out of spatial storage containers and rapidly assembled.

In under two minutes, an earth mage created a boulder and placed it in the sling. The missile was instantly slung at the city wall.

The first shot was way short, so they calibrated the siege engine then launched a second. This one looked like it would miss to their right, but as it reached a dozen feet from the wall, it slammed into an invisible barrier. The city's shielding flickered into visibility for a moment, but as the boulder shattered and fell, it quickly dissipated.

Everyone on the wall flinched and instinctively ducked down. A mage launched a [Fireball] at the attackers, but they were well out of range for a single Tier 8 spell. It traveled only a hundred feet before the mana sustaining it weakened, and it sputtered out like a candle in a tornado.

It didn't even reach a quarter the distance to the enemy forces.

Having found their range, the attackers adjusted the counterweight slightly and lobbed a flaming chunk of stone at the wall. Unlike last time, this stone hit at the top of the wall. Or it would have, if the shielding didn't block the attack.

It still made Matt wince. They were going to run out of mana eventually. Unless Matt kept the city charged…He shook that idea off; he wasn't going to reveal more than his Concept.

A ballista next to them fired, but the large bolt didn't even reach halfway to the line of trebuchets that were being put together.

They got a message from Juni a moment after the impact. "You're here? Good. Take control of the Pathers. Please. Organize them into QRFs and get them ready to reinforce the walls or repel wall climbers."

Liz started issuing commands, getting the quick reaction forces set up. Matt asked, "What's the situation? And how many reinforcements can we expect?"

"Depends on how many we can shove through before the anti-teleporting formation goes up. I doubt you have a spell that goes that far, but if you see them setting it up, try and break things."

"What about the prince?"

There was a pause before Juni's response. "He will be gathering an overland response force and harrying the attackers from the rear."

Matt almost said that the man was a coward since he had stayed in the rear during the golem battle as well. But this time, things were different. If the prince died, they would be out of a commander for two weeks. And worse than that, if he died, they wouldn't be able to spend points for the duration either. An outside force able to keep pressure on the enemy wasn't a bad idea when he thought about it.

It just left a bitter taste in Matt's mouth. Still, it gave him everything he needed to know to start feeding information into his AI.

After two minutes and nearly 10,000 mana, he had an answer. At least for some of their problems.

He called Juni back up. "Get me a mana cannon."

"What?"

Realizing he hadn't explained at all, Matt backtracked. "If I have one of the siege cannons, I can tamper with the runes a bit and increase the range." He debated explaining fully but, in the end decided to be forthright. "Warning though, it will significantly decrease the lifespan of the cannon, and its stability will be shit after a few shots."

Juni answered him after a worryingly long silence. "How many shots are we talking about?"

Matt reran his modification simulations and gave a conservative estimate. "Five, if we're unlucky. Ten is when I'd be really careful about firing them. After that, they'll turn into bombs if mana is poured through them."

"I'll send you two of them. Don't worry about the siege equipment. The shielding can last a while. You need to take out the formation pillars that are going to be set up to lock down real space. The smaller the circumference they have, the cheaper the mana cost. If you let them mostly set up and then break it, we can force them to dig it all up and relocate. That will buy us more time. The more time we have the more we can funnel reinforcements, the better our chances of defending are."

There was a pause and he thought Juni was done, but the man added, "Please don't waste the cannons. They are fucking expensive. But if you can stall for a while, it will be worth it."

Matt failed to find a flaw in that reasoning and signed off the command channel.

Not five minutes later, two people ran up to Matt with a wooden crate between them, carried on poles.

By their sweating faces and trembling muscles, they were carrying quite the load. After Matt identified himself, they scurried away. He pried open the crate and found that it was spatially expanded. Inside, a singular mana cannon and its disassembled stand were nestled in straw.

Matt needed to activate [Mage's Retreat] to lift the heavy metal tube out of the crate by himself. Conor, seeing him struggling, quickly moved to help. Carefully, they set it down and assembled the stand. Once it was all put together, he carefully inspected the runes on the weapon.

Or at least, he tried to. It was far, far more complicated than anything else he had ever seen. There was no way that this Tier 6 cannon was made by anyone less than Tier 15. Matt knew without a doubt that even Kelley couldn't create runes this small or interlocked.

The runes were like twisted braids of rope the size of a human hair, and they crisscrossed the entire length of the barrel. It didn't help that obscuring runes were also placed throughout the rear of the cannon, where the mana conversion happened. Thankfully, he didn't need to affect those runes.

His target was the barrel.

Normally, the barrel simply focused the mana in whatever spell was used. The propulsion was all handled at the base of the cannon, where the spell was generated. He didn't need to, or want to risk modifying those runes. What he intended to do was empower the spell throughout the entire length of the cannon.

It wasn't a new strategy, but it was rarely done, as it increased the mana cost by tenfold *and* reduced the life span of a cannon. It would go from being able to sustain thousands of shots to a few dozen. It was a textbook example of what *not* to do with sensitive equipment.

Matt was only willing to do it because the enemy was outside of cannon and ballista range. The Tier 6 trebuchets had a greater range than their defensive equipment, but that was to be expected. Their effectiveness was pretty much limited to walls and battering them down. They were mostly useless against small and mobile targets.

With his AIs help, Matt carved runes into the free spaces between the braids of runes that lined the weapon. He was fairly confident that he hadn't messed anything up, but his clumsy work was far worse than what it could have been. Each of his runes were crammed into the space between formation lines, and more than one had bled over. If the change wasn't a simple, singular, empowerment rune, he would have never been able to get this to work.

The empower rune would just add more mana to the attack spell as it traveled down the barrel. Which, in theory, should increase the range, since the spell could travel farther before it dissipated. As he was carving, he also realized that he only knew the Tier 5 version of the empower rune. It only made everything worse, as the Tier 5 rune was a mismatch for the rest of the runes and material.

A second team of men brought up the second cannon, but he only made the modifications then stored it back into its crate. He was essentially going to be the only one able to fire this thing, and not just because of the mana cost. That could be made up for with more mana stones.

He was much more worried about the likelihood of the cannon exploding, and [Cracked Phantom Armor] had a pretty good shot at resisting the worst case scenario.

Half an hour later, Matt and his party watched the first column go up. It was a fifteen-foot tall metal structure that was sunk into the ground. There was a slight glow as it was placed upright, and it felt like the air became more restrictive. He almost felt like the air was resisting his movements.

When each subsequent pillar went up, the pressure increased as they locked down real space.

Matt was watching as the readout from the teleporter showed the mana cost for each teleport increase. When it was getting to the point that teleportation was becoming unstable, he charged the cannon and readied it to fire.

It took nearly three and a half minutes and 15,000 mana, but the cannon drank it all in and started to glow. As the glow spread up the barrel, he winced.

There shouldn't be that much wasted mana to make the metal glow like that.

Having already aimed the cannon in the general direction of the pillar they were targeting, Matt fed mana to his AI. There was no way he was going to trust himself to fire at a target he could barely see, especially with a weapon this unstable. He wasn't Tara; he didn't have a Talent for these things.

He made minute corrections to the aiming equipment in the cannon as his AI registered everything in his spiritual sense. Air temperature, air density, and wind speed and direction at the top of the city wall. Angle and elevation, the rotation of the planet, and their latitude were calculated over the course of a minute.

Matt made the corrections that his AI indicated, and then waited for the conditions to line up.

Liz called out to him as he seemed frozen with his hand hovering over the firing rune. "Everything okay?"

"Just waiting for the perfect moment."

As the wind slowed, his AI flashed green once the parameters lined up, and he sent mana into the fire function.

A [Mana Bolt] the size of a horse raced out of the cannon in a gentle arc, and into the base of the space locking tower.

It seemed almost gentle as the light blue mass of mana lashed out from atop the city's walls.

That image only lasted until it landed.

The explosion from the overcharged [Mana Bolt] was so large, it blew down the nearby copse of trees as the impact released its stored energy.

I hope the army was ready for that one.

Matt sincerely hoped so, because there wasn't even a blade of grass left in the explosion radius. The trees that survived looked as if a giant had a tantrum and stomped on them. Their shattered and splintered trunks lay in haphazard piles.

Emily, who was closest to him, whistled. "Ascenders' balls Matt. Fuck! I want one of those."

Hoisting the cannon and moving to the next location with Conor, Matt grunted out, "Get your own [Cracked Mana Bolt] to hold a few thousand mana."

"You're a monster, though. I could do it at half the cost, given enough time to modify the skill. Or use it on the seventh or eighth combo. Ohhh, that's a good idea. I bet I could make a bigger explosion than you if I got my streak high enough."

Annie parted the troops who were manning the walls around them, creating a clear path for them to shuffle through. Thanks to her, they made good speed to the next location. Liz followed up with Aster, assisting her with moving the other cannon with a mix of ice and blood, helping to lift the weight and slide it along.

When they reached their second position, Conor hauled the ballista out of position, to the displeasure of the crew manning it. But when they saw Matt setting up the cannon, they quieted down and moved to the side.

After calculating the shot and charging the mana cannon, Matt destroyed the second pylon. They repeated the process three more times, missing only once before Matt had to switch out the cannons, thanks to his shoddy work. It was also enough time for the queendom to pull back their structures and start setting up the formations farther out.

Matt didn't know what each of those massive formation pillars cost, but he doubted that they were cheap. They might have made the better sacrifice, with one cannon gone for four of their formations.

Still, they underestimated the amount of mana Matt was charging the cannons with, and he was able to repeat the feat a second time, just as they were almost done setting up the formation farther away. The queendom moved significantly faster in pulling up and retreating with their space-locking pillars this time, and he could only hit two pillars before they truly were out of range.

This time, they moved nearly two hundred feet farther back. His last shot with the cannon was sent at a too slow trebuchet, and even that was at the very edge of his range. Watching the strut of the wooden siege engine shatter, then the entire thing collapse, earned a cheer from the defenders around them. They had been the ones watching stone after stone be blocked only feet from where they were standing.

He got a message from Juni, who sounded near jubilant. "Fantastic work. Once we're back from the dead, remind me to throw you the largest party I can fucking plan."

"Whoa, whoa. You expect us to die?"

Juni was distinctly less happy when he said, "Not intended, but there are a million plus troops moving to take this city. I don't know if we can hold out, but we don't intend to give up or go out easily. 'Ours is not to reason why, ours is but to do and die.'"

"Don't you fucking quote Albertson at me, Juni… Juni?"

The prince's right hand man had already ended the call.

Matt growled out at the surrounding besiegers. He didn't intend to go down quickly, easily, or at all.

17

Matt and his party stood together on the wall by the main gate, watching the dozen queendom trebuchets fling boulders at the shields.

They had been at this for a full day now.

The siege engines assaulting each entrance was the queendom's way of battering down the shield reserves, and it was effective. The first attacks had been more about frightening the defenders. After that, the artillery was carefully hitting the walls with standard rocks, no longer bothering to set them ablaze.

They observed the enemy command tent with the telescope they had linked to their AIs. Meanwhile, Juni was leading negotiations with the besiegers from on top of the battlements.

The discussion was going about as poorly as Matt expected. The opposing general was demanding the immediate surrender of their city and the entire defending force. Juni was countering with an equally absurd offer of letting all the standard troops leave uncaptured and unharmed if the queendom commanders surrendered.

Neither side expected the other to comply but, apparently, dick-measuring contests were a part of defending a city.

That neither side had slowed their siege preparations was telling. The attackers were assembling siege towers as if they were children's toys. Meanwhile, earth mages formed smoothed out tracks for the towers to advance on. The mages ventured as close as they could to the wall without the defenders being able to shoot them.

The miniature roads were a worrying testament to the lengths that the queendom would go to for the capture of the city. It was also a clear indicator that they didn't intend to simply batter the city to rubble with their artillery. No, Princess Sara intended to take the city intact. After all, they'd need to pay for any repairs once it was in their control.

Matt looked back over the wall into the massive city. The streets were packed with fighters. Most were uniformed kingdom soldiers, but there were smaller clumps of fighters in oddly colored, mismatched armor. They were the quick reaction forces that Liz commanded, comprised mostly of Pathers.

He had already run simulations for most of the possibilities with his AI. They were going to have to play this almost perfectly to successfully defend the city. His estimation of a million queendom troops wasn't far off. Around their city, there were eight hundred thousand queendom fighters setting up camps and their own additions to the fortifications.

So far.

To his surprise, the prince had done as promised. There were bands of kingdom fighters harrying the attackers and creating chaos. They weren't getting firm numbers, but the queendom had dedicated a substantial force to taking out the kingdom's guerilla forces.

It was the prince himself that led a raid deep into the queendom encirclement, where the team he personally led tore down two of the formation pillars that were locking down the city's teleporters. With their assistance, the city's defenders had managed to reinforce themselves, and now stood at nearly five hundred thousand fighters in total.

Eight hundred thousand attackers versus five hundred thousand defenders wasn't an impossible matchup for the defenders. It would just be a challenge. According to conventional wisdom, a three to one ratio was the minimum an attacking force should be comfortable with for besieging a city of this size. It was why the time they had bought with the cannons was so crucial. The kingdom might now be able to defend against this siege, if they were able to execute.

The problem was time. They were running out of it. According to Juni, the city's mana reserves were nearly spent, and the attackers clearly knew it. The rate of trebuchet fire was slowing down to a sprinkling of boulders, compared to the torrential rain it had been before.

Ten minutes later, the inevitable finally happened.

A flying boulder slammed unimpeded into the city walls. The *useless* prince had spent a lot on city reserves, but it all eventually proved ineffective. Looking around, Matt wished that their leader had spent even more points on the city's fortifications. While their defenses were adequately equipped, they clearly were not enough.

There was a joyful roar from the attacking army as they saw that the shields were finally disabled. On the other hand, the mood turned markedly somber around the defending command center.

A stoic Juni turned to face everyone and said, "So it begins. You all have your orders. Those queendom bastards will be on us quickly, so move to your positions. We don't know if the first attack will be a probe, or a dedicated assault. Show no weakness."

With that, he spun on his heels, climbed to the highest level of fortifications around the city's main gate, and started to give a more energizing speech to the amassed kingdom troops below.

Team Bucket turned to the side and raced along the clear half of the wall, moving to their positions. Their team had been assigned to the eastern city gate, along with a mostly Pather force.

As they approached the large fortification around the gate, Matt swallowed. It was a harrowing picture to see all the faces turn to them as one and lock on. Some had unmasked expressions of greed and hope, but they were in the minority. The resounding majority of the faces shared looks of fear and uncertainty. These were feelings that Matt understood all too well, but he worked hard to disguise them.

This wasn't a rift or a single fight. This was a siege against nearly a million enemies, and they were a small but key piece of the defense.

Matt was poked from behind by the dreaded 'Finger of Doom' and turned to see Liz. She whispered to him that he should speak with his troops. He still felt that she should be the one to speak, as she was the nominal leader. But she reversed the logic on him by pointing out that he was their in-battle commander and strategist.

He couldn't think of a good counter for that.

As he mimicked Juni by climbing up the fortifications, his mind blanked, and his many prepared speeches flew from his mind. His mouth was left without direction, and started moving on its own.

"We aren't here because we have a stake in the war." His throat seized up, but he swallowed hard, and forced himself to keep speaking. "Either war. What do we care if two vassal states fight over a Tier 20 planet? We're on The Path; it's irrelevant to us."

Matt had no idea where he was going with this and scrambled to bring the topic around to something applicable. He could see it on the faces below him. People were questioning his competency from this speech alone.

"Except that's bullshit! This isn't irrelevant to us. We walk The Path of Ascension, and this whole mini-war was set up for us. Us! Not the vassal kingdoms. What does a Tier 50 get out of letting us play make-believe in a little sandbox war?"

People started to look interested, so he decided to throw out something that he had learned from Liz's brothers and various news broadcasts.

"War is coming to the Empire. We're a part of the same Path that has succeeded in creating one monster-among-men already. Duke Waters. And a second pair are only a few decades away from repeating that same feat. I'm sure you've all heard the speculation. Once we have two sets of Ascenders, the other powers will target the Empire because of its success. Any of you could be the third, and now the Emperor is letting us experience a part of what's coming in a safe environment, before it becomes all too real."

Matt paused and looked around at his fighters. His mind frantically calculated how far he wanted to take his next statements.

"How many of you have died already?"

He raised a hand and watched as others raised a hand, some with confidence, and others with shame.

"We've died. And I'm glad for it. If this was a real war, then that would be it. The end. No coming back. This is an opportunity to learn from our mistakes. Ambushes that take down a stronger foe can happen to you as easily as it can to the enemy. I just stabbed a Tier 7 who thought I was a mage. He was dead before he knew to fight at full strength."

Matt winced internally. He was rambling.

"Don't let that be you. Take this as what it is—a learning experience. *Babies' first war*. Don't try to die but, if you do, learn from your mistakes. Make damn sure the other side learns from theirs, too."

He flung out an arm, pointing at the opposing army as they formed into ranks that seemed to go on forever.

"This is our chance to fight real people and learn. As the battle goes on, follow your orders the best you can. And try to learn something. The next time we do this, it could be for real."

He hopped down and activated [Cracked Phantom Armor]. He wanted to hide the shakes that started overcoming him as he'd realized how awful the speech was.

Then he realized his prepared speeches were in his AI. He wanted to slap himself. He could have just read off his HUD and been fine.

Liz rubbed his back, "That was good. People are more motivated, and a lot of the fear is gone."

"That was awful. I forgot all my speeches and forgot I could read off my AI. Then started spewing that shit out."

Annie shoulder-bumped him. "It wasn't that bad. Really. It was fine. Look at it this way; Once the fighting starts, no one will remember a word you said."

Conor shrugged. "I've heard better. Maybe worse. But who cares."

That actually helped.

Liz kicked the tall man's armored shin and glared at him.

He repeated his shrug. "I call it how I see it. Matt doesn't want us to lie."

Matt turned his attention to the queendom forces and watched the square formations start marching forward with shields raised.

The siege towers rumbled onwards in between each formation, keeping the same pace. He didn't miss the ladders and knotted ropes that some of the footmen held either.

As the enemy's vanguard neared the three-quarters point, Matt called out through the command channels, "Catapults with anti-personnel ammo, aim for the troops! The mana cannons and ballista will take down the siege towers! Hold till my command!"

His AI was noting everything and was being relayed information from the city AI. He called out a minute later, and his message went to the appropriate teams on the voice chats. "Cannons and ballista, fire!"

Changing channels, he barked out, "Long-range archers, take out the earth mages if you can."

If they could stop those damn earth mages, the soft ground would at least slow the massive siege towers.

"Catapults, fire!"

As he watched the various spells and mundane munitions being flung out, Matt felt a rush of power. This wasn't the power of an individual, but the power that came from dozens of coordinated attacks against a similarly coordinated foe. The power of an army. It was a whole new rush, unlike anything he had ever felt before.

Just as the rush peaked, it came crashing down when he realized that for all their preparedness, they were sorely outnumbered and outgunned. Even as a dozen fist-sized ball bearings slammed into the queendom formations, only a few handfuls of people were teleported out, and their spots quickly filled in with reinforcements from the rear.

Their most powerful weapons were still only like throwing pebbles into a pond.

One of the siege towers suddenly stopped. He looked and noticed that the ground before it stopped turning to smooth stone. The earth mage was gone. One tower down out of five was a great start.

The attackers soon reached the halfway mark, and he sent out his next command. "Archers, fire at the marked locations!"

A breath later, the sky darkened as thousands of arrows were loosed in near unison. They arced up and then down to slam into the upraised shields of the advancing formations. The next volley was a little more ragged, but gaps started to appear in the enemy formations.

"Mages, when you're in range, take your shots. Prioritize the targets your skills deal with best."

[Earth Spike]s and [Water Spear]s lashed out at the siege towers to Matt's right. A barrage of [Fireball]s did the same to his left. They splashed against the large, reinforced siege towers to little effect, but they did hinder the advance of the attackers.

From behind the first row of infantry, a contingent of archers drew their bows. Matt bellowed out on the open channels, "Prepare to receive counterfire!"

Defenders started ducking under the parapet, but Matt stood his ground. At this range, there wasn't a chance of an attack making it through his armor.

His fighters' shields were raised just seconds before the archers started to fire.

Having seen their own arrows fly over his head and darken the sky not moments ago, Matt thought he was prepared to receive a similar volley. He was dead wrong.

As the storm of arrows hailed toward him, he fought the instinct to duck and cover. Before him was a wave of glinting steel, crashing down upon a shore of flesh and dread.

The projectiles landed with a heavy push of air. Half a dozen of them bounced off his pale blue armor skill with plinking sounds, but that wasn't all they hit. The screams started just afterwards. Some lasted mere moments, but others lingered. Most wounds weren't severe enough to demand elimination.

His AI confirmed that his team was fine, and he dismissed the injury reports after glancing at the tallies of wounded. The numbers weren't pretty, but they were better than he'd feared.

"Healers, start getting the least wounded back on their feet."

Seeing the formations starting to move from a walk to a jog, he called out, "Anti-personnel squads, their formations are advancing. Stop them!"

It didn't look like the queendom was going for a probing attack. With this many resources at play, they obviously wanted to try to gain a foothold on the wall.

Arrows and spells flickered back and forth as Matt called out commands he received from his AI. Most were only what was obvious. It was like a game. You counter what the enemy tried to do while hampering them as much as possible. There were only so many orders that could be given, after all. The rest of the orders were just trying to counter or preemptively cut off problems.

The first of the three remaining siege towers slammed into the fifty-foot walls with a rumble. The second and fifth towers were stuck in mud and on fire, respectively. He didn't know when either had happened, but it was good news.

"Prepare to repel attackers! Don't let the towers distract you from the ladders and ropes."

His command felt unneeded, but it was better to make sure that everyone was on the same page.

Giant doors opened downwards, creating ramps to the top of the wall, where dozens of attackers flooded out.

The first wave consisted mostly of Tier 7 melee fighters in heavy armor.

Matt entered the fray for the first time.

With his staff in hand, he put his full 80 mana into the initial cast of [Hail] and let an avalanche of ice pour in front of the front gate. His staff didn't just empower a single skill. It empowered any skills that had an initial cast cost.

The battering ram that was being wheeled up suddenly had no way to advance. There was an ever-growing pile of ice raining down before the gate, blocking its way.

The hill of ice reached the top of the door and became dozens of feet thick. Matt turned off the skill, then started launching [Fireball]s at the invaders. He was aiming for those with ladders and grappling hooks.

People screamed, and attacks bounced off his armor as he leaned over the parapet to get a better angle on the queendom soldiers.

They quickly realized that their attacks were ineffective against him, and that he'd set those attempting to climb the walls aflame. The opposition quickly began focusing their efforts elsewhere.

Taking a moment, Matt looked over to the three siege towers that had reached the walls. His team was contesting the middle one to a halt. Conor stood poised at the bottom of the ramp with [Demon Zone]'s crimson hue whirling around him, inviting anyone foolish enough to step foot onto his grisly dance floor. Behind him, the team's mages only added to the chaos, playing a symphony of spells to a chorus of screams.

Yeah, that tower was fine.

Matt looked left and right to the remaining towers.

The third was mostly bottled up, but the first tower was gaining a foothold on the wall. It was small and burgeoning, but it couldn't be allowed to grow any further. He really didn't need his AI screaming at him in glaring red letters to know that much.

"QRF-Alpha, move to support against the left-most tower."

He cast a scattering of [Fireball]s at the stream of people flowing out of the tower. After seeing three among them vanish, he checked his surroundings again.

For some odd reason, the battering ram team had brought the covered ram to the edge of his ice field. They seemed to be trying to dig a path forward.

With a shrug, he cast [Hail] a second time, and entombed everyone and everything under another frosty mountain.

He needed to be careful about piling the ice too high. If an ice mage was out there, he was just stockpiling ammunition for them, or providing materials for a ramp. Regardless, it was still effective, and it was worth it to prevent the ram from reaching the front gate.

A [Fireball] slammed into Matt a half-second later, quickly followed by an arrow. He cast half a dozen [Fireball]s of his own in retaliation and watched as part of the archers' division poofed away.

His head swiveled, but he had no idea where the pesky mage who hit him was.

Before he could search further, his AI sent him a warning that a quick glance confirmed. A pair of competent swordsmen from the third tower were overwhelming that section of the wall. Matt leapt down from his vantage point, and dashed over while calling for the QRF-Beta team to converge at his location.

Sliding his staff into his spatial backpack, he summoned his sword into hand and charged into the two swordsmen, whose blades now gleamed with a sanguine red glow.

Both were Tier 7 and prepared for his charge. He met their flashing weapons with his own glimmering longsword, and used its greater reach to cover half the wall's walkway. He blocked two hits before taking a strike to his armor.

It increased his mana draw to nearly the max of what his armor Skill could handle, 45 MPS. But it enabled him to confidently take the glancing hit.

Knowing that, Matt started moving a little more recklessly.

Ducking a sinister looking slash, he half-stepped to the right and brought his blade up from below the rightmost attacker's guard. The swordsman pivoted to block, but as their weapons met, Matt unleashed the mana stored in his blade. [Mana Charge] detonated on collision, sending the smoking and charred intruder stumbling backward.

Before Matt could follow up, his prey's partner was already retaliating. They landed a walloping blow along his left side. The attack sliced through [Cracked Phantom Armor], and dug into his leather armor beneath.

Yet another heavy slash came at him, but Matt's under armor withstood the blow this time.

"Fuck! Why won't you go down!?" The attacker howled with the swing of their third blow, but Matt prepared his own counterattack. He took the incoming hit on his armored forearm while cleaving down savagely into the attacker's forward leg.

He didn't cut through their armor, but it dented inwards, and he felt the bone crunch as the man toppled. Matt quickly pivoted, planted his weight on his left leg, and anchored it to the ground with his Concept. He raised his right leg for a stomp with all his weight and [Mage's Retreat] empowering the attack.

His skill-clad boot cracked into the stone walkway as the remaining swordsman was whisked away.

With a few hacks, he started cutting down the charging queendom regulars who were marching behind the elite swordsmen duo. His reinforcement from QRF-Beta soon arrived and overtook his position. They surged forward and took hold of the area, again buying time for the kingdom's standard troops to hurry up to the top of the wall.

Returning to his vantage point at the gate, Matt inspected the battlefield before revising his orders.

"Team Bucket, stop advancing on the third tower. Do not enter the tower."

His team had pushed forward enough, he was worried they'd enter the tower, which was a monumentally bad idea.

They receded slightly, and Matt checked on the rest of the battlefield. "Get the long sticks to push off the ladders. Don't just clear them of men. Push them over if you can. If you can break or burn them, even better."

"Stop tossing their grappling hooks back over. They can just replace the severed rope. Toss them on to our side of the wall after you cut the rope off. Force them to buy new ones."

He then took stock of his own condition. His AI reported gashes in his armor and flesh; surface-level wounds that he could quickly solve with [Endurance] running at full blast for a moment. He was more concerned about the unexpected damage that the swordsmen's weapons had done to his armor. Their attacks had included an effect that had corroded it, both physically and spiritually. The affected portions of armor were only rags at this point. So, he stripped the ruined pieces from his arms, but left the chest armor in place, as it was only damaged on the left side.

His left bracer, which had broken bones, was mangled. It was irritating as could be, but there was nothing to be done, so he tried to stop dwelling on it. He still had the right bracer at least.

The assault lasted a full hour. Matt was forced to leave his command post two more times to personally take action and prevent breaches.

As he intervened for the third time, Matt resorted to using five consecutive [Mana Charge]s to break the ramp from the siege tower. Without the ability to march down, the attackers were forced to jump. Only a few tested the prospect before they decided to withdraw the crippled tower and reinforce the remaining two.

Matt dearly wished that he could have prevented them from pulling the tower back for repairs, but had no way to do so. The defenders did their best to damage it further with spells and mana cannons, and were able to give the queendom's crafters more work. By the time it retreated beyond their range, the tower was smoking, and its top two floors were collapsing inwards.

The final exit of the broken siege tower seemed to signal a larger retreat, as well. The queendom forces started to pull back.

"Everyone, fire! Don't let them retreat unscathed. Bombard them with everything you have left."

Most of the retreating formations were frayed and disorganized compared to when they first advanced. However, some were retreating virtually unscathed, with shields raised and returning fire in perfect coordination.

Matt, breathing heavily, looked around from his lookout perch. The top of the wall was covered in blood and soot, but there weren't as many wounded as he expected.

"Healers! Get the wounded to the healers!" Matt looked around then added, "Rotate in the second shift of teams. First teams, once they're up here, get down, grab a meal, and recharge."

Matt walked over to his team and clapped Conor on their shoulder, before sliding over to pull Liz and his panting bond into a bear hug.

"How were things?"

Liz was huffing between gulps from her canteen but wheezed out,

"Fine. We held on with minimal help. Just a few nicks from stray arrows. We're good."

Matt checked their mana levels and activated his Concept. While he listened to them debrief and discuss what they could improve next time, he sent out orders and directed the new troops to their positions.

They had been in reserve under the wall, and unable to see anything, but they could hear the attacks and repelling of borders. The wide eyes of each person who cleared the top step and saw the carnage was almost amusing. If Matt wasn't struggling to keep from plopping down on his ass and passing out, he might've even found it funny.

Realizing how tired he was, he channeled [Endurance] and let the skill wash away his fatigue.

He barely had five minutes before the reports started to come in, and Matt checked their casualty numbers. The defenders had lost around four hundred people in his section, against an estimated two and a half thousand lost on the attacking side. It was a great ratio, but the battle had still taken its toll. They still had to account for the fact that the city was outnumbered to begin with and wouldn't be getting any more reinforcements.

Once his team was topped off on mana, and their reserve stones were filled, he moved to the healer's tent set up near their position.

A harried woman with a healer's armband looked up at him and said, "We don't have time for walking wounded. Is there something internal?"

Matt shook his hand. "I'm not here for that. Get me the healers on downtime."

"We don't..."

Matt lacked the patience to explain, so he flexed his Concept. As her eyes widened with understanding, he continued, "I can't control the range, but the more people there are, the less each one gets. So, I want to prioritize the healers."

The woman looked ready to kiss him, and eagerly pulled him into what seemed like a recovery room just for the healers. They were all strewn about and pressing cold packs to their heads. At the entrance, most apprehensively peeked up as if expecting terrible news.

Before anyone could ask, she nearly cheered, "Get up! This guy can refill our mana!" The sudden noise caused the spent healers to wince in unison.

That wasn't a good sign. They must have all repeatedly drawn themselves dry to have mana headaches that serious.

Matt noticed the racks of personal mana stones, where a pale nurse seemed to be dumping regular mana stones into the charging base. The stones were quickly drained away into nothingness, and new ones quickly replaced them.

"I need proximity for this. The farther away anyone is, and the more people included, the less effective my Concept gets. It's already mostly internal, so I need to get every bit of effectiveness out of it to help you out."

Matt tried to undersell the efficiency of his Concept as much as he could before triggering it for the first huddled group. There was a wave of relief-filled moans. As each healer felt their mana pools reach maximum, they uncoiled themselves from the circle to make room for someone new.

Half an hour later, the entire healing staff was back on their feet. Matt moved to the rack of healer's crystals. He placed a hand into the bowl and dumped mana out. It would still need to be converted from his personal mana to un-aspected mana before it could be absorbed into the healer's personal mana stones racks. So, he donated 10,000 mana over the next ten minutes. He could've done it in a little more than two minutes, but he purposefully drew the process out, and dramatically staggered out of the tent as if the ordeal had exhausted him.

He wanted to help, but he still wanted to conceal the true scale of his abilities. Besides, that 10,000 mana was already far more than an average person could have donated.

It also wasn't a complete lie. He was dead tired from running, and his willpower was low. He didn't have to fake the strain that part put on him.

Messaging the mage groups, he offered to help them recover their mana in another half hour.

In the meantime, he returned to his vantage point on the wall to keep tabs on the enemy forces as they reassembled and started repairs on their siege equipment.

Contemplating the descending sun, Matt let out a long-held sigh. This would be a long restless night.

Only the second of the siege so far.

Four days. They lasted four long days of bombardments and repeatedly repelled the attackers off their walls. The advances were blending together so much Matt wasn't sure when one ended and the next began. Sometimes the queendom got a foothold, but they were always able to push them back. It just cost lives.

The defenders were all tired and wounded.

The queendom had attacked them twice daily, before trying a more subtle attack last night, when both sides usually settled down.

That hadn't worked either. This morning, they had resorted to endlessly using their trebuchets to battering at the walls.

That would have been manageable on its own, but the queendom didn't stop there. While the city's teleporters were inoperable, the queendom had no such restrictions. Another million fresh troops arrived to reinforce the siege.

Their encampment was starting to look like its own city, only wrapped around the one that Matt and his team currently occupied. Tents were set in rows around the city that stretched beyond eyesight. The small forest that was nearby was clear cut and used to improvise rough housing for the multitudes arriving around the city.

The rest were used to make more trebuchets, which added to the number of projectiles slamming into their walls.

Right now, they had the earth mages trying to counteract the damage, but it was a losing proposition. Matt was drawing his Concept thin, trying to keep their mages and healers functional while also directing his section of the wall.

Sleep came only in bursts but not for him. Matt mostly relied on [Endurance] to keep him going. Others didn't have that option and found sleep when and where they could. It had been a hectic few days, and now that the queendom had given up on taking the city cleanly. They wanted to end this siege soon and were willing to throw the necessary numbers at them to ensure it would.

With well over a million troops already encircling them, they received reports from outside the city that the queendom was preparing to send another million fighters to ensure the siege was broken soon. Apparently, they had intended to isolate the city early, before the prince could adequately reinforce the defenses. That plan had crumbled with the early and unexpected destruction of so many pylons from both Matt's efforts and Albert. Rumor had it, Princess Sara was fuming at the failure.

It was now clear she'd intended to quickly take the city and from there immediately move to siege another city at a natural choke point deeper in kingdom territory. Now the additional queendom forces they would have teleported directly into this city for the next siege were being redirected to their city on foot. Matt felt proud at their stalwart defense, but seeing one and a half million people surrounding them put things into a new perspective for him.

Knowing that there were another million fresh opponents marching to them left everyone with a sinking feeling.

This would not end well.

A boulder slammed onto the city wall just to Matt's right, and he winced. They had actually taken most of their defenders off the wall after a stray boulder clipped the top and eliminated a few dozen people. But the queendom was still trying to limit damage to the city and were being extra careful about hitting the expensive infrastructure inside.

The defending leaders were grateful for it, as they had little recourse if the queendom decided to launch rocks inside the walls and flatten the city. They would need to move the trebuchets closer, which would put them close enough to retaliate, but nowhere in the city would be safe for their troops anymore, who were packed in tight.

For now, they were okay with letting the queendom chip away at their walls.

A disheveled earth mage raced up to Matt, panting. "The structural support pillar is cracked. We don't know how much longer we can hold it."

Matt stuffed a bit of mana into the man with his Concept, and then reported to Juni, "One of our support pillars is cracked."

"Wait? Only now?"

The man sounded astonished, so Matt asked, "Yeah. Why do you ask?"

"I just thought you weren't reporting it. Everyone else already has cracks. More than one for most of us."

Matt shook his head. "No, I've been using my Concept to keep the earth mages going."

"Fucking damn it! By the Emperor's balls, Matt, our speculation didn't think you could put out near that much mana. You should have said something earlier! Fuck!" Juni took a deep, audible breath. "That's unfair of me. But I'll be sending you more earth mages. Do what you can for them. Please. Even if the walls are doomed to fall, it's better we drag it out as long as possible."

Matt almost felt guilty, but it was his secret, and he'd honestly expected that Juni would have heard about it from the various groups he was keeping topped off. The kingdom having a limited idea of his capabilities wasn't surprising. While he hadn't advertised his Concept or Talent, there were clear anomalies in his team's combat records for anyone looking to find.

Half an hour later, a stream of exhausted earth mages started huddling around Matt. They each lumbered away once they were full, and another would roll into their place. There were just so many of them. Too many. Finally, Matt had to start setting them aside and telling them to wait for his willpower to restore itself.

He was beyond spent and didn't have time to sit and meditate. As always, he had situations to resolve and orders to give. It never stopped, not even for a moment.

They were currently demolishing all the buildings near the most probable breach points and setting up a series of fortified fall back positions. The queendom would break through the walls sometime soon, and they needed to be prepared.

Matt hadn't seen his teammates in two days. Their AI readings showed that they were alive without serious injury at least. It wasn't enough, he wanted to see them and spend time with them, but it was all that he had.

The city AI sent him a request for a scan of his area, which he completed, and then got directions for his building crews. The city AI had apparently lost many of its cameras during the bombardment of the walls. Why the surveillance system was connected to and ran information through the walls at all was a mystery to Matt. Seemed like an awful design flaw. From experience, he could confirm it was.

The city AI now needed personal AIs to feed it information about the situations near the walls. Also, his crew of workers needed to clear two more rows of buildings and create rubble barricades.

He highlighted the buildings in question and relayed the orders. He swore that he could hear their groans from atop the wall but was pretty sure it was just the wind. He knew that they *were* groaning at the additional work, he just doubted that he could hear it from up here.

His AI pinged him with a new idea. He reviewed it and then passed it up to Juni and the city AI coordinating the defender's overall strategy.

He received half the answer he'd expected.

"Only take down half the ballistae and mana cannons. Leave everything else up on the walls."

Not willing to double guess the city AI, he ordered half of the siege equipment to be brought down and stuffed into their fallback positions. He assumed that the AI intended to recall the second half down right before they retreated from the wall. It would be imbecilic to leave them for the attackers to take and then simply turn around after all.

A boulder slammed into the wall next to Matt again.

They just needed to weather the storm for now.

18

Eleven hours later, as the sun was rising over the horizon, the first wall crumbled in on itself. It was the western section, the one directly opposite from Matt's position. The light coming from the east gave him a spectacular view of the destruction. The wall now had a slope where the rubble slid down, creating a natural ramp.

Matt wasn't surprised. No one was. They had expected this for the last few hours. During the next two, the remaining walls fell one by one. They stopped bothering to have the earth mages reinforce them a while ago. They had since been commanded to conserve their mana and energy for this pivotal moment. Now, they would form smaller cliffs out of the rubble, so the attackers would have to slowly scale them instead of marching down an easy path. During that climb, they would be sitting ducks.

Detached stairs had been prepared on their side, to be attached if the defenders needed to sally out. They weren't going to create a stairway for their enemies after all.

Around Matt, archers and mages stood shoulder to shoulder. The attackers probably wouldn't bring siege towers this time, when they had easier options. There was always room for surprise though, so they kept the walls manned. Best case scenario, they would be left free to rain down fire on the attackers as they funneled through the breach, turning it into a potent kill zone.

As they expected, the enemy lines started to trudge forward in a steady procession. These looked like fresh troops to Matt, but he couldn't be certain. The queendom had brought in a substantial number of reinforcements.

Formation after formation moved forward with shields raised high. They weathered the storm of arrows, spells, and siege equipment that the defenders rained down on them.

Matt was hoping to inflict enough casualties to force them into a retreat, but it was a futile ambition. This had all happened before. Only a handful of individual divisions had ever been broken, and only after being completely decimated.

There was no such luck this time.

The first formation was accompanied by skilled earth mages who shaped ramps out of the rubble. It was an oddly satisfying sight. The disorganized rubble shifted and formed clean, precise steps out of the jagged slope. They were a drop of order splashed into a city that had housed only chaos for days.

"Drop."

At his command, the buckets of boiling pitch they had heated with mundane fires were pushed over. The boiling black liquid sloshed into the opening, and the attacker's screams were brutally short. Matt saw people clutching their scalded flesh, and others trying to peel off the soaked clothes that clung to them and burned them.

Matt didn't enjoy their pain or let it linger. At this point, he was too drained to feel much of anything.

"Fire!"

Every mage with a fire spell, including himself, launched their spells to ignite the black liquid. What was boiling before was now a raging fire.

For a moment, it was as if a new sun was born. Everyone but Matt flinched back from the flash and wash of heat. The heat didn't penetrate his armor, but he felt the burst of the air as it rushed past.

He hoped the wall of flames would earn them a reprieve, but the invaders had clearly expected something of this nature. The earth below rumbled, and the fires were quickly put out as the stone shifted to swallow the pitch and flames.

The next wave of attackers marched up the fresh stone stairs like nothing had happened.

Matt messaged the first fallback position and its accompanying ranged positions and squadrons.

"Prepare for enemies."

He was still launching [Fireball] after [Fireball] as quickly as his spirit allowed. He paused only to recharge a mana stone with 200 mana, so he could immediately drain it dry and start the process over again.

Their enemies constructed their own ramp to the ground, not deigning to traverse the makeshift cliffs once more. Their ramp was steeper than what was ideal, causing more than one attacker to slip and fall under the rain of arrows. He cast [Hail] for a moment, but the earth mages hastily created a roof, giving them cover from the onslaught of kingdom attacks.

With a quick check, Matt verified that his melee fighters were protecting the outer wall and the stairs leading to their positions. Good, that gave him some breathing room. He threw himself over the edge, and landed just behind the first fallback position. The men above should be able to keep the invaders from climbing the outer wall, or taking advantage of the stairs. He wanted to be in the thick of the action.

He was just in time. The attackers were racing forward with a deafening roar. Matt screamed back wordlessly.

Each side clashed with a cacophony of epic proportions. [Cracked Phantom Armor] dampened the noise to a tolerable level, but with his own scream rattling in his ears, it was difficult to tell.

Matt leaned slightly forward over the small fortification and smashed down on a head peeking toward him. His target vanished without a sound. He struck down a second, and then a third queendom soldier in rapid succession.

An ally two people over was pulled forward over the barricade. A warhammer was already descending right to where he would crash down.

Without a thought, Matt launched himself at the hammer wielder with a [Mage's Retreat] empowered leap. He body-slammed the man in the back as an ax feebly attempted to cut into his armor from the side, only to propel him forward harder.

Standing over the man, Matt swung his longsword in vast sweeping arcs that left trails of blue from the mana charging his weapon. The pressure of the advancing forces pressed the front lines forward, but Matt stood his ground, sundering metal and flesh as if they were one and the same.

When a mere Tier 7 shield had the audacity to block his attack, he let loose his sword's stored mana with a [Mana Slash]. The bright slash arced out in a crescent moon that jettisoned the queendom fighter and their shield backward into the crowd.

That gave the fallen kingdom soldier that he stood over enough leeway to scramble to his feet, reach up, and be pulled back up to the fortification.

Matt looped his left arm backward, and was met with four outstretched hands that grabbed it and hauled him up as well.

"Don't let yourselves be pulled over!"

The situation here seemed in hand for now. Matt took a moment to survey the battlefield and located his team. He ran over to join Conor in the clear area that had formed around him. Allies knew better than to willingly walk into the red glow of [Demon Zone]. Enemies that took their chances received a free teleportation ticket to the hospital, as did those who were forced forward by the endless march of the queendom.

Together, Matt and Connor culled the swaths of enemies who had no option but to move forward. Aster, Annie, and Liz also made sure to attack the enemies in the range of the skill, too. Every target hit was a chance to trigger the skill's reflected attack, and strike everyone else in the zone, too. With the mages outside of the affected range, they didn't have to worry about reflection damage. Nor did Conor.

It was a devastating combination, and it was how the small team had managed to repeatedly hold a siege tower on their own.

In a moment of clarity, Matt also realized that he should use his Concept, and he let it billow out around him. The enemies that came into range were dead in seconds, before they could meaningfully benefit, so there was no reason not to use the small amount of willpower that he had accumulated.

With that extra mana, Aster prowled to the front, just left of [Demon Zone]'s aura. There, she dug her paws into the ground and reached out with Winter's Embrace. In a flash, the thicket of ice branched out, and the frontmost dozen attackers became tangled ice sculptures. They shattered as the occupants were whisked away. The embrace didn't stop growing there. More and more people were forced into Aster's chilling garden as her area of effect grew.

The stones loudly cracked under the cold. Matt recognized that Aster was using the cold collar he'd enchanted with separate runes. One for her own ice mana, and the other for slowing ice mana. The rune made from her mana increased the ice damage of any spell she channeled through it. Now, he could finally see the fruits of his labor, though they had tested it earlier.

While not a conventional skill, Winter's Embrace still qualified for the added damage from the collar.

As their comrades forced them forward, the frontmost queendom fighters were shoved into a frigid, flowering jungle that wolfishly devoured them whole. Their fate was sealed after simply stepping into its domain.

The downside of such a natural treasure was that it guzzled mana as if it was endless.

With Matt as her bond, it was.

He crossed over to her and slipped a hand through her spiky armor. Burning extra mana to convert his own mana to her personal signature faster, he charged the mana stones around her neck. Simultaneously, Matt's Concept surged forth in a tight circle just broad enough to include only his bond.

Mana rushed into Aster and kept her going, expanding Winter's Embrace, and allowing it to gorge on enough invaders to be self-sustaining, even with its meals being stolen. If the army rescuers left people inside for any longer, the skill could have sustained itself from merely one or two ensnared victims. Aster wouldn't have had access to that mana, but the skill itself would have continued on its own.

At a diameter of nearly fifty feet, a large enough number of troops were ensnared by the wintery jungle of roses to keep it sustained with a little help from Matt. The push of the queendom's advance only led more lambs to the slaughter at Aster's paws. They were so eager to get out of the chokepoint through the wall, they rushed forward into another zone of death. And only the first in line were able to see it.

The best part? Aster was an adorable little fox, and thus shorter than the berm they used as a parapet. She was sheltered from retaliation.

An hour and a half of fervent fighting later, an order went out, which instantly gave Matt pause.

'All forces, Charge!'

Matt thought someone had gone crazy but relayed his orders as was his duty.

"Charge!"

Taking the lead, he leapt over the berm and swung his sword in a downwards arc. After a second of bewilderment, everyone else followed. They collided with the momentum of the attackers, with each side stalling out for a moment.

Then, Matt heard it. Echoes where there had been none before.

A glance up revealed that the city shields were active once again.

That madman Juni had lied about the amount of mana they had and saved some. Now he was using that final reserve to trap the invading forces.

Matt snickered at the pure audacity of the move.

The queendom fighters, who had been taking heavy casualties before, were now on their heels as attacks rained down from the outer wall and archery positions. So *this* was why the city AI only wanted half of the artillery brought down from the wall.

Death and destruction showered down from all sides. Ballistae and mana cannons tore lines of death into the panicked attackers, as fast as they could reload.

With refound vigor, the weary kingdom defenders sheared their way through rank after rank of the opposition. Liz was a golem of bloody death, scything her way through the trapped attackers like ripe wheat waiting to be harvested.

Lightning thundered so powerfully, Matt knew that Emily had to be at his side. As the blinding flashes flared out, half a dozen people blinked away while the [Bolt] arced its way through multiple bodies. The spell was empowered enough to chain through and eliminate swaths of enemies in a flash.

Matt and his forces minced their way up to the breach in the wall, to find an open spot free of enemies. At first, Matt thought that their retaliation ended there. But then he saw them.

The real prize.

Matt looked over the breach to discover a formation of Tier 7 elites with their backs against the shielding. The way their equipment looked, he suspected that they carried Tier 8 arms and armor. A hail of arrows from them caught Matt and his people off guard.

They were backed up to an invisible but sturdy wall. Matt pondered his options. Only for a moment. Now wasn't the time for thinking, it was the time to pay them back for each and every raid.

He launched a max-powered [Hail] with a wave of his staff. It started to batter at his opponents, but they were a Tier higher, and not as threatened as he'd imagined.

Too tired to think straight, he latched onto the simplest option, and ordered a charge into the enemy position.

As he exploded forward with his sword aglow and a berserk roar on his lips, Matt flew through his [Hail] and into the mass of elite troops. He crashed down with a dry-then-wet crunch of someone else's mangled armor and bones. His reckless blitz prompted enough of the fighters to turn to face him, allowing his allies to charge without immediate reprisal.

A spear pierced through the side of Matt's leg armor. Luckily, it was a glancing blow, half stopped by his under armor. He managed to step away before it drew more than a little blood.

His own people slammed into the raised shields of the Tier 7 formation. It promised to be a hectic, bloody fight where they were out-Tiered in both cultivation and equipment.

He kicked and lashed downward with his sword as he cut into metal armor. His sword was heavy for its Tier, but not sharper, so the wounds weren't fatal.

Matt expected the melee to last a while, as it was a brawl in close quarters, when suddenly the air went white.

A huge explosion of cold consumed the area as the air itself seemed to solidify, and ice from the still falling [Hail] started to elevate. The world around him seemed to slow then stop, as if space time had been flash-frozen. The fighters surrounding Matt all stilled.

Then, just as suddenly, they were gone, and the illusion shattered.

Nearby, a wheezing, quivering Aster collapsed onto her side next to a field of ice, blood, and churned earth, with Matt at the center.

His lungs heaving, Matt slumped to the ground. He felt boiling hot despite his armor blocking external sources of heat. He hadn't noticed the heat until just now.

Deactivating it sent a shock through Matt's system as the still freezing air washed over him, jolting him fully awake from what now felt like a bad dream. That had been stupid. Monumentally stupid.

What was I thinking?

He had troops holding the breach, and the enemy was pinned against a wall. That made them fish in a barrel for the mana cannons and ballistae.

There were zero good reasons for his reckless decision.

Liz leaned down to quickly check on Aster, but soon stormed over to him. He expected to be either punched or slapped, deservingly so. But she just kneeled and felt him over for injuries while demanding, "What were you thinking!?"

"I wasn't. Sorry, I neglected to wake myself with [Endurance] for too long and got tired. It's been a long few days, and it keeps wearing off faster each time. I'll…"

"Stop. What was that? Have you not slept recently? When did you sleep last…? Wait, have you not slept *at all*?"

At Matt's shake of the head, she grabbed and shook him. "You idiot! You need to sleep. Right now. Matt, you can only go for so long without some proper sleep." Seeing him open his mouth, she shook her head. "No. The rest of us have all slept since this started. While I hadn't personally seen you sleep, I assumed you were just sleeping when we did. I'm taking over for the next few hours while you get some rest. Things will be easy enough with the shields up."

Matt shook his head. "I need to recharge the earth mages."

"No, stop! They've been resting for nearly a full day now. You need to sleep. We all need you to sleep. Go grab Aster and find a bunk to crash in. She severely overextended herself rescuing you from this insane stunt. Juni sent us a message about this *that you ignored.* He already knew about the Tier 7s here, and an equivalent division of our own Tier 7 elites was already on their way to deal with them. We didn't have to take this risk."

Matt didn't have it in himself to argue anymore, particularly after seeing the state of his bond and hearing her worried pleas. After messaging Juni that he was going to sleep, and being chewed out again for not sleeping, he found a cot and his world went dark before he had time to adjust.

With Aster in his arms, Matt was out cold in seconds.

Liz prodded him awake after what felt like only minutes, but a check of his AI showed that it was closer to seven hours.

"What's wrong?"

Liz pushed him back onto the cot slightly as he tried to stand. "Nothing. We have about three hours before the shields fall for real this time, and I knew you would want to be up. I've had everyone resting and recovering their mana. The healers are even ahead of the casualties, and we're…" She paused. "Well, we aren't at one hundred percent, but everyone is mostly healed and ready for the next engagement."

Matt laid a groggy Aster down on the cot and picked up his sword from where he'd apparently dropped it on the floor, returning it to his spatial ring.

"Thank you."

He kissed Liz's sweaty, soot-covered head.

He walked outside to see that the area around them was cleaned up, and any debris was added to the defensive berms.

Quickly climbing the stairs, he surveyed the attacking army. Their numbers had grown again during the time he was unconscious. While observing the besiegers, Matt called Juni.

Before he could say anything, Juni cut in with, "You're an idiot."

"We went through this yesterday. Yes, I am. No, I won't do it again. Though I think we'll be dead before I need to sleep again anyway. Oh! How many Tier 7s did we get? Was it worth it?"

Juni snorted, "Nine full battalions of Tier 7s with Tier 8 items. I wish I could have seen the princess's face when she found out. After they realized we tricked them, the queendom restarted the bombardment for real. Clearly, the plan to take the city intact is dead and gone. Just like their elites."

The queendom had moved half their trebuchets forward to within range of the city proper and was battering at the shield with a vengeful intensity that could only be born from being made a fool of.

"What's our strategy?"

"Hold as long as we can and make them bleed for it. We intend to hold until they take the outer walls, then try to sally forth out of one of the gates. With the prince's help, we should be able to break through their lines and escape."

"Think they'll happily let us walk out of here?" Matt didn't think it was likely, as boulder after boulder shattered on the invisible shielding.

"No. We'll need to fight our way out. Are your troops ready to ride out the bombardment?"

Matt peered over the edge of the inner wall and surveyed his side. "As ready as we can be. All positions are within the protection of the wall, but outside of its collapsing range. Are we going to hold the wall this time?"

"If we can, yes. But orders will change as we progress."

Suddenly remembering something, Matt asked, "What about the remaining crafters still in the city?"

Juni groaned. "I've gathered most of them that weren't able to catch a teleport out, but some are refusing to leave their workshops, even though we know the queendom will be pummeling the city center."

With that ominous note, they ended the call and waited, with only the pounding of rocks on shielding to give them company.

It wasn't good that all the crafters hadn't gotten out of the city. They were able to get in the teleporter, as it was a swapping function between locations, and they were trying to bring people in. There was nearly no demand to leave except from the civilians. Even then, some of them had simply refused to evacuate without the large, expensive equipment in their workshops that they couldn't pack up in time. Losing that equipment would financially ruin many of them, and if it wasn't stored on their person, then it wouldn't be 'looted but returned' to them when they died or were captured. The ones who fled without any equipment wouldn't be getting it back either because it would either be destroyed during the siege or claimed as war prizes afterwards.

It was a shitty situation for everyone.

Three hours later, the first boulder sailed over the wall and smashed its way through a city block. Then, the queendom started lighting the rocks on fire before launching them. Teams ignored most of the fires, unless they ate their way to their positions, where bucket brigades and mages would handle the flames.

One landed close enough for Matt to smother the flames with [Hail].

He looked over the kingdom casualty list as he waited for the attackers to move in again.

Things weren't looking good. They had lost nearly half their troops in the various fights and while repelling the siegers. On the bright side, they had taken out nearly eight hundred thousand enemy troops already. If the queendom hadn't gotten reinforcements, they would have won the siege, but there were another million and a half troops out there waiting.

With the enemy's new willingness to level the city, Matt hoped that the prince had a decent extraction force ready to help them break through the encirclement.

They would need large numbers to break through and avoid being chased down and killed out of hand.

Five long, agonizing hours later, as the sun reached its zenith, the queendom troops started moving forward.

Matt readied his men. "Form up! The enemy approaches. Let's see if we can bring the tally up to a million casualties with this wave."

There was a loud but wordless cry from the fighters at his command. Most were Pathers, but around a third were kingdom troops who were filling in the gaps from their losses. Even with that help, there were still thin spots on the walls. Matt tried not to think of what would happen once they were unable to repel the assaults.

There was a scream from below, and Matt looked down to see a woman pointing up. He followed her finger and nearly looked into the sun, but then he saw them.

"Air assault! Dropships incoming!"

He repeated the message on all the commander level channels. Though it was already too late.

Dozens of giant, flying battalions were using the sun as cover, and had flown up miles into the sky. They hovered beyond the edge of the anti-flying formations with their immense, needle-like packages, each carried by a hundred plus people with various flying devices.

They let them go, and nearly as one, the fifty-seven dropships arrowed down, spelling doom for anything in their way.

The dropships were crude, angular cones, designed with minimal thought given to anything but reducing drag and preventing rotation during descent. The ones Matt had seen in movies were dropped from low orbit and had fins to allow mundane flight for bypassing anti-flying runes. They always caused devastating damage when they landed behind enemy lines.

Matt heard orders for the QRF teams going out but ignored it to give his own.

"Second and fifth companies. Turn and guard our rear. Lookout only. Get the QRF teams to deal with the fighters. They'll all be Tier 7s, or at least fight like it."

The enemy vessels slammed down into the empty city center, where it was mostly just wreckage from the attacking trebuchets. They landed with ground-shaking rumbles as the heavy metal drop-ships punched into the ground. As Matt and his troops tightened their grips on their weapons, the heavy steel doors smashed down, creating ramps that teams of a dozen people poured out of.

"Annie?"

"Is it time? Am I free?" She sounded eager.

"You still have the giftboxes I made for you?"

"Yes!"

Matt was almost worried about the exuberance in her voice. "Then do what you do best."

He moved his position down after seeing that the queendom wasn't trying to take the half-crumbled walls and gathered his best fighters from the QRF teams. They were all Tier 6 Pathers, but they fought like monsters. They had to, as they were the ones used to defend the worst case scenarios and plug breaches in the walls.

"Be ready to deal with the airborne troops. Each pod seemed to carry a dozen people in it but be ready for larger or smaller teams. I don't know if they'll try to gather together and attack one position or harry us all around. Maybe both. Don't go down needlessly and call for help when you engage. We have the numbers here, let's use them."

The next hour was hectic, as other sections of defenders reported hit-and-run tactics over and over. They were targeting valuable structures and facilities like the healing tents. The drop ship forces' coordinated strikes gave the other teams time to protect the more vulnerable areas, but both sides incurred heavy losses as the day crept along. All the while, they had to defend from a continuous assault from the queendoms main forces.

Even with the sound of battle just in front of him, something felt off to Matt. Things got quiet, and he turned to the rear to ready both his team and the other QRF teams. Something wasn't right. This felt like the times in a rift when a monster stalked in the shadows. You never knew when it would strike, and the feeling slowly wore away at you.

Matt widened his eyes and watched for movement, not focusing on any specific thing. His arm shot left, and he let loose a [Mana Slash]. A scream quickly followed the explosion. A few seconds later, a much larger explosion rocked the entire courtyard.

Annie skulked through the shadows cast by the noonday sun in the rubble-strewn city. Streets were more vague suggestions now than actual clear paths.

She was stalking the queendom drop-troopers as they made attempts at hit-and-run tactics. They were all foiled by her sending messages to any group of kingdom fighters they tried to approach.

They still succeeded more than once, simply because they were Tier 7 and could move so quickly through the rubble. But the greatest damages were mitigated.

She saw they were about to move again and raced around their projected path. They always moved back into the central, deserted portions of the city between strikes.

They were about to hit her team's location, and now was her time to strike.

The army assassination test had given her far more than she expected. Going in, she thought it would just be a practical test, one and done. Instead, it was a series of puzzles that she had to solve in real-time, while stalking and killing a foe. There were dozens of tests with a theoretically infinite number of possible solutions.

She failed the first dozen scenarios, but eventually she adapted and started succeeding. By the end, she was almost always killing her target without being spotted. She knew her Talent made it easy for her to do some of the shadier things in life, but she learned through the training that she had quite the knack for it, too.

Worse yet, she *enjoyed* it.

But that was a problem for future Annie. Now, she got to revel in it.

The group of Tier 7s moved forward to attack her team, and she waited on top of a collapsed roof.

Loading Matt's golem crossbow with a special bolt, she waited for the right moment. Matt, the competent idiot, launched an attack at one of them, causing the attackers to charge, so she was rushed.

As the Tier 7s came within proximity of her traps, she launched the detonator bolt at the bomb wedged into the rocks. She was already sliding down the roof when the explosion went off.

In a white-blue flash, one of the mana bombs Matt had charged for her detonated.

Using a shadow to conceal her, Annie waited as a retreating Tier 7 ran past her so close, she could reach out and touch him.

So, she did exactly that.

Grabbing a shoulder pauldron, she pulled and jumped, raising herself onto the stumbling man's upper back. A quick flick of her knife ended the man's time in the war, before they both tumbled to the ground.

Rolling off, she broke into a sprint, off to find and hunt the other teams.

She tried to remove the smile from her face.

Somehow, it kept slipping back.

Matt looked toward the explosion and concussion force coming from an area behind their defensive lines and shrugged after ordering two teams to watch their rear.

If Annie was handling it, he could worry about other things. There was a frontal assault to deal with. He doubted that this was the last time they would try this strategy on them either. So, they needed to prepare more substantial countermeasures for the other teams out there. It wasn't as if the queendom sent only one drop pod of fighters, or that they wouldn't send more.

The work never ended.

Three days later, Matt sat in a command meeting with the remaining staff. Their forces were down to seventy thousand men from their original five hundred thousand, and they were exhausted.

The queendom had battered them down with sheer numbers.

There was no respite from the waves of enemies. Even after adding another million to their casualty count, they were still outnumbered and outgunned.

At first, they had defended themselves well enough. Then, the queendom tried four more frontal assaults, before sending another larger wave of drop pods yesterday evening. Those troops focused on a concentrated push to take the city's west entrance. Between the combined tactics and dwindling defenders, they were unable to plug the breach, and the invaders started taking the city. With attacks from both sides, Juni was forced to call a full retreat back to his fortified position.

That was where the kingdom went from bleeding numbers, to hemorrhaging them uncontrollably. Under the waning light and with a swarm of Tier 7 hit squads running amok, there was little that anyone could do to make the retreat intact. The dropship teams had learned from Annie's ambushes and set similar explosives along the defenders' most likely avenues of retreat, further increasing the casualties.

So, they withdrew to the southernmost wall, and were holding a small fortification hastily created by the few surviving crafters that had joined Juni's group.

They had thrown in the towel. The city effectively belonged to the queendom at this point, and they were preparing for their breakout run.

The kingdom had bled the enemy, and made taking the city a living nightmare, forcing a little more than two million casualties. Four dead enemy combatants for every one of theirs lost wasn't a bad ratio by any means.

Even with the prince gathering a large force to harry the besiegers, they were still looking for an opening to break through. This would be their final shot. The enemy knew where they were pinned down and had excessively reinforced the opposite side of the city gate that they were pinned against. Attempting to retreat through there would be a suicide mission.

They were stuck.

But they had an idea. One born more out of desperation than solid planning. It wasn't remotely perfect, but it was their best chance.

Juni turned to Matt. "Is everything ready on your end? Annie is in position and the platform is made?"

They had been over this three times already, but the man was worried to the extreme. This was another risky plan after the previous two had failed, and it would be the last. It was imperative that they get the remaining fighters out of the city, as they had earned an absurd amount of points in the last week and a half. If they escaped, anyone here would only come out stronger, with possibly hundreds of thousands of points to spend.

That was something the queendom was keen to prevent.

Juni pulled back the tent flap and, not able to see much, said, "The sun is about to rise. Everyone, get to your positions. You know your jobs. I'll take the front. Follow my lead and stop for no one."

Matt and the other surviving leaders funneled out of the tent with somber expressions. Their odds of getting out of this weren't great by any means.

Nodding at the troops he passed, Matt climbed aboard the nearest wooden platform housing a mana cannon.

As the sun started to filter through the cracked stone walls, everyone stood without being ordered to.

Matt started charging the mana cannon. Most of the glow didn't escape the blanket covering its surface, but it lent an almost eerie glow in the predawn light. He had to spread his legs a bit to remain steady while the platform was lifted off the ground.

Ten men were responsible for carrying the makeshift weapon platform, with another thirty as backup. Two hundred men were in a block formation around them, to prevent the enemy from attacking the most vital aspect of their escape plan.

Everyone fidgeted as the seconds ticked by, but a massive explosion in the wall that the queendom had created to box them in signaled their time to move. They ran in the opposite direction with quiet steps. Screams and shouts echoed across the nearby portions of the city as they moved to the other side.

Matt lined up his cannon and fired.

The wall in front of them disappeared. The sparse queendom soldiers, unable and likely unwilling to throw their bodies in front of the remaining kingdom defenders, left them a clear path out of their encirclement.

He reached up and pulled the burning cloth off the mana cannon and readied his next shot. He held the cannon at full charge as they rounded a corner and reached the street that led to the western gate. They turned right and ran to the northern gate when the western gate exploded as well.

Annie had set the two modified mana cannons near each location and charged them with a few mana stones after Matt had gotten them most of the way there. A remote device that charged them with even more mana essentially became a massive improvised explosive, placed in distracting locations.

They were hoping that with the prince hitting the western city gate's defenders, they could clear the northernmost gate. The idea was that the queendom troops stationed there and at the southern gate would be moved to reinforce the western gate. The prince's charge would be the distraction they needed to escape.

In what felt like seconds, but was closer to twenty minutes, they were blasting through the half destroyed northern gatehouse and into the open air. They'd escaped the city, but they weren't safe yet.

The remaining encirclement was sparse, but that was only relative to the queendom's forces previously, at multiple millions strong. There was still a line of defenders that they needed to get through.

Matt and his cannon cleared a path through the defenders as best as he could. He aimed his shots at the biggest clumps of people in rapid succession.

Still, they were being bogged down.

At the front of the formation, Juni cut his way through the queendom fighters with a seemingly plain-looking stick. It clearly wasn't; it smashed its way through armor like it was wet paper, but there were no visible markings on it.

As they moved farther away from the city and deeper into the ring of enemy troops, their pace slowed even further, from a jog to a shuffle.

Between firing his cannon, Matt saw a fifteen foot tall wave of blood wash over troops in swirling patterns, freeing their men from being ensnared in a melee. Liz wasn't exactly going for subtlety with her attacks.

Person-thick bands of blood lashed out at anyone who strayed too close to her blood wave. Archers shot at her, but nothing seemed able to stop the juggernaut of a blood manipulator on a battlefield. Aster was clearly with Liz, as shards of ice were forming at the tips of the tentacles and attacking anyone trying to flank the golem.

Juni was also performing beyond Matt's expectations. He fought in a circular field of what Matt guessed was heavy gravity, from the way everyone around him moved sluggishly, and the grass flattened around him.

The prince's right hand man moved like a dancer with a grudge. He wove between attacks and used his stick to kill anyone within reach. A group of six Pathers charged him, and in the time it took Matt to charge and fire his cannon twice, they were dead.

Conor was near Juni at the front. A clear area slightly larger than his [Demon Zone] helped relieve the pressure slowing the kingdom fighters down. Based on the space being given to him, the man was clearly a well-known threat. No one wanted to enter his airspace, knowing that their own attacks could hurt them, while the man in the center was unaffected.

Annie was using her crossbow, but disappeared off Matt's HUD from time to time, so he assumed she was using her Talent when she could.

Like Liz, Emily was a tyrant, ruling the area around her. Just like during her time defending the berms and fallback points, she started with a [Cracked Mana Bolt]. Then, she rotated through [Water Bullet], [Fireball], and finished up with a truly massive [Bolt]. The electric spell jumped from person to person, devastating the enemy numbers. It also made her an obvious target, but she had six melee fighters as guards. They were hard at work keeping ranged attacks and other melee fighters off her.

It was an impressive sight.

Everyone on the kingdom side was fighting with everything they had. Matt saw abilities he had no record of, along with flying and weapon skills he had no choice but to envy.

But *he* had his mana cannon. Shot after shot raced out while he refilled the mana cannon as fast as it would cycle. People vanished with each shot.

As Matt attacked, more and more people started to target him. His carriers and defenders tried to help, but they were a long line trying to avoid being cut off and encircled. Firing backward to help the rear most kingdom fighters helped, but it wasn't enough. They were still slowing down.

Liz, in her blood golem form, roared past where Matt was shooting and smashed into an equally large stone golem. He worried that the fight would go the other golem's way, but Liz seemed to flow into the rock and annihilate it from the inside.

After her victory there was a cheer, and he turned to see that the leading element of their group had punched through to the edge of the anti-flight barrier. Juni was already turning around and moving back into the fighting. He made a beeline to secure the gap along with Conor and the other imposing fighters in the front lines.

Matt, atop his platform in the middle of the pack, was constantly taking arrows and spells. But he ignored them as best as he could. One spell dealt enough damage to [Cracked Phantom Armor] to break down the spell structure. Meanwhile, several arrows and a [Fireball] washed over his under armor and scorched his back. The only one he felt was the arrow that struck his side.

Not bothering with it, he kept firing. Time after time, groups vanished under the blue light of the mana cannon. Where he aimed, death followed.

His AI flashed as members of his team took wound after wound, helping to keep the breach open. Liz's entire head was flashing red with a myriad of wounds, but she wasn't in the worst shape. Emily was missing a leg and an arm but was being carried away with the retreating team.

Annie was mostly fine, with only a few minor injuries, along with Conor and Aster. None taking anything more than scratches.

As the midpoint of the retreating kingdom fighters was nearly through the opening, his instincts screamed at him to get off the cannon, and he threw himself back with a tumble. Snapping off the arrow still lodged in his side as he fell off, he saw a ball of purple blackness tear its way through the cannon and where he had been standing.

Matt followed the trajectory to see a lone mage with a staff capped by two orbs on each end. They were racing to close off the gap the kingdom had created and was holding. At the center of the staff was a light-swallowing darkness so black, the man's hand seemed to be holding space itself. Toward the ends, the orbs were a light blue and seemed to have sparks arcing off them toward the center.

Another ball of void simply deleted another swath of the few remaining kingdom fighters holding the line.

Matt rolled to his feet and rushed the mage. If he didn't take him out fast, the man might wipe them all out on his own.

Another ball of void gathered at the center of the staff and launched outward.

Matt threw himself under it and felt at it with his spirit sense as it raced above him.

It wasn't actually void. Or at least, not true void, like the mana he had gotten from his advertisement for exotic mana types. This was more like his Concept.

It was a black hole.

As Matt scrambled to his feet, he crossed the remaining distance to the man while another ball of black hole void magic formed.

He was two strides away; it was too late, and he was too close to change his trajectory.

The mage launched the orb at him, and Matt threw his left hand in front of the attack. It was a desperate move, as his armor was only partially effective against void aspected attacks.

He fully expected pain, and the rending of his armor and flesh to follow.

To Matt's surprise, the attack felt cold as it hit his palm and ate right through his armor. He almost thought it would be painless, but the agony was just delayed. When it did hit him, it was worse than anything he'd ever felt before. It was like pain boiled down to a concentrate and injected into his very being.

Feeling the spell hit a little resistance from his armor, he redirected all of the armor's power to his left gauntlet, just like he did when forming knuckle spikes. It seemed to help, but it really just slowed the spell down a little. The pain was immense and all-consuming as the spell progressed down his arm. It grew to such an intensity that Matt blindly threw everything he had into it.

His Concept's repelling power flared to life and countered its inversion's pull with its own push. The clash of his will against another told him the mage had a Concept of his own as well.

Matt refused to lose, he refused to go down after so much struggle. He pushed everything he had into his left arm, and the spell stalled from its racing speed to only inching forward as it ate away at his armor, Concept, and arm.

It seemed like no matter what he did, the attack kept creeping forward.

To the inevitable end.

Time slowed, and his attention narrowed down to just this single moment. He tuned out the battle around him. Gone was the lost defense of the kingdom city. Gone were his AI's blinking damage indicators for his friends.

None of it mattered anymore.

It was just him versus the void.

If he died, they all might die. Void mages were *that* dangerous.

The fact that the mage wasn't in standard armor and had a Concept told Matt that he was a Pather. It explained why he was having such a hard time overpowering a Tier 6. Only another exceptional Pather could make him struggle like this.

Matt refused to listen to the pain radiating up his arm, or the weariness of his Concept.

He was endless, and would not give in.

Luna, Kurt, and April watched Matt take the void attack head-on.

Luna lost control of herself, and a toothy smile snaked across her face. April was wringing her hands with worry, but she would learn. These moments of danger were how you pushed children to be the best they could be; to reach their true potential.

With an effort of will, she blocked the army watcher from interfering. They should know better by now. She had prevented several true deaths in this siege already.

She earned this moment.

This was the perfect opportunity to see how far the boy could reach inside of himself. She couldn't have asked for a better match-up if she had set the fight up herself. Black hole versus white hole Concepts. It was perfect.

It was a battle of will, determination, and grit.

There wasn't a chance in the multiverse that she would let the army interfere with this moment. Matt wasn't at any real risk, and she had better speed and control than any of them. The rescuers removed people when *they* could save them. At her Tier, she could ride the edge so much longer, especially with someone as durable as Matt. Besides, his little healer friend was somewhere on the planet, so Luna would whisk him away before his head or heart was completely vaporized. She was ready for every possible outcome.

He wouldn't die. But he might feel like death if he lost this contest.

Her newest protege let loose a scream of weakness, hate, and defiance—a scream against the world. She had heard it so many times before as people found where their true limits lay. Most people had far more to give than they thought.

Luna strained to keep her tail from materializing and swishing. If he dug so deep on his own, she could only dream of what he would accomplish with her…*loving* guidance.

One day, he would look back at this fondly.

Eyes wide, she watched with [Perception] draining her massive mana reserves, and her mental cultivation dilating her perspective. She wanted to catch every microsecond of this; every detail.

Flesh and blood vaporized as she looked on. She was ready to step in if need be.

But she expected a better outcome.

Matt could feel the ball of void growing weaker and weaker. The will behind it lessened until he pushed the black hole back long enough to expend its power. He stood there, utterly spent.

His Concept was beyond empty, and he felt like a towel that had been wrung to the point of tearing.

But he had won.

One arm was outstretched and gushing blood at the concave point where the orb had eaten at his flesh. The wound was causing him to get more and more light headed with each heartbeat.

Matt met the eyes of the mage in front of him, who stood panting with pale disbelief written across his face and gave him a grin of victory. He reactivated [Cracked Phantom Armor], staunching the blood loss, and pulled back his sword. He moved to drive it through the man's unarmored chest, when a familiar blood-soaked spear blew a hole straight through the mage's heart.

Liz's golem ran past him, smashing through another line of queendom fighters.

Turning to face the enemies around him, Matt roared at them and charged, sword glowing as the mana he was storing with each step increased. He raised his weapon, but no one was willing to meet him. They all scrambled away to clear his path.

With that, the last defenders of the kingdom city cut their way free of the fallen city.

19

Prince Albert watched as his surviving defenders streamed out of the north gate once he retreated from his decoy attack on the west gate. He was glad for his helmet, as it hid his smile. The smile felt impossible to remove, but with effort, he kept it off his face to issue a few commands.

After a week and a half of brutal bloodshed and determination, the queendom had finally taken the city. Despite the loss, things went far better than he could have ever hoped for, with the escape of his top earners, too.

Things were looking up.

His grin slipped out as he watched the soldiers filing into the rubble that was the razed city. His enemies had fought, bled, and died for the city. After such a costly victory and rebuild, they would naturally treasure it, and hold the city close.

Exactly where he wanted them.

Albert smiled and turned to leave the anti-flying formation with his men.

This had been a great success.

Princess Sara stood outside a daunting metal frame. It was the door she'd been staring at for the last ten minutes. This meeting would not be pleasant.

Finally, she lifted a heavy hand and tapped on the door twice. The gesture didn't even echo. The door behind her slid shut, and the one in front of her opened as the seal completed.

Her mother sat at a plain wooden table, watching a projected map of the planet spin at its center.

Diana smiled at her daughter and lightly patted the seat beside her. "Come sit, honey."

With considerable effort, Sara resisted the instinct to slouch down and slink toward the couch. That would only make this worse.

Her mother popped a brush out of her storage ring, and as she was reaching to brush her daughter's hair, she paused. "Dearest, when was the last time you showered?"

The affectation gnawed at Sara. Her mother's Tier was so high, she'd known the answer was 'days' the second the door was unsealed. When it was just family, the queen always pretended that she was no stronger than anyone else. As a child, that was wonderful. As an adult, it grated. Preferably, her mother would have just called her out instead of babying her like this.

"Mother, it's been incredibly busy the last week. I…"

The queen tutted at her. "Ah, ah, ah. Young lady, what do I always say about appearances?"

Sara let out a heavy sigh. "One's appearance is a weapon like any other. And only a fool allows their weapon to rust."

"Go enjoy a hot shower. Then we'll discuss your latest plan."

Diana sent her off with a gentle smile that made this whole debacle a million times worse. Resigned to her fate, she headed toward the side door.

Normally, raiding her mother's bathroom was a great time. Compared to most people at her Tier, Queen Diana cared little for the trappings of wealth or power. Even this temporary apartment housing her during the war lacked even a single piece of decoration. There was one major exception though. The plain walls outside were in stark comparison to the opulent white marble lining the bathroom, and the luxuriously thick high-Tier rugs felt like standing on clouds, almost literally.

Her mother always splurged on one same thing. Sara wasn't surprised to see the bathroom decked out to a degree that more than made up for her mother's frugality elsewhere.

Stripping her clothes and armor, the items vanished before they even hit the ground. Sara still wasn't sure how that worked. Maybe it was her mother or some automated system in the bathroom. All she knew was that by the time she was done with her debrief, everything would be immaculately cleaned and returned.

Sara stepped into the gentle rain pitter-pattering down in the spacious shower. Turning on the jets, she gradually increased the pressure until the hurricane pounding down on her started to hurt a little. For five minutes, she stood there brooding until she was able to tear herself away to actually clean herself.

It felt…good. Better than she'd admit. The shame of her disaster of a plan wasn't gone, but it felt marginally less important. It was over, and she needed to accept the outcome of the siege and move on to the next plan. After choosing from among the dozens of soaps and shampoo pairs and finishing her shower, she exited the room in the fluffy bathrobe that was hanging next to her mother's.

Right before leaving, she'd poked her mother's high Tier garment, but her finger indented instead of the light blue fabric. Phooey, that meant it really was her true robe, and not a prize for Sara to steal. The higher Tier material was light as dust, but her mother rarely let her steal it.

The queen sat waiting for her daughter to finish. As soon as Sara appeared, she patted the chair in front of her combs and brushes. They were at the ready, hovering around the spot where her mother wanted her to sit.

Sara sat and let the queen mother her for a good five minutes. She relaxed into the soothing feeling of the brush gently working its way through her hair.

Sensing she was ready, her mother asked, "So, what went wrong? What went right? Start from the top."

The lack of condemnation rankled. She felt as if she deserved it, and its absence only made her guilt even worse.

"We took the city but lost over one thousand important small forts that guarded strategic resources. Seven hundred medium forts and thirty large forts." Sara ground her teeth until her jaw hurt but finished her summary, "The city was leveled and will take at least four million points to start the rebuilding process. And their final defenders escaped with their points. It was a disaster, Mom!"

She hated how petulant she sounded at the end. Her mother's gentle brushing of her hair and the comforting pat on her arm were like nails scraping down a chalkboard to her guilty conscience.

"Where did it go wrong?"

Sara wanted to blame Albert and his overly competent second in command, but that was petty and unhelpful. *She* should have anticipated everything better. That was her job.

"I was overly ambitious with the idea of moving so much earlier than in a normal war. I thought if we could take that city fast, we could spread out and hit multiple places at once. Possibly even surround a second city and siege that down as well, over a longer period of time. If I'm being honest, I was far too greedy."

That wasn't actually true, and she corrected herself, "No…I was overconfident. On paper the plan was sound, but didn't account for the Pathers, and things like the modification of equipment." She chewed on her lip and continued on. "I only thought in terms of standard specifications, which doesn't account for the chaos of a real battle. That's what led to the formation pillars getting destroyed, and the Kingdom of Seven Shits being able to fill the city to the fucking brim with troops."

"What else can you say? Both the good and bad. *Be objective.*" The last was the gentlest of reprimands, but it stung.

Sara thought over her decision leading up to this point and sighed. "I shouldn't have gotten hung up on taking the city with minimal danger after the initial plan failed. Our losses were heavy, and we… No, I…" Sara took a deep breath. "I should have ordered them to fully bombard the city and just accepted the point cost to fix it. Because of my inflexibility, now I not only have to pay the rebuilding cost, but also have two million soldiers cooling their heels in recovery."

"Good. Now dearest, what are your next plans going forward?"

"We hunker down and wait for the numbers to even back out. We just need to survive this next week. Once all of our troops are back in the field, I'll take back our forts. With a few exceptions, I doubt Albert plans to hold on to them. Almost all of them are too far outside of his zones of control for a permanent transfer to be feasible. It was a way to punish our concentration of forces, nothing else. But it worked. They took a huge portion of our highest-earning locations." She paused and said, "And we probably won't get them back in a functional condition. Shit, I need to be ready for that."

Queen Diana poked her in the rib, causing Sara to jump and glare at her mother, who ignored it. "Don't get distracted, honey. Anything else?"

Sara thought about keeping her thoughts to herself but finally said, "The Pathers. Their performance was well beyond my expectations. They were pivotal on both sides. They made the city much harder to breach and were also the ones responsible for finally breaking through the kingdom's defenses. Though our dropships played a large part in that as well."

Her mother just hummed at her to continue, so she did. "Their leaders were monsters, one of them in particular. And the other Pathers were a much tougher nut to crack than expected. I have good combat analytics on most of them, which honestly might be worth the cost of all the dead soldiers."

She flicked a finger at the projector, and a collage of the two dozen most influential Pathers appeared on the screen for her mother to view with her. This entire apartment was locked down to prevent her mother from interfering in the war, and information was strictly controlled. The only exception was what she brought in during these reports. Her intelligence teams had scoured all over to find out what they could about the most notable Pathers. All that information was listed under each picture.

Sara had already reviewed the information, but not much stuck out. So, when her mother visibly stiffened, she spun to question her.

"What!?"

Her mother smirked at her and said, "That explains a lot."

Sara started poking her mother back, but the woman didn't even notice it. The woman wouldn't have noticed if Sara had fired a mana cannon in her face.

"I was wondering why they slapped me so hard. This explains it."

"Slapped? What?"

Diana reached up and parted her robe to expose her upper chest. Sara gasped when she saw her mother's beating heart through a perfect, handprint shaped hole. The flesh around the hole was imbued with purple-tinged, void-aspected mana that gave the wound an ominous feeling.

A hand around her mother's heart was not a subtle threat.

"What the flying fuck is that!? Who did that to you? Mom!"

Her mother closed the robe she wore and tried to soothe her daughter, but Sara was far too shocked and angry at seeing her powerhouse of a mother so injured.

"What did I say about language!? And honestly honey, it's fine. I tried to peek out of here when the war settled into a rut. I'm a higher Tier than the general, so I figured the risk was minimal. Well, I was wrong, and someone instantly put me in my place." She pointed at the gaping hole where the wound was. "This is my spanking, so to speak."

"Who could have possibly hurt you, Mom?" Sara knew her mother was strong. The queen was one of the strongest fighters of her Tier and was known to punch up a full Tier. Not once had she ever seen her mother with an injury that lingered. This was disconcerting.

"Well, I'd assumed the Emperor sent a few hidden watchers, but your report makes the real reason obvious."

Sara turned to see a redhead's picture expand until it filled the screen. She analyzed the picture like she hadn't done so half a dozen times before.

Elizabeth Moore. The woman headed the Pathers' Union, as they called themselves, and was a blood manipulator. She had way more than her fair share of kills during the siege. She was certainly attractive enough, if you liked sharp features and yellow eyes, but that was about it.

Her record seemed remarkably ordinary.

"That's Elizabeth Moore. Youngest daughter to Leon and Mara."

Wait, what?

Sara stilled and reviewed to make sure she hadn't misheard her mother. But upon replaying the words in her head a second, and then a third time, she realized she had indeed heard correctly.

"What!? How? I thought they hated each other. How do you know? I found nothing like that from our reconnaissance." She didn't doubt her mother, but she couldn't believe it. How had her intelligence teams failed to find something like *that* out?

"I was there when they introduced her as a baby to the court. Our queendom is one of the ones that report to Leon, after all. It was a massive affair. The celebration lasted a full month. Good times."

The screen changed to show an older, feather-headed, clone of Elizabeth holding a little baby with a wide beaming smile and showing the infant off to a crowd.

"I gave thought to getting you betrothed to her, but I changed my mind after Mara threatened to cook and eat alive anyone who made such an offer. Apparently, they've had problems before with people hounding their children, and I fully believe she would have made good on that threat, so I kept quiet."

Diana shrugged, unconcerned. "It definitely explains a lot. I wondered who could injure me like this so easily, and Elizabeth's presence explains it. You know we wondered why we were given leave to start this war. It was a long shot; we didn't actually expect the Emperor to approve, but it cost us nothing to try. When he did approve, I figured that the kingdom had angered the Emperor somehow. Then it was announced to be a Path War, and I had to assume that was his reason to allow us to attack. But couldn't discern the true reason why for the life of me. But now...now, I think this entire war actually was allowed as an excuse for the Pather training. All so *she* could get some real experience."

For a Path War of this size, Sara couldn't imagine the expense. When this had first been announced, she'd asked her mother about the costs, and was informed that the entire queendom couldn't have afforded the expense of transporting everyone across the Empire like this. They couldn't have even gotten everyone here, let alone paid the cost of the rewards. She corrected herself, the greater than average rewards. The Tier items weren't that much of a surprise, but the item from Madam Renaissance was a shock to everyone, including her mother. That was above and beyond any normal rewards. And then, add on the expenses from having an entire army battalion watch over it. But, apparently, the Emperor was doing it for the daughter of two royals. That was mind-boggling.

"But why would they attack you, Mom?"

"If this was set up to give her experience, they really don't want interference from higher Tiers. If I meddled in the wrong way, it could have ruined their entire reason for the war. Knowing what I do now, I'm glad I wasn't just killed out of hand."

"But she's on The Path. How can they have the help of someone strong enough to hurt you?"

Her mother laughed. "Oh, honey. Mara and Leon are Tier 48. If they want a few million Tier 35s to do something, they will flock to their cause. Even their table scraps are worth more than our queendom. Sending a Tier 40 to protect their daughter is the matter of murmuring a suggestion, or expressing an offhand concern. That's all it would take for Elizabeth to have enough protection to fight off another Great Power. I was potentially going to spoil the point of this exercise with a little good-natured cheating, and they weren't going to tolerate that. So, technically, they didn't help her. They just enforced the already established rules."

She exposed her wound again and poked it. "Originally, I was under the impression that only a Tier 37ish was sent to watch over the event, and they used all of their power to pull it off. But with the control and damage done, I'm pretty certain it was a Tier 40 or higher."

Sara's mother grinned at her green daughter. "Look at this. This is how you properly warn someone. Attack without being seen and without explanation. You proclaim to the target that their life is in your hand. The wound is so slow to heal, it will take a few years to completely recover from it. This lingering void mana is just a hair less damaging than what my regeneration can deal with. A perfect message."

"But what do we do, Mom? Should we avoid her, or surrender?" Seeing the incredulous look on her mother's face, she continued, "I get that the watcher doesn't want you to interfere, but what if Elizabeth throws a hissy fit at us and decides to run to her parents? We can't survive that kind of disfavor. Even if they didn't move themselves, people trying to get in their good graces would crush us. It might be better to just lose and back out of this."

Diana smiled and caressed her daughter's face. "You always think ahead. That's why you are my heir. But while your concerns are valid, I doubt it will come to that. I'll have to ask a few of my contacts, but last I heard, the youngest daughter was trying not to lean on her parents. She wants to make her own way. She *did* run off to The Path, after all."

Sara scoffed at that. The woman had 'lucky' encounters where people in the shadows placed items for her to find. The same tactic was used by her own nobles. It gave the heirs of their houses a false sense of pride and accomplishment to earn rare rewards after delving dangerous rifts. It wasn't as if a Tier 5 could sense a Tier 20 staging a play around them from the shadows.

She abhorred that kind of willfully ignorant noble. They were the worst kind of privileged, and she strove for a higher standard. Her glory would be her own, not earned from riding on the coattails of her mother. Elizabeth had impressed her before this, but that was now tainted by the knowledge that everything was handed to her.

"Don't look so suspicious. Even the Emperor wouldn't dare to cheat in The Path, he's too invested in it. Start a war that benefits everyone which just happens to include her right now? Yes. Let her break the outright tenets of The Path? Not a chance in the multiverse. He cares far too much for the sanctity of The Path to let anyone, even his royals, interfere. Since Leon and Mara came up on the Path as well, they're unlikely to undermine the rules either. If anything, they probably see this as Elizabeth following in their footsteps. Given their personalities…"

The queen's cheek twitched ever so slightly. "Actually, let's not go into that. As for how to handle young Elizabeth, act as if she's anyone else. Don't single her out for special treatment, good or bad. Worst comes to worst, we rid ourselves of blame and suspicion by having acted no differently. It would look awful if her parents were to be mad at us for simply playing our part in this act. At their level, they can't open themselves to criticism from their political opponents so easily. Act no different, and do not share this information with anyone under your command, so they won't either. The only reason I'm even telling you is so that you can make subtle moves to improve her impression of you, and by extension our realm, when the opportunities arise. She will be an excellent connection to have. No one stays on the Path forever, and you should sow the seeds for a better relationship a few centuries from now."

Her mother pointed off to the side. "But I warn you…do *not* make it seem like you know who she is. Better to give no impression at all than one of sucking up. A royal darling like her doesn't run away to The Path because they *like* sycophants."

Her mother lazily ran a finger down her chest over the wound that was now hidden to Sara, and patted the seat in front of her as the brushes hovered back into easy reach.

"Moving back to the battle for the city, what do you intend to do now?"

Shifting mental gears took Sara a moment, but she dutifully allowed her mother to start plaiting her hair as she organized her response.

"I have no intention of letting what I did to Albert happen to me. Starting immediately, I'll have the cities act as hubs for the troops instead of the neutral city. It will increase the overall teleportation costs to move them, but it will also prevent a single city from being overwhelmed in a surprise attack. Next, I'll move to take back our forts and prevent the kingdom from tanking our point generation any further. Then, I'll prioritize rebuilding the conquered city, so it isn't a point sink. Simultaneously, I build up our troops and prepare for a larger defense. I'm sure Albert will be on the offensive soon."

"All good starts. What did you personally learn?"

Sara thought over what she had learned from this debacle. If one of her tutors was asking, she would just say what they wanted to hear. But her mother wouldn't judge her, even if she said everything she had done was perfect. She'd lose some respect for her daughter and express her dreaded disappointment, most certainly, but she wouldn't seriously reprimand her. Sara never had a problem admitting her faults, whether to herself or others. Mistakes were only a bad thing if you repeated them.

"I need to be more flexible with my commands and plans. That includes having more contingencies and giving my generals more freedom. When they insisted taking the city without damage was a lost cause, I should have listened."

Sara felt a kiss on her head and her mother pulled her into a hug. "Excellent, dearest. You know where you want to take things next, now you just have to work for it. I have dinner coming in an hour, and a new episode of Samantha Siblings came out, so let's watch that."

Matt was having an awful time, even as they were met by relief teams lying in wait at the edge of the anti-flying zone. All of the remaining defenders were picked up and carried off, while a screening force blocked the still floundering queendom forces from pursuing.

On top of missing an arm, again, he generally felt like shit. After seeing his team's health readings, sitting still just made him feel even worse. After struggling his way free of the confused woman evacuating him on her flying cloud, Matt pulled out his own flying sword and bulleted off to check on Liz.

She was currently in the makeshift flying infirmary that the evac team had brought along. In reality, it was just a flat platform with an angled wall to block the wind, being carried by six people on flying devices.

A man tried to stop Matt from stepping onto the platform, but Matt ignored him. When the man started getting confrontational, he waved his stumpy arm as an excuse, which seemed to settle things down. Before hopping off his flying sword, he ordered it to fly next to them, and went to find Liz. She was being tended to with a miserable looking, soot-blackened Aster in her lap.

Multiple healers were working on her, but Liz looked awful. Whatever they did, it didn't seem like it was doing much. The left side of her face was seared to the bone, and the remaining flesh resembled melted plastic more than skin. It was gruesome, and a hate erupted in Matt's chest. He wanted to go back and massacre whoever had hurt Liz so badly. With effort, he forced those feelings down. He had done just as bad, if not worse, to others.

For her part, Liz just grinned at him with the intact half of her face. "Seems we both got fucked up right at the finish line."

"Are you okay?"

That felt like a supremely dumb question, but Liz shrugged lightly. "An exploding fire arrow went through my blood pool and hit me. I still blocked most of it, otherwise I wouldn't be here. Damn good shot though. Luckily, it doesn't hurt that bad. Most of the nerve endings aren't there anymore."

She reached up and prodded his still armored form and hovered her hand over his stump. "I'd imagine that hurts worse than this."

Her comment seemed to have caught the attention of a healer nearby. Matt waved them off when they stepped forward to help him. "The armor keeps me from bleeding out and I can maintain it long enough. Help someone else who needs it now."

Aster peaked an eye open, yawned silently, and then sniffed his arm. She said, "Smells like empty." She then sneezed a small cloud of ash, startling herself and all the healers around them.

Matt scratched his bond and comforted her. "It's okay. It will all be okay." He wasn't sure who he was really reassuring.

The three of them sat together until the flying convoy reached one of the large forts that the kingdom controlled. The prince had bought a teleporter upgrade for it and used it as the staging ground for the assaults around the fallen city.

Matt was just glad to be done flying on the jury-rigged infirmary. Now they could head to the neutral city and be transferred into the care of professional healers.

The worst injured were the first teleported out. Emily was wheeled into the first teleport, right alongside Liz. She was missing two limbs, and in dreadful condition.

Juni stood next to the teleporter and talked to everyone in line. He was mostly thanking them for their efforts and cracking small jokes about how rich they all were now. Smiles followed him, even though the ones he talked to were being carried with crippling injuries.

Matt hadn't bothered to check his points yet, and finally pulled up the screen for war contributions from the army AI.

Prior Total (last updated 11 days ago): 21,587 points.

TEAM MERITS:

(Calculated for Tier 6 Combatant).

- Enemy vassal killed, Tier 5. Worth 1 point. Performed 15,574 times.
- Enemy vassal killed, Tier 6. Worth 5 points. Performed 12,692 times.
- Enemy vassal killed, Tier 7. Worth 25 points. Performed 914 times.
- Repelled major assault on ally city. Worth 1,500 points. Performed 23 times.
- Destroyed major enemy siege asset. Worth 500 points. Performed 13 times.
- Constructed minor emergency fortification, crude quality. Worth 1 point. Performed 53 times.

PERSONAL MERITS:
(Calculated for Tier 6 Combatant).

- Enemy vassal killed, Tier 5. Worth 1 point. Performed 4,745 times.
- Enemy vassal killed, Tier 6. Worth 5 points. Performed 1,907 times.
- Enemy vassal killed, Tier 7. Worth 25 points. Performed 182 times.
- Repelled major assault on ally city. Worth 3,000 points. Performed 17 times. Leader bonus (lieutenant general, acting): 2x multiplier.
- Constructed minor emergency fortification, crude quality. Worth 1 point. Performed 19 times.
- Destroyed major enemy siege asset. Worth 500 points each. Performed 9 times.
- Delivered rallying speech to raise troop morale. Worth 2 points. Performed 1 time (limit 1 per day). Audience size bonus (2 divisions): 1.5x multiplier. Quality penalty (substandard): 0.5x multiplier. Effectiveness penalty (substandard): 0.5x multiplier. Reward of 0.75 points rounded to 1 point.

ARMY MERITS:

- Items and equipment looted but returned. Worth 27,874 points.

UNACHIEVED MERITS: For reference purposes only.

- Defend an ally city against a siege successfully. Team contribution (estimated): 50,000 points.
- Defend an ally city against a siege successfully. Individual contribution (estimated): 25,000 points.
- Play a major role in defeating a far superior enemy force (509K vs 2,949K). Awards 5.8x multiplier to all merits. Defensive advantage penalty: 0.5x multiplier. Final reward: 2.9x multiplier to all merits.

SUMMARY OF GAINS:
Team Merits:

- **Raw Total:** 127363
- **Team Multiplier:** 1x
- **Category Total:** 127363

Personal Merits:

- **Raw Total:** 120605
- **Personal Multiplier:** 1x
- **Category Total:** 120605

Combined Merits:

- **Sub-Total:** 247968
- **Total Multiplier:** 1x
- **Grand Total:** 247968

New Gains: 275,842 points.
New Total: 297,429 points.
Pather Team Ranking (Kingdom of Seven Suns): 1st place.
Estimated Daily Stipend: 5,000 points.

Matt whistled. That was a whole bunch of points, no matter how you cut it. The war was a little more than a month in, and he'd earned nearing a quarter million contribution points. Suddenly, the 1.5 million cost for the [Cracked Breach] skill felt within his grasp. His team had put in the work and were now being rewarded heartily. The double-dipping and the steady, albeit small, percent of the kingdom's total points would earn them quite a bit. But they earned more with grand feats of fighting.

That didn't even account for their first place in the Pather ranking. If they kept their position, they would earn around 150,000 total points each month just from the daily stipend. That was over half of what they'd earned for unsuccessfully defending the city.

When he scrolled to the merit for 'deliver a rallying speech', he was slightly mortified. Immediately, he decided to never mention that exact merit to anyone and moved onto the section for unachieved merits. The first two missed opportunities listed were straightforward enough, but he was slightly confused on the multiplier mentioned. As he focused on that item, a more detailed description was offered.

For fighting a significant battle (participants on each side exceed 1,000) as part of a far disadvantaged force, a multiplier is applied to merits earned during the battle. For fighting on the defending side from a heavily fortified position, this is multiplied by a defender penalty of 0.5x. Participants: 2,949,377 attackers versus 508,892 defenders. Final multiplier of 2.9x points applied (after defender penalty). Multiplier was not applied to point total as battle did not result in a victory against the enemy forces.

Now that *would have been amazing.*

If they had managed to hold out defending the city, Matt would be nearly halfway to earning the perfect skill for him. His musing of single-handedly blasting down city walls was cut short by their turn at the teleporter.

Juni clapped his hands together and nodded deeply at Matt. "Thank you all for your help. Without your team, I don't think we could have done nearly as well. I've already talked to the prince, and he intends to compensate you for the mana you supplied. If you were willing to help generate mana in the future…"

Juni trailed off, and Matt shrugged but nodded. "My Concept is beyond dry right now, but I'm happy to help for an hour or so a day to get some practice with my Concept. If the price is right."

The prince's right hand man just nodded, and offered him a genuine smile before patting Matt on the shoulder and moving down the line.

On the other side, they were quickly met with healers who rushed them toward individual rooms on wheeled beds. A woman with snake eyes smiled from under her mask and asked, "Is the armor keeping the blood restricted, and do you have the arm?"

"Yes and no. It was a void attack. The arm is gone."

She patted his still armored shoulder. "Well, don't deactivate the armor just yet. Once we get you in the room, I'll let you know when we're ready. Have you taken painkillers or had a pain reduction spell cast on you?"

When Matt said no, the healer put a glowing finger onto his shoulder, it sank right through [Cracked Phantom Armor]. It was an incredibly weird feeling. He instinctively knew that he could have resisted the spell, but it felt like healing, and the woman was strong. If he resisted, she could have shattered his armor.

But as the energy settled in, Matt yawned.

He was so, so tired.

As he heard the healer tell him he could deactivate his skill, he crossed his legs and passed out.

Matt woke up feeling good. Really good.

He checked his AI, and saw that only an hour had passed, but the healer was done with her work. A new left arm was back where it should be. Looking around, he found himself in a large room, with dozens of others in hospital beds identical to his own. He debated rolling over and falling back asleep, but then thought to check up on his team. After reading a message from the hospital AI, he rolled off the bed and onto his feet.

Per the hospital AI, 'You are on a two-week healing cooldown for the arm. Do not stress it with more than light activities for at least two days. Regular exercise can be resumed after one week. If you need to see staff for trauma, they are available now, or later at your convenience. Otherwise, you are free to leave when ready.'

His AI notified him that Conor, Annie, Emily, and Aster were together and not far away from him, so he moved over in that direction.

He found them loudly and aggressively whispering in the recovery room next door as soon as he opened the door.

Annie wanted to keep her twin sister in the bed, but Emily was struggling to get up. It was almost comical to watch. Annie tried to gently keep Emily down without jostling her sister's newly regrown limbs, while Emily tried to squirm out of her hold like a fussy toddler.

Seeing Emily's own fresh, pale-pink limbs, Matt rubbed his own left arm and sighed as he found no hair. That would itch like hell when it started to grow back in.

Aster leaped from Conor's arms to nuzzle into his. "Feel better? You smell better."

"Thanks, Aster. I do feel better." He dramatically swooped up his bond and smooched her on the forehead, getting a playful lick in return. He was impressed that she didn't even ask for ice cream and was worried for Liz.

"Matt! Tell Annie to let me up." Emily sounded frustrated.

Taking in the situation, Matt instead ignored the woman's plight, and joined Conor in watching the spectacle. A sibling argument was neither his business, nor something he was particularly interested in getting involved with.

He turned to Conor and quietly asked, "How're you feeling?"

The larger man nodded. "Just fine. I got off easy. The healers cast a spell and moved me right along. I saw that void ball attack. I was just too far away to help. Ballsy move, trying to catch a giant ball of death. One-handed, no less. Fucking impressive that you took that on, and shocking that they didn't pull you out immediately."

"I got lucky. Nothing crazy."

Conor rolled his eyes. "Sure, man. Nothing 'crazy.' Okay, those two are getting too loud, let's get them out of here. People are still sleeping."

With that, they herded the bickering sisters out of the room, to Annie's animated displeasure. She maintained that her sister needed to remain in the hospital for at least a few days after losing two limbs to a flaming sword. And while she did, Annie could get some assassination practice in, on a totally random and definitely not related target.

They reunited with Liz when she was wheeled out of intensive care an hour later. She wasn't asleep during her healing like Matt had been, and once the healers left, she pulled herself out from under the sheets and sat on the side of the bed.

She had the rest of her face back, but was bald where the skin had been regrown. The new skin was glossy smooth like his arm, but her other side was buzzed down to nothing, too.

She saw him peering and sighed. "Ugh. I'm going to need a hair regrowth elixir. I look like a ten-year-old boy."

Matt pulled her into a hug, only saying, "It looks fine. This is just different. Buy the elixir if you want, but who cares."

Their team moved out of the hospital at a tired pace, but in good spirits. Together, they ate a heavy dinner at a nice restaurant. It was amazing, though that could have been from eating something other than military rations for the first time in over a week.

Aster, having eaten her fill of ice cream and a beef shank, claimed to be suffering mental trauma and demanded a visit to the recovery ward. A worried nurse had apparently spoken to the young fox about mental trauma, and what they could do to help her. Aster hadn't cared much until one *particular* option was mentioned—animal therapy. When Matt heard Aster's claim, he immediately outed her for only wanting to chew on indestructible bunnies. To which she retorted that the bunnies were her friends, and he just didn't 'get' it.

No one else had the energy to stay up late, so they retired to bed early, with Aster whisked off to enjoy chewing on her 'friends'.

The predawn light was seeping through the windows when Matt woke up to use the bathroom, only to find Liz already out of bed and hogging it. After they both finished up, they slid themselves back beneath the covers.

Matt snuggled up to Liz, it felt so good to be able to hold her. After the hell they'd been through in the siege, feeling someone close to you, and knowing you were both safe was everything to them. He leaned in, giving her a modest peck on the lips. "We've been on the verge of death for days, and that's the best you can do?" Liz teased.

He brushed his hand up to her cheek before he pulled her in tight. "Not even close."

The next kiss was the most passionate he could ever remember. They both felt worn down by all the days of battle, so to feel something like this…they needed it. As their passion built up, they didn't stop each other. Not this time.

Matt reached for her shirt, trying to pull it over her head, and she smiled devilishly in response. "Sir Matthew, you dare threaten a princess's virtue?" she scoffed.

His lips curled in response. "I do."

In Liz's amber-yellow eyes, a flame lit. No longer caring for the silly restrictions they'd placed on themselves, she reached back for Matt. Her hands didn't even bother with his shirt, going straight for his pants.

It was a while before they came back to themselves, both sweaty and smiling. It was the happiest Matt had felt in a long time, embracing the closeness that they'd skirted around in the past, but now fully dove into. "I love you," Matt said.

"I love you, too," Liz replied.

Matt wasn't sure who moved first, but their lips started to meet. From there, hands slipped under shirts. Soon, the offending clothing was off and hitting the walls and floor, leaving them struggling in a tangle of limbs.

They didn't leave their room until well after the sun rose.

20

When Matt and Liz finally got out of bed, they ambled over to the shower and lost themselves for another good while, enjoying each other's company until their rumbling stomachs finally drove them into polite society.

Things felt new and fresh as they walked to run errands and pick up Aster from her sleepover in the recovery ward. Even the most mundane things felt brighter and more vibrant. Despite Liz stopping to get a hair elixir, and furiously scratching as her hair grew out nearly a foot, the morning was turning out to be enjoyable. The salon trimmed her hair back to its former length in short order, while Matt ducked out to collect his bond.

When he arrived at the hospital, a woman with slitted eyes, similar to the woman who had healed Matt the last time, was waiting for him. Their eye colors were substantially different, with this woman's being purple instead of green, so he was pretty sure that this was someone else. She didn't look particularly unhappy, just stern.

Matt immediately became worried just thinking about how much his favorite fox loved to chew on her rabbit 'friends.' He was right to be concerned, just for the wrong reasons.

"Are you Matthew Alexander?" The woman's tone wasn't necessarily unfriendly, but there was a tinge of something he couldn't place. Maybe disappointment.

"Yes. Is everything okay? Did Aster hurt one of the rabbits? I am so sorry if she did."

The woman sighed a little and seemed to relax at that, confusing Matt further.

She gestured backward through the door and around a tree in the recovery area, where Aster was pouncing on a cluster of rabbits. The critters took an opportunity to scatter when one presented itself. Two even teasingly jumped on Aster before scampering off to reset the game.

"The rabbits are fine. I'd be impressed if she even *could* hurt them. I have concerns about Aster though. She's very young, and everything I've seen suggests that she needs far more socialization with people her own age. Both mentally and physically. She's starved for that kind of companionship, friends on her own level. Her life needs to be more than just fighting."

Matt opened his mouth to protest but caught himself as he watched her prance after the rabbits. She looked so thrilled to be there, so young. He felt a pang of guilt. Had he robbed her of a childhood like he had been?

"Oh, fuck. I-I…"

Matt ran his hands through his hair and his mind blanked out. He had no idea what to do. Aster was always ready to fight and seemed to love it, but she was always with him and Liz. Always.

The woman softened further. "Take a deep breath. She's fine… mostly. Bonds from rifts tend to be more resilient than natural-born beasts. However, it's still critical to her long-term development for her to interact with people of her age. It's part of growing up. Honestly, I wish you hadn't given her the Fruit of Perfection. For all the benefits, she'll be at a weird place developmentally compared to other beasts. Still, I understand it was too good of an opportunity for you to pass up."

"I was sure that it would be a good thing. That it would make her a full member of the team, you know? Not that she wasn't before, but she wasn't able to…decide things for herself a lot of the time. If I left it up to her, she'd just eat ice cream all day. Did I hurt her?"

The woman patted his shoulder, and he thought to bring up her profile with his AI.

Healer Kelsey, Tier 17. Empire-registered healer specializing in beast medicine and psychology.

It made sense that she was bringing this to his attention.

Kelsey said as she pulled him forward, "She's fine. I was worried that you saw her as nothing more than a tool to use in fighting. It's rare, but I've seen it before, and with how quickly she's advanced... Well, I had concerns. Especially when I realized that she was faking mental trauma just for a chance to play with some other beasts without her bond around."

Matt opened his mouth to speak, but the woman continued before he could form a word, "Aster needs regular recreation time with people of similar mental and physical ages. Those two things normally work in lockstep, more or less. However, Aster's mental and physical development are off-kilter due to the Fruit of Perfection. That's going to make things trickier for her. Due to the fruit's effect, she's mentally more comparable to other beasts in the Tier 10 to 11 range. Meanwhile, the beasts in her own Tier are the ones she is best fit to play with physically, since higher-Tiered beasts could accidentally hurt her too easily. It would need to be a higher Tier beast that specifically knows how to safely handle a youngster, like our rabbit volunteers. She can't safely wrestle a normal Tier 10 beast, but that's who she'll best connect with emotionally and make friends with."

Matt felt the pit in his stomach continue to drop. Aster was like the little sister he never had. Realizing that he was failing her felt awful.

"Healer Kelsey, what can I do? I didn't know this was a thing at all."

"You just need to find other beasts, bonds or not, for her to interact with as you advance. Set up playdates and let her be the kid she is. Us beasts can grow up faster in some ways, but she still needs time with others who get her. Honestly, she's better than I expected, given her history. But still..."

Kelsey looked at Matt with an unsaid, 'If you care, you'll make sure she gets what she needs.'

Thinking about it, Aster was probably only doing so well because of Liz. That realization made Matt feel like a terrible person.

"Do I need to do anything else? Or better yet, is there some reading I can do about this? Maybe a raise a bond for dummies who got far too lucky at Tier 1?"

Kelsey looked at him and patted his arm again. "Relax. I'm grateful that you're taking this seriously, but this isn't a massive problem. Yet. Just get her a friend or two. Find the others with bonds around here, both on The Path or from the vassals. There are several groups that meet up for their bonds to socialize."

Matt brought them up with his AI, noticing that one was meeting tomorrow and in the Tier 6 range. He signed them up immediately.

"Otherwise, Aster is a very healthy fox who was even willing to let a few people in need cuddle her up. They didn't realize that she was in here for treatment as well. It speaks volumes of her character, and yours as well." The older healer sighed. "It's not often, but some people only see us as tools to be used." She didn't glare at Matt, but it was a near thing as she said, "Don't be one of them."

Matt normally wouldn't explain himself to a stranger, but the woman seemed to be worrying for Aster's best interest, so he answered in kind.

"She's like the little sister I never had. I grew up without my own parents, so I get it. I don't really think of myself as Aster's parent but as an older brother who needs to help her until she can take care of herself. Like how the orphanage brought us up. It was the best they could do. But I don't want her to lack anything she needs." He sighed as his bond nosedived a pile of bunnies, who scattered like leaves in the wind.

"So, thank you for bringing this to my attention."

Kelsey turned to him and proffered her hand. "If you have more questions or concerns, message me. I'm happy to help."

Matt nodded but was again cut off as Aster finally noticed his presence through their connection. She barreled into his arms and started recounting all the adventures she'd had with the bunnies.

With the guilt still eating at his gut, Matt gave the healer a quick wave and nodded along.

Liz was tired of paperwork. She was tired of people complaining to her.

Most of all, she was tired of Talous trying to hit on her. She needed to work with him, as he was the leader of the queendom's Pathers, but the man would not take the increasingly blunt hints she kept dropping about dating Matt.

Such comments were simply brushed off with some blithe response, and he would immediately compliment either her work ethic or her battlefield persona.

She was one more comment away from snapping at him, but she tamped it down. After all, she was a representative of all the Pathers on her side. If communication broke down between the Pathers on both sides, they would lose a lot of their leveraging power. Negotiations were currently in progress, and they couldn't afford to be disunited.

Talous had rushed at the opportunity to sit next to her, Over the course of the meeting, he had inched his chair closer and closer, until their arms brushed. She was one more scooch away from picking him up while still in his chair, and tossing him away with her blood.

Albert sat on the other side of the table with a majority of the people in his retinue surrounding him. "We don't like how people are surrendering. Specifically, the Pathers. We put a stop to it within our own troops, but I want to enforce a two-week ban on anyone who just gives up."

Liz repeated her prepared speech. "That only encourages fights to the death. I agree that ransoming them for half their points isn't the proper measure, but encouraging pointless death isn't a habit that anyone should be getting into."

Princess Sara glanced over to Liz. She had caught a flash of something, but it was too faint and gone too quickly for her to identify. Irritation was the most likely answer. Neither leader was pleased about Liz pushing back on this so much. Talous was urging her to accept their demands, but Liz adamantly disagreed.

While she hardly wanted to encourage surrendering at the first sign of danger, fighting to the death at every turn was just stupid. The stipulations that the vassal states had added to the rules made retreating without orders to do so count the same as a surrender. No exceptions. That was the main point she was fighting against.

Capture wasn't unheard of in real Tier 15 or higher wars. Ransoms and such were common enough and were easy ways to siphon wealth and resources from the enemy without bloodshed. Wars rarely devolved into outright slaughters where surrender wasn't accepted. Trying to keep the fighting somewhat civilized was the reason for rules of war in the first place. Even the Tier 40s refrained from killing everyone and being done with it.

Never accepting surrender was a step backward, in her opinion.

But, apparently, it was only her opinion.

"What do you propose then? We can't have people simply waving the white flag at every opportunity." The queendom's leader sounded exasperated.

Liz calmed herself and refocused. "I think enforcing a two-week cooldown on top of half the points is just too much. I also will not accept any change to the retreating orders. That's neither in line with real military operations, nor logical. If you don't want people to constantly surrender, you don't want them to recklessly throw their lives away either."

Prince Albert looked less interested than Sara, but it was one of the princesses' aides who pushed Liz. "What do you know about real war? None of us know how anything really works at that Tier. Yes, this is a game, but we must fight as if it were as real as possible, if we want to learn anything from it."

Liz actually agreed with that logic at its core and said so. "If we want to get good experience out of this war, yes, we need to take things seriously. But in a real Tier 15 through Tier 30 war, people surrendered if they were hopelessly outnumbered, or if there was no way to win. They are then usually ransomed back to their side. Look at any real war in history. Gastor the Valiant was captured some three or four times in the last Sect war. Each time, he was returned after a ransom was paid. That last time, The Sects forced him to sign a contract saying he wouldn't fight in that war anymore. But they still let him go, since he surrendered peacefully when there was no hope. He's just a *single* high profile example."

Liz really wanted to say her brother was in the army and had been captured twice and ransomed back the same way. Being the son of royals hadn't been the reason either, as his entire battalion had been captured and ransomed back. It happened back when he first joined the army and was only a private. It was also before their parents had passed Tier 35. They would have had zero influence if he had been killed off then.

Admittedly, it was true that wars played a part in population control, but no one wanted to create avoidable animosity and unending blood feuds. Even the Sects, who forbade their rank and file from surrendering, still readily accepted surrender. It was easy profit, after all.

Prince Albert shrugged. "If people stop surrendering at the very sight of the top Pathers, I'd be happy. I care little for how that gets done, though. We just can't have people taking the easy way out anymore, especially when they have a clear chance to win."

Liz nodded at him. He was offering her a bit of help, which she had mostly expected. The kingdom would be in dire straits if she asked the Pathers on their side to stop participating, even temporarily. But neither of them wanted to see that card played.

"I propose that we simply add in an addendum stating that if people want to come back immediately, they need to pay half their points back. But they can pay a quarter of their points if they wait two weeks. They can choose how they get back in, and the idea of waiting is already pretty painful."

Princess Sara shook her head. "It's not enough. There need to be firm repercussions for giving up."

Liz leaned forward and said, "I don't think that's accurate or necessary. It sets a bad precedent."

Talous shrugged as if it didn't concern him. "Anyone who can't fight and chooses to fight anyway but isn't willing to die like a true fighter is a coward. They deserve to be punished. I personally think that we should make surrendering worse than dying. Anyone who doesn't like it can leave."

Liz forced herself to not grind her teeth, but it was a practice of sheer will. Before the meeting, Talous had mentioned his thoughts, but had acquiesced to her suggestion.

Sara leaned forward to jump on the opportunity. "I'm happy to increase the punishment even further. It won't hurt you personally. We made sure to add a clause that anyone with a certain number of points is able to retreat. We wouldn't want the top people to get angry at us. We just want the rank and file to fall in line."

Liz looked to Juni, then Albert. "That's a short-sided idea that will only push people away. Remember why and for who this war is being held."

That caught everyone off guard, and most people looked around.

Talous leaned back in his chair until it groaned. "Who cares what the weaklings think. If they had the power to change things, they wouldn't be the ones affected. If they simply become strong enough, the detriments won't apply to them. It's a perfect way to keep the vermin in line and make sure the fighting is good."

For the first time, Alyssa threw her opinion out there. "The Crafter Coalition is quite unhappy with both sides right now and won't take any change like this lightly. Granted, most of the stipulations don't apply to them, but the restrictions on retreating are vague enough that they could be forced into staying during a siege. That's why they're fuming, by the way; they saw *twenty* crafters lose their lives because they couldn't get out of the city in time. On top of another two hundred that lost all of their workstations and crafting tools. That's a devastating loss to anyone not born to royal families, and not a single crafter on either side is looking forward to the next siege. If you wish to include a clause, then there either needs to be clear exceptions for all support roles, or I'll have to oppose it."

Liz was not pleased to be getting more support from the woman representing both sides' crafters, but she had to take what she could get.

Internally, she was surprised that Alyssa managed to keep her position. Apparently, the replacements sent to take over the queendom's crafters all refused to go through with it after talking to Alyssa. Rumor had it, she and Prince Albert had worked something out with the other side's crafters, but even Liz couldn't find any proof.

Liz shrugged as if she didn't care. "I refuse any agreement like this, hands down. Talous, I doubt that you'd have enough support to enforce a change like that. Some of the top people would agree with you without question, but most won't, because they'll be the ones screwed over. Without overwhelming support from the top, it won't pass without repercussions."

Albert tapped a crystalline finger on the desk. "Then we need to come to an agreement. I don't mind the proposed change." He nodded to Liz.

Now they were once again at a stalemate. There were two on each side, with Alyssa dancing in the middle, but leaning toward Liz. It had shifted from the Pathers Union working together to the opposing sides in the war teaming up against each other again. This wasn't the greatest precedent to set, but the situation couldn't be changed.

The argument spun full circle.

Liz could say, without a shadow of a doubt, that she hated politics.

———

Matt and Liz lounged together, watching Aster play with the other beasts and bonds around her Tier. At the healer's advice, Matt had immediately sought out a local play group. His bond was currently trying to extinguish a flaming lizard in a good-natured way, and stopped on her own if things got too close. They seemed to be enjoying themselves.

A bat with gossamer wings chased both of them, sending out little gusts of wind to harry the two from above. It was all incredibly adorable.

At first, Matt had felt slightly peeved at how hard Kelsey had come on to him about Aster. He took good care of her. But seeing her play, he could see how much good it did her, even if it wasn't as perilously necessary as she'd made him feel. Rather than ponder it further, he just thanked the woman with a short video of Aster playing. He was able to admit when he had faults, though failing here had particularly hurt.

Jeremy, the bat's bond, laughed and said, "Jasper always has a blast, but he's fixated on Aster's tail. It's quite funny to hear some of his thoughts."

Matt smiled. "Aster wants to put out the bad fire. She's quite adamant about it, but she's at least being careful."

He nodded to Rita, the fire lizard's bond, and she shook her head in response. "Chelsea will be fine. She can reignite or extinguish herself at will. She's enjoying the attention. A little ice will just slow her down a bit, nothing else. Honestly, I'm surprised Aster is so well-behaved. Both of our bonds are natural born, and we've found that some of the rift reward bonds can be a bit too aggressive in their play."

"Aster is a bit further along in the mental aspect than most, but she's always been playful. She loves to fight, yes. But she knows the difference."

Liz scooped up a snack and munched on it. She had just gotten back from the meeting in a poor mood. Though she went through the motions of making polite conversation, for the most part, she was noticeably quieter than usual.

The trio of bonds ran over to another group and started to pester four other bonds playing with a ball. A little tussle broke out when the three of them stole the ball, then dared the others to take it back, creating a new game.

Matt made a note to talk with Aster about bullying. Playing was fine, but he didn't want her to get in the habit of taking from others. Some harsh years in the orphanage had taught him that it was better to address it now, before it could become a real problem.

Eventually, as the bonds wore themselves out, Matt and Liz walked home with a stumbling, panting Aster. She was worn down from her afternoon excursion.

"How did the meeting go?"

Liz sighed and flopped into him. "Fine mostly. It took hours of debate, but we finally reached a resolution. The Pathers who surrender will have to pay half their points and stay out for two weeks, but I removed the blanket retreat clauses for everyone. Running away from a foe won't get anyone punished unless the AIs report it as a clearly winnable battle. It was the best I could do. Talous was less cooperative than I'd hoped. I'm pretty sure he and Sara are cooking something up. Seeing them join up, Albert took my side, and it went back to being the kingdom versus the queendom. Though, his disinterest in the argument was clear, which hurt our position."

"It seems like that was better than nothing."

Liz just kicked at the sidewalk. "It is. I know it's not a bad compromise. But that shithead Talous keeps hitting on me, which is beyond frustrating. I've told him more than a few times that I'm not interested."

Matt wavered over what to say. He trusted Liz, but wasn't exactly sure where it was his place to step in. She was more than strong enough to handle Talous, but it felt wrong to leave her to deal with it on her own.

"Can I help? With either issue?"

Liz patted his arm, "No. It's fine, just aggravating. The idiot was arguing that the top Pathers should get special treatment at the expense of the weaker Pathers. He's a short-sighted fool. His flirting would be easy enough to handle if I was willing to walk away, but I don't think anyone else on our side's upper echelons would be as pragmatic as I am. It feels like I'm the only one willing to make sure the weaker Pathers don't get screwed over. It also pisses me off that Alyssa made out the best of everyone. All the crafters will get reimbursements if they're trapped in a city like that again. But not for their materials at least, unless they earn it. If they don't willingly stay and don't help out, they only get paid out for their death, nothing else. We also put out a bounty on all top teams for both sides. If you manage to kill the top team, you get 10,000 points, as of now. That might change, but for now, our team members all have bounties on our heads when our healing cooldown times out."

Matt didn't see the problem there. "Seems fair enough. If the crafters don't help in the defense efforts, that's not unreasonable." He thought about the second part with the bounties. "I like the bounties. It can earn us a lot more points if we're careful. Sure, it puts a target on our backs, but that was inevitable after the siege. If we die, we lose access to our points, and that's a win for the queendom. Then, we won't be able to use them to power up during the war."

"It's not. But it's still bullshit that I was only able to get the agreement through with her help. Talous should have been on my side, but instead, he was deliberately fighting against me."

"Do you have a plan to handle him?" Matt assumed that she did. Liz wasn't as mad as she'd be if she was helpless against the man.

"Another bad thing. I had to make an open-ended deal with Alyssa to help her once in the future. But in return she's going to sow discontent with the crafters and lower-level Pathers by spreading all the bad ideas that Talous was spewing today. He'll lose a lot of support with that, and Princess Sara will be forced to either replace him, or let a dangerous element grow inside of her forces. Either one is a win for us."

Matt, wanting to lighten the mood, suggested, "We could always punch him. It might not help, but it would probably make you feel better."

Liz paused, then laughed so hard it woke Aster up. She questioned, "Who? What?" Then seeing no one, put on her best pleading face and asked, "Get ice cream?"

Still laughing, Liz scratched Aster and said, "Sure, let's get some for after dinner. But that's funny. I've been thinking about beating his ass all day. He's strong, but he's a melee fighter focusing on attack. I'm pretty sure I could take him." She smiled up at Matt. "We think alike."

After that, they kept things simple and light, just enjoying their time together.

Their two weeks of forced downtime were busy after being checked over by Melinda, who gave them all a clean bill of health, along with a little Overhealth to secretly remove the healing cooldown.

Not letting the time go to waste, their team trained as hard as they were allowed. They started with Concept-focused, minimal contact sparring. As they came off their healing cooldowns more, they ramped up to more practical sparring.

To everyone's surprise, Conor was the first to get his phrase, "Reflection." It wasn't the word that surprised anyone, just the fact he found it out of nowhere, during a break from being battered down by Matt and Aster's Concepts. The phrase gave him a bit more reflected damage to his opponents, while still taking none of his own.

That synergized lethally well with his new skill, [Parry], which let him deflect an attack's physical force back at an opponent, if timed correctly. Making him even more deadly was his second purchase, [Blade Arena], an expensive Tier 14 skill that made it so anyone wielding a bladed or sharp weapon took reflected damage whenever it moved. It made the man a true monster to face. Even Matt struggled with the barrage of attacks, though Conor quickly ran out of mana if he used both of his AOE skills simultaneously.

Conor's success gave Annie and Emily a kick in the butt that Matt wasn't sure was entirely good. They both redoubled their efforts, saying that if he got it, they should be able to get it as well. Emily was in a slightly better position, as she had touched upon something. But Annie was still in the dark, which wasn't helping her mood.

She spent all of her free time either meditating or training. A whopping 50,000 of her points went to hiring an Army stealth specialist to train her in assassination, counter-assassination, and espionage. Annie returned to their suite with a variety of bruises most days, but she seemed to be enjoying it.

Even with that as a springboard, she found nothing to resonate with, which only seemed to piss her off more and more.

Emily banked most of her points after paying everyone back, stating that she was saving for something. Rather than tell them what, she just smiled wickedly, telling them to wait and see. Matt did notice that she bought [Earth Spike] but figured it was just to increase her combo of chaining mana types. Her firepower was already scary with four aspect types. He worried that she'd actually kill someone with five if it got twice as strong. But during their sparring, he found that while the fifth hit was notably stronger, it wasn't exactly double the strength of the fourth spell.

After seeing his teammates spend some points, Matt wanted to buy the [Cracked Breach] skill all the more. But even if his team loaned him their remaining points, it still wouldn't be enough. Not that he had the courage to ask that in the first place. They all had items they were saving up for, and he couldn't ask them to put their own growth aside for his own.

It would be selfish and unfair for a skill he wouldn't even be able to cast in this war. [Cracked Breach] had an initial cast cost of 100 mana, which was 20 mana more than his current maximum. Ascending to Tier 7 was the only way to be able to cast it, and only Tier 5 and 6 Pathers were allowed here. He couldn't ask for help buying something that wouldn't help any of them get more points.

He was debating getting [Flamethrower] for 50,000 points instead. The Tier 14 skills were incredibly expensive, but Matt figured that the average Pather would be able to afford one if they saved all their points throughout the war. A channeled spell like that was perfect for Matt, but the price was prohibitive.

He also wasn't sure if he wanted to spend the points on [Flamethrower] when he also wanted the enchanting repository. But that also cost half a million points, and he wasn't sure that he could feasibly get both the repository and [Cracked Breach]. The only positive was that the repository could be purchased by any number of people, so he could try saving for the more expensive item, and then get the repository if he fell short.

Missions were on the horizon again, and that was his path to earning the vast amount of points needed. Things like the kingdom paying for his mana, and their slowly decreasing stipend padded his total, but wouldn't take him the distance. A part of him looked forward to the assassins coming. With Annie's help, they might just have a passive form of income via counter-assassination. Cashing in the points on an extra attack skill now might help him earn more points in the long run. And [Flamethrower] suited him perfectly. Over and over again, it all came back to points.

Liz kicked his leg. "What are you thinking about?"

He sighed and said, "I don't know what to do about our points. We have three days left till we come off the healing cooldown, and we have so many points on the line. We're good, but everyone is going to be gunning for our bounty, and then there's the tactical advantage of killing us. It's incredibly risky to hold this many points for the more expensive items. But not saving now might cost me [Cracked Breach] later. I want [Flamethrower], but is it worth getting it now for the added damage it will give me? The skill is also strong and could mean the difference between life and death. I'll lose a lot more than fifty thousand points if we die now."

Aster hopped up and headbutted his chest. "Noooo! Fire is bad. One fire, enough."

Matt reached for her, but his bond flopped over and rolled out her tongue, sending pretend 'dead' thoughts at him though their link.

Liz started rubbing her belly which caused a tail wag while she still pretended to have been betrayed by his propensity for fire spells.

"Aster, you realize that you have more than enough points to get a new ice spell on your own, right?"

Still with her eyes closed she responded, "Yes. I got one." She then sent him a mental projection of the skill she got. He was half afraid that it would be [Create Ice Cream] or something like that. But luckily, it wasn't. It was actually [Ice Pillars], which created a small area around the caster where pillars of ice rose to create some cover and concealment.

"I got fly!" He received a mental image of a flying fluffy cloud that acted like a Tier 7 flying device. That was actually a good purchase, so he sent proud thoughts to her. He ignored the fact that she got it because it looked like ice cream.

Her next purchase was less impressive. "I got. Ice cream maker!" A picture of a little box that created ice cream out of milk and mana came to him.

Matt rubbed his face. That was exactly what he expected her to spend points on.

"Anything else?"

Aster seemed to think it over, then nodded upside down. "Training. With Ice Wolf!"

Matt made a note to get her a little storage item that she could wear. But overall, he felt that she spent her points as well as he could have hoped for, and far better than he'd feared. She was still a kid at heart.

With her settled, Liz turned to him and said, "Get [Flamethrower]. It's a great fit for you, and it gives you a heavy hitting close range spell that you can just blast forever. Fifty thousand points is nothing to us right now. If you get it now, you'll probably earn more points in the next year or two."

Matt knew she was right, but if he didn't get the [Cracked Breach] because of it, he'd regret it forever.

Still undecided, he returned the question, "What are you looking to get?"

"[Crystal Armor], I need some more defensive skills, and something to stop me from getting exploded by an arrow would be nice. Plus, I'm optimistic that a crystal-based skill won't break from my Tier 1 Talent. At least, that's my hope." She considered Matt with an odd look and asked, "Have you ever heard of the skill [Torch Sprite]?"

Matt had not. Her expression piqued his curiosity though, so he immediately looked into it. [Torch Sprite] was a Tier 14 spell. It was both rare and expensive, not because it was strong, but because it was only found in a few known rifts. That, and no one farmed it because the skill was practically useless. For the cost of 100 mana, the caster summoned a single dim light 'sprite' that floated around feeding on fire. When fed enough, it would multiply and gradually spread out. The sprites were actually fairly autonomous, and if left to their own devices, would seek out new sources of fire to feed on when it got too crowded around the original torch. The spell was great if you only had a torch and needed to light a large area over a period of time. However, the Tier 14 skill [Light Orb] could be cast for just 10 mana, was immediately effective, and would hover anywhere you wanted around you.

There just was no comparison in their usefulness. Even then, [Light Orb] was more expensive than a light-rune flashlight which could run for hours on a little mana. Some night time festivals and outdoor venues used [Torch Sprite] for the ambiance, but that was about it.

No ifs, ands, or buts about it, [Torch Sprites] sucked. Except, Liz's Talent might change that. There was a possibility the skill would be shifted into creating an autonomous, self-multiplying, blood monster that sought out more blood sources to feed on. That was a pretty scary thought on a large battlefield. The skill could multiply nearly endlessly, just for the skill's initial cost of mana.

It all depended on how her Talent changed the spell. For that potential reward, it was still worth a chance.

"That would be interesting if it worked out the way I think it could."

Liz batted at his feet with her own. "Yeah. It's a gamble, but I think it could pay off big time if we get into another fight like the last one. I just wish there was more information about how much control the caster had over the sprites. The description is light on details, but the festivals that use it seem to keep the sprites contained and evenly distributed within designated areas. That's something at least."

Matt rolled back and forth in his chair. "It sounds like you're going to roll the dice on it regardless. Me, I'm still not sure if [Flamethrower] is the right thing to buy. Or at least not right now."

Liz poked him with her toe. "Just get it. You need the skill anyway, and the [Cracked Breach] isn't affordable." She lounged back and said, "I'm ordering my skills, do the same so we can save someone a trip."

With a sigh, Matt decided to take the plunge.

As a box with their skills fell from midair, she added, "We can always earn more points."

That was true, Team Bucket just needed to get back into the field. He and his AI had a plan.

21

Team Bucket cheated. Slightly.

They left the neutral city before their healing cooldown was technically over. They just walked out the front gate and flew to where they needed to go.

It was skirting the rules, if not outright breaking them. Anyone with a healing cooldown was to remain in the neutral city for safety, but with their contribution to the city defense, they were sure that half a dozen people were ready and waiting to kill them as soon as they were fair game.

Watching Annie have a conniption as she tried to assassin-proof their suite had been amusing, until they realized the implications. Subterfuge was the better part of valor, so they slipped out of the city the night before their designated time.

After hearing Matt's plan, the prince and Juni were more than happy to have them out and about. So, the team donned some half-baked disguises, made their exit, and were currently flying through the night.

Matt glanced at Aster and held back a sigh. His bond had gotten a custom-ordered flying device with a few interesting features. It was a cloud that radiated cold, which would help to keep her comfortable during warm summer nights. He liked that idea. He also liked that her cloud could compress into a snowflake brooch that she could clip to her collar.

The only downside was that the flying device distinctively looked like a scoop of ice cream, and apparently faintly tasted like it. His bond spent more time trying to nibble on her cloud than fly straight. After watching her fly in a way that would make a drunk seem like a reasonable driver, he requested access to link his and Liz's AIs to the flying dessert. It was just easier for everyone to have it fly in formation between them while the fox played around.

After an hour of circling while looking for pursuers, everyone gathered within a foot of Matt's flying sword and under an air shield, then hooked themselves up. Once everyone was in position, Matt flew them as high into the atmosphere as he could before breathing became a problem.

The Tier 7 sword was geared for high performance over efficiency, so it was faster than the average Tier 7 flying device, even when carrying everyone in their team. Between the air repulsion shield and the decreasing air resistance as they climbed, the team quickly reached their desired altitude and moved from there. After two hours, they stopped above a barren patch of low mountains hidden in a cloudbank.

After halting, they dug through dozens of spatially expanded bags to find the right one. Within the desired pack were the parts to their cradle, which was carefully assembled midair. Once it was finished and double checked, Matt flew his sword into a specially-made harness, which held the contraption aloft, and dropped down to the platform suspended underneath the sword. It swayed uncomfortably on impact. After a few quality checks, the others quickly affixed the short walls that would provide some measure of protection for the ten by ten platform.

As everyone else hopped on, Matt swished his hands in the water vapor that made up the cloud.

"Home sweet home."

Emily was bundled up in winter gear and glaring at him. "Put up the barrier, you dick. It's…it's freezing for everyone else here."

Matt noted their foggy breath mingling with the cloud and activated the air barrier embedded in the platform. It would keep the cold out, and with the heater that Liz was already setting up, it would get more comfortable shortly.

Everyone else besides himself and Aster was huddling up. He

brought out one of the two reprogrammed golem harvesters, linked it to the flying sword, and set it to hover above the cloud as a lookout. They could keep hidden, and their automated sentry would warn them if their cloud cover was going to dissipate.

Since the temperature was only tolerable to Matt and Aster, he started setting up the two tents that they had. He and Conor needed to share the twin's smaller, two-man tent, much to their consternation. The tent was suitable for the two shorter women, but it was downright cramped for even one of the two men. They both had debated buying another tent, but ultimately, they couldn't risk raising any suspicions about their plan.

Instead, they agreed to try 'hot bunking' the tent by sleeping at different times and swapping in and out. To that effect, they volunteered to take opposite watch shifts as much as possible.

After everything was ready, Matt brought out a utility belt filled with mana stones, ensured they were all full, and hung the belt under the flying sword from one of the cables. Someone on watch would have to refill the sword with 200 mana every hour, and the repurposed harvesters every two hours. Each pouch on the belt contained enough mana stones for one refill. He started the timer and sent them to everyone else.

He felt half tempted to try making a rift on the platform, but he didn't want to give that ability away, even to his team. Plus, it would create a spotlight on their hidden base for all to sense, defeating the purpose of all their preparation.

Aster was prancing around and pouncing off the platform, only to be caught by her new cloud. She then raced around, trying to munch on the clouds surrounding them. Seeing that she was keeping herself preoccupied, Matt slid over to the others' huddle and pulled out a camping chair.

"How's everybody doing now?"

Chattering teeth were the only answer he got back, until Conor made the effort to flip him the finger with a shaky hand. Matt laughed and sat back, waiting for the little area to warm up. Finally, the platform reached a bearable temperature, and the rest of the group started to perk up.

Matt asked, "Everyone gonna be ready tomorrow? Skills absorbed and new items checked? Let's go over our build changes so we can all be prepared."

They'd been through this already, but Matt wanted to double check that the team was on the same page. Annie answered first, "Nothing left for me to absorb. My trainer made me buy both [Lunge] and [Piercing Stab], which was absurdly expensive, even for a Tier 14 skill."

Still rubbing his arms, Conor spoke up. "[Lunge]? Seems a bit weird."

Annie rolled her eyes while cupping her hands over her warm breath. "That's what I said. I also ate those words. It's one of the better movement skills available for stealthier builds at our Tier. You know, before proper phasing and short-range teleports become a thing."

Everyone nodded at that and looked past Annie, right at Emily.

"I picked up [Earth Spike] and a new staff that emptied out the rest of my points. This baby heavily reduces mana cost, the speed at which I can cast, and the strain on my spirit from casting such strong spells. All of which will let me hit harder, faster, and longer. I also got some new armor, but that was relatively cheap."

Matt took his turn next. "I got [Flamethrower] and new under armor to fit under my Talent armor. Other than that, not much changed."

A still shivering, Liz still glared at Matt in his [Cracked Phantom Armor] and chattered out a terse explanation. "[Crystal Armor] and [Torch Sprites]. The armor is already absorbed. And tested. It worked as I thought, and I've got [Blood Crystal Armor] now. It gives me some much-needed defense. [Torch Sprites] hits my inner spirit tomorrow. We'll see how my Talent changes it, then. I'm glad they don't need to go to the core. Just inner spirit. Saved a day on each."

Matt had been present when [Crystal Armor] had reached her inner spirit, and she stopped cycling mana into the skill, causing it to settle into its new home. Once the skill came to a rest in her spirit, Liz received an automated message from the Emperor about the skill's effects. These messages were incredibly convenient, as they let her skip the painstaking process of carefully testing the skill and getting readouts of the new effects. Some skills could be dangerous to use after being converted with Liz's Talent. They'd yet to stumble on any truly harmful skills, but the possibility was always out there.

Skills were easily examined as skill shards, but once they entered the cultivator's spirit, it was exponentially more difficult to analyze the skills with the testing machines. With the equipment available to them, it was nearly impossible. It meant that Liz would have needed to meticulously test the skill and have broad preparations ready to counter any potential side effects. Matt was still worried. If any new skill targeted the blood inside her, she might not live through the adverse effects.

That was why Matt begged Melinda to be on hand during Liz's first use of [Blood Crystal Armor]. Thankfully, everything worked exactly as the message had said, and a reddish-gold armor that was half crystal and half-blood grew around her. Unlike with the original [Crystal Armor], she was even able to individually dissipate any damaged portions of the armor, and perfectly reform them with blood around her. It completely circumvented the usual drawback of needing to recast the skill from scratch when it was damaged.

No one was sure why the armor's color was tinted gold, but they speculated that it might be a reaction between the crystal and the Blood Iron she'd absorbed, possibly creating iron pyrite, better known as fool's gold with the mix of natural treasure and skill. Matt endlessly teased her about the double princess having golden armor, causing Liz to flush and give him the silent treatment for a good ten minutes to Melinda's amusement.

"My other skill will be ready by tomorrow morning." She finished by scowling at Matt, "You're a terrible boyfriend. I can't even steal your warmth."

Conor forced out through gritted teeth, "[Blade Arena]. [Parry]. New shield."

Since they had all trained with the man and his new skills, it was enough.

Seeing that Aster was still chasing the cloud cover, Matt spoke for her. "Aster got [Ice Pillars], which will give us some terrain manipulation powers."

He refused to talk about her ice cream maker. Everyone already knew about it, as she had sat in front of it hour after hour, eating bite after bite of ice cream until she ran out of milk.

They sat around for an hour or two, and finally, it was just him and Annie left awake. They had the first watch, and it was finally warm enough for Matt to deactivate his armor.

He asked, "What was it like training with the army?"

"Ugh. It was awful. The instructor they had was everything I could have asked for and more, but he was incredibly demanding." She smiled into the cloud cover. "I already booked more training with him in another two weeks. I can't pass this chance up. He refused to tell me his Tier or really anything about himself. Even his name. He just told me to figure it out myself. But I bet he's Tier 30 at least. He's a ghost. The scariest thing is, he doesn't even have a Talent for stealth. He did show me that much. His Talent is just that armor protects him more completely."

Matt raised his eyebrows and said, "Seems like a weird Talent to go stealthy with."

"That's what I said. He proved his point, though. He's making me run the assassination and stealth operations without my Talent. It's hard, and I thought it was impossible until he limited himself to half my cultivation and ran all of them perfectly." Annie laughed. "I said he was cheating, so he had me devise a custom scenario for him to run. He's good. Really good. But he's also the biggest hardass I've ever come across. The man's standards aren't just high, they're damn near impossible. Still, he's a good teacher, and he actually explains what I'm doing wrong."

Matt thought about who he could get training with while he had the army personnel around. Even with his management team coming, he doubted it would come with free training from experts. The cost was sure to be heavy, either in Empire Contribution Points or raw currency. Either way, it wouldn't hurt to get some instruction earlier with the relatively easy to earn war points.

They continued chatting as their shift passed without incident.

The next morning, they put their belongings away and headed toward their first target. As they hovered at the edge of the anti-flying formation two miles up, everyone looked to Matt.

This would be suicidally reckless for anyone but him. His AI had run the simulations half a dozen times, but he still felt anxious to jump without his flying sword to catch him. Even having successfully executed the same stunt at Tier 5, his hesitation wasn't lessened.

After his team landed and crept into position at the edge of the formation, Matt checked his AI and rolled off his sword, hurtling to the ground.

Eric walked his post with the usual boredom that came with long periods of repetition. His squad was deep in queendom territory and guarding a Tier 6 gold mine. It was a functional mine, and the metal was actually there. With the kingdom having taken over a lot of forts that their side was trying to reclaim, he was left standing guard as a Tier 6.

It wasn't beneath him; it was actually a good example to set for the soldiers under him. But it was *dull.*

As he was turning to inspect the outer perimeter, he prepared to ask Janet if she had seen anything out of the ordinary. But suddenly, a loud boom accompanied by a wave of dust rushed out and covered him.

When the air finally cleared enough for him to see, there was a recognizable glowing figure before him that he had only heard rumors about. He never dreamed he'd ever cross paths with the real thing. The armored monster rose from the cracked paving stones and sprinted toward the gate.

Realizing what he was going to do Eric screamed, "Stop him!"

He put actions to words and charged. He didn't expect to survive, but the punishment for not trying would be far worse than a traumatic trip to the hospital.

An arrow bounced off the man as he brought a glowing sword down on the crossbar barring the door shut. The strike exploded outward in a flash of blue light.

Shrapnel peppered his face as the man parried his sword. Eric sidestepped and used the momentum to sweep low at the man's forward leg.

His Tier 7 blade just scraped along the armor, but that didn't stop him from ducking a return strike and backstepping.

Eric was about to re-engage when his world became awash with flame. He screamed from the pain, sucking fire into his lungs. Soon everything was black.

Matt kicked at the crossbar still holding the door shut while he bathed the area in front of him in an inferno.

[Flamethrower] was traditionally a spell that cost a minimum of 1 MPS, but he had modified the skill when it entered his spirit. He tweaked it to accept more mana throughput, rather than lowering the initial cost like most people did. He was currently pushing 15 MPS in the skill, which was the maximum it could handle before destabilizing.

That was more than enough.

The skill started as a cone of fire thick as his fist and expanded to a circle seven feet in diameter at the maximum effective range of thirty feet. He would need to narrow the aperture of the initial flame to increase the range farther, but that wasn't what he needed right now. The door just needed to be opened long enough for his team to join him.

Soon, a message came in stating that they were at the door, so he cut the mana flow to the skill and let the flames dissipate. The stones around him glowed red hot. Matt cast a quick [Hail] to lower the temperature of the gateway. Due to the rapid cooling, the ice popped and bounced, but Matt raced out of the interior front gate to rush the exterior door. The stonework could be heard cracking under the thermal shock, but it didn't sound dangerously bad, so he ignored it.

His team followed him up noisily enough for him to tell they were there. Judging by the loud cracks followed by screams, he assumed Annie was using her crossbow to good effect. Conor quickly came up alongside him, and together they battered down the door. The six of them rushed the fort, ignoring the defenders in front of them. Instead, they rushed to the stairs leading down to the mine. Half the team secured the stairs while the other half went below.

In all of thirty seconds, they found the storage bag for the Tier 6 gold that was mined here.

After checking the room-sized bag and seeing that it was more than three-quarters full, Matt shouted, "Got it! Move!"

With that, they charged back out of the fort, only returning fire enough to avoid being pinned down. When they reached the edge of the anti-flying formation, everyone mounted their flying devices and rocketed high into the sky, away from the now bustling fort.

Matt laughed over their channel as they celebrated their successful raid. This deep in enemy territory, they were basically attacking unprepared defenders. It was only meant to be a smash and grab, but they had made out like bandits.

We sort of are bandits, now that I think about it.

The thought amused Matt enough. When they stopped to rest high amid clouds, he was still chuckling.

"Let's get our bearings and hit our second location." Annie sounded as excited as he was and bobbed in the air.

Clustering around Matt, they used his faster sword and kept warm in the air bubble as they rose to three miles above the ground. The lower air pressure and resistance only allowed them to soar even faster. The next target, a Tier 6 iron mine, was a hundred miles away. They would be in place to raid it in about an hour.

This mine wasn't directly connected to the main fort, which was good news. The fort was large, but the mine was a quarter of a mile away, on the side of a nearby gully.

They repeated their smash and grab tactic, which was made easier by the fort's more remote location. Team Bucket was in and out in under two minutes, hauling an incredibly heavy bag of iron slung over Conor's back.

Their third target that day was a Tier 6 titanium mine. The mine wasn't actually real, as the element could rarely be found in a pure state in nature. Instead, the army planted a machine in the location that provided titanium chunks every hour to those holding the 'mine' long enough.

Of the three locations they'd chosen, this was the most challenging to assault. This raid required more than a simple smash and grab. But the prize would be worth it, if they could hold the point long enough to qualify as holding it.

Watching from the air, they scouted the fake mine and the stone wall around it, as well as the fifteen guards overseeing it.

It sat well inside the anti-flying formation, and they didn't have a well-hidden path to take advantage of like last time. The lookouts would spot them from nearly half a mile away, and Matt suspected the large fort would be much quicker to respond than the others.

Emily asked, "Should we maybe wait for night? We could probably get a lot closer to the walls that way."

Annie answered before anyone else could. "If it's anything like the last place we hit, that won't be possible. They'll have light runes to set up. This area will probably look like it did at midday, all night long."

Liz pointed to a section of the wall, which their AIs highlighted in their vision. "I can probably vault over the wall in my full golem form, but that means I'll be alone with Aster on the inside."

Matt asked, "Think you could carry us up with your blood?"

Liz hesitantly nodded. "If I have a few seconds to concentrate, yes. But I don't think I'll get it."

Annie offered, "I think I can get over the wall unseen. It's only ten feet up, but I don't know if being on my own will be enough to count as a steal."

Emily shrugged. "If you can get in, you could open the door for us if nothing else. That will make it a lot easier for us if we need to rush in hard."

Matt worried she might not be able to slip in with patrols walking the wall, but he had to trust his teammate to do her job. So, after getting a few reassurances, he nodded his approval to her.

They quietly landed, and Annie started slinking to the larger simulated mine. The five of them readied themselves to rush out to her defense. But after two nerve-wracking hours, Annie popped out of invisibility on the other side of a slight rise.

In her hand was a glass-like slate a little larger than her palm and waved it at them.

"The Army watcher slipped it into my hand after I sat next to the miner simulator for half an hour. Some kind of stealth penalty, I think." She shook her hand in anger, "Which is a crock of bullshit, but I worked it out. Nine days' worth of the mine's output, right here." She wiggled the slate with a cocky grin.

Matt had to give it to her, she had earned the right to brag.

Aster hopped into her arms and received a kiss, but the fox was more interested in the clear material than receiving adoration. Annie deflated a bit at that, but they quickly snuck away and took to the sky, with no one the wiser for their theft.

None of them wanted to stick around, so they flew to the nearest kingdom city to exchange their loot for half of its value. They earned a little more than fourteen thousand points apiece.

With jubilation, they moved back into a cloud for the evening and glided back over to the queendom territory. They planned to repeatedly raid overly full mines and strategic resource locations.

They never held a location for more than necessary, but the increased defense that they encountered each time was a good sign that they were forcing the queendom to stay on the defensive. To protect their mines, they had no choice but to redirect troops recapturing the many forts they had recently lost.

After four days, incredible resistance awaited them at every outpost. For the entire fourth day, they had to contend with ambushes set up inside of mining locations that had been cleared out to use as traps. After being baited a few times in succession without finding any loot, Team Bucket decided to call it quits. The goods were either well-hidden or already moved to the nearest queendom city.

That was when phase two of the operation started, and they started to hit the caravans of materials being shipped overland to the ruined city for the rebuilding process.

The kingdom's spies had learned about the shipments and briefed the leadership about it. The materials needed for the rebuild were so substantial that teleporting them wasn't remotely cost-efficient. The queendom was forced to haul them overland to keep costs tolerable.

Matt and his team burned two caravans to the ground, with the materials going up in flames.

They avoided engaging the defenders, focusing on doing maximum damage and creating chaos. Matt's [Flamethrower] earned its keep a thousand times over during the two weeks they spent sowing mayhem behind enemy lines.

Their nights spent in the clouds gave them the cover needed to remain undetected and rest without worry. They even watched as search parties combed the surrounding areas below them where they thought Team Bucket was holed up.

When they'd seemingly run out of targets, they found rift clusters and started ambushing the Tier 6 teams exiting the rifts, forcing the queendom to start stationing guards around the rifts.

The raids were nerve-wracking work that eventually stopped turning such amazing profits. But the disruption and resource losses they were causing the queendom was worth it, since the kingdom was giving them extra point remunerations for their efforts.

No single mission was continued for longer than they were able to handle the queendom forces. They always moved to an alternative soft spot before the opposing forces became too much of a problem.

Ambushes happened, but they were able to either spot them beforehand or fight their way out. They were careful to never over-commit, and became proficient at using their new items and skills to maximum effect. Two and a half weeks into their guerilla warfare tour, they were preparing to finally pull out when they received an unexpected emergency call from headquarters. A kingdom team was trying to retreat from a large fort and needed immediate reinforcements.

The request, in and of itself, wasn't unusual. Kingdom teams had repeatedly been retreating from untenable positions for the last few weeks as the queendom retook forts. Some people were eliminated. Which was unfortunate since they usually earned quite a few points for holding a fort deep in hostile lands. This time was different. The defenders had apparently been delving the cluster of rifts in the area around the fort and had acquired an item that couldn't be lost.

Matt asked what the item was, so that it could be secured and wouldn't be teleported out with someone's personal belongings, but he never received an answer. That made the team all the more curious.

So, they detoured to the last reported location, only to find a massacre in progress.

The kingdom fighters should have numbered around five hundred with the normal garrison for a large fort, but they were being besieged on all sides by queendom Pathers and regulars.

Many of them tried escaping into the air, but that didn't seem to do them any good. They were stalled, unable to move as a group, but smart enough to know that breaking ranks would only spell their demise further. One by one, they would be picked off. Matt and Conor took the lead and smashed into the outside edge of the flying mass of queendom forces.

Matt cut down some people from behind, even as the formation shifted to respond to their flank. Their enemy's slow reaction mattered little. Even while flying, he and Conor were much deadlier than the standard Tier 6s they contended with.

The resistance picked up as Matt engaged a Tier 7 scythe wielder. She must have had a Talent for it; she moved like a dancer with the unwieldy weapon. It didn't help that the scythe was Tier 8, and masterfully crafted. The edge screamed danger to his spiritual sense in a way he very rarely encountered.

She didn't fight like he expected such a strong melee fighter to fight. Instead of using smooth movements to guide the fight into positions where she could use her scythe to best effect, she seemed to be letting her weapon dictate her actions instead. It worked well enough; she was able to slip the curved blade around his longsword and cut a line into his under armor. The weapon left a noticeable gash along his shoulders as it sliced through [Cracked Phantom Armor] with only moderate trouble.

From that moment, he knew quickly dispatching her was beyond his abilities. He quickly disengaged and requested that one of the mages remove her while he turtled up.

A sudden bolt of lightning fried her and bounced to Matt, causing him to be jolted when the damage broke through his already stressed armor. His new layer of under armor blocked most of the lightning damage, but his hair stood on its ends. He reminded himself to not ask Emily for help if his armor was stressed, the woman just hit too hard now.

Taking only a moment to reset his armor's skill structure in his spirit, he started to cast and cut his way through the leading edge, trying to free the encircled kingdom fighters. When they finally broke through and made contact, a woman with bloodied armor nodded at them in thanks while directing her fighters to help widen the gap before joining the fray as well.

Matt turned away from her as he saw Conor take the opposite side and simultaneously activate [Demon Zone] and [Blade Arena]. Matt unleashed his Concept to keep the drain on his teammate from being too prohibitive. Together, they wedged a path through the queendom troops.

[Blade Arena] was a Tier 14 skill that created a field of phantom blades. When crossed, the blades dealt physical damage to that person. Conor was safe in the maelstrom's eye, and the ghostly blades resulted in several triggers from [Demon Zone] every second as people tried to pass through. Matt ignored the sharp, but relatively weak impacts. He could manage, as long as he wasn't forced to deal with a ranged attacker. But he was the only one who fared well against Conor's new combination.

Anyone else who crossed the threshold was continuously cut with the static blades. As they tried to move in or out, they would only take more cuts from reflected attacks.

All was going well, until a man with darker hair started shooting [Mana Bolt]s at them while keeping at the edge of their range. Matt did his best to block the shots, but staying on the defensive would only tie them down. Eventually he took an opening and flew out of Conor's zones to rush the Pather mage.

His charge was met by a revolving ring of shields that blocked his first [Mana Charge]. A tiny mallet in the man's hand expanded to ridiculous size as it was brought down in a now deadly arc.

Matt threw his weight to the right, and using the greater speed of his flying sword, evaded the mallet, which quickly shrunk back down to pendant size. After re-engaging, Matt concluded he would be unable to break the man's defenses with melee attacks before that expanding mallet would be swung around again.

Giving up, Matt refilled his pool with a mana stone and cast [Flamethrower], directed the full brunt of the attack at the man. The floating shields were overwhelmed and broke, one by one, in a series of popping sounds. To Matt's surprise, the Pather actually slipped away, albeit charred and with their clothes smoking at the edges.

Matt turned his cone of flame on the surrounding queendom forces and watched as the unprepared attackers were set alight and teleported out in quick succession. Matt scorches a hole in their lines.

That was, until a swordsman in distinct armor hurtled toward him. As the warrior closed in, Matt recognized his newest opponent, Talous.

He blasted his stream of fire at the man, already knowing that it wouldn't have any effect, and raised his sword with his right hand. After hearing Liz's complaints about the man, Matt did some research on him.

Talous was a melee sword fighter. By all reports, he either had a Talent for piercing armor, or a powerful enchanted sword that could. Combined with a suspected growth item that blocked ranged attacks, both the magical and mundane variety, the man was a lethal opponent for both melee and ranged combatants.

Based on his research, Matt suspected that the man had a Talent set similar to Tara's, but more limited. Matt believed he was benefiting from increased blocking power and armor penetration when he was specifically wielding a shortsword and shield combination. The hunch came to Matt after discovering the man had only been publicly defeated in a single duel once, when his shield was broken and he seemingly faltered. It was pure speculation, but his guess paired well with the threat assessment reports put together on the man.

His whole team was deadly with their various builds, but Talous was the major standout. He had yet to die in the war and had taken at least two forts with his team in just the first week. A gust of wind signaled that his second teammate, Oliver, was nearby. The other two fighters from his team were less flashy, so Matt wasn't able to spot them. The fifth and final member never actually fought on the front lines. The reports speculated that he was a Seeker or a crafter, but little was known of them other than the fact that they were Talous' younger brother and viciously guarded by the team.

Matt deflected the first blow, but nearly took a mana infused shield bash in return. He flew higher away from the general melee and used his longer weapon to keep the other swordsman from striking at his feet.

Once high enough above the large engagement, Matt stopped rising, and using the flat of his longsword, blocked another flurry of attacks as Talous rose to equal footing.

For all of Talous' conduct as a pushy asshole, he clearly knew how to fight. Matt was kept on the defensive, even as he retaliated with any opening he was able to make or find. It was frustrating for Matt, even though he was only bottom Tier 6, he was still stronger than the peak Tier 6 opposite him. His full physical allocation of essence and [Mage's Retreat] gave him the edge in brute force.

Talous was just a better melee fighter, able to counter Matt with his shorter ranged combo. Matt considered himself one of the better melee fighters in the Empire at his Tier. He had fought enough people, and rarely found an opponent at his skill level, but Talous was a step above. He read and reacted to every move Matt made, even with his own AI using 5 MPS to predict the man's moves.

In terms of raw ability, Talous was a better mundane fighter.

Simple as that.

The man slightly edged out Matt's strength and the reach advantage from his longsword with pure skill. It was the first fight Matt had fought where he felt so disadvantaged in years.

If he didn't want to break every bone in the man's body, he might have actually enjoyed the fight.

As they exchanged blow after blow, Talous kept his shield up and at the ready. He used it as a wall, redirecting Matt's mana-infused attacks with ease. The dust from falling mana stones explained why he was unable to bash through the Tier 6 shield with [Mana Charge]s from his Tier 7 growth item. The attacks should have bypassed the effects of the man's growth item. His greater strength meant little when Talous never took a hit full on. The opposing Pather let attacks slide off his angled shield or the flat of his blade, while using the flying sword under him to cushion the blows' force.

Matt took more and more slight grazing blows, while unable to maneuver the man into a position where he could fully take advantage of his superior strength. He kept the injuries to a minimum, but they slowly added up as the fight dragged on. Talous' talent rendered him essentially defenseless. If not for his proficiency at parrying with his longsword, the queendom Pather would have carved him to pieces long ago.

They didn't say anything to each other during the entire fight, but from the glint of Talous' eyes through the gap in his armor, Matt saw pleasure— even glee at his state. Matt sensed the man's thoughts. Judging by what he read from the reports, along with what Liz had told him, Talous believed that combat prowess was the only way to measure a person's worth. He presumed to be better than Matt because he was keeping the armored kingdom Pather on the defensive.

Matt decided to break him of that notion.

With a surge of speed, he sidestepped a shield bash and struck out with a heavy blow of his own, forcing Talous back on the defensive. He made sure to keep his attacks at the man's center of gravity, so he would have to absorb each blow with his own strength, instead of letting the force slide off. The shift in momentum allowed Matt to start battering the man around. With his reach advantage, he was able to drive Talous to turtle up behind his shield. He also noted that the spent mana stone dust increased as the man directly blocked consecutive heavy blows from [Mana Charge]. If he had to spend mana stones to fuel his defense, Matt was sure that he could outlast him, if he could keep the man on the defensive

Matt took a slashing strike along his flank, which sliced straight through both [Cracked Phantom Armor] and his physical under armor, as if they weren't even there.

Matt ignored the searing pain and cut down on Talous' extended arm. When you were fighting an opponent with effectively no armor, you had to accept wounds to give them. That, or remain purely on the defensive. But that wasn't how Matt fought.

He could take a few wounds. It was just pain. Matt was old friends with pain. He would outlast this arrogant prick, and show him that he was endless.

The move seemed to surprise Talous, as he was barely able to retract his arm in time to avoid getting it cut off. Still, a furrow was scored in the metal armor where Matt's Tier 7 longsword met the Tier 6 metal.

Talous roared at the hit and lashed out. The duo exchanged a flurry of blows that drew blood on both sides, but with functional armor, Talous had better protection. Matt would have been leaking enough for Liz to kill everyone present, if it wasn't for [Cracked Phantom Armor] staunching his wounds.

Intent on staying on the attack, Matt rushed forward and then backward, battling to maintain his reach advantage over his opponent. He was trying to use his longsword's advantages to their best effect, and was battering the queendom Pather from the edge of his range. But the man was slippery and was always able to slip in close, forcing Matt to be constantly retreating.

In the next exchange, they were again both able to draw blood from each other. Talous snuck his shortsword under Matt's defensive stance, and cut a deep trench into his hip. They both felt metal scrape bone. In return, Matt broke something in the man's shoulder when blocking an attack. He could tell he had injured Talous from the way the man was unable to raise his shield arm. That opening allowed him to land two hits onto the man's left leg, where he tore through armor without resistance. The wounds left blood running down the man's leg, despite the potion he had poured on it during a retreat.

They were both panting heavily when Talous went in for a heavily telegraphed strike. Seeing what was coming, Matt was grateful for the armor covering his face.

He had been waiting for the man to grow wounded enough to get desperate and charge. He readied his blade as if he was going to ignore the attack and try to take Talous down with him.

As they both charged, Matt met the man's eyes behind his armor. He was sure that the glint in the peak Tier 6's eyes was reflected in his own.

When Talous was committed and only inches away, Matt used his bonded growth ring to teleport six inches forward, with his blade already aimed for Talous' face. The other Pather's suddenly working shield would have blocked it, but Matt was behind the barrier and blade before he could react.

With a crunch of teeth and metal, Matt nearly cut the man's head off at the mouth. He might have managed to kill him with the [Mana Charge] he was unleashing, but the other fighter was already gone before the mana had a chance to fully release.

Matt stood straighter and stopped pretending to be as badly wounded as he let on. Sure, he was hurt. But with [Cracked Phantom Armor] useless, he had reduced its mana drain to 1 MPS. He put the other 44 MPS usually reserved for his armor into [Endurance]. With the skill running at such high throughput, his wounds were already scabbing over. The only reason he kept his armor active was so Talous couldn't see his wounds heal faster than they should have.

He had prepared for this fight and knew the only way to win was with trickery. Anyone with a Talent as good as his could fall into arrogance. He had seen it with Tara, though she had her friends to keep her level headed, and Melinda to outshine them all. He only hoped that the asshole would learn to keep his mouth shut after Matt's unsubtle finishing blow. But he doubted it. If Matt knew the type of man Talous was as well as he thought he did, Talous would take the loss personally, and come for revenge.

Matt would be ready if he did.

With a painful yell, Matt rushed into the melee and started to attack anyone strong on the queendom side.

He continued to do so, until a hand-sized sparrow made of blood that flickered like flames flew up to a wounded man and started draining the blood from the wound on his shoulder. The man swatted at it, but the sparrow had already split into two. The duo started to feed off the man's wound even faster. Killing one wasn't enough; he needed to kill all of the sparrows on him. But every time he managed to dispose of one, a second had already formed. Soon, he was encased in an entire flock of pecking [Blood Sprites]. As their sources of food were teleported out, the flock of sprites flew off toward the nearest opponents and repeated their harvest.

Matt had to admit. It was a scary spell to watch work. The battle was quickly over, as the blood sparrows grew in number and overwhelmed the opponents.

Once half the queendom's numbers were gone, the rest called a general retreat, leaving the kingdom fighters free to enjoy their victory. There was a moment of tension as the blood sparrows had nothing else to feed on and turned to start flitting around the kingdom soldiers. But Liz squinted at them and clapped her hands, causing the sparrows to disintegrate into a mist of blood.

Matt flew over and laughed in relief. "Seems like the skill worked."

He didn't know that she had no idea how the skill would actually function before she used it. Apparently, the Emperor didn't think they would try this particular skill, so Liz had gone in blind. Thankfully, it didn't seem to have any negative side effects, though Matt wished she hadn't risked it. But with the spell being external, he knew there was little risk.

"It worked well enough, though the form is annoying." The bitterness in her voice caught Matt off guard, until he pieced it together.

"They look like your mom did, don't they? Like flame sparrows?"

Liz's face twisted in response to Matt's question which caused him to start laughing so hard he tore open a few of his cuts.

"It's not funny! She's going to give me endless shit about this. Matt! Don't laugh!"

He continued to tease her about the birds as she swore she would never use the skill again, until she could change the shape. They both knew she was lying about that one, but he didn't call her out on it. The skill was too useful and powerful to waste.

The rest of the flight back was uneventful, with no one willing to challenge them for the last few dozen miles back to kingdom controlled territory.

As soon as he was safe to do so, Matt quickly checked the points they had earned in the last two and a half weeks of looting and pillaging, with the army rewards and kingdom rewards totaled up.

New Gains: 110,671 points. See point breakdown?

Matt smiled as they flew in formation. That was nearly half the number of points for the unsuccessful defense of the city. With the increased resistance, they earned less per subsequent day, but they were double dipping with the stolen goods and army points. Matt still didn't know which one was more dangerous; banditry had its own worries and risks that a defensive battle lacked.

Ignoring his points, he focused on [Endurance] and healing his wounds. The burn was still lingering, and he was sure he'd need a true healer for the hip wound.

Overall, he was happy with how the outing turned out.

22

Much to his surprise and delight, Matt wasn't placed on cooldown after being healed. He was close, but not quite over the edge.

The good news ended there.

The very night, after they arrived back into the city, they were welcomed with an assassination attempt. Someone was blending in with the wall along a corridor to their suite. A knife slid into Emily's throat, killing her before anyone could react.

Annie lost her mind. She beat the assassin until they were teleported away in a flash. They were sure that she would have continued until their skull caved in, had he not been rescued.

As soon as the hitman was gone, she swore bloody vengeance on him.

That trend continued during their time in the city. On the way to visit Emily, they were hit twice more. After the third encounter, they stopped caring for social niceties, and brandished weapons and armor as they walked.

The next two attacks were thwarted by Conor reacting in time to block an arrow shot from the top of a statue, and Aster smelling someone creeping up on them using some sort of invisibility skill. Liz flooded the area red, revealing the individual standing not four feet away.

They tried to run, but Matt was faster, catching up with two bounding steps. He grabbed them, placed his hand over their face, and squeezed. The message was clear, and the sound of their cracking skull served as the army's signal to remove them.

None of them were in a good mood when they found Emily leaving the hospital, cursing up a storm.

They got back to their suite without incident, but it set the tone for the remainder of their stay in the city.

Team Bucket was forced to wait two weeks for Emily's healing cooldown before they could go back into the field. They technically could have gone on missions without her, but everyone agreed to wait. With time on his hands, Matt shelled out 50,000 points to hire a melee instructor from the army.

The instructor was not what he expected. He arrived at the training room a few minutes before the appointed time and, at first, he thought he was in the wrong room. The only other person there could be mistaken for a child at first glance. She stood a few inches over five feet, if Matt had to guess. But his AI registered them as the instructor he was supposed to meet.

Sheila Benson, Tier 22.

That was it. No other accomplishments or titles listed. But Benson was the instructor listed, so he shut the door behind himself and deactivated his armor.

"Hello?" Matt called out, but the mass of brown curls didn't so much as twitch.

Matt continued to stare at the motionless woman for what felt like an hour but was closer to five minutes.

Finally, at some unseen signal, the woman pivoted on a heel and strode over to him with purposeful steps.

She got within inches of Matt and glared up at him.

Her first words to him were, "You were early. I didn't ask you to be early. I said 7 AM. Not 6:55."

Matt was at a loss how to respond but tried anyway.

"I didn't know if you intended to move locations, or something like that. I figured a little early was better than late."

"A weapon is no good if it's not where it needs to be, *when* it needs to be. A strike should land precisely when it is best applied. Not too early. Not too late. On time."

Matt saw where this was headed, so he attempted to avoid a lecture. "My timing was right where I wanted it, which is control. The most important aspect of handling a blade."

Sheila smirked slightly at his response. "A weak answer, but an acceptable one. You hired me for two weeks. What do you want out of it?"

Matt had listed this on the request but assumed that this was another test of sorts. "Primarily, I want to work on my longsword skills. And maybe polish up my general weapons expertise, if time permits."

The Tier 22 strolled around Matt and poked various parts of his frame. As she circled him, she asked, "Who trained you, and under what schools of bladework?"

Matt shook his head. "I didn't have any formal education at any martial house or school. I was orphaned, and we were taught basic stances. I moved beyond that with the training aids. I also learned from a few of the trainers at my PlayPen."

The woman knit her brows slightly. "Well color me surprised. You have the frame of someone trained under the DaResh school of greatswords. I've reviewed your last several fights, and you fight like it as well, if a touch sloppily in places. If you say you haven't trained with a proper school, then we'll start there. Let's see how much is natural ability, and how much is training."

A longsword sized to her smaller frame settled into her hands out of nowhere. She stepped back and took a defensive stance.

"Start attacking me. Once I get a feel for your abilities, I'll start retaliating."

Matt summoned his sword and took his own stance opposite the tiny woman.

Ten minutes later, Matt had a bruised hand, arm, and face to match his bruised ego.

He expected to lose. The woman was Tier 22 and in the army. An ice cream bunny had a greater chance of escaping Aster than he did to even scratch her. What galled him was that she had spanked him while lowering her cultivation level to *below* his. During the spar, her speed, strength, and proprioception were all significantly weaker than his, but she still treated him as if she was playing around with a kitten.

As he rubbed at his swollen jaw, Sheila motioned him to sit down, which he gratefully did.

"You're not bad. Better than I expected when you said that you haven't actually trained under anyone. Sometimes, people just imitate moves and such, but they don't understand what they're doing. You could go far if you want to lean into the art of the blade more."

She waved her hand, and four swords appeared in a row floating between them. The first three were of a similar design, but the final was noticeably different. The first and last were both made from bronze, but the second was iron, and the third was polished steel.

"I participate in the mundane blade competitions, and I'm pretty good." She tapped the last blade, whose shape contrasted to the other three. "Got thirty-second place in the Empire-wide Tier 20 competition for short swords." She waved a hand over the others and said, "Worked my way up in the Vassal level fights to first place. It took over three decades before I even placed in the Empire-wide rankings."

Matt knew of the mundane blade competitions; anyone who enjoyed melee fighting did. They were duels where no skills or personal gear were allowed, only cultivation. Even powerful Talents would be removed from play by giving participants armor and weapons that precisely counteracted their benefits. If the Talent was too broad or all-encompassing and unable to be countered or turned off the cultivator was unable to participate.

They spanned from Tier 1 to Tier 40, and were held regularly, though not all at the same time. Tier 1 competitions happened every five years, but Tier 40 competitions were only once every ten *thousand* years. It wasn't considered a serious competition until the once-a-century Tier 15 competition, when participants had eons to perfect their craft.

The fact that the woman had won a kingdom-level tournament was incredibly impressive. That she'd then gone on to place in the Empire-level tournament? Just scary. Even if she hadn't taken first place, she'd proven to be in the top fifty fighters out of millions of master competitors from thousands of planets.

Inadvertently, he straightened his posture. From just that information, the dark-skinned woman in front of him was someone to respect. It also explained why she treasured the last bronze blade more than the steel one. Getting a top fifty trophy in the Empire was a wide step above getting a first-place steel weapon from any kingdom. Matt also made a note to search for her fights and review them tonight. They would be somewhere on the EmpireNet, and he wanted to watch.

I wonder if I can get an autograph? Would that be weird?

He hadn't known the woman existed before this, but he was already thoroughly fascinated.

"So, what can I do to improve?" He was eager.

Sheila grinned at him. "We'll start with the basics and work our way up. Today, we'll go over various sword forms with a variety of weapons."

She popped to her feet with an alacrity that Matt couldn't match and started directing him through sword forms.

The next two days were both the best and the worst of times. Sheila repeatedly pushed him to the brink. And if he didn't show the results she wanted, she kicked him right off the edge more than once.

A healer had to be called in twice when she cracked bones to punish him for repeatedly overextending.

Similar to Annie's instructor, Sheila was fair but exacting in her demands. From the way she composed herself, and the videos of her duels that he watched during the small breaks he was given, she expected more from herself as an instructor than she did from him as a student.

He strove to meet her own expectations, and she responded by pushing him even further. For the first day and a half, he didn't sleep at all, just relying on [Endurance] to carry him through. When he began flagging despite its assistance, Sheila booted Matt into a corner and commanded him to sleep.

Five hours later, she woke him up and kept pushing him with renewed vigor. From there on out, she forced him to rest for exactly five hours a day. During those two weeks, he lived and breathed the training room, not seeing the outside at all. His whole existence was endless drills and exercises with Sheila.

Matt was torn between feeling he'd made zero progress and seeing massive improvement. When he was dueling the Tier 22, nothing made a difference. She toyed with him while continuously calling out instructions. When he fought training aids or simulations, he performed at a completely different level than he had before.

His instinctive reactions were being honed, even if it was slightly. He could tell that his predictions of moves were just a hair more accurate.

The training only lasted for two weeks, so the improvements were small, but Matt was feeling good.

Liz felt like shit.

Her boyfriend had all but vanished for the last week and a half, only responding to messages once a day before passing out. Being away from him for so long with nearly zero contact was a new inconvenience, but it was one that she could accept. Although Matt didn't say it out loud, Talous' greater melee skills had been a wakeup call for him. She was glad that he was working to better himself.

To her endless annoyance, Talous' reaction to their duel wasn't quite as mature. At first, he hounded her to find Matt so he could challenge him to another duel. Liz didn't need to see the reports of him raging around once he got out of the hospital to know why he was mad.

He told everyone himself. Loudly.

At every opportunity, Talous told anyone who would listen about how Matt had cheated in their fight, and if he didn't duel him fairly, he wasn't a real man.

Liz found that funny. Matt had zero problems cheating in a fight, and using a trump card wasn't cheating by any means.

No, what she minded was Talous taking things personally, and creating a rift in the Pathers' Union.

He and the princess had contacted all the kingdom's top Pathers and offered them a better deal. In and of itself, that wouldn't have been a problem from her perspective. The problem she *did* have was that their new deal changed the formula with which the Pathers' general point share was distributed. They halved the one percent that went to everyone and redirected it to the top contributors. Now, the bottom half of the Pathers would get relatively fewer points for their contributions, and the top would earn more.

Talous spun it as a great service to everyone, even the people he was screwing over.

Few bought it, and there was an outcry about the unfair treatment. But enough of the top Pathers on the kingdom side were swayed over by the promise of greater earnings and switched sides. Albert was public about his anger toward the situation, and refused to make similar changes, calling it a greedy mindset. Privately, he seemed pretty pleased with Talous' changes. The kingdom was being flooded with requests to switch sides from lower ranked queendom Pathers and independent crafters.

Albert and Juni were happy with the trade, as the mass defections were nearly crippling the queendom's crafting economy. All the independent crafters, still under Alyssa's guidance, refused to work with the queendom. More and more, the queendom needed to rely on their own crafters, slowing their development plans. On the other hand, with a greater share of the top Tier Pathers, the queendom forces were now hitting harder per person. Ultimately, the Pather split flipped into a forty sixty split, with the kingdom having more people but the queendom having the higher quality troops.

Liz was still ticked off. Anyone with two brain cells knew that the queendom was up to something, as they siphoned away a good portion of the kingdom's above average Pathers. But as days went by, no one made any major moves. The leadership eventually eased back their alertness to normal levels. Eventually, part of her figured that maybe Talous just couldn't handle a loss, and this was his payback. But that seemed too simple and easy of an explanation.

The truly amusing part, at least to Liz, was that the top fifteen Pather teams on the kingdom side flatly refused to switch. As more mid-tier Pathers defected, the opportunities to earn points increased, and there was less competition for the highest spots. Sara tried to sway them with gifts and bribes, but none of them budged from the kingdom's side.

Liz was still inundated with work, trying to get all the new people into rooms and fending off assassination attempts. She was only caught unawares once. While walking to a meeting of the Pather Union, a potted plant turned into a person and stabbed her. Fortunately, she was able to twist enough to make it a nonlethal blow.

She just wished Matt would finish up with his training. His steady presence would make all this stress easier to handle.

Luna idled above the neutral city and watched as her newest…*challenges* worked on improving themselves.

Liz mostly dealt with politics, while training with her new skills and learning their limitations. That was acceptable for the present situation. Her new [Blood Sprites] skill was a surprising and creative addition to her arsenal. She was looking forward to seeing the results during the next siege. Although, she made a note to have Liz work on her control. As devastating as the skill was for her enemies, without proper control, the skill could easily backfire and harm her allies.

Aster was still dealing with her burgeoning intelligence. Switching back and forth from animal to child. The play dates were helping her settle in, so she crossed that off her binder of to-do's for the little fox. The training with the Ice Wolf was a good call for her. The older canine had even mentioned [Ice Form] and its ability to counteract Winter's Embrace's shortcoming of being rooted to one spot. It was always better when information was seeded by others before she needed to step in personally. People tended to be more receptive that way.

Matt was training in mundane swordplay. Not the worst idea, after fighting someone who was actually better than him at it for the first time. She would have found him a better instructor, but Sheila was adequate for his current skill level, so she left it as is.

No need to interfere too early.

She *had* pulled a few strings to get Annie the help she needed with her skill set. Luna recognized the enjoyment that the girl got out of performing a perfect assassination. She had seen it before, and those types often went into the deep end without realizing it. The thrill of executing a flawless plan mutated into the thrill of execution.

Luna had no problems taking small measures to prevent the birth of a sociopath when it was happening right in front of her.

So, she'd called Victor, one of the Empire's better assassins. She had no idea what they were calling themselves these days; they always had a new, clever name that she couldn't be bothered to keep up with. Mechanics, fixers, bureau of adjustments, and the like. They were state sanctioned killers who operated in the shadows. Who cared what they called themselves?

Still, Victor seemed very pleased with the girl. When Annie fell off the Path, Luna was sure that he would quickly be there to recruit her. Victor had even admitted to thinking about stalling the sisters so they would fall off the Path and he could get her early. But Luna just laughed at him and told him that if he wanted to train the girl sooner, he should just become a part of the twins' management team at Tier 10. If he didn't, someone else would take the reins on Annie's training.

He grumbled, but Luna knew that he'd take her warning seriously. He'd already started gently pushing Annie into specialized therapy, which she agreed with. Better to head these issues off now, before they grow to be a bigger problem. An ounce of prevention was worth a pound of a cure.

The other two were each honing their skills, but it was mundane. Her charges had lucked into an interesting bunch of Pathers, but her team was usually *so* much more interesting. Now, Luna was bored. The days were turning into weeks with nothing new happening. After rechecking her training notes for the 9,234th time, she checked on her charges with her spiritual sense.

Again.

Liz was still politicking, so she tuned that mostly out, while watching Matt get toyed with by the little girl. At least that was mildly entertaining, so she settled in to watch.

Matt heaved on all fours while he spat out shards of a tooth and phlegm-filled blood.

Sheila stood over him with a presence that belied her physical size. "I told you to keep your guard up."

He just nodded. As always, she'd warned him exactly twice before she broke something. Grunting, he forced himself back to his feet, to an approving smirk from his instructor.

"Again." The words were agony to spit out, but they earned a nod, which was enough.

Matt blocked two strikes before lashing out for a probing strike, only to have it blocked casually.

Sheila's follow-up strike was aimed at his jaw again, but he kept his composure this time, and deflected the blade off his own. He stepped forward and around her, attacking her less protected side.

But she was already gone. His instructor had mirrored his step forward with her own and swung at Matt's back with her smaller longsword.

Matt barely managed to raise his own sword up in time. The worst part was, she didn't even consider herself good in longsword techniques. As much as it rankled, it rang true. In comparison to her skill with a short sword, Sheila was almost *bad* with her longsword. But only in comparison to her skills with a shortsword.

With the shorter blade in hand, it didn't matter what her opponents did. She danced through them, rending flesh with every twist and turn.

Regardless, she was still more than good enough to teach Matt about every weapon he could ask for help with. Even about his longsword.

Only two days were spent training with other weapons. Blunt weapons and axes were the focus, as they covered enough of the damage types that his longsword couldn't.

Sheila also questioned why he was walking the line between longsword and greatsword. It was an unusual line to walk for a swordsman. With his height and reach, his comfortable blade length for any weapon was longer than most. So, he told her how he had to make do with a cheaper weapon at the PlayPen, and adapted to it. Then, there was the addition of being stronger than most at his Tier, which changed his style further. She listened quietly through his explanation and just nodded along. Seeing that it worked for him, she encouraged him to stay the course and create his own style.

While breaking for a quick meal, Matt worked up the courage to ask her why she was even there. That question had been bugging him. She was a good instructor; too good to be babysitting Tier 6s. He was sure that she could have sold her skills instead of joining the army.

She laughed at him. "I'm doing a three century tour with the army to pay for a straight shot of rift locations and spots to Tier 35. Fastest way to advance."

"Surely a noble or a guild would have gotten you the slots?"

She scoffed at that reply. "If I wanted to sign my life away, sure. For a deal that big, I'd be given an incredibly strict contract with exit clauses I could never afford to pay. It would keep me leashed to them forever. The bigger the reward, the stronger they bind you to them. With the army, at least I can pay them upfront and owe them nothing when it's over. Most of the time, it's easy. I train the troops who want or need help in between combat missions. Matty boy, if you fall off the Path, make sure you don't sign anything without reading the contract over well. Pay a lawyer if you can. Everything has to be in plain language, but that doesn't mean you'll understand the implications of every phrase."

Matt just nodded, remembering the contracts he looked over after first receiving the detrimental rating for his Talent. While the contracts were on the surface easy to understand, there were enough ambiguities that made Matt nervous.

"Why do this, then?" Matt waved around at the training room and himself.

"Ha. This makes me more than training some noble brat. The Empire offers tax breaks to anyone who trains kids on the Path, and your contribution points also turn into 5,000 army merit points. For two weeks of doing chores away from babysitting duty, that's pretty decent remuneration. So, I get to pay half the taxes for one year of my choosing, per lesson I teach. It'll save me an assload if I do it when I'm advancing."

She popped back to her feet and, with a wave, the trays of food vanished.

"All right, I want you to run simulation seventeen, but this time, every kill needs to be with a single blow."

Matt readied his blade and linked his AI with the simulation room as he walked into it.

Matt, Liz, and Aster sat curled up in Melinda's suite, having finished watching a movie with the other team, when Matt noticed the orbs in their hands.

"Is that an essence stone?"

They looked baffled at his question, but Sam, who was closest to their love seat, extended it with two fingers. "Yeah. Haven't you been using them?"

Matt turned to Liz, who turned to Aster, who just turned back at Matt. None of them had any idea.

"No. Where did you get them?"

Kyle slumped forward. "Dude, they're five points apiece on the shop. How have you not seen them?"

Matt flushed slightly as he realized what might have happened. "Well, I mostly sort by cost from highest to lowest."

That earned him a round of boos from the team. Tara even threw a piece of popcorn at him, which Aster snapped up. He patted her for her rigorous defense of his person, but she was more interested in getting more of the popcorn from Tara and left to join her.

Melinda stared at them. "So, you just haven't advanced at all in the last four months or so?"

"Not really." Matt shrugged, with Liz looking just as embarrassed.

Vinnie flipped them off, saying with a teasing tone, "Must be nice to be *that* far ahead of the curve." Kicking his feet up, he asked in his normal voice, "Haven't you seen your teammates using them?"

Liz shook her head. "They're peak Tier 6, so they had no need either. I just kinda figured that stalling a bit was a part of the whole war game. None of the books I read mentioned anything about it."

Matt could already see the nasty letters she'd be writing to the authors of all the Pather war books she had read. What a detail to leave out.

Mathew leaned forward, showing off the little orb in his hand. "The ship's captain we were transported here with said that there's a secret in these. None of us have found anything yet, but it's fun to look for while we advance."

Matt looked down in question. In the corner of his eye, he saw Liz doing the same. Neither of them had any idea what secret he was talking about.

"Who said this? And have you looked it up anywhere?" Liz hesitantly probed.

Melinda nodded. "The ship captain. And we did, but we only found rumors, nothing concrete. Figured it was a secret."

Liz pushed off Matt's shoulder to sit herself up. "I've never heard that one. And I feel like that would be something my parents would have mentioned. Or at least not be able to keep a secret. Even my siblings, for that matter."

Matt nodded along, but froze as Kyle asked, "Why would they know?"

Next to him, Liz tensed, but only for an instant. He was about to make an excuse for her, but she sighed and said, "It's dumb to hide this. You shared your secrets with me. I should reciprocate. My parents are Leon and Mara, the two royals."

Her words took a few seconds to register, but everyone's faces started melting into shock. With one exception; Melinda simply bounced around. "Ohhh! That explains the double princess nickname! I thought it was just a weird pet name, or inside joke, but that's sooo much funnier!"

Liz spun and glared at Matt. She poked him in the ribs, "You said that in front of her? You're such a butt!"

Matt had to think back, but he *had* teased her about the double princess having golden armor in front of Melinda. He hadn't even thought about that.

Tara interrupted them. "Wait, wait, wait! You're the daughter of two Tier… I don't even know…" Her eyes flicked to the right. "Two Tier 48s. Holy shit. Forty-fucking-eight. Two of them. That's crazy! Why are you even on the Path?"

Liz pointed back at Tara. "That is exactly why. I didn't choose my parents. I don't want everyone thinking all of my accomplishments come from them. It sucks to be under their shadow. Or having people always trying to be my friend so they can cozy up to them. Nothing ever feels real."

That sobered up the room, and Tara wilted slightly.

Melinda brought the conversation back on track. "Well, thank you for trusting us."

Liz just beamed at them all, including Tara. "Thank you for being my friend before you knew. I hope it doesn't change anything, but I don't like lying to my friends, so I'm happy to have it out in the open."

Kyle shrugged. "Yeah, super parents are cool and all, but I'm way more interested in you being half beast. Does that mean you will have a beast shape? I'm sooo jealous. I'd love to have one." He kicked at the ground slightly. "Stupid humans."

That brought out a round of questions that Liz answered happily. No one seemed to judge her, and when Tara went to go get more drinks, Liz followed her. They came back with smiles; Liz's happy, and Tara's relieved. Matt suspected that she apologized for the rude question earlier.

As his essence stone crumbled to dust, Vinnie finally asked, "So, there's no secret in these?"

Liz put up her hands. "Maybe. But I've never heard of it. Doesn't mean that it doesn't exist."

Matt quipped as the thought entered his head, "Maybe the captain was trying to keep all of you quiet on the trip."

Kyle jumped at him and put him in a headlock. "I'll show you 'keep quiet on a trip!'" And started to rub his fist into Matt's head.

As they devolved into wrestling, the party's mood returned to what it was before Liz's revelation.

When they finally walked home, Liz was jubilant. "They didn't treat me any differently when I told them."

She clung to Matt's arm before bouncing off into a skip and a jump.

"They like me for *me*!" Her shout echoed off the building and was eaten by the mostly empty streets.

She came back and stole Aster to start a little dance with her as she jumped along.

Finally, she settled down enough to walk normally next to Matt. "Thank you for having great friends to share with me."

Matt just put an arm around her. "What's mine is yours."

Liz finished the quote with a devious grin. "And what's mine is only mine!"

She tried to flee, but he caught her and started tickling her until she corrected herself with a lingering kiss. "What's mine is yours." She pecked his nose before hugging him and saying, "You already have my heart. What else is there to give?"

To Matt's relief, the assassins left them alone to enjoy the walk home. Nothing should have ruined their moment.

The war settled down, with each side having taken the easy measures to earn points, and then blocking the other side from doing the same. As the weeks stretched into months, there were no large movements on either side, with only the occasional fort exchanging hands. There was also the odd skirmish that turned into a larger battle as more people flooded in from each side.

All in all, the largest thing that happened at the six-month mark was a grand auction.

The auction was once again held in the same underwater location as before, where they all sat in their auction booths. There were screens displaying various scenes of them fighting throughout the months. Nearly everyone had a moment where they shined, and anyone who rated a private box let it show.

Talous still irritated the hell out of Matt. He hounded him both privately and in public for months about a rematch. To get back at him, Matt widely shared his recording of him nearly cutting the man's head off. Above their auction booth, it was shown on a large screen, playing on a short loop. There were more dramatic and visually impressive clips that he could have shown from the siege, but none so satisfying to share as Talous' execution.

He'd already received seven threats from the man, and each one brought a petty smile to his face. After everything the jackass put Liz through, he wasn't above showing off the man's only death to everyone watching.

Of course, Talous wasn't one to sit and do nothing in response. He retaliated by having Matt's single death displayed above the box of the man who'd killed him. Considering that Matt sat on the top floor now, and that fighter was near the bottom, he didn't mind. Besides, Matt was pretty proud of that death. It showed him killing two people and beating a third to death while being repeatedly stabbed in the back by a half dozen people.

The impact wasn't the same as having a sword shoved through your head in single combat.

If the man weren't such an asshole, he would have happily accepted the duel. Matt had learned a lot with Sheila, but he needed to fight opponents nearer his own level to truly realize his gains. Talous would have been the perfect sparring partner.

But with how vindictive the man was, and how mad he was about not getting his way, Matt enjoyed refusing the requests all the more.

He smiled and waved over at the box where he knew Talous was, then chuckled as the man scowled and flipped him the finger.

They were all relaxed in their box; assassinations were strictly forbidden during the auction. Not that it mattered. The attempts had come to a halt after Annie personally and viciously took revenge on anyone who tried to take them out. She didn't just hunt down anyone who attempted to make a hit on them. She hunted their friends, their family, and their bosses. All without mercy. Each time, she made sure that her victims knew *exactly* why they were suffering in the slowest and most torturous deaths she could get away with, before the army would step in and extract them. After two weeks of knife-work on her part, the constant attempts on their lives had completely stopped.

Emily's assassin had, very publicly, opted to leave the war right before his two week healing cooldown ended. His nerve had broken after watching his teammates, friends, and commanders end up in the hospital, mutilated and screaming for mercy. Each one had carried a message for him from Annie, with promises of his fate to come. This had earned her a title from the queendom fighters: "Calamity Annie".

At the entire team's insistence, she started seeing a therapist. None of them were comfortable with just how far she'd been taking the kills. Annie had only acquiesced when her sister confronted her about how hard she was taking Emily's death and how extreme the level of revenge was.

Matt could understand Annie's feelings, but definitely agreed with the group. Her methods dove a little too far in the revenge category for his taste. At the same time though, she had watched her sister get knifed through the throat for a tiny bounty. That wasn't something he'd handle any better, so he could sympathize with her.

If this wasn't a game with army watchers, Emily could have actually bled out right then and there. As would Annie's later victims. There was a good lesson here for the other side; anyone they killed might have loved ones willing to go to extreme lengths for revenge.

Matt just didn't want to see his friend lose herself in the shadows.

Annie's attitude improved after some time away from her personal wetwork, particularly with the end of the constant attacks. Here at the auction, they were perfectly safe. The army made it clear that any violence on the auction house's grounds would result in the perpetrators being kicked out of the safety bubbles, and no one would be rescuing them. The only place people were allowed to fight was the dueling arenas.

That rule allowed everyone to relax and focus on the auction, which was the entire point. No business wanted their potential customers too afraid to buy things.

Emily was still bitter about her point loss but had come to accept it. Her death meant that she only had about 200,000 points from the team's passive gains, along with a few missions, by the time the auction rolled around. However, the rest of the team had offered to help pay for any items or training she wanted, so she wasn't left destitute.

As item after item passed by the auction block, they mostly ignored them. Prices had skyrocketed with the accumulated points people now had to spend. Items that went for 5,000 points in the first auction raked in ten or more times their previous value. Other people were still spending their points, but Team Bucket needed little. Their team never left the top five earners, ensuring a good flow of points from the daily stipends. But with the lack of large movements on the war front, they were unable to save up enough for what they really wanted—the chase items.

Annie was gazing longingly at the store entry for [Side Slide]. But at a cost of one million points, she was still a ways away. Additionally, she and her sister were aging nearer to twenty-seven as each day passed, pushing them ever closer to needing to Tier up to stay on the Path. The moment they did, the twins would be Tier 7 Pathers, and booted from the war. Having just had their twenty sixth birthdays last week, they only had a year left.

Matt made a note to send Annie a [Side Slide] if one ever appeared during his rift experiments. She was a good friend, and the skill would do wonders for her.

The auction closed out with a gauntlet that increased melee damage. As that last item was wheeled away, the junior auctioneer in charge of the auction gave a flourish. In his place, Javier, the Tier 29 representative of Deep Sky Auctions, took the stage.

"Good evening, my friends! Good evening. Today is a special day." He paced around, nodding. "Yes, it is. It *most certainly* is.

Today marks the six-month anniversary of the start of this vassal war!"

A slight cheer rose, but Javier waved his arms, prompting the crowd into a roar. "Yes, my friends, you have worked hard! You have learned! You have died."

The crowded hall quieted at that, but Javier just grinned. "Around this time, in most such wars, things tend to be slowing down to a grind. To help push past this, the Empire likes to provide a little extra encouragement. For the fighters on the ground, there are new rewards in the contribution points shop! Next month, even more new surprises will appear in the auction house. I'm sure they will interest a great many of you. As for your daring leaders…"

He waved, and both Sara and Albert were highlighted with orbs of light that raced from his hand. "To the two young generals of the war, the Empire offers these…"

On the podium next to him, two Shards of Reality sparkled into existence on a plush cushion. "Two perfectly preserved Shards of Reality. For those that don't know, these are the echo of an Ascension, preserved for later use. Anyone who cultivates under their influence is all but guaranteed to form at least part of their own Concept."

At the murmurs of appreciation, he nodded. "But that is not all! Not remotely. We will also provide the chambers needed to ensure that the maximum benefit is squeezed out of them. This is a rare treat! Yes indeed! Shards of Reality are not cheap. No, they are not! Ascensions are rare, and Shards of Reality do not last forever, no matter how much we may wish for it. But the Empire has purchased a few just for this vassal war."

Javier nodded at the two rulers as he said, "Just ask the king and queen. I'm sure they tried to purchase one, but only a thousand or so are produced per Ascension, and they're quickly snatched up by those there. These treasures are not easy to get your hands on."

Both royals nodded in affirmation at the man's words, but they didn't look particularly interested. On the other hand, both Albert and Sara stared at the two shards like ravenous wolves being held back by sheer will.

"What is required of my young friends to earn these prizes? Now *that* is the question, isn't it?"

He grinned. "Simple! Just fight. Move your troops and make

progress. When each side earns twenty million points from *new, active* sources, these are yours. Send your people out to raid! Send them out to take a city! Prevent a city from being taken! You simply must *do*!"

Matt grinned as well. This meant that things were going to kick back off, which meant more chances to earn points. These last three months had been far too slow for his taste.

Javier turned as if to leave, before pausing and adding, "Oh! I almost forgot about these beauties in all the excitement." The two royal rewards, the staff, and the gauntlet, flashed into place on either side of him. "The two grand prizes for the benevolent rulers!"

He displayed what Matt could only call a predatory smile. "Each respective side is just under halfway to earning these trophies for their monarchs."

With that, both he and the items poofed away. The queen simply placed a hand on Sara's forearm, but the King turned his head toward his son like a loaded cannon ready to fire. Both of their reactions were still visible on the projection. The look aimed at Albert was borderline hostile. That face held more than simple, naked greed; there was a rabid hunger there that made Matt shiver.

Matt opened and flipped through the new additions to the contribution point shop, still sorting them from most to least expensive by default. The first item he saw froze him solid. Tier 14 upgrade orbs were available for the low cost of half a million points. They were limited to one per person, and only fifty total for sale. A minuscule number for the millions of people participating in the war.

He couldn't believe his eyes. A lot of contradictory things was said about these orbs, but one thing known for certain was that they were incredibly rare rift drops. Luckily, the store description provided more information directly from the Empire. The Tier 14 upgrade orbs only dropped from Tier 14 to 25 rifts and could upgrade any Tier 8 or Tier 14 skills to improve them.

They appeared every two ranks of skill shard drops and were able to upgrade any skill at an appropriate Tier or equivalent once. Each upgrade used made the Skill eligible for the next available Tier of upgrade orb, too. So, a Tier 8 skill like [Cracked Phantom Armor] could be upgraded up to four times. First with a Tier 14 upgrade orb, then with a Tier 26, then a Tier 38, and finally with the theoretical Tier 50 upgrade orbs.

The level types of the orb were only theoretical, because there were no Tier 50 rifts to delve, and thus no Tier 50 rewards to earn. If previous trends held, the Tier 38 upgrade orbs were dropped until Tier 49. But the Empire's highest rift was only Tier 47, so there was no way to know for sure.

Matt was close. With the passive points he had earned from being in a top five team, he sat on about 450,000 points. But if he was so close, that meant others would be, too.

Even as he was looking, the number available dropped to forty seven, a gut wrenching decrease that spoke volumes for how fast they would disappear.

Using the reference provided in the store description, he quickly researched how upgraded orbs affected cracked skills, and checked the most common upgrades for [Phantom Armor].

Cracked skills could be upgraded but didn't have set rules they followed like standard skills. Their upgrades were far more varied, and hard to precisely predict. Generally, though, the upgrade would somehow parallel one of the upgrades available to the base skill.

[Phantom Armor] was a historically popular choice, with a single, well-established upgrade. The first orb always granted the ability to store a second distinct charge in the skill, which gave the user the chance of blocking up to two life-threatening attacks in one fight.

Matt wasn't sure what that would mean for [Cracked Phantom Armor]. The upgrade could range from something that forced him to reset his entire fighting style, to something that made him invincible. There was just no way to tell beforehand.

Even with risk in the randomness, he salivated at the thought of upgrading it.

As the group headed to the dining hall, Matt checked the known upgrades for the rest of his skills, to cover his bases.

[Mage's Retreat] added a large increase to running speed. The skill's name was actually derived from this upgrade. At one point, an infamous mage demonstrated this upgrade so thoroughly and effectively, it was widely reclassified as an escape skill for spellcasters. Matt passed on that for now.

[Endurance] simply helped enhance the body's physical fitness while in use. The user could get a 'workout' simply by channeling mana into it.

No other effort needed. The effects were permanent, but not something Matt needed, so he put it to the side as well. He already went to the gym and enjoyed it. Getting fit through a spell wasn't on his radar of needs.

[Hail] was a weird one, with a trio of possible upgrade paths. But Matt couldn't find any information on how to choose, or if you even could. Two of the options were particularly common though. The first made the chunks of ice 'sticky,' causing them to bind to an opponent and slow them down as the weight of the ice chunks gradually built up on them. The second made it so the shards of ice contained pockets of hyper-cooled liquid water and would rupture on impact. It would soak the target in freezing water and cause severe frostbite. A third and much rarer upgrade made the hail blades sharper and interspersed the storm with massive chunks of ice. However, it would lower the diameter of the spell.

One excelled at crowd control, the other increased the cold damage, and the last upgrade made the skill great against unarmored opponents. The first two were interesting, and possibly very useful for Aster. None of them were anything that Matt particularly cared about more than boosting [Cracked Phantom Armor].

[Fireball] had an increased range, damage, and explosion size on impact. That was more tempting, but still not amazing for Matt as he currently stood. He intended to eventually replace the [Fireball] in his spirit anyway, once he had enough mana to afford a version with the increased base cost and damage. It would outpace the lowered cost version he had now by miles.

[Flamethrower]'s upgrade made Matt pause in deliberation. It increased the fire damage a little, but more importantly, it changed the nature of the fire. The skill's output gained the quality of a sticky, flaming liquid that lingered on anything it touched, and could be spread on contact. Now that was a nice upgrade that Matt could see a million uses for.

Matt warred with himself over the options. [Cracked Phantom Armor] was his primary skill that had taken him so far, but the cracked nature made it a risky and random choice. The improved [Flamethrower] would be a solid, immediately useful, all-around upgrade. The fact that he intended to shift to a more mage-like style just made the decision more difficult. [Flamethrower] was a short-to-mid range skill that he wasn't willing to use without [Cracked Phantom Armor] anyway.

He pushed the thoughts to the back of his mind and enjoyed his floating dinner with his friends. There was no point stressing over it until he had the points anyway. He would talk it over with Liz and Aster as well. This was a big purchase that could affect them as well.

He added the rest of Team Bucket into the conversation. With the upcoming push, he was sure they could all afford it sooner than most.

23

The action immediately picked up when the auction officially ended. Matt was pretty sure that the prince and princess didn't stick around long enough for the smaller side auctions to end or the banquet. They quickly flew out of the bubble and started getting things ready.

Team bucket didn't linger either, but they didn't exactly rush out the door. Once they finished their meal, they left at their own pace.

None of them thought that the fighting would start immediately. But their assumption was incorrect. Both sides had already sent out teams to take forts through any means necessary. Matt figured that would be it for the first day, but both sides were emptying the outlying cities to mass troops in a pretty transparent attempt to take new cities.

They were going to rush into the fray, but as soon as they surfaced, a warning went out.

Assassins were out in full force, attacking anyone suspected to have a large number of points. At first, they thought the attacks were all sanctioned hits. But it was soon confirmed to be opportunistic Pathers trying to remove points from the general point pool and collect bounties. The upgrade orbs and the rumored auction next month were surely motives for the attempts. They all wanted to ensure that they had a greater chance at the more expensive items. No matter their motives, their pursuits were causing a ruckus.

No one targeted them in the time it took to make it to their rooms, but they were all on high alert. A quick message to Juni registered the team as ready for new missions, and they immediately received a standby order.

Liz started pacing. "The upgrade orbs and the promise of new items appearing in the auction are going to cause a fucking disaster."

Conor rubbed his hands together with a hungry look on his face. "Upgrading [Demon Zone] increases the likelihood to trigger the reflected damage, and the percentage of damage reflected increases while upping the range. It's just too perfect for me. And I'm so close."

The large man paused. "Well, there is the chance that the skill will get the rarer upgrade that increases attack speed with each successful reflection of damage, along with an increase in area of effect size. But that's so rare, I highly doubt I'll get it."

Everyone nodded. Matt felt the same way. He was only 50,000 points away from the orb, which could mean quite a significant change in his fighting style.

Liz chimed in from next to Conor, "Same. My manipulation skill gets cheaper and easier to use. That alone would be worth the price. Otherwise, I have no idea what my skill would turn into after my Talent goes into effect. But that one should be safe enough."

Liz nodded to Conor. "Granted, any manipulation skill can be upgraded so it's instinctive to use, just like a limb. Zero effort required to direct it. That would be great, but that's like one in a trillion. They're more well documented rumors than anything else. There are tons of theories about ways people have changed their skills into Talents, but Talent scanners haven't figured out how to predict it. Like I said, everyone is searching for the secret to recreating the unique upgrades, but no one has found it."

Annie shrugged. "It's not like we're banking on that effect anyway. What are you thinking of using it on Matt?"

Everyone looked to Matt, who said, "I could risk it on my innate skill—" He meant [Cracked Phantom Armor], as he was still lying that it was a Talent. It was a slight, sudden change to his story, from a Talent to an innate skill. But it was one he hoped they overlooked. Although, he was getting tired of lying to his friends about it. "—but that could backfire, since it's a cracked skill. I honestly have no idea what it could turn into. I also have [Flamethrower], and that upgrade is amazing without the risk. Honestly, I don't know which I would choose, but it would be a worthwhile investment either way."

They all turned to Annie, who wiggled her hand back and forth. "Not sure if I really need it. It would be better for me to save up. My skills are less magical and more mundane for the most part. If I could get [Side Slide] *and* the upgrade orb, it would be great. But as of now, I don't really need the orb on its own."

Matt agreed with her logic. The orb would be nice for her, but it wasn't as vital for her as for the others.

Everyone turned to Emily, who nodded to her sister. "It would be great for [Bolt], but the upgrade only slightly increases base damage, and adds the ability to jump to more targets. If I use it on [Cracked Mana Bolt], it might let me get more aspects, or maybe give me the ability to choose. But I really can't be sure since the upgrade for the base skill only increases damage and range. It's such a gamble with a cracked skill. The upgrades would be nice, but I'm so far away right now, I doubt I'd get an orb before they're all gone." Her eyes flickered off to the side before she said, "They're already down to thirty-one."

Checking for himself, Matt saw the counter on available upgrade orbs and verified what his teammate said. It was a heartbreaking realization, but Conor put a voice to the frustration and started cursing out loud.

Matt clenched his fist. The precious orbs were just going too quickly.

He was so wrapped up in his thought he missed the looks Annie and Emily passed to each other. He didn't miss what the twins said afterwards.

"Take the points you three need from us."

"You already gave me points once. I'm happy to return the favor."

It took him a long moment to register what they had said.

He opened his mouth to speak, but nothing came out. It was just too large of a favor for him to accept, but it was too valuable to decline.

Matt felt frozen in limbo from indecision.

Conor wasn't so afflicted. "We can't take that. It's too much."

Annie rolled her eyes. "Just take it. We know you're all able to pay us back. We don't need the orbs, but with them, the whole team will be stronger. If you three are stronger, *we* can earn more points.

I'm sure this is exactly what the other teams are doing. Besides, we're friends."

That last bit sounded so simple, but it wasn't.

Liz slowly shook her head. "I'm not sure what to say. It's a lot more points than the few thousand points we gave you. I…"

Emily waved her off. "It was a larger percentage of your points. Just take it." Seeing their reluctance, she said, "I still want an orb, so if we can pool our points together to get me one after the next few engagements, I'd call that repaying the favor. if it makes you feel any better. We just think that our team could use the upgrades now."

Annie jumped in. "We already agreed to pool our points if we needed to in the auction, so this is really no different. Don't be weird just because you're on the receiving end."

That seemed fair enough to Matt. He checked Aster's point total and saw that she was at 230,936 points. Where exactly she had been spending her points, he didn't know, but while the others bickered, he impressed on the fox through their bond that she should save up her points. Getting her an upgrade orb now would be incredibly useful, even if she didn't use it right away.

He tuned back into the conversation after Emily called his name twice. He rejoined the world of the living while she rolled her eyes. "Ugh. How many points do each of you need?"

Matt checked. He needed 47,291 to reach the half-million marker. "I can't thank you enough. I'll take it if you insist, but just know that we can do this without the upgrade orbs."

Seeing both twins wave him down, he imprinted this favor into his heart and said, "I need 47,291 points to buy the orb."

A heartbeat later, Emily flicked a finger at him, and he received 47,292 points. He now understood why Emily had been so grateful when they gave her the points she needed at the first auction.

She grinned. "One extra, just in case you die right here and now."

Matt clenched his fist and carved their generosity deep into his memory. He knew they weren't doing it for favors to be traded, but he was determined to repay both for their friendship, trust, and generosity.

Conor nodded slightly at Matt before half-bowing at the twins. "Same as Matt. I am incredibly grateful for this. Since you both have made up your minds, I won't hesitate anymore. Just…thank you. I need 71,013 points to buy the orb."

As Annie repeated her sister's gesture of point transfer, and Conor whispered another thanks.

Everyone looked to Liz, who flushed and said, "I need 91 points."

"What!?" Everyone exclaimed in some fashion.

Matt actually couldn't see Liz's point total. After all, they were dating, not actually married, so some things were restricted. He could ask, and she could send him an updated number, but neither bothered with that.

Liz's blush deepened to a crimson as she sputtered, "I never made any large purchases besides my two skills, and I get a stipend for doing most of the actual leading of the Pathers. So, I have a bit more points left over. I was just going to borrow what I needed from Aster."

His fox yipped a response at Liz, who blew a raspberry at her in return.

Emily flicked a finger at Liz and quipped, "Here's 100 points. Keep the change."

The three of them quickly purchased the orbs. In under a second, three black boxes with silver ribbons tying them shut hovered in front of them. Matt plucked the box out of the air, but immediately stumbled at the unexpected weight.

A quick scan with his spiritual sense revealed why the box was so heavy. Both the box and its contents were Tier 14. Matt activated [Mage's Retreat] to control his stumble. He barely landed in the chair with the heavy object pressing down his lap.

Liz and Conor learned from his fumble, and just removed the lids of the floating boxes. The covers floated next to the box as if that was their intention.

Matt flicked his box open with some effort. Nestled in the black, silk-like cloth was a thumb-sized orb of silver, with pulsing streaks of black running through it.

It was much smaller than he expected.

He picked up the little orb and marveled at its weight. The box and its lid vanished, presumably back to where they had come from.

With a trickle of essence, he still had from an essence stone he'd recently used, Matt connected to the orb in his hand.

Unlike a skill, this object vanished into nothing. But he felt the change immediately in his spirit. There was no cycling needed. A new kind of energy sat in his spirit, waiting for direction and eager to be used.

Matt reviewed his choices, but [Cracked Phantom Armor] won out in the end, despite the risks. [Flamethrower] was handy, but he didn't need the upgrade when he could simply keep the heat on his opponent endlessly. After all, upgrades were rarely bad for cracked skills. From everything he had heard and read, the upgrade would be a net neutral at worst.

He expected some sort of significant change, but no. There was a brief rush of energy that wrapped up his first and most important skill, and then the change was over. The whole ordeal was done in an instant.

With fear building, he inspected the skill and found that there were no immediate changes. Focusing in further, it almost seemed as if there was a second copy of the skill, situated in the same place as [Cracked Phantom Armor]. He attempted to move his skill, but the original skill structure and the other copy moved in unison.

With trepidation and a hammering heart, he poured mana into the skill. Everything functioned as normal. He searched around himself to see if anything else changed, but he couldn't find anything out of the ordinary. His armor was its usual, smooth light blue. Meanwhile, the second, illusionary copy of the skill structure was still sitting there, untouched.

Carefully, he poured more mana into the skill, to the point where it would typically start to overload its structure. The mana was instead redirected to the illusionary copy of the skill. Matt inspected himself as he put his remaining 34 MPS into the other side of [Cracked Phantom Armor]. His AI took the last bit of mana to analyze and record everything that he was doing.

Nothing hurt, or warned him of impending doom, so he inspected his arms a second time.

The changes were distinct.

His armor had thickened, and changed from its simple, smooth design to add an elaborate filigree that lightly lined his armor. He twisted his hands, marveling at the thicker gauntlets, and at his idle thought, all of the extra armor flowed to his fist. Both gauntlets grew incredibly detailed, and the plating became denser as he focused on the area.

All of the extra decorations glided from the rest of his armor to fill out the gauntlets. It was almost overly detailed when it was finished. He was worried that the ridges would give enemy blades purchase, but they were just a slightly different color of mana, instead of actual engraving.

"Huh…"

Everyone was looking at him, so he shrugged. "The skill seemed to grow a second layer that's really easy to shape."

With a thought, he imagined a shield connected to his left arm, and the second layer of armor rushed to create the image. The mana around his left hand simply traveled from his fist to his forearm, creating a ghostly image of the medium kite shield he had imagined. The mana from his right hand crossed his chest before filling in the armor and making it more solid. It was harder to hold this shape than the gauntlets, which were almost natural. From a little testing, he discovered that the farther away from his body—or maybe the original [Cracked Phantom Armor] layer—the harder it was to keep the shape of the image in his head. Even when just six inches away, the skill started growing slightly hazy.

As his thoughts drifted off, the shield fell apart.

"Interesting."

An exasperated Liz hollered, "What!? Give us the details!"

Matt didn't have them to share. So, as he tested and confirmed his hypothesis, he said, "It seems like another channel for my skill. Its default state bulks up the armor all over. But if I concentrate, I can make the second layer reinforce one area in particular."

He met Liz's eyes with his own. "Hey, can you stab me, please? I want to test it."

A tendril of blood rose, and Matt could feel that it was full of Liz's Concept. The darker tinge spoke to her using the blood iron as well, "Sure, my initial mana cost is lower, so I didn't get lucky it seems." She didn't seem upset at that at all as she nearly vibrated as she couldn't stand still.

He stopped sending mana into the second channel, and the extra mass of the armor vanished into nothing.

Liz carefully drove her blood tendril into his armor until she broke through.

"Okay, I know how much that took. Feels about normal. I didn't notice it being harder than before."

Matt reformed the skill but added the rest of his mana regeneration into the other channel. With 45 MPS in the original skill, he sent the rest of his 80 MPS into the second layer, and let it settle naturally in the full body armor configuration.

Liz tried to drive into the skill, but he could see the visible effort it took her. She finally broke through with a grunt, and the outer layer of his armor shattered in his spirit. It only took her a moment to drive through the normal armor underneath.

Matt checked what his AI registered and nodded at Liz.

She inspected his unarmored arm for wounds before finding none. She said, "That was about twenty-five percent stronger. Or it took twenty-five percent more effort for me to break through."

With [Cracked Phantom Armor] having settled down in his spirit, Matt reformed both spells and then redirected the entire second layer of the skill to cover his forearm, where Liz was testing.

Liz had to bring considerably more effort to break his armor, even leaning into the attack while directing her blood with a hand.

Finally, the skill shattered when Matt felt her do something different. He flinched out of the way as a drill of blood slashed past his quickly broken inner armor layer.

She quickly stood straight and nodded to Matt, with everyone else watching. "That was the hardest I can hit, and I had to use a drill to get through it."

A private message reached him. 'I had to use my full Concept to break through the thicker layer. Can you keep that up all the time? I was breaking Tier 7 defenses at Tier 5. I'd call that top quality Tier 8 armor if it's all concentrated.'

Matt thought out loud, "Nope, can't manage that. Too expensive. That eats everything I have. It takes a lot of focus, too."

Conor gave him an evil grin. "Nice. Now we can just stand there and beat anyone who comes to challenge us."

The large man hugged Annie then Emily in quick succession as he thanked each of them again.

Matt nodded to them as well but was thinking more internally. The upgrade wasn't his worst fear; [Cracked Phantom Armor] still functioned as a pseudo-channel skill and was fundamentally unchanged. But its direct application right now was limited. If he wanted to use the skill, he would need to drop every other spell to use it. That meant no [Endurance] or [Mage's Retreat] to increase his combat ability.

The ability to manipulate the skill so easily was great, but it didn't seem to transfer to the original skill. The first layer felt firmly anchored to his body. Whereas the second layer felt loosely anchored to the mana of the layer below it.

With that thought, he reactivated the skill and tried to create his spiked gauntlets with his new layer of armor. It flatly refused to form the spikes. In a panic, he tried to create them with his standard layer of armor, and they formed as quickly as before. Then, and only then, would the second layer cover the spikes, lengthening them a hair. It was still far less than the changes he could do when making it a shield.

That was an interesting limitation, but not one that bothered him a ton. He continued to test the new portion of his skill, but anything that wasn't strictly armor was impossible to create. Considering that the skill was called [Cracked Phantom *Armor*], he wasn't surprised. But it would have been nice to have a backup weapon that couldn't be taken away or stolen.

Still, having a shield that couldn't be stolen and didn't need to be stored could be useful. He wondered if it would fulfill the requirements for a skill that needed a shield, like [Shield Charge] or [Shield Bash]. It would be quite handy if it did.

His second test was a simple one that didn't work. He was unable to activate the second layer of [Cracked Phantom Armor] without putting at least 1 MPS into the base layer. At the same time, the amount of mana he fed into the bottom skill was apparently the max he could channel into the second layer. It was another interesting limitation that unfortunately prevented him from gaming the system, as it seemed that the second layer of armor was directly tied to the first.

All in all, Matt was happy with the upgrade. It added further defense at only the cost of more mana. While just increasing the overall effect of [Cracked Phantom Armor] would have been simpler and cleaner, he was pretty sure that this would allow the skill scale with him even more. The second layer was far less mana efficient in terms of pure defense, but the increased flexibility made the skill more adaptable. It was a worthy tradeoff. Eventually, he would have millions and trillions of mana generation, which meant that taking twice the mana was a great long-term upgrade. It was just somewhat less useful in the short term.

He'd still need to focus on increasing the mana throughput on the skill, but it wasn't anything new. He worked on that every day.

The only problem was that his current maximum mana was only at 80, so he only had 80 MPS to spend on channeled skills and his AI. When he Tiered-up, he'd double that. But as of now, he had more skills than he could afford to keep up at once.

Realizing that he was complaining about having too many skills, Matt laughed at himself. Most people were happy to have a single skill or two at Tier 6, and he was complaining that he didn't have enough mana to power all the skills he had.

He rubbed his face with a self-deprecating smile.

Idly, he checked the number of upgrade orbs left. Twenty-six. He peered at the twins, who smiled and chatted with the other three as he tested his armor.

He owed them. Massively.

That evening, they were called to martial up, but not through their AI. Instead, they were summoned in person by a nervous looking aide. They asked Team Bucket to assemble with everyone else. Over the course of an hour, the team and nearly a million others were funneled through the teleporter, and into a large fortress on one of the other continents.

During their down time, Matt and the other fast flyers were asked to scout the area. This was one of the few new large forts that the kingdom had managed to hold on to from their mass invasion into queendom territory in retaliation for the first city's capture.

They were actually closer to the second city that the queendom had taken. It was the larger of the two cities situated on this continent, and the queendom had made their headquarters, as it held the inter-continental teleporter linked back to their main holdings.

Matt didn't see much of anything during his time scouting; neither enemies, nor anything else out of the ordinary.

Their intention to hit a less prepared city was for naught. They had been flying for most of the afternoon in a loose formation, and their scouts reported that the first small fort they were meant to engage was already garrisoned and on alert. Not only that, but a million extra troops were spread out around the base of the fort, too, positioned well inside the anti-flying formation.

For what must have been the third time in the last hour, Alastair, the top general for this mission, stood around with his own entourage of people and nodded toward the enemies. "What are we going to do about them? Suggestions?"

Matt suspected he was only in charge because his father was a kingdom duke, and that his two aides were the real brains of the operation. Finding an equally sized force shouldn't have stumped the man this much.

With each side fielding massive armies and sending them to cause mayhem and destruction, Matt hadn't expected this to be easy. From the reports coming in, the queendom was already trying to invade kingdom territories and attack a city of their own. If the kingdom could anticipate that move and set up blocking forces, there was no reason that the queendom couldn't as well.

One of the aides, Philip, said, "I see zero reasons why we should fight this battle. There aren't even any notable strategic assets in the area. We just need to go around them and clear a path to the city we were supposed to attack."

Olivia countered his point. "No, we need to weaken the enemy troops now. That alone would be worthwhile. Remember, we're here to siege a city down, but they're probably planning to do the same. If we don't engage them now, they won't simply disappear. Best case scenario, they march on one of our cities that can hold them off long enough for reinforcements to arrive. But most likely, they'll ambush our supply lines, flank us in the middle of the siege, and then partially reinforce the city. That would be utterly disastrous for us. The princess might be desperate for new gains, but only a *short-sighted idiot* would pass up such an easy opportunity to decimate the enemy like that."

Olivia sighed as she rubbed her brow under her helmet. "Were it not for the prince's *very firm* directive to not concern ourselves with reinforcing the cities, I'd say that this should be our plan, too. Either way, convention states that every potential defender we kill here will be worth three of our attackers during a siege. Let's take the opportunity to cull their forces now, in the open, before they have surprise on their side or walls to hide behind."

Phillip tried to counter what Matt felt was a good point. "Yes, but we're only the first million of several waves of troops on the way. We're meant to clear a path, not get bogged down with a battle against a random small fort that we could've bypassed."

Matt just watched the mass of queendom troops with a careful eye. They sat there, but something felt off about their movements around the top of the hill. He just couldn't pin down what was bothering him about it.

He wasn't alone in noticing. Alastair interrupted the squabbling aids and said, "What are they doing? Does anyone have binoculars? I don't like the way they're mucking about."

The loose formation had been shifting around in seemingly random patterns, but it was too smoothly coordinated to truly be haphazard.

A minute and a half later, the long barreled mana cannons were revealed.

"Take cover!" The scream echoed half a dozen times but, even as everyone scattered, it was too late.

Matt tackled Liz and activated [Cracked Phantom Armor], putting everything into the skill and covering his back. Liz didn't sit on her ass either, and a bubble of blood surrounded them. For a moment, the evening sun went dark.

Until the mana cannon shots landed.

The world lit up in bluish-white, even overpowering the deep crimson of the blood wall. Despite having his eyes squeezed shut, he could make out the color clearly.

Well, I can't say I like being on the other side of a mana cannon.

Matt looked around himself and breathed into Liz's face.

After a second of silence, she asked, "Think it's safe?"

He shook his head. It was more instinct, but he expected a second volley.

Liz repeated her question, and he realized that she couldn't see him, and must not have been using her special sense. So, he repeated himself. "Not yet. My gut tells me there's another volley on the way."

Thirty agonizing seconds later, he was proven right. Another all-consuming flash and world-rocking explosion washed through the area around them.

Instantly, Liz deactivated the dome around them, and they scrambled up to their feet. He had been monitoring his AI, and the rest of their team was fine, still where they had been with the general troops.

The command area was a crater, blasted ruin of holes and smoke.

Things had gone to shit with most of the leadership decimated, and the general troops had rushed forward. To his bewilderment, they were charging on foot.

They were in an anti-flying formation from the nearby small fort, but he had no idea why they would just rush into the enemy army after their leadership had been taken out so quickly. It would have been far better to pull back out of range and formulate an actual plan. Now, the best move was trying to instill some fragment of order back into the chaos.

When no mid-level commander responded to his messages, he had to give up and face reality. There was little else left but to simply throw himself into the fray and find his team.

Matt barreled into the front line with a roar and a torrent of fire that roasted half a dozen people as they cooked inside of their armor.

Still trying to keep his cover, he cut the spell once he cleared a hole in the defender's shield wall.

Half a dozen people followed him into the gap and started to hack and slash, before enemy reinforcements tried to close the breach and push them back. The Tier 6 defenders were led by a Tier 7 who engaged with another giant of a Tier 7 on Matt's side.

After they were forced back out, Matt traveled along the frontline to find his team. Liz had become separated from him at some point, but he had no idea when. Nonetheless, all six members of Team Bucket had responded to the situation in the same way. They rampaged their way to the front lines, causing massive damage, and eventually found each other. Conor and Matt reunited first and converged to create and hold a zone of death that none dared to enter.

The upgrade for [Demon Zone] was a massive improvement. The general reflection chance had doubled to three percent. Now, everyone in the area took an unexpected and unblockable attack once every thirty or so hits. Considering that the range was now close to ten feet to a side, the skill was able to hold down a significant number of attackers.

The twins appeared behind their position, with Emily carrying Aster in her backpack. Moments later, Liz joined them from a tidal wave of blood, and collected her partner in crime. Led by Conor, Team Bucket scythed into the enemy ranks. With Aster, Liz, and Emily unleashing a bombardment of spells from behind their front line, their advance was nearly unopposed.

The enemy's situation devolved further once enough blood had been spilled to soak the ground, and Liz had enough to cast [Blood Sprite]. As the first sparrow appeared, it dropped to the ground unnoticed and feasted until it split, over and over again. As Matt and Conor hacked their way through the queendom troops, even more food was left behind for the little monsters to feed on.

When Liz finally directed the flock to attack the queendom troops, pandemonium ensued. Except, it didn't last as long as last time.

A purple-haired woman with a guitar strummed a cord that splattered all of the little sparrows and left everyone around her clutching their ears. Everyone except her defenders, who seemed unaffected. But the odd attack had worked and had prevented [Blood Sprite] from cascading farther and overwhelming the defenders.

Annie tried to pick off the woman with a crossbow bolt, but one of her guards intercepted the shot. With the threats taken care of, the musician went back to buffing the people around her. Visible energy rose off her instrument and into the people around her as she worked.

The tide of battle ebbed against them, and Team Bucket was once again broken away from each other. They had to struggle against several waves of queendom fighters before being able to file back into a formation. The fighting only grew fiercer as each side endured more and more casualties. Annie eventually slipped away, pretending to be hit with an arrow and falling down, just before activating her invisibility and disappearing.

She later reunited with them and reported that she'd returned the favor, executing two of the queendom's top brass before having to escape from the small fort they were using as a headquarters. Their top general was out of the picture.

With Matt's Concept keeping the team charged, they battered their way forward until their enemies broke.

Matt and Liz lay next to each other in the smoking ruins of the battlefield, panting from exhaustion. Aster was sprawled out across them, with her thumping heart beating in lockstep with Matt's own through their bond.

They had been one of the final groups to take out the lingering queendom forces. The bloody and disastrous fight had only been won because the enemy commander hadn't expected anything as dumb as a full frontal assault. Under no circumstances was that a reasonable response to their leadership being beheaded in the opening salvo, especially not for a measly fort. The queendom hadn't bothered to set up significant forward defenses, which cost them dearly when things got to melee range.

With only one hundred and some odd thousand troops left, the force Team Bucket had come with was effectively destroyed. They were now fit only to be absorbed into their reinforcements, which were already funneling through the nearby portal and flying the long way over the ocean separating the continents.

Now, Team Bucket laid in the wreckage of their final encounter, where they'd chased down the last few queendom soldiers unable to flee fast enough. It was a disaster for the kingdom, but their team was too tired and exhausted to care.

Emily, lying at their heads, groaned as she sat up and spat. Her coughs squelched with a wet sound that couldn't be healthy.

Annie flopped over and asked, "Whose bright idea was that charge?"

Matt had to clear his throat twice to force out, "Everyone was already moving when we came up from the first shots. No one responded to my hails either."

Emily cursed as she started inspecting her face with a broken sword that she'd polished. "Are you fucking kidding me!? This is gonna take a healer to fix." She poked the deep gash and screeched. "Fuck! My face…"

He didn't need to get up to see what she was looking at. That blow would have taken her head off if Matt hadn't been there to block it. Well…most of it. Her face was split with a gnarly scar that cleaved through her helmet, grazed her head, and ran down part of her face. Bone was visible, but only gently scored. While not life-threatening, the wound was damn ugly.

The bit of sword dropped as she deflated, "Still, thanks for the save guys. I'd be dead if not for your help. What a disaster."

Matt nodded as he sat up, it had been a disaster of epic proportions. Even for the 'winning' side.

But it had earned them quite the number of points.

Prior Total (last updated 0 days ago): 1 point.

<u>TEAM MERITS:</u>

(Calculated for Tier 6 Combatant).

- Enemy vassal killed, Tier 5. Worth 1 point. Performed 141 times.
- Enemy vassal killed, Tier 6. Worth 5 points. Performed 8,592 times.
- Enemy vassal killed, Tier 7. Worth 25 points. Performed 7 times.
- Enemy general assassinated, Tier 7. Worth 1,000 points. Performed 2 times.
- Items and equipment looted but returned. Assigned worth: 7,874 points.
- Captured a heavy artillery asset intact, long-range mana cannon. Worth 1,000 points. Performed 3 times.
- Eliminated enemy general(s) in the middle of a major engagement (each side >500K units). Reward: 1.4x multiplier to all team merits.

<u>PERSONAL MERITS:</u>

(Calculated for Tier 6 Combatant)

- Enemy vassal killed, Tier 5. Worth 1 point. Performed 21 times.
- Enemy vassal killed, Tier 6. Worth 5 points. Performed 1,272 times.

- Enemy vassal killed, Tier 7. Worth 25 points. Performed 2 times.

ARMY MERITS:

- Defeat a major enemy army of equivalent size (975K vs 997K) in a defensive position, field fortifications. Reward: 1.2x multiplier to all merits (applied after other multipliers). Note: All leadership bonuses (brigadier general) forfeited due to loss of command over subordinate troops.

UNACHIEVED MERITS: **For reference purposes only.**

- Capture a fortified enemy position defended by an equivalent force, small fort. Worth 250 points. Leadership Bonus (brigadier general): 1.2x multiplier to all merits.
- Reestablish the command structure of a major army (>500K units) after the sudden loss of >90% of top leadership. Reward: 1.5x multiplier to all merits. 'Victory from the Jaws of Defeat' Bonus: 2.0x multiplier. Final Reward: 3.0x multiplier to all merits.

SUMMARY OF GAINS:
Team Merits:

- **Raw Total:** 56,150
- **Team Multiplier:** 1.4x
- **Category Total:** 78,610

Personal Merits:

- **Raw Total:** 6,431
- **Personal Multiplier:** N/A
- **Category Total:** 6,431

Combined Merits:

- **Sub-Total:** 85,041
- **Total Multiplier:** 1.2x
- **Grand Total:** 102,049

New Gains: 102,049 points.
New Total: 102,050 points.
Pather Team Ranking (Kingdom of Seven Suns): 3rd place.
Estimated Daily Stipend: 1,250 points.

He sent 47,292 points to repay Emily while they lazily chatted for a bit. The points would only actually be sent once they went back to the neutral city, but he felt better knowing he had cleared his debt. It put his total at 54,758, but he had repaid his friend after just one disastrous battle.

A quick check of the market showed that there were still twenty-six upgrade orbs remaining. Anyone who could have bought one had done so quickly, and the second half seemed to be waiting on those who could earn the most points over the next few weeks. He still wanted to get Aster her own orb, and then help Emily get one for herself. But the rush for the orbs seemed to be mostly over. That, or no one was in the neutral city anymore, so they were unable to purchase items for the moment.

As he recovered his energy, Matt realized that he had to pee something fierce, and stood to find someplace slightly out of sight. A deeper crater fit the bill, as no standing trees were nearby. After fighting through the entire night and into the morning, his body was finally alerting him to its needs.

Seeing him up and about, the rest of the team wobbled to their feet with various grunts and moans. They were all drained, but everyone started to address their own waylaid needs while groaning at stiff muscles and pains. Only their fading adrenaline had kept them upright.

The highest-ranking commander to survive was Olivia. She'd stepped up and directed the battle as best she could, despite losing both her legs to the mana cannons. Even now, she was still barking out commands from her newly cobbled together command tent.

Half a dozen new orders awaited Team Bucket that still needed to be acknowledged.

24

Their remaining troops gathered together, and a debriefing was conducted by the still wounded Olivia. Matt listened in while he acted as a mana battery for the healers, who were hard at work getting the survivors combat-ready.

They had moved into the small fort, and she was permanently stuck on her flying device, as her legs would need to be regrown before she could walk. For now, while under the anti-flying formation, she was carried on a stretcher. That still didn't diminish her contributions to the earlier fight.

Olivia had regained consciousness from one of the blasts that took out the rest of the command staff, and immediately started issuing orders despite her charred off legs. She quickly found that all of their comms were jammed and began working on a solution. As it turned out, an opportunist spy hidden among their mid-level commanders had taken the opportunity to sabotage their comms, after starting the charge himself.

It had taken her half an hour to even be able to send messages at all. But once she had regained some measure of control over the system, she ordered all the troops she could reach to organize an offensive.

Matt and the other Pathers in the army were totally unaware of the situation, as their comms had remained obfuscated until there was a complete wipe of the system. It had only taken place close to the end of the battle, when Olivia felt secure enough about a victory to slacken her micromanagement. The entire process took about two hours.

After reviewing the telemetry of the battle, Matt had personally messaged the woman with how impressed he was with her orders. Her commands and decisions, while only communicating with a fraction of her forces, hadn't simply been practical and smart.

They were inspirational.

She had predicted everyone's moves; even her own unreachable allies. She moved her few troops to counter enemy movements, while also assisting faltering sections of their ranks during chaotic and brutal melee. The disparate forces that should have been beyond her control were seemingly shepherded into place.

The meeting started with Olivia relaying orders. "We won the fight, but our unit has been rendered combat ineffective, so we're going to be absorbed by General Lupis. We did well, but our overall mission was a failure. I'd like to thank the Pather Annie, who took out the enemy leadership early enough to let me direct our troops mostly uncontested."

Matt sent Annie a thumbs up in their private team chat, but there was grumbling from half a dozen indistinct voices transmitted over the AI. Olivia let the remaining mid-level commanders vent for a minute, but she quelled the moderate dissension shortly after.

Her voice cut through the murmurs, "I don't like it either. And that's why we won't be sticking around for reinforcements or another enemy unit to come finish us off."

That only caused another round of questions, which she answered with a casual, "I intended to get started on our original objective. We're down to one hundred and fifty thousand combat-capable troops, which is more than enough to start the initial push. We won't be able to secure as much ground as I'd like, but we only need to keep things going for a day or so before our reinforcements arrive."

There was more chatting, but Matt tuned it out. He was concerned. They had nearly twenty thousand heavily injured fighters who only needed time and mana to get back on their feet. This didn't seem like the best course of action in his mind, and it was at odds with Olivia's earlier decisions.

"Our preliminary scouting shows that the medium forts and large forts are reinforced, but not to the degree that this fort was. They're just doubled up in defenders. I want us to surround them and keep their forces contained. We won't be engaging, just clearing the way for our reinforcements."

That seemed a far better use of their time, and Matt nodded along with the questions being asked. Nothing jumped out to his AI or his own experience. The plan seemed sound enough.

The wounded were going to be shifted into the fort, and its defenders would be the kingdom fighters who were too injured to fight and fly but could stand on a wall on guard.

Olivia ordered Team Bucket to join the fourth squad, which was more of a quick reaction force than anything else. They were to stay with the command structure and be ready to intervene any time the fort's defenders tried to sally forth and break free.

Matt hoped at least one fort would try and break the siege, but none sent their troops out. They had a boring day of easily advancing. They moved forward as a unit, flying when they could, but dismounting and jogging when they couldn't. It was slow, but their numbers ensured that no one could easily attack them while they engulfed each fort on their way.

It was late evening when their reinforcements arrived. Matt saw them approaching from the rear, not by sight, but from the pillars of smoke that rose in the air. They were from the splinter groups that dropped off to siege down the surrounding forts. It was a fiery testament to the devastation that a million-strong force could muster.

Matt and his forces had already arrived at the city's edge, and were busy setting up a small camp, while the general troops were digging defenses and preparing the siege engines.

When the leading elements caught up with them, Liz and the rest of Team Bucket were unpleasantly surprised at what they found.

Alyssa was leading the force in an armored skirt while twirling her obnoxiously colored parasol. Their team followed her into the command tent.

"Good afternoon, everyone. You all look spiffy after losing most of your forces." She beamed at them like she had just given them the greatest of compliments.

"Where is General Lupis?" Olivia seemed suspicious, and Matt prepared to summon his sword from its ring at her shift in demeanor.

"Little Wolfe will not be joining us, unfortunately. An unexpected guest arrived and sent him on a vacation. I'm the new general. How convenient! It seems the queendom was quite upset about someone killing their generals in the middle of a major battle and took revenge. Or maybe they were just *so* impressed with how effective that tactic turned out to be, they decided to copy it."

She shrugged as if none of it concerned her. "Either way, our generals all seem to have a number of assassins gunning for them now. Between that, and all the major movements happening, there just aren't many generals available to step in for poor Wolfe and Alister. The only other candidates are all leading smaller forces right now, and they each seem to be *thoroughly* tied up at the moment. They simply wouldn't be able to get here in time."

Alyssa's mouth stretched from ear to ear as she finished, "Which leaves me the highest-ranking commander for this siege. Wonderful, no?"

Everyone present knew that absolutely none of this was a coincidence. There was no chance that every available field strategist could be simultaneously held up. But if she was rightfully in charge, she wouldn't be removed easily.

Seeing the looks on their faces, Alyssa continued with a laugh. "Oh, don't be like that. Ever since the auction, it's been chaos out there. Combine that with a few of the wrong wild mushrooms being cooked into some meals, and a very messy incident between a member of the peerage and their less-exclusive-than-expected mistress… Well, our beloved kingdom finds itself with a shortage of high level commanders to send our way. Nonetheless, I'm confident we will prevail."

To Matt's shock, Liz beamed right back at Alyssa. "Wonderfully said. We have all the leadership we need to win right here. I'm sure then you're prepared to suborn yourself to General Olivia and her orders?"

Everyone froze, particularly Alyssa and Olivia. The latter of whom made a face like she'd swallowed a bug.

Alyssa looked ready to spit fire but played it cool. "My, my. I don't know what you're talking about. I'm the only person here with a general's title."

Liz's smile grew sharp, and her yellow eyes glittered. "Ah, but you yourself said that Lupis was your original general. If you took over from him, then you're technically just an acting general. No?"

Matt could see Alyssa debate lying, but she finally shrugged and asked, "So?"

His girlfriend looked like the cat who ate the canary.

"Then, when two *acting* generals meet in the field, the acting general who was on site first retains command. Per section 9 subsection 14B of the kingdom's articles of war."

Her words were accompanied with a smile that could cut glass, and an AI message listing the relevant passages straight out of official kingdom protocol.

Alyssa just glared at Liz. "As a representative of the peerage, even the younger generation, I have the authority and responsibility to take over battlefield command from someone I deem unfit."

Annie shrugged and said, "I don't know. Is someone who can't stop a fire in their closet better than someone who single-handedly salvaged a disastrous battle?"

Alyssa stilled, then pivoted to stare Annie down. With bared teeth, she smiled before closing her eyes and biting down hard on her lower lip. Taking a deep breath in through her nose, she twirled back around to face everyone else with a gentle smile.

"I will, of course, follow the *letter* of the law. My troops are at your disposal. Oh, and should things get a little too tall for you, I'm ready to step in and shoulder the burden. Best of luck to you, *General*."

As she made her exit and passed the command tent's anti-listening bubble, Olivia spun to Liz and nearly roared, "What the fuck was that?!"

"I..."

"No! You just threw me under the bus as a political tool to get back at her! Everyone knows how you hate her, don't pretend differently. We all know the laws, but everyone *also knows* they aren't applied equally. Alyssa can ruin me *and my family* if she wants. Easily. I would have happily agreed to her command to avoid that kind of trouble."

Liz looked crestfallen and worked her mouth for a moment before she cleared her throat and tried, "Sorry. I..."

"No, don't. Just don't. That situation was about as nuanced as a rift break. That stunt you pulled? You're either politically braindead, or knew exactly what you were doing, and just didn't give a fuck about the collateral damage. And if the Pather Union negotiations Alister brought to me were any indication, it sure as shit isn't the former."

Olivia looked ready to puke, but Matt stepped forward. "This… this isn't all bad. You can foist blame on us. We can handle the little pressure anyone in the kingdom can put on us. But remember what Alyssa said; she will follow the letter of the law. If you don't show gross incompetence, she can't oust you." He clapped her shoulder lightly. "We believe in you. You can do this."

"I'm not qualified."

Emily scoffed. "We don't believe that for a second, and neither do you. Everyone could tell in ten minutes that you and what's-his-name were the real brains behind that other idiot."

"Alastair isn't dumb. He's just…busy." Even Olivia must have heard how weak that sounded because she wilted in a bit. "He has other strengths. He's nice, at least."

Liz looked subtly chastised as she nodded to Olivia. "You're right. That was wrong of me to put you in the middle of our pissing match, and treat you like a pawn. I'm sorry, and I'll make sure to head off any fallout from it."

Matt looked around to the few command staff in the tent and said, "I know who I would rather have commanding me. If we do our job, we'll have a much better chance of getting through this." He knelt down and said only loud enough for her to hear, "Remember that you're being watched, and if you impress the right people, she can't touch you. You've already proven that you can do this."

Olivia got a hard look in her eyes. Keeping her voice low, she responded, "Fine. But I still need to hedge myself against the political blowback you've brought down on me. If I'm going to foist the blame on you as suggested, then I need to make it publicly clear I think you're to blame, and don't trust you now." Raising her voice once again, she continued, "Effective immediately, you're no longer officially part of senior command. Your presence in the command tent will be by invitation only from here on out, which I will still provide for the daily strategy meetings. It'll cost you your leadership bonuses, but it will also probably placate Alyssa enough to keep her from taking the first opportunity to smother you all in your sleep and blame queendom assassins."

She almost looked as if she enjoyed the thought of the last comment. A hand snapped toward Liz's face. Only Olivia's lack of legs kept the pointed finger at bay. "But if you ever play games with me like that again, I will personally see to it that your whole team spends the rest of the war on latrine digging duty. Now, get the hell out."

With that, Team Bucket moved to exit the tent as Olivia started barking orders. Matt doubted that Olivia could follow through on that last threat, but he wasn't going to call her out. The last thing they needed was for him to dig the hole Liz had dug even deeper.

He could only sigh as he heard Liz berating herself under her breath as she stomped past him. "Fucking fuck. I didn't even think about Olivia when I made the move. I just saw an opportunity to get back at Alyssa. Birdbrained idiot. I can't fuck up like that."

Matt wanted to console her, but she had messed up. And she didn't need or want to be lied to. All they could do was move on.

By the time they moved out of the tent, the new troops were already on the move. It was frightening to see over a million troops begin to engulf the city. The space locking pillars were set up at the maximum range of standard anti-siege defenses, but they were also paired with semi-portable shielding units. If the queendom tried to recreate Matt's prior success, they would find the pillars a much more resilient target.

Their scouts who flew out at the edge of the anti-flying formation reported two million troops in the city from their best estimates, using the best telescopes they could carry.

That wasn't ideal. If they wanted to take the city, they would need three times their current numbers at a minimum. They would also need to worry about any troops in the surrounding area. The queendom would surely try to perform hit and run tactics, as Prince Albert had.

Matt was assigned to handle that eventuality, and with a team of earth mages, they raised a fifteen-foot wall around the entire city. It took them a day and a half, even with their use of mana crystals when he was forced to take a break. But eventually, they had a passable defense set up.

After that, they created a five-foot berm to render sallying forth a more dangerous decision for the queendom defenders. Several mid-level commanders balked at what they called 'overly cautious behavior,' which meant they would earn fewer points.

Matt and Liz privately thought that Alyssa was behind that little cabal, but she publicly defended Olivia's actions.

On day three, the trebuchets started launching their payloads. They were being built and staffed as fast as possible, once the first siege weapons found their range. Olivia had already given an order stating that they wouldn't be trying to take the city intact. Instead, they would be battering it to rubble before they fell for the ploys that the kingdom had used in their defense.

Team Bucket covertly agreed that it was much better to be on the attack and not the defense. It was a lot less stressful to watch the giant rocks fly away from them instead of toward them.

It took half a week to batter through the shielding. Despite their greater number of trebuchets, and no desire to take the city intact, the queendom had extra months to perform various upgrades. Those enhancements now allowed them to hold more mana, and as they learned when the shields faltered, improved the Tier of the wall's stone to 7.

That caused their summoned rocks to be nearly ineffective, but that was when Olivia pulled out her plan. She wanted to bring down the walls from underneath.

Half a dozen teams were given orders to start digging, and Matt was assigned to try and keep the earth mages full of mana, so they could reinforce the walls and move the dirt to the side. It worked until the kingdom sappers approached the walls, where they found that the enemy could feel the earth mages work and resist their efforts. The mages played a game of back and forth, while the queendom defenders tried to collapse the tunnels. Meanwhile, the kingdom sappers tried to punch through the queendom forces and reinforce the tunnels they dug.

Despite her critics, Olivia gave orders to keep the plans intact and move forward. They also criticized how she flatly refused to create siege towers or ladders to take the walls, calling her a coward, among worse things. Her counterpoint was that they were more worried about their individual points, and less about the overall situation, which put a halt to anyone questioning her decisions.

Matt personally felt the sapper plan was a lost cause, but when publicly asked, he backed up her decision to keep up the attacks. They could receive reinforcements and resupply, on top of his own mana contributions, which weren't insignificant. He remembered well enough how mana became a valuable commodity on the other side of the siege, as the days ticked on and supplies dwindled.

As Alyssa stated, all of their reinforcement generals had various accidents, leaving them indisposed. Since they were unable to make it to their camp, it left Olivia in command with no appointed general to supersede her. Matt found headquarters' response of shrugging it off concerning. But when the third wave of troops arrived without a general, putting their numbers at four million, he assumed that Alyssa had worked things out so she could remain in command.

A week after the start of the tunneling efforts, Olivia sat outside watching the wall and smiled at all the important commanders.

"You said my efforts were wasted, but here we go. Perfectly as I predicted."

Someone interjected, "The only thing perfect is the condition of the walls!"

Olivia turned in her chair, and Matt had to give her credit. She sat and still managed to glare at the man. "Do you know how saboteurs work, Claudius?" When the man just wilted back, she pointed down. "Normally it's a battle of earth mage versus earth mage. But what happens if you dig with mundane forces?"

That stumped everyone. Even Matt had no idea.

Olivia spun her wheeled chair and pointed back at the wall. "I used our earth mages as distractions, and now the walls will fall. If they had been paying attention to their surroundings, they could have felt us. But they were too focused on our own mages working to dig through the walls. They completely missed the mundane diggers."

As she spoke, a deep rumbling sound and backdrafts of dust rushed out of the grass-covered areas without sapper tunnels. At first, nothing of consequence seemed to follow. But as the ground in the middle of the closest wall slumped down, the wall bent slightly. It buckled forward, and then, as if trying to resist the pull of gravity, crumbled inward.

"Now, we have access to the city proper. Or at least, one out of four sections." Olivia tried to sound calm, but her pride and smugness shone through. It was as if she was calling out everyone who questioned her early actions.

She had lied to everyone, but with their recent spy problem, he had to give it to her. She had planned her deception perfectly and pulled down the walls with the queendom caught totally unaware.

"Now, we move forward with phase two, which is us bringing down the other three sections of wall. Then, we'll create a breach head. But first, I worry about being harried from our rear, and the defenders saving enough mana to bring up the shields when we have troops inside."

The other three sections of wall came down with water.

Olivia had the ground soaked, turning the area at the base of the hill that the city was built on to muddy slush. They then flooded the existing tunnels to create enough instability that the walls collapsed once explosives were set at the ends of the tunnels. It normally wouldn't have been enough to take down the walls, but the weight of the stone, combined with the weakened ground, caused the walls to slump outwards as a portion of the hill collapsed.

It was an impressive feat of structural de-engineering.

Olivia's prediction proved true as well. The night the walls fell, they were beset from their rear with arrows and other distractions. The attackers didn't show themselves, nor did they stick around long enough to see the siegers muster a response. The kingdom forces didn't need to worry themselves too much. The large rear wall they had set up greatly limited the amount of damage that the queendom could inflict through guerilla warfare.

That only lasted until a million-strong army approached, hoping to force their way through the east side of their fortifications and reinforce the city. They were repelled with minor casualties, but when the assaults repeated day after day, it became an ominous sign. The queendom even set up their own siege weapons to bombard the kingdom army. Olivia responded by mustering twice that number of troops and sending them to harass the enemy with Alyssa in command.

The tactic was ineffective, and Alyssa struggled to pin them down long enough to accomplish anything of note. Her forces spent most of their time chasing the enemies between the forts that they controlled in the area, while trying to limit their own casualties. They had to contend with ambushes, traps, and battlefields of their opponent's choosing.

As it turned out, it had been a distraction from the start.

With the million queendom troops keeping their two million pursuers occupied, the city's defenders attempted to break the siege. With yet another reinforcing army of two million troops arriving on the outside, they tried to pincer the kingdom at the weakest point in their encirclement and rout them.

They were fighting off a major push against their rear berm when the front gates of the city clanged open behind them. A massive wave of troops charged into the field to flank the kingdom forces amassed on the berm. Olivia ordered her forces to ignore them and focus on repelling the greater number of enemies flooding in from the outside.

Matt felt like he was back in the first city siege. He cast spell after spell and repulsed the queendom fighters as they scaled the smooth and steep berm. The flanking army worried him, but he followed his orders and kept the enemy fighters from gaining a foothold in their defenses. He had his team travel from breach to breach, plugging them once the enemy made even slight gains.

Team Bucket was handling an enemy formation that cleared the top of the wall when a series of explosions rocked the world and rattled the air.

Everyone instinctively came to a halt and turned to see. The city defenders were falling to shambles just short of their targets. More and more explosions went off at their feet, which were soon accompanied by a devastating synchronized barrage of cannon and catapult fire right on their location.

Matt's attention was wrenched back to the fight behind him as an arrow plinked off his armor. He threw himself into the still wide-eyed defenders as the melee resumed.

Once he was deep in the enemy ranks, Matt filled his mana pool and cast [Flamethrower], letting the flame wash over the queendom attackers around him. Screams followed, and his team secured the breach, only to migrate and do it again as the battle raged on around them.

As they were fighting off a dedicated charge from an earth mage who broke down their berm, screams started to be heard from the rear of the enemy's formation. There, Alyssa was busy tearing a hole through the defending ranks while attacking from the rear. The queendom army was caught between the berm and the two million attacking troops led by Alyssa. Unable to advance or retreat, the enemy fought like monsters, turning to try and overwhelm the attackers in their rear. But when they did, Olivia called for a general charge.

That signaled the end of the enemy army, as they shattered and ran. Alyssa's forces must have been prepared for it, as they opened a hole for the enemies to retreat out of. Any who stayed were cut down, savaged by the kingdom troops.

Nothing was held back, and no quarter was given.

More than one of the commanders said that it was dumb to let over half of the two million-strong force retreat out of the ambush. Most of the level heads agreed that forcing them to fight to the death would have cost them far more troops than necessary. After all, there was already a million man unit out there, which could have hit Alyssa's force from the rear as well.

That night, the army celebrated their success. The massive fight had earned everyone a large amount of points, and the general troops were happy to see the increase in their balances. Matt didn't bother to check. He wanted to see a massive increase at the end of the entire siege.

With the city missing half of its defenders, Olivia turned her attention back to the main siege. The next morning, the first probing attacks were sent in.

Matt and his team wanted to be in the first wave, but they were told under no uncertain terms that they wouldn't be a part of any initial waves and would instead be saved for the true push with the rest of the elites.

So, they had to watch as the first wave moved up under withering fire from the intact portions of the walls. It was a long and brutal fight that inflicted heavy casualties on both sides, but the first wave retreated after the well-protected earth mages created even steps for the next wave to climb.

It was far worse to watch the others go and fight. Matt felt like he should be out there, leading the troops in each attack and watching them come back with far fewer troops than they went out with.

After two days of attacks, along with the trebuchets constantly battering the city, they were ready to launch their true assault. Their scouts reported that the inside of the city was flattened, and the defenders had lost most of their anti-siege weapons atop their walls from the bombardment.

Matt and his team were a part of the assault formation, and he had to calm his nerves as they neared the city walls. They were so much larger from this side. Even as arrows and spells rained down on them, they ran forward with disposable shields raised.

They hit the stairs, and Matt took them two at a time, throwing himself off the cliff that the defenders created in the stonework. He launched into the defenders standing at the base of the tower.

It was a similar scene to the formations he had constructed when he was defending the kingdom city.

To their side, a flurry of mana cannons and other long-range spells lashed out at the attackers as they tried to take the breach. They pushed through the enemy fire as they closed the distance to engage in melee combat, where the ranged weapons had the chance to hit their own troops.

As Matt landed, he swung his longsword and let loose a [Mana Slash] that created enough room for Conor to land next to him and activate [Demon Zone]. Together, they cut a path to the stairs, trying not to get bogged down.

Team Bucket fought their way up the stairs to the portion of still intact walls with Conor in the lead. Matt reached around him to unleash a never-ending torrent of flame on anyone attempting to prevent their ascent. Liz and Emily took care of protecting their heads from attacks from above, with Liz creating a roof of blood and Emily blasting anyone that stuck their heads out to fire.

Together, they cut their way to the top of the wall and created a beachhead as Annie anchored and lowered rope ladders down the other side of the wall.

They were attacked by what Matt expected was a QRF team, but they couldn't stand the onslaught of Conor's [Demon Zone] and Matt alternating between [Flamethrower] and his blade. They held their position long enough for reinforcements to scale the ropes, even as they were attacked from all angles.

A massive Tier 7 with a hammer that had to weigh in the dozens of pounds made his way to the front. With his heavy armor, he was able to shrug off both Matt and Conor's attacks. As the fight drew out, the man seemed to increase in size until he was nine feet tall. Liz called for them to retreat once the hammer wielder shrugged off one of Emily's [Bolts] as if it didn't even affect him.

Liz glided forward on a streak of blood as more and more of the ruby liquid poured out of the glove on her hand, and she grew to equal the man's size. The Tier 7 brought his hammer into Liz's golem form, sending a spray of blood everywhere, until Liz activated [Blood Crystal Armor]. Her golem form subtly shifted, growing solid and angular, with its ruby hue acquiring a tinge of gold.

The next hammer blow only cracked the solidified blood, which quickly melted and reformed back to full defensive power. In ten seconds, Liz's liquid form enveloped the man, and he was gone. How she killed the Tier 7 in Tier 8 armor, Matt had no idea, but she used her already formed golem to start clearing off the top of the wall.

Seeing that she was fine, the rest of the team waited for the reinforcements to climb the rope ladder and set up another three. They spaced them a dozen feet apart, creating enough room for more and more people to flood the top of the wall.

Matt, Aster, Emily, and Annie climbed partway down the stairs and started peppering the makeshift barrier that the defenders had erected from above. It was a long, bitterly fought battle of attrition, where they whittled down the defenders. Without the high ground provided by the walls, the defenders couldn't stop the never-ending waves of kingdom soldiers.

Liz joined them half an hour later, as they were resting at the first makeshift barrier. They were busy scouting the queendom defenders at the second layer of fortifications. The kingdom's assault had devolved into more of a stalemate. The queendom's position was fortified by mana cannons set up and ready to hit anyone who poked their head over the edge.

The kingdom set up their own fortifications and troop stations in the breach as they flooded in. They had managed to take three out of the four holes in the wall, and the fourth was falling, thanks to a concentrated force that punched through with an extra unit of elite troops.

Matt had to marvel at how much better this siege went when compared to their first one. When you didn't care about the collateral damage, and smashed everything with siege weapons from the start, things went a lot easier.

Once they had captured the city walls, Olivia gave her most controversial order yet. She ordered them to man the walls with their own mana cannons, and simply blast the defenders away from their entrenched positions from range.

Some mid-level commanders called her a coward, along with everything else under the sun, because they were losing out on potential personal points since they weren't fighting themselves. It was a selfish complaint; the overall strategy was safer and inflicted greater casualties without risking themselves.

Nonetheless, it pissed off enough people to nearly inspire a coup, as the commanders openly spread their discontent to the rest of the troops. But to almost everyone's surprise, Alyssa again backed up Olivia's decision, and forced the malcontents into a simmer.

As they pushed the defenders to retreat deeper into the city, they were forced to endure more and more casualties. The opinion of the kingdom general soldiers shifted as they saw the wisdom in the decision to bombard the queendom from afar.

Finally, the defenders tried to break out for a second time and repeat the kingdom's tactic from the last siege. They tried to break out from the gate opposite of Team Bucket. But unlike when the kingdom made their escape, the defending troops were defeated in earnest.

Three and a half weeks later, the city had finally fallen. It was a massive victory.

Matt knew he had made out well from the siege, even without engaging in the final battle. He had his AI check his point total for taking the city.

Prior Total (last updated 25 days ago): 102,050 points (47,292 pending transfer; 54,758 available).

<u>**TEAM MERITS:**</u>

(Calculated for Tier 6 Combatant).

- Enemy vassal killed, Tier 5. Worth 1 point. Performed 784 times.
- Enemy vassal killed, Tier 6. Worth 5 points. Performed 22,877 times.
- Enemy vassal killed, Tier 7. Worth 25 points. Performed 215 times.
- Items and equipment looted but returned. Assigned worth: 15,214 points.
- Played a major role in capturing an enemy city. Worth 50,000 points. Performed 1 time.

PERSONAL MERITS:
(Calculated for Tier 6 Combatant)

- Enemy vassal killed, Tier 5. Worth 1 point. Performed 174 times.
- Enemy vassal killed, Tier 6. Worth 5 points. Performed 3,741 times.
- Enemy vassal killed, Tier 7. Worth 25 points. Performed 35 times.

ARMY MERITS:

- Defeat a major enemy army of quarter-size (6.32M vs 1.91M) in a defensive position while besieging a walled city. Reward: 1.05x multiplier to all merits.
- Successfully besieged an enemy city (6.32M vs 1.98M). Reward: 1.1x multiplier to all merits.
- Won a major engagement using only sound tactics. Reward: 1.05x multiplier to all merits. Note: Merit awarded based on recommendation of Army observers.

UNACHIEVED MERITS: For reference purposes only.

- Capture an enemy city without causing significant damage. Worth 250,000 points.

SUMMARY OF GAINS:

- **Team Merits:**
- **Raw Total:** 170,544
- **Team Multiplier:** N/A
- **Category Total:** 170,544
- **Personal Merits:**
- **Raw Total:** 19,754
- **Personal Multiplier:** N/A
- **Category Total:** 19,754
- **Combined Merits:**
- **Sub-Total:** 228,358
- **Total Multiplier:** 1.2x
- **Grand Total:** 312,324

New Gains: 312,324 points.

New Total: 414,374 points (47,292 pending transfer; 367,082 available).

Updated Pather Team Ranking (Kingdom of Seven Suns): 2nd place.

Estimated Daily Stipend: 2,500 points.

The points for the siege, along with their team keeping third place in the kingdom rankings, earned them 36,000 points. It put Matt a little over a quarter of a million points. It was exhilarating to know that they were back over the points needed to buy the upgrade orb that Aster still needed. By his rough estimation, even Emily would be able to purchase an orb with a little help.

The troops partied like crazy with the influx of points that first night, as they started to rebuild the destroyed infrastructure. They wanted to get the city in good enough shape to get the teleporter active. But to everyone's surprise, the queendom pulled off the kingdom city that they were besieging and were now making a beeline toward them.

They were ordered to abandon the city after only holding it for three days. It spoiled the jubilant mood that everyone had after such a massive victory, but with the queendom's estimated seven million troops to their remaining four million, there was no hope of holding the destroyed city.

With their forewarning, they were able to leave the city without resistance, but not before they set explosives to drop the remaining walls that had survived their initial bombardment. With the city leveled, they made quick time back to the coast, and flew over the ocean and back to the closest neutral city.

Matt and most of the general troops expected to find the prince upset, but to their surprise, he was exceedingly happy at their return.

So happy, in fact, he even called all of the top commanders to watch as he made Olivia a peer of the realm and promoted her to a Baroness. He didn't even wait for them to enter the city proper and did it in front of the entire army.

"For her inspiring work securing us a city before the queendom was able to repeat the feat! For forcing them to retreat without earning the points we have from such a victory!" the prince's voice echoed out over the field out of the neutral city, causing near-endless roars of approval and cheers for the kingdom's newest noble.

Matt just smiled and clapped along with everyone else as they stood in the long grass that surrounded the gate to the city.

Even without her legs, Olivia seemed to stand tall as she received her reward, and clearly suppressed tears as she repeatedly thanked everyone and anyone who came close to her. She even thanked one of the waiters that the prince had brought out to serve everyone, to her embarrassment. When she realized her faux pas, she nervously stammered an apology.

Alyssa walked over to where their team stood and sighed with a glass of champagne bubbling in her hand. "What a lucky girl." Still in her armored skirt, she bumped Liz's hip with her own. "That could have been me up there."

The 'you took that from me' seemed unsaid, but Matt heard it loud enough.

Apparently, so did Liz. "What do you need to be made a peer for? Your parents are already nobles."

Alyssa sighed. "Yes, yes. They are. But there's a key difference between earning my own peerage and gaining it through my parents. Namely, that all decisions related to said peerage *also* go through my parents. That title would have granted me power that belonged to me, and nobody else." She didn't look hateful or angry, just tired. "Oh, well, there is always the next plan."

The colorfully dressed woman's voice gained some heat as she turned to Liz. "You know, considering that favor you owe me from getting the Crafters to back your little Union, I expected you to back me up, too. Or at least not get involved. Dirty of you to flake out like that."

Liz nibbled on her lip before she said, "I didn't even think about it. If you had messaged me, I would've kept my mouth shut to return the favor."

Alyssa sighed and sipped at her glass. "It would have taken a favor for you to simply not *actively* sabotage me? At poor Olivia's expense no less. Well, I guess I expected too much of you, that's on me. Here I thought we'd been quite friendly these last few months, with each of us keeping out of each other's way. *One* of us even lending *the other* a much needed hand on multiple occasions. Clearly, I was mistaken. That's not the type of relationship we have. Not at all. I'll be keeping the favor in my back pocket for now. Be warned; when I do call it in, I won't be holding back. Not anymore."

Another cheer went up, and she raised her glass to where Olivia received congratulations, then downed the glass and walked off to the main gate.

The last thing Matt heard was a muttered, "Lucky girl."

Their team moved to get in line and congratulate Olivia. Matt wouldn't call her a friend, not with how they had foisted her into this position unwillingly. Still, there was no denying that she had done well, and had earned her rewards. Adding a little bit of camaraderie to a celebration never hurt.

25

The city was bustling when they filtered in. It was a long walk to their rooms through the massive city, and they couldn't help but notice the divided populace during their trip.

The rightmost half of the city, the side where the kingdom headquarters was, was filled with celebration and cheer. In contrast, the left side of the main boulevard was home to a decidedly dejected populace. The queendom general troops, along with quite a few Pathers, were glowering at the partying kingdom side. But none dared to cross the street, thanks to the Army personnel hovering over the dividing line.

Matt just kept to his side of the street and tried to get back to their suite. They had ordered a taxi, but with millions of troops filing into the city at once, all forms of transportation were overwhelmed. After walking for nearly an hour and realizing they hadn't even traveled a quarter of the way to their suite, he called it quits. He walked straight into the next hotel that they came across on the main road.

When he could hear himself think again, he said to his inquisitive team, "Okay enough walking. We deserved a bath and a nice meal yesterday." He waved around at the marble and gold-trimmed lobby. "So, hotel!"

It was expensive to get a suite of four bedrooms; a Tier 7 mana stone for a single night was a hefty price, even for Tier 6s. But the room came with an all-you-can-eat menu prepared by a Tier 9 chef.

Matt would have paid that much for the shower, let alone everything else. So, paying the bill and taking the elevator to their suite was easy.

Each room in the suite had an individual shower, which they promptly took advantage of. It was slightly crowded with two people and a fox in the shower, but the shower was as large and fancy as the rest of the suite. After soaking in the overhead spray, Matt sat on the floor and started scrubbing his bond, who was more irritated at the dirt in her fur than the hot water.

To soothe his whining bond, who treated the hot water as if it was personally hurting her, he turned the sink on its coldest setting and let her lounge in the icy water.

He and Liz were too tired to do anything more than clean off and flop on the couch. They threw on a random show while luxuriating in the fluffy bathrobes that the hotel provided. Their dirty armor was piled up on a cart, along with the rest of their team's, to be cleaned and returned.

After seeing that the armor was already piled up, Emily came out of her room and said, "Thanks for clearing that up."

"Wasn't us." Liz half-yawned as she slumped over into the side of the love seat.

Annie and Conor came out of their respective rooms in near unison to join them around the living room.

Annie opened her mouth while looking like she wanted to bring up something important, so Matt cut her off, "Food first. Important shit later."

He refrained from grumbling that the camp cooks had sucked and should all be fired. They had already grown tired of his complaints about that, but he still wanted food. Good food.

They ordered a full on buffet, and even Aster left her ice bath when the food arrived. To everyone's amusement, the hotel had even provided her with a bathrobe as well.

When they were finally done eating, Emily brought up the topic her sister almost had. "I want to buy an upgrade orb."

Conor, who had at some point fallen on the floor, said, "Is that the best idea with an auction coming up?"

Emily flopped her hand around. "I don't know, but there are only thirteen left, and even if I have nothing to use it on now, I might later.

It's too valuable of a prize to pass up. And I could always risk it on my cracked skill, and hope it leans into the cracked, random mana type aspect of the skill."

That felt a little too risky for Matt's taste, but they were her points to spend.

Liz rotated until her feet were in Matt's lap, and after sighing as he rubbed the sore spot, she said, "Could always sell it. I doubt the army will let you change the price, but I bet you can return it or sell it for…" She yawned and paused, "Half a million."

Speaking of the points, he checked Aster's total and saw that she was over the half-million mark. He rubbed her until she woke up and said, "See this listing, this is what we talked about before. It will help you out and boost your ice manipulation."

The fox was half out of it, but the black box appeared next to her. He instructed her on how to absorb it and what to upgrade. She did as instructed, and was the proud new owner of upgraded skill, [Ice Manipulation]. As it was her Tier 1 Talent, Matt hoped that she would get the rare variant that acted on its own. From the two seconds of Aster's testing though, that didn't seem to be the case. It was just stronger, cheaper, and easier to use.

Still, it would boost her growth potential.

The same black box appeared in front of Emily, but she queried into the air, "Can you hold on to that for me? Not sure if I want to actually use it quite yet."

The box idled there for a moment but was then replaced by a slip of paper. Emily plucked it out of the air and read out loud, "If you decide you don't want this item before the remaining stock runs out, it can be returned to the store for a full refund. If and when you want the orb for yourself, simply message the reward AI and it will be retrieved from storage. Should you fail to either pick up or return the item before leaving the war, it will be logged as a charitable donation and added to the Army's contribution store."

Annie, who was the only one still eating, mumbled, "At least that worked." She dropped the clean rib and sighed, "I'm going to save my points. We have five months left before we need to Tier up, and I think if some more cities trade hands, I can get [Side Slide]. It's at least a possibility."

Matt checked his own points. 367,082 wasn't a small amount, but he still wanted to save up for some of the larger prizes. At least with Aster having her upgrade orb, he could look at other things.

He idly used his AI to check the other new additions to the reward shop.

The first thing he noticed was a fresh batch of cracked [Healing Touch]es and [Ranged Heal]s. They were both Tier 14 skills, but they would be incredibly helpful for the team to have. The problem was, the base price was 200,000 points apiece, and most of the cracks were either worthless for the healing spell, or incredibly valuable which drove up the price accordingly.

One [Cracked Ranged Heal] had the bonus effect of increasing the strength of the target for ten minutes. That skill went for half a million on its own. It was damn near one of the chaser items, but it wasn't the most expensive skill on the list.

That honor went to a [Cracked Healing Touch] that had a doubled effectiveness and whose price sat at a whopping one and a half million points.

The rest were cracks that had no real benefit to the healing spells. A healing spell with the added effect of changing one's hair to a random color for its duration was just effectively a normal healing spell.

Getting one for his team was on his list of priorities, but the real question was, who should get it and which spell? It would technically be best on him, until the healing cooldown applied. But until then, he could cast them all day without issue. When he hit Tier 7, he would be able to cast both as well. Unable to decide, he read the description of each normal skill.

[Ranged Heal]: Spend 150 mana to heal the target over five seconds—range of fifteen feet. If the target stays in range of the caster, the spell can be channeled for half effectiveness. As this is an undirected healing spell, it does not require knowledge of the human body to function. It cannot heal more than what a Tier 0 body would naturally be able to heal. It simply functions at an accelerated pace.

[Healing Touch]: Spend 100 mana to heal the target over ten seconds. If the target stays in contact with the caster, the spell can be channeled for three-quarters effectiveness. As this is an undirected healing spell, it does not require knowledge of the human body to function. It cannot heal more than what a Tier 0 body would naturally be able to heal.

[Ranged Heal] had more versatility in its range, since the mana cost wasn't really an issue to anyone on his team. But the lowered effectiveness of the healing meant that they would hit the healing cooldown much faster.

He also wondered if Liz could change one of the skills to something useful. But considering the point cost, he wasn't sure it was worth it to test his theory out. Healing skills were Tier 14 after all, and not cheap.

Either way, he couldn't cast the spells yet, and they had other things to save up for.

He joined his friends in their comatose conversation as they came down from their time in the field, and the talk of points turned to general chatter.

The auction was a wild affair. There were half a dozen items previewed, with most possessing hidden effects or special promises. It was shaping up to dwarf the first auction twice over. Everyone was excited, but the queendom was more subdued. With their failed siege of the city, they were at a distinct disadvantage in the upcoming auction.

With fewer points overall, the queendom was a much more somber crowd. It only increased the fervor of the kingdom fighters, who had a surplus of points and less competition. The noticeable absences were the prince and those closest to him, including Juni. It was in stark contrast to Princess Sara, who sat with a moody expression. It didn't take a genius to see the missing Shard of Reality, next to the queendom's unclaimed shard. The princess glared at the podium as a tribute to her failure, it only drove home the disparity in points from the recent failure of the city sieges.

With his usual flair, Javier strode out onto the stage and waved. "Ahhh, my friends! It feels like it has been *so* long. But my, how you've fought!"

He pumped his arm up in cadence with the roaring crowd. "I hope you are all flush with points! If you are, tonight is the night to spend them. Indeed, it is. You will find items crafted by the masters of the Empire proper here tonight."

He waved, and five mannequins were rolled out with dark brown leather armor. "These beauties are a Tier 7, squad-level formation armor. If you wear these and remain within two hundred feet of one another, you can share strength between each wearer." The high Tier man raised a finger and said, "And if one of you is hit, the damage will be dissipated between each suit of armor. A truly formidable starting item! We'll begin the bidding at 100,000 points."

The first item set the tone for the rest of the auction. Extravagant items were brought out as if they were commonplace.

Nothing particularly interested Team Bucket, so they only paid half attention to the auction as they conversed amongst themselves. Halfway through the auction, their box's door smashed open, and Alyssa waltzed in. She shut the door with her foot and came in with glasses of alcohol in both hands.

Annie spun and growled, "What the fuck do you think you are doing?"

Alyssa interrupted her with a raised hand and said, "Please, just stop. I needed a place to crash, and you were close. After you fucked my plans over, you owe me this much." She paused to finish the half-empty drink in her right hand before she leaned on the wall and slid to the floor. "This doesn't cover your favor. Just call it interest."

The thoroughly drunk woman let her head thump against the wall and just sat there with her eyes closed.

Aster hopped down to investigate the new person in her space, and Matt readied himself in case the drunk woman tried to hurt his bond. But Alyssa just scratched her ears. Aster was more interested in the drink in her hand and started lapping at the concoction before shaking her head at the dark beer, then going back in for more.

Matt and his party warily watched the sitting intruder as the auction continued on in the background. Alyssa set the cup that the snow fox had taken a drink from onto the ground, which Aster took as permission to continue drinking with gusto. She gave a halfhearted glower at the party staring her down before setting her own empty cup down as well.

Alyssa grabbed Aster as soon as the fox had finished the drink. The peacock blooded woman laid down and curled up into a ball around the tox bond, murmuring, "Wake me up when the auction is over."

Matt gave Liz a look, and she could only shrug at the newest development.

They turned their attention back to the auction, which then had two surprising items go up for sale.

The first one that piqued Matt's interest was a collapsible, Tier 7 smithing station. It was only the size of a fist in its collapsed form, but it expanded to a room-sized, fully functional forge. It gave him the idea to get one made up for cooking. Until they had a portable and flying house, the stations would be quite useful.

At the very least, he wouldn't be forced to eat the slop that the army cooks served.

The last item was the most valuable; it was a growth storage ring. Javier brought out the ring on its own stand, but left it covered with a velvet cloth.

"This, my friends, is our final item. And let me warn you, if it doesn't hit our reserve price here, it will be sent to the Empire proper for Tier 15s to fight over. A Tier 6, *growth* storage ring, obviously still unbound. This beauty will not be shown, so don't fret about becoming a target! But know that its growth aspect is that the size massively increases with Tier. But that's not all! No, not in the slightest As this miracle of rift creation Tiers up, it will gain a stasis effect applied to stored items by Tier 20."

The auctioneer laughed, and with a self-deprecating smile said, "Even I don't have a ring that can completely stop time, and I'm Tier 29! That enchantment makes the ring so large, they're measured in square feet, and reserved for Tier 35s or higher."

Hearing that the general audience lost their minds. Even Matt leaned forward to get a better look.

"For our guests' safety, we will be conducting this auction through AI only."

The starting price was half a million, but in seconds, the anonymous bids had it over a million. From there the bidding slowed, but it didn't stop. The final price was one and a half million points, which just caused Matt to sigh in appreciation. A top team must have put every point they had into the ring.

They tried to wake the two drunks, but Alyssa and his bond were dead to the world.

"I'll take her wherever she calls home."

Matt offered to help, "I'll come with you."

Liz patted his chest. "It's fine. I'll do some work at the office once I drop her off. Enjoy the dinner."

"You shouldn't need to babysit her." Matt tried not to whine. He was looking forward to his night out with Liz.

Liz grinned at him, reading his thoughts. "It's fine." Seeing his doubt, she laughed and looked down on Alyssa. "Despite her attitude at times, she *has* helped me out. I owe her at least a little common decency."

Annie stepped forward with an evil grin. "I can take her to her room."

Emily rolled her eyes. "Stabbing her and sending her to the hospital isn't the same as getting her to her room."

Annie shrugged. "She'd get there. Eventually."

Liz just laughed, and with a drunk in each arm, she walked out of the room.

Matt chuckled to himself as well. "Yeah, I agree. But If Liz wants to help, who am I to interfere?"

They moved to eat dinner and enjoyed their time floating amongst the heights. It was a novel way to eat, with their servers floating to each person and their meals trailing behind them.

Everything was going smoothly when Matt heard a voice call out from behind him.

"I see you finally came out of your hidey-hole." Talous' voice echoed over the buzz of conversation.

Matt sighed as he turned to face the man. "What do you want? You must have something better to do than follow me around throwing challenges left and right?"

He really wasn't in the mood to deal with the persistent Pather.

"Yeah, I'm here to challenge you. You're a coward who hides behind tricks and would have never won in a real duel."

Matt sighed, he was tired of this game, and he didn't really care about petty insults to his honor. He knew what mattered. This insecure man wasn't it.

Turning to leave with his team, he paused when he heard Talous' next words. "Where are your two women? Didn't have enough to pay for their time?" He laughed like it was the funniest joke ever uttered and said something about companionship. "Or are you trading down to these two? I guess twins can be fun."

Matt had to restrain himself. The asshole wanted to fight, and giving in would only further whatever plan he had. The smartest move would be to just walk away, which was exactly what he did, even though he was sick and tired of the man and his badgering.

Already walking away, he froze when he heard Talous' follow up remark. "Didn't your parents raise you with any pride? Or are they just as cowardly as you?"

Those words drilled deeper than Matt was prepared for. Rage bubbled up and drowned out his control.

Matt turned toward the opposite direction of the smart move.

Talous was desperate. The irritating man wasn't accepting his challenges no matter what he did. And he *needed* the man to accept his fight.

Being perpetually annoying to Liz, and the plan to challenge her team had started just as a way to drive a wedge into the Pather Union. All on Sara's request, of course. If he could bait either Liz or her boyfriend into a public challenge, he could humiliate them, which would only further his own goals. Neither of them had risen to the bait, no matter how disrespectful he had acted, and he'd resorted to tracking them down in the field instead.

But after that first fight, he was desperate to challenge the man again. He had been so close to understanding his Concept during their first bout, and the cowardly piece of shit had cheated to end the fight, just before he grasped it.

If he had just a *few minutes* longer, he was sure he could have solidified it—both the Phrase and Image in one shot. But, no, the man had to surprise teleport and cheat his way to a victory, stealing Talous' chance to advance.

The war had been nice enough and had earned his team some easy wealth. But that was nothing he couldn't earn with his brother's help. A Concept would stay with him forever.

When Talous completed the Path, he would prove that he was the best, and would earn the accolades he was due. From his birth, his parents had forged him into a warrior, and he had met every expectation with flying colors. He was the perfect son. Unlike his brother Malous.

Where he was strong, Malous was weak and frail. His younger brother wasn't meant for the sword, like the generations of his family that strived to perfect the art. So, it fell on Talous to maintain the family's honor.

The weight was something that both of the brothers should have carried together. Despite everything, Talous loved and tried to protect his brother, but he not so discreetly resented him more and more as time went on. Their parents made no secret about the extra training and brutality they put Talous through stemming from his brother's lack of drive. It was as if they blamed *him* for his brother's failings. But Talous knew the truth.

"The weak have only themselves to blame."

The younger man stopped even trying by the time they were teens, which was the most infuriating part. If Malous had given it his best effort, their parents would have let Talous off with minimal training. But no, the selfish slouch had refused altogether. He sat back and left it to Talous to earn enough of their parent's approval for both of them.

It only meant that Talous had to work even harder to appease them. They were ecstatic when his Awakening revealed a Tier 1 Talent for true ambidexterity, and the ability to split his attention.

When his brother received a Talent for meditation, they cast him out and threatened to banish him. Some part of Talous never accepted that. When his parents convinced an acquaintance to sponsor him on the Path, he demanded they make it a team with Malous.

It was a spontaneous decision that brought the brothers closer than they had ever been before. But they still weren't friends; not by any means at all. Neither of them really understood why he had made that decision. But it paid off when Malous' Tier 3 Talent unexpectedly made him a Seeker, albeit an odd one.

It was his brother who had found two new friends that could keep up with them. At first, Talous had felt indifferent. But they formed a team which, over the Tiers and trials, gradually bonded. Now, Talous was the last member of the party without his Concept. He could not stand for being the dead weight of the group. Never.

And the bastard who could give him what he needed simply refused to fight him. Talous had tried fighting half a dozen people at once, but none of them stimulated the spark that he needed. He even went as far as spending 100,000 points for two weeks of army Concept training. They tried to force the realization out with their power, but he felt nothing. Their only suggestion was to repeat the actions that got him close last time.

So, he'd tried to recreate the moment. When the ever-calm Liz was out of the picture, he'd sling some of the crassest insults he could think of to try starting a fight. Once again, as usual, nothing he said worked. Then, just as he'd given up, he offhandedly threw out a *mild, half-assed dig* at the guy's parents. Somehow, *that's* what did the trick.

The man *finally* turned and lunged for him.

Talous had forgotten how damned fast the man was. He moved like a Tier 7, even at the bottom of Tier 6. Along with that insane armor Talent and Concept, Matt was a frustrating opponent. Exactly what he needed.

Before Matt could close the distance, a towering bald Pather in monk's robes reached over and stuck a huge melon hammer between them. The charging brute reached to rip the weapon out of the way, but stopped when the monk reminded, "Do battle, but not here. Or you'll get a long swim to the surface."

A second, much tinier and equally bald monk glided up next to his larger counterpart. He traveled on a gust of wind while excitedly waving his staff. "Yeah, what Tito said! Take it to the arena, where everyone can enjoy the show. The whole planet has been anticipating this matchup for months."

Talous made a note to thank the men. Drowning to death would have put a hamper on his plans. He hadn't actually expected the man to accept his challenge after all this time and was mostly just mouthing off to blow off steam. If he had known that mentioning the asshole's parents was all it would take, he would have done so months ago.

Matt spat at him over the hammer blocking the way, "There are lines you don't cross."

He would have passed the statement off as idle chatter, but the man's eyes were flat like a corpse's. Apparently, a certain someone had mommy or daddy issues. Not that it mattered anymore. With Matt already giving him everything he wanted, there was no point taunting the man further.

They made their way to an arena that was already crowded with spectators watching the ongoing fight. Matt just threw himself over the railing and into the waiting area, landing with a thud. Talous expected him to shove the two people waiting aside, but he just took his place at the end of the line and glared at Talous the entire time. His gaze never wavered as the other matches progressed.

The fights seemed to drag on forever, as the army changed the arena between each fight to clean up. He also noticed an increase in the number of spectators sitting in the viewing stands. Word had been spread. The bubbly little monk was still calling people over, too, making a show out of the impending fight.

He smiled to himself under his helmet. The more people who witnessed him beating the large Tier 6, the sweeter the victory would be. Matt had humiliated him by playing that death over and over on his banner, but Talous would make it a million times worse. He would make the man quit the war with the humiliation he was going to deal out.

There was clearly something wrong with Matt. Even as they climbed the ring and the shielding went up, he never broke eye contact. It was almost unnerving.

Talous had fought many people. Some were amazing, and some were passable. The man in front of him was irritating.

His own Tier 3 Talent gave him increased armor penetration with his sword and blocking power with his shield. Along with his growth belt, he should have been the perfect counter to the man. The problem wasn't Matt's decent skill with the blade, but his damned Concept, which gave the man near-endless mana.

Some digging into Sara's records had explained his anomaly. The crazy bastard was suspected of using [Mage's Retreat]. At least according to one of the spies that the princess had stationed in the enemy camp. They had heard Liz reference the skill twice in private conversations with Matt.

[Mana Strength] was a better option for most melee fighters, since it was a flat reserve skill. You didn't have to lose too much of your mana to use it effectively, hence its consideration as a mainstay skill. Talous himself used the skill to good effect, but if he wanted to match Matt in strength, he had to increase the reserve to at least 400 mana.

He felt it was bullshit that the man was able to increase his strength so much with an unconventional method. Anyone could be exceptional with endless mana. But Talous had counters prepared; he would not be losing this time.

Matt stood there as the countdown was called, and his Talent-made armor flickered to life around him. Talous shook his arms to settle his armor and weapons. His pouch of mana stones reserved for feeding his shield was ready, and his blade coursed with mana as well. His enchantments were humming with power.

Talous settled himself as the referee counted down to two. At one, he was ready. When the referee began the fight, he was moving at the instant of command.

A trait his parents drilled into him.

If you moved first, you often won, and he needed to win. His Concept was on the other side of victory.

He stimulated his bottled Concept the best he could, and the strength increase allowed him to close the distance between them in a heartbeat. He was able to duck under the crosscut from his opponent's longsword thanks to his enhanced speed.

Talous let Matt's sword deflect off the flat of his blade and activated [Shield Bash]. His left arm glowed with mana as he lunged forward with the spell propelling him.

He met armored flesh and tried to drive the man off balance but was unable to get Matt to even budge. The ghostly form felt rooted to the ground.

He brought his blade down on the armored man's glowing leg. The poison on the weapon would slow Matt as it worked its way into his body. There was no way the man had a healing spell at this stage. And even if he took [Endurance] like Talous suspected, the man wouldn't have the skill modified that far yet. If by some miracle he did, the man would eventually run out of willpower to fuel his Concept. The poison was perfectly calculated to linger and draw this fight out.

When he won, he would have his Concept, and then he would show this cheater what true power was.

They exchanged blows half a dozen times, and Talous had to reassess. Matt had gotten better. Not a ton, but some of the gaps in his style were closed or turned into bait.

He was able to get in a few light wounds that he could have turned into finishing blows if he didn't need to drag the fight out. The man was angry, and it showed in his fighting style. As they exchanged attacks, Talous noted Matt tightening up his form, but not before he just barely avoided a diagonal slash where he expected an opening.

Talous sidestepped a chop and licked out with his blade, cutting into the flesh of Matt's left arm. He took a kick to the shield in return that sent him skidding backward, followed-up by a sword slash that burned a Tier 5 mana stone to keep his shield charged.

Talous kept the wince off his face. That was his portion of an old delve reward stolen away from blocking a single blow. The man was too strong for his own good and wasn't afraid to use it. He had no doubt that the man used that advantage to bully most opponents into disadvantageous spots. That tactic wouldn't work on him, his parents had never trained him to fight an equal opponent, this was just another day of sparring for him.

An over-extended leg let Talous get another cut in, but it didn't seem to faze the man. Why Matt wasn't slowing down, he couldn't answer. But he didn't need the poison— that was just a backup. A way to ensure he could control the fight.

A necessary precaution.

Talous was careful to never fully engage like last time. He wouldn't let the man teleport himself into a victory. If he could bait the item's use out, that would be ideal, but he didn't expect that to happen. There was no way Matt could win once he did, any teleport item had to be incredibly limited at this Tier. Otherwise, it would be used at every turn instead of saved and hidden.

He just had to be careful of the move.

Talous took a nasty kick to his knee that nearly sent him sprawling. He was able to roll backward, dissipating most of the blow before he was wounded, but it was a reminder that the man wasn't a training dummy.

As he was unable to end the fight without his Concept, he grew more frustrated. He was *ready*. He had prepared for every contingency. He should have earned his Concept by now. He was defeating the man in their exchanges, which should have brought on the realization of his Concept, but it lingered like a spark in the dark. It was glowing and dimming to a rhythm he couldn't quite hear.

There was something there, a flicker of sorts in his spirit, in both the Phrase and Image. He was prepared to strike and defend…

He was pulled out of his reverie when a spiked fist landed on his shield and crumbled more mana stones to dust from dissipating the force.

Talous thought the fight was won when he cut deep into the man's ribs, and he felt the ember of his Concept flare up. But a massive glowing gauntlet gripped his forearm and held him in place, stopping the nascent Concept from fully forming.

A hand raised, and flame gushed out at him just inches from his face.

Talous could feel his growth belt's reserves start to dip, and hurriedly connected it with a pouch of mana stones. He linked them one after another to his belt, preventing the man's ranged attack from landing. It was an expensive way to fight, but it was his best counter to the cheating mage. What the belt didn't stop, however, was the flames burning all the air away from his face.

Matt only let go after the third shield bash, and Talous stumbled back.

Why isn't this working?

He had planned for everything. His Concept was so close, he could feel it.

Talous set himself to block and deflect a sword thrust that would be followed by a slash, but it was automatic.

He just needed to find his Concept.

He was ready for it.

The tingling grew.

Talous was ready.

The world grew sharp, and everything clicked into its place. His bottled Concept shattered and vacated the spot in his magical and physical cultivation cores to make room for his new Concept.

His Image was simple. A sword and shield in his hands. Each with a single opposite purpose that could be swapped at any moment. They were all he needed. He was prepared for every encounter. Most importantly, he was ready to strike and defend at any time.

With wild glee, Talous threw himself into Matt, and with his Concept empowering him, he deflected the sword with his shield and stabbed the man in the heart. Or he would have, but there was a repulsion force that resisted his blade long enough for the man to twist out of the way.

Talous laughed out loud and rushed forward to re-engage.

The longsword caught his first blade thrust, but he was fine with that. If his sword was acting as a shield, his shield could be a weapon. He was ready.

He knocked the man off balance and expected to end the fight there, but Matt teleported closer and, just like last time, brought his blade to Talous head.

Still smiling, Talous flexed his Concept and used its added power to get his shield up, just in time to lash out at Matt's chest. With his Concept empowering his enchanted blade, he felt it slice through the man's feeble attempt at armor and bite deep into softer flesh.

The larger man kicked out, and again Talous was barely able to roll with it.

He came back up ready to fight, and brought his blade down on his opponent's own, trying to maneuver it out of position. It worked, but Matt was able to dodge his first slash. He was too slow to fully dodge the thrust to his flank that followed, and Talous felt the enjoyment of whittling down an opponent who had once bested him.

He was better. And now he would show everyone.

Matt readied his sword one-handed, and to Talous' surprise, a shield formed on his now limp left arm.

So, the man could improvise. That was surprising, but nothing he couldn't handle. The length of the blade was good for two-handed styles, but it would hamper a one-handed and shielded style.

Talous' victory was assured.

Then the man's other skill, [Hail], made its first appearance, and thumb-sized chunks of ice littered the floor, until they were a hazard to good footing. Then, the armored man followed up with a torrent of water.

"Stop the coward shit and fight like a man!" He wanted to punish Matt for withholding his Concept from him for so long, and he intended to finish the fight in the same humiliating manner that he had lost in.

But now the man was flooding the floor with chunks of ice and water. A cowardly ploy.

Talous understood why Matt made such a move when he saw the armored man standing *above* the ice and water near his feet.

Talous measured his steps carefully and shuffled his feet, trying not to step on any ice. But it slowed him enough that he was forced to rely on his Concept to block a portion of Matt's heavy longsword. With his return swing, he found the new shield did little more than the original armor and ignored it to hack away at the man's already injured arm.

If he had to cut the man to pieces, he would. Talous would pay him back for the humiliation of his first loss. He would make Matt pay even more for not giving him this duel sooner.

This was Matt's fault. He was only getting what was coming to him.

Talous had to rely more and more on his Concept to counter the water walking. He thought it was a weird skill, but in one of his brief respites, he could feel that it was actually the man's Concept.

How's that fair? Nobody their Tier can do that.

Talous didn't have time to curse. Matt refused to die.

Two more heavy hits to the torso failed to put the armored giant down, and he could feel himself tiring. His new Concept fit him perfectly, but it was draining his willpower like a leaky bucket.

He refused to give in and forced himself to remember his parents' lessons. Losing wasn't an option.

They exchanged blow after blow, with Talous' blade coming back red each time, but Matt's armored form did not waver. The amount of poison he'd been dosed with should have put him in a coma by now.

When Matt teleported again, he was caught off guard, and his left knee buckled as the larger Tier 6 stomped on it.

Talous could feel tendons and ligaments tear under the blow. He was sent sprawling but rolled to his good foot with an agonized scream.

Fuck! Two teleports in one fight?

No item at their Tier could manage that. It had to be [Side Slide]... No, wait...an upgraded [Side Slide]. One of the possible upgrades would have been coming off its shortened cooldown right about now. The copy in the store was still there, so the cheating bastard must have lucked upon the skill even before the war and bought an upgrade orb for it from the market.

He struggled to dig deeper into his Concept, but his cores felt like sponges wrung out one too many times. Just trying to tap into it was giving him a splitting headache.

He had nothing left to give.

That was fine. He had fought his entire life without a Concept. He didn't need one to finish this.

While Talous feebly tried to shake off the pounding in his head from overdrawing his Concept, Matt slipped in a thrust to his chest that glowed with an impending [Mana Charge]. He had to rely on his new skill to stop it. [Phantom Armor] flashed into place around him, and blocked the blindingly explosive blow, just long enough for him to cleave deeply into Matt's left arm, leaving it lame.

With his Concept drained, Talous found it harder to punch through Matt's now ornate armor. The thicker plating was resisting his Talent more than last time. Talous panted between their exchanges. For all he was slicing the man up, he was growing exhausted while Matt stood tall as ever.

His flagging energy was only weakened further when a heavily embellished shield appeared on his opponent's left shoulder, and almost completely blocked his next attack. In a flash of clarity, he realized that the armor must get more effective the more detailed the armor's molding became. Otherwise, that slash to Matt's lame side would have ended this, surprise shield or no.

How is it fair that his armor is so much stronger than even Tier 7 armor? Why does he cheat so much?

In their next exchanges, he was forced to burn more mana stones, as he was drained of mana trying to re-stabilize [Phantom Armor]'s still fragmented structure. It was destroyed after it saved his life from Matt's exploding blade. He was hoping to piece it back together quickly enough for a second activation, but that massive [Mana Charge] had stressed the skill too much, and it had shattered more thoroughly than usual.

He wasn't used to skills needing to be rebuilt, and it took valuable mental concentration to reform the skill. Let alone filling it with mana while fending off an opponent who could now block some of his blows.

As the fight dragged out further, Talous drew blood twice more in rapid succession. Suddenly, Matt teleported for an unbelievable *third* time, and shattered his sword arm with a heavy chop. Only his armor stopped the blow from severing his arm. If his leg wasn't crippled, he knew he could have dodged, but he was slightly too slow.

It had been maybe three minutes since the last teleport. Not even an upgraded version of [Side Slide] could be used that quickly in succession.

What the fuck is going on?!

Talous screamed as he was tackled, and the larger man's heavy form landed on his destroyed leg. He wedged his shield between them, but Matt grabbed the other half of Talous and twisted. He was forced to let go, as the shield acted as a lever, and threatened to snap his other arm. The man was still unnaturally strong.

How is he not out of willpower yet?!

Sacrificing the shield, he quickly drew a dagger and plunged it into the man's kidney with all his strength. To his horror, the armor's lower back suddenly became much thicker and more decorative as the blade arced in. The dagger's enchanted tip simply skittered off the glowing, Talent-made armor, and a spiked gauntlet smashed into his chest.

Talous could feel his breastplate cave in as the spikes penetrated the Tier 7 armor and dug into his chest. The gouges hurt, but the shattering ribs were tortuously painful. His arms crumpled to his sides as one of his lungs collapsed, and he started bleeding out internally.

The fight was over. There was no coming back from this.

He tried to get out a final quip, but he couldn't even take the needed breath as Matt relentlessly slammed down with his one working arm over and over. He crushed Talous' ribs to powder, mincing his heart and lungs with the splinters. Finally, he was pulled out of the ring as his vision faded.

The last thing he remembered was the cold faceless visage of his armored opponent, reeling back for yet another killing blow. Talous saw a monster pretending to be a man, who'd uttered not a word as it was sliced to pieces. A beast that would not fall.

In that final moment, the ghostly mirrored helm reflected his own dying eyes straight back at him. Talous shuddered as the darkness claimed him.

26

Liz hoisted the two drunks as she made her way through the underwater auction house to the platforms that would take them to the surface.

She didn't like Alyssa, but the woman was in a pretty bad state. She originally thought the woman was faking it when she barged into their room, but as Liz carried her, she got a whiff of the woman. She positively *reeked* of booze. Even for a Tier 7, the woman was well beyond drunk, and well into hammered.

Her bloodline still thrummed with oppression due to Alyssa's purer bloodline, but she shoved that down to walk her back home. The imposing presence whenever she was around Alyssa put her in a constant state of anxiety. Bloodline suppression was something that she never thought she would have to cope with but spending time with Alyssa during the council meetings had slowly helped her adjust to the feeling. At this point, it wasn't very difficult to ignore.

They were on the surface when Liz finally said something, "You're lucky I'm willing to drag you all the way home."

"Not as lucky as you are. Such a lucky little bird."

Liz looked around for a moment before realizing that Alyssa had been the one to answer her. Both the condescension and overly friendly attitude had been absent from her voice. The woman almost sounded sincere.

Liz warily asked, "How so?"

Alyssa just laughed as if it was the funniest joke, even as she stumbled in an attempt to walk on her own.

"It's nothing. Don't worry about it."

Liz didn't let it drop. "No, really. Explain. And why are you this drunk? In all our late night council meetings I've never even seen you take so much as a sip of the complementary wine. You being this hammered is out of character."

Alyssa gave Liz a long look before she replied, "Out of character. Yeah, how right you are. I just found out I'm getting married to a handsome young Count from the Empire."

"Congratulations?" Liz responded with a questioning lilt. "It's what you wanted right? To move up in the nobility. Play the game. Gather political power."

"Not this way. Not by selling my bloodline. It makes sense to use it as a lure to gain power, but I am *more* than my bloodline. When I pushed back and told my parents I would rather die than play their game, they lost their minds. Called me ungrateful and everything else under the seven suns."

Liz was taken aback at that. She had put Alyssa in the same category as the rest of those social schemers that she was unfortunate enough to deal with when she was younger. The type that would do anything and *anyone* to get ahead. She figured Alyssa would jump at the chance to marry up, given how she flaunted all the gifts she had received from other suitors. Apparently, she had the wrong idea.

Perhaps I've been too harsh?

"You must know what it is like? I can feel your bloodline. Mine is perfect, *better*, but yours is close. Plus, I know a noble education when I see one, even in the way you hold yourself. I'd bet everything and anything that you had just as many people sniffing around you as I had." She tripped on nothing, and Liz paused as Alyssa ominously held her hand to her stomach. "You joined the Path, though."

Alyssa panted for a moment at Liz's lack of response before she got herself under control and tried to walk. She tilted so far, Liz had to scoop her back up and start guiding her again.

"I didn't get that lucky."

Liz hesitantly asked, "If they were just trying to sell you, that would violate the Empire's laws. You can't be forced into a marriage against your will."

The drunk Tier 7 barked a mocking laugh. There was no humor in it, only pain. "Forced? No, but pressured…? Absolutely. They are my *parents*, after all. And oh, how they pressure. And how little I'll be left with if I refuse. No money, no home, no title, *no protection.* Besides, you think the Empire really enforces its laws in the kingdom? Has no one told you about the 'privileges' given to the high nobles here over the commoners? The royals aren't even subtle about it, and yet not once has your great, benevolent *Empire* even bothered to sniff around. They couldn't care about any of us. Now…if you will excuse me for a moment."

Alyssa jolted to the side to finally empty her stomach into a bush. The acrid stench rolled over Liz and Aster like a wave. Even while unconscious, Aster squirmed to get away.

Wiping her mouth, Alyssa said, "Much better. Honestly, I shouldn't have such a pure bloodline. My mother and father are both third-generation Peacocks. No, no, no, I should have been a normal human. By some fluke, I popped out with a completely pure bloodline. Perfectly, freakishly pure. A curse more than a blessing, really. The vultures were circling from day one, and my parents only worried about finding the highest bidder. Duke Asfodel's Tier 17 son is now in the lead after I rejected the Count. So, I might actually be headed to your precious Beast kingdom. Not that I'll ever leave their estates. But my parents could care less."

She scoffed, then groaned. "Fucking worthless. They can't even break through Tier 14 and become real immortals. Their clocks were already ticking down when I was born. They were *desperate*, and fate simply handed them the prize they needed. That's why it was a fucked up thing to remove me from command. Especially after all the free bits of help I kept giving the Pather Union. I only asked for a favor in return when you wanted something really big."

Liz shook her head, even though the other woman couldn't see it. "Albert would have never given you a Barony. Not after how you try to counter him at every turn."

Alyssa gave Liz a sardonic look. "It was worth a shot at least. Rumor had it that Albert had a title or two for the new planets tucked away in his back pocket, ready to motivate the generals or buy an important traitor with. He was desperate enough to get that Shard of Reality to give a barony to anyone. Even me. Figured if I paired a big accomplishment with a promise to step out of his way, he might bite. You're probably right though, that ship sailed a long time ago." She shrugged. "But once you pick a side, it's not easy to change."

Liz felt sympathetic but worried that this was just a ploy to garner said sympathy. Either the woman was a controlled drunk, or she was playing her. Were it not for the vomit and boozy stench still clinging to the woman, she wouldn't have picked out drunkenness as the source of her sudden personality shift. Alyssa didn't even slur her words. The question was, just how used to being drunk was she?

Maybe she was getting a view into the *actual* Alyssa.

"Why not leave for the Beast Kingdom? With your bloodline, you could have found a sponsor to one of the royal academies. I was offered a spot, and it boasts one of the best educations in the Empire, along with rifts for advancement all the way up to Tier 14."

Alyssa scoffed in response. "Sure, then throw myself into the arms of a random benefactor who would have just as much control as my parents, but even less reason to care about my well-being." She spat off to the side. "No, I'll make it to the Beast Kingdom when I'm Tier 15 and can play the political game for real. Then I'll be an adult by any standards. Only then will I be able to show them how wrong they were."

"There are a lot of strong people there, and not everyone is as civilized as they could be. Without a backer…" Liz didn't know how to say the woman's idea was pipe dream politely.

Alyssa snorted in a less than ladylike manner. "So what? Hardly any different than here."

After a few more minutes of guiding the shuffling girl, they arrived at Alyssa's room. It wasn't what Liz expected, though she couldn't have explained why it felt off. It was a simple room. The only addition that seemed from the woman herself was a multicolored bedspread.

Otherwise, the room was the same as the one she and Matt shared, just not connected to others in a suite. Though, she did notice a dark smoke stain over the closet. A remnant from Annie's act of arson.

Right where her own side table was, she gently set down Aster before maneuvering Alyssa over to her bed.

As Liz dropped the drunk woman onto her bed and yanked off a boot, she thought over what Alyssa had said. When she was done with the first one, she asked, "If you were nicer, you would have more allies. You had never even met my team and backstabbed us. If you do the same to your own side, it's no wonder they aren't very happy with you. You killed how many generals exactly?"

Alyssa scoffed as she covered her eyes. "I didn't kill shit. All I did was use the queendom's plans and get myself in the right position to take advantage. Or at least try to. Their plan was to remove the competent generals and then slowly siege down the city, while sending massive forces to kill off most of Albies' troops. Little did they know, Olivia was smarter than all the generals they killed combined."

That surprised Liz. It also piqued her interest. Alyssa had proven herself an apt political player, but that was information that she really shouldn't know, so Liz pushed slightly.

"So, you didn't kill the generals?"

Alyssa rolled over and buried her face in a pillow. "If I had the influence and resources to pull that off, I wouldn't need a barony to escape my parents. No, I only sent the message to Happer that his mistress was cheating. He's in an unhappy arranged marriage and actually loved the girl. I felt bad for him. It's not my fault that he sucks at combat, and Misty's other boytoy didn't. Timing was just lucky."

"Still, being nice to people rarely hurts." Liz was surprised that the woman had cared enough to try to help someone, even if she then tried to publicly make it seem like a master plan. It wasn't who she thought the woman was.

Alyssa's next words dashed any hope she had for the woman being a nice person. "Like I need to attract even more dumbass suitors. None of the twits around here matter anyway. A bunch of useless losers."

Seeing that the woman was resigned to being a dick, Liz scooped up the passed-out Aster off the table as she said, "Don't sleep on your back. You might choke to death."

"I know how to sleep drunk." There was half a heartbeat's pause when she added, "But your boyfriend might die. Talous finally got his wish."

Only a second later, Liz received a message from Annie

confirming Alyssa's statement, and an attached recording of the insults to both her and Aster, then Matt's parents.

She put Aster down into Alyssa's arms and raced out of the room. She didn't like the woman, but she wasn't evil enough to hurt a sleeping beast bond.

She had the fight streaming to her AI as she tore her way down the halls and into the street. Even as she grabbed a taxi to reach the loading platforms quicker, she watched as Matt was cut repeatedly.

Liz had every intention of making Talous pay for the slanderous things he had said. Emily had filled her in, and seeing the flat angry look in her boyfriend's eyes as he turned to attack Talous filled her with rage.

Win or lose. She was going to make Talous pay.

When she arrived at the platform loading and unloading area, she nearly tore her hair out, seeing the massive line.

She needed to get down there now. She didn't doubt that Matt would win, and she knew that she'd have to do damage control if things were as bad as she feared. His parents were a very sore spot for Matt, and she wouldn't forgive Talous for poking it.

Malous stood there as he watched his brother's mutilated body vanish. He had let his attention slip, and the fool had run off to challenge Matt in another misguided attempt to get his Concept.

That was fine. Annoying, but fine.

Talous losing? Probably for the best, honestly.

What wasn't acceptable was the fight not ending when it was clearly over. His brother should have been pulled out after the first punch to the ribs.

Malous could see his brother's ribcage crumple and flatten with each extra strike. That was far too long to allow the fight to proceed.

It was incompetence. Or deliberate interference.

He looked at his team and saw the same looks. They all suspected that the referee and army watchers were playing favorites.

Malous turned to leave. Without a word, his team followed him to the platforms that would take them out of there. His brother needed him, and he had to do damage control while investigating who had let the fight drag on so long.

He and his brother didn't have the best relationship before joining the Path, but they were closer now, and he really didn't care for seeing him punished over something so minor. The already brutal loss *should* have been enough.

The watchers and referee *should* have been impartial.

As his blood boiled, Malous tried to decide how to handle this. Someone needed to be held accountable.

Luna smiled as she watched the broken body vanish. Her notes hovering nearby were filled with critiques, but she was happy.

Matt had thoroughly impressed her. He had resisted the referee's standard attempts to remove Talous long enough that the army watchers stepped in before the referee could do so physically. The referee didn't have the skill to extract Matt's opponent without destroying his Concept; it was still long enough to get in a few more blows. He was so angry, he probably had no idea that he had accidentally locked down the space around him, preventing the referee from executing their standard removal procedure.

The Talous boy would be fine, too. She had seen his type many times before. Knowing he wasn't the best would just motivate him more. He would come back stronger if he didn't let this get to him. Plus, countless people that she'd mentored would have taken a thousand of those beatings for their Concepts. One day, he'd count himself as the clear winner here.

From someone with his Talent, drive, and proficiency with a blade, she expected good things. She even had a pile of notes ready for his manager when he inevitably got his own team at Tier 10.

Her tail swished, and she couldn't wipe the grin from her face.

Her new protege just kept surprising her.

Oh, she was going to mold Matt into a *monster*.

Conor watched as Matt dueled Talous and winced at the earliest stages of the fight. Matt was raging, and it showed in his combat style.

He hated to admit it, but Talous was good with his chosen weapons. Better than anyone else Conor had personally met.

As the fight progressed, he had to reevaluate Matt several times. He had fought and dueled the man in training, as well as fought beside him dozens of times. For all their time together, he still underestimated the man and his will to fight.

He flat-out refused to go down.

There was something in that tenacity that he could learn from. Conor wasn't the best. He knew that. But he was good. Maybe he didn't need to be the best; he just needed to outlast everyone else. With his defensive style, it wasn't the worst idea.

Conor took note of the way Talous moved for his own purposes. He was a more defensive fighter, but he still wanted to try replicating a few of his moves with his shield later while sparring. They both used a single handed weapon and a shield, after all.

Annie leaned over and cheered as Matt kicked Talous' leg out from under him. Conor took a moment to double-check their wagers, now that the fight was turning.

The initial odds had leaned slightly in Matt's favor, as he had won their first encounter. But during the beginning of the duel, Talous had clearly been taking the upper hand. After a sudden onslaught by Talous a few minutes in, the odds shifted heavily in his favor. At that peak, shortly before betting was closed, Matt winning offered a two-to-one payout.

Annie dropped every single point she had on Matt. Conor had put all but two points in the fight, and transferred the other to Annie. If she died with no points, she was out of the war, and it was better to be safe rather than sorry.

A few minutes later, Emily had arrived and done the same. Her tardiness had actually netted her a much better payout, since Talous had become the major favorite. At the end of the fight, they cashed out with nearly two hundred thousand extra points.

It was a nice reward, but it was quickly soured. When Matt deactivated his armor, his clothes fell away in bloody strips, showing the damage inflicted on their friend. His body had more bloody gashes than unharmed flesh.

The sight of him spoiled their good cheer. They rushed to their teammates' side, but were held back by the referee as a healer rushed forward.

Matt was quickly treated. A week-long healing cooldown was prescribed, but the healer didn't seem overly worried.

Matt was clearly out of it. He looked off into space until Emily asked if he was okay. The question seemed to bring him back to the present.

With a shake, Matt stood up and nodded. "Sorry, guys. He really pissed me off. I was stuck in my own head for a minute there."

That was an understatement, but he wasn't going to tell them that he had snapped at the repeated insults and was about to kill the man. The only reason he hadn't gone for the man's head was that he wanted the pain to last. He was afraid that if he damaged his head, the army would step in before he could dish out the sort of agony that he wanted Talous to feel.

Matt laughed like it wasn't serious, but he could feel his eyes still flat, despite his voice's forced cheer.

Annie didn't seem to notice and lightly elbowed the man. "Great fight, and we won an assload of points from betting on you."

"Oh, that's good."

He wasn't sure what else to say. Regardless, he was happy for them. The more points they had, the stronger they were.

His AI notified him that his winnings from the duel were transferred. He was entitled to thirty percent of the house's take. It was an enormous sum, a little under 750K points.

They tasted like ashes. He hadn't fought for the points—he fought because he got angry, and Talous' smug attitude only made it worse as they fought.

The points were tainted, and he didn't want anything to do with them.

"Hey Annie, how close are you to buying [Side Slide]?"

She was startled, but he spoke before she could say anything else. "Here, take the points I won from the fight and see how close that gets you."

He was relieved when they were out of his point balance. It felt like a weight off his shoulders.

Annie spluttered, "Matt, I can't take these. It's just too much."

Without ruining the mood, he tried to explain. "Annie, I didn't fight for the points, and I really don't want them. Just take them, please."

She turned to her sister and pleaded, "I need one hundred thousand points. Pleassse."

With an eye roll that could only come from family, Emily flicked a finger at her sister, transferring the points over.

Annie poked at her AI's interface, and a second later, the listing for [Side Slide] disappeared. A nondescript skill shard sat in the air directly in front of her.

She turned and hugged Matt. "Oh, thank you! Thank you, thank you, thank you!"

With a smooth motion, she snapped it into a band around her wrist to ensure it couldn't be stolen during the time it took to absorb the skill. As soon as it was in place, she started to dance right there.

Seeing his friend so happy helped to thaw Matt out of his icy mood a bit.

Talous had irritated him with the insults to his friends, but when he'd attacked his parents, Matt snapped. He shouldn't have. Compared to the disgusting slander Talous had stooped to before, that final comment had been rather tame. It had just rubbed him the wrong way.

He wasn't happy with his actions. He should have walked away from the fight. It was dumb and unnecessary, while also playing into Talous' own plans.

Matt wasn't dumb. When he felt the queendom Pather form his own Concept, he understood that was Talous' plan from the outset. The realization that Talous had used Matt's dead parents as a ploy to earn his own Concept still burned at his gut.

He wanted to rip the new Concept away from the man. It felt like he had stolen it from his parents' graves.

As Emily and Annie bickered playfully, he met Conor's eye and nodded slightly to him. The man gave him a concerned look that he appreciated, despite wishing he noticed less. Right now, he didn't want to deal with questions of a more delicate nature.

All he wanted to do was relax.

Liz's messages blinked at him from the corner of his eye, and he read through them. They were mostly asking if he was okay. Clearly, she had seen the duel.

Her last message said that she was coming down as soon as she could get a shuttle. He messaged her back, telling her to wait.

He was going home now, whether the others were or not.

The bustle and cheer of the auction house didn't sit well with Matt. On the platform above, he could already see people cheering for him. If he left the auction house, he could get away from most of this.

Having made up his mind, Matt said, "Hey guys, I'm going to meet up with Liz. Why don't you continue the party? Enjoy yourselves."

Even Annie, who was in her own world, stopped to give Matt a weird look.

Conor slapped his shoulder, "Nah. The last thing you need is to be alone right now. We'll all go back up. We're a team."

There was a finality to that statement that was comforting. Emily pulled him to his feet and patted his back. "We aren't assholes like Talous. If you want to talk, or even be alone, let us know. But we aren't going to let you run off on your own after something set you off so badly."

That brought a real smile to Matt. He might not have any blood relations left, but he had a family.

Sara lurked next to the chamber where Albert was using his Shard of Reality. A special item let her seamlessly blend into a large potted plant in the room. An actual fortune, most of her very generous allowance from her childhood, had been paid to a Tier 12 crafter to make it. But it would fool any Tier 7 not specialized in breaking illusions.

She was getting desperate and needed to make her move. Two days had passed since the auction, and Albert should be coming out any moment.

She was doing this personally, as she could only trust herself to handle this particular mission. The queendom's next moves depended on this fight. On taking out most of the kingdom leadership in one fell swoop. The massive reward for personally killing her rival commander was secondary.

Half an hour later, Juni approached with a contingent of guards.

Seeing him caused Sara to stop and reevaluate. Juni should have been in there with Albert. Their spies had seen him enter the formation, and no one had seen him for the last week.

It could only mean one thing. The man already had his Concept.

That hampered her plans. By every report, Juni was loyal and strong. His performance in the war so far had been stellar. If he could perform at that level even with his Concept hidden, then he might be able to prevent this assassination with it.

With a steadying breath, Sara refocused her mental wellbeing. She could die for this kill. Her orders were given and plans already in motion. Her people could make do, as long as Albert was unable to give orders or buy upgrades to his cities. She had already spent all her side points in the perpetration phase.

The queendom needed a win, and they needed it now if their larger plans were to succeed.

The door swung open, and she tensed her hand with the specially made storage ring for her lance. The ring would be useless when she Tiered-up and got a new weapon, but she needed the utility right now. Speed was of the essence, and a six-foot lance would be too large to quickly draw.

When Albert stepped out, she targeted him with her Tier 1 Talent. As he was well within her fifteen-foot range, she immediately teleported to his side.

She didn't thrust at him or attack him with her lance. She didn't even summon it from her ring. The man was too well armored for that to guarantee a kill. No, she stuck an explosive to his face. Even as it made contact, she changed her Talent's target and, with an effort of will, appeared beside them fifteen feet away.

The bomb detonated almost instantly. A shock-wave rocked the hall that threatened to blow out her eardrums. Her AI pinged to report the death of the enemy vassal's leader with a fanfare of color and points. Doing it herself merited a million points. Better yet they were personal points with no restrictions on their use.

Now, she just needed to sever the last of the hydra's heads.

The only important survivor was Juni. When he stood up and caught her eye, madness stared back at her. Bits of debris scarred his face and blood poured from his ears, but he looked manic. At the sight of her, he lunged with a gravity assisted leap.

The gravity around Sara multiplied a dozen times, and the surprise almost caused her to stumble, but she changed her target and teleported out of the range. Her spirit was on fire from changing targets so many times and so quickly, but seeing Juni's stick land on her previous location with an explosion of stone, she forced the pain down.

That blow might have ended her. She checked her AI's combat evaluations. Her mother had gifted her a nearly perfect copy of her own AI skill, just scaled down to work for a Tier 3. It's starting capabilities were massively beyond what the typical blank slate AI began with.

The AI assured her she could win this fight, if she didn't fuck up. With her emergency backup plan, she could win even without a fight. But that had other costs.

Juni immediately lowered her chances by half as a wave of gravity sent everyone around them flying. With no one else in range, Juni was the only viable target for her Talent. Which he no doubt wanted.

With his gravity manipulation, fighting in close quarters was ill-advised.

Sighing, she resigned herself to using the backup plan. This was something she'd only readied in case the bomb didn't finish her Albie. A last resort.

Sara removed her belt and tossed it to the ground, where it started spewing smoke, and moved left to dodge a thrown knife.

This needed to happen quickly. Reinforcements were no doubt on their way, and it would be dumb to die from archers while trying to kill a secondary target.

Under the concealment of the smoke, she targeted Juni and teleported directly in front of him. Her lance's thrust felt slow as molasses as she tried to push through the repulsive force emanating from him. As her weapon nearly stopped, she activated the enchantment on her lance's head. In a blue explosion, a Tier 8 mana stone between the shaft and head discharged. The front of her weapon bulleted forward, covering the needed distance while simultaneously supercharging the piercing enchantment on the tip.

Her beloved weapon was destroyed, but as she walked out of the now normalized gravity zone to confirm her kill, she found Juni standing there with her lance *through* his chest. He was still standing somehow.

With a sudden, manic grin, he brought his stick down at her head.

The deactivation of his gravity field had been bait.

Sara rolled backward and drew her daggers from her back sheaths, but the tip of the weapon caught her in the head even as she tried to avoid it. She felt the bone crack, but ignored it as the split skin wasn't leaking blood into her eyes.

She was ready to fight.

Thankfully, she didn't need to. Juni disappeared just seconds later, as he moved forward to engage her. The watchers must have decided the lance head through his chest was life-threatening enough to warrant removal. Him holding still was probably the only thing keeping the bleeding in check enough.

Seeing the kingdom guards rushing her, she dashed down the other hall to an exterior wall. With a final burning effort, she targeted the man waiting outside of the building and teleported next to him.

As soon as she was outside, she sprinted to where her own people were waiting and checked the reports coming in.

Her armies were in their places and making their moves. The ambush teams for the kingdom's top Pathers were already engaging. Two armies that had been moving in the open were already engaged and encircled.

Things were finally looking up.

Now she needed to focus on their other plan. It needed to go well, just as much as this one had. She checked her timer. Two weeks and six days.

That was when they would end this war.

And they would be taking far more from the kingdom than the prizes. Hopefully, Albert would forgive her one day.

27

Matt spent the evening with his team, casually watching movies and dining in. He wanted to cook, but the others wouldn't hear of it, and ordered a spread of dishes before they even reached their room.

On their way back, they picked up Aster from a groggy Alyssa, who only opened the door long enough for them to enter before she shuffled into her bathroom and into the running shower.

Aster was happy to see him but was still mostly out of it. So, when they got back, they put her in the freezer until the food arrived. Unsurprisingly, she miraculously revived at the smell of roasted rabbit.

She was still feeling the alcohol and only nibbled at her food until Matt cut it for her. She whined a mental, "Thank you," before projecting an image of her being fed by hand.

He was happy to do so. It was cute and nostalgic to see her so helpless. It took him back to when she was a newborn, when she needed him to help with pretty much everything.

His introspection ended as they watched a comedy movie, and he went to use the bathroom. He noticed how Liz wouldn't take her eyes off him and was tracking every movement he made.

When he went to fetch a drink from the kitchen, she took the opportunity to descend on him.

She rubbed his arm, and when that wasn't enough, leaned in for a hug. Then, holding him tightly, she apologized, "I'm sorry I wasn't there. I—"

Matt rubbed her back while in the embrace but cut her off. “Don’t worry about that. Even if you had been there, I still probably would have snapped on him. I’m more mad at myself for giving the bastard what he wanted.”

Against his conscious desires, his body tensed at the mention of Talous and his Concept.

Liz noticed and pulled back. “What do you mean?”

Her eyes were sharp, and Matt understood how it felt to be a rabbit with Aster eyeing them from a bush. It was unnerving to know that a predator had their full attention locked on to you.

When he didn’t answer quickly enough, Liz prodded again. “He wanted a fight, but your tone tells me that’s not all. What did he want?”

Her tone was gentle, but there was a hardness in there that spoke of the pain and anger just waiting to be unleashed. Not willing to lie to her, he debated a half-truth, or something less revealing. But, in the end, he decided to just let it out.

“I think the reason he wanted to fight me so badly was that he was close to finishing his Concept and fighting me got it for him. Halfway through the fight, he finished forming it and started using it. I expect he was just a hair away, and needed the final push.”

He tensed up again, but tried to shove it down. Liz noticed, so he finished his thought. “It pisses me off that he insulted my parents to get me to fight, and that’s what earned him his Concept. It feels like he besmirched their memory.”

Liz was clearly concerned, and he noticed that his knuckles started to pop. Realizing he was tensing, he shook himself in an effort to relax.

“It’s fine. I just need some time to cool down completely.”

His girlfriend and teammate looked at him like he was stupid.

“What?”

Her look of incredulity only increased to near comical levels.

“Matt, you need to talk to someone.” When he opened his mouth, she spoke over him. “A professional. Talous threw some hateful shit at you, and you’re just pushing it down and bottling it up. Have you even messaged your therapist at all?”

Internally, he winced. He had thought about it but had decided against it. He just wanted the incident behind him.

"No. I haven't."

She hooked an arm through his arm and started to drag him out of the suite. She called over her shoulder, "We're going for a walk," to the rest of the team, who was watching them leave.

Aster jumped off Emily's lap and padded after them on her slightly wobbly feet. He leaned down to scoop her up and carry her after he probed their connection. Her head was hurting enough. He felt bad about her not resting, but kept his mouth shut.

The Tree of Perfection's fruit had nearly completed its mental effects on her. She was self-aware enough to decide what she wanted to do herself. If she wanted to come, he wouldn't stop her. And he wanted her close. She was a balm to his spirit.

His fluffy bond sent peaceful thoughts to him, which stopped him from resisting more than anything Liz had said. Aster had a direct line to his emotions, as did he to hers. Despite her pain, she was more worried about him than anything else. Even rabbits and ice cream were distant thoughts for her right now.

They didn't talk much as Liz led him to the hospital and into a check-in section. Seeing she was going to sign him in, he gently put a hand on her arm and handed off Aster to do it himself.

After checking in, he was barely able to sit down before his AI pinged that he was able to be seen.

A man in nurse's robes escorted him to a room situated along a hall filled with doors next to each other. Behind the doors, his spiritual sense could feel blocking wards and spatial expansions. From the spacing of the doors, they should be closer to closets than the spacious room he was led to.

He had waited in a stuffed chair for only a few seconds when an older man came in and smiled at him.

"Healer Lester, Tier 18 with seventy years of mental health expertise."

"Matt." He had no idea what else to say and waved slightly, which just caused the older healer to smile and ask, " And how do you think you're doing today?"

Matt wanted to say he was fine, but tried to be more truthful. "I snapped on someone after they insulted my parents to get me to duel them, and then proceed to beat them to a pulp."

The healer took that in stride and started to talk to Matt.

They conversed for a little more than an hour and a half, before the man escorted Matt out and back to Liz.

He felt slightly better, but realized it was still too soon for him to really be okay. He was angry, and the only way to start healing was to let that simmer down a bit.

He and the healer had scheduled a follow-up meeting for the following week.

The three of them wandered the city for a good hour, just window shopping and seeing what they could find. Aster was feeling well enough after a passing healer threw a healing spell on her. Now, she was bouncing around and reveling in the attention she garnered from the crowds.

They made it back to their room just as everyone else was getting ready to go to bed.

The next day, Matt found a reason to escape his teammate's watchful eyes thanks to Melinda, who asked to inspect his body once more. With that excuse, he spent another few hours in this hospital, being poked and prodded by Melinda and her mentor, Baxter.

Most of what they said went over his head but, finally, when they both seemed happy, Melinda asked for his help.

"I think I was able to get my Talent to latch on to the spirit and make the changes."

When he looked confused, she punched his arm.

"If I can figure this out, I can heal people to have a perfect body like yours."

Matt sat up. "I didn't think you would get it to work. What changed?"

She looked awkward as Baxter smirked.

"Well, for one, I've been practicing my Concept. And, secondly, I'm getting a lot of practice, since you keep getting injured."

Matt opened his mouth to congratulate her, then closed it with a confused *click*. He had no idea how to respond to that.

"You're welcome?"

At his question, Baxter snorted, and Melinda laughed as she explained, "No, really. The Tree of Perfection works by changing the spirit, then providing the energy to the body for the transformation. When you get limbs cut off or whatnot, the new flesh that grows back *is* the perfected flesh. All of your injuries have allowed me to observe the changes and see the different stages as they appear in different parts of your body."

Matt was taken aback. "Wait, wait, wait! Is that safe for me?"

Matt started looking for parts of his body that were distinctly better than any of the other parts. The arm he lost to the void user was completely regrown, but it felt mostly the same.

At least he thought it did.

"Relax, Matt. It's not dangerous. Your body is just more perfect than before. It's not physically a Tier 15's body. It's just that any imperfections are fixed, and your body runs a lot more efficiently. It's also primed to start using essence as a fuel source."

"So, it's not dangerous to have bits and pieces in different stages?"

This time it was the mostly silent Baxter who answered. "It's not. The rich will start cutting limbs off and regrowing them to speed up the process. It's not dangerous. And even if it was, Melinda would keep you alive."

"That last bit isn't comforting."

The older man rolled his eyes and flopped into a chair that wasn't there a moment ago.

Melinda refocused his attention. "So, I want to try to *heal* you into the point of the Tree's process being finished. But I'm pretty sure it's gonna take absurd amounts of mana."

That was something Matt had in abundance, so he stuck out his hand. "I can keep you going with my Concept, while also refilling the mana stone rack things your healers all have, if you want."

Baxter just watched as Melinda cast a spell. They were both staring at something Matt couldn't see or feel as thousands, then tens of thousands of mana was drained from Matt into Melinda.

It cost him nothing and was a good willpower exercise. After an hour and way too much mana, Melinda stopped casting and dropped into her own chair next to the examination table.

"So?"

She just grinned at him, so he asked, "It worked, then?"

"It worked like a charm. I was able to improve the furthest-behind portions of your body by fifteen percent."

That didn't sound like a lot, and he said so, to both of the healers' derision.

Baxter pointed at Melinda and shook his head. "Kid, she just proved that it worked, then demonstrated it. That's huge."

"Yeah, but that took over half a million mana and two hours. While I don't mind providing it, it seems ineffective."

Melinda stepped in. "Only because I was providing the energy for the physical change. The spiritual one is already done. Now I need to test on someone without the spiritual changes. If I'm right, making the spiritual change won't be anywhere near as hard."

Matt put up his hands. "Back up for a second. Did you say the Root of Perfection provided the energy? Wouldn't it be bad if that was lacking?"

He was worried that she'd hurt herself.

"Relax, Matt. Worst comes to worst, I've already proven that I can fix that with enough mana." She pointed at the older healer and said, "From other tests, Baxter and I theorize that at worst, it will siphon off a small bit of mana regen, or steal a bit of the essence we absorb until the changes finish."

Seeing that the two far more knowledgeable people were in agreement, he again provided mana to Melinda in an endless stream, and she cast a healing spell on herself.

It took hours, but eventually, she came up from her casting and started to look at herself, while Baxter walked around and did the same.

Matt, having no idea how things went, asked, "So?"

Melinda grinned at him. "I was able to convince my spirit that the changes were its natural form, and even jump-started the process a bit."

He smiled. "That sounds great." He paused and asked, "It is great, right?"

"It's amazing. This will let even Tier 5s live for centuries longer than normal. It's a step to healing old age itself. To turning back the clock."

He had no idea what she was talking about. The two things seemed completely unrelated. Letting someone live longer wasn't reversing aging, and it wasn't like she could heal people one at a time.

When he said that, Melinda explained, "My Tier 3 Talent is the 'you know what'. It's still a Tier 3 Talent though, which means it's a growth Talent. It will grow as I push it. When I Tier up, I should be able to rely on it doing the hard work and making changes if I want to. No going inch by inch to convince the spirit to accept the changes."

"That doesn't sound that hard. Why couldn't a normal healer do that?"

Baxter snorted, "It's what her Tier 3 does. It's still doing most of the heavy lifting. I wouldn't trust anyone else with that type of detailed work. Even the healers who *do* manipulate spirits mostly do so with Tier 44 specific healing spells. They rely on those spells to do the heavy lifting." Seeing that Matt still didn't believe him, he continued, "Imagine trying to demonstrate an entire ecosystem with only your hand, while blindfolded…and drunk. And without having hands."

Melinda cut him off from further diatribes. "It's hard, Matt. My Talent makes it so I don't have to worry about the little details. I just need to think about the ecosystem in general, instead of every detail. If someone else tried and messed up one little thing, it could be quite dangerous. At the PlayPen, when I was still learning before acquiring my Tier 3, it was explicitly stated a million times to not mess with the spirit."

"So, when you Tier up, you'll just slap a normal healing spell on someone, and it'll just make the change? What if someone doesn't want that?"

Melinda shook her head. "I have control over things like that. I can't turn off the general Overhealth, but I can turn off the things I've added to it. And it still won't be that easy. It will require a lot of mana to do, but I'll be quick. I still need to convince the entire spirit that the body should be more in line with what the root did to you."

Matt changed the topic. He was thoroughly lost in all this medical talk.

"You said that you worked on your Concept. You've been cagey about it. What did you figure out?"

That caused Melinda to sigh. "I've learned to accept that it's what I have. Death isn't who I want to be, but it is what's shaped me. I wish it was something like life, but that's a hard ideal to embody."

That was something Matt had experience with.

"I feel you. Did I ever tell you what my Concept image was?"

At her head shake, he explained. Matt didn't miss that even Baxter seemed interested. But if the man worked for the Emperor personally and was sent to watch Melinda, he expected the man to know how to keep his mouth shut. He might even get the higher Tier man to talk.

"I knew my phrase was, 'I am endless,' but the image gave me a lot of trouble. I didn't like how a wellspring felt, even if it was easy to make."

Baxter nodded silently as Matt continued, "A sun was a lot harder to make but felt way better. Suns live forever with essence, but the knowledge that they die without essence kept cropping up in the back of my mind. Weirdly, going with hotter and shorter-lived suns worked better for me. They were less endless, but they had power."

Seeing Melinda's interested expression, he explained, "With the Ascension, I was able to form all of those images, but what I settled on was a black hole. Those are endless…or so it felt."

Matt paused to gather the right words. "It felt perfectly wrong. Like a mirror image. So, I inverted it into a white hole. They aren't necessarily real, but the image was perfect for me. Endless energy outflowing."

Melinda looked interested but stayed silent.

Baxter nodded respectfully to Matt before saying, "Thank you for sharing. A person's Concept is a glimpse into their truth."

He raised a hand, and a greenish energy mana flowed out into a tree. "My Concept was the idea of growth and renewal."

The tree bloomed into a green explosion, but he smiled as it withered. "My Intent wasn't what I expected. It was the night that let some rest, and others hunt. A time for healing and pain."

The tree's leaves drooped as a white moon rose out of the mana and took center stage, casting its light down on everything it touched.

Matt leaned forward, "No one I've talked to really knows Intents or Aspects. What about you?"

Baxter leaned back, and his solemn aura vanished. Suddenly, the relaxed man who took nothing serious was back.

"No one can tell you anything because it's a personal journey. I can't tell you about you." Matt opened his mouth to protest, but Baxter waved him down. "I'm not trying to be cryptic. You can't even start on your Intent until you've converted all of your essences to resonate with your Concept. I've already heard that you learned about mana aspects. That's an extension of expanding your Concept. When you've fully converted your cores, things will be clearer."

That was actually helpful, so Matt nodded at Baxter before asking, "Is it the same for Aspects?"

"Not really. Even Intents are different to form, but there isn't a one size fits all way to go about it. You'll still need a phrase and image, but beyond that, it varies from person to person. Don't worry about it now. You have plenty of time."

As the older man said time, Matt had a thought and blurted it out. "If you said I need to convert my essence to resonate with my Concept, I shouldn't advance."

Baxter shrugged. "That's a strategy. More than one person has used it. If you convert everything to resonate with your Concept early, it's easier. Any new essence added will automatically convert. But it's not like you have to stop. Your Concept is already doing it. It's a passive thing. The more your Concept fits with you, the faster it spreads."

He pointed at Melinda. "She didn't even mean to get her Concept, and it's *perfect* for her. Her essence is already converted. It only took her weeks. But your phrase and image are massive and complicated. The white hole is a brilliant move, but it's still a huge idea. Death, or at least how Melinda sees it, is simple."

Matt and Melinda both looked at each other with confusion. Baxter rolled his eyes and stood. "You have until Tier 24 before this becomes an issue. That's why this information isn't widely available. Focus on the next step. Not the one ten steps down the line."

With that, he walked out the door and was gone.

Matt and Melinda chatted a bit about their Concepts and their experiences with them. He was slightly jealous of the idea of a passive part of her Concept.

It seemed incredibly useful. He had no idea what he could do with a passive version of his own Concept, but he liked the idea.

They eventually both had to leave for their team training, but it was nice to spend time with his old friends, and even help them grow. Even if it was just giving them the mana to try wacky things, like reversing old age.

Team Bucket's Concept training was going well. Emily felt closer and closer to her Concept with each training session and was hopeful that she would fully manifest it in the next month or so.

Contrary to the norm, she actually already had her image. It was herself standing on a growing pyramid as her Talent increased the power of each subsequent spell she cast. She just couldn't pin down her phrase.

Annie was growing frustrated with her lack of progress, but Conor was closing in on his own image, after already having his phrase.

Matt almost felt back to normal as the evening rolled around.

The next day, he was still on a healing cool down, so the rest of his team was sent on an escort mission without him. The army was moving a large number of troops who would have normally taken care of such activities.

Unable to participate in the mission, Matt encouraged them to go while he went to work on crafting with Kelley, after receiving a message saying that the man had something to show him. He was glad for it. With all of the sub-aspected mana he had accumulated over the length of the war, he was ready to try new things.

Most people were happy to give him a bit of mana for a few points. It cost them nothing, and the points meant little to Matt.

Still enjoying his new Tier 11 status, Kelley was strutting around the room when Matt walked past his nephew manning the desk.

When the crafter saw Matt, he beamed, extending his hand with a familiar-looking ring to the one Matt had on his finger.

"Look what I got!"

A quick inspection showed that it wasn't a growth item, but a standard item.

"I see that. What does it do, and how did you get it?"

Kelley let Matt take and examine his ring while he explained, "I've been putting every point I have into hiring Tier 5 teams to run that rift for me. Me and every other crafter who learned of your ring. I finally got lucky."

Matt nodded along. He and Kelley had talked to other crafters after discovering the changes to see if it affected their own products. It did for everything that took mana. Tailoring, smithing, and every other trade were all improved with the proper sub-aspect to the mana that the crafter used. It even improved the quality of the finished product.

Items that went through more than one crafter's hand were improved as well. A sword that was smithed with hardness sub-aspected mana was better than one without. If paired with an enchanter that also used hardness sub-aspected mana, or even strengthening, the blade was nearly unbendable when an actual hardness enchantment was embedded into the weapon.

The effects compounded. It was an incredible revelation, and everyone wanted the ability to store the sub-aspected mana types without having to imprint a personal mana converting stone for each type.

The number of needed stones quickly got out of hand.

Matt knew that Kelley had a spatially expanded storage crate made that held all of his tools and materials. It was a huge boon for whenever he wanted to move locations. He had heard the man bitch often enough about how much it cost and how unwieldy it was. But it was much larger than a standard backpack and was the only way to store as much junk as the Tier 11 pack rat kept.

He, along with every other crafter, had another crate made for the mana stones, and they quickly filled them.

They had all wanted a ring like Matt had, and while no one said it, he was sure that they wanted to buy or steal his own. Fortunately, the ring being a bound growth item put a stop to all of that.

Kelley stroked his ring with his thumb. "It only holds one hundred mana types, but its efficiency in converting the mana is nearly perfect. About ninety-eight percent."

That was much higher than the normal converting mana stones available, making the ring an amazing tool for saving mana.

Matt brushed past the shorter man and asked, "How many people have tried to buy it from you?"

The Tier 11 laughed as he, with his greater cultivation, shoved Matt back. "Nearly all of them. Even had a few assassination attempts from real contract killers."

Matt looked to his friend, but the man waved it off. "Nothing new. Nothing new about that at all. I'd be more concerned if they *weren't* trying to take it."

"Still, killing you? That seems excessive."

Kelley still seemed unbothered, "Not at all. I'd at least try the same. Most of the things we pull from that rift are trash." He showed Matt a familiar dual mana stone that his own team had gotten from the rift. "These things are interesting, but they're ultimately useless. It's just pre-aspected mana. It doesn't even have a sub-aspect, and once you empty the stone, it breaks just like any other mana stone. This is mostly what we pull out. Tiffany is trying to figure out how to use them, but she isn't making any headway at all."

That lined up with Matt's own experience with the rift, so he brought them back to the ring. "And you're the first to get a ring like that?"

Kelley shrugged and responded, "I'm the first one to make it public."

Seeing Matt's look, he scoffed. "Idiot team I hired to run the rift started celebrating as soon as they left the rift and were showing the ring off. I still paid them, but I would have paid more if the idiots didn't broadcast it to everyone else. So, every crafter knows I have it."

Only able to trust that the man had it handled, Matt offered, "Do you want the rest of the mana samples I've gathered then?"

"Of course, I do. In the last teleport from off-planet, I had another two hundred personal mana stones brought over. Damn merchants are jacking up the price, so that's all I can afford right now."

The crafter moved to the shipping crate that held his mana stones, and they ducked into the waist-high box to enter the expanded space, where shelf after shelf lined the six-foot-tall space.

Every three inches was a slot with a mana stone, labeled with a single mana type held in each stone. Matt filled each of the new stones with mana types that the man didn't have already.

Matt had nearly five hundred various mana types and sub-aspects, all gathered from the people who were willing to give him mana. Kelley could have fit all of them in his newly constructed container, but every other crafter was trying to do the same. The competition drove up the price of mana stones to the point that he couldn't buy them.

After Kelley got the mana types he wanted, they started crafting various trinkets.

Kelley was convinced that he could make a fireball staff with water aspected mana, along with a sticky sub-aspect. So far, he had gotten nowhere, but the man was determined, and Matt enjoyed the tinkering enough to join in.

They were in the midst of an attempt when Matt's AI blared a warning that all but one of his team was now in the hospital.

He quickly told Kelley what happened and started running out the door to get to the hospital. As he did so, the general messages started flooding in, painting a larger picture.

Everyone of importance to the kingdom side was taken out at the same time. Everyone from Prince Albert, to Juni, Alyssa, and even Olivia wasn't spared.

Anyone with any authority was hit during the coordinated attack. Assassins made most of the kills, but reports were coming in that more than a few spies took the opportunity to break cover and take out valuable targets.

The top ten Pather teams were all attacked. Ambush squads hit a few teams, but at least one of them was reported to have been bombed in their room. There were even reports of another team turning traitor at the same time.

From the brief messages from Liz, the attackers had hidden in a mass of normal soldiers, and were perfectly picked to counter their abilities.

She had fought a man who had simply absorbed her blood, and by the time she realized the problem, he was already on her with a spear through her chest.

Emily had been countered by a woman who turned all spells near her to fire, regardless of the original mana aspect. It completely cut off her advantage and let her opponent, who seemed to be immune to the element, waltz up to her and slit her throat.

Aster, who had been with Emily, has suffered a similar fate. All of her spells were at best hot water, and at worse, actual fire spells. Neither of them had lasted very long.

His heart hammered at his bond's condition, but he could see her AI, and despite a cut to her chest, she was fine after being teleported out. Even now, he could see the report that said the wound was closed, and that the scarring was being removed. She was still unconscious, but he expected that had more to do with a healer than her being hurt.

Conor was the last one to fall. The enemy had peppered him with long-ranged attacks, while sending waves of Tier 6s in heavy plate to keep him pinned down.

Annie was the only one to survive the hit, with her new skill giving her an advantage that the enemy hadn't prepared for. With her Talent, she was able to escape into a forest and hide, but she was currently on another continent, avoiding enemy troop movements.

Once the area calmed down enough, she was going to fly away but she couldn't risk it until she was sure she could escape detection.

As bad as his team's situation was, the general situation seemed worse. Two armies were caught out in the open and were being whittled down. Reports were already coming in about how both generals were taken out right at the start, along with their command staff.

People were demanding answers as to why the armies had been out in the first place, when it came to light that the queendom had gotten wind of their movements through spies and had planned the ambushes well in advance.

From the stream of information, things didn't exactly seem perfect for the queendom. At least two teams had fought off their attackers while sustaining only minor losses, and one Pather had survived the room bomb. Apparently, he was in the shower during the explosion, and it protected him well enough that he had only needed minor healing.

Matt was approaching the hospital when the news came in that the queendom had two of the kingdom cities under siege.

Pushing away the things he could do nothing about, Matt waited with dozens, then hundreds of others for their friends and teammates to come out of the healing ward.

Matt paced, unable to do anything. He was out of the war until his healing cooldown elapsed in five days. Waiting in the crowd for his friends like so many others, he felt very alone with only Annie's unending stream of curses through their team chat to give him company.

28

Albert nodded to Juni in his private hospital room as he walked in the door.

"What's the report?"

Juni looked purposefully blank as he relayed the information. "Your highness, it's better than we feared, but worse than we hoped."

That hardly clarified anything. Albert cursed Sara and her little stunt with the bomb. He was impressed, but still irritated by her methods.

Even with the army watcher's intervention, the explosion nearly took his head off, and he was under observation for the next day due to the concussion. They had slapped an AI restraining bracelet on him that prevented the skill from interacting with him, forcing him to get updates manually so he didn't strain his brain.

His right-hand man kept his professional demeanor as he said, "We've identified most of the spies in our structure. Not just the ones who moved, but the others who were complicit in their endeavors. As we predicted, they immediately moved two armies to surround and siege down two of our cities. Cities two and four. As we expected, Sara pulled most of her troops out of her teleporter city to make up the numbers. Our elites are ready to move out, and the general troops will be ramping up while the survivors try to hold the situation together. When we make our move, they will be ready."

There was a slight pause before Juni added, "Nothing else unusual has been noted, except Alyssa was also assassinated and is recovering herself."

Albert nodded along until the last. They had their own spies and informants in the queendom hierarchy and had early warning of the queendom's attempt to take out the leadership. They were also well aware of the queendom armies' larger movements brewing behind the scenes.

They still didn't know why the queendom higher-ups were pushing for a lightning-fast end to the war, but it slotted nicely into their own plans. No, Albert forced himself to be honest—

His father's plans.

It was risky but having the queendom on the offensive was exactly where they needed them. Them taking the queendom's teleporter city and cutting off their supply lines meant that they only needed to take a single, undermanned city.

If the queendom wanted to end the war in under a standard year, they were prepared to respond in kind. It was incredibly unusual for co-opted vassal wars to host Pather wars, but not unheard of.

The Emperor wanted a place to train his youth, but he only put down a few laws regarding how that would happen. He gave out various rewards and reimbursement for resources spent, which meant the vassal wars were usually milked for years.

It was unusual, but they weren't close to the shortest Pather war, even at a year. No, that honor went to the Ascender before Duke Waters; the yellow dragon, Lila Worldwalker.

The young dragon had killed three-quarters of the enemy troops in the first two weeks, before being forced to retreat from serious wounds. That massive number advantage allowed her side to win in under a month, creating an Empire-wide shock.

A year would raise a few eyebrows, but it was nothing on that level.

Albert still wanted to know why the queendom was pushing so hard.

He came out of his musings and realized that he'd let Juni stand there for far too long. He was engrossed in pondering the ramifications of the rapidly approaching end of the war.

Of all his people, he had thought Alyssa was a spy with how she always seemed to be in place to take advantage of both sides' actions.

While you might kill a spy to keep their cover in a situation like this, her death made no sense to him.

If Alyssa was left 'alive,' she could have taken control of his side's troops. If she were a spy, she could have handed them the victory with that move. He had orders for his own assassins to take care of her if she had survived.

She was a contender for one of the high level spies they hadn't been able to find and negate or remove. They left the lower level spies so they could report curated information the kingdom mostly controlled. Their worry was spies in the highest position that they hadn't identified and Alyssa had been their number one suspect.

He nodded for Juni to continue, and the man delivered the rest of his report in short order. He quickly left once excused.

Albert's father reappeared in the chair next to him as he watched the door that Juni just left through.

"The boy always knows when I'm nearby. What an exceptional commoner."

The gruff man straightened his shirt before standing. "I don't have much time left outside of my box." He spat to the side, "Fucking army."

Before Brice could exit the room through a spell or other means, Albert called out, "Have you figured out why the queendom is rushing? Any word at all? And is Cori okay?"

The king paused, and the air grew heavy. Albert could see the man's thoughts as he considered punishing Albert for his impudence but, in the end, he decided to humor his son.

"Nothing from either front. They keep me in a fucking box to limit interference. The real war is going fine. Your sister is competent enough and is fighting in a *real* war." He narrowed his eyes at Albert in a not-so-subtle threat. "And she's winning. But there's nothing I care to share with you otherwise. Focus on your own war, and don't lose me my item crafted by Madam Renaissance."

Albert wanted to complain. He had earned his father the staff by earning enough points but had never heard a word of praise for the act. His father only complained that it took him too long.

The king must have seen the bitterness in Albert's eyes because he appeared at Albert's bedside, either teleporting or moving so quickly that Albert couldn't tell the difference.

"You knowingly decided to let that bitch's plan go off unhindered. If this little stunt of yours loses me the war…" The king's pointer finger pressed into Albert's ribs, and he felt bones crack, but tried to keep it off his face.

Showing weakness only invited more punishment.

The king growled, "Well there is a price for disappointing me. If you do fail…I. Will. Have. Your. Head."

With that, he was gone. Albert coughed up blood as his shattered, crystal-like skin had punched through his lungs in a few places.

The alert by the room's monitoring system brought healers running.

Albert resolidified his hate for everything his father and everything he stood for. The man controlled his actions at every turn, then when his own plans might yield detrimental results, shifted any possible blame to Albert.

If the king wanted to set up contingencies that cost Albert his lead in points, those plans were going to be used.

As he was being healed for the second time, he wished his father would just up and leave the kingdom already. Even if he didn't get the throne, he just wanted the man gone.

Matt was finally able to see his friends when the four of them were let out of their recovery rooms.

Aster threw herself into his arms with a whining yowl. It drew attention, but he didn't care, and shoved his face into her soft fur.

"They hurt me. It's not fair! I didn't take *their* ice cream."

Matt paused at that and squinted his eyes at his bond, who realized that she had given up too much.

Putting her ice cream theft off for a later conversation, he pulled the now approaching Liz into the hug before Conor and Emily neared them.

After a whispered check-up with Liz, Matt hugged both of them eliciting an eye roll and light punch from Emily.

"Damn, Matt, you didn't get like this last time."

She did return the hug, which took any possible sting out of her words.

Matt unashamedly shrugged. “I wasn’t with you, and that makes it a lot worse. I probably couldn’t have saved us all. I’m not arrogant enough to think that, but I couldn’t do anything at all, and that sucks.”

Emily gave him another half hug before they all turned to leave. “That’s fair enough. Annie is still pissed.”

Conor laughed. “Yeah, I can see the chat log. Two hundred and nineteen messages.”

Emily scoffed. “That’s less than half the personal messages she sent to me.”

“At least she got away and is on her way back. That’s the important bit.” Liz had an odd tone in her voice that made Matt look at her in worry. She was only half-paying attention, and from the flickering of her eyes, he assumed that she was reviewing the information from the last few hours.

He had already taken in the information one piece at a time.

Things weren’t as disastrous as the initial outlook had appeared. A decent number of individual survivors from various sources were gathering together and trying to salvage the situation.

That didn’t prevent some commanders from trying to further their reach and take overall control. It caused some chaos, and no one knew what to do while the established leadership was out of the picture.

With five days left on his healing cooldown, Matt had watched the situation carefully but was unable to take any action directly.

In theory, he could act as the Pather liaison, but that meant little. It was a position that allowed people on a healing cooldown because they didn’t have direct authority. They only had veto power to send the Pathers to battle.

And Liz could perform much better in that role anyway.

They were back in their suite when Matt started to interrogate Aster.

She denied everything, but her furtive glances toward the fridge gave Matt all the confirmation he needed. They kept ice cream on hand for the fox, but usually, the freezer was safe because she didn’t have thumbs or a way to get that high up.

When he opened the door, everything looked to be in its proper place, but when he popped open one of the ice cream containers, he found it filled with ice. Not ice cream, but ice.

Aster wilted and plopped down at his glare.

"So, that's why you only nibbled at your dinner?"

Through their bond, he got, "I was hungry, and it smelled too good."

Really, Matt wasn't that upset. Honestly, he was more impressed that she had gotten into the packages, and had the foresight to fill the containers to keep their shape and weight.

He kept that off his face as he gently reprimanded the fox.

When he told her that they wouldn't be buying her more ice cream until they would have if she hadn't eaten it all, she flopped over dead and yowled.

"That's not fair!"

"My cultivation will backslide!"

"I'll starve."

He had to interject at that complaint. "You ate three pounds of ice cream. You won't starve."

Matt tried to prevent a smile at her caterwauling, but froze when Aster paused and stood up with her ears and tail perked up, as her sadness turned to happiness.

"I'll just buy my own ice cream!"

Matt opened his mouth, then shut it, finger still outstretched. He had no counter to that, but tried anyway. "You can't live off ice cream."

"I'll get hearts. Ice cream and hearts."

"You still need a balanced diet." It was a weak excuse, but it gave him his second idea, "Will you not eat my cooking? No more braised rabbit."

Aster's tail flicked, then dropped slightly.

She turned and met his eyes with her ice blue ones that glimmered with tears. "But I like the rabbit..."

Her questioning tone seemed to long for reassurance that he wouldn't take her favorite dish away.

"Well, I won't cook it unless you can enjoy it. And if you're full of ice cream, you can't enjoy it."

That seemed to convince her, and she happily pranced away to the living room.

Shaking his head, Matt promised himself to never have a real kid. A little sister in fox form was bad enough. And she was rapidly aging thanks to her Tier advancement and the effects of the Tree of Perfection.

Dealing with an actual child seemed like torture.

Annie came back late that night and was visibly happy to see her sister okay along with the rest of the team.

Matt didn't miss the awkwardness when she hugged Conor, as Annie came out of the hug a light shade of pink, which everyone else pretended not to notice.

The next morning, Matt found Annie coming out of her room with an array of blades strapped to her while he was cooking for everyone.

Matt tried to stop the determined woman with a, "Wait."

It mostly worked, and she paused long enough for him to get his piece out.

"What's your plan?"

Annie looked at him like he was dumb as she said, "I'm going to stab Sara a few times, then work my way down her organization." She tapped her bandolier. "I've got a knife for each person. Knives for everyone!"

Her smile had none of the cheer on her face.

Matt had been busy with Liz that night. Things didn't sit right with either of them, and they had spent most of the night reviewing the kingdom's survivors. They were pretty sure a good few were queendom spies.

Liz shuffled out of their room, and when she saw Annie, asked while holding back a yawn, "Did you tell her yet?"

"No."

"Tell me what?"

Liz looked into the pan while Matt answered, "We were reviewing information last night and think we've identified a few spies in the kingdom hierarchy."

Liz set down four plates full of eggs while Aster took her own chair and started digging in. She had found their investigation boring, and quickly went to sleep.

They explained their findings over breakfast while Annie nodded along. She wasn't dumb enough to disregard them, and eventually agreed with most of their reasoning, while also setting a few targets of her own.

After eating, she was out the door, ready to spy on a few commanders and remove them if they turned out to be dirty.

Considering that her plan was already to pay back the people who ambushed them, she was happy to add more targets. Though, it was harder to get her to stick to only gathering information until Matt came off his healing cooldown.

She wanted them punished immediately.

With her promise to only watch, she went out the door as she faded from their vision.

Matt and Liz informed the rest of the team about their plan when they woke up, and the five of them tried to scour the kingdom command structure for more suspicious targets.

Annie stood next to her latest suspect and listened to her conversation.

The woman was in her bath while lounging. She was actively plotting against her own people, but not with the queendom, just with other opportunists in the kingdom.

Annie slipped out of the bathroom, and after checking her mana, teleported past the door. It was much easier than having the door shut on her when she entered behind the woman.

She had to drain three mana stones to deal with the rapid drain from making her intangible. Invisibility from her Talent, and even a minor level of intangibility, was free. But moving through hard, impassable objects drained her quickly.

As she made her way to the next target, she contemplated her assignment, with her mind drifting to her Concept. She had discovered her phrase weeks ago, but hadn't told anyone, not even her sister.

It was just too shameful.

She even had a good idea about the image that worked for her. Not the one she wanted, but the one that fit. She could make her Concept at any time but resisted letting it solidify.

She didn't like what she had learned about herself.

That was part of the irony.

I do what's necessary.

She had an idea of her image. Annie was the blade in the dark, the blade *of* darkness. She was the one who spied on allies to find traitors.

She would get her hands dirty. Where others shirked away, she threw herself into the challenge.

If it was a reluctant realization. She could've tried to force something else, but the reality was that she *enjoyed* all of it. The skulking and hurried movements gave her a rush like no other.

Taking her target's life and then escaping was better than any thrill she could imagine.

That felt wrong.

She did what others didn't want to do, but she didn't think she should enjoy it. The uncertainty was making her hold back.

In the end, she knew that she would need to make a choice, and it felt as if she was at a crossroads. Before she had found this realization, she had been able to get sharp and the image of a blade to mostly work.

She could always form a Concept around a standard sharpness idea, and fight like a generic rogue for delving rifts. But she didn't like that idea any more than the second option. It could work for her, but it wasn't the perfect fit.

Doing what was necessary fit her like a glove, but its related image did not.

As she found her next target, Kepler, she followed and watched his interactions.

She could tell he was a spy almost immediately.

The idiot wasn't even trying to hide it. Or had gotten careless in the extreme. While taking a queendom man on a date could be innocent enough, his half-assed attempt at stealthily handing his date a sealed bag was beyond obvious. Especially when the date ended soon after.

It sent every sense she had on high alert. She didn't really know Prince Albert. She had met Juni more than once, and from Matt and Liz's recounting of their time on the planet fighting the golems, the man was anything but dumb. She had seen as much for herself when under his command during the first city's siege.

There was no way that she could believe someone that competent didn't know about the rampant corruption in the middle ranks of his commanders. The only options she believed were either he was a traitor himself, or they did know, and her team wasn't privy to whatever he had planned.

That possibility sent her on a searching spree for the next two days, whenever she wasn't trailing a target. The only time she rested was when she went and got her mana stones refilled by Matt.

She would rest while he dumped endless mana into fast converting mana stones, then transferred the mana to her stores. She took naps while that happened but kept pushing herself otherwise.

It was finally when she started following Alyssa that she found the proof she was looking for.

A kingdom spy was following the woman. They were good, but Annie was better. She could admit that she might not be as good without her Talent, but she *did* have her Talent, so she followed the watcher as they observed Alyssa's every move.

Over the next few days, she unraveled the kingdom's counter-espionage operation. For an organization that had just been decapitated and was now floundering, they had a thorough network of watchers.

It wasn't obvious, but she found dozens of people who worked at static locations, or were responsible for covering a modest area with limited movement. They reported information through secure pads while keeping a low profile and limiting their exposure.

The kingdom seemed to have one in every position. With that knowledge, Annie could identify the queendom spies by noting the people who weren't being actively watched. It seemed that the kingdom wasn't wasting manpower watching those they knew were turncoats and, instead, were dedicating resources to ferreting new ones out.

Liz and Matt repeatedly asked her to not kill anyone until they were ready. But when the man with too much mana had one day left of his healing cooldown, they finished vetting their targets, and she rested for the fun that would follow.

Matt and Liz prepared for their next moves as they painted a picture of the corruption. They quickly all agreed that the prince and Juni had a plan after Annie's information came back in, but they didn't care.

The spies and traitors were making sure that the political situation remained turbulent, and the remaining top Pathers were barely able to hold things together. The two intact teams were leading troops in harassing actions, while trying to get reinforcements to attack the armies surrounding the kingdom Cities.

The other Pathers who were single survivors from decimated teams were less cohesive. Their inexperience in politics was only further increasing the disunity.

Matt had let them know that when he came off his healing cooldown, he intended to add some order back to the situation.

When the team asked how he planned to do that, Liz answered for him and said that he'd use the same tactic anyone else would use in a power struggle.

Overwhelming power.

That, and an invisible, stab-happy trump card didn't hurt either.

Really, they were going to heavily rely on her gathered information. And after killing a few of the spies, they expected that most people would fall in line.

The crux was killing the right people without setting everyone against him. The last thing he needed was to unintentionally unify the leadership against him.

Matt was incredibly nervous, but with Liz reassuring him that he couldn't mess things up *that* badly, he was ready to at least try.

The next morning, he came to the area that had turned into the 'command center.' In reality, it was just where the surviving leadership argued with each other every day.

Matt felt like an idiot as his armored form kicked down the door. That was Annie's demand to go along with the situation.

He knew that it was purely theatrical; he'd never actually do something so obnoxious. The door, frame, and wall were all made from reinforced Tier 7 materials. He would run out of mana before he kicked the door down.

Annie promised that she would handle that, and after she convinced the rest of the team that it would set the right tone, Matt gave in.

Considering the door nearly flew off its hinges at his [Mage's Retreat] empowered kick, he relaxed and stepped through the now empty metal frame.

Annie had done her job. Now it was his turn.

Someone stood up and shouted, "What the fuck are you doing!?"

Matt punched him in the face as hard as he could. The man crumpled, and before he hit the floor, he was gone.

They had used Annie's contacts with the assassination reporting function to let the army know that they were going to clean house, and to be ready to take bodies out.

Seeing the numerous shocked faces, Matt took the temporary silence to hop onto the table and shout at everyone present.

"You are the dumbest group of people I've ever fucking heard of!"

"That's not fair. We…"

Matt kicked a pad at the speaker. They weren't highlighted red like the known spies, so he didn't kill them out of hand, and continued speaking.

"The queendom kills most of the leadership to stop a coordinated response, and you all bicker for individual power. They already have breaches in a wall. *In less than a week.* All because you can't unify to put up a resistance."

A wave of sound hit Matt as everyone proclaimed their innocence.

Matt ignored most of it until a woman highlighted in red copied his action of standing on a table and shouted, "Exactly! Like I've been saying for days. We need unity."

She reached out a hand toward Matt and said, "We need to gather our forces and strike out hard."

Matt reached out and took the proffered hand in his armored own.

Annie didn't need to be told, and a message of the woman talking with a queendom higher up and receiving a pouch of mana stones played for everyone who watched the video.

There were sounds of surprise or laughter as Matt's grip tightened, and he pulled the woman toward him and drove a spiked fist into her chest.

Jenifer gasped out a last burble of blood as Matt shoved her away to be taken by the army.

He shouted, "None of you can trust each other because you're all a bunch of lying, traitorous pieces of shit! There are nine other traitors with us here, right now. Or at least nine that we have proof of."

As the noise level tried to pick back up, he shouted over it, "No, this is my time to talk! All of you need to listen. You have had days to talk, and you've gotten absolutely fucking *nowhere*."

Linking his AI to the larger wall screen, he played the other traitor's videos in rapid succession. Those around the spies quickly restrained them, and Matt shouted to get everyone's attention once again.

"They aren't the only ones! We have more spies that need to be disposed of. But until Prince Albert is back from his healing cooldown, I'm in charge. I don't give two shits about your kingdom, or this war." He patted his armored chest. "I'm in it for the points, and I'm not going to let your stupid fucks screw this up for me."

"That's not right! You have no power over us!" a larger man shouted. Matt shrugged, then punched him in the chest.

He had retracted the spikes, but he still felt things shatter.

"That's your first and only warning. The next person to complain will be sent for a two-week vacation."

He paused to let that settle in, then sarcastically asked, "Would anyone else like to voice an objection?"

When no one said anything else, Matt started passing out his orders. It was mostly him reiterating the plans that they and their AI had come up with, but it got people moving.

All the while, Matt felt like absolute shit. He felt exactly like the Healer Iris, who tried to steal Aster's egg what felt like a lifetime ago. He was using his greater power to enforce his desires on those weaker than him.

Liz and his team had convinced him that with the Pathers outside of the normal command structure there was nothing they could do except crush everyone's resistance with physical might as they had no political power in the situation. At least nothing they could do and resolve the situation quickly.

The fact that it was for their own good didn't alleviate his concerns or make it any better. It somehow made the pill harder to swallow.

These people were his peers in Tier and power. But with his greater than average fighting prowess, he bent them to his will.

Still, he shouted his orders, and when a woman balked at merging her force with someone she hated, he didn't stop Annie from driving a knife through her chest.

His teammate had said something that stuck with him when he expressed his concerns for their plan. Sometimes, you needed to do what was necessary instead of what you wanted to do.

It reminded him of killing Zoey in the golem war. The woman endangered those weaker than her and had to be removed. Matt had killed her to prevent further harm but worried that those incidents would only become more frequent.

He had done what was necessary, but while he shouted orders, he was worried that this wasn't *really* necessary. He had no stake in this war.

Even earning more points didn't feel like a justified reason to lord his power over those weaker than himself. The whole thing just left a bitter taste in his mouth.

But he didn't stop giving orders and turning his armored form to anyone who resisted and intimidating them into following his orders.

Albert and Juni were sitting and watching a show when their informants reported that Matt and his team's assassin were taking over. They watched the recording of them storming the room and throwing their weight around with bemusement.

That indifference turned to worry as the man started killing spies and traitors.

They needed some of the spies and traitors to enact their own plan.

Albert looked to Juni when someone they didn't have registered as a spy was outed.

Juni cursed as he threw popcorn into his mouth. "Well, fuck. We missed one at least."

Albert glared at him. They had spent a massive number of resources to not be surprised. It was far too late in their plan to have unknown actors.

Juni shrugged. "Edward is a small player. He didn't matter, so us missing him is fine. Our digging teams were well-vetted, and he had no contact with any of them. We're fine, Albie."

His friend chewed, then said, "The die is cast. The chips have fallen—" He waved his hand, "Other cliche sayings. Yada, yada, yada. We can only do our best now. It's really a good thing. It will take them at least a day or two to get a sizable army to face the queendom, and I doubt they will immediately engage. When we get back, we can reroute them to the queendom main city."

Albert tried to relax, but the king's threat loomed over his head. He really didn't want to be killed by his own father because the Pathers suicided all his troops in a stupid battle.

All he could do was wait, so he snatched the bowl of popcorn from Juni and went back to watching the show. Try as he might, he couldn't stop shifting his focus back to Matt, watching as he distributed orders.

29

Matt wasn't doing what he expected when he took over the kingdom's military affairs.

He had expected to lead troops into battle without any other real considerations. He was wrong.

So, so wrong.

He was trying to figure out the logistics of moving a million people spread throughout squads of ten thousand. Without the ability to spend kingdom level points, he could not provide for so many people, and he just didn't have the personal points to spend. To add insult to injury, he could watch the kingdom level points accumulate, but couldn't touch them. They could solve all of his needs in seconds.

It should have been easy. Just hand them food and water and give them their orders. That was all his team needed for extended stays in the wilderness or rifts. They had done it, and when he suggested that to the others, they looked at him like he was an idiot.

They were right.

Throughout all his campaigns with the larger armies, Matt hadn't realized one simple fact.

People always needed mana.

Logically, he knew it was a concern for most people, but he hadn't realized how much the kingdom spent in resources to move any number of fighters.

Every standard flying device cost a little more than 10 mana per hour to maintain the average flight speed for efficient Tier 6 devices. That number multiplied out of control if they flew at max speed for any length of time but he ignored that.

For one or two people over an hour or two, that was nothing. But when you needed to move a million people in a group, the mana cost became enormous. For a ten-hour flight, which was conservative to get an army in position to engage with the enemy, Matt needed one hundred million mana. *One hundred million* mana just to engage.

It was impossible.

The cities were surrounded by nearly all of the available queendom troops, and each siege had at least three million soldiers participating. As the soldiers completed their healing cooldowns, they moved to reinforce the armies.

So, Matt needed more mana in order for their troops to perform hit and run tactics. Otherwise, they would be susceptible to counterattacks and end up getting decimated.

One hundred million mana would take Matt a little over fourteen days to produce with just his Talent, but that didn't account for the extra mana needed to mobilize afterwards. Even if he sat around only generating mana, they didn't have the storage to hold that much mana.

The thing that pissed him off the most was that even a Tier 6 melee fighter should be able to cover their mana costs with just their regeneration. But they flatly refused, on the grounds that they needed it to practice and train with. He was fairly sure if the prince had given that order they would have complied, but it was another way people resisted his orders.

Then there was the food. Matt had learned that each side hadn't bothered to procure rations the usual way and were simply purchasing it in bulk from the army.

That had baffled him. Even his backward shithole of a home world used rifts to farm. They had a team go in and clear a rift with sunlight and decent soil, and once it had no threats, they let loose farming robots to seed and water crops. Then after however long it took for the crop to grow, the robots harvested the crops and trundled out of the rift with a full load of produce.

Other, higher Tier planets just used plant mages with the Tier 8 skill [Grow]. Or, better yet, the Tier 14 skill [Farm]. With a single Tier

8 mage, they could grow acres of crops, only having to worry about soil fertility and harvesting.

With the Tier 14 spell, they didn't even have to worry about that. The skill rapidly planted, grew, then harvested the selected crop in seconds. It even provided the needed nutrients for the soil, leaving no impact on the ground for a mana cost.

The army had neither skill for purchase; he'd already checked. He had been willing to buy the skill, just to get the army moving, but he didn't even have the option.

So, he was forced to find other workarounds for each of the problems.

Matt had mostly solved the mana problem through the expedience of lying.

He had simply told everyone to break out their savings and buy the mana stones themselves, and the prince would pay them back double when he was able to spend the kingdom level points.

It was his fault that Matt had to deal with this shit, and he could pick up some of the cost himself when the time came.

The food was still a question, but he thought he had an answer to that as well. They could steal it from the enemy. He wanted to hit a queendom reinforcement caravan and steal their food.

It was their fault as well that Matt had to deal with these problems, and stealing from the enemy was never a bad thing.

He looked over his numbers for the third time, and had his AI run the numbers for the tenth time.

Things didn't look great.

If they successfully took a resupply party, they would get mana stones and food, allowing their teams to run rampant and harass the besieging armies.

But if he could think of that, so could the queendom.

That was why Matt was considering a riskier option.

Of all the kingdom military operations that had fallen to bits when the leadership was taken out, the scouts had remained fully operational. They were even willing to fall in line once Matt reaffirmed that he wanted to give up command as soon as the prince was back.

After that, he had a half-decent idea of how to get all of his needs met. It just remained to be seen if he could pull it off.

Annie stalked around the queendom headquarters, just as she had been doing for the past two days.

She was going to kill Sara. It wasn't a question of if. It was only a matter of when and how.

The woman was hiding somewhere. A panic room of some sort, she assumed. If she was taken out, the queendom would have the same problems that Matt was bitching about.

She had made her way into the headquarters by carefully following behind people, giving her free reign of the building. It was identical to the one she knew.

The problem was, she couldn't find Sara anywhere.

Annie had followed her right-hand woman. She had followed food carts. She'd even managed to scale the building to find the room that should have been hers. The princess just wasn't in there.

The room didn't look inhabited at all.

Annie was running out of ideas and time.

She wanted to take Sara out before the first army moved out, but with each passing minute, it looked like she wouldn't be able to.

That fact had started to eat at her, and a whisper in the back of her mind, she affirmed that she would be able to find Sara with her Concept. She just needed to finalize it and embrace that she was a monster in human skin.

It would be so easy to fall into that rabbit hole, but she denied herself that. Her image wasn't perfect. She could make it work, but she wasn't a mindless monster, and trying to create an image like that was incredibly hard.

She couldn't deny that it would make things easier. Sara needed to die, and Annie believed that conviction would allow her Concept to assist her in finding and ending the woman.

Still, she resisted.

Annie was currently hiding in a garden, where she watched a young man trim the various vegetation. She was pretty sure they were various herbs as she remembered the smell from Liz on a few occasions. When he finished making perfect spheres of the decorative hedges, he started checking something with the soil, and then watered a few of the plants.

It was pretty soothing to watch the man work. He was completely engrossed in his task, and seemed happy.

There was something about the way he guided the plant's growth. The tending and pruning she found intriguing, but as she thought on it, she wasn't able to put her finger on why she was drawn to it.

The sight was a nice distraction, but she moved on.

She had the urge to kill Talous and his team if she ran into them. With the beatdown Matt put on the man, there was no way he wasn't on a full two-week cooldown.

Talking shit about her friend's dead parents wasn't something she was willing to overlook. She continued skulking around the base, careful to conserve her intangibility by dodging obstacles and people. She didn't want to waste mana either. Eventually, she found Talous' team suite and waited.

The army watchers approved a hit on the rest of the man's team, so she inspected the lock to plan her best entry method. She wasn't planning on killing them until after she killed Sara. No reason to give up her presence.

She was listening to the muffled sounds inside the room when she heard footsteps.

There was something about the pace that caught her intuition.

It was the speed of the footfalls.

The walker wasn't walking briskly with an urgent task. No, that pattern of steps had speed, but surety.

This walk was the near run of someone who wanted to move quickly, but quietly. It sounded like they were running crouched and on the balls of their feet.

Annie trusted her intuition.

Her still-unnamed trainer had hammered that into her.

Anyone doing undercover work needed to trust their gut. When she asked when it was wrong, he just laughed. He told her that in those rare cases, success resulted when combat skills and evasion skills met proper planning.

If any of the three weren't up to par, you died.

It was as simple as that.

She had understood that quite well, to her own surprise. There was a freedom in knowing that only death awaited in true failure. It took some of the pressure off.

Emily didn't understand that in the slightest, but Annie embraced it like a warm blanket.

When she turned the corner, she found a man skulking through the halls at a low crouch.

He reached a corner and rounded it with a tray in hand.

Annie moved forward like spilled water, and caught a brief whiff of balsamic vinegar.

Princess Sara was said to love salads, and no salad was being served in the communal dining hall. She had already stolen a meal from there. They were eating some vegetable pie thing.

She was sure that Matt could tell her a million uses for balsamic vinegar, but she only knew that it went on salads.

More importantly, her gut told her that she was onto something.

The Pather quarters were a perfect hideout for a princess trying to lay low.

She followed the man as he made two circles around the spatially expanded quarters. Finally, he went into an unremarkable door.

Annie was far enough back that she couldn't follow him into the room, so she positioned to get a good view into the room as the man exited.

He was just as furtive when he opened the door and ran out of the room while crouching. Annie got a half-decent view inside, and that little glimpse was enough to give her pause.

Nothing was wrong. Not overtly, at least.

The only thing out of place was the missing alcove that was normally at the entrance of each room she had been in. It was meant for people to drop off jackets or coats as they entered their rooms.

It was missing here but was standard issue for every room.

She could think of a million reasons why it was missing, but none were good. Or at least it triggered her paranoia regarding small details that she'd learned during her training missions.

She would assume that it was just broken or moved in a normal situation. But there was no reason for the space to be filled in like that.

Annie hunkered down and waited. She was patient.

Whoever needed to have food delivered would eventually have it delivered again. Then she would make her move. Until the moment came, she would watch.

There was no need to rush.

Matt moved his troops out en masse. They didn't have the mana reserves to use the teleporters, so they were forced to trek the long and slow journey.

They quickly ran into their first roadblock when their scouts discovered that they were being followed. Matt ordered them to wait and observe their watchers. The queendom scouts had their direct route to the armies under surveillance.

That wasn't a surprise to anyone. Their options were limited, which meant they were predictable.

The only thing the kingdom troops had on their side was that their enemy had no more troops to throw at them. Most troops were holding their cities as they tried to race down its walls in retaliation or were reinforcing the notable forts.

With the remaining troops surrounding the kingdom cities, they had no real way to counter Matt's army's movements.

Not unless they wanted to give up a siege.

Matt could hope, but only an idiot would give up their progress on taking such an important objective, when there was only a smaller force unaccounted for.

That was why he wanted to change the paradigm.

When they were nine hours into their flight, and about to reach the continent where the queendom was attacking the two cities, the million-strong army split apart. They formed ten units, each one hundred thousand strong, and scattered.

Matt would have preferred that they only broke off into a few units twice that size, but he had to bow to practicality. If the queendom gathered enough troops to wipe out one of his teams, they would have a warning at least. All of the teams had orders to retreat at the first sign of being engaged on. Their purpose wasn't to fight land battles, but to hinder the queendom's ability to reinforce their troops.

Burning mana, everyone sped up and started to hit their large fort targets. They were acting as supply points, and the teams were each assigned smash and grab missions.

Matt and his team were landing at the farthest section of the forts.

They would be attacking last, and therefore would be in the most danger, as they were the closest to the armies engaging the cities.

After seeing the performance while the kingdom leadership was dead, he didn't trust anyone else with the job. He also wasn't entirely sure that he had weeded out all of the spies.

His men landed like a wave of locusts. Their positions were already set, and everyone jumped into action. Matt had the remaining Pathers that weren't acting as hit and run units with him.

He hit the ground and started running toward the front gate; he wanted to shoulder check the door and knock it down like some great hero. Instead, he skidded to a stop as he was peppered with arrows through the slits in the gatehouse tunnel.

Matt responded with fire.

Lots of fire.

[Flamethrower] washed over the stone, blackening it during the brief exposure, and the arrows stopped for a heartbeat.

He rushed to one of the windows and let his torrent of fire loose inside of the building. He could hear the screams, and when they stopped, he moved to the other gate and repeated his actions.

The follow-up teams quickly advanced, and they started hacking at the gate.

They were mostly a distraction.

Their long-range scouts reported that the defenders were sending everyone to the gate, and the general troops rushed forward in a wave. In seconds, ladders and ropes were secured, and their numbers crushed the unprepared defenders.

Two minutes later, the door opened from the inside, and Matt strode in over the blood of the fallen.

Matt sent the next wave of orders, but the inner keep was barred up tight.

Two mana cannons were brought out and assembled next to Matt. He blasted his Concept and had the men fire them into the front door.

It took six shots, but the doors finally exploded, and Matt repeated his [Flamethrower] trick with the same results.

The spell was a death sentence to anyone unlucky enough to be stuck in an enclosed space.

They had the front room clear, and started to take the boxes of provisions that hadn't burned. A few of the spatially expanded storage containers had been too close to the heat and had caught fire.

When the enchantment broke, the space returned to its normal size, and items were scattered everywhere.

As they pulled the boxes out, Matt could see his other teams setting explosives along the inner walls of the bottom level. All of their first targets were large forts that had been upgraded with teleportation formations.

They intended to cut off the queendom's easy access to reinforcements and goods to start. Then, when they attacked the besieging armies, they wouldn't be able to reinforce and re-supply as easily.

They took the fort in under ten minutes and set the explosives off. The building crumbled in on itself and down.

Matt cheered internally as he watched their supplies numbers tick up. Their casualties were painful, but they hadn't lost enough to materially affect their combat capabilities.

For now, they just needed to move to the next large forts that they believed had teleportation formations and batter them down.

Everyone's orders were to do so from range, instead of directly assaulting the forts. They only needed to last long enough for the prince to reinforce them.

Two weeks of supplies were more than enough.

They just needed to slow down the queendom. Not kill them all.

Sara sat in her bunker of a room and cursed.

The damn Pather connected to Liz was ruining her plans, or at least slowing them down. It was the same thing really, when things were going this poorly.

He had taken out her large fort's teleportation with eerie accuracy. It only built on the stress of being stuck in a tiny single room with nothing to do.

She was losing her mind being cooped up.

How her mother handled it, she had no idea. The stress was brutal.

She turned to comfort food when it grew too bad for her to cope with. She hadn't thought to take anything besides prepackaged meals, and if she ate another one, she would drive her head through the wall.

As she watched another fort fall, she gave the order. She needed to force the cities to fall quickly. She only had a week and three days before Albert was able to come back and launch a point-funded counter attack.

She figured that the inability to spend kingdom level points would have stopped any coordinated counter-attack in its tracks. Apparently, Albert had known of a number of her spies, and set countermeasures in place with the Pathers.

It made her wonder if he also knew of Liz's background, but that didn't feel right.

She expected it was more Juni, and his previous relationship with the group.

The problem was, Matt was keeping his troops out of direct combat. If she pulled off enough of her own troops to take him out, she'd be reducing her sieging units to dangerously low numbers.

That was if she could even get him to engage. He had already proven, from one skirmish, to be unwilling to fight head on.

She had ordered her generals to ignore the Pather and his army, in favor of taking the cities faster. That didn't mean she didn't give them orders to protect their rear. Each city had a barricade around them to avoid recreating the disaster that had befallen her own city.

With two weeks and two days remaining before the real war was supposed to be over, she needed to keep to her own deadline and end the Pather one.

Casualties didn't matter as long as they won, but if they lost too many troops now, they wouldn't get them back before the end of the war. If that happened, then they would be truly dead.

It was a delicate line to walk, and she wasn't sure if she could manage it.

Time.

She needed more time.

After deliberating, she ordered an agent to lay a trap for the Pather, and activated a few spies.

Sara checked the time. She wanted another good meal, but forced herself to open the packet of cold pasta and heated it up.

She craved a fruit plate, or anything that didn't taste like it could last a few dozen years and still be considered food.

Still, she resisted the cravings and choked down the food.

She'd get a good dinner tomorrow.

As she controlled herself, she reviewed her intelligence on Matt and his team and her spies reports.

Her eyes lingered on the goals section.

Her people suspected that Matt was a perfect fit for the [Cracked Breach] skill. It was such a good fit that with the knowledge of who Liz's parents were she suspected that it was placed there for him personally.

It only reinforced her conviction that this entire war was for Liz and her partner's benefit.

She had the personal points to buy the skill. It would make a good bribe to remove him from the war or even to just have him lead a less effective counterattack.

She only needed to stall him for a little while.

Sara nodded and decided to buy the skill if her trap didn't work. If he refused, she could sell the skill to a queendom noble for a hefty profit.

Matt and his hundred thousand troops set up on a bluff near the encircled city and rained down fire on the queendom attackers.

It had been irritating to his own besieging army when it happened to them, and with the queendom trying to take two cities, they didn't have the numbers to properly manage their force.

They had been chased off twice already by a unit three times their number, but they hadn't set down tents or anything else that couldn't be rapidly packed, so they were able to retreat quickly. The hit and run tactics were making it rough for the queendom.

To that effect, they weren't able to use their mana cannons. They took too long to set up, and using them immediately always provoked a reaction, until now.

Their newest spot was a much better one, and the bluff was just inside the anti-flying formation, which meant that the queendom army had to go around, or fight up a sheer, hundred-foot cliff.

One of his Pather members, Adam, had noted that the shape of the valley indicated that the cliff was inside the formation, despite the standard sphere suggesting it wasn't. It was like the area they had found the queendom secret base in on their first mission. A slight variation on the standard formation.

It was the break they needed to put some more significant hurt on the queendom armies.

So, they set up a more permanent camp with heavy rear defenses.

Matt sat on one cannon and let it fire at the speed that his Concept should be able to refill his reserves. It wasn't nearly as fast as he could have actually fired the weapon, but every minute, a blast of blue licked out.

The damage was beautiful. Spots in the enemy camp simply vanished when the shots landed.

But, like all good things, it ended all too soon.

From their rear, warning alarms rang out, and Matt turned to survey the situation as he gave orders for his rear guard to brace for a fight. They had a decent position and could bleed some of the queendom troops during a defensive engagement.

His looking back was the only reason he saw Adam taking off on a flying sword at the edge of the formation.

Then the explosion went off.

The hill under Matt crumbled, and the mana cannon he stood behind crumbled with him.

Matt put every bit of his mana generation into [Cracked Phantom Armor]. 40 MPS went into the normal layer, and 35 MPS went into the secondary layer. The remaining 5 MPS went to his AI to figure out how he was going to live through this and give orders before he died.

His first order out was to hold the line, as he could see the explosion only affected the top of the cliff, and not the entire thing. The second was to reinforce the chain of command.

As Matt fell into darkness, he read the report that showed he'd most likely survive the fall. It was only a question of if he could dig himself out of the rubble before he suffocated.

When the world stopped rumbling, Matt oriented himself from the AI connections with his men and tried to feel around himself.

He started digging as best as he could when he hit something hard. Feeling around, he found that it was a metal tube.

He smiled as he checked its orientation, then checked his AI.

The odds looked pretty good. His AI also noted the 'anomaly' that let this area remain in the anti-flying formation had disappeared. It wasn't hard to realize that it was just a part of the queendom trap Adam had set.

Matt filled the mana cannon with mana, then put everything he had into his armor.

The world rumbled, and Matt felt [Cracked Phantom Armor] break under the close explosion. But despite his ringing ears, he was alive. He coughed out what he was pretty sure was blood but ignored it.

His flying sword that had been at the edge of the only anti-flying formation raced to him and hovered around his head. With one hand, he gripped the blade and hoisted himself up out of the crater in the landslide.

Using his flying sword and [Mage's Retreat], Matt pulled the mana cannon out of the rubble as well and started charging it as he rose into the air.

The queendom troops, who were flying up the side of the mountain, froze for a second after seeing the flying mana cannon fully charged and ready to fire.

Matt let it loose.

The world went blue for a second before he slammed into the ground from the kickback.

While he had [Cracked Phantom Armor] to protect him, the queendom troops did not.

He started charging the cannon while he unstuck himself and flew to his troops, where his most recent orders to get into the air were being followed. Together, they flew out of the trap, with an enemy force keeping a *very* respectful distance behind them.

Anytime they got too close, Matt let loose a blast from his cannon. He also wondered if he could build a platform to carry their two other cannons, and just fire them from the air.

Their squad ran until they met up with another team of equal size, and then turned to chase the queendom soldiers.

Or at least they tried.

The queendom troops didn't hesitate long enough for Matt's forces to turn on them. They quickly retreated back to the safety of their greater army, instead of fighting it out with a force that they only outnumbered by fifty percent.

Once they landed, Matt began giving orders while healers came to tend to him. He wanted to ignore them, as his wounds weren't too bad, and some of his men had far worse. It was only after a quiet and uncomfortable reminder that he was the only reason they were out here that Matt let the healers do their jobs.

The man quickly left, but not before Matt topped him off with his Concept. They needed their healers in the best condition, and he did feel better from the healing. At least one rib had shifted uncomfortably during the process, which only confirmed what his AI had been telling him.

Their teams harassed the enemy armies while avoiding conflict for the next week. Seven brutal days of little sleep and being constantly on the move.

Still, their hard work paid off in the following days.

Neither city had fallen, despite the queendom bombarding them night and day. The defenders were able to repulse every attack, and rumor had it that Prince Albert was preparing for a grand campaign when he came off his healing cooldown, in four more days.

While they were all tired, their presence had slowed the queendom down enough to have a fighting chance at relieving one of the cities.

Their chances were so good that a large portion of the general troops even clamored for it. They were easy points, they said.

Matt and the other commanders all believed it to be a trap.

The queendom had only reinforced one of the cities the entire time. It wasn't as if the queendom hadn't had traps before and something so obvious made them all wary.

In the end, Matt's threats and presence had placated the dissenters. He didn't have to kill anyone, but he had to go and give some friendly chats to a few mid-level commanders. A few questions about their loyalties were enough to stop any more of those complaints.

After the traps and betrayals, any hint of being a traitor was enough to merit an instant killing. No one disagreed with the method after the third poisoned camp stew, and a bomb planted under the command tents.

The bombs had been ineffective because Matt refused to hold any personal meetings, insisting on only using their AI. He purposely avoided gathering everyone together. It made things harder for him since half of his authority came from the threat of him kicking someone's ass if they refused his orders.

He had to substitute in threats of giving generals and commanders personal visits to keep them in line.

That was, until they got the news.

Sara had been killed, along with a number of her higher officials, in the chaotic aftermath.

Someone, presumably Annie, had finally killed the woman.

Annie had grown tired.

Not just physically, but mentally as well. Standing watch on a random door had been too much for even her after two days, and she looked at other methods.

She trusted that barging into that room would mean her death when she had an idea.

Do I really need to stab her?

A quick message to Liz had provided her with the name of a particularly subtle poison, and she had spent 200,000 points on a small vial of the stuff.

The list of ways the little vial could kill someone was longer than her forearm.

Even the fumes were toxic if breathed in too long. The advantage of the stuff was that it was odorless and tasteless to humans. Most beasts could smell it, but Sara wasn't a beast, so Annie expected it to work.

She stalked the kitchens for days, following the one man who brought down the food the first time. He was a mid-level manager, who was unremarkable besides delivering the princess's food.

When he started cutting a cheese and fruit board, she knew that she had the right person. It was also not a part of the general menu.

Annie also noted how he tasted each piece of food before he started walking down the hall.

She shadowed him until he was about to enter the same door as last time, when she put a drop of the poison on a halved grape as he went through the door.

One drop was all that the little vial contained.

With things already in motion, Annie ran to one of her marked locations, and watched key members of Sara's side.

She was only one woman. She couldn't operate like a dozen assassins and take out their entire command structure, but she could take out a few key people. Or at least, people that she thought were key.

When the panic started, she began stabbing.

Blood ran as she worked her way through the ranks.

When people started bunkering up, she concluded her bloody work and ran.

She had to use a bomb to blow out a window, as they had an anti-teleportation formation active after the first murders. Also, her mana was too low after all the time she spent behind enemy lines, and without Matt to refill her.

Her escape was messier than she would have liked, but after two and a half hours of mingling in the shopping district, she was happy with the operation.

Victor smiled as he watched the chaos Annie had caused.

She had a knack for assassination.

So many young recruits got overly attached to one plan and couldn't pivot to another when the situation demanded it. It would have been better if she had changed her plans faster, but he was still happy with the results.

He was going to turn her into another Blink. Her Talent wasn't as good as the elusive man's, but Talent wasn't everything.

Annie enjoyed it. He could tell.

A predator recognized a fellow predator.

A dark-haired woman appeared out of nowhere next to him, and Victor had to repress the urge to stab the intruder.

Luna was a menace with her void element. She was able to erase her presence better than nearly anyone, and when she appeared, it made him jumpy.

The infamous manager shook her head without looking at him, her attention on the piece of paper she was writing on.

"You won't get what you want."

"Why do you think that? She's perfect." Victor was actually curious. He knew when he was outmatched, and in predicting young

Pathers, Luna was one of the best. Listening to her was just good business.

"She's going to settle on a more cause and effect Concept. She realized something with the gardening she saw earlier." the delicate nose wrinkled as she sniffed. "Smells like it at least."

Victor shrugged. "If her phrase is still the same, it will fit well enough. I can work with that."

Luna paused and met his eyes before the orbs of obsidian wandered down his body in a slow path.

It made him shiver.

"I guess you have grown up, Vicky." Luna's attention then drifted back to the paper she was scribbling on.

That was closer to the truth than he liked to admit, so he tried to play it off. "It's been a long time, and even immortals can grow, if given sufficient incentives."

She just nodded along before asking, "Are you about to leave?"

He nodded. "I intended to. She's a good candidate, and I need to get my affairs in order before she reaches Tier 10."

Luna tsked. "The final show is about to happen. Stick around to see it."

Victor shook his head. "I've already noticed and extrapolated. I don't need to see the aftermath. We've all seen *her* tantrums. I don't want to get caught in the crosswind."

Luna smiled a toothy smile. But she didn't say anything, just wiggling her fingers in a half-wave.

Victor hadn't been lying. *She* was going to be pissed, and he didn't want to be in the same sector as the madwoman. It wasn't the first time she had done something like this, and after the events that had occurred on this planet, anyone who knew her could predict her intentions.

It didn't mean the Emperor wouldn't be pissed as well, even that wouldn't stop her.

The time to leave was now, while the getting was good.

Victor took one last look through real space at the king.

He *really* didn't envy the man.

30

Liz paced around their shared living quarters. She was restless and irritable. Matt had been gone for so long, and she was stuck here. The days had passed agonizingly slowly, with nothing to do but observe.

She just hated being forced to sit around, unable to act.

At first she tried to lose herself in alchemy, but she could never keep focused long enough, and kept ruining her mixtures. Even Conor and Emily tried to keep her distracted in their own ways. The party's healing cooldown was just over halfway done but she *needed* to start moving again. Now. But there was still a long way to go.

The situation outside wasn't looking entirely awful, but it wasn't anywhere near good.

It may have been self-centered or egotistical, but Liz believed she could make a real difference. She just needed the chance.

Albert was doing hanging crunches when his AI pinged.

He tried to ignore it as he concentrated on his form and aching abdominal muscles. Out of habit, he flicked his attention to the message to skim the subject at least.

In sudden shock, his legs slipped from the bar, and he plummeted to the ground.

The impact didn't even register as he started to laugh.

Sara was dead!

He smiled as he flexed his newly formed Concept from his time with the Shard of Reality.

Things were looking up. Now she would be in the same situation he had been in. She might have contingencies set up, but he doubted she would have counters in place for what he intended.

———

Sara cursed as she popped in the hospital above a bed. A cracker stacked high with cheese and meat half hovered an inch in front of her open mouth wiggled ominously.

"What the fuck!?" Realization hit, followed up quickly by, "How did I die!?"

The healer pressed a hand to her arm before nodding a few times as his eyes flicked back and forth.

"Simulated poison in the cracker before that one." Seeing her confusion, the healer explained, "No one is going to risk actual death with something *that* dangerous. No actual damage done, so you're free to go."

Sara glared at the cracker in her hand before asking, "Simulated poison? So, is this safe?"

At the healer's nod, she chomped down, making sure to savor the flavor. It was the only enjoyment she was going to get out of her day, after all.

Thankfully, she'd prepared for this scenario. Her subordinates knew what to do next. And while she couldn't command her own people during her healing cooldown, bribing the kingdom's hierarchy was another matter.

Proper planning prevents piss poor performance.

This inconvenience may slow her down even further, but she could recover. She had multiple layers of contingency in place for a reason.

She started at the bottom of the Pather and kingdom personnel who weren't a part of the greater plan.

Sara only needed to stall for another week and a half.

Amber should already be making calls now that Sara's death was reported. While she was on her cooldown, she might as well give her mother an update and see how the real war was progressing.

———

Matt sat in his command tent with half a dozen of his most influential officers, listening to a brief from their scouts. Suddenly, a message from Princess Sara's right hand woman, Amber, came in, asking for a conversation.

He was going to dismiss it out of hand but thought better of it. Making a quick excuse, he backed out of the room while everyone discussed the ramifications of this plan or that plan.

It was fairly moot. The kingdom forces currently lacked the manpower to accomplish anything truly significant.

When he accepted the call, he found a smiling virtual head waiting for him.

"Hello, Matt. I know you're busy and don't appreciate the normal political wordplay, so I'll cut to the chase. I want to talk with you about coming over to our side for the remainder of this war."

Matt should have expected it, but he was still taken off guard by the request.

Amber seemed to take his speechlessness as permission to continue her pitch.

"I'll ensure you are well compensated. After your win in the duel arena, we noticed the [Side Slide] skill vanished. With your teammate Annie's survival of the ambush, we can put two and two together."

Matt nodded slightly at that. It was an easy enough deduction, so there was no point trying to hide it. But he wasn't sure how that related to him and the queendom.

Amber continued, "Obviously you used your own duel winnings to help her get such a high value chase item. Which would mean, with your team's recent deaths, that you're all rather low on points. So, I took the liberty of buying [Cracked Breach] myself."

He internally panicked as he checked the points store to find the skill, along with several other high-cost items, gone.

"We would be quite willing to give you the skill. All we're asking in return is that you use it to help us level the final cities. It would be a double win for you, since you'd earn a queen's ransom of contribution points in the process." Amber finished with a beaming smile.

Matt could feel the temptation bubbling up inside of him. It was an incredibly generous offer, and with a few notable exceptions, the kingdom had not enamored itself to him. That skill was perfect for him. He honestly hadn't considered that anyone else would buy the skill. It was a cracked skill that needed massive amounts of mana to properly use.

Any normal mage would have to wait *at least* a few Tiers before they had enough mana to make it consistently useful. Technically, anyone could use the skill if they had enough mana to initially cast it, and others fed them converted mana afterwards. It was just that most people didn't have a spare 10,000 mana to throw away on a single shot of a skill, or a battalion of support mages to feed them more mana.

But that was the problem. Amber, and through her Princess Sara, wanted him to cast the spell *now.* Matt had a maximum mana of 80, and the 100 mana was needed upfront to cast it. Nothing he could do would allow him to cast the spell without Tiering up first to double his maximum mana again. But that wasn't an option, since he'd be removed from the war the moment he became a Tier 7.

He was also afraid to try and brute force the skill to lower its cost, considering the skill's additional cracked effect preventing the initial cost from being lowered further. He wasn't sure if it was a hard limitation, or if it meant that the skill couldn't stabilize with less mana. An unstable siege skill would be like an unstable mana cannon. Every shot came with the risk of just exploding instead of firing at the target, and he didn't want the equivalent of a mana cannon detonating inside of him.

Matt couldn't accept the bribe, no matter how much he wanted to. When he couldn't follow through on casting [Cracked Breach], it would reveal that his Concept wasn't responsible for his insane mana generation. It would raise questions that Matt couldn't afford to have people asking.

Fighting to keep the disappointment off his face, he decided to play it straight. "I'd never change sides for something as simple as a bribe. How would that look on me as a person to the Army watchers?

A supposed ally any enemy can bribe away with a sufficient enough trinket? No, I'm sticking with the kingdom."

Amber raised an eyebrow but didn't seem phased. "We're willing to sell you the skill for half-price, on the condition that you don't absorb it until after the war. You just have to stall the counter-attacks on my sieges and let the two cities fall." She smiled and continued, "Even if those two cities fall, the kingdom will still have one left. It won't end the war."

Matt was even more tempted and regretted the excuse he'd chosen. Having made such a hardline stance about moral appearance, he couldn't take this offer either without revealing his lie. Sabotaging the kingdom from within would look even worse to the Army than openly switching sides. He shook his head. "That's another generous offer, but I'm unwilling to sell my morals."

Amber seemed unbothered and just nodded. "Then best of luck to you. I know we don't need it." The call ended with a grin on her part.

Curses started to flood from Matt's lips, drawing widespread attention to him as he debated what to do.

Finally, he decided to report to Juni that Sara's people contacted him in an attempt to bribe him away. This mess would look much worse if he didn't get ahead of it now. Sara could send carefully edited recordings of everyone she messaged to Albert and destroy any trust the kingdom's leadership had in him and the other top Pathers.

Even with AI proof, suspicion would fall on them, creating doubt.

Juni picked up nearly instantly. Matt rushed to explain the situation.

Juni only nodded along before saying, "With the restrictions in place, all I can say is that we trust you to do your job."

With that, the connection cut out.

Matt's mouth dropped open before shutting. Reflexively, he just shrugged. There was work to do.

Sara tsked as she listened to the call with Matt. She'd hoped at least one of the propositions would have enticed the man. Having Matt at her side would have given her an incredibly useful, not-at-all suspicious connection to Liz. With some subtle leveraging, she could have gotten closer to the woman in short order.

Tapping her fingers, Sara nodded at Amber, her second in command.

The woman was still engrossed in her pad. She didn't look up until Sara tossed the [Cracked Breach] skill shard onto the table, along with all the other failed bribe items. Even if she couldn't bring the perfect matches for her plans over with these items, she could use them to motivate her own people.

Thankfully, the pile of accepted bribes dwarfed the discarded pile. That made things easier.

Sara pulled [Cracked Breach] from the reject pile and slid it toward her second in command. "Amber, for your years of loyal service, please accept this skill as a gift to absorb and use *as you see fit.*"

Sara immediately felt the weight of a higher Tier being pressing down on her spirit like a wet blanket. The army watchers were warning her. That barely disguised order pushed the boundaries of what she could do while on a healing cooldown.

Amber was smart and understood her liege's meaning as soon as she reread the skill's description. Without another word exchanged, Amber bowed slightly and left. She'd be blasting holes in the cities' walls. A bag full of mana crystals from the supplies should ensure that they could end the sieges quickly.

It was best to give such a dangerous skill to a loyal subordinate, rather than someone who might turn on them after acquiring that kind of power. By the time Sara's own healing cooldown ended, the war would already be over.

Both of them.

Cori stood in front of the mirror and contemplated her actions for the millionth time.

She came to the same conclusion she always did.

Betraying the kingdom that she grew up in didn't bother her. They had done nothing for her and deserved nothing from her in return. She was pretty sure the common people living under her few noble supporters would lead better lives under the queendom's rule.

Her motivations for this weren't just personal.

Or they weren't *only* personal.

Personal grievances may have started her down this road, but she'd come upon a plethora of other reasons to continue along the way.

Cori traced the half-inch scar on her temple where her father had backhanded her.

An old rage simmered back to life, but she tamped it down as she thought of her childhood.

The daughter of the king from one of his many companions, she was the first possible heir he had produced.

Not the last. Nor the most valuable.

Just the first.

The testing bed for how he raised all of her other half-siblings.

A series of nannies brought her up, being rotated in and out as soon as they made the slightest error. Even the most minute slip ups sent the Tier 35 king rabid.

Her own mother abandoned her as soon as the agreed payment for birthing a child to the kingdom's ruler was transferred. Cori loathed her mother for that as a child. Now, she understood the choice, even if she refused to respect it.

The king offered a handsome reward to anyone who birthed him a child. No one could stand the man long enough to stick around for any significant amount of time after that, let alone consider marrying him. The same song and dance had played out for each of her younger siblings, too.

Only one of the mothers had reconsidered and protested, trying to secure a better life for her child. But poor Maria simply vanished one night, never to be spoken of again.

Cori was certain that she'd been killed off, likely quite brutally. Her father didn't tolerate people questioning or interfering with his affairs, particularly regarding how he chose to rear his children.

She had met her father only half a dozen times in as many years. He barged into her wing of the palace one day, shoved a miniature sword in her hand, and physically dragged her out to a training yard.

With the bastard's cultivation pressing down on her, she was scared and confused. She didn't react fast enough when he pointed at the training dummy and commanded 'strike'.

Her ten-year-old self hadn't even properly heard the command. Only when he backhanded her and sent her sprawling did she realize exactly what their relationship was.

In the early months, she thought something was wrong with *her*, and repeatedly cried herself to sleep. At the same time, she just hoped that someone, anyone, would save her.

After the first year of training, she grew hard and realized that the only way to survive was to meet the madman's expectations.

So, Cori threw herself into martial training. With a Tier 1 Talent for balance and a Tier 3 Talent for proprioception, she dedicated herself to combat and Tiering up to advance. All for the sake of winning some sliver of her father's approval.

When she reached Tier 15 in record time, and was rewarded only with a dismissive sneer, she realized that she'd never make him happy.

He had called her to task for not creating a political base, and instead rushing through the Tiers. She had done exactly what he had taught her to do, and then he had called her an idiot for doing it.

Cori despised fighting; it had never resonated with her. But, for him, she had forced herself into it when she could have had a more normal childhood, or at least a less horrific one.

She left that meeting with a drive to correct her mistake, but it was too late. Branch family members showing promise had been adopted into the main family, and had poisoned the well with most noble families. Their birth parents had given them the political lessons her own father had neglected.

Her noble peers wouldn't work with her, and she was cast off as an heir who would never ascend to the throne because all she cared about was fighting. So, she embraced that persona and entrenched herself into the kingdom military.

It had taken decades, but she had worked her way up, and was now in the perfect position for revenge.

The original idea had been to just kill the bastard when she matched his Tier. But perspectives change. Once she was released from her sheltered life in the capital, and was no longer focused solely on delving to advance, she witnessed the rampant neglect and abuse in her kingdom. The system was broken beyond repair. It needed to be shattered, melted down, and completely reforged if anything good was going to come out of it.

At the kingdom's outskirts, people didn't even bother to hide their contempt for the heavy taxes, neglect, and disgusting privileges taken by some nobles.

That was where she found people who were desperate for change but lacked the power to act against the higher Tier nobles pissing on them from above.

So, she made use of the political skills her father claimed she didn't have. Bit by bit, she gathered the disparate groups and few decent nobles under one banner. Like-minded individuals slowly rallied around her.

It wasn't easy or fast, but the right person noticed. A queendom spy eventually contacted her. At that time, her plan had been a mass defection to create an independent splinter nation. When instead offered full membership into the Alliance of Allied Queens as a queen herself, Cori could not refuse.

A deal was worked out.

Under her command, a large swath of border worlds would defect to the queendom, stealing away twelve percent of the kingdom's current territory. Centuries worth of expansion would disappear overnight in a single, devastating blow.

To give Cori leeway in winning over additional nobles in the targeted area, the deal included a provision that all kingdom nobles that willingly defected would retain their titles in the annexed territory, so long as they fully adhered to queendom law. The rules as such had been explicitly laid out in no uncertain terms.

Paired with a chance to escape the kingdom's inevitable war of succession among her siblings, that guarantee was all many of the nobles needed to hear. However, there were several nobles that no one believed would jump ship, and her people employed various methods to remove them from power in the area.

Some were just killed, but that tactic had to be used sparingly to avoid attracting notice. Only the vilest and most pigheadedly loyal could be put in the ground where they belonged. A few even found themselves unexpectedly promoted to better territories on the other side of the kingdom, after Cori and her supporters secretly cashed in all of their political favors. Most of the other potential holdouts were simply challenged, and quickly saw reason when they realized that they were surrounded and outnumbered by nobles intent on defecting by any means necessary.

Their actions caused some turbulence, but nothing that wasn't smoothed over easily enough with copious amounts of wealth. Bribes could get you nearly anything in the kingdom. For all it made the ordinary citizen's life a struggle, the very corruption she hoped to cure made planning the rebellion much easier.

So many people flocked to her side for a reason. It was why she was able to embed so many of her own troops in the war, despite the measures her father took to ensure that only soldiers loyal to him were under her command.

When the new, higher Tier planet had been found in the neighboring sector to her little rebellion haven, she had hardly believed the luck. It set them up to take an even larger portion of the kingdom with them when they left. As she and the other queens had hoped, the Emperor allowed them to declare war on the kingdom for the land, which would let them cripple the remaining loyalists.

Careful planning ensured her own people suffered fewer losses than the most loyal regiments. The difference wasn't enough to tip her hand, but enough to hobble a few critical assets in key areas. Her traitors knew the risk, and put their lives on the line for a better tomorrow.

Some died willingly for that. Unlike little Albie's Pather war one planet over, this wasn't a game. Death was all too real.

Cori traced her scar again. She kept it as a reminder for all these years.

With an effort of will, she convinced her spirit that the scar wasn't a part of her true self anymore. Over the next hour, she watched the mark gradually vanish.

It had been a reminder of another life.

Today, she was free.

She withdrew her helmet from her spatial ring and strode out of her tent, into the bustling camp that her army had set up.

Assembled around her were 200,000 Tier 20s and 75,000 Tier 21s, along with a smattering of Tier 22s.

Less than half were on her side. Most were loyalists from the personal armies of the dukes, the most sycophantic of the king's supporters. That was fine. Most of this army was destined to be slaughtered in the mass ambush that she had waiting.

She started sending orders to gather everyone up. Within half an hour, the tents were stored, and everyone hovered in formation on their flying devices.

The army flew over the mountain range where the queendom lay in wait. The scouts were some of the first to be infiltrated, and reported what she wanted. At her request, a token queendom force had been moved a little too far out of position, leaving a supposed crack in their defenses. When her generals predictably clamored to attack, she let them gather the majority of their forces and led them to their doom.

Her countdown timer ticked down, and when it finally hit zero, she struck out with her true power. In an instant, she went from the apparent weakest leader, here only because of who her father was, to one of the strongest.

By law, the queendom couldn't have a Tier 20 ruler, the Tier her peers had successfully stalled her at. As a sign of good faith, they had secretly given her resources and time slots in their own rifts to advance. At Tier 24, her power allowed her to cleave through the two strongest kingdom generals highlighted. They were also Tier 24, but the element of surprise allowed her to slice clean through their heads. There was no surviving without a brain, and she ended her largest threats in an instant.

Two of her compatriots, highlighted blue, assaulted the nearest red generals. They weren't overwhelmingly strong, so she gathered a bit of mana and sent out a [Mana Thrust] at each of them.

The strikes hit true. They slumped over on their flying devices before falling, with a mist of blood flowing from the holes in their heads and residual energy dissipating into the air.

Chaos surrounded her. A rainbow of spells and skills lit up the sky with flashes of light and death.

Kingdom loyalists fighting kingdom traitors. Only she and her forces could see the difference, and more than one of her troops fought alongside their own brethren to integrate themselves into a group of kingdom loyalists, before attacking from the inside.

They'd trained for this.

Her command channel sang with a chorus full of panicked and contradictory orders. Captain Michels was trying with mild success to reinstall order, so she found him in the melee and directed a free squad to gang up on the man.

Things would have looked bleak with the loyalist's numbers advantage, but then a wave of queendom troops arose from concealed locations in the mountains, and only now were they apparent to her spiritual sense. Like a tidal wave, a multitude of queendom elites flooded up and around her men, even as entire battalions of snipers began felling their preselected targets.

In under ten minutes, the final kingdom loyalist fell.

Milly soared up next to Cori where she hovered.

"I half-thought you wouldn't go through with it."

Cori met the younger woman's eyes. Milly held her gaze for longer than most were willing to, but she looked away and down. She was the third daughter of the sixth and newest queen of the Alliance of Queens.

Or rather, her mother was the second newest of the current queens. As of this moment, Cori was the latest, though she needed to push her cultivation to at least Tier 30 in a hurry. Her Intent was close, but she needed something else, even beyond her phrase and image. The Intent refused to crystalize like her Concept had.

That information was one of the many things she intended to ask from her peers at the first possible opportunity.

"I never break my word. Are your other troops taking the locations I specified?"

Milly nodded. "They made their move at the same time. The teleporter formation should be under our control as long as your people don't back down."

Cori checked her AI and the reports. The situation looked acceptable so far, but there were a few pockets of resistance that she directed troops to. Controlling the queendom troops as well as her own gave her a thrill of pleasure.

She didn't miss the voids in communication from certain locations. That signified some of the loyalist troops had already ditched the standard combination channels. It was smart of them to realize that the lines were compromised, but dumb of them to reveal that and make themselves high priority targets.

Looking to Milly, she sent her the locations. "Have troops check these locations."

Before she could respond, Cori finished focusing her will, and ripped a hole through reality into chaotic space.

She was immediately buffeted by the energies that made up the realm between realms. It took most of her power to keep the corrosive energies at bay.

Without reality to help it travel, her spiritual sense didn't cover even half the distance it usually did. That was still enough for her to scan around the spark of light in the void that was the essence-full world. Seeing no one around her trying to escape, Cori changed the location of her focus, and punched back into the world, halfway across the planet.

That stunt had cost her nearly half her mana and most of her willpower, but she was still confident in her combat prowess.

Damien and Kristen came to a halt, sensing her presence as she entered real space and hovered behind them. To avoid breaking the rules of engagement, Cori needed them to attack first as she was the stronger party. The Tier 22 man and woman were her most significant problems. They were a Marquess and Marchioness, respectively, and die-hard loyalists.

They were also capable tacticians, which was why she was going to take them out herself. Or that was the excuse she had briefed the queendom on.

In truth, she detested the pair. They were willing to sell anyone out for personal power. Starting as unlanded nobles, they had schemed their ways up the ranks. At every opportunity, these two sociopaths were held as shining examples of why her father's methods worked. They were loyal enough to have eagerly performed violent loyalty purges of their domains, often unprompted.

While they had officially only killed heads of state, they had taken out any political opposition they could get their hands on. More than a few people were executed on charges that were later revealed to be lazily fabricated. Her father adored the pair.

Everything they embodied; Cori abhorred. Wiping them from existence would be a public service.

They also took every opportunity to talk down to her, claiming that their power was only their own because they had earned it, and not squandered it. The unspoken 'as Cori had' was always hidden in their smirks and the glints in their eyes.

The tall, pale man summoned his war ax, and the woman readied a staff that cracked with lightning, water, and eddies of air.

Kristen spat to the side. "You sold us out to the queendom!? You are fucking bitch! When the king hears of this, he'll have your head on a platter!"

It was hardly a question, but Cori smiled under her helm in response.

She activated [Flexibility], [Endurance], and [Mana Strength]. Moving at full strength normally drained her rapidly. It was really a question of whether exhaustion would set in, or she would tear a muscle first.

The buffs allowed her to fight with neither constraint nor worry. A Tier 26 mana stone was already being pumped into a rapid mana converter to slowly recover the mana from her trip through chaotic space. The expense was ruinously wasteful, but she had her own sources of wealth. The underground fighting arenas paid obscenely well for deathmatches. It was how she could afford her new weapon.

The rapier gleamed a glossy green in the setting sun.

It was an exceptional weapon that she had ordered from an Empire crafter. Most considered a plant mage weaker in the air, but Cori disagreed. You just needed a little ingenuity to make the spells work effectively.

There was little point in hiding her abilities anymore. It was time to put down the rabid dogs who thought themselves her rivals.

Damien lost his patience first and used [Blink] to close the distance.

There it was. All the provocation that she needed to engage. They had attacked her first, after all.

Cori rushed forward to where she could feel the spell targeting. In the split second it took the spell to transport the man, Cori struck with a [Mana Thrust].

She was still too slow and only grazed the man's chest armor instead of timing the attack to land inside of him.

A disappointing failure, but nothing to worry about. She ignored him to rush the mage. Kristen was already summoning a storm. The entire horizon was being gorged with rapidly darkening clouds.

A bolt of lightning struck out at her, but she cast [Entangle]. The vines absorbed the energy. The electricity fried the plant life, but it let her close the distance.

Kristen wasn't stupid and was already retreating on a gale of wind. But she was too slow. She wasn't a real storm mage. Not yet.

The enemy mage had yet to merge her three distinct mana types into a solid, unified whole. Instead, she was pulling from carefully portioned areas of her mana pool. Not only was the practice slower, but it was also dangerous. If the woman lost concentration, her unstable mana would mix, and the result wouldn't be a storm, but an unusable mess which she would need to purge to fix.

That necessity made her slower, which ensured her death.

Cori, with her higher cultivation, was nearly on the Tier 22 mage. Her rapier was only feet away when she felt Damien close the distance with a [Shield Bash] used in conjunction with a [Lunge]. Interweaving skills required a delicate blend of magical control that he wasn't able to properly achieve. She could feel the mana spillage from the spell structure radiating around Damien. For it to be this bad indicated the shoddiness of his efforts.

Unfortunately, it still allowed him to close the remaining distance in an instant.

With her Talent and passive skills helping, Cori bent backward and under the chopping ax. Her bones and ligaments screamed with the sudden bend, but she hardly lost any momentum with the maneuver. Still, even that slight hesitation was enough for Kristen to cast [Tornado]. She was clearly mixing water mana with wind, and the funnel of wind quickly grew to monstrous size as it absorbed the clouds around them.

Kristen retreated into the cutting vortex of wind, a place where Cori would have to expend a lot of resources to reach, leaving her open to the couple's retaliation.

Instead, through her rapier, she cast [Spore] and [Seed]. Tiny motes of plant life flaked off from the green blade, and were sucked up into the tornado. If Kristen had been able to merge lightning with the skill, she wouldn't be able to pull this off. But, as it was, Cori was free to pump the tiny plant life full of mana.

In seconds, the pinhead-sized motes of [Seed] swirling around Kristen were massive tendrils of greenery.

Suddenly, the defensive tornado became a trap.

Damien struggled to cut through the magically strengthened vines, but he was two Tiers below her, and a full three Tiers below her weapon.

Kristen scrambled to race up and escape out of the apex of the spell, but Cori was prepared, and she was faster. She had ensured that her spell spread out well above and below the mage.

Damien spun to attack her, hoping to break her concentration on her spell. To his growing alarm, she avoided each of his attacks simply by leaning on her training and physical advantage.

Finally, a vine wrapped around the Kristen's leg. Cori smiled. The woman was in her grip now.

The resistance stopped, and she paused to find that she no longer had a hold of the mage. Not all of her at least. Her growing vines searched to find the leg severed at the knee.

It was a shrewd move. One that may have worked if not for [Spore]. The spell was already in the air, and she could now feel Kristen's location. A Tier 15 or higher could keep the tracking spell out of their body as long as they concentrated. With a gaping wound to infect though, it was already too late. The skill was *inside* the woman.

With a mental effort, she bent around another heavy mana-infused ax strike and changed the skill that was still connected with her blade.

Through her rapier, she merged the still active [Spore] skill with [Toxin]. Combining an active skill was incredibly hard and painfully slow, but it had the desired effect.

In Kristen's body, the skill slowly turned poisonous. It was already hard to break through the mage's Concept, willpower, and spirit. Dodging Damien's attacks on top of that was taxing and forced her to split her attention. Still, she managed it.

Long ago, Cori had learned that her Talent made it far easier to dodge a blow than to block the hit. She was a small woman. Dodging was easy, and only risked injury if she couldn't move out of the way fast enough.

As she felt Kristen abandon her active control of the weather, Damian finally earned both her full attention and a counter thrust into his chest.

[Phantom Armor] appeared, and for an instant helped his own

armor resist the strike. The force of her attack sent him flying upward and out of the atmosphere.

Not letting the opportunity be wasted, she rushed toward Kristen, who sat shaking and vomiting. A bored slash took the woman's head off.

It was almost too easy.

In her spiritual senses, Cori felt Damian going utterly berserk. Music to her ears. He unleashed his veil and shockingly started burning essence to empower his attacks.

A massive, twenty foot wide [Mana Chop] forced her to both activate her own [Phantom Armor] and wrap herself in a ball of vines to block it.

Using essence in your attacks was possible after Tier 15, but it had two major drawbacks. First off, it permanently damaged the skills used, and would destroy those skills if used too much. Using essence also permanently damaged your cultivation base as you ripped it away. As far as she knew, there was no way to use loose, non-allocated essence to attack. It had to come from one of your cores, which meant you lost that progress forever.

New essence didn't go to fill those voids, it went to advancing. All that power was just gone.

Most people weren't willing to sacrifice that much, even for a lover. For immortals, spouses were often temporary. Personal power was the only thing that couldn't betray you, after all. And it was the only thing that could drive you forward.

If the couple hadn't been such vile pieces of shit, she might have almost found Damian's dedication touching.

Cori was still rebuilding [Phantom Armor] in her spirit to charge it again, when another [Mana Chop] lashed out. Unlike last time, she was prepared, and got out of the way in time. She felt a mountain explode behind her from the impact of the spell.

She could now personally attest to the power of essence-fueled skills. Despite her two Tier advantage, that first strike had punched through two of her defensive skills. Her armor was still smoking from the impact.

Still, Cori's confidence didn't falter. At best, this put Damien at her level, and only until his diminishing cultivation and crumbling skills caught up with him. She had never had issues fighting people at her level.

Only stronger fighters ever provided a challenge worth enjoying. An equal was nothing to get excited about.

Cori unleashed a normal [Mana Slash], causing Damien to twist out of the way and interrupt his next attack. By her estimation, he probably had two more casts of [Mana Chop] before the skill fell apart.

She closed the distance and slashed out with a heavy blow. The haft of his ax rose to block it. The blow still sent the larger but weaker man flying into true space.

Cori refused to let him take advantage of the momentum she'd provided him and flee. She would keep close here; her higher cultivation gave her the flat advantage over the dedicated melee fighter.

They neared the planet's largest moon when she caught up with his larger form. In her brief but rapid approach, she felt someone watching.

She had an inkling of who it was. If she guessed right, she wasn't sure if she should be insulted or flattered. Either way, it was time to put on a show.

To show her worth.

Damien slammed into the moon with a crash, sending debris spraying everywhere. Right before impact, an essence-fueled [Flame Barrage] shot toward her. Two dozen person-sized fireballs exploded out and homed in on her.

Cori weaved her way through them without letting a single flame lick her. But she cut it close enough that her armor heated up, even though the vacuum of space.

Damien was ready and had a [Mana Chop] charged with essence building on his blade. She met the attack with magic and steel, as her own full power [Mana Charge] flashed to meet it.

As their attacks clashed, a wash of energy surged out in all directions as the two opposing forces tried to overpower each other.

She had to use her Concept to brace herself in place with plant life on the moon, but soon, their attacks dissipated. When she saw Damien, she trusted the fight was over. He was bleeding from the backlash of their clash, and each drop was evaporating in the vacuum of space. Despite neither having nor needing air to breath, he wheezed with undeniable effort.

In contrast, she kept herself controlled and poised. Even if she wanted to vomit after the effort that repulsing that attack had required, she was a queen now. And, honestly, this was the most fun she'd had in decades, from the thrill of a fight that she actually believed in.

Plus, Cori loved to put on a good show.

To her surprise, Damien glowed with the ominous crimson aura of [Berserker's Rage]. The red color was taken over with white as essence was cycled through the skill, and the aura became massive. She could feel how it skyrocketed with power. The increase was absurd, too much for even burning essence to explain. Shaking off the initial distraction, she took the whole of him in. With her own eyes and spirit, she could both see and feel the damage the skill was doing to the man.

More than just cultivation was being devoured. It was burning away his spirit.

That was mildly concerning. Best to end this in a hurry.

Damien lashed out with [Mana Slash]. It was empowered with essence, but it was far weaker than the [Mana Chop]s he had been using before. His weapon wasn't a great match for the skill, and he had clearly neither modified nor mastered [Mana Slash] as much as [Mana Chop].

Cori flexed like a tree in the wind, and dodged the arc of energy that tore across the moon's reddish surface.

Increasing her boosts to the maximum, she let her Talent fully take effect. With three rapid steps that tore at her bones and ligaments, she arrived next to Damien. She reached up, grabbed his burning head, and yanked it back to where she could run her blade across his neck.

It was a pointless gesture. She felt his spine snap on the initial yank alone. But this was supposed to be a show.

Her watchers stepped out of chaotic space, clapping metal hands.

Verona, the fourth queen in the alliance, strode over to where Cori stood. Through AI messaging, Cori received, "Well fought. I thought I'd have to step in when he started using essence to power his attacks."

Cori just stared her newest peer down. "If you intervened, he would have had to be let go. No, I wanted him dead. So, he died."

Verona shrugged. "He already crippled himself, so it was no bother. Your life is more important, my newest sister."

The ebony-skinned woman's smile was sincere.

Cori didn't trust it on principle. But she didn't show that. That would be rude.

Verona seemed to catch that regardless, and just silently laughed in the void.

"Worry not. We may never be the best of friends, but we are sisters of a purpose. That is something beyond mere friendship." Still seeing Cori's expression not soften, she added, "There is no rush. We have time. Speaking of which, we have an appointment to catch."

That caught her attention. Something like that was distinctly not a part of the plan. Cori grew wary. "What do you mean?"

The Tier 31 shrugged one shoulder, "Our eldest sister was wounded severely when she tried to peek into the little vassal war. In retaliation, someone put their hand through her chest and around her heart. She's not exactly in the best shape to go up against your father, so we will all gather to support her."

That caused Cori to pause. No sane person would tell their direct subordinates they were seriously wounded. That was begging to be stabbed in the back. But why else would they change their plans so suddenly?

And who could casually injure a Tier 35 like that?

Then Cori understood.

The Emperor had clearly sent a hidden powerhouse to watch over the war. If they were that strong and that trusted, the queendom could use them as an official witness to the willing rebellion of her side.

An official treaty would prevent retaliation of any kind.

Cori nodded to Verona, who smiled and stuck out an arm. "Come, come. We have a turbulent path ahead. Something strange is happening in chaotic space. The currents are muddled; it makes travel slower and more unpredictable."

It took a moment, but she realized that her new peer was offering to carry her there like a baby. Not thrilled at the prospect, she still recognized that this was the only way to get to the neighboring Tier 6 planet without using the teleport path. Cori reviewed the situation, sighed and sent her orders to the troops still on the planet. She didn't miss Verona's grin widening at that.

Neither of them trusted official routes that her father set up. It was why the queendom invaded using chaotic space vessels instead of using the established lanes. No one had missed the fact the kingdom stopped using them too after the war was declared.

But even she wasn't sure if the lane was tampered with. They'd need to be thoroughly and carefully inspected later.

Gathering her power, Cori prepared for the trip. She thought of her father. She thought of the face he'd make when he lost a huge chunk of his kingdom. That put a smile on her face that just refused to leave.

31

Matt had once again just finished leading his troops to attack a portion of the queendom's defensive fortifications. Scores of soldiers were surrounding the second of the two cities under siege. The other city was receiving constant reinforcements, and he got news that a new skill was being used on the quickly falling walls.

As the reports filtered in, he started to curse. Amber had clearly gotten [Cracked Breach] after he refused it, and she was using it to devastating effect in the siege of the second city.

They had managed to knock down two of the three standing walls in just hours. The city was quickly falling as they lost defensive position after defensive position. The highest-ranking officer had ordered his remaining troops to attempt to sally forth, but they were stopped on the rampart of dirt that the besiegers had set up.

He watched two shots of [Cracked Breach] obliterate nearly half the kingdom personnel in the recording.

The siege was officially over when the queendom troops rose in a wave, and cut down the few scattered and disoriented defenders. It left the kingdom with a single unmolested city, and another under siege.

That report was only minutes old, and the new information implied that the queendom was moving to take the city with most of their wounded and less than ambulatory troops. The remaining troops were being organized in formations that Matt expected to be moving to end this siege.

He felt so helpless. It was a combination of knowing his perfect skill was gone because he couldn't immediately use it, and envy at seeing the skill in action. If he had that, and could use it, he could finish this siege in an hour. Two at max. It would be like having a perfect mana cannon ready at any time.

If Matt had that, he would be unstoppable. And he doubted that there was another version of that particular crack on [Breach] around. Now he would need to wait until Tier 9, when he could afford the initial cost of 500 mana for the original skill.

Still, he couldn't say that he regretted upgrading [Cracked Phantom Armor], or giving Annie the points from his win in the dueling arena. He had good reasons for each of his decisions, and while they had cost him an amazing skill, he didn't think he would choose differently in either scenario given the chance.

It just hurt to see a skill that would let him eventually fully utilize his Talent go to someone who was surely being stuffed with mana crystals.

Still, he had a much more important job to do: slow down the reinforcements as much as he could. The prince only had two days left on his healing cooldown, and they needed to try and buy time to prevent the second to last of their cities from falling.

After he was able to pass off command, the army couldn't blame him for any losses. As much as he did his best, he was sure that the army AI would be handing out critiques left and right for his performance.

Still, he shook off the morose thoughts and set his AI to create a plan to slow the enemy down. That was on top of dealing with a woman who could take down city walls in quick order.

There were two distinct possibilities. Either they tried to hide Amber because of the value of her new skill, or the armies flaunted her and the prowess she represented, while she blasted through any defenses his side set up.

Matt felt like pulling out his hair as he failed to develop a suitable counter to the [Cracked Breach] skill. His best option was to call on Annie to assassinate the woman, but it was a pretty obvious plan that he was sure the queendom would expect. Especially after taking out Sara.

But he didn't have an adequate way to remove Amber besides

throwing a ton of people at her, and hoping one of them could take her down between blasts of her skill. It wasn't an ideal anti-personnel skill from the recordings, as it was relatively slow, but that was only relative to other spells. It would be challenging but not impossible to dodge a well-planned shot if directed at you given the normal distance the skill was cast at.

Their only other advantage was that it took Amber nearly ten minutes to charge up each shot. Still, they would need to know exactly where she was and be aware of her forces' movements. To that effect, Matt gave orders for the scouts to carefully shadow the city and the troops that were forming up as he predicted.

The army didn't immediately move out, to his surprise. So he started sending out his own orders in the time that the queendom's inaction bought him. The two cities were separated by a mountain chain, which he could use to set up defenses and hopefully slow down the queendom's advance.

He and his troops quickly abandoned their camp and moved to the most likely passes the queendom would take, setting up skeleton fortifications. They didn't want to commit until the queendom troops had established their route.

Matt was digging out the side of a mountain late into the night, when the report came in. The queendom was finally moving. Even with their head start, the task was less than ideal. The queendom was moving nearly three million troops, but they weren't staying grouped up. They were splitting in half.

To make matters worse, the two formations went in opposite directions around the mountain chain.

The scouts had no idea which formation Amber was in.

The whole situation brought her last words back to mind. "Then best of luck to you. I know we don't need it." Her little proclamation felt like a slap in the face now.

He calculated the odds of which formation she would be with, and had his AI do the same. He had no better way to determine the path she took than a fifty-fifty chance.

His AI was better at processing information, and had seventy percent odds on the southern formation. The northern procession was too obviously centered around a single individual that was careful not to be seen. That in and of itself hadn't given the AI sufficient information to make such a call, but it had noticed an anomaly in the southern procession. A much smaller selection of individuals revolved around one person.

It was a detail that was easy to get lost in the movement of millions of people, but his AI was able to use his full mana generation of 80 MPS to analyze each person. His AI finally found the hidden anomaly, and he trusted it enough to order his forces south.

They needed to at least slow Amber down.

He was hoping that Annie could get out here quickly and would be able to pull off another miraculous kill.

She was still on her way from recovering in a hidden location, after killing Sara, and would take another two days by her estimation. Apparently, there was a city-wide hunt for her. The queendom hadn't taken kindly to their princess being assassinated, and had placed a sizable bounty on her head.

With the queendom having to travel for ten hours to reach the mountain range, Matt and his men rapidly built fortifications. Sadly, this area had a lack of small forts that would have anti-flying formations, but they were able to set a few mana cannons up. They hoped they would be able to quickly strike into the heart of the troops and kill Amber.

If they did, they would come out on top no matter the losses they suffered. Or at least, the prince would heavily reward them for their sacrifice.

The wait for the queendom unit to appear was agonizing. But eventually, as the sun rose over the horizon, the mass of flyers breached the curve of the planet. They were right where their scouts' report said they would be.

Matt could feel the morale of his troops plummet like a stone, and he couldn't blame them. They were currently flying in range of the mana cannon emplacements for support, but almost unconsciously, his troops retreated slightly.

Wanting to put a stop to that as the queendom formation swung wide, he said over the general command channel, "This isn't the time for retreat. We need to force our way into the enemy formation and break their spirits."

That was clearly the wrong thing to say, as he felt the air shift. His side's spirits were breaking, not the queendom's.

He was tired of all the responsibility landing on his shoulders, and the ever-building murmuring of the troops who increasingly disliked their ability to decisively end the sieges.

Without thinking, he added, "Okay, fuck that. We need to kill the woman with the siege spell, and it doesn't really matter how many of us die to do it. It has to be done, or we'll die when it's used on a city instead. We rush in there to watch for the blast, then focus on that location. The reports say that it takes her ten minutes to charge back up, so that's our window of opportunity. Find her and kill her."

While that didn't improve the general mood, people tightened their grip on their weapons. Seeing that it was the best he was going to get, he called out the general charge.

His remaining three-quarters of a million troops rushed forward like a wave into the prepared flank of the flying enemy.

Spells and ammunition raced across the distance in a multi-colored rainbow of death. Matt kept the lead position until a pillar of rock smacked into him, sending him spiraling until he steadied himself.

To his mounting trepidation, Matt felt the mana in the area building, signaling Amber's charging of [Cracked Breach]. He raced back to the lead position quickly, but a hole opened up in the queendom formation as their sides were about to clash.

Out from it came a figure with glowing hands, who launched a bus-sized arrow of mana.

Matt reacted with everyone else and scattered.

Most of the flyers were able to escape the projectile's path, but the mountain and their embankment weren't so lucky. So, when the [Cracked Breach] shot landed, there was a flash of light, and a rumbling sound accompanied by an impact of wind.

Matt felt like he was kicked by a mule as the wave of wind passed.

He internally cheered when his AI reported that the shot missed the majority of his troops. When he ordered a follow-up charge, he found that a portion of his troops refused to listen and retreated.

That still left a sizable wave of men and women all desperately rushing to where the [Cracked Breach] shot came from.

Matt parried an ax while he spun on his flying sword, trying to rush forward. The queendom soldiers were just throwing their bodies at the rushing kingdom troops in an attempt to prevent them from reaching Amber.

He was hemmed in by five people as he charged a [Mana Charge]. As soon as his weapon hummed with power, Matt brought his glowing longsword around, into the flying sword of a queendom fighter.

There was a faint scream as they started to fall, and he slipped through the gap created with his faster flying device.

Once he was through the barrier, he found a few hundred kingdom fighters trying to batter their way into a knot of queendom troops. Tired of this farce, Matt rushed forward and cast [Flamethrower] at anyone in a queendom uniform. The spell was fairly short range, but even the thirty feet was more than enough to send people running.

Matt was peppered by a rain of glowing arrows a moment later, but when he turned to look, it was one of his Pathers using [Arrow Storm]. It was a Tier 14 skill that, for 200 mana, created a mass of mana construct arrows in a cone around the original arrow. He was simply hit from the expanding cone as the archer took out a number of other fighters.

The archer created a tunnel in the queendom defenders that he didn't need to order people into. It was mostly other Pathers, but the kingdom fighters streamed into the gap and closed the distance with Amber.

Matt was intercepted by another four fighters who hacked and slashed at him while trying to dodge his [Flamethrower]. They disappeared as he washed the jet of fire over them, but they still slowed him down. He was now at the trailing end of the forces chasing Amber down.

The ten minute countdown timer was nearing its end, and Amber started glowing again as the ambient mana started reacting with the mana being converted and pumped into her.

She must have decided that she didn't need a fully charged shot, because with three minutes left on the timer, another large arrow of mana lashed out. It was significantly smaller than the first shot, but much faster.

It cut through a number of her own people who stayed engaged with the kingdom troops, taking them along for the trip to the hospital.

Matt rushed with everyone else to fill in the gap, when another team curled around and attacked from above. A man with tiger ears sticking out of his helmet swooped down, and with a gust of wind that swirled around, accelerated to blurring speeds as he tore into four of the defenders around Amber.

A second member of the team started throwing [Fireball]s that froze their targets instead of burning them, creating a gap large enough for the final man to rush forward.

Matt paused in his rush at the sight before him.

As the final man approached, the defensive spells and magical attacks all seemed to lose cohesion and fall apart before they could hit him. The arrow that slammed into his neck only slowed him down as he got within arm's reach of Amber.

The Pather cast a [Fireball] inches from her, and the resulting explosion caused them both to vanish.

After confirming that they had actually taken out Amber, Matt called for a general retreat. He and the others who made it deep into the enemy formation had to fight their way out, but no one held anything back. A wave of spells created enough of a gap for them to slip up and over the flying queendom soldiers.

"Everyone fall back and watch our rears. The queendom might decide to engage while we pull back. We killed Amber. Now we need to make it out of here."

That actually seemed to help slightly, as the middlemost troops slowed and formed slight defensive walls as they continued their retreat. Forming up allowed the rearmost kingdom fighter to catch up and have some modicum of protection.

Matt was afraid that they wouldn't get away safely at all when the queendom moved to pursue them for longer than he anticipated. He was concerned that they would be unwilling to let their ace being killed go unpunished and wouldn't relent in chasing them down to finish the remaining troops off.

Considering that he was down to nearly four hundred thousand troops, he sorely hoped not. They had killed Amber, removing her and the [Cracked Breach] skill from the war for two weeks. But they didn't have the numbers to fight off the queendom's army. They started out with a numbers disadvantage, and it was only growing as they were picked off.

At some point, the queendom must have decided that pursuing them deeper into the mountains was a losing proposition, and contented themselves with their advance to the besieged city.

Matt called for the end of the retreat twice before the leading elements of the unit stopped their advance.

They landed in the mountains, and he started barking orders to set up a camp, but he didn't have any plans other than to wait for the prince to finish his cooldown timer. They would rest until he mobilized the entire kingdom army with his *actual* authority.

He and his people had done their part trying to hold everything together, and had even taken out a vital asset.

They had earned the break.

Albert watched the timer tick down and smiled as it hit zero.

He sent out his orders to his elite units and the remaining troops. He added Matt and his forces as an afterthought. At less than half a million troops, they mattered little. They were farther away from the queendom capital, but he could use the extra manpower in their rush on the queendom's port city.

He also didn't want the top Pathers caught in the fallout of his father's plans. They had done more than he could have hoped for by stalling the queendom, and he didn't want to repay that trust with a death right before the end of the war.

Albert had already pushed their trust with his seeming failure to stop Sara's surprise attack. Since he couldn't go out to reassure them, and could only communicate with those who came to him directly, many were despairing about the outcome of the war.

When you had the win condition and could trigger it at any time, what did games matter? And having nearly seventy percent of the queendom troops in or around the cities was exactly where he wanted them. He couldn't have gotten Sara to more perfectly place her troops if he had asked her to.

She was so concerned with holding the cities, that by all reports, she had stripped her forts to avoid weakening any of their defenses.

She was concentrating her forces exactly where he wanted them to be. While he only had a single city that wasn't under siege left out of the six, he was fine. Even if they moved to siege that one down as well.

The only city with a variable that he didn't control was the queendom port city. As long as that fell quickly, he had the victory of this war in his pocket.

As much as he hated his father forcing his plan on him, it had worked out well. The queendoms' greed to end the war quickly had driven them to swallow poisoned pills.

He knew that he could have prevented quite a bit of his nobles' bickering with some simple calls, or some 'casual' face-to-face conversations. But that indecision let him keep most of his troops safe while the two armies were all on healing cooldowns. He would need them to swiftly take the final city. So, letting his troops sit around without risk was ideal for his plans.

More than a few of the nobles and generals who weren't in the loop had contacted him, asking for whatever guidance he could offer. He was able to placate most of them, despite the seemingly worsening situation, without giving away the larger plans. He wasn't sure how many were spies trying to ferret out information for Sara, who must have suspected that something was wrong, or who were truly loyal and worried.

Still, a few carefully selected top generals and their personal retainers knew about the plan. They were the ones who had done most of the hard work in preparing the cities. Olivia had been a massive help in that effort, which was a part of the reason why he rewarded her so heavily.

But all of these games were going to come to an end in the next day or two. It was only a matter of choosing the *perfect* moment to end the war.

With Amber dead, trying to take down the much better walls of the second city would be a much more difficult proposition. Even the most conservative estimates put the queendom at half a week out.

Things were going perfectly.

———

Matt and his remaining troops were told to move to the queendom's port city the very minute that Prince Albert was off his healing cooldown. They met up with a large force that was moving in that direction already. It was an odd order, but he was happy to no longer be the highest authority on the kingdom side.

The only positive was that they had successfully stalled the original force and whittled down their numbers for long enough. Their city was in much better shape for it.

Through preventing the pounding that Amber could have delivered, the kingdom still held the city. The queendom would win, that much wasn't in doubt. But they were going to have to bleed for it.

Matt still had no idea why Albert wanted them to go to the queendom's capital city. It seemed like a stupid move. He was unable to figure out their plan, but with Liz, Aster, Emily, and Conor on the attacking force, he was fine with just following orders and meeting up with them.

The last week had been far too stressful for his taste.

The new army quickly absorbed his remaining troops into the standing army of five million, bolstering their numbers by quite a bit. He pulled Aster and Liz into a sweaty hug when he saw them for the first time, once he found their tent in the sea of similar, spatially expanded tents.

Liz pushed him back to examine his face and said, "You look like shit!" She got a much more perceptive gleans in her eye when she asked, "When was the last time you slept?"

"Last night, after our failed attack. It's been a disaster the last few weeks."

Conor clapped his shoulder and said, "From everything we've seen, it looked like you did the best anyone could have asked of you."

Aster wiggled to make her presence known.

"Yeah! You did well!"

Matt had his doubts that Aster had any idea what he had actually been doing, but the encouragement was nice, nonetheless.

"Thanks, Aster." He kissed her head before squeezing her a bit. That was apparently a signal to play, as she yowled her distress, and Matt started to spin her around and rubbed her all over.

The pleas that she had just gotten her fur the way it should be sounded more like encouragement to him. As he played with her, he listened to Emily while she idly informed him about the general disposition of the neutral city.

"Odds are heavily in the queendom's favor for winning the war with the latest developments. A lot of middle-level Pathers were even wondering if the kingdom could hold onto their final city. Others wondered if there were more points to be had in changing sides." She kicked at a partially visible stone until it was free as she talked, knocking it away and out of the standing area in their tent.

"So far, the more restrictive point distribution and the cost to change sides are keeping people over, but I think this siege is the important bit. Rumor has it, Sara stripped most of the forts she had of troops to fuel this attack without weakening the city." She pointed through Conor to the city under siege.

Matt shook his head. "What's the plan, then? Why not relieve the siege on the other city?"

It wasn't Liz who answered, despite her open mouth.

Juni's voice answered from outside their tent, "I can explain that if you'd let me in."

Liz turned her head and glared. "Come in. I'm so glad you are listening in on our conversations."

Juni ducked under the flap and shrugged. "I coughed twice and messaged Matt three times. I had to make my presence known somehow."

Matt checked to see if that was true as Juni continued, "Generally, commanders come to the headquarters tent to report in. They normally don't have the leaders track them down."

He cringed at that as Juni turned an icy and tired gaze at him.

"Yeah, sorry. It's been a shitshow with the last attack." Matt tried to sound apologetic, but he wasn't sure it worked. He really didn't care.

Juni looked nonplussed as he waved Matt's statement away. "That was fine. You were able to take out Amber, which was the true victory. No, we need you to help with the next attack. We have been digging a trench forward and have a fortification of mana cannons set up with a clean shot on the front gate."

Matt interrupted, "And you want me to fuel the attacks?"

Juni just nodded, to which Matt asked, "What good does that do? There's no way we can take the city quickly, even if the gates fall."

The prince's right-hand man shook his head. "Taking the city through one entrance is risky, yes, but it's a start. We're in a rush, but we can't be stupid. We won't throw our troops away. Once we have the gate down, we'll start battering down the walls. But they're upgraded, so it will be harder. Speaking of which, we'd like you to charge up the mages with whatever willpower you have leftover."

Matt just looked at the man with tired eyes. He just wanted to relax. He may have been able to sleep, but it hadn't been as good a rest as he needed.

Juni seemed to understand that, and offered, "Take a few hours. We can wait that long."

Matt just nodded at the man and turned to his friends, which Juni took as the dismissal that it was.

He needed to recharge from them in a way that had nothing to do with mana.

The war just felt so distant and unimportant.

Liz didn't leave his side as they sat around and talked, except when she brought out a stew from a heater next to their little sink.

It tasted amazing. Matt wasn't sure if that was from his only eating cold rations, or if the person who cooked it was just that good.

Listening to his friends washed away the lingering self-doubt and endless questions of the past week. Having Liz close was even better, though she barely said ten words, content to simply intertwine their fingers and soak in each other's presence.

Aster yammered on through their connection about all the fun she had playing with her beast friends and chasing the bunnies during her downtime.

This is what matters. Not the war. Not the prizes. Friends and those close to me. I can't lose sight of that.

Matt vowed to keep what was truly important firmly affixed in his mind as he went forward. He knew he would have to fight, and taking the city would be anything but easy.

Five hours later, Matt was back in action with a team of mages who rotated off, feeding the mana cannons with their personal mana and mana stones. Their underground bunker only had slits for the cannons to stick out, but it protected them from the return fire with minimal losses.

If the dust from the destroyed mana stones didn't vanish into nothing, they would have been hip-deep in the stuff. Sack after sack of their crystalized mana was brought up and emptied.

Still, they had managed to destroy the front gate in short order. What was taking longer was blasting through the rubble that the defenders had set up behind the inner gate.

Two hours later, they were finally through, and their entire bunker was ordered to halt their attack and move to secondary locations.

Matt was going along with them, when he was called to rejoin his team for an attack with siege towers. He thought it was suicide but didn't think Juni would throw their lives away on a foolish attack.

He was right. Mostly.

Plans had shifted with new information that their long-ranged scouts had discovered. The exact nature of that information was kept quiet, but it necessitated a faster siege.

Their team was part of a coordinated effort to attack from fifteen metal clad siege towers at once. The majority of his tower consisted of the other top Pathers, as well as a battalion of Tier 7 men and women equipped with Tier 8 weapons or armor.

He felt quite a bit better seeing that. These had to be kingdom elite, who were in no way disposable.

When they arrived, they were given a position inside the tower, to all of their surprises. Normally, people didn't ride the tower for the approach, as any added weight simply slowed them down.

Matt laughed when he reached the top of the tower and found a mana cannon already set up on a swivel.

It was exactly what he wanted to see.

The kingdom had to have splurged on spending, because each of the towers were set up with a portable shielding unit. While weaker than the city-wide version, they were enough to protect the towers on the approach.

With an ease that belied what Matt knew to be true from the other side of this tactic, they slammed into the wall and dropped the tower's ramp down. They were met with a rain of arrows, along with a wall of shields.

It meant little when Matt sat on a mana cannon in the entrance.

He didn't even flinch as the first arrows and spells slammed into him, while the cannon lit up and blew away the front-most troops.

Quickly, he charged another shot and swiveled right as he fired again. Scores of troops vanished in the expulsion of mana. When there was a clear area, the Tier 7 troops moved out in a shield wall and set up small barriers. Meanwhile, Matt and his team removed the mana cannon from its mount and carried it to the roof of the tower.

There was a second mount there, where he was able to shoot over the heads of his allies.

During the quieter moments when the queendom was unable to take the offensive, he saw the kingdom's mana cannons firing from each of the siege towers.

The expense boggled his mind. Albert must have put every point he earned in the two week healing cooldown into this siege. Mana cannons weren't cheap by any means, and the non-castle versions were only more so.

Liz acted as his spotter, along with his AI, allowing him to target problem areas in his range. Eventually, they decided to move to the wall to get a shot inside the city, but Juni flatly refused that request.

Liz even asked to use [Blood Sprite] to set upon the enemy but was similarly refused.

Matt didn't understand that, since things seemed to be going well. At least, until he accessed the command channel and looked at the overall casualties. Things were looking awful. The kingdom had taken nearly half a million casualties in the last push.

Their side of the city had either gotten lucky, or they were stacked with stronger people, because they were holding their section without much issue. The only thing they had to worry about was the queendom troops shooting anyone who stuck their heads over the parapet, into the inner city.

The other side of the city had had three towers repulsed and set ablaze, along with a higher concentration of anti-siege weaponry. They had bled to take a single section of the wall and hold it, while reinforcements streamed up their tower to replace the losses.

Things were slowly stalling as the sun set, and the night that was still sweltering went on, ensuring that anyone without magical armor was uncomfortable. Liz and his team, with little else to do, cursed up a storm the entire time.

They were waiting around for more orders when Matt felt the ground rumble. He looked past the besieged city, over the northern horizon. It was like a new dawn was born over the wrong horizon.

He turned to look along with everyone else, and saw a massive fireball rise into the air.

It didn't take a genius to know that location was one of the queendom cities. He still had no idea what was actually going on when he found himself standing in the sunlight with millions of others. Instead, he blinked to clear the bright sunspots out of his eyes. It was nighttime where he was last, and the sudden translation to mid-day was jarring.

In those few blinks more and more people appeared around him.

He was still confused and looked to Liz and the rest of his team standing in the shadow of the neutral city's wall.

"What just happened?" He asked the open air, but he was hardly the only one.

Liz looked around and shrugged and messaged him through their AI, to be heard over the growing rumbling of a confused crowd. 'I don't know, but I thought I saw Juni.'

Matt jumped with [Mage's Retreat] empowering him, and as far as he could see, queendom and kingdom troops mingled.

Liz ducked away into the crowd for a moment, before pulling Juni back by the arm, with Alyssa following close at his heels.

"What the fuck is going on!?" Matt, Conor, and Emily asked variations of the same question as Juni scanned the air.

When he found what he was looking for, he pointed at the sky with an armored hand. "Look."

Hovering in the air were three distinct factions. One of them only had two people. It was hard to see exactly who they were from a distance, but the figures were dressed in the kingdom's dark red and gold.

The army was in the other corner of the triangle, with a mass of people hovering behind who Matt suspected was Colonel Thorne because their uniforms seemed to blend into their surroundings.

The final section was a mass of at least two hundred people in various forms of the queendom colors of silver and light purple. The mass of people seemed hostile toward the two lone figures.

His questions of what was going on were only partially answered when his AI bleeped at him,

'Kingdom Victory by surrender of Queen Diana; rejoice as your side has won!'

Matt looked back to the sky as a broadcast streamed to his AI.

What is going on?

32

Albert was in his command center reviewing the information stream routing through Juni's AI when he felt the world tremble. No one else seemed to notice, but he was sensitive to his father's comings and goings. That experience had honed his skill in detecting the fluctuations created by higher Tiered beings when ripping through the veil of reality when entering or exiting real space.

His father came to mind first, but it only took a second to realize that it was someone else. The tearing didn't stop quick enough to be a single person. In rapid succession, half a dozen presences flickered into his awareness, presumably members of the Army.

Things soon returned to normal, so he shrugged it off and turned back to the ongoing sieges. Juni had cut off the last queendom city with the space-locking formations already. Ending this war was just a question of when the ideal time to detonate the bombs would be.

According to his scouts, the queendom was stripping their forts to skeleton crews, as they funneled all available personnel to either repair the conquered city, or to speed up the next siege.

Once enough people gathered in or around the cities, the kingdom would win the war in one fell swoop.

His daydreams of future glory and prestige were shattered when a much more violent tear rippled out around him, this time causing *everyone* to flinch. Albert prepared an emergency query to send out through his AI, asking for any related information, but he felt space ripple around him before he could send it out.

This power was familiar—his father's. He was yanked through space, only to find himself hovering above the neutral city. Facing him was Queen Diana, flanked by four other stern looking women.

One was Sara, who stood slightly behind her mother. A Chaotic Space ship behind them drew his attention before he could inspect the other women more closely, as it disgorged dozens of his father's nobles. But then, his brain picked up on a familiar figure standing beside Queen Diana.

Cori. His sister.

Has she been taken hostage? How did the war go so badly?

The last reports from the Tier 20 world had indicated that while the real war was slowing down, the situation leaned in their favor. Then his brain took note of the colors that Cori wore, and the complete lack of shackles on her.

His older sister wasn't simply standing near the queens. She stood *with* them.

A woman amongst equals.

He scrambled to write her a message when Queen Diana broke the silence. Her voice resounded in the air around him and his father.

"This war is over, King Brice. I will accept your surrender now." She gestured behind herself at the kingdom nobles behind her.

Albert corrected himself mentally; they were new queendom nobles, which Diana confirmed. "I, First Queen Diana of the Alliance of Allied Queens, have accepted oaths of fealty from these nobles on behalf of themselves and their subjects. They have renounced their allegiance to the Kingdom of Seven Suns. Apparently, they desired finer leadership. For their own betterment, and that of their people. These are just a portion of your nobles who felt they could do better under a new ruler."

Albert peeked up at his father. The man smiled as if everything was going according to his plan.

The king barked out a laugh. "I don't see how that changes the outcome of this little Pather war. Why should I surrender?"

The queen was clearly prepared for the question and looked to her right at the empty space beside her. Suddenly, Colonel Thorne appeared, flanked by half a dozen other officers.

Queen Diana smirked at everyone. "With the annexation of the territory these nobles represent, we control all spatial routes leading up to this series of worlds, and all adjacent territories. On behalf of the Alliance of Allied Queens, I hereby request this war be ended, on the premise that the kingdom has no remaining claim to the Tier 20 planet. In accordance with Chapter 6 Section 2 of the Empire's Articles of War: a war between vassal states must have and maintain a valid casus belli. The new borders place kingdom territory too far away from the original war claim to justify their continued involvement. Therefore, I ask that both wars be concluded."

The Colonel nodded. "As I have confirmed the noble's willing allegiance change, we can move forward. The law does state as much. In the absence of higher interference, I, Colonel Thorne of the Imperial Army, as His Eternal Grace's most senior representative present, confirm that the Kingdom of Seven Suns no longer has sufficient connection to the Tier 20 planet to stake a legal claim. Therefore, the real war between the vassal states is declared over, and ownership of the contested Tier 20 planet is awarded to the Alliance of Allied Queens."

The queen's smile widened, but Thorne held up a finger. "However, the Pather war is a separate matter. The casus belli for this was an Imperial Mandate directly from His Eternal Grace, which is independent of the larger war for the Tier 20 planet. Unless the Emperor himself revokes said mandate, the Pather war will not conclude until at least one of the victory or dissolution conditions set forth has been met."

For a heartbeat, Queen Diana paused, before shrugging and glaring at Albert's father. "As my daughter will soon conquer your kingdom's second-to-last city, why don't you just surrender and save yourself the shame of a protracted defeat."

King Brice smirked outwardly, but on the inside, he was fuming. His traitorous little bitch of a daughter had sided with the enemy. Worse yet, she had seduced a flock of his nobles over to her side as well.

He didn't care about the kingdom one whit, and had one foot out the door anyway, in preparation of leaving it altogether. He was ready to reap his rewards from the Empire for expanding his territory, and, by proxy, the Empire's land.

That reward would compensate him for the five millennia of stalled advancement. The main factors regarding his compensation were the quality and quantity of the planets he subjugated under the kingdom during his expansion. In theory, his expansion efforts were sizable enough to warrant the resources required to pave his path all the way to Tier 39. Maybe even Tier 40 if he was lucky.

With his firstborn's treason, his expansion rating would probably be slashed down by half, if not more.

His reward would be equally reduced.

Taken away from *him*.

No one had taken *anything* from him, not since he had ascended to the throne. He was the one who took from others.

How dare they.

He stared at his daughter.

How dare she?

The anger blazed like a coal, and he was already planning his revenge; how he would kill his daughter and any queens he could get his hands on. After ceding the throne and Tiering up, he would lodge a long-term stay in a rift, using the excuse that he needed a few decades of seclusion to settle himself.

It was a common enough practice that no one would question it. To avoid blowback from the Empire, he would need to change his identity. That would necessitate changing his face and destroying his AI before absorbing a new one. But, after a few years, he could exit the rift with no one the wiser.

Then, he'd stalk the chaotic space around the queendom, kill his daughter at the first opportunity, and start picking off the remaining queens at his convenience. His cultivation was only a breath away from Tier 36, which meant he'd overwhelm any single ruler with it alone, not even taking into account his combat prowess.

After all, people went missing in chaotic space all the time. If he destroyed his AI for a second time after he finished, there would be nothing to connect him to their disappearances.

But for now, he needed that reward from Madam Renaissance. Anything crafted by her was worth far more than the slots to advance given by the Empire. That item would be the lever he would use to fight above his Tier and advance through the last few Tiers faster.

He just needed to reach Tier 45 and complete his Aspect. Then, he could ascend to new lands and advance farther.

Grow stronger.

Before leaving, he wanted to twist the knife. Spread some distrust.

With his best shit-eating grin for Diana, he faced his useless youngest son and ordered, "Detonate the bombs."

Sara noticed Albert's repeated shocks and felt terrible. The naked confusion when he saw his sister on their side made her feel even worse.

She was contemplating how their relationship could advance past this when the king's words froze her brain in its tracks.

"Detonate the bombs."

What bombs?

Albert swallowed hard and looked to Colonel Thorne. She followed his gaze to where the Colonel glared daggers at the king. The soldiers around him flickered away. A slew of Army announcements arrived through her AI. None of which were good.

The general order to stand still and halt fighting for immediate evacuation caused her stomach to roll.

The king backhanded Albert and repeated himself. "I said detonate them! That means now! Not when you feel like it."

Without so much as a ripple of power, a shorter woman with finger length, midnight dark hair appeared across from where the Colonel stood creating a square.

With a purring voice, she asked the king, "Are you not willing to wait for the evacuation to finish before enacting your plan? The kills will still be rewarded without the need for bloodshed."

Albert's father spat off to the side, "It's mostly kingdom and queendom personnel. The few thousand Pathers are an acceptable loss. Deaths are expected with this war."

The woman, who Sara couldn't feel at all, just cocked her head as if she was studying a particularly interesting specimen before dissecting it. Her pose held for a long moment before a flare of light, like a new sun rising over the horizon, drew Sara's attention away.

When she looked back, the woman faded away without a ripple of power. But from her place in the sky, Sara witnessed millions of people pop into existence at once around the neutral city. Her AI was too overwhelmed to identify them all, but her gut told her that this was *everyone* from both sides in the war.

The kingdom and queendom sides were intermingled, but if the woman had moved close to forty-two million people at once, it was a massively impressive feat in and of itself. Sara instantly knew that this was the woman who had so casually injured her mother and left behind a wound so dire that only the queen could survive it…as merely a warning.

Queen Diana said that only a true powerhouse could have managed it so flawlessly, and that it was a display of power like none other.

Considering that the woman hadn't reprimanded the king, Sara feared that she may side with him, and possibly interfere with the queendom's expansion. But the woman was just gone.

The total death tolls rolled into Sara's AI, and she blanched. Nearly seventy-five percent of her troops were registered as "dead". Even the city that the kingdom had only held for days was obliterated.

Her only city left standing was their port city. The one that was locked down, and actively besieged.

Sara's mother cursed at the king, "You would set explosives that large? And you added depleted copper to make them dirty bombs? Are you insane?"

Hearing 'dirty bombs' drew her up. Sara had to look up what depleted copper was. Her AI reported it as a byproduct of mana enriched copper, which was unusually common on this planet. The list of side effects was long enough that she had to scroll for quite a while. But the short of it was, anyone who was unlucky enough to breathe the stuff in would be facing chronic mana problems, depending on the severity of the exposure. It could also linger in the air and soil for decades.

Huge swaths of the planet were now uninhabitable.

The smug bastard smiled and said, "I'll accept your surrender now." He obviously took great pleasure in throwing her mother's words back at her.

Diana just shrugged. "So be it. We lose the Pather war. With most of our troops dead and our final city locked down, Prince Albert only needs to blockade the entrances to the central city. He'll easily be able to hold the planet for the required month. I'm not too prideful to admit defeat. The Alliance of Allied Queens officially surrenders in the *Pather War*."

Sara's mother nodded to Albert. "Well played, young man. I—"

The king's laughter boomed "You think this sniveling idiot had anything to do with this!? No, I wouldn't trust him to empty a boot filled with water even if I told him the instructions were on the heel. I ordered this at the start because I didn't trust the little idiot to win himself! If it wasn't for the blood test, I'd have thought his mother was sleeping around. He's worthless."

For the first time, the king looked for Cori. He actually smiled kindly at her. "No, I only have one heir. My only true daughter. The only one willing to do anything for power. As is proper." He laughed, and this time it was deep and sounded genuine. "No, Cori is the only one of my spawn who measured up. Most of my children ended up as only whining pups, but she's a wolf like me. Vicious, and willing to do anything to seize what she desires. I knew of her plot long ago, when the other contenders froze her out of the throne. It was only a question of when she would make her move."

Sara turned enough to see Cori look nauseous, but the king kept talking, "And you, my once nobles. Did you think I wasn't aware of your little plot? No, I knew, and it's why I was willing to poison this planet. What do I care for a wrecked world I won't have to deal with?"

Diana cut in, "You should care, because you violated half a dozen treaties forbidding deliberately harming habitable worlds. They'll have you slaving away in an asteroid belt for this."

This time, the king pointed at the now returned Colonel Thorne. "That's a stretch! No, ask him. When a war is declared, the planet's *current* habitability rating is locked in until the war's conclusion, to keep the rules of war from swinging with the population of soldiers. This shithole was still well under the population threshold needed to be considered an inhabited planet at that time, and so it remains 'uninhabited'. I can do anything I want to an uninhabited planet. They are explicitly outside of the rules."

He looked back as he turned away and called over his shoulder, "Oh, and do watch out for my little daughter. She won't be content with last place. Eventually she'll start picking you all off. One by one. I would know, since that's how I ascended to *my* throne, after all."

With a final laugh, he vanished.

Albert hovered over to Thorne's side. He hadn't taken the king's disparaging of his abilities well. His dejection was mirrored in Cori, who looked physically ill.

Sara thought over the early parts of the war and started to piece things together.

Albert had spent a reckless number of points on mana, which she now knew went toward charging those massive mana bombs. They must have been ruinously expensive, which explained the discrepancy in spending that her side had noticed.

It also answered where Olivia had come from. A strategic mind like hers should have been making waves much sooner. After the first week of the war, her and her noble liege had barely been seen before they vanished off her spies' radar. Her intelligence officers had written them off as a lazy noble and his retinue treating the war like a vacation. If they were in charge of digging the hiding spots for the bombs, that would explain what they'd actually been up to.

There was just one thing she still didn't understand. None of that explained how her earth mages hadn't discovered any of the bombs. When they took each city, large portions had to be completely rebuilt by them. The mages should have felt the lingering signs of other earth mages' work.

It made so little sense, she had to ask Albert.

"I don't understand how you planted the bombs. I just don't get it." Her message was private enough, as she asked through their AIs instead of in the open.

He replied through the same method, without meeting her eyes. "Mundane digging teams. No magical residue to give them away. We also put the bombs under the teleport pads. No one but the army is dumb enough to mess with them. And they knew of the plans beforehand and didn't interfere."

Albert looked at his hands. Even from where she stood a hundred feet away, she saw his hands tremble as he clenched them into a fist. But it didn't stop the shaking, only increased it.

Sara might have lost the Pather war, but she wouldn't switch places with Albert for anything, not if it took her mother treating her like that.

That was far too cruel.

"He just said those things to hurt you. He was just trying to be cruel."

Albert shook his head. "I don't know. Was he? I just leaned into his plan. I made excuses to myself that you wouldn't be willing to siege any of my cities if you found out, so I let you take the first city. Maybe if I had played my hand better, I could have won on my own. My side may have won, but I don't feel like a winner. I'm just tired."

He looked to the side at the Colonel, and a second later, he vanished.

Sara turned to her mother, where she stood with Cori. The newest queen had composed herself again and looked no more shaken than she had when they first arrived. The only difference was she had a frigid edge to her now.

Sara only knew the woman in passing. They had spoken only once, at a private dinner several years back. So, she might be wrong, but Sara suspected that the king's parting words had marred Cori as much as Albert.

Most of what she knew about the new queen was second-hand through her mother, but everyone knew Cori hated her father with a burning passion. She could understand why, after only interacting with the man once. He publicly demeaned Albert, and even went as far as to hit him.

In public, no less. The abuse was no doubt far worse in private.

That level of disrespect was hard to believe. Her mother never publicly reprimanded her, let alone physically assaulted her. Considering the level of thirty Tier strength discrepancy, keeping a blow nonlethal required a minuscule margin of error. The slightest slipup would leave his son in pieces.

King was almost asking for an accident to happen. Or simply didn't care.

With nothing else to do, Sara began organizing her people. The planet needed to be secured. The queendom might have lost the Pather war, but they had won the real war, so this planet was theirs by proxy.

A mountain of work needed to be completed, starting with quarantining the contaminated areas around the cities that had been hit with depleted copper.

Hopefully, her mother would step in to assist in the clean-up. Otherwise, large swaths of the planet would remain dangerous for decades. The army reported the wind patterns to her and expected fallout zones. The predictions were troubling. The city locations had been selected to maximize rift access, but now they were untraversable wastelands. The rifts themselves would be unaffected, but they were nearly impossible to safely reach for now.

With more and more messages piling up, Sara asked her mother to send her back to her headquarters.

Overall, today was a cause for celebration. Despite losing the Pather war, the queendom had a new queen, and a new Tier 20 planet.

The future looked bright.

Alyssa stared blankly into the sky as the recording played through her AI.

The betrayal and treason were hardly news to her. She had caught wind of that early in the Pather war. Or more accurately, she had been approached by the queendom early in the war with an offer. If she fed them critical information, there would be a permanent spot in the queendom for her.

Initially, Alyssa had refused the offer off hand. Spies took on massive risk while being largely expendable. She refused to needlessly put herself in such a precarious position. Plus, massive effort had gone into establishing good connections in the kingdom. Among this generation, her information network ranked second to only the prince's, despite being born to the lower nobility. Losing all that work for a 'spot' in the queendom? No, that pitiful reward didn't remotely justify the price.

On top of that, there was all the effort that went into creating contacts among the independent crafters and various Pathers, too. If word got out she had been a spy, they would assume she was only using them to sabotage the kingdom and the trust she built up would sour. No, she had worked too hard to build her position in the kingdom to lose it all for so little gain.

Then, the letter from her parents arrived. Once again, they were trying to sell her off. The pretext of her being able to approve her suitors was fading away with each attempt. Eventually, she might just disappear in the night and her parents would publicly announce she'd accepted a marriage offer outside the kingdom.

After careful deliberation, she realized she was running out of time to escape her parent's machinations and decided to throw her lot in with the queendom. It would take more work to rebuild her social standing, but she was confident that she could make it happen. With her access to kingdom information networks and her own rumor mill, she could earn enough political clout to gain a better starting position when she officially flipped sides.

That same night, she had gotten plastered in an attempt to make her decision easier to swallow. With one message to Amber, her future was set in motion. Immediately afterwards, she panicked and resorted to drinking herself into a stupor to dull the feelings. She had given up everything she knew for an even greater unknown, with only blind hope to comfort her.

Ending up in Liz's room was more of an accident than on purpose. Alyssa had just needed to move, and her desire to avoid all of the people she decided to betray led her to Liz's room.

That night, she feared that she had slipped up, but Liz hadn't seemed to mention that she had called the kingdom *losers* to anyone. She kept a wary eye out for the following few days, but either Liz hadn't picked up on the slip or she just hadn't cared enough to report it.

Which was why she didn't balk at the news that she would be killed in the assassination wave, after giving Sara the hidden location of Albert's meditation room and making sure the woman had an entrance to the secure building.

All of her work was now gone. On both sides. She had burned her bridges with the kingdom by betraying them, all to escape into the queendom away from her parents' authority. But even that work went up in smoke. Her parents were *here*, still with her under their thumb. There was just no winning, or no escape at the very least.

She stared up at her parents with horror and disgust, as the implications started to settle in.

They had long been planning to jump ship without informing her. It made everything feel so futile. If she had remained loyal to the kingdom, she would still have been forced to join them in the queendom anyway. No one would trust the daughter of two traitors.

Even with her AI to prove that she hadn't known about the treason, they would always suspect her of being a plant. She would never be trusted and would be under constant surveillance.

From the very start, her parents' opportunistic cowardice had screwed her over once again.

Her only hope was that the goodwill she had earned with Princess Sara might be enough to prevent any marriages without her consent.

Alyssa was a peacock. She wasn't necessarily choosy about her future mate, unlike what her parents claimed. They just had to meet her criteria. At least, not really. Was it so much to ask for someone who was beautiful and powerful in their own right? Someone *she* chose.

She didn't even mind if they had other spouses. The company might even be nice. She could share, so long as she was number one.

What she wanted to avoid was being stuck in some loveless marriage of convenience, like her parents had. She intended to stick it out with her spouse forever—none of those timed contract marriages.

Is that too much to ask for?

Alyssa didn't think so, but her parents waved away all of her concerns as the pointless whining of a child. She figured it was because neither of them had a strong bloodline and didn't feel her instincts. They didn't feel the pull to act as the primal, unthinking portion of your brain guiding them.

Her mother's eyes met hers, and after nudging her father, the two of them started to fly down to where she stood. Her stomach dropped as they, and the inevitable fate they would press onto her, once again loomed over her.

Juni had already run off after Albert's scolding from the king was broadcast to everyone, and she was thoroughly alone in the mass of people. She didn't feel like she belonged to either side.

Her mother landed gracefully, with all the bearing that someone flying with their Concept would have. Or it would have been, if it wasn't so obvious that she was trying to hide the flying device around her waist. Her father mirrored her mother's movements, and they settled down with faux smiles and flares of their power to clear a space for themselves.

"Oh, good, we were worried that you would struggle with making a connection when we changed sides. It was gratifying to hear that you had already jumped ship. It also smooths a lot of our hurdles in introducing you to a new generation of suitors. While this switch will be a benefit to us in the long run, we'll have to start making alliances. We..."

Her father only nodded along as he added the occasional, "Good, good." His attention was more on a Tier 15 noble who flew under her own power. Alyssa had no idea if he was talking about her taking the queendom's side, or the woman's body.

Her mother must have noticed, but she said nothing. As usual.

Alyssa's mind raced in circles that turned into ruts. She tried to find a way to use this to her favor, when Liz slipped away from her team, deliberately showing her back to Alyssa's parents.

Her bearing was tight, as was her posture, suggesting Liz was bringing news someone didn't want to hear. She had seen that expression enough in their various meetings and verbal duels. It usually meant some good fun, but now Alyssa didn't know if she could handle someone else kicking her while she was down.

Alyssa's mother moved forward to continue their conversation when Liz started speaking and halted her with her voice.

"This wasn't how I expected the war to go. Or, for you to have been a part of a larger plot to change sides." The redhead looked at her parents with a withering glance that took all of them aback. "Or for your parents to be such pieces of shit."

Alyssa stood up straighter at that direct provocation. Pather or not, that was an insult few nobles could let pass without a response.

Her mother opened her mouth, but her father barked out, "Now, you listen here..."

Liz ignored them, but Alyssa didn't miss Matt shifting his weight and taking a subtle ready stance. The rest of their team fanned out slightly, but it would do them little good. Even as worthless as her parents were, they were still Tier 14.

No Tier 6 could fight through that much of a power gap.

It was touching in a way. Alyssa knew that they weren't doing it for her, but seeing others disagree with her parents' attitude felt good.

"I recognized my owed favor to you after our little talk, but we never had the opportunity to make that even. Thankfully, I prepared for such an opportunity."

Liz coughed slightly, and a woman appeared out of nowhere.

Power radiated off her nearly see-through skin, and Alyssa's bloodline resonated with the woman's power.

She spoke with a whispery voice that was somehow lulling and grating to Alyssa's ears and spirit at the same time.

"I am recruiter Felicia, Tier 22 of Red Feather Academy, the Beast Kingdom's preparatory school for exceptional youths. I am here to offer you a full scholarship. Our program will take you to the peak of Tier 14, and there are classes to help you find your own Concept. We boast a nearly seventy-five percent success rate for our charges discovering their own Concepts while enrolled. After our unluckier charges leave our halls, they still have a ninety percent success rate, through the skills we teach and connections they make while walking our illustrious halls."

At the slight pause, Alyssa shook her head. She didn't want to be under someone's thumb with that large of a favor. The statistics were also probably carefully selected and curated to show such high percentages. Even seventy percent of people getting their Concepts was unheard of.

Still, she wanted in.

She expected that Liz might have gotten her this little opportunity, but the cost might be untenable. Nothing was truly free.

"I can't afford the price that comes with someone offering that."

Felicia nodded slightly and grinned, revealing thin black needle-like teeth. "A perfectly astute first observation. A young lady should always be wary of the potential unspoken price of any gifts. But no, this favor isn't one that comes with a price tag. Possibly the only such one you'll ever encounter in your life. Your sponsorship comes directly from Queen Mara herself. Considering she funds most of the school herself, she is allocated a number of spots per year to give away however she desires. There is a standard contract you can have reviewed, but there is explicitly no repayment clause."

Alyssa doubted that it was as simple as that but changed her view of Liz. This wasn't a favor equal to her helping Liz set up the Pathers Union. If she took this favor, she'd be firmly in the woman's debt.

"Why? And how?" She needed to know before seriously considering the offer despite how tempting it would be to jump in feet first.

Liz shrugged. "The why is rather hard to explain, and less important at the moment. *How,* on the other hand, is quite easy. I'm a young Phoenix with an exceptionally pure bloodline. When my Talent came to light, I was concerned that it might present dangerous complications. So, my family requested an evaluation from Queen Mara. She has a well-known soft spot for Phoenix children and granted our request. I met her at that time."

Liz shrugged as if that wasn't a monumental occurrence, but Alyssa figured that it made sense, given they were both Phoenixes. She could imagine the woman's bloodline allowing her to meet someone so powerful and above her station.

"Her Majesty told me to message her if I ever needed anything. Considering she offered me a position in this very school, I figured I might be able to get you a spot in my stead. I never wanted it, but I suspected you might be interested, so…"

The Tier 22 nodded. "Once we were made aware of you, your bloodline, and your other"—she drew out the word with a hiss, as if she was searching for the right thing to say next but Alyssa felt that it was purely for dramatic effect—"achievements. Once you came to our attention through more standard means, the academy would have extended a scholarship offer anyway. Perhaps not a full ride, but the amount would have been substantial by its own merit—your merit."

Alyssa swallowed. If they knew of her playing both sides, they might have been watching her for quite a while. That was unsettling.

Liz finished off with a half-smile, half-shrug. "Now, back to the why. I thought that it would fuck over all of your scheming and planning, while also clearing our favor. It's everything you wanted, while rendering the networks and connections you've made over the years useless. I know how much you care about those things." The smirk grew slightly evil as she added, "And I don't think you're ready for the level of pettiness and layers of intrigue you'll find there. It made me happy to imagine you getting eaten alive by people who are a million times better at these little games than you."

Alyssa had no idea what to think about that. She knew—or she *thought* she knew—Liz pretty well. But even she had to admit, that was quite the devious gift. It was everything Alyssa ever wanted, while, just as predicted, also ruinous to every last one of her plans.

A favor equal parts gracious and cunning.

It was also a challenge. Alyssa didn't fear the others at the school. She wasn't arrogant enough to think that she'd be better than them, but she knew that she'd be able to hold her own. And if the recruiter was to be believed, her backer was Mara, the queen of beasts herself. No one would push things too far, even if she fucked up and got herself on the wrong side of a bad bargain.

Alyssa could see herself thriving in that environment, and she tingled at the thought of battling equals.

It was thrilling.

Even at its worst, decades of work beat a lifetime as a broodmare.

Looks of shock and horror slowly crept across her parents' faces at the realization that their greatest prize might escape their clutches. Seeing that only sweetened the deal.

She just nodded. "I'll take it. I—"

Felicia cut her off. "Good! Now that you have decided, we must be off immediately. Your current education is years and six Tiers behind your peers. We will need to work on forming good habits and erase all these bad ones. As Elizabeth said, your peers will eat you alive if you enter as you are now."

A ship descended from the sky, hovering over the crowd, and detaching a small platform, which swooped down to pick up the two women, "I only have a month and a half while we travel to personally get you up to snuff. That isn't nearly enough time. First, we need to…"

Alyssa carefully listened as she glanced back down. Liz had a smile that said Alyssa would hate what was to come.

Liz was wrong; good or bad, this was exactly where she wanted to be. She tried to convey that in her return smirk.

The Pather just laughed and waved as their platform rose into the air.

"And if you want to send messages with just a look, you need to be far more subtle. You don't need to shout with your face. It's uncivilized and you give far too much away. Instead, you should have…"

Matt watched Alyssa leave with poorly hidden amusement. The fact that Liz had called her mother to get Alyssa the scholarship, while presenting the exact same tale about only knowing the queen, was quite funny when he knew the truth.

Having been on the other side of that lie, he could appreciate the delicate web of truths that Liz had spun to give the impression she had.

He looked at the grinning Liz and asked, "Seems like she won that round, no?"

Liz shook her head. "No, not at all. She thinks she's going to do fine, but I was serious when I said those other kids are going to eat her alive. Everyone who enters the Academy thinks they're hot shit. To make matters worse, the cliques have already formed for her year group. She's going to have an awful few decades."

Alyssa's parents turned as one to Liz, and the woman roared, "How dare you!? You little viper! I'll have your head for this!"

She started to lunge, but her husband blocked her and frantically started talking her down.

He at least caught that Liz had a good relationship with one of the royals. Attacking her was suicide, and he kept repeating that to his wife. The army was still here and watching, after all.

With that dealt with, Matt and his team started to move into the neutral city with the rest of the crowd. It felt odd. Even with the queendom technically losing the war, they celebrated on their new planet. Meanwhile, the kingdom troops were in poor spirits.

Matt saw Conor and the twins huddled up and whispered together as they walked through the crowd.

Finally, when they had just exited the tunnel through the outer wall, Annie swung an arm over his and Liz's shoulders and asked, "So, what are your plans?"

Matt shrugged. Right now, they were just waiting for their management team to be created and to start directing them. They didn't really have control of their travel plans for the foreseeable future. His speculation of what Annie wanted was confirmed when she asked, "We're going to form a permanent team. After Tier 3, our

Sponsor gave us permission to add anyone we wanted. We want to officially or unofficially team up with you three."

Emily and Conor nodded along.

Matt was touched. They may have met through random chance, but they had become good friends. He just didn't know how to turn them down.

Liz took care of it first, but through their group chat. "We appreciate that offer. We really do. But we have a management team waiting for us in the wings somewhere."

Emily cocked an eyebrow while saying, "I don't know what that is?"

Matt filled them in. "After Tier 10, if you show enough potential to excel on the Path, a support team is put together for you. They help you press your advantages and shore up weaknesses. Seekers, or people with seeker-like abilities, can get it early if they can fight above their weight class. Think about my mana Concept in terms of charging rifts. It lets us advance without the normal time restrictions, so we were offered the team early to prevent us from falling into a rut. It came with strings attached, though. I'd love to have you guys join, but our path is a lot more restrictive now."

They didn't press, which Matt was grateful for.

Annie punched his arm as she laughed out loud. "Well, we'll expect great things in the future then. It's not like we won't see each other again. The three of us are close to finishing our Concepts, and once we have them, we're going to race ahead."

They idly chatted before they separated with hugs all around. The trio were taking one of the soon to be leaving Empire ships out to the other side of the Empire. They had agreed on hitting a Tier 12 planet for the abundance of Tier 7 rifts. They wanted to get used to being Tier 7 before they moved to the much more profitable Tier 8 rifts that would drop skill shards regularly.

Matt had little worry about them running into issues. They were strong individually. Together, they would make a fantastic delve team.

They wanted to stay and chat, but their ship was going to be the first one to leave. Their scheduled departure time was quickly approaching, as the ship was going to the farthest reaches of the Empire.

Hugs and slaps were once again shared as the new trio turned and raced away. Matt was watching them go when half a million points were transferred from Annie, with a note of thanks for the loan.

Matt smiled as he brought up his own points total.

Prior Total (last updated 24 days ago): 365,751 points.

TEAM MERITS:

(Calculated for Tier 6 Combatant).

- Enemy vassal killed, Tier 5. Worth 1 point. Performed 541 times.
- Enemy vassal killed, Tier 6. Worth 5 points. Performed 20,274 times.
- Enemy vassal killed, Tier 7. Worth 25 points. Performed 748 times.
- Enemy leader assassinated, Tier 7. Worth 50,000 points. Performed 1 time.
- Items and equipment looted but returned. Assigned worth: 50,447 points.
- Assisted in the elimination of a critical enemy strategic asset, siege mage. Worth 5,000 points. Performed 1 time.
- Eliminated enemy general(s) in the middle of a major engagement (each side >500K units). Reward: 1.4x multiplier to all team merits.

PERSONAL MERITS:

(Calculated for Tier 6 Combatant)

- Enemy vassal killed, Tier 5. Worth 1 point. Performed 541 times.
- Enemy vassal killed, Tier 6. Worth 5 points. Performed 20,262 times.
- Enemy vassal killed, Tier 7. Worth 25 points. Performed 732 times.
- Victory achieved! Top 100 contributor. 500,000 points.

ARMY MERITS:

- Successfully seize command of vassal kingdom forces. Leadership rating: poor. 1,500 points.

- Lead a long-term harassment campaign against a superior invading army. Reward: 1.3x multiplier to all merits (applied after other multipliers).
- Took charge and led remaining troops while infighting delayed proceedings. Reward: 1.5x multiplier to all merits (applied after other multipliers).

UNACHIEVED MERITS: For reference purposes only.

- Conquer the final enemy city. Reward: 2.0x multiplier to all merits.

SUMMARY OF GAINS:

- **Team Merits:**
- **Raw Total:** 226,058
- **Team Multiplier:** 1.4x
- **Category Total:** 316,523
- **Personal Merits:**
- **Raw Total:** 620,151
- **Personal Multiplier:** N/A
- **Category Total:** 620,151
- **Combined Merits:**
- **Sub-Total:** 936,632
- **Total Multiplier:** 1.8x
- **Grand Total:** 1,688,713

New Gains: 1,688,713 points.
New Total: 2,054,464 points.
Points transferred from teammate: 500,000.
New Total: 2,554,464 points.
Pather Team Ranking (Kingdom of Seven Suns): 1st place.
Estimated Daily Stipend: N/A.

He had well over two million points now. If [Cracked Breach] was still on the market, he would have bought that without a second thought. But now, he really didn't know what he wanted. He knew it should be things that he currently couldn't afford on the Empire Market, which meant Tier 14 skills, or other obscure skills that were made cheaper for the war.

But as he had told Annie, Conor, and Emily, they had a management team that should be here shortly, and it was prudent to wait for their input. There might be some super underrated skill that he was overlooking.

Matt and Liz stopped by Kelley's to say goodbye. The man was ecstatic about the end of the war, and what it meant for the expansion of his craft.

"Me and a number of other crafters are staying. Really, it's most of us. We will work for the queendom for a while, with the condition that we get first dibs on the rift that makes these." He rubbed his ring. "It's a fantastic deal."

The older man brightened. "Speaking of which, we're starting our own little informal guild-like structure. It's mostly to just trade unique mana types. You'll join, won't you?"

Matt was already looking over the sent-over information and nodded as he accepted. The rules were fairly straightforward and fair. Mana types were rated and shared but had to be posted on the open forum for everyone to browse. Selling was done in between the parties involved, and any restrictions could be applied.

"This is perfect. I'm happy to add to it. I need lots of weird types to experiment with."

Kelley grinned. "Oh, I know. With the war over, the queendom is happy to host a number of Pather crafters and is already moving resources over. We'll be making things with nearly no profit margin, but that's fine for now."

Matt knew the resource in question was more personal mana stones that could be imprinted to hold a mana type. Kelley and all the other crafters would need massive numbers of them, even in a place as small as the queendom.

"Let me know if any more good growth items pop out of the rift."

Kelley laughed. "That's what we're hoping for. It's not even close to likely, but we're hoping nonetheless."

They chatted for a few more minutes before Kelley got called into a meeting and had to go.

The three of them were moving down the street, when suddenly, they were floating in the air amongst the clouds. Aster yowled at the lack of ground. She tried to jump into his arms, but was only able to spin herself, which only increased the yowling.

"Good day, children." A woman appeared with short, black hair so dark that it looked purple. She had slitted, gleaming purple eyes, and smiled at them with two others flanking her.

She gestured and said, "I'm Luna, your new team manager."

Seeing no reaction, she pointed at a man who held up a sign that had, 'Hello! It is good to meet you!' written on it.

"This is Kurt. He's mute, so you'll need to read what he says. If you want to use AI, that's fine, but only as long as I'm not around. Kurt is my assistant, and he's damn good at his job."

The short woman pointed at the remaining blonde woman. "This is April. She is our liaison. In a normal management team, she would be the one who interfaces with you, while we—" Luna gestured between herself and Kurt, "—work with a number of different teams."

She shook her head. "I don't work that way. I only work with one team at a time, and most of your primary training will come directly from the two of us. April will be helping with our scheduling, PR, and making you new public personas. None of those are easy. She will also be taking care of your day-to-day needs. That doesn't mean she'll be wiping your asses for you, so don't push her willingness to help."

Kurt pulled up a sign asking, "Can you please share your Talent information with us?"

Matt was surprised that they didn't have access already, but the mute man shook his head while Luna explained, "Talent permissions are *absolute*. Nobody can see your talent records unless you allow them to. Without it, we're limited to vague guesses from feeling your spirit."

He, Liz, and Aster silently communicated for a few seconds. They came to the agreement that if they were doing this, they had to do it right, and their trainers would be better with hard numbers instead of guesswork.

Together, they shared their information, which caused quiet murmuring and note scribbling from Kurt and Luna.

Finally, the two came up for air and Kurt wrote out, "Matt, it's good that your mana is a true double. We feared from our observations that it would drop off. It gives you amazing versatility after a few Tiers worth of growth, and you'll eventually make one monster of a mage."

Luna interjected as he flipped pages and started to write, "But that's a problem as well. You'll need to put in even more time to grow your skills and learn how to use them, but this isn't a bad problem to have. It just means that you need to put in more work."

Kurt flipped up his board. "Mana Concentration will hurt you going forward, but if you can recreate that rift again, we can handle this. It will be expensive and time consuming, but we don't want to let you fall too far behind on that."

A page flip showed the next text. "Mana control is something else you'll need to work on. It's going to get harder and harder as your mana pool starts to expand massively, and in sudden jumps. We're also looking into ways for you to deal with your mana doubling issue, but it's unlikely to be a problem in the long run. We have a few potential solutions lined up, but they're not even relevant until at least Tier 25."

Luna then pointed to Liz. "Your Talent is more straightforward, but it has potential that Matt's lacks. You should be trying to understand and truly be one with blood. Also, you should be trying more unorthodox skills like [Fire Sprite]. That was a good roll of the dice."

Kurt held up a sign for Aster. "You are fairly standard, but your Concept is a variation on the normal ice bloodline, which is useful. You can do anything you wish to with ice or water magic. That gives you less room to grow, but you can become a master of your element."

Luna held up a finger. "Speaking of growing."

Around the woman, dozens of paper notepads appeared and then hovered before the three of them in piles. Matt's was taller than himself, and from what he could see, the other piles were just as large. To make matters worse, the notes were written in a small but neat hand that filled every available spot on the visible pages.

"These are the notes that I've accumulated over the past year of watching you three."

She pointed a finger at Matt, with her tone turning a bit more severe and chastising. "You have too many options and versatility in combat. While your mana pool limits you now, it won't forever. We need to do a lot of work with both your melee and magical combat if you don't want to be shoved into a dark hole and forced to power a planet. Or twenty."

Luna seemed to ripple as she appeared in front of Aster, who was between Matt and Liz.

"And you, miss 'wiggles her butt a lot.' It's to set your grip, not to show off. You need to pick a role in the group and start working toward it. You can't remain in a backpack forever."

Aster cut the older woman off with a yip and a growl. "I like my backpack! It's comfy."

Luna grinned evilly. "I don't care. If you want to be useful, you'll have to *be useful*. You have a massive advantage with your intelligence, and we need to press it for everything it gives us."

She turned to Liz. "And you. You're a short to medium range mage, with your boy toy and the glove. Good idea to make that, by the way. That was a creative use of your time, though you got shockingly lucky as well." She nodded back to Matt and Aster. "You don't have the problems that most other elemental mages have. You carry your resources with you everywhere and can just kill something to get the ball rolling."

Liz opened her mouth, but Luna held up a finger that demanded no interruptions.

"You need to decide if you want to remain a mage or turn into a more melee-oriented style. Or, you might tread the path of both, so you can be more versatile and cover more situations."

Liz raised her own finger in question, to which Luna nodded her assent.

"I was just wondering who 'G' was. The first message you sent was signed 'G,' and none of your names start with a G." She shrugged as she added, "Seems weird."

Luna barked a laugh, and Matt didn't miss Kurt crack a smile as well.

"I was afraid that you might recognize my name. When you didn't react after I introduced myself, I realized your parents must not have told you about me. Even if you did, I could have worked with that. But really, if you knew who I was at my first message, you would have known that I'd be watching you the entire time. I didn't want that."

All three of them must have had looks of confusion because Luna grinned wide, with far too many teeth showing.

"I've been retired for a while, but I was your parents' manager a long time ago."

Liz groaned. "Does that mean they'll be hanging around? I have a deal with them to not show up until Tier 10. But I wouldn't put it past them to say that they're visiting you to see me."

"Ha! No, not a chance. Your parents wouldn't even be on the same planet as me if they could avoid it. Last I saw them, they ruined my nap with one of their little foreplay sessions, so I made your mother play heat lamp and your father water my garden for a few years. Haven't seen them since."

Liz's eyes grew wider and wider as Luna spoke, until it was almost comical.

"I'm honestly surprised that your parents never complained about me."

Liz leaned forward and laughed. "Oh, they did. I know that story, but all they called you was that 'bird eating bitch'."

"Ah, yes, your mother was still a mouthwatering little flame sparrow when I took on their team. Catching and eating the other birds around her proved to be great motivation for her to train harder." She caught Aster's eyes. "Will I have to do the same with foxes?"

Aster shook her head violently and deflated.

Luna turned back to Liz. "Your parents were giant failures, which I intend to rectify with you. They were lazy, and more concerned with goofing off. I will not tolerate that in any way, shape, or form. Not again. Not with *any* of you."

Liz shook her head. "No, this is perfect! I hate how they just gallivant around and refuse to take anything seriously. And if you being here means that they won't spy on me, I'm all for it. I'm pretty sure they have been. I've gotten the feeling of being watched more than once."

She looked to Matt, who still had reservations but about a separate topic. "So, how long have you been watching us?"

Luna shrugged. "A month or so after that investigator, whatever his name was, reported in."

Matt winced. It meant she had fully seen his Talent at work. His initial reaction was to tense up at that, but he had already shared with her the exact details. What did it matter if she watched him make rifts? Which led him to his second question. "And how often did you watch us?"

"All the time. I'm over Tier 40. I can see an ant on the other side of the planet fall off a branch while sleeping."

Matt blushed at that thought. Luna apparently understood and just smiled. "Yes, I watched you two have sex. Notebooks seventy-three and seventy-four have notes where you can improve on that for the both of you."

Matt felt himself flush to the point that his ears felt hot. He had to resist the urge to activate [Cracked Phantom Armor] to hide. Knowing that a higher Tier being could sense you was one thing. Having her critique their sex and write suggestions down was another thing entirely.

Wanting to change the topic, Matt asked "Why notebooks? Why not just send us an information packet?"

Luna grinned at the question and said, "I have some *problems* with people over-relying on their AIs, it makes you lazy and predictable." She turned to Kurt and batted a small stack of notecards out of his hands, the first of which seemed to have a transcription of what she had just been saying. "I'm not doing the full rant, we only just met. Besides, showing the cards for the speech as I say it got old after the twelfth time you did it. Try to be original."

Matt looked at April, who had been silent up to that point, and asked, "Do you know what our plans going forward are? What are we supposed to do? I don't know how a management team actually works."

April had a soft voice that carried on the wind. "I know we have a few recommendations for you but, in the end, you aren't forced to take our offers or orders. In reality, they are simply strong suggestions. I do know that they want you to travel back through the queendom, and head to a Tier 10 planet for your initial…" she hesitated for a second, "training. We found an individual that we feel can help the three of you with melee training, first and foremost. After that, we have a list of people for you to visit. With your age and Tier, Luna says that it's better to have you work on the fundamentals than to Tier up. Once we cover some bases and basics with you, I believe she intends to have you Tier up to Tier 8 rather quickly and start with your—" she glanced over at where their island was, "—rift experiments."

"What about the rewards for the war? We have quite a few points left over, but the item I wanted was bought." Matt tried to not let his longing for [Cracked Breach] leak through, but he could tell he failed.

Luna turned around and jabbed a finger at Matt. "I wouldn't have let you use the skill much, even if you had bought it. It's too strong for your current prowess. No, it's better that you didn't get it. Besides, the regular version will be better for you soon anyway."

Liz leaned forward. "Wait, did you tell Sara to buy it?"

Luna shook her head. "No. I didn't interfere in the war a single time for or against your benefit. My only actions were to observe and prevent true deaths."

That actually made Matt feel better, until Luna said, "If you want my opinion, Matt, you should buy all the Tier 8 and Tier 14 elemental manipulation skills. I don't expect you to ever get the finesse a focused mage should have, but I want you to be able to out muscle or out mana any mage in the small bit of space around you. It will help prevent you from being taken out of a fight too early. Also, get [Mana Charge] and [Mana Slash]. Stop relying on the runes residing on your sword. You're leaving too much damage on the table and, at Tier 7, you'll be able to cast them. Plus, you're wasting space on your sword that can go to enchantments there aren't skills for already. Spend your extra points on whatever you want. I don't care."

She pointed to Liz. "You need to get the same things. Keep them in your outer spirit, so they don't get changed by your Talent. You don't need to be amazing with them. Just have them. Also, get any skills you think might change to be useful."

Aster received a look that said she needed to get the same things, and from Aster's ear flick, she understood.

Luna turned back to Matt. "If you have any points left over, just trade them for Empire points, even with the awful conversion. Then buy [Ranged Heal] because the war shop is out. I intend for you to need it."

She looked down and to the side as if someone called her name, and she listened for a minute before turning back to the trio.

"As I said earlier, we will be making new identities for you all. Masks alone aren't secure enough. Also, Baxter intends to point his kids in the same direction. Treat the travel as a vacation, because it's the last one you'll get until you meet my standards or reach Tier 25 and complete the Path."

With that, they found themselves in the crowd that they had disappeared from. Matt looked around and, not seeing anyone they knew, sent a message to Melinda's team stating that they were apparently traveling together.

Taking Liz's hand in his own while carrying Aster in the other, Matt made the suggested purchases along with the repository of runes up to Tier 25.

They all made sense, and it wasn't like they couldn't afford them. Money would never be an issue, and he needed to get over that particular hangup. Buying Tier 14 skills was still out of his price range but knowing that rare Tier 8 skills sold for Tier 14 prices was enough to ensure that it was at least possible.

Add into that the things he had learned about crafting and using aspected and sub-aspected mana types for making items, he was sure that he could repeat his success with making new skills like [Copper Skin]. It was only a matter of reaching Tier 7 or Tier 8, so he could rapidly make and charge rifts to Tier 8, and guarantee skill drops.

Even with the disaster of the war ending in what felt more like a loss than the victory it was, he felt like things were looking up. They were getting a break and could relax with friends for the next few months. It was a shame that Conor, Annie, and Emily were not along for the trip, but he had the feeling that things were going to change up once again.

His life before the Path of Ascension was repetitive and dull. It had been anything but since he stepped foot out of the PlayPen.

He was looking forward to the future, no matter what it brought. They were just challenges to be overcome, and he was coming to truly believe that the three of them could triumph over anything life, the Path, or Luna threw at them.

33

Emmanuel looked around his office, lost in thought.

He had cracked thousands of healing skills, to no effect, before he started looking elsewhere.

More than one person had taken to collecting odd, cracked skills for a variety of reasons. Some did it more as a hobby, just trying to find or create unique cracks that completely changed the skills' function.

Others, people he disapproved of, used the rare and unique cracks as recruiting tools. They functioned as bribes, used to entice people that the new skills perfectly fit over to the creator's side, along with stringent contracts.

It was never illegal, but the contracts could be restrictive. They essentially stated that the person accepting the contract was given something genuinely unique and incredibly valuable. That definition allowed the skill owner to bind people to their cause nearly forever.

That was where he found the answer to his Melinda problem.

Duke Frederic Macheteuil was the cause of quite a few of the Empire's current problems. He was a part of an old house of nobility that had remained neutral when Emmanuel's grandmother took the throne from the previous dynasty.

The loyalists had all been purged or forced to ascend during his grandmother's rule. Still, her supporters and the neutral parties had been given special compensation, along with exemptions from the rules that had been implemented.

His grandmother was a monster and might have been able to give Duke Waters a run for his money. At Tier 48, she had an inspiration that pushed her to Tier 49, allowing her to kill the Emperor of the time.

The gaps between Tiers only grew more prominent as a cultivator ascended through them. The Tiers where you earned a Talent or needed a Concept were always watershed Tiers, where it was even harder to close the gap.

Grandma Agatha had been a force that few could compare to. He only had recordings of the woman, but she had dethroned a corrupt dynasty, then struck down the internal strife that nearly led to a civil war. Most of the vital Ducal families tried to seize the throne, causing chaos amidst a struggle for power.

It had come to a head when a noble had secretly met with the then slightly stronger Sects and proposed an alliance. He had convinced the Tier 50 ruling them to assist in his take-over plot, for some unknown compensation.

In an at-the-time realm shaking event, his grandmother cut the Tier 50 in half, causing him to retreat in a panic. Agatha then proceeded to cull the families that backed the coup. That event cemented the Empire as a power not to be trifled with, but it also painted a target on their back.

The Sects didn't take their loss lightly, saying that their Tier 50 was about to ascend, which he did in short order. The new Tier 50 was incredibly aggressive to the Empire, and declared nine wars on them during their thirty thousand-year reign.

Most ended in draws, with no land exchanged on either side, and only spilled blood to show for them. But in order to fund those wars with both money and bodies, his grandmother had to make several concessions to convince the remaining noble families to back her.

She instituted many new changes, which would eventually be the foundation that the Empire's success rested on. But those changes came at a cost.

In exchange for amending the Path of Ascension to allow commoners, and reducing the stringent requirements to recruit new people, she was forced to reform the tax policy and replace those funds with her own delving profits.

Preventing newly raised noble families from excluding all but their firstborns from seats of power and allowing anyone to challenge a noble to their position caused even more backlash. In response, she had to write an exemption for the nobles of that time. It declared that they, their houses, and any land they directly settled were exempt from those rules.

As was the case today, the nobles of the past subtly threatened to go to the other great powers and split away from the Empire. His grandmother could fight one Tier 50, but if there were two…

She never wanted to find out, and thus refrained from pushing the nobles too hard. A trend his father had followed. So did he, for that matter. But he was slowly trying to chip away at their power bases, and the noble families knew it.

That threat had caused Agatha to turn to the then similarly powered Conglomerate of Guilds and offer a truce, treaty, and official defensive alliance. It was rare for two of the Great Powers to ally, since they usually contested each other for territory and resources. It was rarer still for two *neighbors* to enter into an alliance, as settled land didn't need to be curated or Tiered-up. To that effect, most alliances were ones of convenience, and lasted for only a single conflict. They usually were formed to knock down a common threat or rival.

That didn't mean that the two Great Powers didn't have their differences, but their alliance had been tested, and had never faltered. Even when the Empire was at its weakest and recovering from strife caused by the multitude of changes that his grandmother implemented.

As they started to rise in his father's time, the two powers only grew closer, and the Guilds were the first to implement similar changes. They only remained the fifth great power due to a string of terrible luck. Both of their most recent territorial gains at the time had yielded nothing but low Tier worlds. The lack of any higher Tier gains caused bottlenecks in their ability to produce similarly Tiered fighters, causing apparent stagnation. Low Tier worlds had their usage, but they were only really settled to create connections to the more valuable, higher Tier worlds.

In truth, the Guilds were nipping at the Sect's heels then, and were about to overtake them in relative power, even if they were significantly smaller.

His father and the Guilds' last Tier 50 had both gone off to delve the far reaches of chaotic space, and together had found and hauled back a Tier 39 world, causing a resurgence in exploration and cooperation.

Power was what prevented the lower Tiers from breaking free and setting up their own kingdoms. Tier 50 was a hard limit in this realm, and as long as there was a single Tier 50, everyone was forced under their power.

Emmanuel was Tier 50 himself, which equated to strength that couldn't be ignored. He could kill any of his nobles without question, and easily. If he wanted them to die, they would. But it would cause the other nobles to scatter into the arms of the other Great Powers and split the Empire.

The other Great Powers were always hungry for new land, and high Tier planets were at a premium. If he pushed changes too fast, the nobles would band together and defect to one of their neighbors.

All of the compromises that his grandmother made were still causing problems today. Despite all the good his father had done, he wasn't a fighter. His grandmother chose him as her heir because of his steadfast personality, along with his ability to network and play politics.

That wasn't to say he was weak. His father was strong, but he simply wasn't the most combat-oriented cultivator. In truth, he was a seeker of middling ability at best. His abilities relied more on his honed skills, rather than Talents.

His father had made great strides in limiting the abuses of those under Tier 15, to the point that the common men lived amazing lives, free from most worries. It had inspired Emmanuel's own personal policy, that it was not the place of higher Tiers to meddle. They were guides and protectors, *The Shield of All*, not petty tyrants trying to dictate the lives of those weaker than them.

After Tier 15, rules were less enforced outside of cities, and to Emmanuel's shame, the rules were treated more like guidelines after Tier 35. He and his forebears had ensured that fighting down without being attacked first was a death sentence, but only living people could report the attacks.

It didn't help that his nobles clung to the old ways, and rarely intervened. Most believed or purported that the law of the strong was paramount, so it wasn't their place to intervene.

Two of his royals were nobles and were backed by the opposition faction while supporting noble causes. Rusty and Tur'stal had been found and backed by noble houses during their advancement, and had pushed back against any reforms that were too hampering.

Harper was deliberately neutral in all dealings, leaving Emmanuel backed solely by Mara and Leon. They were excellent friends, and steadfast in their support of his changes, but they were flakier in their duties than a fresh pastry. Getting them to show up to a meeting of royals was like pulling teeth, as if they were actively hiding.

That worked well for the nobles aligned against him, but it was also why he was able to allocate them rifts to reach Tier 48 so quickly. The nobles didn't mind his having two allies that couldn't be bothered to participate in court politics. Even his most fervent opposition wanted the Empire to remain strong, and no one could deny the couple's fighting prowess. And with Great Powers limited to having only two Tier 48s, he was happy to have them on his side.

The pair just worried more about their personal entertainment than directing their entire being to the betterment of the Empire.

Emmanuel sighed. That wasn't fair. They dedicated all of their profits from delving to him and to taxes, and their presence wasn't entirely needed at meetings, since they had standing orders to always vote with him. But it still left him at a distinct disadvantage in those meetings.

He, as Emperor, had three votes. One for each of the kingdoms he presided over, and an extra vote for being Emperor. With Mara and Leon's votes he had five, against the two from Rusty and Tur'stal, and the single abstained vote of Harper. In theory, that should allow him to push everything and anything he wanted through. But Rusty and Tur'stal's kingdoms accounted for nearly forty percent of the high Tier planets, and were far and away the largest powerbases.

It forced him to need at least their tentative support for most things. And to their credit, they were incredibly supportive of reforms that didn't affect noble power or privileges.

Duke Frederic Macheteuil was the reason he was in a pickle. The Empire had grown so large in such a short amount of time, it was already time to raise another royal to the council. Duke Frederic Macheteuil was the strongest non-royal who was interested in politics. At Tier 46, he had the strength to fill the role, and he was widely popular amongst the old blood families for his desire to retain noble power.

In one of his few mistakes, his father had given Frederic's father the dukedom of one of the outer systems, in which a Tier 35 planet was found. At first, the deal seemed terrific, as the noble family had to give up their current holding to take the new land. At the time it was a reason for celebration, but now it was a thorn in Emmanuel's side, letting Frederic campaign to be raised to a royal position.

Emmanuel's father had refused to grant the request, on the pretense of the sector not being built up enough, which Frederic and the other nobles accepted. There was a long-standing tradition to only award royal seats in areas that met the inner worlds' standards. Frederic's ancestors had used this reasoning to prevent a rival's ascension to power, so his faction couldn't balk at it now.

In an expected move, but one he couldn't prevent, they poured massive amounts of resources into the sector. They rapidly attracted settlers under Tier 15, along with quite a few higher Tiers, over to the new regions.

They even followed his laws and edicts to the letter about under Tier 15 treatment. Things were going as well as he could ask for, which was the problem. Frederic, for all his faults, wasn't an evil or stupid man. He was a supporter of the reforms that Emmanuel pushed through when he took the throne, to once again increase noble taxes so the proceeds could be reinvested into their worlds and for the Path.

What Emmanuel worried about was creating another royal that would work on the old system, making this another prime position for a corrupt noble to take over after Frederic ascended to the higher realm.

Emmanuel sighed as he debated whether it was worth it to go see the man.

In the end, he had to. He had so many useful skills for when his current hopefuls fell off the Path or participated in the Tier 10 tournament.

Melinda particularly was too valuable of a resource not to cultivate.

Her growth with her Talent was one of his highest priorities. He wished she would focus on things other than healing old age, as was her current obsession, but he wouldn't interfere. Not only would it betray his principles- he was no tyrant- it ran serious risk of stifling her, something he couldn't afford regardless.

Still, he had consistently made trips to her the moment she Tiered-up so he could get the newest version of her Talent. It was so potent, it replaced his Tier 3 in situations where he wasn't in direct combat. Assassins weren't expected, but they rarely were and could strike at any time, and the ability to save someone's life around him was too useful a power.

The skill in question was [Cracked Miasma].

[Miasma] was a Tier 20 skill that created a massive area of effect noxious gas when cast. It was formidable in and of itself, but nothing exceptional. Mostly, it was paired with more dangerous poison skills to increase their range. The skill lingered in the cast area for hours or days, depending on the initial mana cost. And unless purged, the toxins remained in the body for up to a week.

The cracked version only had one single change that made it useless for other people. It was a healing skill that acted the same way as the original skill. In theory, all AOE healing skills were amazing, but this one was as weak as it was long-lasting. While not usually a problem, healing a body already under the effect of a healing spell was dozens of times more difficult. It wasn't impossible, but it was an unnecessary added effort for subsequent healers.

Melinda's Overhealth didn't have that problem.

He had Moon check a dozen times.

For Melinda, a healing skill that lasted a week would be a game-changer. Instead of the active skill interfering with subsequent healing spells cast after the fact, any healer treating someone with the spell active inside of them would get the benefit of Overhealth. It would let Melinda cast the spell on entire armies, who could then walk through the lingering miasma and become practically immortal for the next week. He hadn't even factored in the lack of healing downtime, which could last decades at the higher Tiers.

Emmanuel needed the skill unless he wanted to wait for Matt to make a new skill with his rift experiments. But while the boy's experiments showed promise, he was unwilling to wait that long, or risk the situation with his nobles changing. While he and his people didn't know the combination Matt had used to make [Copper Skin] they could brute force it with enough mana and attempts. Mana he didn't really have the budget for.

Perhaps Alex would be able to coax it from a Rift if they knew where to look…but, no.

The Empire needed the skill.

He just didn't know how to get the skill without tipping his hand and revealing Melinda's existence or backsliding on millennia of progress. Frederic was known for his hard bargaining.

Emmanuel sent a message to his wife to let her know that he was leaving. Once she responded, he ripped through reality and into chaotic space.

For him, the angry winds of the corrosive energy weren't even an annoyance, and he could see farther than nearly anyone else through the swirls of power. Orienting himself, he plotted the most direct path to Fredric's duchy, and ignored the lines of power connecting the linked worlds. It was faster to go through space directly.

In only a month, Emmanuel was inspecting the linked worlds of this new region. With his Tier 50 perception, he could blanket and inspect half a dozen worlds and all their inhabitants at once.

He needed to change his Tier 25 Talent to one that let him split his mind into portions, allowing him to comprehend the information at a reasonable pace. But he was quite happy to see the progress.

There were no overt abuses of power, and no signs of commoners being mistreated. The worlds around him were thriving and proliferating. It was everything he could ask for.

Crime and such happened, but that was just human nature. The worst offenses he observed were recorded and sent to the proper authorities, ensuring that the guilty would be punished. There was nothing egregious to be alarmed about.

Emmanuel repeated his actions with each new world he passed during his month-long journey. It would take someone in a state of the art chaotic spaceship a year to traverse this distance, and longer if they tried under their own power, but that was a benefit of being on top.

If he wanted to, he could snuff out any of the worlds around him with a thought.

Power was dangerous, and he wondered if it would be better if there was no cultivation for the millionth time. His wife, Carissa, thought he was crazy for even trying to contemplate the idea. But he figured that if everyone was similarly weak, they would be truly equal, and no one would be able to abuse their power.

When he arrived at a bright speck of light in the void, he politely sent a strand of perception, and deliberately brushed upon the strongest perception on the planet.

He could have, with his greater power, inspected the planet without being noticed, but it was the politest way to contact someone on their home planet.

A strand of perception punched out of real space and offered an open but questioning invitation.

Emmanuel noted where Duke Frederic Macheteuil was and ripped through space to meet him in a sitting room. It was clear that he had just teleported into the space to meet Emmanuel upon his arrival, as maids were scurrying to prepare delicacies in the nearest kitchen.

Duke Macheteuil stood and bowed deeply at Emmanuel's arrival. He kept the position held as he said, "As always, it is a pleasure to receive you, my liege. My home is your home."

Emmanuel waited for the proper timing and responded in the traditional response, "Rise, my loyal retainer. I protect what is mine, either by proxy or directly. Only together does the Empire remain strong. Rise, and let us speak."

They both sat as tea was brought in, with the formalities out of the way.

This being a Tier 35 world, Emmanuel didn't have to worry about accidentally tearing an uncontrolled hole into chaotic space and destroying the planet, but he still moved with more control than Frederic.

As they sipped the tea, Frederic probed slightly. "It is always a pleasure to have you visit your grace, but I must ask if this is an official visit or a personal one."

"Both. It was time to inspect this region of my territory in preparation for integration to a kingdom. I was also looking for some practical skills in your collection."

He was trying to offer the carrot to get what he wanted, rather than the stick he was willing to use.

Using his father's Tier 50 Talent, he checked the next few seconds of time and reviewed the various possibilities in descending likelihood. Seeing nothing out of the ordinary, he observed Fredric's reactions.

The duke nodded. "I was sure you would see the progress that we've made in the last few thousand years, and grant our request in short order, but it is good that we have met your expectations."

Emmanuel wanted to scoff. The man was essentially saying it was good that Emmanuel would be forced to elevate him and this region of worlds to a proper kingdom sooner or later. Whether he liked it or not. And it wouldn't buy him any favors to do it early.

"I am glad that you and your nobles have worked so diligently and kept any excess in check."

Frederic just smiled. "We always strive to do what is best." Clearly seeing Emmanuel's disagreement, he temporized, "Not all of us are so conscious of our obligation. I do admit that, but no system is perfect. I keep a strong leash on my nobles, unlike other locations."

The Tier 46 scoffed. "There are no uncontrolled rift breaks on any planet I control."

Emmanuel nodded to the man. That was true. It had only been with Frederic's support that he had been able to push through reforms against such negligence, after the disaster at Lilly. It was also only with his interference that the law passed with the clause that nobles would only lose their title and privilege if subsequent disasters were at least sixty percent as destructive as the break on Lilly had been.

Still, it had been a good reform. Emmanuel could admit that.

"Yes. I inspected your worlds and only found the normal crimes one would expect. I must commend you on your control over your retainers."

The small talk continued as they talked about expansion routes and various resource exchanges—normal and mundane things between kingdoms. Most deals were fair and equal, but they each got the upper hand on a few key items. Emmanuel had two kingdoms worth of resources at hand, compared to Frederic's single new kingdom.

When that was settled, Frederic broached the second topic after leading Emmanuel to his vault.

They passed through layer after layer of restriction to reach a massive door made from Tier 47 steel. Even Emmanuel would need time to physically break through that much metal, which was all that it was meant to do. Nothing could stop a desperate cultivator except for someone stronger.

The vault only needed to slow anyone foolish enough down, so Frederic and his guards could rush in and subdue them.

The spatially expanded space was massive, and they meandered around as Frederic showed off the various things he had collected throughout the years. Most were unique rather than useful, but that was to be expected. Useful things were used.

They finally reached the section of the vault where the cracked skills were kept.

Frederic waved and said, "And so, we finally arrive within my most prized collection. Unique cracked skills with various effects. The more unique or specialized, the more I prize them." He sighed in a way Emmanuel believed was genuine, if rehearsed.

"And the same ones that you use to bind people to you."

Frederic shrugged. "I don't force anyone, nor do I prevent them from growing in power and ascending. That breaks all contracts, and they keep the skill. When something is perfect, what is a little service? I treat those in my employ with generosity and all due consideration, it is rare for any to truly complain." Seeing they were going to tread down a long-rehearsed path, he waved. "I welcome you to look around if you aren't sure what skills you need, but if you want to pick the ones you need, I will be happy to start negotiations."

They started with more common skills to bargain for. There were two dozen promising youths Emmanuel was preparing to reward with special, targeted rewards in the next Pather tournament, and it would help obfuscate the skills he actually wanted to get from Frederic.

Vince and Adam both just needed cracked skills with lower spiritual strain. Easy enough to get but hard to find good ones that matched their hybrid fighting style.

Tiffany was a void melee fighter who needed [Cracked Heavy Punch] with a void aspect to really shine, and he intended to get it for her here.

Very few Skills could withstand part of their structure being twisted to Void, and given the *immeasurable* rarity of true Void Skills, this was a perfect reward for her.

Bradley was steadfastly trying to get his lava-aspected skills to work for molten metal instead, and a [Cracked Metal Manipulation] that allowed the material it controlled to be moved like a liquid would help him immensely once he succeeded.

The others would either get specialized items to further their advancement, or Tier 20 skills. Adding to the numbers would hopefully hide Melinda's skill.

Emmanuel had already found the skills he wanted, and with an effort of will and a show of power, broke the restrictions around their cases and brought them to hover in between them.

He wasn't stealing them, but he was showing that he had a distinct advantage and wasn't going to deal with bad faith bargaining.

The first ones were easy enough to bargain for, as they were there more so to round out Frederic's collection than anything else. They were hardly of any true value. To Emmanuel's irritation, the man latched on to [Cracked Miasma] with much more enthusiasm.

"Yes. [Cracked Miasma], truly a rare crack. A damage skill turned to healing. One of a kind."

They both knew it wasn't one of a kind. Just rare.

"Yes, it's a great find indeed, though no rarer I would say than [Cracked Heavy Punch]."

Frederic smiled. "If it is your majesty who needs the skill personally, I will be happy to give it as a gift. But…" He trailed off, seeing if Emmanuel would lie.

The man was probing to see if there was a new rising star in the Empire that had a Talent the Emperor could use to his advantage. The free gift wouldn't be free, but instead a favor, which was far worse. It was also a way to see if Frederic could make the cost too high, and then try to rope in the young person the skill was meant to synergize with.

Emmanuel would kill the man before he let Melinda fall under his thumb.

He still needed to avoid lying, though. "No. As you suspect it is for a young person who can make good use of it."

Seeing the man's smile turned predatory, Emmanuel flexed his power.

Slightly.

Reality trembled for an instant, and the expanded space grew disjointed as the enchantments started to fail under the stress.

"Do not try to play games with me on this, Frederic. I will not tolerate it in this instance. What do you want for these skills?"

Even under the power, Frederic remained calm.

"I would like to know who the young up and comers are. I like to do the same as you. Bring them to my side early and raise them up. Don't pretend you're doing anything different. I just don't hide my bindings. And you say I'm the worst."

"I'm nothing like you. I don't force anyone into my service." Seeing the man about to object, Emmanuel raised a hand, "I won't argue that you don't treat your people well. But I don't force anyone to accept my leash. You should know with how many of your guards were on the Path. You snatched them all up as soon as they fell off."

Frederic nodded at that. It was true, after all. The Path of Ascension was a fertile recruiting ground for noble houses and guilds, and Emmanuel let them take freely from those that fell off. His only restrictions applied to approaching the youth that were looking to complete the Path. Those were national assets, and not to be touched.

He had killed more than one noble for trying to tempt Light and Shadow off the Path.

Frederic sighed. "If you want the skills with no strings attached for your prospects, I want you to halt all of your reforms targeting the nobility for the next five thousand years."

Emmanuel resisted the urge to curse. He was hoping, despite knowing how unlikely it was, that the man would just ask for his own royal title and leave it at that. Still, that was too far. Emmanuel only had thirty thousand years as a ruler, and a thousand were already gone. Losing one-sixth of his time to get a single skill was inexcusable.

He wanted to have the old nobles well under control, and a balance for the guilds, while the new meritocratic nobles who were more loyal to him and the central government held more of the power.

Emmanuel shook his head this time. "That's too long. Two thousand years, and I'll immediately raise you up to a royal during the session."

Frederic tried to retort that the deal was too unfair, but Emmanuel held firm.

"It is not enough. These are one of a kind skills. I can't part with them so easily."

Thinking, Emmanuel brought out [Copper Skin]. It, too, was one of a kind, at least until Matt made more of them. If the boy took too long, he would start tasking other people with it, but his mana budget was already held together with promises more than anything. Everything cost mana, and there were always places to use more of it.

"This is [Copper Skin], a unique Tier 8 skill. A seeming variation of [Iron Skin], but a Tier lower. One of a kind."

Frederic's eyes glinted with interest, but he tried to play coy. "But the skill will be pulled out of rifts in the future. It's only rare now. Not forever."

Emmanuel shook his head. "No, the skill wasn't thought to be unique at the time, and with its birthplace being only Tier 6, the rift was either Tiered-up or dissipated. They aren't sure, as it was a part of a batch increase. Regardless, the rift is gone, and the skill is the only one that remains."

That caught Frederic's interest, and Emmanuel knew he had him on at least that.

Eventually, they settled on two thousand years of no changes to noble privileges without Frederic's approval. A condition they both agreed on easily enough. Change needed to happen, and if Frederic approved it, the nobles that followed him would fall in line. The deal also came with Frederic's immediate rise to royalty, with Emmanuel assisting him in a few public speeches, and shows of support for his new kingdom. [Copper Skin] was the final touch which let him keep the years of the condition down.

Frederic was a collector after all, and the skill was a prize he couldn't pass up on easily.

Neither were happy with the deal, which was how they both knew that neither was being screwed.

He believed that before two thousand years had passed, Matt would be a high enough Tier to change the face of the Empire. Then, he could turn this deal in on the nobles, and hold the benefits of unlimited power to those loyal to him.

Emmanuel was touring the new kingdom while meeting and greeting various local nobles and commoners, when the report of the Pather war ending came in.

Things were normal enough, until he saw what Mara and Leon had done.

He had to resist face palming in front of the crowd when he got the high priority report. They loved to create problems for him.

Brice, former king of the Seven Suns vassal state of the Empire, as he had sent his abdication order as he left real space, flew through chaotic space with the rage still burning hot in his chest.

The amount of turbulence currently in chaotic space didn't help, his one-man ship being tossed to and fro in the not-winds until it settled down.

His anger only increased as he left. All of his recent troubles had started from Pathers. *Pathers* had gotten tangled up in his idiot family members scheme of taking indentured workers and then the *Pathers* had caused the war to be allowed in his territory.

He thought it was a good sign when he noticed the chaotic space warping into the semblance of flames, in response to someone strong enough to impose their will on the untamed space.

Not willing to interact with someone that strong, he started to fly out of the area when he noticed that the flames grew hotter and started to follow him.

His worry turned to alarm, and he flew ahead at full speed, only to turn and see a woman with flaming hair feathers chasing him down.

Realizing that he couldn't escape, he began to ask why he was being chased down, only for his ship to be seized within a giant talon. The next moment, his ship had broken around him, and the claws were wrapped directly around him.

His ribs and arms shattered like dry twigs, as the crushing power was accompanied by a cultivation pressure that threatened to extinguish his very spirit.

He tried to ask why but was unable to even concentrate enough to use his AI.

The woman looked at him with a tilted head that reminded him more of a bird of prey, wondering the best way to pick out the soft bits of its meal, than a human. It was then that he put the pieces together. This was Mara, queen of beasts and evolved humans. A Tier 48.

"Are you King Brice?"

"I…"

The talon tightened. "Don't bother. I already know. I'm quite upset with you."

The chaotic space around them flared to orange and flame.

As Mara expected an answer, her talons lessened their pressure, and Brice was able to say, "You attacked down Tiers. The Emperor will kill you for this."

She shook her flaming hair. "Nah, I don't think so. More like chewed-out. I've been chewed out before."

The claw around him tightened as she leaned forward. "I'm debating just eating you now. It would solve so many problems. But I won't. I'm sure you have plenty of enemies lining up to take your head. Your own family for example. I can't believe you actually treat them that way. As if they're disposable."

The flames roared around them, and even Brice's' full power couldn't keep them at bay. The inferno started to char his skin.

"I treasure my children. They are the most important thing to me. Now how do you think I felt when my youngest daughter asked for a favor from me to help a friend?"

The crazy bitch clapped her hands and smiled. "I was ecstatic! Friends! She had so few growing up that I worried for her. Then there was the whole mess with her Awakening, but she's moved on from that now, and now she even has a friend good enough that she requests a favor on their behalf. How wonderful! She also formalized her relationship with my soon-to-be son-in-law on that planet. I was going to memorialize it and add it to my collection. So, how do you think I reacted once I found out that you detonated depleted copper all over the place!? It's going to take *years* to return to its pristine condition! It can't be a part of my collection if it's not pristine, can it?"

Brice tried to speak, but the talon tightened. "From the report, I saw that you were even willing to kill quite a few people with your little plan. You're lucky the army had overrides for your son's detonators to the explosives. The poor boy was panicked enough to actually do it."

With a monumental effort, he wheezed out, "There are always losses. I…"

The talon tightened even further. "Clearly, you are much too stupid. Maybe I should just kill you after all. People disappear in chaotic space all the time…" Mara seemed to really ponder it for a minute but shook her head. "No. I have a much better punishment."

The power radiated off her, and there was an authority in her voice as she said, "Former King Brice of the Vassal Kingdom Seven Suns. I, in my authority as a royal, am ordering you to serve on a clean-up crew on the old frontier to help re-terraform them from the last war. This is nonnegotiable, as I find you guilty of using planet-harming munitions on a soon-to-be habitable world. You may have followed the letter of the law, but I find you in violation of the spirit of said law while risking the lives of thousands of Pathers."

Unwilling to be forced to clean planets for who knew how long, he tried to protest. "I am due my reward for growing the Empire by proxy. I…"

Mara cut him off. "Yes, you are, and even I can't touch that. But with my authority, I am postponing your compensation until after your punishment is complete. If you fail to report in, you will be treated as a criminal and will be hunted down." She smiled a hopeful smile as she finished, "Please do run. I'll chase you down, even into another Great Power. Test me. Please."

Brice was flung away and slowed in the uncontrolled chaotic space while he focused on healing. He intended to flee into unsettled space to get away, but that was only an initial reaction.

He would lose too much. No, it was better to report her, and try to use the physical attack as a lever to reduce the punishment. It was also far more likely to work. The woman had gone overboard and had broken half a dozen laws. Even if laws were less enforced when between two people over Tier 15 she had broken them, nonetheless.

She was probably right, and wouldn't be killed, but he could fight to reduce the punishment on the grounds that she had already punished him.

He was still focusing on healing when the chaotic space started to change again. He feared it was Mara coming back to finish the job, as he would have, when he noticed that it was a lightning user.

To his bafflement, he saw a single man hauling around an entire world. It felt like a Tier 7 planet, and they were clawing their way through chaotic space. They were pulling a *world* against the current. Brice couldn't pull a world through chaotic space *with* the current. At least, not more than a few feet. He had done so once with a Tier 2 world as a show of power and had needed years to recover his over-taxed spirit.

It didn't take his reading the message that was sent for him to figure out who the man had to be.

"When I get done hauling this, I'm gonna kick your ass for ruining my daughter's fun!"

Brice decided that it was much better to report into the terraforming location, and shelter somewhere even those two maniacs wouldn't dare act against him.

After the party and commiseration, Queen Diana was positively sloshed with her newest sister.

Her father's parting words still bothered Cori, but they convinced her that they were all bluster, and that he was only trying to hurt her.

It had mostly worked, and they had gorged themselves on good food and better wine for the better part of a week.

Even their immortal bodies could only take so much punishment and abuse. Coupled with her almost gone, but still lingering wound, Diana was feeling sore, but good.

That was, until she and all her sisters were ripped through chaotic space, suddenly standing in front of Mara.

Diana immediately bowed deeply while sending messages to her sisters, who followed suit.

Technically, they were peers as they were both queens. The only noble she technically had to bow to was the Emperor, and Leon, her direct liege. Mara's husband. Even the land they ruled was of different quantity and quality. Diana's entire queendom was the size of maybe two duchies in the Empire proper. And Mara controlled dozens of duchies. Only a fool wouldn't bow in front of true power.

That wasn't even to mention the difference in Tiers. A Tier 35 might as well be a child in front of a Tier 48.

"Stand up! Stand up." Mara sounded in good cheer, which relieved most of Diana's worries. The fear that her daughter had said something still lingered but lessened.

"How can I assist you, Queen Mara? We will do…"

Mara waved an arm that slightly turned into a wing. "Please, hunnie. I don't care about the formalities. I want to buy the planet."

Diana paused as she replayed the words that the queen in front of her just said. It made no sense.

"We will happily give you sovereignty over the planet if that is what you wish. I…"

"No, no, no. I want to take the planet. My daughter had quite a few first experiences here, and I want to add it to my collection. I want to take the planet home with me. She made real friends here! I can't let this place go."

Diana started to panic. This planet was the only tether to the Tier 20 planet next door, and if they lost the connection, the Tier 20 planet would start to drift into chaotic space. Then, they would have lost everything.

Trying to figure out how to deny the woman without pissing her off, Diana tried, "We would give you the planet if we could, but there is a Tier 20 one jump over. We will lose the other planet if you take this one. Great lady, please, I beg of you not to make us lose something we have fought so hard for."

Mara scoffed at her. "I'm not an asshole. My hubby is bringing a replacement planet over as we speak. A fresh Tier 7 planet. We'll just plop it in place before we leave."

They stared at each other for a long moment as Diana questioned if she heard her right. She knew Leon. The man was strong. He had to be to remain a King but moving a Tier 7 planet over more than her range of perception should be nearly impossible.

She peered upstream to see if he was just guiding the planet over. That would be much more believable, but her spiritual scene showed her the opposite. There was nothing there.

She did, however, find him pulling a Tier 7 world from *downstream*.

Diana was speechless as her mind ground to a halt.

Mara shoved a bag into her chest, along with each of her sisters.

Diana took it out of reflex, and nearly drifted away as the higher Tier stones had enough spiritual prescience to try and drift off, it was more than she could easily stabilize. Her lower Tiered sisters weren't so lucky, and she felt Mara assisting them.

"Five Tier 45 mana stones apiece. I'll also be paying everyone on the planet a mana stone fifteen Tiers above them."

Seeing the woman pause and look at her with a cocked head, Diana nodded.

"This is more than generous, great lady. We will immediately start evacuations. I…"

Mara waved her off. "When we get the other planet in place, I'll move everyone over." She also looked at the connection between the Tier 6 world and the Tier 20. "I'll also clear the traps through there. Did the idiot do that?"

Not waiting for an answer, Mara continued, "Maybe I should have killed him."

At the same time, a series of explosions rang out in chaotic space. She turned to Cori, who had passed off her bag of mana stones to remain with them, instead of drifting off into chaotic space.

"Hey, girl. Your dad's a proper dick. If you plan to kill him, you need to get a lot stronger, and soon. I ordered him to planet clean up duty for this little stunt, but it won't prevent him from advancing forever."

Cori opened her mouth, but Leon arrived, puffing with exertion. "I'm here." He panted more before continuing, "Did we make a deal?"

Mara transformed her battle garb to a skimpy maid's outfit and started patting his forehead with a small cloth while shoving her chest into his arm.

The comical scene was offset by the weighty words, "Yup! All sold. I'll do the swap and move the people."

There was a flash of flames, and the two worlds seemed to merge in space for a second, before the Tier 7 replaced the Tier 6. Even the connections were transferred over.

Mara froze as Diana felt a powerful perception inspecting the people on the new world and Mara looked at Diana. "Ummm, did you happen to get a note with training instructions on it?"

Diana paused. She actually *had* gotten one. Everyone on the planet had. They were quite good and addressed everyone's singular greatest weakness while giving them things to improve on. The instructions for Sara were so good, Diana was genuinely impressed. Concise information about her general fighting style, and tips for her budding Concept. That didn't even account for the note for her, which hinted at what she needed to do to get her own Aspect.

"Yes, would you like to see it?"

Mara screamed, "No!" Even her feathered hair stood straight out.

Leon looked like he would be sick as they turned to each other.

"Tell me they wouldn't do that to our baby girl!?" Leon seemed to be asking anyone for reassurance, while Mara looked as if her flames would gutter out.

"How are we supposed to spy on her if the crazy cat is there? She's going to try and make us work hard!"

The two looked stricken as they peered around, like they knew someone was watching them.

Finally, they said in unison, "Let's get out of here."

Mara, with an effort of will, moved everyone on the planet over, and then the two flew off, with Leon dragging the planet away.

"Squawk!"

Mara's last word confused Diana further. The woman had *said* squawk. Not actually made the noise but said the word.

Those two were…weird.

Still, as Diana inspected their new planet, she smiled. It was lovely, but the Tier 45 mana stones would pay for quite a lot. They would both increase the value of her queendom and her own personal equipment.

Overall, they had made out well.

She wondered if there was another planet that the crazy couple wanted to buy.

The story continues in Book 4!

THANK YOU FOR READING THE PATH OF ASCENSION 3

We hope you enjoyed it as much as we enjoyed bringing it to you. We just wanted to take a moment to encourage you to review the book. Follow this link: The Path of Ascension 3 to be directed to the book's Amazon product page to leave your review.

Every review helps further the author's reach and, ultimately, helps them continue writing fantastic books for us all to enjoy.

Also in Series:
Book One
Book Two
Book Three
Book Four

Want to discuss our books with other readers and even the authors? Join our Discord server today and be a part of the Aethon community.

Facebook | Instagram | Twitter | Website

You can also join our non-spam mailing list by visiting www.subscribepage.com/AethonReadersGroup and never miss out on future releases. You'll also receive three full books completely Free as our thanks to you.

Looking for more great LitRPG?

Trapped in a Dungeon. There's only one way out. Kill or be killed... *An AI calling itself Schema has assimilated earth into its System. As a consequence, everyone gained access to status screens, power-ups, and skills. This AI turned these concepts from fiction to fact. It's easy to become intoxicated with leveling up and becoming stronger. To some, it's too good to be true like living out a dream. For Daniel, however, it's closer to a nightmare. He's in a bit of a predicament. Cracks in our dimensional fabric have unleashed terrifying beasts from dark, abyssal places. Schema organizes these cracks into dungeons, giving the native species of the planet a chance to fight back. Daniel finds himself stuck in one of these dungeons. It's time to break free, by any means necessary.* ***Experience the start of an action-packed LitRPG Apocalypse series with nearly 15 Million views on Royal Road. For the first time, The New World is coming to Kindle & Kindle Unlimited, completely revised, re-edited, and loaded with new content.***

Get The New World Now!

Stack your Deck. Climb the Gaia Tower. Defeat its Guardians. *Almost half a century has passed since prison ships en route to Australia discovered the mysterious Tower rising out of the Indian Ocean, known as Gaia. Monarchies, republics, and trading giants came together to build a city around it, and contain the monsters spilling out of the rune-covered structure. The few that dared enter and climb it learned the magic of Gaia's runic cards. Now, most people enter the tower seeking fame, fortune, or power. Not Diya Sen. He climbs hoping to find clues about his missing brother and to solve Gaia's mysteries. However, the warring noble houses stand in his way. His mission won't be easy. Many sources of power are outside his reach as an ordinary man. But if the direct approach doesn't help Diya achieve his goals, perhaps the talents of a Spell Thief will.* ***Don't miss the start of the TOWER OF CARDS series from bestseller J Pal. This is Progression Fantasy utilizing a runic card-based magic system with tons of customization. Perfect for fans of All the Skills and Towers of Heaven, as well as games such as Slay the Spire, Hearthstone, and Gwent.***

Get Spell Thief Now!

Alone. Surrounded by Monsters. Armed only with his Fists... Time to fight. *Jack Rust was a disillusioned biologist with a PhD—almost. When an extraterrestrial AI calling itself the System invaded Earth and thrusts it into a world of aliens and violence, the least Jack hoped for was gaining access to magic. Nope. Even worse, the System also spawned a forest dungeon around him and a goblin in his face... Armed with nothing but his fists, Jack must grow strong enough to survive hordes of monsters. He needs to return to civilization and find out what the heck is going on. He might also get magic—or not. Surprising himself, Jack discovers that violence is fun. In this battle-ridden new world, Jack finds the life he always dreamed about. He won't just survive. He will thrive.* ***Don't miss the start of this action-packed new LitRPG Apocalypse series from Valerios. Join Jack the Brawler as he pummels everything that gets in his way with his fists on his road to mastery and power. It's perfect for fans of Primal Hunter, Defiance of the Fall, and lovers of all things Progression Fantasy and LitRPG.***

Get Road to Mastery Now!

For all our LitRPG books, visit our website.

Made in the USA
Middletown, DE
18 September 2023